THY TEARS MIGHT CEASE

Thy Tears Might Cease

Michael Farrell

HUTCHINSON OF LONDON

HUTCHINSON & CO (*Publishers*) LTD
3 Fitzroy Square, London W1

London Melbourne Sydney Auckland
Wellington Johannesburg Cape Town
and agencies throughout the world

First published November 1963
Reprinted before publication
Third impression December 1963
Fourth impression January 1964
Fifth impression October 1972

Printed in Great Britain by litho on antique wove paper
by Anchor Press, and bound by Wm. Brendon,
both of Tiptree, Essex
ISBN 0 09 113840 X

To Francie

Contents

'If thou and I could by a tale
Some hours of wand'ring life beguile,
Thy tears might cease, and we might fail
To mind ourselves awhile.'

      Anon. (Lines from a lady's album)

'. . . tush man, mortal men, mortal men.'

    FALSTAFF (*King Henry IV*, Part I)

Introduction

by

MONK GIBBON

I

When Michael Farrell died in June 1962 his publisher may not have felt a sense of relief; the news nevertheless came as the solution of an almost complete impasse. Most authors live for the moment when they will see their work in print: this one, for five years after his book's acceptance, had clung steadfastly to the typescript, refusing to believe that it was yet in a condition to be shared with others. It had been given back to him at his own request for cutting and final revision, and the artist continued to cling protectively and defiantly to what the man had for years longed to see given to the world. Letters remained unanswered, or were answered by excuses. Tactful approaches through a friend would only produce an explosion of impatience highly undesirable in a sick man. Financial sanctions might have been applied. They would have been accepted without resentment. But neither they nor any other form of pressure would have made Farrell disgorge his book. It was not ready for publication. It was not yet the work of art which he wished it to be.

What kind of a book was it? It was a large unwieldy novel almost in the Victorian mode. In many ways it stood a great deal nearer to Emily Brontë, or to Thomas Hardy, than to James Joyce. It was Irish, but it was concerned not with the peasant Ireland of Synge's plays, nor with the shabby-genteel, sordid Dublin of Joyce which Shaw in a letter to Sylvia Beach calls 'that foul-mouthed, foul-minded derision and obscenity', but with the bourgeois, middle-class, county-town Catholic Ireland of the

9

time of John Redmond. And it overflowed from those peaceful
oratorical days to the desperately serious, bloodstained Ireland of
the Bad Times. A breadth of sympathy, a refusal to allow class
labels, sectarian labels, political labels, racial labels to colour its
treatment of events, make it—in spite of touches of semi-romantic
eloquence—a remarkably truthful record. But it is not an
historical novel. It is an intensely personal and subjective one,
linked throughout to the consciousness of a single individual.

Thy Tears Might Cease is full of real life, but it is not a realistic
novel in the accepted sense. As Mary McCarthy has recently
pointed out, that sense is almost always pejorative. So-called
'realism' rules out both the noble and the lyrical. 'Such figures as
Othello and Hernani', she writes, 'can never be the subject of
realistic treatment, unless it is with the object of deflating them,
showing how *ordinary*—petty or squalid—they are. . . . We think
of Turgenev and Mrs. Gaskell almost as pastoral writers, despite
the fact that their faithful sketches have nothing in common with
the artificial convention of the true pastoral. We suspect that there
is something arcadian here—something "unrealistic".' It is not
the least of the merits of Farrell's novel that it combines extreme
realism of the accustomed sort with a degree of poetic apprehension, an awareness that life has its overtones of destiny, even
though we may never fully understand them, which lifts it on to
a plane where fate and vision are relevant as well as the actual
event. Fate is stressed by the reappearance, at long intervals, of
certain minor characters. Vision is the whole theme of the book,
the ecstatic, over-sensitive, egotistical and over-hopeful vision
of boyhood, and the embittered, angry and soured vision of
disillusioned adolescence. These successive phases of youth are
the audience, and it is history itself which determines the play.

It is difficult to say when Farrell first began to write the book.
It may have been in the early days of his marriage, but his brother
Sean believes that it might have been considerably earlier that
he was shown some of the school portion. Farrell had used the
emotions of his own childhood and some of the experiences of his
schooldays as basic material for a panorama of youth of exceptional vividness; and all through the book there are touches and
episodes which suggest that he was drawing in some measure on
what was factual. For example Farrell's own career as a medical
student—he had begun to read medicine at the National Uni-

versity—was disrupted in much the same way as his hero's by
the arrival of the Bad Times and by imprisonment. He was not
deeply involved in the troubles, but he happened to have offered
to take charge of some banned periodical or circular which was
being returned to Dublin for revision, and when this was found
in his room he was arrested, tried and sentenced to twelve months
in Mountjoy prison.[1] When the hunger-strike of prisoners took
place there he was excused participating in it by his colleagues
on the score of health; and, for the same reason, the length of his
sentence was shortened by the authorities.

But he had made himself suspect with the county officials who
had given him a university grant. He did not return to the
National University. Instead he went for a prolonged walking-
tour on the continent with a young woman who had been his
fellow medical student. When they returned to Ireland both he
and she taught for a time in a private school at Killiney. Later he
obtained a post as a Marine Superintendent of Customs under the
Belgians in the Congo and would have liked her to accompany
him as his wife, but she refused. After some years of service there
he returned to Ireland, relatively—for him—well off. In later days
he never spoke much to his friends of his Congo experiences. In
1930 he met and soon afterwards married Frances, younger
daughter of Frances Cahill, wife of Dr. Frank Kennedy Cahill,
a woman of considerable energy, who had founded and was
running, with the aid of her daughter, a hand-weaving establishment known as The Crock of Gold. Farrell now resumed his
medical studies, but in the other and older of Dublin's two
universities, Trinity College, Dublin. There he distinguished
himself in the various college societies and by helping to edit the
undergraduate periodical *T.C.D.*; and won a medal for oratory
in one of the inter-university debates. After his death *Trinity*, the
official annual record of the university, could write of him: 'In his
lively enthusiasms he appeared sometimes restless and impulsive,
but they were the reflections of a mind both talented and generous.'

His medical studies were not making much headway. For a
time he and his wife lived in Herbert Street and were well-known

1. His landlady was called to give evidence at his trial, and being asked by
the prosecution to say what the colour of her politics was, made a reply which
many Dubliners might have made at that time, had they possessed the necessary
frankness: 'I am all things to all men'!

figures in literary circles, but in 1932 they moved out to a house
in Co. Wicklow, above Kilmacanogue and almost on the slope of
the Big Sugar Loaf. He was still in Trinity at this time, but now
he decided to abandon medicine and to devote himself to
literature. He had as neighbour in Kilmacanogue the writer
Sean O'Faolain and there was constant coming and going
between the two households. Here, in the mid-thirties, he set to
work seriously upon his novel and also began work as a compère
for Radio Eireann. When, at the beginning of the war, O'Faolain
founded his monthly, *The Bell*, Farrell was asked to write on
aspects of theatrical activity in Ireland and to contribute a series
of outlines and analyses of the plays most popular with amateur
dramatic societies. He adjudicated at various drama festivals and,
when the series of drama articles ended, his editor could write of
him in October 1940 that for fifteen months 'he has recorded the
theatre up and down the country'.

In April 1943 *The Bell* started a regular feature which was to
run for a number of years. It was

The Open Window
by Gulliver

A Monthly Perambulation

It took as its motto, 'This is Liberty Hall, gentlemen; you may do
as you please here', from *She Stoops to Conquer,* and it was a literary
causerie in which Lemuel Gulliver (Farrell) discoursed freely on
whatever happened to interest him at the moment, set translation
and other competitions for his readers, and generally revealed his
anonymous personality as that of a highly cultivated and
generously-minded European. O'Faolain could not have given
him a task more to his liking. All his love of literature stood
revealed in this monthly symposium. In his conversation Farrell
loved to be slightly fanciful, to put on an act, to show off—the
elation of a child rather than of a genuinely vain individual—and
now with his identity a carefully guarded secret he delighted
many of us by his monthly revelation of an urbane and scholarly
mind. One turned to Gulliver's three or four pages of smaller type
at the end of *The Bell* each month in very much the same mood

that one would feel when drawing the cork of a bottle of wine whose bouquet was already well known and highly appreciated.

At the same time that he was writing for *The Bell* he was also working regularly for Radio Eireann. The poet Robert Farren has told how for six or seven years Farrell was his colleague— 'a spare, slight figure with a brown face, lively eyes and a moustache, and oceans of talk. Limitless oceans of talk . . . Every week in my office we were at it hammer and tongs for hours on end—and for other hours on end just talking amicably and at large. The talk kept us both very late but we seldom minded. We respected each other—or at least I deeply respected him. And when he was criticized I tried to defend him.' Farren was able to perceive the genuine ore of idealism behind his compère's torrential flow of loquacity. 'Like all Irishmen who got us our freedom—at least all those of them whom I have met—he was a fighter; a fighter for ideas and freedom to express them. He fought everyone who tried to restrict freedom of speech, and mostly when the Second World War was limiting freedom of speech even in neutral countries. He fought me vehemently, torrentially, not about freedom of speech, but when he thought I was stupid and wrong-headed, and I thought he was intolerable, unpractical, wrong-headed to the point of nonsense. . . . He was a complicated person, but a charming one. He could have played a safe game in order to ensure his place in broadcasting, but he didn't. . . .'

But though a poet some years his junior can speak of him in this fashion, literary Dublin as a whole either ignored Farrell or treated him as an amusing irrelevance. No one believed in the great novel which he was writing. He talked about it too much. A complete stranger, who did not know Farrell, was told by some friends in Paris: 'He intends to write his book in Greek. No other language is worthy of it.' In this way did sly Irish malice poke fun, as is its habit, at a scheme too grandiloquent, it was thought, to come to anything. Even to O'Faolain, who in the thirties had taken an early portion over to London and shown it to a publisher, it must have seemed that its chances of completion in any final sense—that is to say as a pruned and disciplined work of art, and not as a vast imaginative quarry in which blasting operations had been going on for years and huge shapeless boulders had been rolling down the hillside to lie there untended and awaiting the stone-mason's chisel which should put shape and polish on them—were small indeed.

Farrell was the sort of man who must spill himself over, spend himself completely, exhaust himself even over trifles; and such men seldom have the staying power for achievement on a large scale. Mercurial, volatile, enthusiastic, he belonged to the tradition of the picaresque novel. If he had had to entertain Don Quixote he would have done so in just the grandiloquent style which would have pleased the knight. Willing to expend a hundred per cent of his energy on some quite trivial controversial issue—that being his nature—the tax upon his nervous reserves was always great, and often wasteful. He had never learnt to conserve his strength, to measure himself out in teaspoonfuls.

To a casual stranger he might seem flamboyant, a little too anxious to assert himself at the first opportunity. To a few close friends, university professors or fellow writers, he was the amusing host, the delightful conversationalist, and they were well aware how generous and magnanimous he could be. But even to them he was a man who must be accepted completely upon his own terms. You might like him or you might not like him but you could not change him. He had something ebullient, something of the caballero, something a little showy in his composition; but at the same time he was devotedly attached to a graciousness of living which he had seen vanish from the Irish scene within his own lifetime. He liked the old ways, he liked the traditional courtesies. He was capable of striking an attitude merely for the sake of re-creating that past which once existed, which he had glimpsed as a child, and which in the depths of his being he felt deserved an imaginative, and if possible a factual, reconstruction in present time. In later years the maid who waited at his dinner-table was capped and aproned very much in the style of her Edwardian forerunners; and the children who, until illness overtook him, used to rush out from the gate lodge to open the inner avenue gate for him, were always greeted with a touch of genuine but at the same time slightly feudal benevolence. They were part of a game which he was still playing after most others had abandoned it.

George Moore has said that if a man talks too much about how he will write his book he is unlikely ever to write it. But Farrell did not talk about how he would write his book; he talked about how he had *already written* it. He loved to hold forth on any subject. I have listened to him as he demonstrated to a young girl at the dinner-table how the part of Viola should be played in *Twelfth Night* and it was like witnessing a full-length Beerbohm Tree rehearsal in which Farrell, 'the one-man band', took everyone's part and dealt with it equally faithfully. And, in just the same way apparently, he used in earlier days to try out a passage or passages from the book on his friends, his talent for dramatization, and especially for self-dramatization, permitting him to put on an act of tremendous and exhilarating vitality. But in Dublin if a man is capable of such a *tour-de-force* it generally ends with his letting the matter rest there. The possessor of a talent of that sort is content with periodic displays of conversational fireworks; but nothing ever reaches the printer. That would be too much like work: it would be an attempt to trap one's versatility into the narrow canal of actual achievement. The novel came gradually to be treated as myth. Like The Man Who Never Was, it was The Novel Which Would Never Be. After his death I found it hard to convince a number of people, who knew him well, that it really existed.

My own acquaintance with him did not begin till the early fifties, and by that time the novel had ceased to be spoken of. He had abandoned his journalism and his radio work, had taken over the management of The Crock of Gold and was showing his customary energy in a field new to him. To his friend Pat Holland it seemed that he had let the literary bohemian die suddenly in him and was determined to carry off his new role of business man and property owner with his customary bravado. But to me, when I met him, he seemed the very type of literary freebooter whose casual conversation—in Ireland certainly—is often richer than half a dozen well-paid articles. He was vehement, volatile, denunciatory and fundamentally kind; and, since I knew by now that he was Gulliver, a certain degree of mild exhibitionism was easily forgiven. Besides, when he staged himself it was as authentic as Cyrano de Bergerac.

The novel by now had been finished, cherished as a masterpiece, reviled and repudiated as a failure, such were the extremes of heat and cold in which its creator viewed it. It was no longer a conversational topic. It seemed to have been forgotten. Then, about 1954, in a burst of fresh energy, he made a new revision of

all the earlier part and had it retyped and bound in pale yellow
canvas covers. He never spoke of it directly, but occasionally,
in front of his fire, he might indulge in a flood of reminiscences of
some admired figure of his schooldays and this—vivid as anything he ever put on paper—was his method of trying it out on
you. In the same way short passages from it had been interpolated
in broadcasts in the past. To my wife he read aloud a few
chapters but she was told that on no account must I be allowed
to set eyes on it.

Then in 1956 came a nervous breakdown and a few weeks of
invalidism in Baggot Street General Hospital. Thinking of him
there, I said one day to my wife: 'You know, what is really wrong
with that man is that he has never had the measure of recognition
which his talent deserves. Couldn't you get hold of his book and
let me have a look at it?' Farrell's own wife was won over to the
plot and I was given possession of the five bound volumes. When
he came out of hospital the books were safely back in place, but
we invited him over to supper and in the course of the evening I
confessed my crime to him and begged him to let me send the
book to an agent. It took a good deal of persuasion, but after
about ten days he brought the typescript back and gave me
permission to go ahead with any plans I had for it.

2

The merits of the book were perceived almost immediately,
even though it was plain that it was still in an unfinished state.
It was accepted, and Farrell, at last, had the satisfaction of
knowing that all the time he had spent on it had not been wasted.
He had been vindicated. His labour had been justified. He wrote
to me: . . . *my deepest satisfaction is for Francie, that she can feel that
whatever happens to the book now for good or ill, it aroused the enthusiastic
interest of good and cultivated judges, and that a publisher was ready to go
so far for it.* . . .

He suspected—quite correctly—that I had read very little of
his book; only enough to form an immediate qualitative estimate
of its merit. And the problem before the publishers now was
how such a lengthy book was to make its appearance: piece-meal
or as a whole. They had seen only the revised earlier portion,

enough in itself to make four or five ordinary novels. There was still a whole later section which had not come under their consideration at all. I would suggest: 'Couldn't you break it off at the Easter Rising? That in itself is an historical milestone.' And Farrell would agree tentatively. But I was offering advice in the dark, as anyone who reads the book now will realize. The 1916 Rebellion, so far from signifying the end of something in Martin Matthew Reilly's life, is really the landmark of a beginning; in fact of two beginnings. The one thing on which everyone was agreed was that the book must be cut. And even if this was done it looked as though it would still have to be subdivided. The publishers handed over as much of it as they had received to an expert; but the expert after making some good general suggestions threw in his hand and the bound volumes of the typescript were sent back to Farrell for him to do the work himself.

And now arose a most curious situation. This man, whose lifelong heart's desire, a mutual friend once said to me, was 'to see his name on the wrapper of a book', pushed the cup from his lips when at last it was offered to him. Fundamentally modest in spite of his superficial ebullience, he told hardly anyone that his novel had been accepted. I rather think that it was I who whispered the information both to Professor O'Meara and to Professor Grene, his two closest friends. John O'Meara had once been allowed to read it in its entirety—a thirteenth labour for any critical Hercules—and had wounded its author by his rather dazed response to its undoubted merits. He was to witness now the author's anguished and ineffectual attempts to put into effect the advice offered on that occasion.

It was not that Farrell was incapable of revision. Periodically he undertook it. But in the same way that Jowett, when Swinburne thanked him for having shortened one of his earlier poems by twenty thousand lines, was forced to remind the poet that, though the surgical operation had unquestionably taken place and been gratefully welcomed, nevertheless thirty thousand new lines had very speedily taken the place of those removed, so when Farrell set out to revise and tighten it generally ended by an interpolation of anything up to a dozen new pages. Page 460 would in the course of nature become pages 460, 460a, 460b, 460c, 460d and 460e. There might be a few minor eliminations but it was the accretions which were really significant.

Undoubtedly there had been rewriting at various stages. But there had never been that ruthless, objective reassessment when an author ceases to be the creator of his own book and makes himself for a time its reader. It is only by this exchange of parts that he can deal adequately with the situation. If he becomes the reader he becomes capable of condemnation on behalf of the reader. If he remains the creator—still inside his book, never for a moment entirely outside it—he may of course still present the world with a work of genius, but it will be a happy accident if he does so. A study of Tolstoy's proofs, or of the proofs which Proust returned to the printer, makes absolutely clear how, when at the right moment the writer allows the critic within himself to take command, a book can reap the benefit of such an exchange of roles. Both these writers were merciless to their own progeny.

Farrell's book had been accepted. Discriminating publisher's readers had acclaimed it. Publishers on either side of the Atlantic had shown themselves enthusiastic about it. The printer was waiting for it. He was, at last, not to see his name on the wrapper of a book, because it was to be published under the pseudonym which he had used from time to time in *The Bell*—Michael Burke—but to have the supreme satisfaction of communication upon a large scale. All that he had to do now—and everyone, including himself, was agreed that this must be done—was to undertake this final revision, to put this final polish on it. When the topic arose between us he would shake his head gravely and say, 'The trouble is if you cut one thing it may affect half a dozen other things later in the book.' And then, after a pause and with a note almost of desperation in his voice: 'It isn't cutting that it needs. It needs boiling down.'

The weeks went by, the months went by, the years went by. It became more and more difficult to mention the subject to him. If you urged him to return the book to London as it was— and the publisher was already bitterly regretting ever having let it out of his hands—he would lose his temper and, no matter how sick he was at the moment, all the old vehemence would return and he would shout at you angrily: 'Impossible! Impossible! It's not finished. It needs to be worked over.' Finally the subject became almost one of taboo between us.

The easiest explanation of his behaviour would be to say that he was already a sick man when the book was first extracted from him and sent to London, and that thereafter, for the five or six years of life which remained to him, he never enjoyed sufficiently good health to make final revision possible. But this is too simple. There were—and in this his friend John O'Meara agrees with me —a number of other much more subtle psychological causes at work. To my wife it seemed that having talked so much about it in the past he was reluctant now to submit the book itself to the possible harshness of critics. O'Meara believes that it was more than that, and that he was loth—when it came to the point —to give the world the inside history of himself. One half of him loved Martin Matthew Reilly with the sentimental affection of a highly indulgent parent; the other half may have seen him, from time to time, as a hateful little chap, critical, conceited and an abominable prig. Unconsciously, he may have dreaded that moment when all his ardours and exaltations, and angry reactions and disillusions, would be part of a printed book and would have to face the world far away from the parental tenderness which had accepted and even condoned certain masochistic aspects in Martin's character.

But Professor O'Meara's second explanation is in my opinion even nearer the mark. He reminds me of the advice which Quiller Couch gives somewhere in one of his lectures to young writers. This was to write full steam ahead while inspiration was upon them, to put down everything that came into their head. Then, when it was all safely on paper, they must wait, and, after a reasonable interval, they must go on a completely different tack. 'Murder your darlings' was the way Q put it. 'Murder your darlings.' But here was an author who found that impossible.

It is doubtful if Farrell could ever have brought himself to put this advice ruthlessly into practice. His darlings were too dear to him. It is true that in a book written over a number of years he may sometimes have deliberately repeated himself—he was obviously aware that he did—intending to decide later whether the passage would remain in this chapter or that. But the type-script which he had bound up was after all a revised one and it is absolutely clear from it that his idea of revision was still a very long way short of infanticide. Rather he would trot his same infant out again and again, dressed up in the identical finery which had so much pleased him when he first put it on, thus endangering some of his own best effects; just as he could

sometimes betray a too obvious delight in them in the first
instance.

His book has been a fatiguing one to revise, but not a hard one.
I have found it mainly a matter of curbing his exuberance and
shortening his dialogue. Certain episodes, which resembled too
closely other earlier episodes, have had to go. But in doing this
I had the consciousness all the time that I was merely carrying
out a little finishing work with a chisel, work which the sculptor
himself knew had to be done, and wanted done, but which
temperament and circumstance had made necessary should be
done by another hand. The statue at the end of it was more than
ever the statue which he himself had intended. This may seem
an insolent boast from someone who has removed well over a
hundred thousand words from the book of his friend. But I can
assure the reader that they do not deserve his regrets and that of
the two hundred and twenty thousand or so which remain I have
not added more than, at most, a thousand. The novel as it is
now is the novel as Farrell wanted it to be. All that is perceptive
and poetic and evocative of its period reaches the reader freed
from literary archness and from that suggestion of 'showing off'
which was a part of Farrell's charm as a conversationalist, but
which was liable to be fatal when it crept into his writing.

His book, even in its massive original state, was never
amorphous or unthinking. Every effect had been thought out and
was deliberate, and it is only when one reads it a second time that
one sees how every episode and often every phrase has been
conceived as part of a total whole. It is the depiction of an epoch
—ten years in all.

Farrell has managed to suggest all the various implications of
a transitional world. His minor characters are never abstractions.
They are types, but they are types so representative of countless
individuals that they live for us vividly in their own right. No
doubt in the Monkstown of the period one could have encoun-
tered not one Miss Peters but at least a dozen; but that does not
make her any the less real. None of his protagonists—apart from
the hero—change a great deal. They are static, part of the
general pageantry of the period. But, because the epoch is one of
transition and radical transformation, we seem to be seeing Clio
herself in the act of changing her robes.

The Ireland in which the book opens is a wholly and com-

pletely different Ireland from the Ireland in which it ends. My
task was made easier because I grew up in a somewhat similar
setting to Farrell's own. The outlook in a Co. Dublin Protestant
rectory did not differ so radically from that of well-to-do business
in a Carlow home. Both presupposed comfort. Both presupposed
a stable world. What Farrell's book does is to show that stable
world falling into disintegration at the dictate of fate. He reveals
it faithfully in its various social strata, and then we see, as it were,
the earth's crust bend and crumple under the stress of some vast
internal upheaval, and a new and quite different geological
formation makes its appearance. Only at the end of the book is
there a hint on the part of Dan, the friendly old bargee, that
human types survive, even when regimes alter. His words to
Martin on that occasion are like a less bitter paraphrase of
Yeats's quatrain:

'THE GREAT DAY

Hurrah for revolution and more cannon-shot!
A beggar upon horseback lashes a beggar upon foot,
Hurrah for revolution and cannon come again!
The beggars have changed places but the lash goes on.'

The panorama is not just one of Ireland in process of political
rebirth. We see a boy passing through the various stages of acute
greensickness, turning his back on the ardent idealism of his
childhood, and experiencing all the characteristic reactions of
resentful youth, brought up in the over-watchful and morbidly
solicitous atmosphere of extreme Catholic puritanism, when he
enters his period of *Sturm und Drang*. It is not a new theme. Joyce
has exploited it to the full. And in *Twice Round the Black Church*
the poet Austin Clarke has made a directly autobiographical and
even more telling use of it. In each case the priesthood are blamed
for terrorizing adolescence with threats which, to some considerable extent, emanated quite as much from current medical
opinion—opinion since repudiated—as from the theologians. But
the theologians endorsed and strengthened the argument with all
the terrors of hell, and it is upon the theologians that the rage of
the writers has subsequently fallen.

Farrell, however, stands a long way from the savage unmiti-
gated bitterness of Joyce, or the restrained but equally lethal

irony of Austin Clarke. For one thing his hero always remains
dimly aware that what redeems life are its moments of lyrical
apprehension. And though his hero becomes a militant atheist,
the author himself seems conscious that in a different setting—
say the Catholicism of Bavaria or Austria and not of Jansenist
Ireland—Martin Matthew Reilly might never have reached that
pitch of embittered disillusion which, after a single unfortunate episode, added to a couple of deeply felt bereavements, led to the complete overthrow of his faith. Farrell never overstates his case against
Mother Church, only against certain of her human instruments.

Martin repudiates his Catholicism, but, like Farrell himself, he
remains in some measure Catholic in spite of the repudiation.
Farrell was very far from being a militant secularist. He had
lapsed from grace. He had wandered about Europe with *une
chère amie* as temperamental as himself; and he had presently
married a devoted wife of Protestant origin, thus putting himself
outside the fold, for she had been married before and had divorced
her first husband. He was alienated, therefore, from the Church
which had meant so much to him as a child. But, like Ruskin, he
refused to regard himself as separated completely from it. Like
Ruskin he would protest: 'I *am* a Catholic. They may say what
they like, but I am a Catholic.' He did not go to Mass; he would
get excited about the arrogance of a tyrannical priesthood and the
iniquities of over-solicitous Catholic teaching upon the tender
conscience of the young, as most lapsed Irish Catholics do.
Nevertheless he was convinced that, basically, the values of
Mother Church were wiser and sounder—and truer—than all
the glib, psychological jargon with which men have tried to fill
the vacuum created by their rejection. Such nonsense angered
him, and the young Catholic boy would suddenly emerge, from
behind the anti-cleric and the rebel, to reaffirm that life is something more than the empty and pretentious generalizations of
minds that flatter themselves that they are being up-to-date.

3

For the last four years of his life Farrell was a sick man. During
the last two he was—probably in his own eyes, certainly in those
of his friends—a dying man. It was his custom to remain in bed

until about six o'clock in the evening, then to dress, make his slow and painful way downstairs, and after dinner to sit for perhaps an hour or two in front of his drawing-room fire. He was in the grip—the metaphor is all too appropriate—of arterio-sclerosis. His leg gave him great trouble and it was distressing to witness his anguished progress, leaning on a stick, across the room to his armchair, or to see him later in the evening take out a little spray, which the doctor had suggested he should use, and blow a stream of air into his nostrils to increase his intake of oxygen.

When one visited him upstairs in his room the coverlet of his bed would be strewn with books. Along one whole wall were shelves with the authors—French and English and a few Italian—which he loved so well. He was not a savant, he was just an enthusiast; one of those readers of books whom every author secretly hopes for, whose soul can be set aflame by words. As time went on he read less, but it was still always possible to kindle the essential man, if one broached the right conversational topic. An idea—one that he wished to endorse or one that he hated fiercely—would suddenly evoke all the old, vehement Michael Farrell, and one would see him coming to life before one's eyes. It is characteristic that—not having been outside the house for nearly two years—he got up one morning, dressed, and had himself driven to the polling booth to register his vote at the general election.

Not that he had any enthusiasm for politics as such. If his novel indicates a violent revulsion from religion, the corresponding disillusion with politics is only less because Martin's faith in that direction has always been less. His patriotism is an imaginative flame in early boyhood. But from the moment that he becomes associated with the movement he is on the way to becoming a cynic where its activities are concerned. In fact what gives a touch of the universal to Farrell's book—and that he realized this himself is implicit in his using as one of his two mottoes for his book Falstaff's phrase 'Tush man! mortal men, mortal men'—is that it reveals how subjective and self-centred the young intellectual, in every country and during any epoch, is, and remains, even in the throes of a political enthusiasm. Too clear-sighted and too intelligent to be taken in any longer by slogans that are already wearing thin; and too much of an egotist to be capable of complete self-donation, he is the least likely of all men to submit patiently to the ordeal of a Procrustean bed, where he must either allow his boyish ideals to be chopped off or his faith in the wisdom and integrity of those with whom he works to be stretched almost to breaking point. For what the intellectual is predominantly interested in is himself, and the setting in which he feels he could do himself full justice. He is not an altruist, even though, like Martin, he may strive hard in his more sentimental moments to convince himself that he is one and feel willing to immolate himself upon an altar of self-sacrifice. His judgements, which were once illimitably hopeful, tend to become more and more negative, as he finds himself up against the rough texture of life. The whole trend of a mind like this is negative and critical. It inclines equally to self-regard and to self-pity.

Such an individual does not escape from himself, even when he is in love. Martin's love for Millie is not disinterested in the way in which hers for him is. It is still irresponsible. She is part of his idea of self-fulfilment. But he must first fulfil his concept of himself as patriot-hero. Millie is already a woman, but her lover has not yet attained the stature of a man. Indeed the book is really a chart of his progress from fervent childhood, through unhappy adolescence, towards that manhood which should be his.

In one sense Martin Matthew Reilly is a typical figure of the modern world. He is plunged into a sequence of events which are far too big for him to cope with, and his whole nature resents the pressure, brought to bear upon him by circumstance, to become an effective cog in a machine which secretly he has come to despise. It is unlikely that he would have been happy in any setting; but he might have flourished better in a static world than in one where all values, philosophic, political and psychological, were in process of being overthrown.

The non-Irish reader should know a little of the historical background. In 1913 Ireland—despite the so-called Curragh mutiny, when certain officers stationed in Ireland let it be known that they would resign their commissions sooner than lead their troops against the intractable minority in Ulster who refused to contemplate acceptance of Asquith's Home Rule Bill—did seem on the point of coming to terms at last with her traditional enemy, England. When war broke out the Home Rule Act, though placed upon the Statute Book, was in effect suspended, and thousands of young Irishmen enlisted to fight against Germany, confident that when the war was over Ireland would be placed in control of her own affairs. The 1916 rebellion—the work of a small and, at first, unpopular minority—changed all that. Anglophiles used it to support their argument that the Irish were never to be trusted. Anglophobes made the fullest possible propaganda use of the subsequent, and highly unfortunate, series of military executions.

Out of those executions was born a new and entirely different spirit. An Irish officer in the British Army could get up—as I have seen happen—in a Command Depot Mess on Christmas night and announce that as soon as the war was over he would be found still fighting, but against the English then, and not for them. Even before the war ended spasmodic military action was being taken and a most complex organization was being built up to direct operations against the forces of England. The Irish discovered and perfected a technique of guerilla warfare and national resistance which the Spaniards who opposed Napoleon might well have envied. They blazed a trail subsequently followed with equal success by Israel, Cyprus and Algiers.

In one sense it was war. In it figured ambush, barracks siege and arms raid. But as well there came into being recognized or unrecognized policies of assassination and counter-assassination, reprisal and counter-reprisal, spy and counter-spy. In an evil moment the English government decided to try using terrorism to repress terrorism, intimidation to counter intimidation. Two forces, the Black and Tans and the Auxiliaries, were specially recruited in England, and these showed none of the moderation shown by the regular army. Though they may not have been official terrorists, they could be as rough in their methods as the trained commandos of the Second World War. But the method defeated its own end, since not merely did it make three rebels where there had been one before, but there were far too many Englishmen who themselves disapproved it and were quite willing to protest loudly and consistently in certain English newspapers. There were atrocities on both sides but the conscience of the more liberal Englishman was with Ireland in her struggle. Against this background we see the sensitive soul of Martin Matthew—in a context that unfortunately for it happened to be both real and melodramatic—swept on its way like so much flotsam before the storm.

I

White Blackbird

I

In the dining-cum-living-room of her home in the town of Glenkilly, Ireland, Mrs. John Reilly, before settling down to her winter-evening avocations, counted the number of 'Valeta' waltzes on the programmes of two approaching balls, the Farmers' Ball and the Cricket Ball, and studied the list of her chosen helpers at her 'Fancy Stall' in the forthcoming town bazaar.

Humming a waltz air, she looked hesitantly from the very tall and bright mending-basket to the bureau which held her husband's ledgers and account books. During her bridal days, eighteen years earlier, she had taken lessons in book-keeping because she would trust neither shop-girl, shop-boy nor clerk to give the care she herself would give to the accounts of the two shops which were to keep her family in the comfort and respect due to the household of a Glenkilly 'citizen merchant'. Once, at a Home Rule meeting in the Town Hall, Mr. John Redmond, successor of Parnell himself, had made a graceful gesture towards the platform where Mr. John Reilly sat with other townsmen and had said, 'Supported as I am by the citizen merchants of this ancient borough . . .'

Those words, and one poem on the death of Parnell, had never been forgotten by Mrs. Reilly. Whenever a certain Reilly sister-in-law tried to indicate that a shopkeeper was socially below a solicitor, farmer, priest, doctor or 'professor' in a secondary boarding-school, there would come into Mrs. John Reilly's handsome face a flush that was at once shy and embattled, and she would lead the talk to the doings of Mr. Redmond and then to the graceful gesture of his hand and 'the citizen merchants of this ancient borough'.

As she hesitated between ledgers and tall basket, she was being watched by her nephew, Martin Matthew Reilly, who at long

29

last had lifted his head from the diary which his Grandmother
Reilly had sent to him for the approaching Christmas. He murmured, 'Aunt Eileen . . .' and stopped, postponing yet once again
the request to be wakened to hear the Christmas waits. In all his
years, now nearing twelve, he had only once heard the waits and
he had often revived in himself the spell of that morning—the
voices and footsteps in the dark street far below his window; the
mystery of the *Adeste Fideles*, coming to him in the cold dawn
through the wail of melodeons; the strange and intimate saluta-
tion which followed; the footsteps fading away into silence along
the icy footpaths.

Mrs. Reilly plunged her arm into the lucky-dip of the basket.
When she saw that what she fished up was a pair of clink-creaking
stays she blushed, and was about to put them back out of sight,
but she hesitated, glanced towards Martin, decided that he was
too absorbed in his diary to notice, and called secretively to the
second of her four children, a girl of sixteen.

'Come here, Rosaleen, and take off your house-pinafore till I
see what can be done with your old stays.'

Rosaleen, smoothing her mouse-coloured plaits, said appealingly: 'Mother, I've a lot of Christmas cards to send yet. Can't we
do it another time, even though my new ones are too tightly laced?'

'Pshaw!' said Mrs. Reilly with maternal boredom. 'If you'd
been a girl when I was . . . !'

As Rosaleen put away her Christmas cards—most of them
'pious cards'—the pointed, pale face of her fourteen-year-old
sister, Bridget, came over her shoulder, and Bridget's black hair
flowed across Rosaleen's mousy plaits. Having made a moue at
a card which held a picture of Blessed Catherine of Siena framed in
holly, she began pirouetting around the room, her skirt, pinafore and
petticoats making black-and-white switchbacks below her knees.

Mrs. Reilly, tugging at the stays, strained widely around
Rosaleen's black school-frock, and glancing to see if Martin was
noticing, said through pins: 'Bridget, you oughtn't to practise
your solo dancing until Advent is over. Even real dancing is not
proper in Lent or Advent! Can't you read Patrick a story?'

Bridget continued to pirouette, but when Mrs. Reilly said
quietly, 'Bridget, do you want us to go upstairs to the cane?' she
stopped, and Martin, who had heard, shut his diary and left the
room, because only once had Aunt Eileen ever called him to her

to punish him and even that once she had not done it. She had
suddenly shot at him the queer look he knew fairly well and had
walked straight away from him, leaving him very relieved. But
she had left him sad also, because he knew that she would have
chastised him, as Aunt Mary did at Moydelgan, had she not
thought him a boy already sufficiently punished by some un-
named penalty. So now, to shake off the reminder of this
Glenkilly difference between himself and all 'ordinary' boys and
girls, he went towards the kitchen.

Pretty Mary Ellen was not there, only the ungainly Josie, her
feet stretched to the range, her cap streamers hanging stiffly
white along her flat back, a leg of a goose in her big hand, and her
bony raw face and red head bent to *Ireland's Own* spread open on
her great white lap. She shook the red head and white streamers
at him, welcoming him with 'Hello, me hearty' and a wink. As
he winked back at her, he thought that she was going to be
'merry' again this Christmas because the wild look was in her eye
and her long horse-face was redder than ever.

He sat over the range with her, explaining to her the longer
words in *Ireland's Own*, taking bites at her cold leg of goose and
telling her of Big Mick Lannigan's triumphs at football, for Big
Mick Lannigan called Josie his 'best pal', and although he had
courted through the years with all the pretty girls for miles
around, he had never married, and good-natured people would
say: 'Maybe in the end it's poor Josie he'll marry! And wouldn't
it be a lovely and grand thing if he did!'

When Josie began ironing he looked long at his grandmother's
high, pointed letters in the front of his diary: *To Martin, my
warmest and dearest grandson. From Lullacreen. For Christmas 1910.*

On the next page he had written: *Martin Matthew Reilly,
5, River Street, Glenkilly, Leinster, Ireland, Europe, The World, The
Universe, under God.* Beneath this he had written:

*I have Matthew from my father, that was his name, he was Aunt
Mary's favourite brother. I don't know where I have Martin from. My
father and mother are dead. I never saw them. One of my ancestors was
Colonel Reilly who sailed away to fight for France with Sarsfield and The
Wild Geese after the Treaty of Limerick which the English broke. He died
at Blenheim, fighting for France, King Louis, the Fleur-de-Lis and Ireland.
God Save Ireland.*

There followed a description of the river during a summer shower by evening, and then:

The Protestant poet in Dublin who wrote the new song that is Aunt Mary's latest favourite must know about a river because the last verse ends with:

> *She bid me take life easy as the grass grows on the weirs*
> *But I was young and foolish and now am full of tears!*

and grass does grow on weirs, lovely bending grass, like Gertrude's hair when she is brushing it before plaits. Nota Bene:—Niave McDowell's does not bend so much.

Under the heading 'Favourite Sports' he had written:

Running—1 butter-dish with rolling top, 2nd prize. Handball—1 decanter; Aunt Eileen keeps her Wincarnis in it. Rugby—touch judge for the Glenkilly Boys' team; my cousin James Edward is the Captain; he is 17 and a bit. Cricket and Racquets—beginning. Rowing—real racing rowing, not just ordinary rowing—not yet.

The extracts ended with a description of the monument, 'Hibernia in Tears beside her Harp'. All of his memories flowed back to the marble runnels of Hibernia's carved robes as she bent in sorrow over her harp, and now, while he brooded over the words, the pages of the diary fluttered lightly back and he saw again: *To Martin, my warmest and dearest grandson.*

On St. Stephen's Day his grandmother would be standing straight and quiet in the doorway of Lullacreen to welcome her twenty-five grandchildren from half the counties of Leinster. And, as always when he thought of her, he thought also of his Aunt Mary, so pretty, so gay, so loving, and he was moved to the need for expression. So, underneath his grandmother's high letters, he wrote the motto: *To the Glory of God and the Honour of Ireland.*

Once, during one of the St. Stephen's Day reunions at Lullacreen, in the afternoon when all the younger children were made to rest, his grandmother had put him lying down in her own four-poster curtained bed and had wrapped her shawl about him.

She had sat at his head and through the gap in the curtains the
gloom of the room had come in to the brown darkness around the
bedposts. Leaning her head against the bedpost, she had said,
'Your father, Mat, used to run to me across the lawn, with one
shoulder up, exactly the way you did this morning.'

He had tried to stare up at her face in the cold gloom. 'Am I
like him?'

'Sometimes, terribly like him.'

Quite easily he had said, 'Am I like my mother?'

'I think you must be sometimes. I never saw her.'

He thought she was crying a little; he could hear her, her head
against the dark post away above him.

'I know she was very pretty; and she must have loved Mat more
than . . . above everything.' He had lain taut in the soft gloom,
feeling her hand on his hair. She had begun to sing, a thin
sound . . .

> '. . . though Autumn leaves may droop and die
>   A bud of Spring are you.
> Sing O, hush-a-bye, low, low. . . .'

Her cold hand stroked his head all the time: the words went
away towards the canopy:

> 'And holy Mary, pitying us
>   In Heaven for Grace does sue . . .'

The song had died in her mouth and instead she had muttered:
'Himself and Mary, the two best of them all. Poor Mat.'

Her head had come down and her cold, wet cheek had lain on
his. He had waited motionless, afraid that a movement might
make her think that her wet cheek distressed him. When he
wakened she had gone and the gloom of the room had changed to
blackness. Beneath him he could hear the shouts and laughter of
the other children in the dining-room and hall. He had sat up in
the bed, going over the scene in his mind, until his Aunt Mary
had called him down to the crowded fun of an early and
enormous tea.

Sitting on the low window-seat in the living-room, Martin

cheerfully reminded himself that Gertrude Jamieson and Niave McDowell would be home from their schools tomorrow for the holidays. At the same time he admiringly watched his eldest cousin, James Edward, reading his American business books at the table. Ah, James Edward was an inimitable boy. During one of the times when money was 'scarcer even than usual' he had avoided being sent away to school by proposing a much cheaper course of studies, so that now, in unschoolmastered dignity, he took Spanish lessons from a man who lived in a caravan and said he was related to King Alfonso, and pored over books having pictures of a well-dressed man in a large circle labelled 'Executive', with lines radiating from him to other men in smaller circles labelled 'Advertising', 'Distribution' and 'Sales'. James Reilly would say: 'Wait till I'm twenty-one! Then you'll all see Papa's business sit up!' He would say: 'Wait till Home Rule is law, then we'll make this a great country. We'll soon deal with job-wangling County Councillors like that Tim Corbin fellow over in Ballow!' James, secretary of the boys' cricket team and vice-captain of the mixed hockey team (the captain had to be a girl, for chivalry's sake), had got the Protestant boys and girls in both teams to write to the *Glenkilly Liberator* saying: *On mature consideration, we hereby support the demand that the anti-Catholic references in the Coronation oath be removed before the approaching Coronation of King George V.* The paper had published the letter but had left out the word 'mature'.

Martin was aware that none would call him 'funny' in James Edward's hearing, nor passers-by smile amusedly if James were with him, but well aware also that James was more than shy of him, that James was afraid of him and never knew what to say to him.

He turned to watch his tall Uncle John, for Mr. Reilly was about to light his pipe-spill, and for several moments the paper spill would be throwing shadows along the downcast face of the 'Queen of Heaven, Protectress of this House'. When flame and shadows had ended, he leaned back against the dark green woodwork and began to sing for himself one of Josie's songs. He had heard it called 'a bad song', but his Aunt Mary had not reproved him for singing it in Moydelgan, so now, shaking his head in imitation of Josie's aggressive independence, he sang softly:

'I must go home tonight,
I must go home tonight,
I don't care if it's snowing—or blowing—I'm going!
I only got married this morning,
And it fills me with delight . . .'

Mr. Reilly's handsome face flushed and he glanced quickly
at Mrs. Reilly, but she was gulping to stop herself laughing as she
glanced secretively at Martin singing to himself and shaking his
head truculently just like Josie. Across the table, James Edward
smiled at his mother as he too glanced at Martin's performance.

'I'll stop out as long as you like next week . . .'

and with a bang of his hand, like Josie's banging, he finished:

'But I must go home tonight!'

Mrs. Reilly looked up and saw her husband's shocked, angry
face. With a sudden blush she sharply ordered Martin never
again to sing that song. And then James Edward, who had
looked at his father, blushed and there was a silence until Mr.
Reilly said angrily:
'You pick up far too many bad, vulgar things, young man.
That's from always having your big girl's eyes poring over a book.
Too much book means too little God! And it is what gives you
your pale face, too.'
Mrs. Reilly said quickly: 'Martin, go and get out your week-
day boots for the cobbler to call for. Go immediately now, child.'
As Martin rose to obey, his uncle muttered: 'Books and
piano-playing all day. That's what sent Mat to——' but he
stopped himself even before Mrs. Reilly had hushed him with
her warning, 'John! John!' and a furtive glance. Mr. Reilly shot
his own queer glance at Martin, who was near to the door, when
James Edward suddenly stood up and said in a loud, strained
voice:
'Books, books, books! Why shouldn't Martin have his own
ways? You wouldn't dare to say a word in Moydelgan about the
hundreds of books. You know the way Aunt Mary would . . .'
He ran to the door, turned and said bitterly: 'All you Sodality
men, you're all the same. The Holy Family! Holy Ireland!' and
he dashed up the stairs to his room.

Mr. Reilly stood with grey face and heaving shoulders. 'The young pup!' he gasped, 'the infernal young pup!' and he made for the door. But Mrs. Reilly sprang to her feet, a stocking dangling from around her fist and her thin gold watch-chain swinging out from her neck. It was his father, Mat, who had given her that lovely chain and watch, Martin knew. She stood up straight between her husband and the door and said: 'No, John! Never!' Her face was white but her voice was quiet, although it trembled. She stood unyieldingly and, catching his wrists, swayed against him before the open door. Mr. Reilly made a lurch and Mrs. Reilly nearly overbalanced, but all the time she held on to his wrists and soon she forced herself up straight again.

'Never, John!'

She had little breath for words, but with words and pushing she held him back.

'It's myself who's always done their punishings and you'll not take it into your hands now. That's my place!'

'He's getting too big for you now,' said Mr. Reilly, still pushing somewhat.

'Pshaw!' she said.

The swaying stopped, but she still held his arms out in the form of a cross.

'Now, John, go off to the Cathedral and ask God to forgive you your anger. Then go on to the Fitzgeralds' or your club and have a game of solo.'

'I wasn't going to play cards tonight.' His arms were still held stiffly out.

'Well, billiards, then!' she said impatiently, as if billiards and solo were one to her with marbles and hoops.

She coaxed him back to a chair and, holding his head in the crook of her arm, she looked down at him and said, 'My poor John.' After a long time he lifted his greying brown head and turned his handsome face towards her.

She said nothing, merely stroked the greying parts of his hair beside the temples.

'You're a good woman, Eileen. I don't deserve you.'

'Ah, stop it!' She laughed and a blush brought colour back into her face.

'You're as pretty as ever you were. And that's saying you're a belle still. Do you remember old Kelly?'

'Old Hunting Kelly? Captain Kelly? At the Regatta Ball? Will I ever forget him! "Young John Reilly will get you," he said to me after that last waltz. "Young Reilly will get you, me upright bright thrush." ' She looked half smilingly into space. 'And you did.'

'Aye, but it was a long job. Do you never regret it?'

She looked away over his head and paused a moment before saying very brightly: 'No, John. Never.'

They were quiet then for a while.

At last he said uncertainly: 'I think I'll go now and ask God to look down on us all. It's a queer world.'

'Yes, do that. Then go to your club. Yes, it's a queer world indeed.'

Mr. Reilly went away and James Edward came downstairs and sat in silent, unhappy defiance at the table until his mother, closing the big ledgers, said: 'James, I told Josie to cook some mashed carrots for you. You said every second night.'

James had read in his athletic papers that mashed carrots were good for the muscles if taken at night. Martin watched him eating this extraordinary dish, marvelling at his enjoyment of it. Then, turning, he saw his Aunt Eileen's fingers kneading the two brands of tobacco in the proportions which his Uncle John best liked. That done, she put on her glasses, and bent her pretty face, her dignified head, to the sewing of the hair fillets on which the girls had set their hearts for the McDowells' Christmas party. Her needle flashed in the steady beam of the lamp. As she sewed, her lips worked silently in one of her secret calculations of ways and means, how to provide this for one person in the house and that for another, and how to do both without offending the opinions of a third, and without making the Bank Manager think they were being too extravagant so that he wrote again about the overdraft. Martin had long ago observed that this working of the lips was a prelude to some expenditure, or the granting of a heart's desire. Later tonight she would have a head-ache and would ask him to comb out her hair and sing to her. Once or twice, she raised her eyes to glance at the bent head of her eldest son as he ate his 'athletic dish', while on the chimney-piece her husband's tobaccos, nicely mixed to his fad, awaited his return.

It was the night before Christmas Eve and Martin's last opportunity to ask to be wakened for the waits. Deciding to postpone the request until his bedtime, he watched Josie who, by pretending to talk to herself as she laid things on the sideboard, was managing to let the room know what she thought of 'them Gaelic brats in Dublin' who had sent down 'a whipster with a raincoat and attachy case'—she laughed her harsh horse-laugh—'to stop the lads from playing rugby football because it's English'. All knew that by 'the lads' she meant one lad— Big Mick Lannigan. The red head tossed arrogantly. 'Dublin Jackeens! Irish-Ireland, how are ye! It's cock them up, I would.'

Martin, seeking Mary Ellen, was about to go to the kitchen when James Edward came in, followed by Patrick, nine years old, plump and authoritative.

'Papa holds up everybody, keeping us waiting for the Rosary,' said James. 'You said, Mother, that I could go early to my committee. After all, the chairman ought to be in time.'

He looked resentfully at the clock. Glancing at the other fretful faces, Mrs. Reilly said: 'I love those new voice-parts for "Oft in the Stilly Night". Start it for us, Martin. Get the music parts, too, and open the piano.'

So they opened the tinny, old-fashioned 'sideboard piano'; because 'the piano', on Mrs. Reilly's tongue, never meant the piano in the parlour, which was 'the new piano', played only for parties, visitors and on Sundays and Holy Days of Obligation. Their voices had begun to mingle and re-flow in the glee and Mrs. Reilly's head begun to nod the rhythm over the big ledgers when Mr. Reilly entered, saying: 'I'm afraid the concert must wait until after the Rosary. Have Josie and Mary Ellen in.'

'Anastasia Josephine's here, mum.' The harsh voice crackled from the doorway and there stood Josie with the flamboyant drinking-look in her red eye. 'And Mary Ellen's not back from Confession yet,' she declared triumphantly.

'Then we'll have to wait for her. She can't be long now.'

'Say the Rosary now, John. Mary Ellen can't say prayers in two places at once. God will listen to her from the Cathedral just as well as from here.'

'The Rosary's not the same thing if there's anyone missing from it.'

Mrs. Reilly nodded her agreement to this; but she said, 'Kneel down, children.' All obeyed her—none ever dared to disobey her —and from the door there came a loud, challenging flop, made by Josie kneeling down in an aggressive way.

While the Five Glorious Mysteries were said, Josie kept shaking her big head truculently and every now and then she uttered one of the responses in a shout, and gave her chair a bang of her hand. The girls giggled at that, and James Edward looked aloofly down his nose.

Putting away his knee-mat, Mr. Reilly said cheerfully: 'I suppose you all think the heaviest work of the day is over now. It's extraordinary how people will grudge giving ten minutes to God Almighty! Mark my words, you'll all find one day that God and your religion are the only things of any value in this world.'

'Now, Bridget, don't smile,' said Mrs. Reilly. 'You see Martin doesn't smile—he knows his Uncle John is right.'

Martin, who had been watching the shadows and light on the downcast face of the Queen of Heaven, came to himself with a start and heard his cousin laugh and say: 'Oh, Martin! Martin was just mooning away at something. When he blushes like that now, he's like a girl, or half a one, anyway!'

'It's lose himself he will one day,' said Mr. Reilly. 'Like a little calf lost at a fair. A half-black, half-white calf.'

Mrs. Reilly said sharply: 'John! Your Vincent de Paul meeting! All the poor people waiting for their coal tickets for Christmas.'

'Yes, I'd better go. I can't have even a small joke without people taking it in bad part.' Out in the hall he recovered his good humour and could be heard humming cheerfully as he put on his outdoor things.

Mrs. Reilly went out to him and could be heard speaking to him in low and expostulating tones, after which the street door banged and Mrs. Reilly came in, sat down to her sewing, gave Martin an unhappy, sideways glance and said crossly: 'Rosaleen! Bridget! Sit up straight.'

Martin leaned his head against the dark green woodwork and above him he could just hear the soft winter rain falling against the window. Its sound reminded him of his grandmother's soft crying coming down from the brown darkness of the bedpost in Lullacreen. Going to the hall, he took from his topcoat the electric torch Aunt Mary had sent to him from Moydelgan, and then stepped quickly into the parlour. The only light was that of the fire, lit in case Christmas-time callers came; and through the lace curtain he could see the rain speckled with street-light which spread weakly into the room until the plush furniture carried it into darkness. On the chimney-piece the clock ticked gently and from the street came the muted sounds of footsteps and the shadow of an umbrella travelling monstrously across the ceiling. He sat in the plush rocking-chair, rocking himself, flashing the light of Aunt Mary's torch upon his diary, and watching the moving line of darkness which he made upon the pale glimmer of the carpet.

Hearing the hall door open, he stepped out of the room and saw his uncle standing in the open hall door. Coming down the hall, Mr. Reilly leaned his tall, thin frame down to Martin.

'Here's something to buy sweets. I don't mean to make you to cry.'

'But I didn't cry, Uncle John.'

'Ah, well, I never know. What'll we do with you at all, with your queer ways, always hanging over a book, and your secretizing with lassies twice your age: Niave, nearly seventeen, and Mr. Jamieson's girl, a few months older still, and a Protestant too! Sure the men in the club often go to the window when word goes about that you're coming down the street with one or both of them.'

Martin said nothing; he was thinking how Aunt Eileen, without one spoken word, had let him see that she relied on him not to let news of the secret 'mixed bathing' come to Uncle John. One day, those Sodality men at the club window might blurt out some remark about bathing costumes seen in their boat.

'Anyway,' added Mr. Reilly apologetically, 'you shouldn't mind a joke.'

He stared helplessly down at his nephew and Martin stared helplessly up at him. Mr. Reilly tapped hesitatingly on the floor with his umbrella, glanced evasively once more at Martin and remarked, 'Your Aunt Eileen nearly killed herself nursing you years ago when you had diphtheria—did you know that?'

Martin nodded miserably.

'Your poor father . . .' Mr. Reilly looked away and sighed. 'Well, if it hadn't been for him the people at home might never have agreed to the match between your Aunt Eileen and me—there's that to it, anyhow.'

They stared at one another for a while until Mr. Reilly said: 'What can we do? What is it you're wanting at all? Come on now. Give up those old books and your chit-chatting with a pack of girls. When I was a boy I wasn't a bit like that.'

His grey eyes were worried and they looked with sadness into Martin's dark eyes.

'If there's anything you want, can't you ask your aunt for it? Haven't we always looked after you as well as we could?'

'Yes, Uncle John. Thanks for the money for the sweets.'

'Ah, you beat me altogether!' said Uncle John, and turned towards the door. When he reached it he looked back at Martin, while behind him the rain flickered. They stared at one another down the length of the hall until Mr. Reilly opened his umbrella.

'Well, good luck to you, anyway,' he said, and banged the door. His steps faded into the soft beating of the rain, and for a little while Martin stood gazing at the closed door.

From the dim passage to the kitchen Martin looked in on the brightness where Josie was kicking the oven door shut with her foot and bustling cockily in and out of the place where the three plum puddings hung near the turkeys and geese which had come from Grandmother in Lullacreen and Aunt Mary in Moydelgan. The ducks and geese from the aunts in Clonglass and Meeldore and the other farms were farther away with some barm bracks, all put aside for Mary Ellen's and Josie's families and the St. Vincent de Paul Christmas treat for the poor.

When Josie turned her head towards the kitchen door, her red face almost blanched and she stopped stiffly in her tracks with a frightened mutter of, 'Mother of Christ!' Sinking weakly into a chair, she said: 'Oh, it's only you! Come in out of the dark, for God's sake, me hearty.' She stared at him. 'What were ye doing standing out there like a . . . like a . . . it's not right to say what! Yer big white collar! Yer white face! And yer eyes!' and suddenly she pulled him to her. 'God, the night I turned to go up the stairs and there ye were in yer nightshift looking down through the banisters—I nearly dropped!'

'I was only looking to see if Mary Ellen was about.'

'Well, ye looked as if ye were waiting for a . . .' She shivered, shut the door and said: 'Here! Would you like a bit of toasted brack?'

He sat in the wicker chair by the range while Josie, crouching beside him with the toasting-fork, winked up at him and shook her head. He winked back at her and shook his head. She began to move about on her big feet, sweeping the floor, although it was quite clean, and, as she swept, she glanced at Martin where he

sat munching his brack and swinging his legs to the red bars, and
she crooned to herself:

> 'If those lips could only speak,
> If those eyes could only see,
> If those bee-yu-tiful golden tresses
> Were there in reality,
> Could I take your hand in mind
> As I did when you took my name . . .'

The plates gleamed, the alarm clock ticked and Josie's harsh
voice sang:

> 'But it's only a beautiful picture
> In a beautiful golden frame.'

Putting the twig broom away, she came to hunch herself before
the fire, and the lamp on the wall threw soft lights into her coarse
red hair.
Looking into the fire, she said, 'If I told ye something, Master
Martin, ye'd never let it past yer lips, would ye?'
He shook his head.
'No, begob, ye wouldn't! Ye're the sowl of honour for the size
of ye.'
He thought that she wanted to tell him something about Big
Mick Lannigan. She said at last: 'Well, do ye know what I'd like
now? I'd like to be sweeping me own kitchen and me own son
ating hot buttered brack by the fire.'
She looked up from the red glow. 'Tell us, would ye give us a kiss?'
'All right,' he said. Taking his head between her hands, she
kissed him and he wondered that raw, bony Josie could have such
soft lips. Her head came down to his shoulder and he heard
something like a sob.
'It's a quare world,' she said bitterly. 'God, it's a quare world!'
When Mary Ellen came in, Josie put on a very cheerful air.
'Wait till ye see the grand letters we'll all be getting from the lad
when he goes to school, Mary Ellen.' She did a few steps of her
jig. 'Begob, Mary Ellen, they'll be half scarifying him for writing
to so many women.' She tucked up her skirts and did a few more
steps of her jig. Then, pointing to herself: 'Bedad, they'd get a

drop if they saw the sweetheart he was writing to.' And then, a
grimmer thought creeping in upon her gaiety: 'A fat lot they'd
care about me. But they'd object to you all right, Mary Ellen.
You're pretty——'

Into the kitchen came a rat-tat-tat from the hall door, the
ringing bell jangled and Josie, drawing an arm angrily across her
eyes, said, 'If that's another Christmas post tonight it'll be the
seventh today!'

When he went back to the living-room his Aunt Eileen looked
up from the ledgers. 'Ah, Martin. I have a headache. James will
be able to do the rest of the books for me and Rosaleen will help
him, won't you, Rosaleen, child?'

Martin fetched her hair-comb and drew out the hair-pins, enjoying the heavy roll of the tresses through his fingers and rubbing
her temples gently. 'That's grand, Martin. Sing a song for us.'

'Will I sing Aunt Mary's new favourite?'

'Yes, sing that.'

Patrick squatted by the fire. 'Sing,' he said authoritatively,
lifting his fat chin; and Rosaleen, tugging at her stocking beneath
her wide skirts, said, 'Yes, sing.'

A silence of waiting fell on the room as Martin held the comb
poised above his aunt's unbound hair. Josie, who had brought in
the letters, turned at the door to wait. The steady light shone on
dark green wood, on white pinafores, on black and mousy hair,
and the soft rain touched the window-panes behind the blinds. . . .

'Down by the salley gardens, my love and I did meet.
She passed the salley gardens with little snow-white
feet . . .'

He could hear the words going effortlessly from him over the
thick folds of hair, as his boyish treble rose, the long notes
seeming to be drawn from him by their own flow of feeling.

'She bid me take life easy as the leaves grow on the tree,
But I was young and foolish, and with her would not
agree.'

Out of the contented silence, there came softly from the door,
'Ah, lovely, Master Martin!'

All turned, and there at last, in the hall beyond Josie and the open door, was Mary Ellen, her pretty face smiling beneath the cornflowers on her hat as the lamplight caught her rosy cheeks. Martin waved to her, his hand beside his face. She lifted her hand to her face and replied with a tiny wave.

Closing the door, she went with Josie, and Martin called excitedly, 'Oh, I have an idea!' and leaping on to a chair he danced with excitement. 'Instead of a separate present from each of us, let's combine and give Mary Ellen a hand-bag with a glass inside the flap and with a hole for eau-de-Cologne like Aunt Mary's, if we can subscribe enough! I'll give one-and-sixpence,' he declared magnificently, and in his enthusiasm he blurted out, 'You see, this Christmas I got a half-sovereign from Aunt Mary!'

The girls looked at him with respect, but Mrs. Reilly said sharply, 'You never told me!'

'You didn't ask me, Aunt Eileen.'

'Well, you should have told me. I always let you spend whatever you get for Christmas and your birthday. But a half-sovereign is outrageous. A terrible amount. It must go into your Post Office book! Go and get it for me!'

He went gloomily upstairs and unlocked the enormous old mahogany tea-caddy which was his store-house. The caddy, pride of his eyes, stood on a carved central leg of great magnificence and had several compartments where he kept photographs and letters, conquering chestnuts, sea-shells from Tramore, hand-balls, Rossetti and Constable prints cut from illustrated supplements, and the many drafts of the speech he would one day deliver to the restored Irish Parliament in the Old Houses in College Green, each draft ending with, 'Gentlemen, I have done!'

The cold gleam of the coin between his fingers enchanted him even in the sadness of failure, of knowing now that he had hesitated too long over his plans which had included the purchasing of extra New Year presents for all of his friends, from Mary Ellen up to Gertrude; and for himself a new dictionary with 'Famous Characters' and 'Proper Names' and 'Great Quotations'; and, lastly, a specially good pair of football boots to be held ready for the day when James Edward might summon him to save the boys' rugby team from defeat in an important match. Going gloomily downstairs, he met Patrick, who had been commanded to bed.

'If you're awake for the waits, call me,' said Patrick in his authoritative manner.

'Oh, yes, I will. It's lovely, isn't it?—the morning, and the voices, and the waiting for them to go away.'

'I don't know,' said Patrick doubtfully. 'I only want to best Paddy O'Gorman. He says he's the only fellow in my school who ever hears the waits!'

'Oh!' Martin said flatly, and went on his way.

He woke with a start and sat up straight in bed. Through the heavy coldness of the room he heard Patrick's quiet breathing. He was rigid with excitement because he knew that, somewhere in the streets outside, the waits were coming to him through the lonely morning. He lifted the blind and, peering through the frosted tracery on the glass, saw the dark windows, the lines of white on the sloping roofs battlemented against the sky. All the town was held in the frosted silence, not a bell for Prime in the convents, not even the distant rattle of a collier's cart.

There was a creak at the door, a dim shape of whiteness sped to him and Mary Ellen whispered straight into his face: 'Oh, you're awake? I came to call you. Josie knew what time they'd be out this morning because Big Mick Lannigan is with them this time. Hush, hush!' and her coat and night-gown hung forward on to the bed.

He was overcome with love and gratitude; Josie and Mary Ellen, without being asked, had remembered. He flung his arms around her: 'Oh, Mary Ellen. Pretty Mary Ellen!'

'Ssh, ssh, alannah, you mustn't do that!' she said, and shivered. 'I must go back now.'

'But don't you want to stay and hear the waits yourself?' He raised the blind cautiously and the hard light of the frost showed Mary Ellen's shining eyes and teeth.

'Yes,' she whispered, 'I'd love to.'

They wrapped coats about them and he made her tuck her feet under the bedclothes and put his own warm feet against them. Leaning forward, he drew his finger along the delicate turrets and spires on the window.

'Jack Frost up to his night tricks again,' he whispered.

She laughed, low and secretively, and nodded.

'I must call Patrick,' he whispered.

Mary Ellen wanted to go then, but was persuaded to stay.
When his whispered calls failed to waken Patrick, he giggled and
hurled his pillow across the room. There was a grunt and Patrick
sat up in his bed, a dim, small shape.

'Ssh, ssh! The waits, the waits!'

They waited a long time in silence, hearing each other breathing in the heavy air. Patrick whispered: 'Hi! Are you sure they're
coming? I think I'll go asleep. You stay awake and call me!'

'Hush! listen!' said Mary Ellen, lifting one finger in the light of
the window. And from far away, faint and vanishing, came the
sounds of music and voices. 'Could that be as far off as the
Jamiesons' now, Master Martin?' Mary Ellen whispered.

'No, much more up the river than that—coming this way.'

Soon the sounds came again, a little nearer. 'That'll surely be
at Mr. McDowell's!' The sounds had stopped altogether, the three
waited tensely.

Then, suddenly, Martin leaned forward and gripped Mary
Ellen's hand—a shuffling had sounded and died in the street
below them. They held their breaths. A step rang on the pavement, voices spoke low. Then silence. Martin and Mary Ellen,
fingers entwined, leaned towards the window and suddenly,
without any warning, the music and song rose out of the silence.

'Adeste, fideles . . .'

The notes of melodeons and concertinas mingled with the
voices while the hymn mounted in waves through the morning to
the last insistent summons:

'Venite adoremus, venite adoremus,
Venite adoremus—Dominum.'

The emptiness of the town sucked the sound away into
nothingness until the sing-song greeting burst forth:

'Happy and Holy Christmas, Mrs. Reilly, Mr. Reilly, all the
young Reillys, Miss Anastasia Josephine McDonnell, Miss Mary
Ellen Conellan . . . Good morning to all in the house, and God
Save Ireland! A fine and frosty morning.'

The 'morning' drawn out into a chant, wailed into silence
which yielded to a hesitant beginning of:

> 'Hail! Queen of Heaven! the Ocean Star!
> Guide of the Wanderer here below . . .'

Louder and more confident, the music and voices rose:

> 'Mother of Christ! Star of the Sea!
> Pray for the Wanderer—pray for me.'

The footsteps rapped away into silence along the icy pavements; the waits were over.

'Won't I wipe O'Gorman's eye properly!' and Patrick lay down quickly.

Mary Ellen withdrew her feet. 'Go asleep now,' and she went, a white shape, to the door.

For a long time Martin sat watching whiteness invade the sky and turn the dark roofs to blackness. The waits had been only nearly, not quite, as thrilling as he had expected. To have waited so many nights during so many years for this moment, and then to find it vanishing so quickly and completely. He thought now that perhaps the presence of others had prevented him drawing from the waits that revelation of deeper wonders which he had expected, now that he was so much older than on the former occasion, and could, as he believed, control his impressions. He thought how, when he himself sang, he never poured forth the feelings which possessed him, nor ever saw in others' eyes the expression of his own emotions. He thought of his Aunt Mary's half-sovereign, of his hesitation and failure; he watched the sky that was heavy now with snow. Far, far, over the roofs, over the river, flowing through the sleeping town, the high, thin bell of the Crucifixion Convent rang the call to Prime, and its tintinnabulation reinforced the frosted loneliness of the world. He shivered and, lying down beneath the clothes, he thought of the dark figures moving along the corridors, the slippers turning into the Oratory and the ovals of fog around the candle flames on the altar.

Weak and vanishing came the dying sound of the waits:

> 'Mother of Christ! Star of the Sea!
> Pray for the Wanderer—pray for me!'

2

'And do ye think, young Reilly man, that every single one of St. Columcille's prophecies won't come true? Be the powers, then, they will! As sure as this is Christmas Eve, this day!' and Tommy Fagan moved the *Freeman's Journals* to one side of the counter to give himself room for a bang upon the Christmas numbers of the *Girls' Friend*.

Tommy Fagan's shop, tiny and dark, was one of the snuggeries of Martin Matthew Reilly. Here, on long winter afternoons, leaning over the counter under the hissing gas lamp, he read every paper which Tommy kept for sale, including *The Grocers' Journal* and the ladies' fashion papers. Here, on those quiet afternoons under the gas lamp, Tommy would engage Martin in discussion of Life, Death and Sin. Half boastfully, half timorously, he would recount the sins of his adolescence.

'Oh, I was a terrible chap when I was about twenty or so. I don't know why I tell a young boy like you these things, but do you know what I used to . . . ? Well, I . . . I used to kiss girls at dances—now! I once even squeezed one! Isn't that a terrible thing to have to confess to a young boy like you!'

'Terrible!' Martin would say, 'terrible, Tommy!' although really he was not the least impressed.

On this Christmas, as so often before, Tommy, with sad, unresigned suspicion, accused Martin of not believing in the St. Columcille prophecies. And, once again, Martin, feeling that he owed Tommy something for all the free reading he did in the shop, assumed an air of awed belief. In vain. His too expressive face and Tommy's jealous instinct defeated politeness.

'Aw, now, them eyes of yours gives you away. All the same now, just listen to this . . .' and he leaned like a conspirator across the counter. 'Listen! "When the birds stand in the sky, let the people of Erin prepare fifteen months for the destruction of the world." ' He smiled at Martin's failure to see the point about the birds. 'And weren't the electric wires black last Wednesday with dead birds standing on them? Weren't they? "When the birds stand in the sky"—that was Columcille's clever way of putting it, but you can see he meant last Wednesday,' and after a mental calculation, he announced, 'That gives us until next March twelvemonth before the end of the world.' Then, struck by the coincidence: 'March! St. Patrick's own month! Oh, that puts it beyond all doubt, once and for all,' and he ran to his prie-dieu in the inner room and beat his breast until two Christian Socialists among the mill-workers came in for their *Pagan-Capitalism*, followed by a shy young servant-girl for 'violet note-paper, if ye have it'.

The afternoon was drawing to its close as Martin went down the street, but the sky, laden with snow, still threw a grey light upon the huddled houses. Along the pavement came Mrs. Jamieson with a young woman friend and, submissively before them, Gertrude and her youngest sister moved sedately side by side, their muffs held with proper deportment to their waists, their backs straight and unswaying because of the two pairs of eyes behind them—and their belted coats buttoned tight to their chins. On the night of her arrival from school, Gertrude had had only a short talk with Martin, and now, with two grown-ups marching her about, there was not time for much during the halt while Mrs. Jamieson and young Miss Morrison offered their Christmas greetings to Martin.

'Thank you, Mrs. Jamieson, and a very happy one to you. Thank you, Miss Morrison, and a very happy one to you.'

They moved away, but Gertrude lingered to whisper: 'I have a secret to tell you; why haven't you been round to us today? I was furious yesterday at being locked in my room and hearing you laughing downstairs. I'm so ashamed for still flying into my temper when I thought I was learning to control it, but I'm glad in a sort of way that I was kept in my room as well as slapped for it. The first time in my life I was ever glad of a punishment. That Philip Wilson was horrid, horrid! This town is full of horrid, so-called manly boys. I hate them. You're different. You're coming to my party, aren't you? You and the

McDowells will be the only Catholics there this year, but you won't mind that.'

He smiled and nodded ardently. How grown-up Gertrude looked even in her school hat, and even in spite of still having not only her ankles uncovered but even a little of her legs. How pleased he was that all the world should see him whispering to this tall, elegant person who treated Rosaleen as an infant! To him she seemed to be even more lovely than ever, because of the occasional seriousness, the sort of 'grown-upness' and gravity which had begun to show itself sometimes in her since last holidays, and which, at times, now, almost overbore her gay 'devilishness'. So far from putting her beyond him, it—or something—had made her want Martin's companionship even more than formerly.

'Gertrude!'

'Yes, Mother!' She bent even closer to Martin. 'Don't forget in your Lullacreen Stephen's Day gathering to get your Aunt Mary's picture for me. Bring it round next day and you can stay after Niave goes home after tea and we'll have a long time up in my room.'

Whistling cheerfully on his way, he looked back and saw Gertrude stoop in a pretence of tying the lace of her high boots until her mother and Miss Morrison had out-passed her. Then she blew him a kiss, waved her muff gaily, and, to his horror, lifted one long, long leg and shook it at him. Swirling about, she resumed her submissive walking beside her little sister, muffs, back, toes and heads set in the correct deportment for young ladies in the street.

'Begod, did ye see that!' said a passer-by with half-admiring condemnation.

'Oh, Votes for Women!' said his companion meaningly, then exculpatingly, 'But, sure, she's only a Protestant girl!'

Martin was not sure how he ought to judge Gertrude's behaviour. It was probably all right in one's home or among special intimates. But to show everyone her knees and petticoats! Every Tom, Dick and Harry! Really, it was no wonder she got into hot water so often.

He was roused by the sounds of the bell-man announcing a coming concert and jangling his bell steadfastly, despite the angry looks of a solitary old bagpiper who, on a beat outside the traps and cars lining the kerb, marched up and down, up and down, his torn coat splaying out behind him, his few hairs fluttering in the raw air. When he had finished the mournful tune he moved to the pavement, hat in hand. The children and corner-boys straggled away.

Martin stood his ground. 'Mr. Piper, please, is it true pipers always walk up and down when they're playing because the British Government is afraid to let them stand still with the war-pipes?'

'What do ye want, young fellah?'

'Why do you always walk up and down when you're playing the bagpipes?'

The piper scratched his head. 'That's funny now! I don't be walking up and down with the bugle, only with the pipes. Begob, that's funny!' He turned musingly away.

'Mr. Piper! Don't all pipers find it easier to talk in Irish than in English?'

'Irish! In the name of God what would the likes of me know about Irish!'

'But didn't you learn the pipes at your mother's knee along with Irish?'

'I did not!' The piper was indignant. 'I learned them from the Sergeant Bandmaster in the Royal Hibernian Military School in Dublin. Here,' he added angrily, 'are ye going to put anything in the ould hat now after keeping me standing here like this?'

Martin put a half-penny in the hat. 'I'd have been able to give you more but some money was taken from me last night. Next week I'd be able to give you a penny if you'll be in this town and play "Lord Clare's Dragoons" for me. One of the officers was an ancestor of mine, Colonel Reilly, my great-great . . .' But the piper was already wandering from door to door, hat in hand.

Somewhat depressed by this encounter, Martin continued on his way until, outside Dr. McDowell's house, he saw the doctor's new motor-car surrounded by a group of children and adult loungers. Dr. McDowell was at his door and greeted Martin with a wave.

'Would you like a ride, young Knight-at-Arms?'

'Oh, yes, please. But I'm only going as far as Mount Leinster Bridge.'

'Well, that's my road. I've had a call from away out beyond Clonadole.'

'Oh, is it a life-and-death case?' and he was beginning to picture
Dr. McDowell struggling through the night to save a dying
child, when Dr. McDowell laughed and pulled his pointed beard.

'Oh, Martin Reilly, Martin Reilly! Your romanticism will be
the ruin of you. Life-and-death case, indeed!' He smiled a little
wryly. 'A country doctor, Martin, knows that in ninety-nine cases
out of a hundred it's a toss-up between cramp and constipation.'

Dr. McDowell went to get his bag, and Martin dashed upstairs
seeking Niave and Muirne or Michael, but the girls were not in
the drawing-room where he was nearly trapped into the task of
holding the frame for Mrs. McDowell's coloured silks. He ran to
the old schoolroom where up to two years ago when he was ten
he had done his lessons with the three McDowells and Gertrude
and her young brother. Although the girls at fifteen had been too
far ahead to need his help—except for 'useful quotations' for their
essays—Michael McDowell, his senior by more than two years,
had not been above seeking his prompting in the unenterprising
answers which he gave to Miss Denham's very enterprising
questions. But, one sad day, the girls had gone to their boarding-
schools and 'Nice English Miss Denham' had returned to
England, encumbered by picture souvenirs of green harps and
Round Towers festooned with shamrocks, by one 'Spanish' hair-
comb labelled 'for Ball dress and in remembrance from your six
respectful pupils', and by one proclamation, drawn up on Tommy
Fagan's best Irish vellum, announcing remorse for all the 'bad
mornings when we made you cross'. Thereafter, Michael, until
he too went away to school, had borne Martin company and
solace in the daily journey to the Faithful Brothers, which Martin
must now do alone until he would go to Dunslane in September,
his only comfort the silent repetition of Dr. McDowell's words
for them: 'Those clumsy bog-trotters.'

Neither the girls nor Michael were in, so Martin went back to
the street and made his way through the little group around the
motor-car. 'Keep back, please. Better keep back. Motor-cars
are dangerous if you don't understand them.'

He climbed to the driver's seat with an air mixed evenly of
bored efficiency and alert sang-froid. This effect was somewhat
spoiled by his tripping over the hand-brake lever outside the door,
and he was in two minds whether to reassert himself by trying to
blow the horn. But it was not always easy to pump a sound from

its big bulb and he decided not to run the risk of ignominious
failure. Instead, he pulled up his gloves with a resolute air and,
hoping that none of the loungers knew him by appearance,
wondered if he might be mistaken for the son of some French
racing driver sent by his father to see if the roads around
Glenkilly were suitable for a big European motor-race like the
Gordon-Bennet. He therefore climbed down from the car and
peered intently at the roadway. When the loungers, gathering
around him, had stared at the roadway and at him, he stroked his
chin and muttered: '*Ah, pour French tyres pas bon. Pas, pas!*' He
climbed back, this time avoiding the hand-brake, and began
prodding the levers with a knowing air until the moment of
yielding the driving seat to Dr. McDowell.

'Will I hold her, Doctor, while you wind her up?' a man
offered, as Dr. McDowell cranked the engine.

'No, thanks, Tim. She doesn't buck, this grey mare.'

The engine started, the crowd parted, giving a little cheer, and
Martin, waving his hand, called, '*Au revoir, mes camarades
Irlandais,*' but softly, so that Dr. McDowell would not hear
him.

It looked as if there would be rain again instead of snow and,
from the high seat of the car, chugging down the street, Martin
saw the spangled Christmas stockings in the toy-shops glittering
through a humid haze. The sound of the motor sent men scurrying to their horses' heads, and from the crowded pavements the
countrywomen gaped at 'Queer Dr. McDowell, God bless him!'
Young men from the villages, labourers from farms, gleaming
from recent shaving, pulled asses' cars, pony-traps or bicycles
against the kerb. They returned to seek in the shops for cherry-
mounted hat-pins and coloured camisole ribbons for their girls,
giggling, plump and bright-eyed outside the windows. Martin
forgot about being a French driver's son in the thrill of rushing
through the hazy air speckled with reflections from tinsel and
glass. It was the hour when the road began to be invaded by
pedestrians. Up and down they wandered with an air that was
spacious and leisurely. The serious shopping of the better-class
people had been completed days before, and now, for their
inferiors, the Christmas Eve expanded into the perfect Saturday
night.

The car passed the Protestant boys gossiping outside the

Protestant Hall and went into quieter streets where, between the street lamps, the greasy roadway reflected no bright shop windows. Here the spire of the Protestant Parish Church rose into the dark sky, aloof and strange, but familiarly across the crowded streets and quiet squares the distant Catholic Cathedral pealed the hour. On and on, to where the river flowed blackly past silent mills and wharves and under the curving arches of the Mount Leinster Bridge. Here some shops reappeared and, as Martin's stomach recorded the car's sharp rise to the hump of the bridge, he saw to left and right the water gleaming far beneath him. The people of the little suburb, streaming across to the brightness of Glenkilly itself, left behind them the witchery of their own low houses running down in lines towards the Crucifixion Convent ever silent amid the flat fields. No light gleamed there; its bulk was dark against the slopes beyond it, but Martin knew that, behind those walls, the first prayers of Christmas were already being said by the ladies whose silken trains he had held up from the processional paths of the public garden, whose wedding veils had billowed across his face amid the flowers and joy-bell sounds of the Profession—the ladies, to him all tall and lovely, whose last look back at the world had ended sometimes in a smile for himself, their page in satin, as he dropped their trains at the closing door.

When Dr. McDowell stopped the car to allow Martin to descend, he was hailed by a stout, red-cheeked gentleman with a clipped white moustache and abrupt air.

'Good evening, McDowell, how are you? My wife wants to know when are we to have the next game of whist?'

'Hello, Moran, old man. Not until after the New Year— too many babies and plum puddings!' Dr. McDowell laughed and pulled his pointed beard. 'Do you know my young friend Martin Reilly? Martin, Major Moran.'

Major Moran said: 'How d'ye do, boy? I know who you are. Met your father, is it, or is it uncle, in the Vincent de Paul.' Turning to Dr. McDowell with many jerks of his stick to mark his opinions, he began discussing the speed of his motor-car and his own special way of dealing with roadside punctures. Then he inquired politely about the doctor's household. 'All well?'

Dr. McDowell gave a good account of his family then he hesitated a moment, and said a little diffidently, 'And Eva . . . ?'

Major Moran's smile vanished. He answered slowly, 'Still of the same mind.'

He turned and looked through the speckled haze at the grey-dark shadow of the convent. Dr. McDowell looked down at his furred gloves, then raised his head and he too looked past the lights and over the low roofs to the outline of the convent. The strained silence embarrassed Martin, so that he, too, began to look towards the convent and once more to regret that some time ago the scandalized astonishment of a rough country priest had put an end to his journeys in the revolving barrel which joined the convent parlour wall to the great wooden grilles, thus completing the division of the parlour into the world's side and the nuns' side; the division that might never be crossed except only by a few fingers pushed through the one interstice of the grille left specially large for the purpose. Ah—but crossed by himself in the revolving barrel up to an age far older than had ever been permitted to any other boy or girl! He thought now how the barrel would turn until the opening in it came round to the nuns' world. Looking down from his crouching in the dark barrel, he would see the nuns' faces uptilted to him and their eyes shining beneath their wimples. Their arms would come swooshing in to him, and he would be lifted down into a crowd of excited nuns who squabbled with whispering laughter and plaints for the privilege of taking him to their garden or the Refectory, where he devoured sweets and cakes, while the nuns, with wooden forks and spoons, had a meal of dry bread and vegetables.

He looked at Major Moran's short figure, stout and rigid in the tight topcoat, and tried to picture Eva, whom he had seen once or twice at the McDowells', but he could recall only a memory of a tall young woman with a large and beautiful mouth.

Still neither of the men spoke. Often when he was small Martin had run from the nuns into the private garden, teasing them and defying them to catch him. Once, scurrying to hide, he had seen one of his favourite younger nuns kneeling and crying outside the Oratory door with her arms held out in the form of a Cross. He had gone to her and begun to dry her tears with his handkerchief, and at that she had cried more bitterly than before and had sunk down with her hands to her face. So he had run away and never told anyone about it, but the picture of the pretty nun, crying with a bar of sunlight along her black

shoulder, was part of his mind now as he looked from Dr.
McDowell towards the high wall enclosing that secret garden,
where often, in his hiding, he had heard the nuns calling: 'Little
St. Martin! Come back to us!' High, sweet voices through the
shrubberies. 'Come back to us,' thinly calling. 'Come back . . .
come back . . . come back to us.'

He heard Dr. McDowell speaking hesitatingly to Major
Moran: 'When does she want to . . . to . . . ?' He left the question
unfinished.

'March,' said Major Moran without turning his head.

Dr. McDowell sucked in his breath. 'So soon?'

This time Major Moran turned his face, stiff and drawn, and he
nodded. 'So soon.'

Martin was astonished—March, so soon? Why, March was a
long way in the future! After the Christmas holidays, a whole
term of the Faithful Brothers to be borne. Why—it would be
Easter!

Major Moran went on speaking, staring at Dr. McDowell and
keeping his stick quiet beside him. 'I was in India when you
brought her into the world for us, McDowell, you remember?
She was five when I saw her first and nearly ten the next time; her
hair had changed to brown then. Always going back to school
until she was nineteen, hardly ever at home during her holidays.
Then that finishing year in Germany!' He looked down at his
feet. 'Barely six months home from that, and now . . .' He lifted
his face into the spangled mist. 'It's a queer world, Mac,' he said
in a frightened way.

Dr. McDowell nodded grimly. Martin, watching the reflections
of the lights in his eyes, saw him studying the short figure on the
pavement. 'Do you remember, Tom, the night in Trinity when
we denounced one another's plans for the future?'

Major Moran jerked his head into alertness: 'God, yes! Often!
In my old rooms in the Rubrics. Huh, I was to be an Irish
military genius, another Wellington.' He laughed without mirth.
'You were a damned Fenian in those days, Mac.'

Martin was astonished to hear Dr. McDowell described as 'a
Fenian' when everyone knew that he was barely a Nationalist at
all, barely a step removed from a Unionist, and with a bitter
word for all the Irish-Irelanders, as bitter in its own way as
Josie's mocking 'Dublin Jackeens, God save us.'

'A Fenian?'

'Maybe you don't remember the night when you dragged us all across to see the rooms where that fellow Ingram wrote "Who Fears to Speak of '98". Heavens, we were drunk that night.'

'Yes,' said Dr. McDowell seriously, 'very drunk!' He looked at his watch.

'I must be on my way,' he said quickly. 'All the seasonable greetings, my dear chap.'

With his chest hunched to the driving-wheel, he drove away towards the darkness, having given an indifferent wave of the hand in response to Martin's thanks for the drive.

For a while Martin stood looking at the dim line of the hills which separated him from Grandmother in Lullacreen, from Aunt Mary in Moydelgan. Through the balustrade he looked down at the dark gleaming of the river where it flowed silently below him.

One day, in his satin breeches and silk stockings, he would attend Eva Moran and page her through the public gardens of the convent amid the flowers and joy-bell sounds. One day he would see the room in Trinity College, Dublin where 'Who Fears to Speak of '98' was written by a Protestant!

> They rose in dark and evil days
> To right their native land;
> They kindled here a living blaze
> That nothing shall withstand.

He whirled about and strode purposefully through the mist until in a lonely road he came to the railings enclosing the plot and the Cross where the Glenkilly men of 1798 were buried. Here to this Cross, in each anniversary month of May, he brought the bouquet which the Crucifixion nuns, locked away for ever from the world, could not themselves bring for the Memory of the Dead. He peered in through the railings at the wan gleaming of the Cross; he tried to imagine what the fighting had been like one hundred and twelve years ago in the streets he knew so well; tried to imagine the ships sailing from France to Ireland with '*Liberté, Egalité, Fraternité*', exactly one hundred years after Colonel O'Reilly had gone to France with Sarsfield to fight for King

Louis and Ireland, and not many years after the other exiles at
Bunker Hill had fought for America. If only one were living in
the days when the American rebels were calling to Ireland for
help, when Wolfe Tone and the French officers were actually
blowing their noses and talking and everything! As he stared and
stared through the railings at the lonely Cross, deserted by all on
the gay Christmas Eve, he murmured fervently:

> 'They fell and passed away.
> But true men, like you men,
> Are plenty here today!'

After all, Bunker Hill and 1798 were only a little more than a
hundred years ago, and Colonel Reilly at Limerick and Ramillies
only another hundred years before that. So the past was really
very near when you looked at it that way, with the Cross actually
there behind the railings and the men under the sod beneath it.
But the future was different and the time until next March was
an age.

Moodily humming 'But true men, like you men', he came back
to the bridge, turned down the steps to the wharf and, having
passed some closed warehouses, came to a low house that fronted
on the river. The ground floor was a kind of shop without a
counter and encumbered with carpenter's tools and half-finished
articles of furniture. Passing under the arched entry, he picked
his way across thick shavings between brown and white cupboards
towards the door at the back, where a dim radiance showed
through the fanlight. The moment he knocked, an angry-sound-
ing discussion ceased within the room, the door was opened and,
against the light of the room, Mr. Burns's spare figure stood
stiffly.

'Oh, it's you, Martin,' and then in Irish, 'Come in and
welcome before you.'

'God and Mary bless you,' replied Martin in the same book-
Irish and, taking off his school cap, entered the room. A kitchen
lamp hung on the wall but its yellow light, dimmed by curls of
smoke from the high grate on which a kettle bubbled, could not
at first reveal to Martin the figure sitting in the high wooden
armchair before the dresser, neatly but sparsely stocked with well-
washed crockery.

From the chair, Father Riordan's clear, musical voice came in the same book-Irish: 'God and Mary bless you, O Martin, O boy of Ireland.'

'God and Mary and Patrick bless you, Father,' replied Martin, and, smiling shyly, shook hands.

From the gloom at the door, Mr. Burns came forward, stroking down the grey hairs from the horse-shoe of baldness on his square head. He took a bandana handkerchief from his tweed jacket and leaned his short body down to grasp the kettle.

'Father Riordan and meself were just going to mend a difference with a cup of tea. We'll put you between us and you'll serve the tea for us and keep the peace.'

He looked over his shoulder from the kettle, his lined face serious.

'You'll be my woman-of-the-house this Christmas Eve, Martin.' He used the Irish *'bean a tighe'* for 'woman-of-the-house'.

He cleared the heaps of books and papers to one end of the table and Martin laid out the spotless checked cloth, and thick Delft cups and plates, then put his topcoat on the books above the flour-bin under the grocer's calendar and the map of Ireland. From the topcoat pocket he dragged forth a small, rather crushed parcel. 'It's only a quarter of a Christmas cake, Mr. Burns, but the whole cake was too dear because something happened last night to some money I was keeping for it. But it's nice, and you know I'd make it the whole cake if I could.'

Mr. Burns took the untidy parcel, shook Martin's hand. 'May there be a thousand thanks at you,' and then in English: 'And Father Riordan has brought another cake, and I've baked a fresh piece of soda-bread. So . . .' he laughed, 'we'll have one of the teas I used to imagine in my cell at Dartmoor.'

Father Riordan stood up, his tall figure stooping slightly beneath the smoky ceiling, as he put his hands under his elegant coat-tails and nodded at Martin. 'You haven't said anything about Mr. Burns's grand holly, Martin.'

Martin, looking above the shelves of books, saw holly hanging in a wreath between the pictures of Wolfe Tone and Thomas Davis.

Father Riordan sat down at the table and Mr. Burns said gruffly, 'Say yer Grace, boy,' and abruptly turned away from the table, while the priest and Martin bowed their heads.

Sipping the strong, sweet tea and munching the buttered hot
bread, Martin looked at pale Tone and gentle Davis with the
holly between them and thought cheerfully that other boys did
not sit like this, with Father Riordan on one hand, so distinguished, so elegant and gentle, and, on the other hand, Mr. Burns,
the Fenian hero who had spent eighteen years in an English
prison, Mr. Burns whose deep voice could thrill Martin with talk
of John Mitchel, of the Fenians; with talk too of later days and of
Parnell lifting his hand over hushed streets.

A silence fell until Martin said, 'I never knew until tonight
that "Who Fears to Speak" was written by a Protestant in
Trinity College.'

Mr. Burns put down his cup. 'Ah, Martin! You were to be the
child of peace between us, but instead you . . .' He smiled grimly.
Then he smote the table heavily with his hand. 'No, Father
Riordan, no! You can never come my road. For me and my like,
a Protestant—aye a Pagan—rebel is worth twenty Catholic
slaves. And the Protestant that's a Unionist even, if he's that way,
out of care for Ireland, as a lot are, he's more to me than the
shoddy patriots, the play-boys, the good Catholics, the . . . ah,
the Slave-Hearts!'

Father Riordan said nothing and Mr. Burns muttered scorn-
fully: 'Aye, you have them here in Glenkilly and you know them.
They're swarming over Ireland now. Look at that fellow Tim
Corbin, over in Ballow. A fine Catholic, they call him, a nice
Party-man, a fine patriot. Tim Corbin of Ballow! Aye, a fine
Slave-Heart!'

Father Riordan would have spoken, but Mr. Burns leaned in
front of Martin and said bitterly: 'Your heart is all right, Father;
and your head would show you the clear road. But between you
and Ireland there's that terrible——'

'Bernard! The boy!'

Mr. Burns bit his lip. 'Aye, you're right.' He rose wearily and,
going to the fireplace, said: 'Martin, did ye come yet in the
Fintan Lalor I gave ye, to the bit about armed resistance? Say it
out now, or maybe it's too long a bit for you to remember by
heart?'

'I remember it all right,' said Martin unhappily, and looked
hesitantly at the priest, who smiled sadly and said:

'Yes, Martin, say it. "Any man who tells you . . ." Yes, say it.'

Martin put down his cup. ' "Any man who tells you that an act of armed resistance, even if offered by ten men, even if offered by ten men armed only with stones, any man who tells you that such an act of armed resistance is premature, imprudent and foolish, let him be spurned and spat at. For mark you this, and recollect it: somewhere and somehow and by someone, a beginning must be made, and the first act of armed resistance is always premature, imprudent and foolish!'

A long silence followed. Mr. Burns's grey eyes brooded over the fire. Father Riordan's head was bent and his hands rested on the table. At last Mr. Burns spoke to himself. 'Grattan, Emmett, Davis! All Protestants and Trinity-men.' Suddenly, he loudly demanded: 'Martin! What was the best thing Hussey Burgh ever said in the Old House in College Green?'

Martin, feeling more like crying than speaking, answered, ' "England has sown her laws like dragon's teeth—they have sprung up as armed men!" '

'Aye!' said Mr. Burns grimly.

'But, Bernard!' said Father Riordan, raising his head. 'You wrong me. I'm——'

Mr. Burns interrupted him gently. 'What's the use, Father? You know it as well as I do. For me and me like, it's Ireland first, last and all the time. For you—something else.' He became less gentle: 'Well, you have had yer way again. You have your new Catholic University now. You've split Ireland there as well as everywhere else and you'll spawn a lot of huckstering politicians out of yer grand new college.'

Father Riordan raised a protesting hand. 'But I was for the one United University scheme.'

Mr. Burns's grey eyes flamed sombrely in the light of the fire. Once he murmured Parnell's name to himself, a loudly bitter 'Parnell! Parnell!' Unhappy Martin could not be sure whether he was reproaching Parnell himself or those who had pulled him down. Beside the fire, the spare shoulders drooped a little. 'Year after year in that cell I kept myself up with the thought of coming home one day to work for Ireland's greatness and freedom, to pass on the things them great men passed on to me. I'm here in Glenkilly now twelve years, and they all say, as polite as can be, "Oh, how are ye, Mr. Burns?" But they always manage to let me name drop out of their committees; above all, if there's a priest there, and when isn't there one? And the *Glenkilly Liberator* is always short of space the weeks I write a letter to it; and they never have room, they say, in the town library for me books. After twelve years in this town the only people I can influence are yourself and that boy there. A child and a priest!'

Father Riordan looked up. 'Bernard,' he said gently, and looked with respect at the old man's figure. 'You *do* influence the priest, I assure you. And as for the child—well, to influence even one child is to have a say in the future. More in this case, because it's a good child and one who . . . well, anyway, in years far ahead, a bit of him will carry our mark.'

He rose, and, going to Mr. Burns, took his hand. 'You know already all I might say. We'll leave it for tonight, and just wish one another a Happy Christmas.'

Mr. Burns nodded.

'Here, Martin,' said Father Riordan, extending his other hand, and drawing Martin to himself and Mr. Burns. Holding their hands in a chain, he said, 'A Happy Christmas to us,' and smiled. 'Come on! Say it, both of you.' Martin, still a little uncertain about this recovered unity, gazed up from one to the other, seeing the firelight flicker on the old man's face and on the priest's high forehead.

Holding hands in a chain, the three said, 'A Happy Christmas to us,' and laughed.

Mr. Burns walked with them across the thick shavings and said goodbye to them at the arched entrance in front of the river lapping in the mist. Looking back as they mounted the steps to the bridge, they saw him still standing at the entrance, gazing out over the water.

At the bridge, Father Riordan said: 'Tell me, do you still serve the Celestine nuns' private Mass? I heard that Major Moran's sister was trying to get it for her eldest lad.'

'She was. And Aunt Eileen was furious. But the Celestines won't ever take the honour from her, until I go away to Dunslane.'

'I think it's you as much as your Aunt Eileen.' He smiled. 'Well, I'm saying the Celestine private Mass tomorrow so we'll be able to wish each other a Happy Christmas again then.'

'Oh, grand! I just love that private Mass before it's real morning!'

'Yes, you *know* that it is beautiful. So used I to know it, too, when I was a boy, and still do. But there's a greater beauty than all that, Martin, grand as it is.' He looked seriously into Martin's eyes. 'Greater than the peace and the flowers and the prayers. The perfect beauty of the Catholic Faith itself! It's just because you do see those other things now that one day you'll see . . .' He stopped and smiled. Then he said in a different voice, 'You must pray specially for Mr. Burns, that he may soon come back to the Sacraments and God.'

He took Martin's arm. 'Come a little way with me.'

Crossing the bridge, they walked side by side in silence for a while. Then the priest said: 'It's years and years too soon for you to have the slightest idea yet, but I hope that when the time comes you will want to be a priest, Martin, because it's the noblest destiny in the world, to be a priest of the Catholic Church,' and, stopping to say goodbye in a quiet side-road by the darkly gleaming water, he said, 'And after that the next-best thing is to be the man who will give Ireland back her old rightful place again.' He looked thoughtfully down at Martin, studying him, then said: 'Do you know what Hofer said to the Tirolese, Martin?'

'Yes, Father. He said, "Men, it is time!" '

'Yes. "Men, it is time!" '

Looking away over the flowing water, he said, 'And who dare to say that the Hofer of Ireland is not among you boys today!' He shook hands, bid Martin carry wishes to his Aunt Eileen, uncle and cousins. 'And we'll see one another in the morning.'

It was a long time before Martin moved from his watching of the water flowing past him to the bridge and Mr. Burns's house. Some priests had called Mr. Burns 'a scandal to the town', but Father Riordan had only said, 'Pray for him and for me.'

To be a priest! To bend over the Host and say *'Hoc est Corpus Meum'*—This is My Body. And over the chalice to say *'Hic est enim Calix Sanguinis Mei* . . .' for this is the Chalice of My Blood, of the new and eternal Testament. And thus to call God Himself to the altar, changing bread and wine into His Body and Blood!

He came out of his brooding to hear his name called and there, across the street, was Michael McDowell looking more than his fourteen years in his new belted overcoat.

Michael's round face was eager with news. 'I say! There's a

chap come to stay with the Jamiesons for Christmas, an English chap, and he can move his ears backwards and forwards!'

'He couldn't! Not backwards *and* forwards!'

'Yes, yes, I've seen them going both ways. And he's got a sister with him who can do reverse turn-overs, much bigger and slower than yours!'

In excitement, the boys set off to Brunswick Drive, the quiet side-street where the red brick houses looked from above their steps at bare plane trees glinting in the light of two weak street lamps. Norburton, a stolid boy between fourteen and fifteen, readily agreed to accompany his visitors to the nearer lamp-post, since the holly-shaded electric light in the Jamiesons' hall was not thought to be brilliant enough for the demonstration. Beneath the lamp-post he worked his ears and Martin had to admit that the ears did move both backwards *and* forwards. They returned to the Jamieson doorway, discussing moving ears, until Michael said, 'What about showing us your sister's backward turn-overs?'

'Well,' said Norburton doubtfully, 'there's a bit of a celebration here tonight for us and she's in her party clothes and things by now, so it's . . .' He blushed and said pugnaciously, 'Look here, does she know you, Reilly?'

'Not yet,' said Martin.

'Well, I'm jolly well not going to show my sister's backward turn-overs to chaps she doesn't know. Especially in . . . no matter.'

At this moment Michael hailed another resident of Brunswick Drive, a fat boy called Hyland. Hyland wanted to inspect the moving ears, so they all had to make another journey to the lamp-post. On their return they found the youngest Jamieson in the hall, a taciturn boy of Martin's age and the one who up to two years earlier had done lessons under 'nice English Miss Denham' with Gertrude, Martin and the three McDowells.

A minute later a group of boys went down the road pushing a soap-box on wooden wheels.

'Hi! Martin! Hyland!' called Michael McDowell. 'The very gang that threw the stones at us yesterday! Dirty lane-boys!'

'Come on,' said Hyland, 'let's pitch their filthy caps in the gutter!'

'What is it?' said Norburton keenly. 'Cads, is it?'

'Oh, cads, are they! Come on, then, let's have at them!'

Whooping 'Dirty lane-boys!' the five boys swooped down the road. The boys with the soap-box were bowled over and their caps sent spinning into the gutter. Doors opened and an infuriated Pomeranian came yelping along the pathway. Mysteriously, the youths of Brunswick Drive smelled battle through the red brick walls of their homes and from the doorways boys ran to join Michael McDowell's force. More mysteriously, boys in the main streets got the whiff of far-off fighting and came running to support the lane-boys, so that in a few moments the quiet street was in uproar. A battle of blows and kicks sent the lane-boys back and they growled in the middle of the road, barring the passage and seeking stones, saying: 'Let's crush them, the bloody college boys! Look at their asses' collars! Mammies' pets!'

Michael McDowell and his followers were now alarmed by the commotion in the quiet road where they were all known; their enemies could return, an unidentified crowd, to their obscure quarters where, in any event, mothers never seemed to think street-fighting a matter for chastisement, but rather for calling round to 'decent boys' ' doors and sending in complaints. Already some of the residents of Brunswick Drive were peering through the mist and it was decided to try to charge the lane-boys to the end of the road and then disperse, each to his own house.

Into the charge Martin put all his venom, for he was charging not just those boys but the sycophantic hordes who cowered before Brother Gannon's rough threats; who sniggered slavishly when Brother Finnegan made a joke about the leather; whose sly eyes on Martin's face watched knowingly his shameful endurance of Brother Kiernan's clear whisper. Down with them, the low, cringing lot! In a flash, the words jumped in his head—the Slave-Hearts! Mr. Burns had said the very name for them.

'Slave-Hearts!' he yelled, and charged the faces gleaming in the pallid light, while the Pomeranian yapped on the pavement, and Michael, throwing prudence to the winds, roared, 'Dirty–lane-boys!' The lane-boys fled, refusing battle, and Martin would have followed them into the crowded street beyond had not Michael McDowell pulled him back. Swiftly, boys vanished into doorways, and back in the Jamiesons' hall, Norburton, animated by a feeling of recent comradeship in battle, moderated his resistance to the proposal that he should put his sister's slow backward turn-overs on show. 'She could tie a string around her clothes,' he said doubtfully. 'I saw a girl, an acrobat, do that in a theatre in London, and really, you know, it was quite all right.'

But now Martin, remembering the conclusions he had drawn about Gertrude waving her leg at him publicly, said: 'Well, I don't know. A fellow's sister is not the same as an acrobat, even with string around her clothes.'

'That's right!' all agreed readily, Norburton adding: 'Besides, if she were caught, she'd catch it. All the same, I'm really very sorry, you chaps. Some other time, perhaps.'

'Oh, that's all right,' they said heartily. 'Thanks all the same.'

There was a moody silence until football was mentioned, when Norburton was told the exact number of tries scored by Ireland in every match against England for the preceding twenty years. The recital droned on until he became somewhat irritated. 'Gosh, Reilly, you talk like a beastly talking-gramophone!' Because Michael McDowell grinned in sympathy with the remark, Martin felt depressed and allowed Norburton to switch the topic to cricket and boast for a while about his leg-break bowling.

'My big brother's jolly keen on the school's cricket and football! I can tell you he lays the cricket stump well into any slacker who tries to dodge football turn-out.'

'Do you mean to say fellows *have* to play whether they like to or not?' Martin asked. 'And a cricket stump—that's a savage thing for a master to use!'

'A master? He isn't a master. He's a prefect.'

'But you said he beat people! How can he beat anyone if he isn't a master, or a grown-up of some sort, anyway?'

'Really, Reilly, I think you're a bit of an ass. I said he was a prefect.'

'You mean just another fellow? But you said he beats other boys!'

'Of course, you ass. Just you wait until I'm a prefect myself. I'll make things hot and heavy for shirkers, I can tell you.'

'What, you? Do you mean to stand there, Norburton, and tell me that other boys will let you give them orders and slog them when you're only a boy yourself?'

Michael McDowell explained tolerantly, 'It's like that in public schools in England.'

'I think it's just downright disgusting! I'd like to see them try it out on *me*!'

Norburton shrugged indifferently, and Martin began to look at him with dislike mixed with incredulity. The way the fellow's jaw had seemed to get bigger when he said, 'Just you wait until I'm a prefect myself.' Why, a boy ought to die first, be flayed alive rather than be punished by another boy. He watched Norburton closely, let him talk for a while, then said aggressively, 'I suppose you're a Liberal, Norburton?'

'Good God, no!' Norburton's expression was horrified. 'Only utter bounders are Liberals.'

'Well, you're a Conservative Home Ruler then?'

'Great Scott, no! I'm a real Conservative. You Irish jolly well couldn't govern yourselves. There'd be a famine again if we gave you Home Rule.'

Michael and Martin were so astonished by this remark, delivered with calm conviction, that they were at a loss for words. Furthermore, they were infuriated by Norburton's 'if we *gave* you', and offended by his 'You Irish', which they privately thought a very bad-mannered way to speak of people. They looked at Norburton's jowl and stolid eyes, his smug plumpness, and Martin decided that Norburton was a very objectionable fellow and very ignorant.

'Well, Holy God!' declared Michael at last. 'That takes the cake! Why, it was the English who were responsible for the famine. And then you say because there was a famine we can't . . . Well! Holy God! You take the cake!'

'Yes,' said Martin hotly. 'Your soldiers marched with fixed bayonets beside the carts carrying away corn that would have fed three Irelands—to ships, of course,' he added.

'Father says,' began Michael deliberately, 'that English boys never learn anything about any other country. He says they're most ignorant of all about Ireland. He says the funny thing is they're good—really good—on Africa and India, and utterly ignorant of Ireland, next door to them.'

'What does he know about it?'

'He does. He was at an English school himself.'

'Oh, was he?' Then after a moment, 'Oh, well, it must have been some rotten little school.'

'It was Rugby,' said Michael with weight.

'Oh, well, I expect he couldn't get on very well, and was jealous.'

'You stinking little cod,' said Michael carefully. 'My father took every prize he went in for. He has some of them at home in a box.'

And now Martin, who had been fairly peppering on the edge of this conversation, burst in with a vicious demand, 'Who brought civilization to England?'

'Civilization? What do you mean? William the Conqueror.'

'Indeed! Time you learnt something. It was Irish monks who taught you first. You were painting yourselves with woad when we were Christians and writing great poems—at least everyone says they were great poems.' He shied away from this because it seemed to be getting a little too near to St. Columcille and Tommy Fagan's ways.

'Of course we taught you first,' put in Michael:

> 'Ireland was Ireland when England was a pup!
> Ireland will be Ireland when England's sugared up!

and if you don't like it I'll give you a puck in the jaw,' ended Michael.

'No, no! Let me!' screamed Martin.

'No, you're too small. It'd suit an Englishman to take on someone a good deal smaller than himself. The Boers——'

'But . . . gosh!' Norburton stared in amazement. 'Why . . . we began the spirit of sport! We *made* it!'

The others hooted mockingly at this and just then George Jamieson, a handsome boy of eighteen, came down to the hall. Norburton turned to him in relief. 'I say, Jamieson. These Home Rulers are saying that English people are very ignorant.'

'Well, so they are,' said George equably. 'Present company excepted, of course,' he said politely.

Norburton's jaw dropped. 'But I thought all your people were Unionists!'

'So we are,' said George pleasantly. 'What's that got to do with it? Everyone knows that the English are really rather stupid. They can't help it, of course!' he added, still polite.

'But you can't say a thing like that. I never heard anyone in all my life say a thing like that before.' He was utterly dumbfounded until a thought struck him. 'Well, what about our Empire? Stupid people couldn't have an Empire like ours.'

This argument disturbed Martin, who had been feeling that

Michael and he had exaggerated their case, that after all nice
Miss Denham could not be the *only* clever English person. And
there was Shakespeare to complicate the case, and he did not
wish Norburton to have any case at all. But George Jamieson's
answer was agreeable to his ear.

'It isn't your Empire,' George was saying evenly. 'It's ours!
The English just did the dirty work. But who won all the battles?'
he asked, and answered himself heartily: 'We did! Who runs the
colonies?—we do. Who has the prettiest girls?—we have! But the
English are good, I admit, at the dog-work.'

'Oh, thank you!' said Norburton with heavy irony. 'I suppose
you'll say we're bullies, too, as well as stupid?'

'Well, you're not very sporting except when it suits you; then
you make a great song about it. The English are pretty good at
blowing the trumpet about being sporting—present company
excepted, of course.' And he went his way.

Norburton looked at the others as if he honestly thought that
they were a little mad. Before he could find words there came
a swishing of skirts on the first landing and Gertrude appeared
dressed in her white muslin for the party.

'Oh, hello, Martin, Michael! Hello, Billy Hyland!' and then a
thought occurred to her. 'Oh, I say, wait a minute, boys.' She
whirled about and ran back along the landing calling: 'Muriel,
Muriel! Quick!'

In a few moments she reappeared with a fat girl who seemed
to be between fourteen and fifteen. She was certainly younger
than the long-legged Gertrude and she giggled her way down the
stairs, beside Gertrude, who was swinging a long broad piece of
elastic, and calling in a whisper: 'Wait till you see this, boys.
Come on. They're all up in the drawing-room. We can risk it for
a few minutes,' and she shepherded them into the room at the
end of the hall. While the boys stood huddled awkwardly near
the door, she helped Muriel to move back the chairs and table,
and fastened the elastic band around her skirts.

'Now, Muriel—quick, before we're caught! Watch this—she's
simply marvellous.'

Stolid Muriel took up a stand at one end of the room and
gravely proceeded to perform a series of slow reverse turn-overs.
The boys, interested but embarrassed, refused to meet each
other's eyes.

Gertrude, however, commented excitedly: 'Isn't she great! Oh!
—did you see that one! She says I'd find it too hard to learn at
my age.'

Norburton coughed meaningly several times, and once blew his
nose loudly, but Muriel did not notice these signals and continued
her display with bovine calmness. The performance over, the
boys mumbled embarrassed congratulations to Muriel and
shuffled from the room. Gertrude came to Martin, looking to him
like a great big pantomime fairy in her short muslin dress and big
hair-bows.

'What were you quarrelling with Everard Norburton about?'

'Oh, politics!' said Martin profoundly, and then suddenly: 'I
say! You're not thinking of falling in love with that fellow, are
you?'

'That infant!'

'He's older than me,' said Martin anxiously.

'That's just what has nothing to do with it. Come on . . .' and
leaving the boys gathered near the door, she and Martin sped up
the stairs to her attic bedroom, where, without turning on the
light, she drew him to the window, set between floor and sloping
roof.

'Martin, I've been waiting to tell you, because you know
you're my secret diary and my brother and sister in one. Oh,
Martin, how wonderful to have you!' She crouched, leaning to
him, the white silk hair-bow standing up like two ears until she
moved between him and the window, when it looked like two
sails on the gleaming river flowing beyond the garden.

'Now this may be difficult for you to understand.' She clasped
her long arms, thin in the long sleeves of the party dress, round
Martin's neck and crouched still more to look straight into his
eyes. 'You remember how it was in October just before I went
back at the beginning of term?'

Martin nodded. Gertrude had still come on the river with
Niave and him, but there had been no more confidences, no
notes asking him to come and read with her, or to take her out,
or just to 'come round this afternoon'; no imaginary travels
abroad with atlas to plot their route, no more talk of the clothes
she would have when she left school. And hardly ever had she
been gay and 'devilish'. And then, suddenly, had come from her
at school one of the most treasured of the letters in the tea-caddy;

only a few lines, but it had begun: *My darling, wonderful brother and sister . . .*

'Well, Martin dear, it's this way. I had just been realizing that I wasn't anything like as near becoming grown-up as I had been thinking. I felt terribly ashamed of being so backward inside myself, compared with some other girls only a year or so older who seemed so sure of themselves. And I was even more ashamed of all that thinking two or three times that I'd fallen in love. You remember?'

Martin nodded. 'I hated you falling in love.'

'But that's just it. It wasn't falling in love. I realize now it was just partly silly crush pash-stuff, and partly merely myself imagining. Everything seemed far, far more serious and difficult than I'd ever imagined, Martin. And, as well, I couldn't think what I wanted after I'd left school. Oh, Martin, dear Martin, I was awfully miserable often. And I so wanted to tell you and have you up here at the window like before, but, you see, I was also beginning to think that I *ought* to be ashamed of needing you to be so close and dear to me, at your age, and wanting you to be like a brother and sister all in one. I *wasn't* ashamed of it, but I thought I *should* be, I thought it was another sign that I was an awful baby. And then the bigger boys flirting and teasing, after one of our hockey matches, when they got you small ones to go off on some excuse or other, that made me so that I could hardly stand boys except when we were doing something with a bit of a lark in it, just doing it, you know. Do say you understand.'

And, because he so ardently wanted to please Gertrude and make her happy, he felt that perhaps he did understand, and he nodded and smiled.

'Other boys were either mushy asses, or boring torments wanting to flirt and kiss, or mostly just horrid, dull, thick, no . . . no I don't know what; no spirit . . . no, not that. No understanding. And yet full of rules, oh, full, full, full, full of rules. But not darling you. But I thought I should be ashamed to be so secret and thick with you, and to want at the same time to look after you. I just told no one, but one day I cried and cried about everything. I thought there was no one there, but this mistress was, Miss Gifford. She said not a word until I stopped crying and I got such a shock when I heard a voice say, "Come here," like that. She teaches science and I never had anything to do with her. No one has. She wouldn't live in the school or supervise, and she hates games. She likes men and—oh, darling Martin, I just told her everything. I couldn't ever have breathed a word to any of the others. They're either awful frumps or the kind that use powder secretly and have girls having silly pashes on them. But I just told her and do you know what she said? I'll give you the bit about you first, though it came last. Are you ready?'

Martin nodded.

'Well—listen. She said that not being a bit ashamed *in myself* of feeling what I do about you was a sign that I had a better chance of growing up one day than most girls! Now, that's the bit I don't fully understand myself, but I *feel* I do. And she said: "Stop leaning forward. Lean back and wait." And she told me that it meant not to think or care when or whether I would be really grown-up inside. And I'm so happy now and I read and read, and I get more fun out of everything, and it's wonderful just to lean back as she said and let things come their own way. And I pick out the little ones, those that look lonely, and I look after them and get up larks with them.

'Martin, listen—she drinks whiskey! I saw the bottle in her lodgings. And she has some man in London she thinks about a lot—I can see that. And she never pretends she and I can be friends yet, she just said once, "one day, perhaps". And, Martin, she sometimes thinks of taking a job in Dublin to see if Ireland would be less stuffy, she says. And if she does, I'll live near her and help housekeep. The way she talks—she's a divil, Martin, a flaming divil, she's wonderful. She says "For God's sake", just straight outright! No tooth in it, Martin. "For God's sake, child, be more punctual or I'll beat you," and she would too. It was after I'd told her that I wrote to you that very night.'

He smiled and nodded. He still found some difficulty in understanding how this could have meant so much to Gertrude, but he had always found it easy to share all Gertrude's excitements, the simple ones and the confusing. She was looking prettier than ever, too, and, in addition, he was anxious to please her and make her happy. She began to laugh.

'That's right. Now you're being lovely. I can always see everything in your face. Oh, Martin, if only all boys would just take people as they are and not be silly with their stupid little rules. Martin, dear Martin, how I wish you could be here in the house

waiting when I come home for the holidays, and you'd sing with
me and like flowers and history, my dresses and Shelley. And
you'd be my brother and escort me to the McDowells' in the
evenings and then I'd be let go see Niave after dark, and you'd be
my sister whenever I was showing you the fashion pictures of the
grand things I'm going to have when I've left school.'

She drew him to her, kissed him and told him in whispers of
her plans for next term, told him how good she had become since
she had first talked with Miss Gifford, and they planned a future
in which Gertrude and Miss Gifford would live in a beautiful
house, with Martin coming in hungry for his meals and putting
up the rods and screws for bright, bright curtains. Once Martin
pointed to the distant shape of the Celestine convent and told her
that Eva Moran was to take the veil in March.

'Yes, I heard it too. And her mother cried about it—even before
us and other Protestants! Oh, Martin, I'm so glad that I could
not be a nun, even if I ever could want to be. A Crucifixion nun!
Don't think I'm saying one word against nuns or convents,
although I could if you start me at it; it's only that I'm so glad
that I'm a Protestant.'

They gazed down at the river and out of its sheeny glitter they
erected the house of the Future with Miss Gifford and the bright
curtains.

'We must keep together again this year at our party, Martin.
And at the McDowells'. But listen—I'll catch it if I don't fly to
the drawing-room.'

On the first floor she whispered her goodbyes. 'And remember
I've told you things I'd only tell a girl except that I wouldn't
trust a real girl,' and, skipping to the drawing-room door, she
smiled back at him over her shoulder, patted muslin dress, hair-
bow and all into demure 'deportment' readiness, winked at him
and, with the mien of sweet and submissive young ladyhood,
entered the room.

Downstairs, Norburton ignored Martin's cold 'So-long, you'
and said, with a meaning look towards where Gertrude had just
vanished, 'I'm always right when I think that a chap is a bit of
a sissy,' but Martin was feeling too elevated to pay any attention
to this indirect challenge.

As he skipped beside Michael's plunging strides, hailing
acquaintances, desiring things in shop windows, the words and

pictures flashed between him and the exciting world about him.
The holly hanging in a wreath between pale Tone and gentle
Davis; the Perfect Beauty of the Catholic Faith itself; Gertrude's
hair-bows like sails before the shining water. And words, words,
words. When, oh when, would he have the new dictionary with all
the lists? Cruiser, Corsair, Nepenthe, Transmute. ' "Quaff, oh,
quaff this kind nepenthe and forget thy lost Lenore. Quoth the
Raven—nevermore!" ' He sang it out, dancing backwards before
Michael's long strides, improvising movements that he wanted
to make like the bending grass of the weirs. 'Transmute the
nepenthe—oh God, Michael, if I could write a song!'

Michael, accustomed to Martin, plunged solidly along, dodging
Martin's flying legs and arms and saying, 'If I honour an infant
of twelve by being seen walking publicly with him, he's got to tell
me what he is saying.'

'Oh, I'm just talking to someone who might understand what I
say even though he doesn't understand the meaning,' Martin said
loftily, remembering something that Father O'Riordan had once
said to him.

Michael stopped dead in his stride. 'Holy Moses!' he said
fervently. Then with abandoned resignation, 'Oh, you *are* dotty,
all right.'

'No, I'm not really, Michael. Don't be stupid like any thick boy.'

A horrible suspicion showed in Michael's eyes. 'Here, wait! Is
all this another of your home-made plays? Because I warn you I
won't be an old woman this time. I'll help with the curtains and
greasepaint, but I won't be an old woman with a shawl and black
skirt. D'ye hear me now. I'm always a poor old woman.'

Martin shook his head and said, 'You need not be an old
woman.'

A wave of loneliness swept over his gaiety and he wondered
again with inner panic if he really was 'queer and funny'. He
answered Michael perfunctorily until Norburton was mentioned,
when both boys heartily agreed that Norburton was 'just the kind
of clown who would be a Conservative'. And when Martin had
left Michael at his door it was of Norburton he thought and,
while he tried to recall the stolid look, the heavy jowl and the way
the jowl seemed to grow bigger when Norburton spoke of being a
prefect one day in his turn, the lineaments of the picture hardened
and he said, 'A bully.'

That night Josie's eye glared, she did her jig and shook her red head and made no pretence of hiding the bottle. Martin sang for her and Mary Ellen, song after song. The ballads, sentimental or patriotic, poured from him, while Mary Ellen, ironing her own lace collar and his second-best surplice for the morning, smiled and nodded prettily, and Josie said: 'Good man, me hearty! Give us another.' Lastly, at their request, he sang the *Adeste Fideles*, and the triumphant rise of the hymn poured from him with feeling.

As he had to get up at five in the morning, he was sent to bed and given the kitchen alarm clock, while Mrs. Reilly, ordering the others upstairs to lie down until Midnight Mass, shut the parlour door on Santa Claus and his secrets of the morrow.

In the bathroom Martin tried to do reverse turn-overs as good as Muriel Norburton's. In bed he drew forward his day and deeds into the interminable Future that held the beautiful house with Gertrude, Miss Gifford and the bright curtains, and many meetings of the restored Parliament in College Green, listening to the great leader, Mr. M. Reilly, worthy successor to Parnell himself.

3

The convent door, opening slightly, made a crack in the morning darkness and from the harshness of the street Martin slipped into the soft obscurity of the hall. As he went up the polished stairs towards the Oratory, the black-and-white figures rustled on their aloof coming and going.

In the little vestry, warm with the incense of many years, he put on his silver-buckled slippers, regretting that his gorgeous red soutane could be worn only for a bishop, but glad that his black one, with its long folds was so dignified and gracefully made. Having carefully put on the second-best surplice with the deep crochet work at sleeve and hem, walked up and down the room to make the well-cut soutane curvet about his ankles.

With quiet superiority he allowed the vestry nun to make the preliminary preparations, but he himself lit the candles on the altar, and cast an appraising eye on the nun's arrangement of the Missal, of the wine and water cruets. He moved the cruets about half an inch from where the nun had placed them, just to show that the final responsibility was his. However holy she might be, however important among nuns, she was below Martin Matthew Reilly this morning. No woman, no nun, no female saint, could do what he was about to do—serve at Mass. No woman could serve the wine, pour water on the priest's fingers crossed on the chalice, nor could she, bending on one knee and holding the Missal itself, feel the priest's chasuble brush the face and hear his blessing pass overhead to the kneeling church. The priest said Mass, repeating in a bloodless manner the bloody sacrifice of Calvary. Beyond the priest was the Bishop, beyond the Bishop, the Cardinals and the Pope, and behind the Pope were Peter and the Apostles, grouped around God. And next to the priest came Martin Matthew Reilly.

When Father Riordan came he gave no greeting other than a
courteous bow, and this, too, pleased Martin. Until Mass had
been said, and Communion administered, it was unseemly to
grin and stutter greetings, as little Father Flaherty did; not
downright bad, as eating after midnight would have been, but
very objectionable, in Martin's opinion. Whereas a bow, a
courteous bow, was just right. And he loved to give a deep, slow
bow in reply. That was one of Father Riordan's many charms for
him. With Father Riordan, he could try those handsome gestures
which he saw done by people in plays, by his pretty Aunt Mary,
by Niave's small, thin mother. Ah, how nicely girls moved
always. Even when tumbling they always managed to come down
in a graceful position. Even stolid Muriel Norburton had not been
ungraceful in her reverse turn-overs; and when Gertrude had
shaken her leg at him it probably had been shocking, but it had
also been very gracefully done.

But, great heavens, what was he doing! Thinking about girls
at such a moment, about girls showing the whole of their legs and
glimpses of their underclothes! And Protestant girls! Good God,
had he gone and committed a sin, just as he was about to serve
Mass? And the Celestines' special dawn Mass!

Was it a sin? He removed a twist from Father Riordan's stole.
Was it a bad thought? He smoothed the end of Father Riordan's
chasuble. Some of the horror retreated from around his heart. It
was not, he felt sure, a bad thought at other times. But could it
be a bad thought just before serving Mass? Could it? He picked
up Father Riordan's biretta. Then relief came to him. Why, even
—'and remember only *even*', he told himself—even if it were a bad
thought, he had not yielded to it. And the sin could only lie in
'giving way to bad thoughts'! Therefore, if it had been the devil
—and he did not admit the point—who had sent the thought, the
result had been a victory for goodness, so the position was
actually better than if he had never had the thought at all! In
happiness, he bowed gently to Father Riordan to indicate that
all was now ready and, going to the door of the vestry, he rang
the little bell.

As with bowed head and fingers correctly joined before his
face he preceded Father Riordan to the Oratory, he prepared
himself to give to this Mass a perfect service. Not once would he
sink on to his heels or droop his back. Not once would he fiddle

with the bell, nor scratch his knees, no matter how weary they
became. Thank goodness Father Riordan would not rush up the
altar steps and come rushing down again, rubbing his neck like
little Father Flaherty, dropping things and saying 'Oh, dear me!'
Father Riordan would move and speak with care and dignity. On
the other hand, he would not take all the morning at it, like poor
old Father Ryan, crawling about all over the place, and making
one wonder if he might not at any moment make some dreadful
mistake. No, Father Riordan was the perfect priest. Perfect.
And he had said, 'The perfect beauty of the Catholic Faith
itself!'

'*Introibo ad altare Dei*,' prayed Father Riordan at the foot of the
altar steps, 'I will go unto the altar of God.'

And Martin answered boldly, '*Ad Deum qui laetificat juventutem
meam*—to God Who rejoiceth my youth.' And under the influence
of the place, the hour, the resolve to give perfect service to this
Mass, he said to himself, 'Yes, I will go unto the altar of God
Who rejoices my youth and Who made the perfect Beauty of the
Catholic Faith itself.'

The words seemed to him to declare an extraordinary revelation, which so filled him with awe and delight that, when he
knelt on the steps after Father Riordan had gone to the Epistle
side, he smiled at the priest's back, at the vases of Christmas
roses, smiled straight at the door of the Tabernacle itself.

This rather excited joy lasted until, while standing behind
Father Riordan, waiting to carry the Missal to the Gospel side,
he remembered his promise to pray for Mr. Burns. While he
prayed earnestly that Mr. Burns would soon come back to God
and the Church, the excitement flowed into a sweet contentment.

Carefully following each sequence of the ordered service,
timing his slow walk to bring him at just the correct moment to
just the correct part of the altar, gratefully making each bow and
movement respond to Father Riordan's care and dignity, he felt
that nothing could excel this quiet Mass, with the nuns' voices
behind him, rising now and again in the Gloria or the Credo. The
Gregorian Chant had now in his ears a sweetness which it lacked
when it thundered from the throats of hundreds of ecclesiastics in
the magnificence of the Bishop's High Mass. Feeling so strongly
this morning a mood which he had always loved, loving Father
Riordan all the more because his presence accorded so well with

that mood, he moved and served in a kind of rapture. When the Consecration came and, prostrate along the steps with the bell ready beside his hand, he looked up at the Host held above Father Riordan's head, it was from a heart full of happiness and adoration that he murmured, 'My Lord and my God.'

He knelt before Father Riordan for Communion and when he received the wafer on his tongue he thought that this was the best Communion he had ever made, that never again would it be necessary to go to Confession before Communion because he would never again have any sins to blot out his state of grace.

With the wafer melting behind closed lips, he held the great silver candlestick beside the ciborium flashing in Father Riordan's hands as the priest moved with the Sacrament from nun to nun kneeling along the step which separated their pews from the Sanctuary. The nuns' pale hands passed the napkin from chin to chin; the upturned faces, thin, broad, plump, might have been the faces in the Dublin waxworks, so cold were they in the light of the candle, so fixed in devotion. One after another, the white faces in line toppled over, as nun after nun bent her head.

Back at the altar, he found the last movements of the Mass coming all too soon. '*Ite, missa est*,' Father Riordan looked down at him; and '*Deo Gratias*' answered Martin, wondering how he and other boys had ever thought it funny to say 'Thanks be to God' because Mass was nearly over.

The Last Gospel having been said, he waited eagerly for the *De Profundis* because he always liked to remember that only in Ireland of all the countries in the world was the *De Profundis* said after Mass and that its purpose was to pray for the souls of all those Irish people whose records had been lost in the Penal Days. Nothing could have pleased him more than to close this Mass with prayers for those far-off countrymen of his who had suffered for God and Ireland under England's laws.

For the last time he raised the hem of the chasuble from Father Riordan's heels as the priest went up the altar steps; for the last time he bowed to Father Riordan's descent. For the last time, with a swinging of his soutane, he measured his pace before Father Riordan coming away from the altar of God.

Back in the vestry, Father Riordan and he shook hands. 'A Happy Christmas to us!'

'If only Mr. Burns could have been at our Mass, Father, and be in here with us now!'

Father Riordan said: 'Next Christmas, we'll have him. We'll get the nuns to allow him to come to this very Mass next Christmas Day.'

Then the nuns came in, laughing and swooping. 'Oh, Martin, you were perfect!' They bundled him amongst them, almost rolling him from one to the other, and he laughed into their laughing faces. The boxes of sweets, the blessed medals and relics, showered upon him, and each toffee-box, each prayer-book or medal, had a special characteristic which had to be explained privately in the secrecy obtained by drawing him behind the open door of the big cupboard. There was a call from the younger nuns, 'Couldn't we have him to breakfast?' But Mother Superior shook her head.

Laden with presents, the praises and smiles still with him, he tried to slide along the frosty pavement. The balance of his presents on top of his Mass-bag was maintained with many delicious threats of disaster, until he reached the door left open for him by Josie and Mary Ellen when they had gone out to first Mass at the Cathedral. At the door, beads and books and sweets came crashing down and he laughed as he ran up and down along the dark hall retrieving them.

He went upstairs and stood at each door, listening to the breathing within each room, at his Aunt Eileen's door, at the door of the girls' room, at James Edward's and, lastly, at his own door, listening to Patrick. He went to the bathroom, longing to turn on all the taps at once and pull the lavatory chain as fast as the cistern would fill up for him, for then the great rushing of water would match the rushing of his heart.

Nibbling sweets and investigating the nuns' gifts, he recited poem after poem, and poked the kitchen fire in accordance with his promise to Josie. Soon, while feet began to move about overhead, Mary Ellen, Josie and he sat with juicy mouths in the lamp-lit kitchen and gazed at the eggs and sausages bursting on their plates.

All day he carried with him something of the loveliness of the Mass and the joyfulness of the nuns, something, too, of the self-confidence and success. It stayed with him through the enormous dinner, the long afternoon of music and games while Santa

Claus's candles guttered dangerously amid broken tinsel and holly. It was with him when he went to bed and was still in his heart when his last sleepy thoughts turned to the morrow and Lullacreen, to his grandmother and his pretty Aunt Mary.

The side-car lurched along the frozen ruts glinting in the sunlight; they were nearing Lullacreen.

Martin watched the landmarks, answered the pleasant little remarks of his Aunt Eileen, straight and dignified on one side of him. Up on the well of the car, with his head in the small of Patsy's expressive back, Patrick slept. On the other side, with their backs to Martin, Bridget half mockingly heeded Mr. Reilly's knowledgeable comments on every field, while James Edward frequently looked down his nose.

The wide fields of Meltone were bare beneath bare trees; there, in summer, Martin lay under the boughs, helping the blacksmith to record the runs, while out in the sunny spaces the smack of the bat sounded and the white fielders ran.

'Aw, come on, now—put a good show on it,' Patsy grumbled to the horse as the first Lullacreen fields spread wide.

There was Paddy Keegan's cottage. How fine Paddy looked in the summer in the lines of men up the ladders, swinging the forkfuls of hay to the blue sky. There was the cottage of Old Tommy, the oldest of all the Lullacreen men. When Old Tommy's grand-daughter had married young Paddy's brother all the uncles Reilly had sat in Tommy's yard watching the dancing under the tree, but the barrels of porter had not begun to pour blackly until the aunts Reilly had withdrawn to Lullacreen. Uncle Edward himself had danced with Old Tommy's grey wife, while Old Nancy, as old as Tommy himself and as long in Lullacreen, had declared that she had never had under her in the Lullacreen kitchen 'a better nor a dacenter girl' than Katie, the bride.

They passed the stile where Aunt Mary, swinging her parasol across her little feet, had told him stories about his great-grand-father blowing a hunting horn on Sundays on the drive to Mass, 'and every horse for miles around, mighty Martin, lepping mad to get out, thinking it was the hunt'.

And there now were the barns, the hay-sheds, the cherry trees bare to the skin, and the clipped circles and pinnacles of Aunt

Mary's own inner box-hedge, where Martin used to say Mass, with an old newspaper for chasuble and his Cousin Molly, dressed as a boy, for acolyte.

'Wait till the horse stops, you mad child!'

'He'll kill himself—pull up the horse, Patsy—quickly!'

But already Martin was swinging from the step, his feet banging along the gravel, the horse slithering as Patsy dragged on the reins. The gates were wide open, the lawn swarmed with children. He let go, whirled around in a stagger and then, through the groups of children and adults advancing to meet the car, he shot faster than ever he did with the ball, and panted for breath in his grandmother's arms.

'My dark angel.' She held him. 'Steady now, boy. Steady.'

'They kept saying you wouldn't be standing in the door this time.'

'Ah, you mind too much what people say; that's why they say things to you. Silly girleen of a boy,' and she smiled, smoothing the net over her hair.

'Have Aunt Mary and Uncle Charles come yet from Moydelgan?'

'Not yet. The youngest and always the latest—Mary. I thought I'd switched it out of her, but there you are! Now, stop thinking she's not going to come. She'll come all right like everyone else. Steady now.'

Her grey eyes and her 'Steady, boy, steady' soothed him. Cupping one hand to her mouth, she called clear and high, almost like a young person: 'The jam cupboard! Grandmother is off to the jam cupboard!' And, as hens answer a clucking call, boys and girls came running from all the corners of Lullacreen and down out of the trees. While they surged around her and she brought from the cupboard her butterscotch, her cakes and boiled sweets, Martin stood on a chair to count the heads in the heaving mass. The task was made more difficult by the compulsion under which he placed himself to count in order of age. Kathleen Reilly from Ardell, she's just seventeen, but now is her brother Jack older than Mary Reilly from Rathdore?

'Ah, stand still and eat while I count!'

He tried beginning at the other end, at the youngest. Tom from Rathdore is only eight... 'Grandmother, I've got it. Twenty here, and Aunt Mary's two little girls to come from Moydelgan, that's twenty-two. And Edward from Malldean and Rathdore Eileen think they're too old now to come for sweets. That's twenty-four only this time.'

'Wrong, dark angel. Twenty-five. You missed my little red-nose.' And behind her skirts tiny Norah peered.

Those who had already assured themselves that the tock of the grandfather clock was as strong as ever streamed upstairs to inspect the corners where they slept during summer visits, and pushed their way through another stream coming downstairs from the same inspection. The dining-room, even in winter, smelled of flowers and sunlit woodwork, and though the front window was bare the back window still had its frame of greenery outside. The lines of boys and girls trooped across the parlour, across the dining-room, down the three thickly-matted steps and on to the kitchen. There the metal doors in the wall swung open and the baking bread poured forth its odour. The settle beds, the ladder to the servants' lofts, the huge bins of flour and meal were as thrilling as ever. Outside, the orchard was bare and black and the big pans in the dairies only half full of milk, but the horses, the ponies, the cows were ranged in their stalls. In and out of farmyards the lines of youngsters went, noting the familiar, disapproving all change. They counted the beehives, went through loft after loft, they worked the well-bucket and swung from the water pump and they raced through the lawn coppice and past the arbour to stare across the five-acre field at the woods and the furzy slopes.

Then Aunt Mary came. Scarcely had the wren-boys marched on to the lawn in their colours, chanting and holding up the bright bier of the wren, than she and Uncle Charles arrived from Moydelgan.

She stood in the parlour door, tugging at the waist-points of her little jacket. What lovely strange clothes Aunt Mary wore, thought Martin, watching her from behind the sofa. Her little jacket made him think of Mr. Midshipman Easy on the deck of the frigate. What elegant skirts; what 'different' blouses, without buttoning or brooch, silky-smooth all the way to the high, ruched neck without a seam or fastening. She patted her little head with its tight curls.

'Well, Mary? Late again!'

'Indeed I am, Mother.'

They stood clasped together before the fire, Aunt Mary's pale pink cheek against Grandmother's pale grey cheek. She slipped back to close the door, then taking the pale grey face in her hands she kissed it. Her two little girls, in their apple-green coats and apple-green muffs, stared at the embracing.

'How's Father keeping?'

'Grand for his age. Seventy-eight's a good age. But he's leaving things more and more to Edward.'

'Mother, Edward must get him a wife. He's forty-five now and soon it will be too late. The eldest ought to be married, there must be a youngster to grow up in the place who's to take it on him after him and Father.' She touched her mother's shoulder ever so gently. 'You're looking a bit tired, Mother.'

'Aye, lately I feel a bit tired. You're right. We must get Edward married quickly. Tell me, does the doctor say yet whether you'll have to go under that operation?'

'Ah, they talk a lot of balderdash, doctors. Possibly in March. But it may not have to be at all. And, anyway, it's only a little operation, no way serious at all, they say. Mother, they're not keeping my hedges, and the rockeries are gone to the divil altogether—do men never bother about anything?'

'Ah, sure the land's the land for men, and all else is nonsense to them. And ye can't blame them—'twas held hard. But it isn't only the men. Bridget has let her hens strip nearly every blade of grass from the Clonglass lawns. That lovely place, not a year married into .it and she's . . . well, the only ones that ever cared were yourself and——'

'Poor Mat, God rest him. And he——'

'Quiet, quiet! The boy's there behind the sofa.'

Aunt Mary swirled about, the little jacket-points lifting out from her waist. 'Well, if it isn't himself popping the old black head over the sofa!' She drew him out, kissed him and danced him around the room. 'Martin, mighty Martin, mighty Marty Martin,' she sang. The tender mouth smiled, the merry brown eyes danced. She swung out an arm and, without stopping, drew the little girls into the round and danced them across to the dining-room where the aunts around the fire broke into waves of fluttering comment.

'How smart you look, Mary.'

'Heavens bless you, this isn't a costume! Just a blouse and a few bits of things. How are you, Father?'

She kissed the old cheek. All the aunts fell silent, waiting for the old man to speak. 'I'm well, thank ye, Mary. Ye're looking well yourself.'

He studied her, his eyebrows wrinkled. On the wall beyond him there hung the framed list of the ploughing-matches he had won. Near it, a picture of a racing horse. People said that before his marriage he had drunk much and 'followed the race-horses', but never since.

'But different, too, Mary. As pretty as ever, prettier I'd say, but different. Tell me, is that veil with the dots meant to hide your face when you pull it down or to call attention to it?'

When Aunt Mary laughed, all the other aunts, sure that the old man had made a joke, not a reproof, laughed also, but with expressive shrugs at one another. Aunt Mary's merry, tinkling laugh ended. 'Whichever it's for, Father, it's nice. Just a fashion for ladies, you know.'

'Aye! For ladies.' The hand, gnarled by the plough and the spade, moved to her shoulder, and after a moment he said, 'Mary,' and touched her pale red cheek with his grey, grim lips.

She drew the veil down over her face, pointed it swiftly under her chin. 'There you are, Father.'

He looked and nodded and, as he turned away, the grey old lips were twisted in a private smile.

He demanded that all the boys and girls be sent to him in the kitchen. 'And at once, if ye please!' Timorously, the biggest and smallest had to follow him. Seated in the big chair by the open hearth, he leaned on his stick and surveyed the great circle that had to spread around all the walls of the kitchen.

'Stand straighter than that, miss. What are they doing with ye in those schools of yours at all! And you, sir, keep your hands quiet!'

They licked anxious lips and waited.

'Now there's one thing in Latin ye all can know, even the girls, and that's the Mass. Maureen, say the *Pater Noster* and say it clear and correct.' Maureen trembled; Old Nancy and her 'girls' looked on commiseratingly from the background.

'Joe, the first part of the *Credo*. Sharp now, sir!'

James Edward whispered to Martin, 'For the love of Moses, how does the *Introibo* start?'

And Martin whispered, '*Introibo ad altare Dei, ad Deum qui*

laetificat juventutem meum.' What would Grandfather think of
Father Riordan? And of Mr. Burns? Martin remembered how,
when someone had said that a priest had ordered Mr. Burns to
stand 'well away' from the gates of the Cathedral so as not 'to
insult a Catholic church by your proximity', Grandfather had
twisted his already twisted lips and asked sourly, 'And did he
budge?'

He was a strange man. Once, walking with Martin, he had
stopped at a small pot-hole in the road and had made Martin
help him fetch earth and small stones from the roadside and
water from a cottage; they stamped until the pot-hole was level
with the road and the old man then said, 'If everyone did that
every time they saw a hole, the road would keep better for
everyone.'

At last he let the circle go. 'And remember yer manners. You,
Eileen from Rathdore, you're a fine, good-looking girl, but I
want none of your new-fangled ways in this house, miss! And,
since you and Edward are the eldest, ye'll please set a good
example or ye'll both catch it. Go now, and God guard ye all and
bless ye.'

In the afternoon Aunt Mary brought her two little girls to the
room where Martin was and put them under rugs, bidding him
to watch them. 'I'd sooner trust them to you than to those big
bounders of girls from Rathdore.' With the apple-green frocks
over her arms, she sat by the little girls, teasing them a little
while. Then with a tinkle of her laugh, she swished away. 'You'll
mind my lambs, Martin, I know.'

Martin, pleased by the trust and the opportunity to read, was
the more pleased because he disliked the uncouth, joking
Rathdore cousins, hated the atmosphere of labour and straitened
circumstances on their farm that was 'too small for the fifteen of
them', and feared, while despising, their judgements, especially
those which labelled himself 'funny' and 'soft but terrible wild'.

They disturbed him later by crawling over him and he sat on
the edge of the bed with them, enjoying the mystery of the vast
room and the sounds from below and inventing dramatic
explanations for some of the sounds.

When later Aunt Mary came and sent the little girls downstairs, he was lucky enough to get a few words with her
alone.

'What's this I've only just been hearing about you so often having a headache when you come home from school in the afternoon?'

'It's the smell, partly, I think. It gets bad near the end of school and I feel sick sometimes. When Brother Finnegan hits my head it's worse, of course.'

In the light of the candle her face wrinkled in horror. 'Look here, you must tell your Aunt Eileen things like that, whenever your grandmother or myself are not about. You'll be off to Dunslane after the summer, but even so I won't have this kind of thing in the meantime. I think I'll go over and stay a night at Glenkilly soon.'

'Aunt Mary, the Rathdore girls were saying in the lofts that Aunt Eileen came from a poor family and was not good enough for a Reilly of Lullacreen.'

'Those horrible girls! What nonsense! And we ourselves just farmers up to sixty years ago. Your Aunt Eileen is a good woman and, let me tell you, John was very, very, very lucky to get her. What nonsense to give ourselves airs. If your great-grandfather hadn't been in the ledger books of the Hoares, he'd have been put out of this place when the Protestants were all trying to grab the last little bit any Catholic had left to him. But the Hoares refused to do it. He was shrewd, your great-grandfather, and he'd taken care to do his banking with Hoare's banker brother. We'd better luck than the Prendergasts over at Melrone. They lost their land and they're labourers now to this very day. That might have happened to us. Do you know, Martin, he nearly *was* put out. It got round that he used to have the men in twice a week to read out *The Freeman* to them. Hoare's bailiffs came to threaten him but he stood down there in the dining-room'—she nodded her curly head towards the floor under his feet—'and he said, "There's a musket hidden here and, if you find that, there's still many a slasher, and the man that puts me out of here won't live long!" Bedad, he must have been great. It was a hanging matter for a Catholic in those days to have as much as a sword or a gun. Oh, the stories there are about him.'

'Go on, go on. Please!'

'Well, they say he got up on his horse and marched the men here and all the men from Melrone to vote against Hoare's man, although they had their sons at the door taking down the names

of all the tenants and how they voted. And he held his prayer-
book in his bridle-hand and in the other hand he held up a stick
with *The Freeman* nailed as large as life to it. Oh, he must have
been great. And he led them all to the voting; himself and Father
Lacey that was home from Louvain.'

'Oh, wouldn't I love to have seen it! When we get Home Rule,
Aunt Mary, we'll give the Prendergasts back their land.'

'Ah, it's not as easy as that now, Martin. It's too late now to
start changing land back again. Besides, the others are different
now. I think they're sorry for the past now, and they'd like to
mix with us now; it's ourselves that are doing the no-mixing
balderdash.'

'But don't you want Home Rule, Aunt Mary?'

'I suppose I do, but to tell you the truth I'm none too crazy
about it. We must mix. And it's with the others that I sometimes
think I get on best, the nice ones, you know.'

Martin was embarrassed. Aunt Mary might be right about
clothes and manners; but she couldn't know anything about
politics—she couldn't even vote. He changed the subject.

'Aunt Mary. You don't like Uncle John very much, do you?'

She turned him about to face her and said gravely: 'Martin,
John is my brother and your uncle and a Reilly, and a family's a
family. If you were staying now at Moydelgan I'd deal hard with
you for that.'

She let him apologize hesitantly, and put up his hand on
the smooth silk of her blouse where it ran up without seam or
button.

'It just popped out—you know, Aunt Mary.'

She sighed. 'That same popping out will make trouble for you
all your life, I fear,' and she kissed him.

She picked up the candle but stayed to look at her reflection in
the mirror over the mantelshelf. She patted the tight, dark curls.
'Martin,' she said into the glass, as she held the candle sideways
to her reflection, 'I once saw three Faithful Brothers walking down
the street in Ballow past the Royal Leinster Arms; the hotel you
and I stayed in that night. They looked like three great black
cockroaches in the sun,' and her shoulders went up and in the
mirror her pretty face wrinkled with disgust. 'I hate to think of
them hitting you. They shouldn't be allowed to wear a Roman
collar.' She looked at him again steadfastly and then said with

sudden vehemence, 'Look here, if the Faithful Brothers punish you in some wrong way, or not properly, or are rude to you, just throw something at them.'

At the moment he treated her remark as a joke, but her words were to come back to him a few weeks later with crucial effect.

All around the parlour, softly bright in the lamplight, uncles and aunts sat. The door was left open so that the communion of revelry might pass across the hall to the tired ones who gossiped in the firelit shadows of the dining-room; open also was the door to the three matted steps and the kitchen passage and, from the dimness there, the faces of servants, labourers and carmen peered, as big cousins and little cousins showed their accomplishments of song or music or tableaux vivants. While big Margaret from Malldean demonstrated that her final year 'at the French nuns' ' was not being wasted since she could do her 'social deportment' lesson without a movement of her back, and could recite gracefully in English and carefully in French, Grandfather's twisted lips were grim and his old eyes utterly mystified and sardonic.

Aunt Mary fetched Uncle Charles's guitar and sang strange little songs, short and with no point to them, which were praised respectfully by everyone and enjoyed by Aunt Mary, who understood them, and by Martin, because they were sung by Aunt Mary. Before they could ask her to sing again, she turned to Martin. He sang 'The Minstrel Boy', and then someone called, 'Martin, "Fontenoy"!' From the steps and kitchen passage, eager murmurs were passed on to the invisible ones beyond, 'Oh, begob, "Fontenoy"!' Even Grandfather leaned forward on his stick to hear 'Fontenoy'.

From the first lines of his recitation Martin was away in that battle, foreign and yet his own, far off and yet so near, in which an ancestor of his own, the revered Colonel Reilly, had fought for King Louis, the Fleur-de-Lys and Ireland. It was Thomas Davis who had written the poem, Davis who hung on Mr. Burns's wall with a holly wreath separating him from Wolfe Tone.

> '. . . King Louis turned his rein;
> "Not yet, my Liege," Saxe interposed.
> ' "The Irish troops remain." '

And from kitchen steps, dining-room, hall and parlour a gasped 'Ah!' of satisfaction sighed into the air.

After that no one wanted to sing or dance and soon it was time to go. Already the cars were being brought round and the top-coated and muffled figures beginning to gather downstairs. The last to come down knelt in the hall and dining-room, while along the kitchen passage, the line of kneeling servants, carmen and labourers stretched towards the back doors. All faced towards the parlour where, amid the muffled throng, Grandfather and Grandmother together said the first of the Joyful Mysteries. The responses rolled along the faces gleaming towards the kitchen, rolled through hall and rooms, rolled out to where, beyond the little lawn, the car lamps hung in the star-lit night and the horses stamped the frozen gravel.

Edward, the eldest uncle, and Bridget, the eldest aunt, shared the first Joyful Mystery. Down the lines of uncles and aunts, the Mysteries went in order of age. But the younger uncles and aunts had no Mystery to say because the last Joyful Mystery was always the privilege of Old Nancy and Old Tommy mingling their voices in the kitchen passage.

The last responses rumbled to silence, and Grandfather prayed: 'O God, we thank Thee for the joy of this day and because Thou hast preserved this house against so many dangers through so many years. And for all the departed ones of this house we implore Thy infinite mercy.' He paused.

'May perpetual light shine upon them.'

'Amen.'

'May they rest in peace.'

And, as the 'Amens', shrill or gruff, passed from room to room, Martin, meeting his Aunt Mary's eye across many heads, saw that she too had been thinking that the last of the departed ones was his father, Mat.

In the darkness outside someone cried, 'Where's Martin?'

Rosaleen and Bridget were calling him.

'D'ye want the ould horse to die on me now with cold?' the pessimistic Patsy was grumbling.

His grandmother's goodbye still lingering in his ears, Martin followed his Uncle Charles as he carried one of the sleepy little girls amid the bobbing lanterns and the calling figures crossing the lawn.

In the shelter of one of her pinnacled box-hedges, Aunt Mary put down the second sleepy little girl. She kissed Martin goodbye and he held her.

'Listen, Aunt Mary, you are definitely coming to stay a night? And you'll bring a photograph of yourself and Uncle Charles for Gertrude and Niave?'

'I promise.'

'Will you wear today's jacket when you come? It makes you look like a midshipman!'

'They always said I had a small touch of a boy.'

'And they say I have a small touch of a girl.'

In the shadow of her hedge, her merry laugh rang. 'Well, so you have, thank God!'

The horse-hooves smashed the frosty gravel. 'Goodbye, good-bye.' On all sides the farewells circled in the darkness—'Goodbye . . . goodbye.'

As he settled himself between Rosaleen and his Aunt Eileen, Martin was seized by a passionate desire that his grandmother should look at him from the doorway. The side-car wheeled so quickly, the house was swivelling away! There, between two of his Aunt Mary's pinnacles, was a gap leading to the bright door, and Grandmother standing there, smoothing her net and looking down at a muffled child. She must look up, she must! She did. He thought that she looked straight through the gap at him but he knew that she could not see him in the darkness. Did she think of him now as the car's sounds came to her from the Glenkilly road? Was Aunt Mary thinking of him, as she sat beside Uncle Charles in their high gig, the little girls asleep in their arms, and the hooves hitting the Moydelgan road?

4

Despite the fact that it was almost nine o'clock, Martin felt himself under compulsion to touch and count every lamp-post and to place his feet evenly between the cracks on the pavement. When he had covered half the distance to school his foot stopped on a crack. He raced back, recommenced his double task and, despite his hurry, carried it out successfully until he turned into the street where the school was.

There, bearing diagonally down upon him, came the Brothers, marching from their Residence House. Slipping into a doorway to allow the black figures in front to gain the school road before him, he crouched back in the doorway as they tramped past, three black figures in front, then after an interval two black figures, then three more. Following them, he watched the broad black boots as they came flatly down on the pavement and thought how in summer the dust lay in the folds of the black trousers. Once again, he pondered the question: why, when boys were formed in a half-circle before his chair, did Brother Kirwan so often swing his foot, so that the toe of a boot kicked into a thigh? Boys were always arguing about what caused the sharp pain as opposed to the feel of the kick itself. Some maintained that the frayed state of the toe of his right boot was because of pushing pins between the sole and the upper; others claimed actually to have seen the pin.

He turned in through the school gate. As often, in spite of all his precautions before leaving home, he had to go shivering to the lavatory. He hated the smelly little row of lavatories, hated having to ask publicly for the key, hated the miserable, useless pain in his belly, worse than the worst 'confession pain'. Stupid with hate and dread, he thought dazedly of Moydelgan and invented incidents which were to happen there, in all of which

92

Aunt Mary tugged the waist-points of her midshipman jacket. As Moydelgan was near to Lullacreen, he would often go to see Grandmother; indeed, he could spend a night there. Coming back to himself with a start, and not knowing how long he had been day-dreaming, he ran in panic. From the upper classrooms the sound of the leather came to him, so he knew that school had begun. Slipping into his own classroom, he met the heavy smell of breath and of damp clothes and thanked his lucky stars that it was Brother Shaughnessy's class. The Brother at the blackboard had his back to the room, so Martin tiptoed cautiously, hung up the key, tiptoed back and would have gained his place undetected had not some boys sniggered and shuffled their feet.

He stood still, he would not slink to his place before them now. Brother Shaughnessy said: 'Reilly, you seem to like getting your hands warmed up good and early. It's the same nearly every morning.' Martin went to him and took the three blows of the leather. He told himself that it was 'fair enough'; he had been late and any other Brother would have given him more. He stared into the watching faces and curled his lip at them, then tried to smile at those boys whom he approved; at that, they sniggered again. Ah, yes: 'The Slave-Hearts, who twist and beg off.' He himself would never ask a Faithful Brother to let him off anything.

Brother Finnegan, later in the morning, seemed to ignore him. But Martin knew very well that he was not being ignored. While the class worked at sums, Martin looked up to find the grey-green eyes fixed upon him. A long reddish hand beckoned and Martin struggled between the packed seats, stopping in the passage to straighten his wide collar and pat his bow. Standing by the tall chair, he heard Brother Finnegan's Cork voice saying very low:

'You little molly-cod! Stopping to titivate yerself in the gang-way. What do ye mean by it?'

'By what, Brother Finn——'

A stunning blackness smote him, the blow on his face sent him to one knee and his head thumped against the leg of a desk. Groping for the side of his face, he stared up and saw the big hand still open, and behind it the Queen of Heaven smiling in the coloured dust beam.

He got to his feet.

'Maybe that'll teach ye not to be impertinent. You're the worst-mannered boy I ever met. "By what, by what." ' The long lips sneered as they mimicked Martin's voice. 'Ye think yourself too good for everyone but you've no manners at all yerself. Talking out to me as if I were . . . as if I were . . . !'

The long face leaned forward, the grey-green eyes bright. 'Ye think yourself very cute. When I refuse you leave to go for a drink in the yard ye go and get leave from another Brother just to show me ye don't care about me.'

Staring in perplexity at him, Martin raced through his memory, seeking an explanation. From somewhere in his throbbing head, a memory came—a very hot day in the stony yard between the high, grey walls. Nearly a year ago. Brother Finnegan would not let him go to the tap. He had been very thirsty, so later on he had asked another Brother.

'It was just I wanted a drink.'

'Ye wanted to best me, ye little hypocrite. "I only wanted a drink." I called ye up to know what ye meant by ignoring the instructions Brother Shaughnessy gave last week.'

'Please, what instructions——'

Once more the stunning blackness smote the side of his face, once more his oblique view dizzily saw the Virgin's smile behind the big hand. Brother Finnegan gripped him by the coat lapels and said straight into his eyes:

'Impertinent! Insolent! How dare ye pretend ye don't know what I mean!'

'But I don't. I don't! I forget! I forget a lot of things!'

'I don't believe ye. Aye, when I passed ye with Miss McDowell and Miss Jamieson, I saw ye all right, smirking to score over me. Big girls that ought to be young ladies. I saw the look in yer eye, I tell ye.' He stopped, the grey-green eyes full of darkness. 'And, anyway, ye've no right to forget. Hold out your hand.'

As he stumbled back to his seat, refusing to nurse his smarting hands under so many watching eyes, he heard the Cork accent say, 'Is there a single boy here who doesn't remember what Brother Shaughnessy said about keeping your hands joined when the Hail Mary's said in Irish at the Hour?'

'No, Brother Finnegan, no . . .' the replies rose heartily.

Low, treacherous cur—he *told* them what it was.

'But smart little baby-boys can't remember, or pretend they

can't. Their little head is so full of itself that it can't remember. "I forget. I forget a lot of things!" '

The mouths opened and sniggered at their master's words.

'Go back and write on the board: "I forget a lot of things. I'm a silly baby. I'm also very impertinent!" Go on. Now sign your name to it: "Martin Reilly". All right, everybody, that's enough laughing now! Back to your books, everyone!'

The hands of the clock moved sluggishly on towards three o'clock and the air grew fouler. It was Brother Kirwan's class now. Martin thought that it relieved his head a little to keep his neck stiff and to look sideways at the cupboard while the others pattered:

> 'There stood two glasses, filled to the brim,
> On the rich man's table rim to rim.'

Since he knew the verses, he kept his neck stiff and stared at the cupboard while waiting his turn to repeat the required lines. Slowly, he began to realize that he himself was the cause of the profound silence; there was a tittering and he bent his head to his book. Out of the silence, Brother Kirwan's clear whisper came along the room in carefully precise tones.

'Dinny Byrne, will you go down and tell our young genius that we all know he has most interesting thoughts and a beautiful disposition and that he need not call our attention to himself by posing. Will you repeat that, Dinny, to see if you've got it correct.'

Big Dinny stuttered and laughed as he repeated the message and his rubber soles came padding down the room. Above Martin's head, the message stuttered between the adenoidal sniffs which half-witted Dinny could not control. The soft padding went away up the room but stopped.

'Oh, Dinny, I forgot to give you the rest of the message. Will you go back, Dinny, like a good boy and—you don't mind all this trouble, Dinny, do you?—that's a good lad. Will you go back and tell Master Reilly in a gentle way, Dinny, so as not to offend his feelings, tell him to come up to me, that I have some nice hard sweets for him. *Hard* ones, Dinny: be sure to let him know that they're good hard ones. Will you repeat that, Dinny.'

Big Dinny's stutter rasped in the silence; Martin lifted his

head, curled his lip at the staring white faces and went forward
to the grey young face and the hand holding the strap.

In the dining-room his Aunt Eileen said: 'But you really can't
do without dinner. Tell me, Martin, has anyone done anything
to you at school? Hit you some way they shouldn't? . . . Mary
Tierney was saying on Stephen's Day at Lullacreen——'

'It's all right, Aunt Eileen. Just I have a headache. Won't you
let me have a cup of tea, please, instead of dinner? Dinner would
make me sick.'

'Are you sure now that no one's done anything wrong to you
at school? The Brothers are good men and very holy monks, but
I sometimes wonder . . . Well, all right; go and lie down on your
bed and I'll get Mary Ellen to bring you up some nice tea and a
piece of toast.' She put a hand towards him, hesitated and
withdrew it. Then suddenly she said: 'Don't do any homework
tonight. I'll give you a note.' As she turned away, he dizzily
thought she muttered something about: 'Once and for all, I'm
going to find out. I won't have . . .'

That night Martin got out of bed and, wrapping his blankets
about him, sat hunched in the window-bay in the shadow of his
great caddy and looked out at the stars beyond the roof of the
town. He thought how fine it would be to trample on the faces of
Brother Kirwan and Brother Finnegan; he imagined the faces
squashed beneath the boots. He invented dramas, in one of which
the people of Glenkilly, over his drowned body, pointed accusing
fingers at the Faithful Brothers. But no drama of revenge or
remorse could satisfy the shame in his soul.

At last his hatred spilled over his lips. 'Bog-trotters, blasted
bog-trotters. Slave-Hearts and . . . oh . . . oh, great black
cockroaches in the sun.'

After that he was able to lie down and his sick spirit discharged
itself in tears.

The following morning, before getting up, he read some of the
letters in his caddy and looked at the photographs. He had re-
read Gertrude's latest letter when he turned to one from his
Aunt Mary, and the words she had spoken at Lullacreen came
back to him: 'Look here, if the Faithful Brothers punish you in
some wrong way . . . just throw something at them.'

While he dressed and all through breakfast he brooded over

his plans. He could not get to school quickly enough and this time, when he passed in through the dread gate, he felt no shivering useless fear in his belly. Several times he said to himself, I should have thought of it myself!

He went about the room until he found the biggest slate in the place with its wooden frame broken to expose jagged edges. This he substituted for his own slate. Well, Finnegan would get it. Finnegan would surely ask for it. It was a pity that Kirwan would not get it also. Come on, Finnegan, you Cork lout, and say something or do something to me so that I can bang this slate into your face. Dear Aunt Mary. She would say, 'Bedad, you were great,' as she had said of his great-grandfather.

Once or twice he took the slate from its hold to feel its strong jagged edge. It would not kill him, but it would smash his face all right! Then, when they arrested him, he would tell the judge everything about the Brothers and Aunt Mary would prove that she had told him to do it, and that would be the end of the Brothers. Perhaps the other fellows would throw their slates, too, when they saw him begin; once, some of them had brought in stones but none of them would throw when the time came; but now with himself to show them the way, this might be a real revolution against the Brothers! He drummed impatiently upon his desk. Hurry up, Finnegan, you lout.

The morning passed and it was only just before the break for lunch that Brother Finnegan's long face leaned forward from the high chair. Martin looked at him across the heads and took a good grip on the slate.

'Well, well, stop everybody and look at our wild young thing.'

Come on, come on—say more than that, that's not enough. He chose the place between the eyes where the slate would go.

'Well, well, what a face our Master Impertinent has on this morning. Or our Miss Baby Impertinent, maybe we should say.'

Martin stood up.

'Sit down! How dare you look at me like that, ye——'

He ducked only just in time as the slate hurtled straight towards his eyes. It whizzed over his ear, crashed through the window beyond and clattered in pieces outside.

Martin stared panting at the crouched, frightened face in the big chair, then he walked to the end of the room and, flinging the door open, shrieked: 'You're a Slave-Heart! That's all you are, a

Slave-Heart!' and went out. He pushed the door open again, put
his head round it and shouted, 'Now do what you like about
that!'

Brother Finnegan's face stared from the chair, the white faces
stared. And, as Martin walked home along the street, he stamped
his foot in anger and muttered: 'God, why did I miss him! He
ducked, and I missed him!'

He wandered about the streets until the late afternoon.

Down at the river he watched its cold flow, surging now with
the pressure of early spring; he drew his hand through the water
among the reeds and watched the long grass bending beneath. He
went then to stand on the river bank behind the Jamiesons'
garden where he looked up at Gertrude's little attic window. He
went away from the sight of the window which looked into a
deserted room, empty of her until Easter. Why, it was only a few
weeks until Easter. It was March now! March so soon! Easter
and Moydelgan with Aunt Mary's daffodils under the dining-
room window! And, thinking of it, he faced homeward at
last.

But he began to be frightened now. Perhaps Aunt Mary had
meant that he was to throw something small and light? Would he
be put in the jail when they arrested him? Would he get any food
there?

He went even more slowly towards the back door of his uncle's
house, but there were no police waiting for him outside the door
as he had expected, nor in hiding behind it, waiting to pounce
upon him, and he was astonished to find himself merely being
scolded for returning so late from school. 'Your aunt has bad news
for you,' Josie told him. For the next hour he waited for whatever
was going to happen, getting more and more frightened and
stuffing himself with food in order to fill up for jail. At last his
Aunt Eileen came to him with a white frightened face.

His grandmother was dead. She had visited Aunt Mary in the
Dublin nursing home and she had caught a chill on the way back.
She had died that afternoon and tomorrow he must travel by
train and car to Lullacreen with all the men of the Glenkilly
Reillys, with his Uncle John, James Edward and Patrick.

The March air was cold and still, the road hard, and Old
Tommy drove the horse smartly from the railway station.

Once, a horseman, galloping around a bend, pulled his horse's chest straight up into the clear air and, with hand uplifted above the rearing horse, he called, 'The old lady?'

'Gone home!' answered Old Tommy with raised hat and whip, and the horseman bent his head.

That evening they brought Martin into his grandmother's room, where the tall candles burned and in the dimness beyond the candles the watchers rustled and whispered. He knelt by the bed until he decided that he had been kneeling for a suitable length of time, then looked at his grandmother and saw her white hands around the black crucifix on the brown habit. Her smooth, waxen face recalled to him the nuns' faces in the light of the candle beside Father Riordan's ciborium. He was certain that at any moment the pale lips would say, 'Steady, my dark angel, steady!' He stared so long that they tipped him on the shoulder and led him from the room.

During the night he was wakened by a noise in the bedroom, where, to his disgust, he was packed in a bed with younger cousins. The noise grew into a blurred shape and light of a candle, and he heard Old Nancy whispering: 'Do you think ye'll be all right on that sofa, with the rugs, Mr. Joe? I'll shake the snow from your things. We never thought you could get across the water so soon.'

A big man struggled on to the sofa and Martin, watching through the bed curtains, saw a glowing cigarette-end and heard a mutter: 'God, what a country! Europe's suburb! The Beauty in the Sleeping Wood! Nothing but the old lady could have got me back, even for forty-eight hours!'

Sleepless now, and with an exciting, queer lightness and heat in his head, Martin lay wondering when and where he would be arrested. The Government might not think it nice to arrest a boy when his grandmother had just died.

In the morning black footmarks pitted the thick snow on the lawn paths. Alone beneath his Aunt Mary's clipped hedges, he threw snowballs at the pinnacles till, realizing that it was not quite right to snowball when his grandmother was lying dead upstairs with her hands around the crucifix, he went indoors and spent his time bathing his hot cheeks and light head, keeping out of people's way and trying to identify faces among the ever-arriving cousins and in-laws of all degrees. Old Nancy called him to her, took him to the kitchen, gave him hot tea and made him dry his feet at the hearth. She said: 'Poor Master Martin. What'll become of ye at all?'

Later on he slipped unobtrusively upstairs and, from the windows, watched the lines of cars lengthening beneath the white hedges, and the arms flapping across the chests of pipe-smoking men. He stepped into his grandmother's room and found it empty. There she was, alone on the bed.

Bending down and putting his mouth close to an ear, he whispered: 'Grandmother! Grandmother!' He looked for a long time at the ear, and although he knew that she was dead, he nevertheless could not believe that the ear was unable to hear. Gradually, however, he began to believe it, to understand that it would be wrong for the ear to be able to hear and he became frightened. He began to understand that he would never again talk to Grandmother, nor ever hear her or be hugged by her. Kneeling down then, he began to pray passionately, until people came in, when he sidled away from the room.

Now that he was pierced by knowledge of mortality, the lines of cars spreading along every hedge appalled him. The figures streamed ever more numerous into the house, while the Rathdore girls took ladies upstairs and bustled about importantly. From a deep corner in the kitchen he watched and saw that people were beginning to come and go in their overcoats. From the top of the three matted steps his Uncle John and Grandfather looked in and down at him.

'Yes,' the old man said, 'you did right to bring him; he has the right to walk after her with all her grandsons.'

'Go and get well wrapped up, Martin. The coffin will be coming down in a few minutes. There now, don't look like that. You're not a bad lad, really, and you were terribly fond of Mother. Mother!' and Uncle John bent his head and a quiver twisted his long figure.

From his place among the grandsons behind the open hearse, Martin watched his uncles' feet pulping the snow on the lawn paths as they carried her from the house, his six uncles with Paddy and two others of the men, Uncle Edward and Uncle John stooping their heights to the level of the smaller uncles. Alone behind the coffin came Grandfather, and, close by, Old Tommy carried Grandfather's second topcoat. Far behind, rows of legs

and flowers moved steadily forward, and in the open door Old
Nancy watched without tear or sound.

The coffin slithered bumpily into the hearse, while the waves
of flapping died along the road as heads were bared in the cold
air. As the Monsignor bustled forward, his plump cheeks
shrivelled by the cold, priests opened their prayer-books. But
Grandfather's hand went up.

'Monsignor, if you please. I'll give you the *De Profundis*
myself; and her sons and grandsons will do the answering.'

He stood alone behind the open hearse. Old Tommy remained
near him with the second topcoat.

'*De profundis clamavi ad te* . . . Out of the depths I have cried to
Thee, O Lord!' His old voice shook but became firm again and clear.

Along the roads towards the village, lines of cars stood beneath
the snow-patterned hedges, waiting to follow after. Outside many
cottages figures knelt on straw and prayed into the thin air.

'May Perpetual Light shine upon her.'

'Amen.'

'May she rest in peace.'

'Amen.'

Martin watched his grandfather's stick striking into the snow
and listened to the steady slushing of his uncles' feet behind him.
Now and again, he looked across his grandfather's shoulder at the
coffin with Nancy's and Tommy's wreaths jogging along beside
it. In there she was, with the ear that could not hear.

He kept his place in the front row of grandsons, big and small,
and trudged behind the wheels and stick. People had often said
that the long street in the village was rather English in the
sunshine; now it was silent with snow and two lines of men. The
men's bare heads made an uneven line before the windows and,
from behind drawn blinds, women peered. From end to end of the
line the sound ran heavily.

'Eternal rest give unto her, O Lord!'

'Amen.'

Within the church they had to wait for the carriages bringing
the aunts by a side-road and someone whispered that the tail of
the funeral was still passing Lullacreen. Was Nancy still watching
there in the open door?

The ranks of clergy intoned the office, their cadences wailing
down the aisle to the thronged door.

He was helped to keep his head by becoming offended when he saw the halts in the service, while the Monsignor and the priests from the town whispered instructions to the village acolytes. Tiptoeing awkwardly about in their boots and looking around them every minute for advice! If only it could have been the Cathedral with its massed peal of voices and the half-light stealing through the stained glass; or the nuns' Oratory with himself serving and Father Riordan the celebrant. But, no, it was not '*Ite missa est*' and '*Deo Gratias*', but the Requiem Mass ending and the Requiescat for the dead.

Around the coffin the plump Monsignor went, sprinkling and praying, and when they carried her out to the street the priests in their surplices made a black-and-white rosette at the gate. Once more he followed his grandfather's stick along the street, away up to the old burial ground on the hill.

Softly the wheels and feet went now in the thicker snow and the air stung the ears although the blood raced burningly in his hot, light head. Higher they went and carried her slantwise across the slope and under the lichened arch which spanned the creaking gate. Up here, wind crept around the ruined Abbey, destroyed by the reforming English, and stirred the moss on the unkept paths. Not down in the hole! Not Grandmother, at least not yet! Suddenly his nerve went. It seemed to him that the police must be waiting to do the arresting as soon as she was down and the earth covered over her. Aunt Mary, save me! Aunt Mary!

The grey tapes were jerked from under the coffin and the priests, being cold, prayed quickly through the creeping wind. When the first clods of earth thumped on to the coffin, Martin stared in unbelieving horror. He saw his grandfather pointing his stick towards him and then felt someone lifting him out through the throng between heads and wet yew branches, and struggling with him down the thronged slope.

'He'll faint, sure as God, he'll faint. Who is it, anyway?'

'It's one of the Meath grandnephews, I think.'

'No, it's a Glenkilly grandson.'

They lifted him into a damp carriage, full of strange women, and he said, 'No, I won't faint, you needn't fear.' And then: 'Let me go back. I must see it again. The coffin.' But they drove quickly to Lullacreen.

Next morning Paddy drove them to the station, and when they got to Glenkilly, Martin was instantly put to bed. He shivered for a long time between the sheets until he remembered about Purgatory. Even the holiest people, even saints, found it hard to escape Purgatory!

Leaping from bed, he knelt and frantically promised God long lists of prayers if he would take Grandmother from Purgatory there and then. Half crazy with horror at the thought that two whole days had already passed, he moaned his prayers. Then he remembered what Father Riordan had said on Christmas Eve by the river. Boys' prayers have a special power because Jesus Christ remembered His own boyhood's beauty and innocence. It would be all right; he would offer for her the Masses he served; he would say Novenas; and he would give up sweets in Advent as well as in Lent. For long he prayed by his bed, repeating his two prayers, one for Grandmother and one that Aunt Mary would come at latest before the end of the week.

Comforted and sure of his power in the matter, he got back into bed and fell into a troubled sleep. Three hours later the maids discovered him sleepwalking in the kitchen. They clustered terrified at the kitchen door in the dawn, afraid to waken him, as he recited by the cold range bits of 'Fontenoy' and scattered phrases from 'Who Fears to Speak of '98'.

Then he wakened and heard their whispers.

'Poor chap. It's the excitement; the funeral.'

Back in bed, the next thing he was conscious of was Dr. McDowell's pointed beard above him, and his Uncle John all unshaven and muffled in the light of a lamp. Beyond them, big, bony Josie and pretty Mary Ellen.

He could hear his uncle saying: 'This happened once before. He's a terribly strange boy—all strung up, like a girl.'

And while the words and faces banged about him, he called: 'Well, don't stand there! Go and get Aunt Mary!'

God would take Grandmother from Purgatory and send Aunt Mary at once. Then the Faithful Brothers would not be allowed to have the Hail Mary said in Irish every hour; only nice people would be allowed to do it. People talked in low voices by his bedside and in his more lucid moments he sensed that something tragic had happened to his Aunt Mary.

He tossed about for days, sometimes tormented by police,

sometimes with falling snow or a monster hand between him and
the smiling Queen of Heaven. Of all that nightmare time the
worst moment was when he imagined he saw an anaesthetist in
Dublin holding up his Aunt Mary's curly head, while trying
skilfully and terribly to draw up her tongue, which had fallen
back into her throat during the operation and was choking her to
death. The man failed, and in his delirium it seemed to him that
he could see her face turn blue as she died with her tongue stuck
in her throat. Afterwards, when the fever had left him and he
knew the bitter truth, he realized that he must have heard the
others speaking of this in his sick-room.

5

Fʀᴏᴍ the heat of the afternoon sun the side-car went into green twilight beneath the trees and out into sun again. The boughs, heavy with September dust, brushed the jarvey's head.

'I never saw the like of it for the second week of September,' he said, craning his flabby neck round Martin Matthew Reilly's box on the well of the car. 'Them hedges are bursting their sides with grass.'

He peered reflectively at Martin.

'Yez not feeling lost over there all be yerself?'

'No, thanks. Are we near Dunslane?'

'Oh, just on top of it! That's an ancient poor ould thing, God help it,' and he took a swinging flick of his whip at a goat standing deep in the roadside grass.

The dust whirred beneath the wheels and, from beyond the shimmering emerald of the pasture fields, beyond the camps of haycocks and the Red Indian wigwams of stooked corn, there came through the haze the tattle of a reaping machine.

'Yer a few days late, ain't ye? Yer a new scholar, I can see. How old might ye be?'

'I'll soon be thirteen. But a Freshman is what you should say for Dunslane, not "new *scholar*".'

'Begob, I've driven hundreds to and from the ould college, and yer the first to tell me that.'

'What's it like here? Did you ever hear any of them say whether the food was good?'

'Oh, lashings of the best! Crubeens—pigs' feet, ye know—crubeens and cabbage *every* day. Oh, fed like fighting cocks!'

Martin decided that this summary of the meals at Dunslane revealed only the driver's own horrible tastes.

'I've never been at a boarding-school before. Is it a hard place? I mean, is there much . . . ?'

'Oh, never a beating at all! I declare there isn't as much as a strap nor a rod in the whole place. Not one!'

'I haven't done any schooling at all for six months. I had a big fever in March. Are there many free days, do you know?'

'Free days, is it! Oh, now you've said it! One every week. Sometimes two, with lashings of fun. Sure it's a grand place altogether; I only wish I was going there meself.'

Martin abandoned all hope of obtaining information from his jarvey. Wishing he was going to school himself . . . ! Does he take me for a fool altogether? A free day every week! Pigs' feet and cabbage—ugh! No cane! The man was an old cod!

'Aw, now,' the driver flicked his whip among the flies on the leaves tied to the mare's blinkers, 'it's a grand ould college altogether.'

'It's the oldest Catholic school in Ireland,' said Martin proudly.

'Begob then, is it now? I knew 'twas ancient, but I never knew that before. Before Dan O'Connell, then?'

'Of course! Eighteenth century,' said Martin, crushingly, because he had not forgiven the nonsense about pigs' feet, free days and no slogging.

'Eighteenth century, eh! Begob, away back to Cromwell, be the Holy!'

Martin set out to enlighten this dark ignorance. Relating the origins of the school, he thought it well to go back beyond the Penal Days and explain the history of the preceding period, but each period seemed to need explanations drawn from a still earlier period, and he was away back at the coming of the Normans and ardently recounting the marriage of Irish Eva to Strongbow at Waterford when his jarvey said musingly: 'Aye, Strongbow. Oh, it's an ancient college all right. Strongbow!'

Martin looked in bewilderment at him.

'Oh, begob, a power of great men have come out of that same Dunslane College. Strongbow—I heard of him!' and he took another flick at a donkey whose rump was projecting from the ditch out into the sunshine. Martin, in great disgust, looked coldly at his own side of the road.

'Aw now, I'll tell you one thing. Last June, I druv four lads away from the college. Leaving for good they were, four big galoomps of nineteen or so. And do ye know what they were doing when I pulled out of the avenue gates? Well, I'll tell ye!

Nearly crying they were and trying to let on to one another that they weren't. So ye see, ye'll be rale fond of it yerself and when yer own time comes to leave, it's likely ye'll be crying too!'

'I wish you'd say definitely how much the fare is.'

'Arrah, I tould ye I'd leave it to yerself. Sure, a shilling one way or the other . . . !' While Martin brooded anxiously upon the difference which 'a shilling one way or the other' would make to his pocket-money the jarvey added casually, 'It's a long ould pull for the mare and I lose the whole evening over it, but no matter; it's a pleasure to do a good turn to any young gentleman from the college, even though it mightn't pay me at all, at all!'

He pushed back his hat, craned the red neck still farther round the box. 'I'll tell ye one thing I *do* know! The head man of it all, Father O'Neill, is a gintleman! It's rarely I've driven a lad who didn't have the high word for him. Ye know, his mother came from a high-class Protestant family away over . . .' He waved the whip in a circle that included the whole of Ireland for all the information it gave. 'She turned Catholic to marry his father, a carpenter or something like that. But 'twas her own people mainly brought up the son. So now he houlds all their fine ways and fashions. But they never breathed a word against the boy's religion! There ye are—when a Protestant plays fair and is a good Protestant, well they're the best in the world! Now, if *you* had a poor ignorant Protestant damned to hell in your house, wouldn't you be trying your hardest to save his poor immortal soul for him?'

'I might. I don't know. He's a Unionist, isn't he? That seems strange for a priest. I wish he was a Home Ruler.'

'Ah, musha, Home Rule! I often think it might be all a cod. Sweating hell out of ourselves passing resolutions at public meetings—and for what?' He gave the mare so disgusted a swish of the whip that she actually broke into a gallop for a few minutes. 'Tim Corbin of Ballow! Jerusalem's primest cut of a do-diddler. And Moran the solicitor is another. Irish patriots—Oh, God Save poor Ireland!' He glowered at the flies, then suddenly growled in anger: ' "The sun-burst over Dublin Bay and College Green" —Holy God! The only burst them fellows know is the cork bursting out of a Guinness, or the bank-book bursting with entries.' With a violent gesture he yanked at the reins. 'Will Home Rule get me the money for the new harness I've been saving up for all

these years, will it? Will it give me another ounce of Cut Plug so
that I won't be scraping to have a fill for me pipe? Will it get
me eldest, Mary Ann, a hat with feathers on it, will it? Will it buy
a new piece of linoleum for the bad bit of the floor?' He stretched
his red neck, until Martin thought that he might stretch it
altogether away from his body. 'Listen! Listen, young chap. If
the Chinamen or the Omdurmans promised me a leg or two of
land and sent me youngest lad to be a National teacher, begod
they could go up to College Green and put their yellow flag up
on the ould Houses of Parliament and I'd salute it for them every
bloody day of the week if they liked.' Then he shook his head
unhappily. 'No, I wouldn't then,' he said helplessly, 'I'd be a
bloody fool. I'd be refusing me bit of land and singing "The
Wearing of the Green" along with the rest of them.' And, facing
straight forward, he said gloomily to the mare, 'G'wan to hell
out of that.'

The sound of the distant reaping mingled with the creakings
of the warm harness, while Martin thought of the night when,
Patrick having truculently taken over the succession to the great
caddy, he had brought to Mr. Burns's care his print of King Louis
presenting the flag to the Irish brigade, and the MSS. of his own
future speeches to the House of Commons in College Green, all
ending with, 'Gentlemen, I have done!'

His trunk and bicycle had gone already to Dunslane and the
box on the car held only the things which he would not trust out
of his own care—the cake baked by Josie; the *Songs of Erin* from
Mary Ellen and his surplices freshly ironed by her; a book of
rugby and cricket rules; Gertrude's pencil-cases and her photograph with *To my dear brother and sister* secretly on the back of it;
Niave MacDowell's unspillable ink bottle and her ivory Rosary
beads; Tommy Fagan's 'Best Irish Vellum Writing-Pad'; and in
the box was Aunt Mary's own dispatch case which Uncle Charles
had sent to him in her memory.

Her prayer-book and the diary from his grandmother he
would not trust to any box; these were with his 'first-night' things
in a little basket which he clutched while he pondered the future.

'Well, here ye are now!'

The car bowled down the slope where, on one side, seats snugly
fitted the trunks of trees spaced in line along the playing fields,
and swerved suddenly through pillared gates. It ran on smoothly

to the first triangles of flowers and white railings where the avenue forked. This must be the Bigger House, thought Martin, looking with pleasure at the shining whitish-grey building.

'See here now, the ould mare has a bit of a dislike to that front door. So, if ye'll just walk on to it, I'll bring her round to the kitchen and get yer box down there.'

Tightly clutching the basket, Martin walked past the flowers towards the main door which was open. Peering in, he saw a cool hall, a wide passage, a brownish staircase and in the back of the house another open door revealing grass, squared bypaths, a robin blowing out his belly in a tree, and a portion of an old, old house, Muire's House, almost for certain: Muire, the special name for Mary when Mary meant the Blessed Virgin. He noted with pleasure that it was near to the river, his own river he knew, which flowed past Gertrude's window.

In the stillness the car creakings died. He walked to one end of the Bigger House terrace which, rounding that end of the house, overlooked a yard with two odorous trees and stiles leading to juicy-looking fields, grazing cows and a chanting weir. He went back to the door, disturbed by the sound of his own steps on the gravel; it did not seem possible that anyone could be alive here. In the whole, wide world there was no sound but the cooing of the wood-quests and the murmur of the weir.

He peered in and wondered what to do.

'Well? What is it?'

He whirled in surprise. There, at the end of the terrace, a priest was watching him, the sun striking red and gold lights from a lock of hair which curved in a careless swoop across his forehead. Martin took off his cap and they advanced towards one another along the terrace. The priest's long, lazy stride set his soutane into slow whirls and the tall stoop had a sideways tilt of shy and whimsical friendliness. As they met the priest's arm slid comfortably round Martin's shoulder and drew him back towards the door. 'Well? What is it? Want to see someone?' The head came down sideways, the roguish red lock swept across his forehead, the whole face giving a puckered lift of conspiratorial interrogation.

'Are you the boy that I saw sitting up all by himself on the side-car that came down the avenue just now?'

Martin giggled into the friendly face. 'I suppose so, Father.

I'm a new boy, please. The Dean doesn't see Freshmen himself, does he?'

'I'm the Dean.'

Horrified to have giggled with familiarity at the Head of the School, Martin started. But the arm around his shoulder pressed him encouragingly.

'You are the last to come, Martin Reilly. You weren't expected till tomorrow. But what does it matter? You *are* Martin Reilly, I suppose?'

'Yes, Father. Martin Matthew Reilly.'

'Oh—Martin Matthew? I see!' The blue eyes studied him, while he held his breath, ready to answer questions the moment they were asked.

'You know, Martin, I'll have to be nice to you because maybe one day you'll be Pope and then I'd be very glad to have you thinking well of me.'

Martin, knowing that his Aunt Eileen sometimes endowed her own children and himself with those qualities which she felt to be lacking in them, blushed and stammered.

'But I'm not really sure that I'm going to be a priest at all, Father, I never *definitely* said that I wanted to be a priest. You see Aunt Eileen sometimes——' He stopped.

'Look—your jarvey is waiting for his fare.'

Martin hesitated.

'How much ought I to give him? Would three-and-six be enough or too much?'

'Three-and-six? Is it a millionaire you want to appear? Oh, it's Danny, I see. How are you, Danny?'

'Middling only, Dr. O'Neill. A bit shook with the long ould drive in the hate of the evening. And the mare's not what she was.'

'Well, here's two shillings for the fare and sixpence for luck . . .' Martin handed over the money. 'Go round to the kitchen and get them to give you a cup of tea. There might even be a fistful of oats somewhere for the mare.'

Martin did not dare look Danny in the face. But he heard him say cheerfully: 'Thank ye, Dr. O'Neill. It's real good ye are.'

'All right, Danny. Good luck to you.'

'And a power of it to yourself, yer Reverence. Goodbye now, young gentleman.' He turned to the Dean. 'That's a marvellous orator, that young chap. Better than Tim Healy himself. He tould me the whole list of men from college, Strongbow and all.'

The Dean's long stride drew Martin towards the Refectory.

'Now listen, there's the very man for you came here only three days ago—Norman Dempsey. Same age to the month. The two of you will likely be a pair of scarecrows up in higher classes with older boys, so you ought to suit one another down to the ground. Or do you know anyone here?'

'No, Father. But my cousin, James Edward, knows a boy called Tommy Callen.'

'Well, perhaps then you'd better start off with Tommy; he'll be more than glad to come out from First Study to show you around. I'll send him.'

Sitting at one of the long tables in the empty Refectory, Martin looked at the tall windows with their flowered curtains stirring in the sunny breeze, at the golden sunlight slanting along the walls. At one end of the room a bowl of flowers flamed, at the other end a picture of the Blessed Virgin hung, different from the Protectress of this House in the dining-room at Glenkilly, this Queen of Heaven glowed palely amid dim, tantalizing colours which could not be named exactly.

A maid in blue and white appeared with a tray. She reminded him of Moydelgan, so he smiled cheerfully at her. In answer to her call of 'Willy', a short young man advanced energetically from the service door. 'Are you Master Reilly? I have your trunk and bicycle safe for you this two days.'

He looked at Martin critically.

'I told the maid to "slip him out a bit of jam on the quiet with the tea". The Dean has taken a great fancy to you. I could see it by the way he spoke about you in the kitchen.'

While Martin devoured his tea the pantry boy stood over him answering his eager questions. 'I tell you this is the grandest college in Ireland, only seventy-seven boys but we can beat most places at anything.'

They were still chatting when Tommy Callen came, but his pleasure at being released from Study did not quite enable him to hide his superiority to a mere youngster.

'Long Dick says I'm to show you around.'

Martin followed his conductor behind Muire's House and down an alleyway between chestnuts, sycamores and beeches. To right and left, water-flags clumped their broad swords together, and in the plantations the leaves of dead water-lilies lay flatly on the dark pools.

On the river bank they plunged through thickets, past the school boats to where a triangle of gleaming sand lay like a picture from *Treasure Island*. By the apex of sand, beneath the overhanging branches, the foam clots rolled from the weir. The satin curve of power broke into white flounces on the rocks below and the thickets threw back the sound.

'This is a grand place!' Martin said loudly, to overcome the roar of the weir.

'Wait till you've been here a month. Lessons, get up early, mind your Ps and Qs the whole time, study every blessed minute, catch it hot for this, that and the other; and the meals, "plain, wholesome diet"—you've read the prospectus, haven't you?'

'But the Dean, Father O'Neill, you like him surely?'

'Oh, Long Dick's a toff all right.'

Tommy picked up a stone and flung it far out into the midst of the falling water.

'Look here, are you *really* a cousin of Jim Reilly's, *really* a *first* cousin?'

Martin nodded, scarcely recognizing James Edward as 'Jim Reilly'.

'Well, I'd never have believed it. Jim Reilly is a fine chap and very sensible.'

Determined to make polite conversation, Martin said ingratiatingly, 'He enjoys staying in your house terribly.'

But Tommy ignored this gambit, and closing his eyes, seemed disposed to take a nap beside the pounding weir. Martin sat gloomily by him, watched the unending power of that satin curve streaming out the long green hair of the grass beneath it, then as Tommy rose he followed him back through fields yellow and white with hawkweed and the big ox daisies which Aunt Mary had liked.

'Tea!' shouted Tommy as a bell clanged; and the sound of a distant storm rushed out into the quiet evening. Sprinting desperately after his one link with this new world, Martin was carried into the Refectory in a stream of gabbling boys and someone pushed him behind a chair as a tall man in a soutane said Grace. A prefect? he wondered.

Above the talk and laughter, Willy's bread-cutter whirred ceaselessly. Martin, dazedly trying to identify Norman Dempsey, saw with relief that some boys at his own table were much younger than himself.

Suddenly he saw the swerving figure of the Dean moving on its uncertain way through the doorway, the red-gold hair shaking, the puckered face lighting up in recognition of this boy or that. Sometimes he stopped between the tables and his hand rested for a moment on the shoulder of a particular boy who flushed with pride during the whispered interview. Martin, because he passionately wanted to be singled out, bent his head, refusing to invite attention but hoping to feel the touch of that hand. But the long lazy stride went past his table.

By the time Grace was said again, the Blessed Virgin had become a mystery in shadow and the last sunbeams had gone below the distant hill at the gates. Down the long corridor they streamed and whooped to the big play-hall. A billiard-table at one side had created a zone of silence around it, absorbing all activity on the part of the onlookers into a watching of the effortless motion of the balls. But the bagatelle-table was a fury of sound; card-players disputed and ring-throwers shouted at one another; the wood of the panelling round the room gave out a smell of hot pipes and paint. Through a door at one end, boys came and went, and when Martin had gone out and closed that door behind him he heard the sounds of the play-hall cut off to a murmur. He found himself staring in the school library, at the rows of books behind glass doors, at the chairs and the leather-covered tables. Story-books, histories, biographies—and dictionaries! Big fat works of reference which would certainly have lists of Dramatic Characters, Proper Names and Great Quotations! 'Gosh!' he exclaimed, whereupon a boy looked up crossly from his book and said:

'Shut up. If you don't want to read, get out to the play-hall.'

As he retreated he saw a fair head raised and bright blue eyes looking at him from a face that was pale-clear with a subdued rosiness behind the clear pallor. He felt in his bones that the boy must be Norman Dempsey.

He returned from the marvellous library to the equally wonderful play-hall. Finding an inconspicuous place by the wall, he wondered if he would ever stand with his hands in his pockets beside the bagatelle-table, whistling and saying, 'Rotten shot!' Would he ever dare to stalk into the library and pull a book from one of the shelves from behind the swinging glass?

Into the hall, the Dean came swooping. He watched the billiards. 'Good shot, Paddy.' He moved towards a ring-thrower, 'If you cocked the fat leg back a little bit, you'd get a better balance for the throw.'

Straight down the length of the hall the long stride came bearing down on Martin.

'Well? How are you getting on? Is Tommy Callen looking after you?'

'Yes, Father,' lied Martin.

He would have liked to ask the Dean whether the handsome boy whom he had noticed in the library was Norman Dempsey. But Willy came just then, saying that the Matron wanted the new boy.

Upstairs she helped him to unpack, uttering threats and showing him the back of a hair-brush. 'It's five years in use now, and better than ever, so you're warned now, remember!'

He was delighted that she was neither old, fat nor ugly; he had always thought that matrons were either stout or wizened. She nodded approvingly over his Aunt Eileen's careful packing and careful provision of all prescribed articles: '. . . forks, one napkin ring, one dessert fork and spoon. . . . Good, all there. And your initials on them. Did you bring a fine-tooth comb? Now as you're here you may as well start getting ready for bed, and not one lark's quiver out of you, or . . .' she pointed to the hair-brush.

He suspected that her bark was worse than her bite, although one could not be sure, because Aunt Mary, who had no bark at all, had had a terribly sharp bite when displeased. Suddenly he noticed that the laundry bag on the next bed to his had the name 'Norman Dempsey' on it. 'Am I next to him?'

'Yes. Dr. O'Neill said you'd suit one another. I daresay you will, too.'

She smiled, and Martin, emboldened by the smile, said, 'I never thought that a matron would be pretty.'

With a sigh, she said: 'Slootherer! It won't work with me, me lad!' but she blushed as she started to make up the bed with the sheets she had brought with her.

When she had gone he undressed, then walked up and down

in his night-gown, looking through the windows and investigating the topography. The Dean's suite was below him, another Bigger House Dormitory across the landing; the other dormitories in Muire's House were near the masters' rooms.

He counted the beds and windows; he worked the taps. His own window looked away up the avenue and, down to the right, the stars were hanging above the weir. He took his diary from under his pillow and wrote: *The stars above the weir.* He read out the words many times: 'The stars above the weir.'

He wrote the Dean's name and nickname 'Long Dick', and his own name under them; and wishing that there had been room to write them on the first page with his grandmother's inscription and his own, *To the Glory of God and the Honour of Ireland,* he slipped the diary back under his pillow.

The young harvest moon slanted on to the row of basins and the long mirror. Fancy having a basin and taps all to oneself. He would lie awake until the others came up from Second Study; it would be great fun to see eighteen boys going to bed all at once, the long ones and the short ones. But when he opened his eyes a bell was clanging downstairs, the dormitory was full of movement, and there, where the stars had hung above the weir, the sunlight was streaking through the tree-tops to lie in bars along the polished floor.

6

Novelty made the term speed by. It was all so different from
the leaden hours in the company of the Faithful Brothers. The
first of the long-awaited free days and the great paper-chase
had come and gone; the first big rugby match was over, and its
subsequent supper party and the sing-song with the visitors. The
new boys had stood equal with the best to sing Long Dick's own
words for Dunslane; the concert in the play-hall had ended and
the visitors, all now jolly good fellows, had gone in their two-
horse brakes up the avenue beneath the branch-patterned stars
while Dunslane's farewell cheers died into the murmur of the weir.

The next morning the school was to sleep late, but Martin
awoke very early and lay quietly, being pleased by the greyness
of the sleeping dormitory. He cautiously brought the beam of
Aunt Mary's torch along Norman Dempsey's bed until he could
see his friend's face. As always, Norman lay on his right side,
with his hands lightly clenched under his chin, and a little
dampness showing around the roots of his tumbled fair hair.

They were inseparables. They would walk arm-in-arm, in
class sit side by side, and sometimes at night they would join
outstretched hands in the space between their beds, entwining
their fingers hard to the sockets, and gripping until bone and
flesh hurt a little; until their two hands made one hand growing
cold out there in the darkness.

But when Martin said 'nice' things to Norman, Norman would
smile with the little pout and head movement which seemed,
while not denying the remark, to deflect it from Norman himself.

'Norman, when I say grand things to you, they just run off you
like water off a duck's back.'

'No, they don't! And it's just because they don't that I wish you
would be more sensible.' He had linked arms and continued,

116

'Sometimes you are very, very nice but sometimes you are not
so nice.'

'Well, if you'll tell me whenever I'm doing something *you* don't
like, I'll stop doing it.'

'All right. Well, firstly, don't argue so much. And don't pay
any attention to fellows we don't like; and, above all, don't let
every Tom, Dick and Harry see what we're thinking about
something or someone. And also, don't give cake to every begging
fellow who asks for it; they're playing on you, and I get disgusted
to see them playing on you. They know *you* will never ask them.
Besides, it's no good for me to keep all of mine for us two if I
only get one slice of yours, and we both have to wait until one of
us gets another!'

Watching Norman now, Martin thought: If Norman died, I
don't know what I'd do, but if I died, Norman would only be
very, very sorry. And that's not the deathless friendship of
Orestes and Pylades.

The thought of death, of his grandmother's face still in the
candlelight like the nuns' faces in the light of his candle beside
Father Riordan's ciborium, troubled him. He took his diary and
began to write the events of the Free Day. As he wrote the date,
he suddenly remembered that this was Aunt Mary's birthday. He
had always refused to think of her with her tongue stuck in her
throat, with an ear that could not hear. And he had never cried
for her. A whole year it would be, next St. Stephen's Day, since
she had said goodbye under her pinnacled hedge. How far away
now, Moydelgan, Lullacreen, the little girls in their apple-green
coats and muffs dancing around the room!

He put on some clothes and tiptoed down the stairs to climb out
through a window which the rain had warped so that it could be
opened at any time. As he went down the natural alleyway behind
Muire's House, streaks of light were beginning to spread along
the rim of the copses across the river and, the cuckoo being gone
these two months, it was the blackbird who abruptly wakened
the other birds. In the growing light he walked by the river that
was still cold-looking and dark with night. Then from a wall he
plucked ivy; it was ivy which people used in order to commem-
orate Parnell and he would keep Aunt Mary's birthday with ivy.

He would put the ivy in Big O'Gorman's handsome shaving-
mug and keep it on his window-sill until rising-bell. O'Gorman

was the largest of three big boys who had returned too late in
term to get beds in other dormitories; he shaved more often and
more ostentatiously than the other two and kept a handsome
shaving-mug in a prominent position on his window-sill.

Having secured his piece of ivy, Martin tiptoed upstairs and
undressed in the colder light. Beside O'Gorman and his mug,
slept McNally, who, although two years older than Martin,
seemed to welcome patronage from anyone. Unfortunately, he
went with Mullins's rotten lot. And, above all, Norman did not
like him!

Martin's hand wavered as he stretched it out now; the mug
rolled on the floor and McNally sat up sharply, but Martin had
already hidden the ivy in the folds of his night-gown.

McNally leaned out of his window and said, 'It's grand looking
out in the morning when no one's up.'

'Yes, lovely. But mind, don't waken Mullins.'

He looked at Mullins snoring with his carroty head fat on the
pillow, then noticed McNally looking curiously at himself.

'You and Norman Dempsey have been slogged a fair lot by
Long Dick already, and yet he likes you both. I wouldn't really
care if someone called me a suck of his. I might pretend to care.'
There was a note of envy in his voice.

Martin's heart warmed. 'Look here, McNally. Why do you
go with Mullins? Do you really like him?'

McNally said bitterly: 'No. He's a fool and he thinks he isn't.
And I have to pretend to——' He stopped and the glance
flickered down to his toes. Martin stared curiously at him.

They leaned out of the window, smelled the dampish morning
air, and were aware of the presence of animals in the fields below
them. McNally murmured: 'They say that Cromwell looked all
over Leinster from the Round Tower of St. Canice's and remarked, "By God, I don't blame them for being rebels; it's a
country worth fighting for."'

The remark pleased Martin. He took a great resolution: 'Look,'
he said, and showed the ivy. 'That's for my dead aunt. It's her
birthday. Like Parnell. Now we'll simply have to be friends.'

There came a rough call from a nearby bed. 'God, the day
isn't long enough for Guffy Reilly to talk, he has to get up early
to do it.' They had wakened Mullins.

Martin pointed to the ivy and laid his finger on his lips;

McNally nodded and Martin smiled, but McNally's glance flickered down. Martin secretively put the ivy in the collapsible drinking-cup which had been Mr. Burns's goodbye present, put the cup in his cupboard and got back into bed. Mullins, yawning out of the window, said, 'Jesus, it looks bloody cold,' in his queer accent, half Lancashire, half Connaught. His father had made his money in a pub in Liverpool before returning to Ireland. Scratching his carroty head, he whistled and hummed loudly.

'Shut up,' said Martin, and unwisely added, 'You'll waken Long Dick down below.'

The shiny, freckled face glowered towards Martin, and Mullins thought hard, assisting himself by picking his nose. His labour having delivered him of an idea, he got out of bed, stamped three times right over the Dean's head, stared challengingly at Martin and catcalled.

'Shut up, Mullins.' Sleepy voices protested but Mullins stood up on his bed and broke wind loudly.

'Bugle Call!' he said.

Out of the shocked silence there came a contemptuous 'Liverpool-Irish!' said indifferently to the ceiling. It was Norman. To answer the bored contempt, Mullins, failing to break wind again, imitated the noise with his lips. Some boys whispered threats of putting Mullins under a tap after breakfast but already Mullins was leaping on to beds, while some fought him cheerfully, a few larked and others protested. Even a better sleeper than the Dean would have been disturbed by the din, but now Big O'Gorman roused himself sufficiently to quieten Mullins with a ferocious threat, and soon, to the relief of Norman and Martin, the bell rang.

They were washing when the door was thrown open and Long Dick, huddled in a dressing-gown, flamed there in red-gold wrath, and began to deal out retribution. It was the prelude to a morning of trouble.

At Mass and breakfast sour looks were given to the boys of St. Brigid's Dormitory, because all feared that the Dean's ill-temper would, like other things, spread from above downwards.

In the good-natured Mr. Regan's class a couple of hours later Martin, as often happened, began to dream, and leaning forward on his desk accidentally sent his books with a bang to the floor.

'Great heavens! What's that—oh, it's you.' And then a determined: 'All right! I've been spoiling you. Go up to the Dean:
say I sent you up for making a deliberate disturbance.'

'Oh—sir!'

'Go on. You and your friend there act as if you owned the
whole school.'

On his slow way to the door, he tried to respond to various
sympathetic winks which indicated, 'Thou who art about to die,
we salute thee'; tried to respond to Norman's apologetic look
which said, 'I told you so'; and, at the door, tried on the young
master the effect of a reproachful glance, intended to remind
Mr. Regan that one day last month Martin had lent him a
bicycle pump.

'No, go on. I've been spoiling you.'

Outside the Refectory, he looked wistfully down on the blue-
and-white maids shaking bright tablecloths below the sunny
windows. Beckoning Willy to him, he whispered, 'Is the Dean in
a bad temper after the row in the dormitory this morning, Willy?'

'Well, I slipped him up an egg-flip Matron made for him; that
helps the liver, you know.'

Outside the Dean's door, he paused, looking towards the
Oratory and the inviting gleam of the sanctuary lamp. No, it
was not right to ask God to interfere with 'Human Order and
Harmony' or with the rules of one's station in life, which in his
case unfortunately would be a schoolboy's for many a year to
come. God did not answer all our prayers because He knew best
what was good for us. But how could it have been for the best that
Aunt Mary should die? How he had prayed!

Norman, every time they had been up together for a slogging,
had just given a squeeze of the arm, said, 'Come on,' and
knocked. Now, standing alone inside the door, he heard the
familiar 'Well? What is it?' and then the changed tone: 'Oh!
Trouble?'

He went to the sofa, gave his message, and the Dean with a
gesture of unhappiness drew his hand along the sweeping lock
of hair.

'Deliberate disturbance, Martin, you said he said?'

'Yes, Father.'

'Mr. Regan is a very decent master. It's not often he sends
anyone up to me.'

'No, Father.'

He was sent to fetch the pandy-bat ferule from the Dean's bedroom and, with his hand on the leather in the drawer, he looked around him, thrilled to be in the Dean's bedroom, to see his shaving things, his driving-coat, a race-card from the Curragh.

Wondering if he would have to take down his knickerbockers, he tried to show in his manner that he knew he must be punished, tried to save the Dean from any embarrassing thoughts that here was one of those innocent sufferers who would have tried to stop the morning disturbance in Brigid's Dormitory if he had been a little older.

A hard blow fell on his palm; a second, less hard.

'He did say deliberate disturbance; he said that definitely, did he?'

'Yes, Father.'

A third blow fell. He bent his head to prevent the Dean from seeing signs of distress.

'Look here, Martin . . . ! *Was* it deliberate disturbance?'

'No, Father. It was an accident really.'

The strap was put aside and Long Dick said: 'I see. Look—just say to Mr. Regan that you have been punished.'

'Yes, Father,' and, seeing the Dean smile invitingly, he burst into tears. Evading the outstretched arm and urgent call, he got to the door, turned and said:

'I'm not crying because you let me off so easy, but only just because you're so nice,' and, with the door open, he stammered, 'Mr. Regan didn't know it was only an accident.' He got out of the room, bathed his face and returned to a defensive Mr. Regan, who avoided his eye for the rest of the class.

When it was over, Norman joined him. Turning together into Jimmy Curran's classroom to watch for his coming across the yard, they found him already there, startlingly there, walking up and down behind the empty benches with a cold, grey little face and not a sniff out of him.

'Martin Reilly!' Martin stood to face him.

'Two weeks ago I mentioned the most important writers of the Pastoral School—English. Name them, please.'

Dumbfounded, Martin stammered: 'But, sir, you never said we were to *learn* them. And it's a fortnight ago!'

'Ah! Why did I mention them? Just to hear myself talk? Brains and idleness make an abominable character. What do you think happens to boys who dream instead of doing?' and his watery eyes glistened coldly.

'I don't know, sir,' stammered Martin.

'Well, I shall tell you. They become life's failures. They write for *The Irish Chronicle*! A daily paper published in a capital city! Capital of a supposed *European* country! Their written words are corrected by the Literary Editors of such papers. Sit down.' Martin sat down. On his desk was a note from Ned Connolly. *Look out. Jimmy Curran got a rejected article back in the post.*

'Dempsey!'

Pale and anxious, Norman stood.

'Principal writers of the Pastoral School—English.'

Without a moment's hesitation, Norman shook his head.

Huddled in the torn gown Curran bore down on him. 'And were you also dreaming in company with your friend?' Coming up close to him he asked, 'Your best and closest friend?'

'Yes, sir.'

'And *you* are *his* friend? Are you, boy?'

'Yes, sir.' Norman's lip trembled.

For the first time Jimmy gave a sniff, not an elegant one, a bitter little sniff.

'Ha! Your father is—or certainly was—a good classical man. Did he ever tell you what Cicero said about friendship?'

'Yes, sir. "Friendship is the discovery of oneself in another." '

'*And* the delight in the discovery—oh, don't leave that out!'

He walked to the head of the class—startling, untraditional deed!

'For the rest of you—you will grow up, work, possibly marry, certainly die. With the possible exception of Seumas Conroy, you will not even get a shake-hands from Lord Rosebery and a dinner from London University, as I have. Not even that! Not even see your chosen words corrected by the Literary Editor of—— Oh, I am going now. Write an essay which I shall carefully examine afterwards. Write on this subject.' And, in a despairing scrawl, he wrote on the board: *Which is the decent life? To be or to do?* and, gathering the fragments of gown about him like a tattered flag, he gave one small, sharp sniff, careened by the door-jamb and away like a leaning black model boat towards his little house among the trees.

Astonishment kept the boys quiet until Seumas Conroy in his saffron kilt jumped to his feet, his long narrow face flushed with the air of one who knowingly faces ridicule and misunderstanding.

'Listen, chaps. Why should two boys much younger than this class be bullied? . . .' In a whisper, the class gave a mocking cheer. Conroy settled his head, brushed back his brown hair. 'My father says . . .' Looking down, he saw his bare thigh, and shook down the kilt.

'Hush, hush. Listen to "my father says". Seumas's daddy rides to give lectures in the University in breeches on a bicycle. He passes Ned Connolly's house in Dublin.'

Conroy went pale. 'I wanted to say that Dempsey and Martin Reilly should not be bullied merely because Long Dick may have bullied Jimmy and . . .'

Martin was up on his feet. 'You're a . . . a . . .' and Josie's mocking words came to him. 'You're a Dublin Jackeen, Conroy, for saying that. Long Dick . . .'

'Sit down, Martin,' Norman's whisper implored. 'Now, you're being just as bad as he is. Up on your feet.'

Martin shook off Norman's hand. 'Seumas Conroy, Long Dick never bullied anyone in his life.'

The class roared, forgetting all prudence. 'Bedad, "Long Dick from Cradle to Grave" by "One Who Was There".'

Conroy's eyes on Martin looked hurt. He sat down, stood up again, and with his eyes on Norman, said angrily: 'It's snobbery and pretentiousness that's having a bad influence on chaps who would be good Irishmen. I like Long Dick. I admire him, too, but this is a West British school in lots of ways. The place had no right to take up hurling whenever it did, if it meant to continue playing rugby and cricket also. My father says that if they don't alter the traditions of this place, he'll . . . he'll take me away.' Conroy on rugby practice days went to the hurling pitch and, lone as a scarecrow, practised hurling all through the rugby period 'as a dignified protest'.

Outside, Mullins accosted Martin, shouting: 'Here's Guffy Reilly. Look at the lip cocked up. You'd think he was Little Lord Fauntleroy. Did you ever see such a puss-face? Supposing Long

Dick knew you were the one who wakened everyone else this morning? Out in the fields at that hour!'

So McNally had told that! Had he told about the ivy? He looked over the shoulders of the neutrals, but Norman was streeling farther away and not now looking back.

Mullins protruded his shiny chin: 'What was your father?'

Martin's heart tightened. Someone said: 'That's rotten. The chap's father's dead.'

'He was . . . he was . . .' Aunt Mary's words about her Charles leaped off his tongue. 'He was a gentleman and a gentle man.'

Mullins roared with laughter. 'Holy God! He talks like a fellow in a book or a play. A gentleman—what do you mean, you eedjit? Maybe he was a duke or something?'

Hatred choked Martin; he was making a fool of himself for this brutish Liverpool-Irish cad. He could see the thick stupidity in the eyes, as he had seen it in Norburton's.

'Your uncle in Glenkilly is just a shopkeeper.'

'He's a citizen merchant. John Redmond called them "citizen merchants".'

His arm was tugged and Norman was saying: 'Don't, Martin, don't! Come away from them. Stop it.'

Mullins snarled, 'Keep out of this, Snotty Dempsey, or I'll break your girlie doll-face.' Martin shook off Norman's hand.

The crowd of boys pressed closer. Mullins's eyes glared into Martin's.

'Oh Jasus!' he roared. 'Ivy! Ivy for me dead aunt's birthday. Like Parnell—did you ever!'

Martin swung his arm and, with all the passion in his heart, sent his fist across Mullins's shoulder straight into McNally's mouth. McNally staggered, hands to his face, bewildered and frightened. Martin dragged the hands apart and once again drove his fist into the mouth. 'You dirty lane-boy. Slave-Heart! I might have known you wouldn't keep your mouth shut.'

Amid shouts of 'A fight. A proper fight,' some of the oldest boys arrived and arranged that Martin and McNally would fight it out properly that afternoon. Martin went alone to the lavatory where he tried to practise in the long mirror the poses shown in James Edward's boxing books. There Seumas Conroy found him. 'I came to tell you that I'm altogether on your side in this.

Mullins behaved rottenly. But why pick on McNally? McNally's not much use but he's harmless and——'

'McNally is a Slave-Heart. And if you don't know what that is I'm not going to explain. Thanks, anyway, for coming and saying what you did say.'

'I'd like to be your second if you would agree to have the announcements made in Irish.'

'No. Thanks, all the same.'

Conroy hesitated, then went away, and Martin was practising knock-out punches in great unhappiness when, in the glass, he saw Norman standing shyly at the door.

'Listen, Martin. Drink three large cups of cold water. That gives speedy muscular action. Our cook's brother read that out to me—and he's an army boxer!'

When Martin had drunk the three mugs of water he said doubtfully, 'Maybe I'd better take four?'

'Well, three was the number. Only, of course, it meant them to be taken every day for a year.'

But the fight was to come to nothing in the end, since Martin after lunch found his name beside Norman's on the notice-board for a rugger practice.

After the game, side by side, and silent, they changed amid the shouting boys and washed at the farthest corner of the wash-house where they would be seen only by one another. A hunger greater even than usual slowed the ever-slow passage of First Study, but the sounds of cups and saucers came at last with lights in the Refectory and a burning western sky beyond the avenue.

As they left the Refectory they saw Mr. Curran waiting under a faintly hissing gas lamp. He stopped them, holding out his hand.

'I should like to have this letter delivered tomorrow, Sunday. Beyond Rodesbridge—a long journey. You have bicycles? Please ask the Dean if you may do this for me.'

He turned away, while they slowly realized that he was giving them a commission which would provide long hours of freedom tomorrow. They looked at each other with amazed delight.

In their anxiety to save Long Dick from awkward memories of the morning, they gave their message too shyly and had to repeat it. Pulling at his lock of hair, the Dean said: 'Certainly, if Mr. Curran wishes it. If he'll excuse you doing your Sunday-evening English essay, you may stay out till eight o'clock.'

Until eight o'clock! 'Oh, thanks. . . . Oh, thanks awfully, Father. Oh gosh, thanks.'

That evening, on the way up to the Oratory, Martin saw through the great landing windows the light in the room where Mr. Regan was probably arguing Home Rule with Mr. Salter over there in Muire's House, limned sharply now under a moon double-haloed with foggy dew. The Oratory lights were not lit and on the Stations of the Cross around the walls the garments of Jesus and his Mother glimmered, while the cadence of voices rose into an air subtly impregnated with the smell of varnished wood, of the countryside by night, of fine linen on the lonely altar. The voices near to manhood rolled a shy, slurred murmur but the voices of childhood were unhesitant and clear.

'. . . and by the intercession of Blessed Mary, ever a Virgin, may be delivered from present sorrows. . . .' The chant of the weir, mingling with the sound of the prayers, made one sound. And then the power of prayer poured forth—'*Magnificat anima mea Dominum. Et exultavit spiritus meus* . . . And my spirit hath rejoiced.' The rising glory of the words remained in him, as he sat beside Norman waiting their turn to file out in the ordered hierarchy, pleased with that order and with his own place in it.

In the dormitory he went to his cupboard to get his best stockings for tomorrow's jaunt. Crouching down to the lowest shelf, he put in his hand and felt a cold, strange object. It was Mr. Burns's collapsible drinking-mug and it held the ivy that he had plucked in the foggy morning to honour Aunt Mary as people honoured Parnell.

After the long Sunday-morning Study, they were pushing out their bicycles when the Dean leaned out of his study window into the frosty sunlight.

'Catch, fielders!' He lobbed down a rosy apple, then another. They called their thanks to him.

They had expected their ride to be a quiet one, but beyond Rodesbridge increasing processions with music and banners began to converge along their road and, when they had delivered Jimmy Curran's letter, they learned that no less a person than Mr. Redmond himself was to address a Home Rule demonstration in the big town of Ballow.

'Let's go! I've been there with Aunt Mary and can find our way about,' said Martin.

From chimney-top to chimney-top, the banners spanned the streets of Ballow—'Remember Limerick' and 'Who Fears to Speak of '98'. Through the sleety whistle of fifes, that mingled with the blare of brass, came the roll of drums, like circling thunder linking side-street to side-street, while above the narrower by-ways the sunlight was slotted by moving insertions of silk and satin, gold-fringed and swirling. A processional banner, 'Ireland Sober is Ireland Free', linked the tops of two public houses above the heads of men jostling to get to the two half-opened doors, barred each by an unshaven man who asked of the clients wriggling in under his arm towards their drinks, 'Bona-fide traveller?' only to receive the gaily ironic answer, 'Oh, bona-fide all the way from the First Orange Lodge in Belfast.'

'We'll go to the Royal Leinster Arms Hotel, Norman. I spent a night there once. We'll have *table d'hôte*, whatever that is. Aunt Mary always said that it was the only possible thing to have in Ballow, although it's just like dinner really.'

In the thronged hotel they struggled to the office counter where two young women in elaborate black dresses and bangles ducked and rose like nervous bathers, the while they pulled corks from bottles of stout which they passed as fast as they could to a perspiring maid beyond the hatch window. When Martin rapped on the counter, the red-headed woman, without looking up from the bottle gripped between her satin knees, gasped, 'And what is it now in the name of God?'

'Please, I want to find a waiter called Paddy. An old man.'

'Carmel, shout down the tube for two more cases of Guinness,' then turning her burning face towards the boys: 'What did you say that time?'

'Where is the old man called Paddy, the nice waiter?'

'Children are not allowed in the licensed portion.'

'But we've come to eat *table d'hôte*.'

'Coffee-room, down the passage!' She pushed her beringed hand through her hair, revealing sodden satin creases in her arm-pit. 'Carmel, did ye screech for the Guinness?'

'I did not!' said the pale young woman crossly. 'This is no job for a lady typist at all. It's bad enough to have to pull corks but I won't shout for Guinness. That's a servant's job.' Noticing the

boys, she dug her elbow into her friend's backside. 'Hey, college
boys; from away over Dunslane,' then said in a very refined
voice, 'Is there anything I could be doing for you?'

'I want to find a waiter called Paddy. An old man with a stoop
who would remember my aunt, Mrs. Charles Tierney of
Moydelgan, near Killan, twenty-two miles away.'

'Which of the waiters would that be now? It's a terrible job to
remember all the domestics and waiters. Are you at Dunslane
College?'

'Yes.'

She did not seem able to help them but on the next floor Martin
recognized a grey-haired chambermaid who had been in the hotel
when they stayed there on their way back from Dublin, after
missing a train connection. He remembered his Aunt Mary's very
gesture, putting eau-de-Cologne on her ear lobes from the bottle
in her travelling case; and her laughter; and how she had said,
'Mighty Marty, Moydelgan, home again tomorrow, and the
children, and my Charles!' The whole scene was clear in his mind.
'And she waltzed, Norman! With a chair! In an hotel, Norman.
In her night-dress! Oh, she was grand, she was just grand!'

The chambermaid took them down the passage to a long room
where women and youngsters were taking luncheon at occasional
tables drawn up to plush sofas and ottomans. Four long windows,
coming down almost to floor level, gave brightness to the
brownish wallpaper, the thick carpet, and the room had a withdrawn, restful air despite the bustling of waitresses.

'The Ladies' Tea Room,' she said. 'We're giving ladies'
luncheon up here today. Down there's no place for them today!'
and she nodded significantly towards the noises of corks and
laughter downstairs. 'No, ye can't leave out the first course. Ye'll
have to take the soup and the cabbage; if yer mothers were here
they'd make you take them. If ye eat all the vegetables and a big
plate of the soup, then ye can have both the apple-pie and the
castle pudding.' She whispered instructions to a pretty young
waitress and went with a 'If ye want anything, ask for Kate—
that's me.'

The pretty servant kept bringing bottles of ginger ale and
extra helpings of the tastiest things—'Kate said you were to have
this.' When she brought them a bill for seven-and-six they waited
until Kate reappeared, then without a word pointed to the bill.

She sighed. 'That Carmel Brannigan young gillyveen down-stairs!' she said tolerantly. 'It's maybe all that new typing-printing makes her such an eedjit,' and she scrawled '2/- *Kate*' across the bill. 'Come along now,' and she led them to a window where people were already seated. 'The best window in the place,' she said.

Already distant music and cheering were heard. Men were rushing from the public houses to join the throngs below, and on the far side of the street the Faithful Brothers of Ballow were drawing up their pupils in two lines. The skirl of bagpipes, the thud of drums, drew nearer as the unseen glory of the procession curved towards the Main Street, until, at last, Eire's graceful body on a green silk banner and holding a harp came surging into view.

The men of Ballow Brass Band always reserved their breath to give their loudest blowing in the Main Street, where their families congregated, and now they sent forth the tune loudly:

> They rose in dark and evil days
> To right their native land.

The drums double-thudded and echoes resounded from the grey old houses.

> Alas! That Might could vanquish Right.
> They fell and passed away.
> But true men, like you men,
> Are plenty here today!

Down below, refined Miss Carmel Brannigan was waving a little flag between the shoulders of the men at the door. The great names went by—'The Wolfe Tone League of . . .' 'The Thomas Davis Branch of . . .' and fife and drum beat out the stories of battlefields and scaffolds not much more than a wren's excursion from the bright, bannered street.

'Martin, isn't it great to be Irish!'

'Great! Just imagine, we might have been born Swiss or Portuguese or something! Even English!'

Now the waggonette with the leaders was drawing near and all the street was roaring, 'Redmond!'

As he went past, the Irish leader looked up and saw them as, waving their Dunslane caps, they leaned straight down to him and cheered, 'Redmond for Ireland.'

He raised himself in his seat and the heavy-jowled face smiled. When they called it once more, 'Redmond for Ireland,' he straightened his shoulders and held his hat out to them as if in salute. The moment the waggonette had passed they made for the door.

Kate made a grab at their flying limbs. 'You're to come back here for yer tea after the meeting, d'ye hear me now! Get up on the wall in the Square; that's the boys' grandstand.'

Safely up on the wall, and equipped with chocolate and the remains of Matron's sandwiches, they watched the great Square changing into a heaving lake of humanity pierced by flags and standards. But Martin stopped cheering when he perceived his Uncle John among the men on the distant platform. It was a pity that Uncle Edward in Lullacreen never went to meetings and that Aunt Mary's own Charles would not have anything to do with political parties. Uncle John was not . . . well, was not the person he wanted Norman to meet.

The lines of priests on the platform shone blackly in the sunlight. And to think of Long Dick swooshing around Dunslane, and probably not even knowing that this meeting was being held here today.

Black hats waved high above the labourers' caps and the shop assistants' hard hats. Down there were the men from Mount Leinster who had ridden many miles early in the morning and who now waved their black felt hats above their heads to greet the speakers.

'Tim Corbin, begob,' said a voice as the secretary of the meeting rose to address it. Martin saw a young man with gold-rimmed pince-nez on his big, fleshy nose. This was the man he had often heard Mr. Burns refer to with such contempt. He had a shrewd face and his grey suit, that looked prosperous and towny, was already beginning to enclose the rotundity of a young-old paunch.

Mr. Corbin's voice came in snatches of expected rhetoric: '. . . at no far distant date the Green Flag will float again over College Green and the sun-burst of Freedom brighten the shores of our Holy Ireland . . . Learn Irish . . . some of us of course are now

too old to learn it . . . but all the young people can . . . our pure
and holy tongue. . . . Here on our platform to welcome our great
leader are two of our oldest and most respected Protestant
families come to make common cause with their Catholic fellow
countrymen.' Mr. Corbin pointed a finger towards two gentlemen, one of whom bowed and raised his hat constrainedly, while
the other hemmed and blew his nose. And all the time Eire's
graceful body swayed to and fro with her harp on the green
silk banner nearby.

Martin's vague uneasiness and sense of disapproval was swept
away when the crowd broke into a storm of cheers, as Mr.
Redmond rose and leaned one hand on the balustrade. Heads
began to nod their approbation of every sentence whether understood or uncomprehended. The boys heard the great man talk
with tired vigour of the vacillations of the Liberal Party; of
General Botha and German sabre-rattlers; of land holdings and
'the British Empire's changing purposes'; and they were a little
relieved to find that he made no oratorical reference to a sun-
burst over College Green.

The next speaker had scarcely begun when an English voice,
a girl's clear and rather beautiful voice, called, 'Votes for
Women!' It was followed by the voice of an older woman with a
rather horsey Irish tone, 'Votes for Women, you melancholy old
humbug!' And, at the same time, two new banners rose into the
air: 'Justice! Votes for Women!'

Upraised near the wall, and holding one of the banners, was a
beautiful young woman, with a white motoring veil falling behind
her upstretched throat like a cascading waterfall.

'Oh, begob, the Suffragettes from England.'

The crowd growled rather angrily to the alarm of Martin and
Norman, who vaguely knew that dreadful things were sometimes
done to the English Suffragettes. In Manchester they had been
beaten and kicked, and somewhere else two girls had had their
skirts torn off in the street. Of course, no decent English person
(and no one at all in Ireland!) would ever do such a thing, but
still . . .

'We must stay and protect them.'

They heard a man nearby comment, 'Begob, haven't they the
pluck of the divil?'

'Mebbe yes. All the same it's not nice to see women making a show of themselves. That little thraneen of a girl looks a dacent young lady.'

A fat, hot Royal Irish Constabulary man—a sergeant—floundered through the packed crowd, and people grinned good-naturedly, 'Old Flanagan himself.'

'Now, ladies,' implored the perspiring Sergeant Flanagan, 'come now, ladies. Sure ye can't behave like this in this country at all.'

'Votes for Women!' shrieked the older woman, and then to the sergeant who had been addressing her so coaxingly, 'We're not leaving here till you make us, you great bully.'

'Sure, God forgive ye, ma'am, I'm not wanting to bully you at all, at all. But don't ye think now . . .'

A tall, thin, district inspector had come through the crowd, and Sergeant Flanagan saluted with relief.

'Two Suffragettes from England, sir!'

'I'm not from England,' shouted the older woman angrily.

'Now, now, ladies—I implore you,' stammered the young district inspector.

From the platform came Mr. Corbin's voice, strained to carry a long distance. 'Mr. Butler, make your men remove those . . . those squawking females at once.'

'Aw now, that's not a nice way to shout about women.' A voice came from the crowd. 'Go on home out of that, girls, and have some sense and decency.'

But the English girl, tilting the lovely line of her neck before the cascading veil, continued to shout 'Justice! Justice!' until, feeling a hand tipping her shoulder, she looked up. Norman had leaned down and touched her shoulder. For a moment she looked from him to Martin in a puzzled way, then smiled, a full flashing smile.

'That's right. You're young and you should be for justice. Come on, shout with us. Justice. Votes for Women!'

The two boys shook their heads.

Sergeant Flanagan gazed up hopefully. The girl turned to continue her calls, but her foot slipped from its hold on the wall. Fat Sergeant Flanagan stooped and gently shook down her skirt over the ankle thus exposed. The girl, still clinging to the wall, looked at him in a puzzled way, said 'Thank you,' and glanced up once more at the two boys. She looked from them to the sergeant, making inviting motions of departure with his arms, then she got down from the wall and allowed herself to be led away.

Mr. Corbin was closing the meeting and inviting the crowd to give 'three boos for Carson and his Orangemen'. Up from the crowd a loud deep voice called: 'Shame on ye! Wrong as they are, they're better for Ireland than such as you!' Martin knew that voice. He looked and saw the bald familiar head of Mr. Burns with its horseshoe of hair. His hat and stick were held up as he forced his way out of the crowd. On the edge of the throng, he turned and shouted: 'Shame and shame again. The Orangemen of Belfast are our countrymen. They were Nationalists once and they might be again. 'Twas in Belfast the United Irishmen began.'

Martin and Norman tried to find him again in the crowd but it was impossible. Their search brought them near to the Royal Leinster Arms Hotel and, remembering Kate, they went up to the Ladies' Tea Room. As they came down from an enormous tea, Martin halted on the stairs and drew Norman back. His Uncle John was in the hall with Mr. Tim Corbin and another man talking to Mr. Redmond. Mr. Reilly's cheeks were flushed and his eyes merry with good humour and a drink or two. Someone drew Mr. Redmond aside and Mr. Reilly, glancing up, saw Martin.

'Well, how on earth did *you* get there?' he called good-naturedly.

Martin went to him, presented Norman, and was introduced to the secretary of the meeting.

'Well, young Master Reilly,' Corbin said with forced heartiness, 'if you're true to the Reilly stock, you'll be all right. Now come along, and bring your pretty friend along too.'

In a stale, brownish room at the back of the bureau, he rapped on the hatch. 'Well, gentlemen? Another round of the hard stuff, eh? The vin de pays of Erin, eh what?' and at his remarkable French pronunciation Martin and Norman cocked the priggish snouts of experts. The hatch revealed the red-headed girl with the sodden arm-pits and the refined Miss Carmel Brannigan hair-preening beside her.

'Four Jamesons, please, Carmel, and a couple of small ports for these two young gentlemen.'

With an abstracted manner, Corbin put his arm around Norman's neck and stroked above his wide collar. Norman stiffened, drew his neck away and came to stand in the background with Martin.

There, sipping the syrupy port, the boys watched through the smoke haze, saw the whiskey and stout dripping on the fingers that clutched the glasses.

'Tell me, John,' said Mr. Corbin solemnly, directing his gaze to Martin, 'it was your second-eldest brother, wasn't it?'

'Yes! Mat,' said Mr. Reilly shortly.

'Well, he's a lucky boy to have you, John, as uncle. John Reilly, my boy, is known and respected in more counties than one.' He took a swig of whiskey and then, adjusting his pince-nez, murmured speculatively: 'Hard, all the same, to lose both parents. Tell me, John, was it in Dublin they died? Or am I wrong in that? I never seem to have heard exactly.'

'Not Dublin,' said Mr. Reilly noncommittally, and made to move away.

Mr. Corbin detained him with an affable, 'Well, here's health, John,' and the two drank, while overhead there sounded women's light steps up there in the Ladies' Tea Room.

'Sad! Very sad. Tell me, John, by the way, was it a Dublin lady now she was, or from where? Or was it in Dublin the wedding was? I was just a chiseller when it all happened.'

Mr. Reilly looked straight at the big, prosperous face thrust towards him and there was a good deal of dignity in his manner as he said curtly: 'Listen, Tim Corbin—you know well or, if not, you ought to learn it now, that our brother Mat's death in the prime of his life is a very painful subject to us, and we naturally do not like to have such memories raised. So we'll drop it now, if you please.'

Mr. Corbin's gestures became wildly apologetic, and a melancholy man nearby said: 'Ah, sure we're all friends here. No disagreements. Let's have another, seeing the day it is, and "God Bless Redmond!" '

'All right,' called Mr. Reilly. 'But it's my round now.'

He leaned over the bar and ordered the drinks and, turning back to his friends, caught Mr. Corbin whispering to his neighbour: 'Wouldn't it be a good one now if the pure and holy Reillys, God's first-prize Catholics, had a skeleton in the cupboard all the time! I've sometimes wondered whether there wasn't something a bit fishy . . .'

Martin saw his uncle flush with sudden anger.

'You pup, Corbin. You infernal pup!' said Mr. Reilly. He brushed Martin aside and struck a heavy blow on Corbin's jaw. Corbin struck back and the two men fought, their feet splattering in stout droppings and broken glass. The red-headed Bridie screamed, Carmel Brannigan whispered, faces crowded to the opened door and, while another glass went lurching from a table, men rushed in and Mr. Reilly was led off to another room.

Martin hurried away. How awful that all this should happen in front of Norman, whose father was a Resident Magistrate and had once dived off a Mississippi riverboat to rescue a lady's wallet and been called 'The Golden-Haired Irish Leander' by all the American papers. Sounds of music and cheering were coming through the yellowing dusky light as the people made ready to see Redmond off, but the boys paid no attention to them.

Away from the cheers and music, they cycled through the outskirts where lighted lamps were hanging mistily in the dusk of the autumnal evening.

Without speaking, they went through the oncoming night and came to Rodesbridge where the houses, deserted for the sake of Ballow's great day, showed no lights, except the police barracks, big enough for three such villages. Below them, the river shone in starlight.

Still not speaking, they rested on the bridge. Martin glanced timidly and unhappily at the side of Norman's face, but Norman was watching the sky where the Milky Way streamed across the heavens, as if Cassiopeia's gauzy scarf had been blown before and behind her gilded chair, while, far down on the left, the eye of the Bull flamed, as he led the torches of winter up the processional slope of the sky.

7

'Y ou're wanted in the Dean's study, Martin.' Martin looked at the Matron incredulously. 'No, don't go yet. You're going to have me look at you from stem to stern. You're not going to that lady with as much as a speck on you, if it is for her you're wanted.'

'But it couldn't be!'

'She arrived in a Swift motor-car driven by a young man with a moustache. I daresay she isn't for you at all. But I know what her stockings are like—I got a glimpse of a bit of them as she lifted her skirt going up the stairs. So just in case.'

'It can't be for me. I wonder why the Dean wants me.'

'Oh, maybe it's to put you in a glass case and throw sugar at you!'

At the Dean's study door Martin began glumly to examine a conscience which held several reasons for expecting an unpleasant five minutes to come.

The 'Come in!' sounded bad. Liverish? Or angry about the delay? No one in the room but the Dean.

'What on earth has kept you, Martin?'

He mumbled from the door, 'Well, for one thing, I was more or less tidying up; in a general kind of way, Father.'

'But Willy couldn't find you anywhere twenty minutes ago. Were you out of bounds then?'

'Well, not exactly, Father . . .'

On his left there sounded a low laugh, instantly checked.

Turning in astonishment, he saw over the edge of the armchair a hat half turned up at one side and a brownish plume lying back along the other side. And, in shadow underneath, a face was watching him. He looked back towards Long Dick.

'You've kept a lady waiting. That's unpardonable.'

'But it was a very pleasant wait, Father O'Neill.'

The low tones, so full of deprecation as she said it, sounded 'nearly altogether English' to his ears. He turned again, the face gave him a welcoming look and he went to the chair. 'Come more into the light,' she said, and with a strong movement led him to the window.

Looking up, he saw the light on auburn hair under the hat, the brownish feather and the upturned veil that was brown and small, not white and cascading like the veil of the lovely English girl shouting 'Justice' in Ballow. Her blue eyes looked seriously down at him, very seriously, studying him, and one long glove rested on his shoulder. In that moment he was sure that once before he had thus stood beneath this tall window with that hand upon his shoulder in a gauntlet glove and the Dean hovering in the background. Awed by the tricks of Time, conjuring impossibilities in Long Dick's room, he stared and stared and then began to smile in forgetful delight, because of the gleam in the auburn hair and the lovely set of her neck as she looked down at him.

The tricks of Time, curiosity about her—all forgotten! He just smiled in bright delight up at her; and in a few moments she began to smile too.

'So this is Martin,' she said at last. She stooped, her face came down to him, a faint scent flitted across his senses, and she kissed his cheek.

'Are you a relation?' Martin asked. She nodded.

'You are? *You!* Really *you?*' he said.

The Dean led the way into the drawing-room. Father O'Neill scarcely ever used the drawing-room, and the fire, which had been hastily lit, had not yet begun to warm the room. Martin's curiosity about her had no urgency; he was quite content to sit here and watch her and the Dean's easy-going deference to her. When she smiled her smile was wider and much slower than Aunt Mary's smile, not so gay either, perhaps almost a little sad. Or was it perhaps haughty? No, not haughty; sad.

Presently the Dean left them. She sat very erectly on one side of the room, he on the other, and there was a long silence.

Martin broke it.

'You are really some sort of connection?'

'Yes.' Another silence. She seemed to hesitate. At last she said, 'I've wanted to see you for a very long time.'

It was as though she were going to add something and then checked herself. He wondered if she thought that since she was the guest she ought not to talk much without encouragement. So he said, 'If you stay until after five o'clock I'll get off First Study.'

She gave a little laugh. 'So that's all it means to you? Don't you even want to know who I am?' And seeing the puzzled look in his face she added authoritatively, 'Come here!'

'You don't know my name, do you? Well, I'm Mrs. Vincent.'

'I'm sure I've heard you spoken of. The last time Aunt Mary took me to Kingstown there was a fat man with an eyeglass——'

'Oh, yes, Mr. Peters. That's right.'

Again they were silent. He said: 'Please. I thought I saw you before.'

She started. 'But you couldn't remember? You were only a baby.' A look of passing embarrassment, almost a sudden twinge of pain, crossed her lovely face. Then she took his hands and said, 'Of course I'm a connection of yours.'

'How near? I hope very near!'

'I'm a kind of aunt.'

'Gosh, that's grand! You're so lovely!' Then, more shyly, 'May I call you "Aunt", because I feel very impertinent calling you nothing?'

'Of course. Call me Aunt Kathleen.' She scrutinized his face once more. 'Everything they told me of you was right. I've heard a lot about you, Martin, you know. A lot. When you came to the door just now the first thing that struck me was that you were quite like Sally, my elder daughter. Not in appearance, of course, just in manner—Sally when she thinks there's a punishment coming. Sally's a year and three months older than you.'

So she knew his age and even the month of his birth. Then she must be a relative. 'Who told you about me? Which aunt? Aunt Mary?'

'Yes. I liked her very much. I only met her twice, but we wrote . . .'

He looked into her blue eyes, and then, at the thought of Aunt Mary, burst out crying.

She drew him quickly to her and he stammered through the uncontrollable tears: 'She's dead and Grandmother's dead. I never cried for them before and lately I've been even forgetting some days to pray for them. And I don't want to forget them, I don't want to forget them.'

'It's sometimes bad for people not to cry when they want to.'

'People were always saying I was ready to cry for nothing.'

'Loving is a great deal more than nothing. Besides, from all I've heard, the opposite would be truer of you. There are things others cry about and you don't.'

'I know. But they never noticed that.'

'Your Aunt Mary did. And your Dean does, I am sure. He's a delightful surprise. I'm so glad that I came before Christmas. I was going to wait.'

She was standing in the window embrasure, and the light was falling along the line of her neck as she looked out on the fields. As she turned quickly, her skirts made a rustling curve and he thought, Matron was right—those are a lady's stockings all right.

'This place has a great charm about it, Martin. I must see it.'

'Listen, please—Aunt Kathleen. I've been thinking. I'm pretty sure you were not at Grandmother's funeral. So you're not a Reilly aunt, are you? You must be related to my mother?'

She gave him a cautious look. 'Yes. Your mother was my cousin. Only my second cousin. But we were more like sisters. We were devoted to one another. We might have been sisters.'

'Well, did my mother die of consumption, galloping consumption?'

'Good gracious, no! What an idea! She died when you were born, just after it.'

'Oh, I'm glad to know about that at last. I often thought that perhaps that was why she was never to be mentioned and I was afraid I might have it from her. What was her name, please?'

She looked pained for a moment and then said, 'Her name was Anne.'

'Did you know my father too?'

'No.' Under his searching gaze, she added: 'I know that he was clever and kind. And good. And he must have loved Cousin Anne very . . . very much indeed.' She sat down, drew him to stand before her and said: 'Martin, you must grow up to be very wise and cautious. You must never forget that the world will not let the heart rule. Even love must be calculating.' Looking gently at him she said, 'Don't look so serious . . . as if you understood everything.'

'Please, Aunt Kathleen, why was my mother never to be mentioned?'

Her clear cheeks paled a little and a quicker breathing made her bosom surge strongly up from the long waist of the coat towards the net-like cravat.

'It's all very difficult, Martin. To begin with, your mother was not a Roman Catholic—a Catholic, I mean, and——'

'What!' he gasped. 'You don't mean to say that my mother was actually a Protestant!'

'Yes. I'm a Protestant.'

He began to nod with comprehension. 'So that's it! So that's why she was never to be mentioned!'

She gave him a surprised look, then said quickly: 'Yes, yes, that would be enough, wouldn't it? Enough for many Catholics; for Irish Roman Catholics. Especially those like the Reilly family, wouldn't it?'

'Oh, they'd certainly like to keep that dark, all right. Aunt Mary wouldn't have minded a bit, though. And I'm sure she was very holy.'

'Do you yourself mind much?'

'I do mind.' He blushed apologetically. 'I don't mean that Protestants can't be holy in their own way. But was my mother —was she the kind of Protestant that says it's blasphemous and superstitious to believe in Transubstantiation?'

She noticed his look of horror as he said this, and her anxious expression changed to a weak smile. She said gently: 'I am quite sure that anything which people really believe can't be blasphemous, whatever else it is. And in connection with Anne the idea is just ludicrous because she didn't think of those things, and neither do I.'

'But you're not a "careless Protestant", Aunt Kathleen? I mean you're a good one?'

'Well, I hope so. It's not so simple as being a Rom—a Catholic.'

'But you would agree that the anti-Catholic bits should be cut out of the King's Coronation oath?'

Frowning in perplexity, and with a little irritation in her voice, she said: 'I've never thought about it. Do all these things *really* seem so important to you, Martin?'

Her frown had changed to a pucker that was half deprecating, half appealing, and he thought that he was making a splendid response to that puckered deprecation when he said: 'No. It's all right really. You see we are taught that Protestants can get to heaven much more easily than Catholics because God doesn't expect so much from them since they didn't have the same chances.'

His reply might seem magnanimous to him but it brought a fretful expression into her face and she said again, rather coldly: 'Does all this matter? Anne—your mother—was lovely and good.'

'Oh, of course.'

'Well, then, if you're so sure of that, does it really matter that she did not belong to your father's Church?'

'It doesn't matter as much as I thought at first, perhaps. But I don't know. It's rather terrible.'

'*That* I simply cannot understand,' she said sharply. 'If it were the other way about and . . .' She rose and looked out through the window like someone who does not know what to do. He was appalled to see how much he had hurt her. Supposing she never came to see him again!

He went to the window and began apologetically to call her attention to sights outside. Trying to study her expression, he looked up at her unhappily and she, looking down, said remorsefully: 'No, don't look at me like that. I'm sorry. Of course it must all be very, very disturbing for you.' And then, a moment later: 'Is it going then to matter that I am not a Catholic?'

'Of course not. That's quite different. I've a great friend— Gertrude Jamieson—who's a Protestant——'

She interrupted him eagerly: 'The older girl who calls you her "brother and sister"? Your Aunt Mary told me about her.'

'Yes. She's awfully nice, you know.'

'When you come to stay with us, you'll have to be "brother and sister" to my girls, Sally and Peggy. They have no brother and I don't want to send them to school again. They hated it when I did.'

'Oh, yes, please. It'll be lovely. Honestly, I don't think it matters as much as I thought about my mother being a Protestant. My father had a dispensation, of course?'

'A dispensation? What is that?'

'From the Pope. To marry a Protestant; to get married.'

'Oh, married!' She turned her eyes away, then said in a low

voice, and without looking at him, 'I'm sure they had their dispensation, poor dears.' Then, turning back to him, she added quickly: 'Now, show me all you can, before the light goes. It's so exciting. Here you are, Anne's very own boy, nearly thirteen, and in this nice-looking school and its nice Dean. It's all even better than we'd hoped.'

She stood at the Oratory door, while he showed her his place in chapel and Norman's. The evening sun was streaming through plain and stained glass. 'It's so airy and bright,' she said.

'Couldn't you ask to see Norman just to get him off Study? He needn't be in your way.'

'Certainly not!' she said curtly. 'That would be quite wrong and dishonest!'

Her rebuke left him chastened and cautious, but when they came to Mr. Curran's classroom he recovered sufficiently to give her a lively imitation of that master in class.

'Once, walking down into Italy from the Alps I saw—what? Norman? Martin? Seamus Conroy? Any boy know? Well, I saw a packet of Murphy's Starch in a village shop window. Oh, Ireland, land of saints and scholars! Walking down into Renaissance Italy—and a packet of Murphy's Starch from Ireland staring me in the face.' Sniff-sniff. Sniff-sniff. And Martin laughed happily.

They went down the alleyway beneath the trees, their feet noiseless on the thick damp leaves. She gave him her hand to be helped on to the river bank and did it as if she really expected his help. As she followed him through the thickets, she stooped to peer out at the water, murmuring several times, 'It's delightful, the whole thing.'

When they came out by the weir, he stood away and watched her as she moved about and turned her head here and there in movements of pleasure, her cheeks russet-toned now in the last glow from earth and sky. Very straight she stood, kilting her skirt at one side and looking at the weir all wild with colour and at the foamy clots which, in their sweep towards the advancing dusk, seemed to hold already their night-time quality of greyish ghost-boats glowing powerfully in silence.

She moved away from him along the grassy bank, while he watched the rooks wheeling with tattered cries of defiance, and, out beyond the weir island, a bargeman muffled beside his rudder,

lonely and cold-looking, as the barge trailed southwards after the
swishing rope, and the red glow went up from the cabin hatch to
the purple air.

'Aunt Kathleen! Quick—look! Be quick or they'll be gone!'
Above their heads the wild geese were streaming, heralding the
coming of night and of winter. Could she be expected to know
that Colonel Reilly and the Irish regiments sailing from Limerick
to exile had been called the Wild Geese? She was almost certainly
a Unionist, and Unionists weren't interested in such things.

'When are you coming again, Aunt Kathleen?'

'You are coming to us first. I've asked that you should spend the
free days for All Hallows with us. And you may be coming
to us for other holidays—proper holidays—as well. I feel that
your Aunt Eileen has had her fair share of you. It's our turn
now.'

He guessed that his visit was to be a sort of trial, and the fear
of lessening the implications of her remark kept him from asking
even one question more.

They went slowly back, up through fields where cows, breathing steamily, watched them from the gloom. Around them the
birds were settling down in hedges and trees; above them, a snipe
was changing his day-time click to his goat's bleat of night-time,
and before them were the twinkling house-lights, while behind
them they heard faintly the murmur of the weir.

'I'm sure it's good for your soul, Martin, to live in a place like
this.'

Two pulsing lights were returning up the avenue. It was the
Swift coming to take her away. His aunt! He looked sideways at
her erect graceful shape in the dusk—his own aunt—Aunt
Kathleen!

To his astonishment, the moustached young man in the Swift
called her 'Aunt Kathleen' too. How could she be aunt to a full
man? Perhaps she was his aunt by marriage. That would explain
it. The Dean had come out on the steps and, oh joy, by some
lucky chance he had brought Norman with him, so they would
meet after all.

When she got into the motor, the young man with the moustache stole the job of holding the car door open for her but
Martin managed to have a hand in the rug-tucking. Norman was
beside him, a slim shape amid the wind-blown scents of fields and

river, his quiet soft voice saying to her crisper, half English voice,
'Goodbye, Mrs. Vincent.'

'No, not goodbye. I hope your parents will allow you to stay
with Martin often; I shall write to your mother when I get your
address from Martin. It's *au revoir*.'

The sound of the motor could be heard after the lights had
vanished. By the time she got home Sally and Peggy would be in
bed and would not hear about him until morning.

'Tea! Martin, come on. I'm hungry and we're losing time.'

'Listen a minute! There's the Swift again.'

It was. A small sound that suddenly came and slowly went,
leaving only the windy night and the flowing of the weir.

8

LAZILY trailing its scarf of smoke along the fields, the train went on its way, leaving the little station once more a part of the country. The station-master was taking off his official braided overcoat and cap and pulling on an old soft hat from his pocket, when he noticed Martin, who stood irresolutely on the platform, holding a wicker travelling-basket. Putting the coat and cap on again, he came to Martin. 'Musha, I forgot. You'll be the young visitor for Keelard? They've sent the big side-car. It's round the bend because the red mare can't abide the smell of a train.'

At the wicket-gate, he said almost apologetically, 'Ye wouldn't happen to have a little bit of a ticket on you, would ye?' When he had got the ticket, he hurriedly took off the braided cap and overcoat and pulled out the old soft hat again. 'Musha, sure I'll take ye as far as the bend myself.'

At the bend, Martin viewed with some alarm the grim expression of his driver who was lean, elderly and stooped. His long head balanced a small hard hat, and from the prominence of his chin, which stuck forward like a shrivelled pear, jutted out a little grey beard.

In two minutes he had made it abundantly plain that he had no use for a thirteen-year-old who needed to be met at the station and who removed him from more essential work in the garden. In fact it was manifest that he had no use for young people at all.

After a dour silence, lasting nearly ten minutes, he remarked: 'Ye needn't expect any pity from me. I'll tell on ye. I'll tell on ye seven times.'

'But what will you tell?' asked Martin.

The driver smiled—a little smile, full of cunning. 'It takes seven times telling on Miss Sally and Miss Peggy before they catch it. So I'll tell on ye seven times.'

145

'But what can you tell? And, anyway, I'm only here as a short-stay guest.'

'Well, short or long, I won't like ye, I'm warning ye. I don't like childer nor dogs,' and giving the mare a brooding flick with the whip he drove on moodily. His silence lasted nearly a mile. Then he remarked abruptly: 'Tell me! Did ye ever have a garden of yer own?'

'No.'

'Or even a flower-bed?'

Martin shook his head.

'Or as much as a'—he gulped in disgust—'a window-box?'

Again Martin shook his head and Hanrahan's expression grew even more alarming.

Beyond a tree-shaded slope the car turned between stone gate-posts crowned with stone balls. They drove with a soft whirr over the dampish avenue, glaucous under high sycamores that already were showing their strawberry shapes at the tops. Hanrahan glowered at the lucent smears of moss on the avenue. 'Will there ever be just one day when I'll have overtook me tracks? I'm no sooner got to one place than it's long past time to go back to another.'

Flashing out from the green twilight under the trees, they whirred between wide pasture fields railed back from the avenue, went through a white gate and made straight for a thick belt of copper beeches dully gleaming in the grey afternoon. Before Martin had time to think, the other side of the copper beeches had become a boundary for a large half-moon of lawn that faced the house.

There it was—but it had not even one castle battlement on the roof! A gentleman-farmer's house near Lullacreen had had *two* small castle turrets but this house had none. He knew that the square house was 'Georgian Architecture' but the queer red-brown addition at the far end was what? A wing? Having 'a wing' was nearly as good as having a bit of battlement on the roof; one could say 'the new wing' or 'the old wing' as the case might be—or even, with a bit of luck, 'the ghost's wing'!

Hanrahan angrily pulled up the mare before shallow steps. Shyness overcame Martin as he saw Aunt Kathleen coming down the steps in a soft dark dress with many folds.

'Welcome, Martin,' and she kissed him.

On the top step a girl in a blue dress and white pinafore was looking down at him, the serious expression of her pale, oval face emphasized by the way her brown hair was scraped back to a blue bow. He knew this must be Peggy because she seemed to be about a year younger than himself. Coming down, she looked at him with an interest both eager and solemn.

'Welcome to Keelard, Cousin Martin. I'm Peggy. We've been hearing such lots about you.' And very coolly and naturally she leaned forward and kissed him.

Up in the doorway-shadow another dress and pinafore hovered shyly; an older girl came out and, as she paused between the shadow and the light, he saw that she was a little like Aunt Kathleen but her hair was not auburn, not brown like Peggy's, but what he called 'dark red'.

'Welcome to Keelard, Cousin Martin.' She did not kiss him and they stood looking at one another. Her eyes, darker and warmer-looking than Peggy's, stared at him with as deep an interest but more penetratingly and at the same time more shyly. 'I'm Sally.' She hesitated. 'I met your Aunt Mary once in Dublin with Mother; she was lovely and she let me ride on top of the tram, not inside.'

Washing his hands in the cloakroom, he found it reassuring to see the cricket bats and croquet mallets in a corner—he knew his way among that kind of thing anyway! It was reassuring also to find that the water tap gurgled and was as hard to turn off as the taps were in Glenkilly, and to learn from Sally that he would have to help to pump the water up to the cisterns.

'In this house, let me tell you,' Peggy said, 'there's no end to the jobs that are put on *sub ferula* people.'

'Oh, do you do Latin? Properly, I mean, not like most girls?'

Yes, they did Latin. Not with Miss Clare but with Colonel Howard, who 'lives in a cottage near here but he's always staying the night; you see, he comes to luncheon and he's not gone by dinner-time, so he stays the week-end'.

In the broad, shabby-dim hall, he was shown the drawing-room door where '*sub ferula* people enter by invitation or order', and the dining-room where 'You'll dinner with us. It's the Jews' luncheon, but they don't have sago, rice and all the other worse-than-Foxe's-Martyrs things,' said Peggy.

'The Jews?'

'Oh, not the real Jews. Not the *Merchant of Venice* kind. G.U. is short for grown-up and just sounds like Jew accidentally.'

The long, shining tubes were Chinese gongs for Jews' meals, she explained, brought home by Great-Aunt Harriet's 'other brother', called that to distinguish him from the poor brother who had no money and spent all his time on 'the green-covered translation of Lucretius—a Pagan'. Peggy talked away, calm, candid, solemn yet eager.

Going up the stairs, he stared at a long picture which looked straight down into the hall from the first landing. Because of a window beside it, he took a few moments to see that the brightness in it was the plum-coloured coat of a man in eighteenth-century dress with his hand on his sword hilt and a very queer, tight smile.

'The Minorca Man. Daddy's great-grandfather. He came home specially to vote against the Union.'

He said hesitatingly, 'And now I suppose you are all Unionists?'

'Well, the family is. Daddy says now he's a kind of half-and-half Home Ruler or getting that way. Colonel Howard says I'd better not go in for it when I'm grown-up. He says I wouldn't stop at that, that I would be worse than the Suffragettes.'

And, laughing, they signalled him to follow through a green baize door that led to the schoolroom where, beside a cracked blackboard balanced on the chimney-piece, biscuits and lemonade in a jug awaited them. He was shown a model house which Peggy had made, and her book-bind tools and press; and he was asked to put by any old magazines or books he might ever be able to spare, in order that Peggy could have them for those old men and old women whom she had taken under her wing, and to whom, twice a week, in the governess car, or on her pony or bicycle, she carried ju-jubes, knitting wool, tobacco, old magazines and yesterday's newspapers. He was shown Sally's illustrated music-sheets; her drawings of ponies and of the house drawn over and over again from all viewpoints; her sketches of things seen upside-down after she had stood on her head; and the cleaned skeleton of a dog and 'Miss Clare's Black Days of Wrath, Doubt and Sorrow Book'. Miss Clare, they explained, could be awfully strict. 'All the same, she's marvellous. Cool as a cucumber, you know: fearfully handsome, and Mother's best *young* friend.'

They asked him not to look through the window. 'You might see across the back of "Kathleen's Garden" and so you must wait; it's a sort of small surprise.' They led him downstairs again to see the new bread. The smell of it was beating along the passage to the side, and there, in the kitchen itself, one iron door was already open, the oven's heat wafting outward in waves, and Aunt Kathleen herself stooping to peer into the dark recess.

'Oh, if only someone would make a song for new bread,' Martin blurted out. They smiled and wiped the sweat from foreheads; and the parlourmaid, carefully aloof in the pantry to avoid the hot baking, laughed; and the cook-general laughed; and 'the slip of a girl', Aggie, laughed.

The baking-boards and tins were left for the girls to clean, and he was led down a passage and into a small ante-room where a young woman with a black tie in her choker collar sat behind a typewriter, with Hanrahan behind her scowling down at a bill in her hand. This, Martin guessed, was Betty, who did all the clerical work of the farm.

In the room beyond they came upon a tall man, with brown hair greying at the temples, stooping to wash his hands at a basin behind a screen. Nodding reservedly but kindly at Martin he turned and shook hands with him.

'I am very glad that you've come. I think it will be good for everyone.'

'Perhaps I could help on the farm? I've helped at calving twice and I could doctor sheep and . . .' Martin stopped, afraid that he might be too obviously asking this new, dull, but terribly impressive, uncle to keep him here.

Mr. Vincent nodded again in that reserved but kindly way, and asked: 'Tell me, do your uncles, the farming ones, take any interest in the Co-operative movement? I'm having Sir Horace down to speak—Sir Horace Plunkett; do they tell you about him and his work at your school?' Before Martin could reply there was a knock at the door and Aggie entered.

'Tom Prendergast wants to know, sir, what about the old drain behind the Four Acres?'

Mr. Vincent turned to where Tom stood waiting beyond the threshold. Sally took Martin's arm. 'Now we'll show you "Kathleen's Garden". Father called it that when he was planning it. Now everyone calls it that.'

Martin, ordered to shut his eyes, was guided into the garden as far as the central intersection of the paths. 'Now you can open them again.'

There, beyond flower-beds, beyond a low hedge, beyond a gravelled walk outside the hedge, a field went bumping down and down to a broad sheet of water.

Beyond the water, trees were massed, silver, grey, gold-brown. 'That's our surprise—the Long Island. No one expects the river here but it's been curving for miles really and then up there it breaks into three forks and this backwater comes right over to us. Listen!'

Through the cooling autumn air he heard a faint rumble. 'The rapids,' Sally said. 'Just shallow parts with rocks. It's only a backwater really.'

'But it *is* the river! It starts curving of course after it has passed Glenkilly.' He looked solemnly at her. 'Just fancy. All this time we've been looking at the same river and we not knowing one another at all.'

'Yes, and now when you see the river at your school you'll remember it's here too.' They smiled shyly at one another.

They turned back to show him the farm buildings. Martin stood at the door of the boar's house and felt the magnificence of a farm that had its own boar kept specially to encourage people round about to breed that kind of pig. And three prize heifers. And a big silo, and a prize herd of sheep! But all other magnificence faded before the glossy power, the curveting strength, of Aunt Kathleen's roan hunter, Dominick, in there in the smelly half-light.

In a blurred exaltation, he followed the girls across the rutted back-avenue, went down the bumping path of the field beneath the elderberries and came again to the water. The shallow current rumpled onward in the centre but an annexe of a creek flowed very gently apart to the boathouse. Peggy took a key from a ledge above the door. 'It's a hiding-place for it but everyone for miles around knows where that key is, "God bless it", as Tom says.'

He looked in upon the sour darkness of the boathouse, heard the lapping at the door-jambs, the gurgle around the keels of the two boats. They had to go in single file along the tiny path which was the only way of circling the wet parts that lay between the

river and the back-avenue, until they came out below slopes
and mossy banks, yellow in the last cold light. Climbing the
slopes, they took branches of hips and haws from the hedges, and
stiff, tinkling leaves from the beeches, and it was nearing dusk
when they came to a belt of trees, railed off from the road below.

'Useful way of getting in and out,' said Peggy as she pulled
herself up to a branch, swung out and dropped to the road. One
day he would find it useful indeed, although he would not swing
so easily as now.

They were walking on the road now. Out of the gloom,
there appeared a small house surrounded, it seemed, by lofty
spears.

'Tom Prendergast's Ambition,' whispered Peggy. This was
Tom's house surrounded by scaffoldings. Tom had planned great
additions to his house which brought all his acquaintances for
miles on Sundays after Mass to look at the scaffolding; that
addition was to be a bathroom.

Holding up their rustling branches, they began to walk close
together through the silence redolent with the evening breath of
resting, well-nourished land. The odorous breath pressed up
against the windows of cottages yellow-lit in the dusk, and
sometimes along the road the lamps of traps went by, effulgent
and benign. They turned between the open gates into the darker
silence beneath the sycamores. 'Higher, higher,' called Sally, in
the gloom, and they strained their golden leaves aloft. Martin
took out Aunt Mary's torch and, in the beam of light, phantom
shapes curled around the berried branches in the faintly luminous
mist. He turned the beam upon Sally; her neck was upturned to
the branches and her face, framed in her arms, was eager, cold-
white and lovely. They curved past the copper beeches, and saw
the lighted house ahead and the dark gleaming of the laurels.

From the garden gate, Tom Prendergast's voice came. 'Well,
well, the quare games ye get up to.'

'Hello, Tom,' said Sally, and then, rather dryly: 'Thinking
how many turnips you could grow in "Kathleen's Garden",
Tom?'

'Aw, now, Miss Sally! All the same, I do say it takes up a good
quare bit of room just for flowers, ye'll admit that.'

Tom called hesitantly, 'I say—Master Reilly?' and when
Martin came back to him, he said: 'I'm glad to see you. Me own

father was born over at Melrose next to your grandfather's place. I was over there once and I a lad.'

'Oh!' So this was one of the Prendergasts Aunt Mary had mentioned: 'Though it's well over a hundred years ago, they're labourers now to this very day.'

Martin wanted to talk to Tom, either in the way Sally and Peggy had just done, or else in the way he himself would have talked to a Tom Prendergast in the Lullacreen yards, swinging the forks of hay to the sky with Old Tommy and Paddy and all the men. But here in 'Kathleen's Garden' a curious constraint seemed to overtake him and he could not talk to Tom in either of those ways.

'Well, so long, Tom. See you tomorrow,' and he ran towards the waiting faces of the girls in the light of the side hall-door. In the cloakroom, where the girls sang as they unlaced their high boots, he refused to admit a vague loneliness which had touched him as he stood in the garden and he set himself to learn the words of the song the girls were singing about an old man who had never seen Carcassonne although his children had seen distant Narbonne and Perpignan.

> 'Ma femme avec mon fils, Aignan,
> A voyagé jusqu'à Narbonne
> Mon filleul a vu Perpignan
> Et je n'ai pas vu Carcassonne.'

They took him to the schoolroom where they found Aggie stirring batter in a white bowl. Peggy took over from her and Martin started telling her of Josie's pancakes; but when Sally with an improvised dance went round the room, seeking places for the branches they had picked, he danced with her and improvised to her humming.

When she left the room he followed, hearing her call to him from the passage. He saw her beckoning from the big window near his bedroom. Looking down, he saw a solitary horseman riding slowly away in the dusk towards the back-avenue.

'Some visitor from drawing-room tea.' She opened the window. The cold air stole in, and, with it, the sound of the horse's steps. The unidentified grown-up rode away into darkness, just one of those who dropped in to Keelard for casual hospitality. Out of the darkness came the click of the gate-latch raised by the horseman's crop. 'Ssh! Listen.' They listened and—click—the crop had let down the latch once more. Like people watching a great play, they gazed out on the milky world; looked at one another; then went to the pancakes.

Miss Clare being away, having gone to spend Hallow E'en in England, the girls had time the next morning to give him one lesson in riding and another in how to sport with the dogs without giving Hanrahan the smallest excuse for telling on them because the flowers had been broken down.

When they went to work in the dairy Martin listened a while to the rumpling rhythm of the churning, then offered his unwanted help to one man after another in the yards. Feeling slightly deflated by their rejection of it, he returned to the house.

He was in the breakfast-room with Mr. Vincent, who was questioning him about his school, when there was a knock at the door and a slight, short, elderly man came in. He had a clear, healthy complexion, hair silvery white and a moustache that was entirely white. He was very neat and precise-looking in a well-made grey suit.

'Well, Brendan . . .' he began; then, seeing Martin, he looked at him with interest and said: 'Well, well. So this is the boy?'

'Yes, this is Martin.'

'How d'ye do? My name is Howard. Colonel Howard. If you come here often I expect you'll do holiday work with me. Have you started Horace yet? I am sure you will be a great encouragement to Sally and Peggy.'

Warming his behind at the fireplace, he said to Mr. Vincent, 'You know, what with your meeting today and the Hallow E'en party tonight, I really think that today I will not go back to the book.' He touched the big, black folder under his arm.

The girls had told Martin that Colonel Howard was writing a book containing an account of those Irishmen who had given prominent, or important, service in India: 'The Army and the Indian Civil; he's sorry he has to leave out all the Railway people.'

'I think, Brendan, I told you about the Hallow E'en party in Madras when——'

'Yes, yes,' said Mr. Vincent quickly. 'You told me dozens of times, Philip.'

'Well, didn't you enjoy it every time!' and he laughed good-naturedly.

Later in the morning several people arrived for the meeting to discuss plans for a village hall. Presenting Martin to the local curate, Mr. Thorpe, Mrs. Vincent said casually: 'Martin's mother was a second cousin of mine. She lived a lot abroad.'

In response to the cleric's greeting, Martin hesitated, worried by a special problem—Mr. Thorpe could not be called 'Father' like a priest, but to say merely 'sir' to a clergyman would surely be rude, so he said brightly, 'How d'ye do, Reverend sir.'

Mr. Thorpe looked embarrassed, and Mrs. Vincent, stooping to Martin as he held the door for her and Mr. Thorpe, whispered: 'No "reverend", just "sir". All the same I call it very clever of you.' Then she added: 'More people are coming to see your uncle. You'd better go away the moment they come.'

'Canon Masterson didn't feel up to attending the meeting this time, Mr. Vincent,' Mr. Thorpe was saying, 'so he asked me to represent him. A sort of watching brief. Hope it's all right?'

'Of course,' said Mr. Vincent, but he sounded depressed as he added: 'And Father Callaghan says he can't come. He writes that his curate is away and he is very busy.'

Colonel Howard looked at his watch. 'Late, of course,' he said disapprovingly, but just then voices were heard and Martin, in obedience to Aunt Kathleen's order, made to leave but stopped sharply when he had opened the door. Out there in the ante-room were three or four men in overcoats, and in front of them, leaning over the typewriter to whisper with twinkling insinuation to Betty, was Mr. Tim Corbin of Ballow.

Martin whirled about and went hurriedly to the window to get away by the garden but, as he fumbled at the handle, he heard Betty already announcing the visitors and, afraid of being seen and recognized by Mr. Corbin, he flopped into the dark space between the wall and the high safe with the screw-press for paper on top of it. Crouching down uncomfortably on the heaps of *Farm, Field and Fireside,* he was hidden from view unless someone came deliberately to peer into the corner.

The men were in the room, Mr. Corbin handing over his hat to Betty with an abstracted air, like one scarcely aware of a servant's presence and not like one who had just been twinkling with jovial insinuations. A skinny man in knickerbockers entered.

Looking at his watch, he said, like a judge summing up many crimes: 'Good morning. I knew it would be useless to be punctual. Nothing ever starts in this country at the time stated.'

Instantly, Colonel Howard, who only a moment before had been saying disapprovingly, 'Late, of course,' said sharply: 'Well, Mr. Binnay, what does it matter? We have our own ways of doing things over here.'

Mr. Vincent shook hands with his visitors.

'This is Mr. Corbin here that we told you about, Mr. Vincent, who took such an interest in our business and now he's come all the way from Ballow.'

'How d'ye do, Mr. Corbin. It is very good of you to come so far to give us your help.'

'Not at all, Mr. Vincent. I felt the least a man with a little influence in the county could do was to give a lead to others.' He said it as if there existed between himself and Mr. Vincent a common fount of power and knowledge not shared by the others of his own party. He twinkled around him, pince-nez shining, young-old eyes noticing everything. 'So here I am,' he said, 'and I hope the poor Nationalist won't be drugged and stabbed.' He laughed but everyone else looked embarrassed.

From the minutes of a preceding meeting Martin learned that Mr. Vincent proposed to convert a large barn into a public hall. He would give the barn and a sports field free, negotiate for reduced prices for the necessary materials and give a generous opening subscription. The Hall was to be managed by 'a strictly non-political, non-denominational committee from among the people themselves'.

Martin, very worried lest his Aunt Kathleen would think that he had disobeyed her, but afraid to draw out now from the corner, scarcely followed the long discussion, which remained lifeless until someone mentioned dancing. Thereupon, a young man with an Irish-speaking symbol like Conroy's, set in his lapel beside a Temperance badge, leaned forward assertively. He had lumpy black curls so high up and so clustered that they looked as if they might float away from his head like a swarm of bees. 'There must be a rule that at all dances in the Hall at least every second dance has to be an Irish dance.'

'But scarcely anyone knows those dances,' said Colonel Howard.

'Well, people will have to learn them, then!'

'But, dash it, if people don't want to . . .' and Colonel Howard looked with dislike at the young man.

'They ought to learn their own dances,' the young man said stubbornly. 'Actually, this is only a temporary compromise. Foreign dances should not be allowed at all by rights.'

'By what rights——' began Colonel Howard, but Mr. Thorpe said in a reasoning, placatory tone:

'But, really now, is there much that is particularly Irish about them? I understood that most of them were invented not many years ago.'

'There was a national purpose behind the invention! The people must be compelled to dance their own native dances!'

A big, heavy farmer said carefully, 'Now that we've mentioned dancing, Mr. Vincent, I may say that Father Callaghan asked me to inform you of his settled opposition to . . .' He took a worn little notebook from his pocket, spectacles from a shiny case and shifting into a reading position, read out: '*No dances on Saturday nights, nor any night in Lent, nor on the Eves of Church Holidays, nor any night at all after 10.45 p.m. and——*'

'But that rules out all——'

'You'll excuse me, Mr. Vincent, but I'll just finish now about the dancing business as we're at it,' and he read out:

'*Father Callaghan won't allow any drinking, and all sitting-out places must be within twenty yards of the hall and open to all observation—there must be no screens! And no palm trees in tubs! Also, Father Callaghan is disturbed about the matter of the platform for Dramas and Grand Concerts. If this stage is to be used also for dancing when the floor below is too crowded, then Father Callaghan will denounce this hall to the people and not allow them to take part in it.*'

Mr. Thorpe, Colonel Howard and Mr. Vincent looked puzzled, the young man with the badges and curls blushed, and Mr. Corbin pursed his lips noncommittally.

'But what is worrying Father Callaghan?' said Mr. Vincent. 'If it's a question of accidents, I can assure him——'

'It isn't a question of accidents, Mr. Vincent,' said the big man with embarrassed bluntness. 'It's a question of immorality!'

'He means immodesty,' the curly young man muttered.

'Immorality? But how . . . what . . .' Mr. Vincent said rather testily, and the big farmer answered with kindly understanding and respect.

'You're a simple gentleman, Mr. Vincent, and you gentlemen,' he nodded towards Colonel Howard and Mr. Thorpe, 'and really it's too delicate a matter to discuss.' He blushed and said, 'We ought to decide on it in silence.'

'But decide on what? What *is* the trouble?'

The curly young man stood up. Blushing swarthily, he said: 'If there's dancing up on the platform and men down below on the floor, well, in the Lancers and other English dances—not, of course, in Irish dances!—ladies are often swung off their feet and even if not, still they're swinging about a lot, and if men are on the floor below, there would be an appeal to . . . to . . .' and with determination he finished, 'an appeal to that which should *not* be appealed to!'

For a few moments there was a bewildered silence, then Colonel Howard said, 'Well, bless my soul!'

Into the embarrassed silence the big farmer said confidingly: 'To tell ye the truth, what do they want with dances at all? If you have no dances, you have no need to discuss—well, the subject we discussed. Can't they have singing and a game of cards——'

'Oh, excuse me.' It was Mr. Thorpe who interrupted. 'Before we go any further, perhaps I ought to say now that Canon Masterson wishes to convey that he could not support a hall where . . . excuse me . . .' and he took from his pocket a sheet of Rectory paper and read out: '. . . *where persons are allowed to take part in Roulette, the playing of cards for money, Sweep Lotteries, Wheels of Fortune, dicing or any of the many pernicious appeals to the evil spirit of Gambling.*'

The big farmer gaped. 'Do you mean to say that the lads wouldn't be able to play pitch-and-toss or have a bit on an under-and-over-seven at a bazaar.'

Mr. Thorpe said apologetically, 'I am afraid that both would be included in Canon Masterson's objection.'

'But that's intolerant!' exclaimed the curly young man with contempt. 'Most puritanical and narrow-minded!'

Mr. Thorpe flushed. 'Canon Masterson does not think so. Whatever my own opinion, it is my duty to point out that his objection is founded on a principle as important as . . . and pragmatically speaking, more . . .'

'Now, do ye know what?' said the big farmer. 'This hall will lead to trouble! Halls and dances always lead to trouble and to . . . well, the subject we discussed. 'Tis best really to let the people go on as they are. They have plenty of football matches and an odd race-meeting and a drink or two now and then, and a bit on a horse. What more do they want? If you have no dramas and dancings and no halls, ye have no need to discuss the subject already mentioned.'

There was a long and helpless silence, broken at last by an elderly little man with a sharp, intelligent face and an angry Jack-in-the-Box way of speaking. 'Tell me,' he said, with grim readiness for opposition, 'have you considered my point about the R.I.C.? Whatever this hall is used for, the peelers must not be allowed to have hand, act or share in it.'

Colonel Howard pushed back his chair. 'I'm sorry, Brendan. But I cannot sit quietly by while the King's police officers are openly insulted. I had better go.'

'Philip—please. Gentleman, surely . . . ?'

'This hall won't pass if Royal Irish Constabulary men are let into it; they have enough opportunities as it is to spy on the plain people of Ireland. . . .'

'But why—why are all these difficulties suddenly raised now?' said Mr. Vincent, wearily and irritably. 'After finding a way around so many real difficulties, this is altogether disheartening!'

'Both the matter of Irish dances and the matter of immodesty due to the platform are *real* difficulties,' said the curly young man, 'and I may say——'

'The question of the peelers is more important. The eyes and ears of England's garrison must not——'

'Brendan, I cannot allow His Majesty's . . .'

Into the rising cross-arguments, a soothing voice called: 'If you'll excuse me, Mr. Vincent, I have a suggestion to make.' It was Mr. Tim Corbin. He had risen and now looked around the group with friendly understanding of everything and everybody. 'Now we're all getting a bit worked up. And really there's no fundamental difference between us at all. Nothing really fundamental.' Over the heads of the others he nodded confidingly to Mr. Vincent. 'All these little points will be easily settled when we are calmer. But to give us a chance to think quietly how we are all to meet one another in these little differences, I propose that we postpone further discussion of them to another meeting.'

'But this was to have been the decisive meeting. We were to open the subscription list!'

'Now, Mr. Vincent, leave it to me,' and he gave Mr. Vincent another reassuring, intimate nod.

'Aye, aye. Best way out of it,' muttered the big man, looking snobbishly down his long nose, 'adjourn it *again*,' and he looked at his watch.

Mr. Vincent hesitated. 'Very well,' he said suddenly and very curtly. 'The next item on our agenda is the Farmers' Co-operative Store. Sir Horace will speak if I ask him and . . .'

Mr. Corbin, still on his feet, stroked his chin thoughtfully. 'Now there again there are a few little points—little things of course—but for today, seeing that we're all a bit worked up, it would be as well to leave that question also till we meet again.'

Mr. Vincent meditated. 'Very well,' he said grimly, and after some lifeless talk about the date of the next discussion the meeting broke up without naming the date.

Mr. Corbin slipped into the chair vacated by Colonel Howard. 'By the way, Mr. Vincent, I've only just thought of a little matter. Some of us were talking of perhaps mentioning it to you and, sure, now that I'm here, I might as well just drop you a word.'

'What is it?' said Mr. Vincent curtly and wearily.

'Well, now then, it's the County Engineer. We feel it's only right to let all those who' are members of the County Council know that there's a great deal of feeling against appointing this man Ryan. The whole county wants Mr. Purcell.'

In his corner, Martin was stung by shamed distress as he remembered what his Uncle John had told him in Ballow on the day of Mr. Redmond's meeting—that 'Tim Corbin was swinging votes today for your Aunt Eileen's cousin, Purcell, because he stands to recover money owed to him by a contractor if Purcell does get it'.

'It's the first I've heard of such a feeling,' said Mr. Vincent, giving Corbin a sharp look.

'Sure a gentleman like yourself would be the last in the world to know the pulse of the people.'

Mr. Vincent winced. 'Have you any evidence of this feeling you say exists against Mr. Ryan?'

And from the fireplace Colonel Howard snapped, 'It's none of my business, Brendan, but I am quite unaware of any such feeling and it would be extraordinary if we had to wait for someone to come from Ballow to tell us it existed.'

The sharp, elderly little man, giving Colonel Howard an angry glance, intervened. 'The fact of the matter is, Mr. Vincent—whatever Mr. Timothy Corbin's private objects may be,' he added sourly, 'some of us are not going to let Ryan be elected because he's known to be indifferent, possibly hostile, to the national aspirations of the plain people of this country.'

'I don't know anything about that. I do know that he has the better qualifications. Much the better of the two.'

'Maybe. But qualifications aren't enough to offset the objections of the plain people.'

'But who is making the objections? I have received none.'

'You're receiving them now, Mr. Vincent!'

'But the people who trusted me with their votes, elected me to administer affairs——'

Colonel Howard interrupted impatiently: 'And Mr. Vincent, remember, was not elected by any caucus. He got in on the combined votes of the Unionists and the best Nationalists of the county.'

'Oh, did he, then!' snarled the fiery little man, giving the table a rap. 'Let me tell you that the Protestants of this county couldn't elect half a member, nor a quarter of a member only that the plain——'

'Heavens, he's going to say the "Plain People of Ireland"!' said Mr. Thorpe loudly, and turning to face the table, he muttered in a helpless way: 'The Plain People. I'm sick of it. It's really the most dreadful cant.' He pulled himself together, glanced apologetically towards Mr. Vincent and turned away.

But the fiery little man jumped to his feet. 'Oh, sick of it, are ye?' he shouted. 'Well, ye'll be sicker let me tell you before ye finish. It gets under yer skin to know that the plain——'

Over his shoulder Mr. Thorpe said, 'As if Protestants were never plain and never Irish!'

'No more are they!' The little man banged the table. 'If it's the truth ye're driving me to I'm not afraid to say it. The Protestants had better make up their minds——'

Rounding on him, Mr. Thorpe said in a shaken voice: 'Don't
dare talk about Protestants as if you knew the smallest thing
about them. Your cant phrase covers everything for you! I'm a
Christian priest and I try to be charitable and yet I can't help
loathing that determined ignorance! I came down here hoping
to work with all sorts . . . well, to work in Ireland and for Ireland
. . . and all you do is shut me out with your "Plain People of
Ireland". Do you know that much'—he snapped his fingers—
'about the history of this country? Name me one, just one . . .'
his voice began to rise '. . . just one inspired leader of your own
political faith who, with the single exception of O'Connell, was
not "a plain Irish Protestant".'

'Intellectually, I agree,' murmured the curly young man with
the badges; 'only intellectually, though.'

'Intellectual me hat!' roared the elderly man, banging the
table and taking a few strides towards Mr. Thorpe. 'Now it's out,
the black Protestant venom! "I loathe your ignorance," he says.
Christ above—who made us ignorant? You and your ilk. Ye've
sneered at the people of this country and drove us into the dust
and now ye're upset because we refused to stay there and you talk
of ignorance—by God, I'll brain ye!' and with an even louder
bang upon the table, he whirled to Mr. Vincent. 'And you, what
do ye think yer doing! D'ye think ye can crawl back into the belly
of the Irish people with yer halls and yer school-libraries and yer
Co-operatives?'

'By God, sir!' Colonel Howard stepped forward.

'Easy—easy on now,' implored Mr. Corbin, who backed to the
door, while Mr. Vincent looked helplessly into the grim face of
the elderly man.

The latter said: 'I'm sorry for you, for you personally. Ye mean
well and do your best, I know. But our day is coming back again,
make up yer mind to that. And by God we'll use it! An eye for an
eye and a tooth for a tooth.'

'You poor ignorant enemy of Ireland,' said Mr. Thorpe in low,
intense tones. 'I pity you.'

'Enemy of Ireland!' shouted the man. 'Me?' and he rushed
forward with upraised arm. A chair went crashing to the floor,
as the curly man tried to hold him back. 'Me?' he roared again.
And at that moment the door opened.

All turned and there inside the door stood Mrs. Vincent, the warm glow gone from behind her cheeks. She stood a moment, then turning towards the ante-room, said in a steady voice: 'Betty, your master's visitors are going now. Find their hats, please.'

She came forward and everyone moved, making a greater bustle than was necessary. The big farmer, giving her an inclination of his head, said: 'I'm heartily sorry you've been disturbed, ma'am. It's a shameful thing in your decent house. I had no part in it, and now I'm going, for one.'

Mr. Corbin advanced, hand held out, his regretful air deprecating everything and everybody, except himself and Mrs. Vincent. 'Ah, too bad . . . tut-tut,' and he kept the hand held out to her. 'I'm Mr. Corbin. From Ballow, you know. You know the Royal Leinster Arms. You may have heard of me.'

'No,' she said.

A little vicious flash passed across Mr. Corbin's eyes. Then, recovering his deprecating smile of a half-mourner, he almost leaned towards her face. She turned away, ignoring the outstretched hand, bowed to the big farmer at the door and said, 'Goodbye, Mr. Regan.'

'Goodbye, Mrs. Vincent. It's a bad business to be upsetting anybody's decent house,' and he went out.

The elderly, fiery man turned at the door and with a jerky nod of politeness, said: 'Good day to ye, ma'am. Me tongue outstripped me manners and I'd ask your pardon. Goodbye, Mr. Vincent, sir. I'm sorry I spoke hard to you or your friends. I've a respect for ye here in this place and me own grandfather got more than one good turn done to him from here. So I was in the wrong in speaking out the way I did.'

The curly young man, blushing and fumbling, followed him, and, suddenly putting his head up high with assertive independence, walked out without a word. Mr. Corbin, hesitating at the door, saw Mrs. Vincent turn to look at him. 'Er . . . well . . .' he began, looked again at her, murmured, 'Grand day,' and slipped from the room like a beaten dog.

When all had gone Mr. Thorpe, who had been standing by the window, turned to Mrs. Vincent. 'I have no excuse at all. I simply lost my patience and my temper. Lately I have been coming up against so much of this kind of thing. You must forgive me. Can I go out by the garden?'

'Of course. And you had provocation, I am quite sure.' She shook hands with him.

When he had gone she turned to her husband. 'Brendan, if you still want to try to work with those people, if you really think that you can, then you must do it somewhere else, not here in the house. Why bring them here—to Keelard? That young boor who nearly knocked Betty off her feet—the one with curls, what is he? One of their new young men, I suppose? Elsewhere, if you simply must go on. But not in Keelard.'

Mr. Vincent, standing with bent head by the fireplace, made no answer. Colonel Howard said: 'Now, now, Kathleen. There's a great deal to be said for Brendan's projects. But, even in small practical affairs, fundamental differences of principle, it seems, are bound to crop up.'

'Oh, please stop it, Philip! All I know is that I simply will not have those people tramping in here, tramping on our peace and quiet. Why can't we just be ourselves and leave all that to others?'

She was silent for a few moments, then said very quietly: 'I'm sorry. I lost my temper also. You see how it is,' and went out.

Without a creak, Martin slunk around the front of the safe into the garden and away round by the side hall-door, up under the Minorca Man, through the green door and into his tiny room. On the other side of the half-open door communicating with the girls' room, he heard their voices as they got ready for dinner, which would be 'Jews' luncheon without sago or rice'.

He pushed mysteries and fears back over the edge of his mind into forgetfulness. Tim Corbin would never dare to come here again—banished! The way she had looked at him! And down in Uncle Brendan's leathery-smelling room he and she would now be talking properly and nicely to one another once more.

It took the Hallow E'en party in the afternoon to restore harmony to the household. When for the last time the silver lamps in the drawing-room had been turned low and in the near-darkness the last sparklers had sprinkled their dust of light on laughing faces, on bright sashes around white frocks, and on black silk knees, someone called for 'A Conger'.

The singing line wound to the hall, Uncle Brendan at the head, and Aunt Kathleen at its tail, and in the line, Martin, his hands

resting on the whale-boned waist of the eldest Stillmore girl.
Then, with crossed hands beneath the dying lanterns in the hall,
they sang 'Should auld acquaintance be forgot'. Then, without
warning, he heard the opening words of 'God Save the King'. In
dismayed flurry, he hesitated. On the other side of the great circle,
Peggy was singing; beside him, there was Sally singing. He looked
round the ring. His Aunt Kathleen's eyes were on him. Well,
Norman's father drank the King's health, and he was a
Nationalist and a great friend of Mr. Redmond. He smiled at his
Aunt Kathleen, and joined in:

> 'Long to reign over us,
> God save the King.'

As the last sounds of wheels, the last high calls of departing
guests, faded, he turned back into the draughty but now warm
hall, and said to her, 'You know, a Nationalist can sing "God
Save the King" all right because he wants the King, Lords and
Commons of Ireland, like Grattan.'

She looked down at him. 'Can he?' she said. 'Well, you were
very nice and good. As I knew you would be.' On the clear skin
her black medallion moved with her breathing, holding, he knew,
his Uncle Brendan on one side and the girls on the other.

From the hall where the candles died in the glass lanterns he
followed her as she went up the stairs, one hand gripping her
dress at the knees.

When for the last time she had rustled in and out of the
communicating door to the girls' room, she picked up his candle.
'You understand, Martin, that it is not always like these few days.
This was a special treat. When you come to us again I'm afraid
you'll find the regime a little stricter. Miss Clare, remember, is
very severe.'

'Yes, I know that. Is she as marvellous as the girls say? And
your best friend?'

'Yes. And really well educated, which I am not.'

'Did my mother come here, Aunt Kathleen?'

She blew out the candle and answered from the dimness, 'Yes.'

'Did Colonel Howard know her? He did, didn't he?'

'Yes.'

'I knew. I felt it somehow when he first spoke to me.'

She said nothing.

'Sally and Peggy said you had a miniature in your lovely day-room.'

She hesitated, then went through to the girls' room and brought Sally's dressing-gown to him. They went through the green door and up the four steps to her little day-room. There she lit a high-standing lamp; and, in its shaded light, the gilt legs of the ottoman gleamed, the leather household account-books, the heavy embossed frames of little pictures, all glowed softly. She took down the miniature which hung with others, looked from him to it and handed it to him.

It was a very small picture, just an oval, serious face of a child with heavy, hanging curls behind her ears and a slim neck disappearing cloudily into the line of a sky-blue dress.

'Haven't you one of her when she's older?'

'Yes, in her wedding dress. She's lovely. I asked for one of her quite alone and . . .' She stopped, sat down at the shining escritoire, and, with a tiny key, unlocked a drawer, and handed him the photograph.

'Her veil,' he said. 'It's turned back, almost like a waterfall, like a girl Norman and I saw shouting "Justice" at a meeting in Ballow. . . . A Suffragette,' he added hastily.

'One day these must be yours, Martin. But not until you are grown-up. Twenty-one or -two.'

'Why didn't you have another wedding picture with my father in it?'

She turned away as if to fasten the drawer. 'I have one photograph of him and her together which she sent. Just a small snapshot, taken by a friend. I shall show it to you one day.'

'Am I going to come here, like Sally and Peggy, and help you with the house and the dairy books and so on? I will, won't I?'

She turned and looked at him, and suddenly stooped to him. 'Yes. Just like the girls.'

The black medallion was close to him, and the lace top of her dress curving from shoulder-point to shoulder-point was like the surf froth at Tramore fringing a sea-shore half-moon of bare skin, sand-coloured in this shaded light. It seemed to him that beauty such as this had never existed on the earth before.

They went back in silence. As they passed the window she looked out at the still coldness of the night. 'All Saints Time,' she murmured.

Chin over the sheet, he watched her standing in the dimness of the communicating door, looking in at the sleeping girls. When she had gone, he planned to lie awake and think what his mother had been like, playing the piano perhaps, down beyond 'Kathleen's Garden' in that drawing-room where the silver horses for ever waited to prance with their silver coaches across the polished tables, and where the Crusader on the ladies' fire-screen flashed like Roland or Oliver. But the plan miscarried and when he awoke, Aggie, with crooked apron, was grinning through spirals of smoke from the hot-water jug, and there, bundling her aside, came Sally and Peggy, unwinding night plaits.

That afternoon, Tom Prendergast drove him to the station. It was nearing dark when Martin left the train. He got a lift in a tinker's cart and, lying comfortably among the pots and pans, heard the adventures of the tinker, until the lights of Dunslane twinkled beyond the fields. He short-cut his way towards them.

Willy met him with news that a visitor had called for him that day. 'She sat there at the table and scribbled a note to you. I have it here for you.'

Dear Master Martin,

It's terrible not seeing you after all the journey. I hope there doing your surplices all right and darning your grand stockings. Dr. McDowell was real pleased with the grand snap photo with Master Dempsey in his football suit and his arm round your neck and the big priest laughing behind your backs. He said Master Dempsey was a botty shelly some kind of foreigner angel but I told him he was Irish with yourself. I'd been hoping to hear you sing again but the Mistress says you'll be spending the Xmas Vakaytion with friends of your own. Josie is gone to live in Dublin, she's never been the same since big Mick Lannigan went and married that girl on her after all these years. So dear Master Martin I put down my pen hoping your well and the same as ever. Things are going nice and easy with me just as ever. God bless you and don't forget me and I mention you high up in my prayers every night.

Your kind and respectful

Mary Ellen

P.S. It will be real queer this Xmas, without Josie and myself having to remember to wake you for the waits.

II

The Pruned Sapling

I

THE quiet years went by; the world was set and secure in spite of Miss Clare in the schoolroom, and Jimmy Curran at Dunslane, both of them saying, 'History goes on making history.'

One accepted it dutifully; one believed it to be true because it was they who said so. But dynastic wars, religious wars, could never happen again to make people do the savage, frightening things of the past. History could now only make a quiet history of goodwill, tolerance, consideration for others, especially the weak and the poor. Never again would people be tortured, or civilians slaughtered in war; never again would a true gentleman defend or excuse callousness in face of injustice or meanness. Even Miss Clare said that. Even Jimmy said, 'The Liberal tradition cannot now be deflected.'

'Write down the date of Erasmus's birth. Oh, Martin, is this all right? Are Catholics permitted to learn of Erasmus?'

'Yes, Miss Clare.'

He still did work in the holidays with her and the two girls. Colonel Howard had stopped talking of the danger that the Balkan Wars would spread. One thought of them as a far-off matter among half-primitive peoples. Sometimes, the colonel would speak uneasily of 'German Militarism', of 'the Dreadnought Race'. But who would dare to challenge the might of the British Empire and of a France growing ever more confident and happy, although, alas, under an 'infidel' government? One ignored the infidel Government and, instead, repeated Miss Clare's 'Every man has two fatherlands, his own and France'. The English genius for tolerance; the French genius for civilization. The two greatest peoples the world had ever known.

'Greater than Greece? Than Rome?'

'Than Rome—certainly. Than Greece—not greater, just more

169

THY TEARS MIGHT CEASE

developed. France and England are the grandchildren of the
Hellenic spirit.'

And, of course, when Home Rule had been finally passed,
Ireland, with its 'King, Lords and Commons of Ireland', would
be an equal partner in that great world. How wonderful!

'It is unlikely—Sally, ankles crossed—decorum, decorum,
you're not a milkmaid—unlikely that men will ever again put
their opinions above their humanity. Martin, are you allowed to
learn about 1848? And the Risorgimento?'

'Yes, Miss Clare.' He was not too sure of it, but he himself could
do things that might be wrong for other Catholics!

Uncle Brendan was more and more 'almost a "half Home-
Ruler"'. Colonel Howard, still very Unionist, would say: 'Home
Rule, when it comes, must be accepted and loyally worked.
Loyalty to the King's laws—that above all.' Yes, how wonderful
the world; and France, Italy waiting out there to be seen.

Thus the years went by in a secure, fixed world that would
never change. Downstairs, the silver horses for ever waited to
prance across the little tables in the drawing-room; up here the
cracked blackboard gleamed.

'Miss Clare, you said that these holidays you would shorten
holiday lessons two mornings in the week. Will you make *this*
morning short?'

She nodded.

Peggy's turn: 'May we go on the river all day, please?'

She nodded.

Sally's turn: 'May we take the potato-boat, please, not the
small boat?'

She nodded.

Martin's turn: 'May the girls take off their stays, please?'

She nodded.

Everyone's turn: 'Will *you* come with us, please?'

Very often she would nod.

There were, of course, black moments; the mornings when
she said: 'Come out here. In order of age,' and picked up the
cane.

One nursed one's palms; three pairs of eyes refused to let the
tears even show; three tongues said later, 'So long as Hanrahan
doesn't know.'

And, as well as his beloved Keelard, which had almost effaced the memory of Glenkilly, there was Tory Hill. When Martin paid his first visit to Norman there he found a household of friendly young women who required only occasional services: occasional company at croquet or 'dining-room billiards', when none of the many varieties of young men had arrived; occasional escorting; occasional silence when they were reading in the evening and occasional bicycle-cleaning. Only Agnes, the eldest of Mr. Dempsey's 'five fillies', as he called them, stood for the Law. Mrs. Dempsey was in failing health and Agnes had given up her post in London to come home and 'manage'.

Even Mr. Dempsey himself bowed to Agnes and when he met her on the stairs might say heartily: 'Well, what we'd do without you, Agnes, I don't know. The house is grand now.'

He was a big man, a powerful swimmer, fond of hunting and very soft-hearted. He sought the company of the boys, and more than once when driving home in the cooling evening he would tell them that he did not much like being a magistrate. 'If I were starting again, I think I'd prefer something less controversial.'

He was very proud of Norman—as were his sisters, but less openly than he—and in the evenings he brought out his old Virgil and enjoyed having his mistakes corrected by the two boys, who suspected him of making some of the mistakes deliberately for the fun of seeing if Norman would notice them.

He had been ready to like Martin before seeing him because of Martin's devotion to Norman. 'I am glad about you and Norman. I was a bit worried about his never making friends here with other boys. But don't fill him up with too much of that God Save Ireland stuff—he seems to be getting a lot of that from you. And for God's sake, Martin, don't make him into a priest on me. The fillies will clear off with their husbands. Even after giving them their marriage shares, I'll have a little left for ourselves and he could have Tory Hill, and the bit of land. There are openings around here for a civil engineer, say, or a decent architect. Or a doctor. It'd be a good life for him here and he'd have all the time he'd like for reading and could pick the wife he wanted.'

He disliked Sessions days because of having to fine people and jail them. Sometimes he himself arranged to have the smaller fines paid. He was very proud of being a Catholic, of being 'a moderate Home Ruler', of having served under three monarchs. 'I served the old Queen, I served Edward VII, and I'm serving

King George. He doesn't altogether sound my sort but he's the King and that's that.'

He took the boys and the 'fillies' to all the local race-meetings and the whole household went up for Fairyhouse Races and met the Keelard people there who had arranged that Martin and Norman should return with them after the races.

On the racecourse they came across one of the biggest boys from Dunslane whose father, a trainer from the Curragh, tipped Norman for the last race a rank outsider who, colourfully in red and blue, came in a winner two lengths ahead of the horse which all the Tory Hill and Keelard elders had knowingly backed. And the great day ended greatly when a press photographer, who had for some time followed them about, took a picture of them standing by the rails. But Mrs. Vincent and Miss Clare were angry when they heard about this: 'What impertinence! Photographing people for a newspaper! And without even permission!

When, late that evening, they got back to Keelard, Martin went with Norman for a night bathe. In the cold evening they plunged naked into the dark pool below the boathouse, then leap-frogged back towards the house, and went up to the schoolroom that was as strange and exciting as a room before a party because of the table laid for a meal at that late hour.

So time went on, in a rhythm marked by term and holiday, the recurring festivals of the Church, the sowing of the crops and their harvesting, in a world where each one knew what to do, and where beliefs and aspirations, even those most opposed to one another, shared a common basis, in which what Jimmy Curran called 'the pillars of European Civilization' were embedded for ever, unshakable, unquestionable!

Many times there was talk of Martin spending some of his holidays in Glenkilly, but circumstances, and a growing reluctance in himself, which he did not examine, postponed his going. At last, during his second summer vacation, plans were completed for him to spend a fortnight in Tramore where his Aunt Eileen had gone, as she had done year after year, for the 'family holiday'.

Two days before he was to leave, Colonel Howard, who had been to Dublin for some days, returned with a worried, grave air. From scraps of overheard conversations Martin gathered that the colonel had been told by friends in his club, the headquarters

of Unionist opinion, that they were so determined to resist Home
Rule that they were going to found a Volunteer Army in Ulster
concentrating on those four counties where they had a majority;
that this would have the tacit support of the highest ranks of the
War Office, and that they would get in arms from everywhere,
even from England's potential enemy, Germany.

'Brendan—you see what it means? If the King signs Home
Rule, they will be traitors to the Crown. Treason, Brendan!
They will have to—and they say they'll do it—shoot down the
King's soldiers. But listen, there's even worse. They say they are
assured that large numbers of army officers will refuse to obey if
an order is given to disarm the volunteers. They will refuse even
to fire on them in order to guard army stores of rifles! Army
officers! Their oath to the King!'

To Colonel Howard the thought that there could be a betrayal
of that simple loyalty which, for him, cemented together all
oppositions, all relationships, was a shock which struck deeply
through him.

At Tramore Martin found that Aunt Eileen had only Rosaleen
and Bridget with her: Mr. Reilly joined them from Saturday to
Monday. James Edward came only twice, and Patrick was
spending his holidays with a school-friend. Martin perceived
that at week-ends his Aunt Eileen tried to keep him and his uncle
as far apart as possible and he was glad to help her in this by
staying out of the house all day, swimming and boating alone
with a book. But every evening he returned and took his Aunt
Eileen for her favourite walk high above the bay.

'Even the Nigger Minstrels sound nice up here, Martin.'

'Yes, Aunt Eileen.'

They walked far beyond the last seat where two lovers whispered cheek to cheek. They could no longer hear the elusive
sounds of the Minstrels, only the Atlantic. On a sloping bank he
spread his raincoat to keep the grass from her grey tailor-made.
They spoke of Glenkilly, of Tommy Fagan and his prophecies,
and of the Crucifixion nuns. 'They always say they never had
anyone to serve Mass for them the way you did.' When Martin
inquired for Josie, she looked grave and said sadly: 'Ah, Josie. No
word about her all this time.'

'And Father Riordan?'

Father Riordan had been moved from Glenkilly to another

parish. Of Mr. Burns she knew nothing and nothing of Gertrude
Jamieson since she had left school a year ago. The treacherous
power of time dismayed him. He struggled resentfully against the
feeling of change. 'People ought to be able to go on for years
being the same without seeing each other.'

They watched the streaky clouds across the moon, listened to
the water. Looking sideways at her dignified head, he thought
with relief that she had not changed at all. 'Do you ever think of
the evenings when I used to comb your hair when you had a
headache?'

'Often. In lots of ways you remind me of . . .' He guessed she
was about to say 'Mat Reilly', but she changed her mind. Instead
she said, 'I mean you were a gentle-hearted boy in lots of ways.'

'I'll comb it when we go in tonight—if you like,' he said
timidly.

'Oh, no. Of course not.'

They walked in silence until she said, 'Have you a holy-water
font over your bed in your friend's house?'

'Yes, Aunt Eileen.'

'Martin, I have to ask you something.' She coughed, embarrassed. 'I don't want to, I told your Uncle John it was not right
but he said he'd ask you himself tomorrow if I didn't, so it's
better for me to do it. It's of no importance at all, but he wants to
know if two girls in that house sleep in a room with a door open
or half open into yours. Something you said a long time ago in
a letter to Mary Ellen made him think it; he heard her reading
me out bits of your letter.'

He hesitated; he could picture her working her lips over her
needle or account books while she secretly planned how to keep
the truth from Uncle John. He knew that she knew it was true;
so when she said, 'Well, Martin, what am I to tell him?' he said,
'Tell him no, Aunt Eileen.'

'Well, one more thing,' she said with relief. 'He wants to know
if you went once to some service, Evensong or something, with
your friends to their church.'

Again he conspired with her in a lie—'Tell him no, Aunt
Eileen'—and was depressed by this denial of the evening when
first he had seen not merely 'a Protestant service' but seen Aunt
Kathleen praying, her chin and neck outlined before the brass
standard of the pew lamp; beyond her, Miss Clare's clear

profile, beside him Sally and Peggy; through the cool dimness
that was so different from the pomp and surge of Benediction,
he had heard 'And bless thine inheritance' in the voices that
were part of his Keelard world as the others had been part of
Glenkilly.

Behind Mr. Thorpe, the only things which had continued to
gleam had been the two candlesticks on the altar cloth. 'Give
peace in our time, O Lord.' And in the pew with Martin the well-
known voices had replied, 'Because there is none other that fighteth for us, but only thou, O God.' He had walked back to Keelard
along the field path in the gloom, thinking that Evensong was 'as
nice as Benediction in its own way' and telling himself that he had
not done wrong in going because Evensong was not the service
which replaced Mass; besides, his mother had been a Protestant
and so he himself might with impunity do things quite wrong for
other boys!

The day of departure arrived, Aunt Eileen came to the station
to see him off on his way to Tory Hill whence he would carry
Norman to Keelard. He knew that she would like to give him the
salute of a loved authority. She knew very well that he had always
received that authoritative salute from Aunt Mary, and that he
was in the habit of tilting his face for it now to 'that Protestant',
the woman 'in that house'. He could see all this, wanted to show
her that she, too, was a loved authority. But, as always, she was
too proud to make an asking movement, too timid with him to
make a commanding one, so that their hands parted and they
said their shy goodbyes without any embrace. Instead she
looked after him a little wistfully, a little remorsefully, as she had
often looked at him in Glenkilly when, glancing up from the
account books, she had seen him cautiously bringing his diary to
the window-seat low down near the floor.

Back at Keelard, the last days of the holidays seemed all the
more precious because Dunslane drew near. Miss Clare continued
to rule the schoolroom with all the authority of a martinet. But
Martin liked her. She was comfortably reassuring. She suggested
all the stability and security of accepted principles. And even she
could be indulgent at times. She was willing for example to
condone, or at least to overlook, his and Sally's attachment to the
bargee Dan Murphy. One evening they lingered on board long

after they should have started for home, in order to finish a game of cards with him.

It was less hot in the little barge cabin now late in the evening, and looking up past the smoky lantern Martin saw clouds going rather quickly before the stars. His view saw the hatch frame oblong, not square, and away beyond the frame Cassiopeia's chair rode steadily.

Dan Murphy, stroking his moustache and looking anxiously from Sally to his assistant, Jim Geoghegan, paused gloweringly over a card, while with a pencil he secretively added the number of letters in the month, July, to the figures of the year, 1914. If the result were an odd number, he would play his strongest card now. 'He has the Ace of Hearts,' thought Martin gloomily. But Sally screwed her eyes at him and beneath the table her bare foot pressed warmly on his toes. Could she have the Five of Trumps?

Suddenly Jim Geoghegan leaned back and, drinking down his stout in one draught, put the mug down on the table with an air of a man who brings things to a conclusion.

'How much is in the kitty?' he asked significantly.

Dan Murphy, his broad nose touching Sally's dark red hair, glanced at him with tolerant suspicion. 'Fippence. And then there's . . .' He paused and looked deprecatingly at the little pile of coppers which made 'the kitty'.

'Yes,' said Sally, 'Martin and I owe it thruppence. We'll pay up on Saturday when we get our pocket-money. Go on, Dan, play the Ace of Hearts; we all know you must have it.'

Excitement gripped them all. Dan looked at the three tense faces, raised a card. 'All right then, Miss Sally, ye high divil! Ye'll never take anything easy, yerself and himself there. Seventeen and as hard after me poor ould Ace of Hearts as if you were twelve again. Well, there it is for ye and if you have the Five, you can put it on it.'

'I haven't the Five,' said Sally, drawing voice and body up with rising emphasis. 'But I have . . .' She rose fully and stuck a bare knee over the table edge. 'I have . . . I have . . . Bang! The Knave, Dan, the Knave!' and the Knave of Trumps smashed down on Dan's Ace.

'Huroops,' shouted Martin and then in dismay saw Jim Geoghegan's arm go triumphantly upward.

'And I'll kill yer Jack, Miss Sally,' roared Jim as he swung down the conquering Five. 'And there's the King after the Five,' he shouted, crushing his great young shoulders against the ceiling, 'and if yez can beat that, yez are geniuses altogether,' and he scooped the kitty to him.

Just then the river gave a little slap against the barge. Sally and Martin heard their boat knocking against the hull like a bored pony fuming to start homewards. While they gloomily watched the coppers between Jim's brown fingers, there came a creaking of the bank plank and steps on the deck. Two long legs came down the ladder. Quickly, warningly, Dan called, 'Hello—if that's Jack Morgan . . . !' and Jim shouted uneasily, 'We've got a couple of young visitors, Jack!'

The man on the ladder stooped instantly and crooked down his head to peer into the smoky cabin. 'Oh, well . . .' he began, then peering along the side of the bunk: 'Oh, it's them two, her with him again, is it!' He laughed, an insinuating laugh. 'Well, I don't know how yer going to get home tonight. Yez'll have a hell of a wind up the river and bloody lashings of rain.'

'We'll be all right,' said Martin curtly.

'Oh,' said the dark man sneeringly, 'isn't that grand! "We'll be all right", sharp and mighty. The real gentleman, to be sure!'

'Would yez like a cup of tea before ye go?' said Dan quickly. Sally and Martin looked at the empty stove.

'No, thanks, Dan.'

'Ah well,' said Jim with great kindliness and heartiness, 'ye'll have yer revenge next week.'

'Yes, and we'll pay the thruppence we owe the kitty on Saturday.'

'Ah, sure that's all right,' and Jim waved his arm magnanimously in the way Tommy Fagan in Glenkilly used to wave away obligations for free reading and a sheet of 'Best Irish Vellum'.

The long man went up the ladder and stood blackly against the sky at the hatch. Turning as Sally reached the deck, he gripped her arm to pull her up. 'I'm all right, thank you,' she said coldly and moved her arm, but the man held on to it. Martin, on the ladder, looking vertically upwards, saw the man's chin chewing up and down beyond the bell of Sally's skirts.

'Yer getting a gorgeous fine girl, Miss Sally. Pushing close to seventeen now, ain't ye?' said the man. She made no reply. 'You know who I am, don't ye?' he snorted.

'No,' said Sally. Her grown-up aloofness astonished Martin by its likeness to Aunt Kathleen's air when she had answered 'No' to Tim Corbin in Uncle Brendan's study.

Indifferently, she added, 'I daresay we may have seen you up and down the river.'

The man laughed, snorting deliberately. 'Be God, I bet you have! The two of ye cavorting about half stripped in shifts and underthings—oh, I've seen ye! Oh, only looking for flowers you do be, oh aye, only flowers! How's that haughty young English lady? Yer teacher, I mean. I've had a dekko at her. She looks as cross as they say she is. Oh, everyone knows how she wears out the rods on the three of ye down there.'

Sally looked down at Martin, so he pushed his shoulders up before her, forcing the man to release her arm. 'Come on, Sally.' Dan and Jim clambered up and all stood on the warm deck in silence. The breeze strengthened, slapping the ripples against the barge. Chill and sweet it came, driving the summer night before it, and blew resolutely from the marshy right bank to the verdure and slopes of the left bank. 'Good night, Danny, and thanks for the game. Good night, Jim.'

'The horses, Martin,' whispered Sally.

They slid down into their boat, Martin scraping his bare legs along the tarry barge side. Getting the sugar from his pocket, he followed Sally on to the bank. They crossed the back stream and went down through the thick, damp grass of the field. In the distance they could hear the horses working their jaws in the grass and could see their dim shapes. Holding hands, they moved on through the grass towards the shapes and the regular sounds. From the framed glow of the cabin hatch behind them there came an occasional murmur carried by the sweet wind that was blowing from far away across cottages and ruined abbeys, blowing chill across the cows and the horses and on over all the haycocks and cornfields until it would arrive at the sea and blow away to all the world. As they neared the horses, he let Sally go forward alone and the rich grass clasped his feet as he stood watching her circle away to approach the horses from in front. She held out her arm, shining in the scudding light.

'Whoa now. Steady now, steady,' she clucked and soothed and slid an arm along the neck of one horse. She could always manage horses without fuss, even strange horses from other parts of the

country. He went forward and now the other horse let him come
and took the sugar from his outstretched hand. Feeling the rough
necks, listening to the warm animal-breaths, they stayed silent
while the horses munched the sugar. Martin put his cheek against
the tough mane and the old work-tired head turned to nuzzle in
his shirt, the soft muzzle nosing into him and pushing him. How
near and intimate was Sally now, silent, and separated from him
by the width of two breathing horses.

They said good night to the horses who made a half-hearted
attempt to follow them. Sally leaned against him and he knew
that she was tired. He put his arm around her to help her but the
thick grass made it difficult to walk in that way so he withdrew
his arm and crooked it that she might hang on to it. With her
hands pulling on his arm, they came back to the barge and there
on the narrow band of deck around the hold were Dan and Jim,
watching them.

Dan leaned to them and whispered so that Jim could not hear,
'Have yez nare a penny left at all after the cards?'

They shrugged resignedly.

'Well, lookit,' whispered Dan. 'There's threepence. Sure ye can
pay it back when ye've a good lot. When ye've made a bit on a
horse at the Curragh or something.'

'Oh, no,' whispered both, 'we lost it. And we still owe Jim
thruppence to the kitty.'

Dan leaned coaxingly to them, the stiff grease shining on his
jersey. 'Arrah, sure, no matter. Take it.'

'Well, make it tuppence and we'll take a loan of it. We wouldn't
take thruppence because that would be exactly what we lost.'

'All right, then,' said Dan, giving them the two coppers.
'Ye're the same pair always.'

From the darkness below the barge came the voice of the long
man and the sound of women's laughter. They could just see the
shape of a small boat down there and the long man coming up
towards them on the bank.

'Are they gone yet, Jim?' he called softly. Then he heard the
thump and the rushes swishing as Martin pushed off. 'Oh-ho!' he
said loudly. 'Good night, Miss Sally.' He laughed, his blue officey
suit glistening before the field which held the horses. His voice
came loudly through the whisks of rain and the scudding moonlight. 'You'll be putting yer hair up in a couple of years, Miss

Sally. Then there'll be no more tricks on the river for ye with yer
so-called cousin. The pair of ye! Quarter past nine now and God
knows what time ye'll get home tonight.'

'Dry up, Jack!' came Jim's voice and then Dan's speaking
authoritatively, angrily. His words, scattered by the noise of wind
and oars, came in fragments. 'If you want me to let you aboard
the ould boat . . . a pair of children.'

'Aw, children, me eye!' answered Jack viciously.

'Good night, Dan. Good night, Jim.'

'Good night, good night. Safe home.'

Then clear along the flapping ripples came the dark man's
laughter. 'Children, I don't think! Sweet seventeen and never
been kissed. You come in to the flour-mills office and ask for me,
Miss Sally. Mr. Jack F. Morgan is the name. I'll help ye look for
flowers, ye bet.' Fainter came laugh and words. 'Tell yer teacher I
was asking for her. The County Clare herself. I've seen her marching
the three of yez about on the road. I bet ye'll both catch it hot from
her tonight for the hour ye'll get home at. The pair of ye!'

Looking up from his oars, Martin saw a belt of gold-white light
between dark sky and darker earth, and black against the belt lay
the lump of the barge. Two women's figures arose from among the
reeds and moved towards the barge.

The boat, driving into the wind, moved steadily along the black
and silver water. The village, with its scattered lights, drew
slowly alongside, swivelled sluggishly into the distance, and
beneath the bridge the current drove the boat onward in a silent
and powerful curve. Sally, at the rudder, nursed the boat into
the narrow channel while Martin crushed his strength into his
back and legs, fighting the side-drag to the weir, a broader weir
than Dunslane's. The drag sucked away from them and the
cavern of the lock enclosed them, silent and black. Together they
closed the upper gates, straining their backsides against the creaking wood. The lighted window of the lock cottage was opened
and through the windy spatters of rain Mrs. Patterson's voice
came thin and high. 'Is that Miss Sally and Master Martin passing
back? Johnny's down beyond cutting rushes. Will ye tell him to
come in before the rain gets bad. And the goat's out in Captain
O'Connor's field.' She held the baby heavily against her shoulder
in the frame of the window.

'All right. But stay in out of the rain, Mrs. Patterson.'

Gripping his boat-hook to the slimy wall and sinking swiftly into blackness, he watched Sally's figure as she bent up there to the cogs of the downriver sluices. The wind blew more loudly up above and the clouds went madly before it, low and furious, but unable to swamp the stars. Splaying rain struck through the wind and Sally swayed on the footboard, her tawny mane glistening and blown, while around Martin the dark water surged deeply, quietened, grew still and held some light from the wild sky that silvered Sally above. The lower gates creaked, the black mass moved, and beyond it lay the broad river and the dim trees sloping up to the stars.

Waiting below the lock for Sally, he took up the rudder and the stern seat, and placed the long cushion on the floorboards. He pushed their shoes and stockings under the end of the cushion, and over that he rolled his jacket into a pillow. When Sally came tiredly lilting down the bank to him she said nothing, but lay down on the cushion and put her head on the jacket. He covered her bare legs with her own jacket and said: 'You snooze now. I'll manage all right.'

'But are you sure?' She smiled up at him, her lips nearly black in a white face. 'Such a long way too to row alone,' and the tones were like Aunt Kathleen's and almost grown-up. Startled, he nodded down at her and smiled.

'Keep well clear of the old sunk tree,' she said and snuggled down into the cushion.

He pushed off and heard behind him a distant waft of song. Pulling out to midstream, he let the boat go with the current. The storm was breaking up into fragments and the vanishing after-glow was being blown into clear night-time. The song came nearer, and with it the swishing of a heavy boat or barge in the reeds. Sally lay with closed eyes, unheeding, apart, her body framed in the shelter of the boat's upcurving ribs. The big boat drew ever nearer and Martin, looking downstream, could see the glimmer of men's white boaters and women's blouses. It was a late picnic party homing.

The last sounds of the big boat upriver died into silence; the noises of the river, its animals and reeds, replaced the sound of song and people. He rowed hard until he saw the lantern among the rushes and heard the cutting of the scythe. Nosing the prow in among the rushes, he called softly: 'Johnny! Johnny!'

Johnny's lantern came sliding towards him, Johnny's flat boat slithering through the rushes.

'Mrs. Patterson said would you come in before the rain got bad, but the rain's all gone now.'

'Aye, I knew it wouldn't be much, thanks be to God. But they'll have had a heavy pelt of it down at Keelard.'

They spoke softly and easily, keeping their boats taut against one another.

'Lookit, what'll they do to yez at all when yez get home, it'll be that late. Miss Clare!'

His lantern's reflection wobbled in the still water beneath the rushes as he pushed Martin's boat out.

'Off with ye, children, in the name of God.'

'Good night, Johnny.' The boat slushed out into the current.

Far away the lantern bobbed now and Johnny's voice came from the distance: 'Safe home, children.'

'Safe home, Johnny,' they called and heard their voices go waste in the air.

Sally snuggled tightly on the cushion and shivered a little as she drew her jacket closer around her legs. Martin took off his shirt and wrapped it around her chest and shoulders, then took off his shorts and tucked them across her middle, carefully closing every little crevice where air might get in at her. That pleased him, to shut her in completely from the air. Tightening up the under-pants which Miss Clare cut out so neatly from the great roll of Lancashire cambric that came every year to her from one of her aunts and that made shirts, shifts and things galore at no cost, he stretched himself to the night and felt its velvet touch on his body and limbs. Moving stealthily, he lit the lantern and fastened it to the prow. Stealthily he rowed with strength, rejoicing in the power of his feet pressing the wood and aware that he was rowing with good style and finish.

The moon rode high, quite sure of itself now, and the wind was only a sigh among the trees. He knew that Sally was asleep now, and the breathing of her half-parted lips pulled at his heart. She must never change, no one must ever change; he would hold them always the same and they would always be together in a free and wonderful Ireland under Home Rule.

Even if one could not be the Hofer of Ireland, one could at

least be a True Man. He and Norman. They could put the Red
Hand of Ulster upon the Green Flag.

> But True Men like you Men
> Are plenty here today.

Above all things he wanted now to be good and noble. He
murmured the words about True Men and they passed over
Sally's sleeping form into the width of the river.

The sweat poured from him and the water from the day's
bathing, belching in his throat, filled his mouth with the muggy
river tang. He was tired now and had to make an effort to keep
his knees steady, to shoot down with the wrists, to drive with the
legs. Clug-thump, clug-thump went the row-locks. The clug-
thump was a lullaby, the moonlight flashed on his dripping
blades; the lullaby was like Grandmother singing above his head
and he nodded with sleep. Then, startled awake, he found that
he had caught a deep crab and he stared anxiously at Sally as he
let the oar slide until the boat righted itself. But Sally slept on.

At length the Long Island pushed its wooded point beside him,
the salley-willows swept by and the shallow backwater raced him
onwards. Shipping his oars, he leaned over Sally, feeling her
breath on his face, and shook her. She wakened instantly, and
sitting up, looked at the massed oaks and beeches and chestnuts.

'The Long Island already?' she said and clambered forward.
Standing up, each using an oar as a paddle, they held the boat
straight down the rushing flow; they ducked beneath tree
branches and swayed to the undisciplined current that swirled
to throw them aside as a pony might do. The air rushed past
them, and far downstream a light of home appeared, only to be
lost again as they swept round a bend. Then, rupple, rupple,
rupple—the low rattling of the 'rapids' came at them. Sally,
jumping back to crouch at his feet, looked up at him over her
shoulder, the tree shadows flickering across her moonlit face.
'The middle rocks?' she called. 'Looked deeper there this
morning.'

Plying the oar on one side and the other, he kept to the channel
as the water rushed bubbling under them and the channel broke
into bewildering crevices of branches; they were in and up.
'Back, Sally, back.' She pressed back on him as he too pressed

back, lifting the prow straight into a narrow crevice between
the rocks. It was in; it shot like a wild thing. 'Forward,' they
shouted together and ran to the prow. The stern lifted but for
a moment it stayed poised and shaken and the sides grated.
Martin made one powerful lunge against the rocks; the stern
went up; it went round and they were away, gliding deliciously
into the wide calm stretches beyond.

Sally began to gather up their things while Martin guided the
easy movement of the boat. On the slope to the left the house
showed against the sky. The party was lasting late—there were
lights in the drawing-room, all its lamps shining across that end
of 'Kathleen's Garden', lights in the kitchen and scullery and
scattered lights upstairs. It looked lovely, the house.

'It must be all hours now,' said Martin.

'Yes. I don't think they will have been worried about us, do you?'

'No.'

'Isn't it queer, Martin, that one often knows like that the way
things will go without having any reason for knowing, even
having reasons to think the opposite?'

'It's instinct. When you know people . . .'

They dressed, except for their shoes and stockings, and went up
towards the lighted house. In 'Kathleen's Garden' the flowers
looked still and white, as they went round to the side which long
ago Martin had hoped might be a ghost's wing.

As they crossed to the front hall, the drawing-room door
opened a little crack of light, and Miss Clare appeared there.
Closing the door, she raised a finger in reproof and, coming to
them, made a severe gesture signing them to precede her into the
cloakroom. There the moonlight shone white and still among the
mackintoshes and cricket bats. 'How late you are!' She looked
lovely in the light and shadow and half of each shoulder shone
bare—this must be quite a big party.

'Martin rowed all the way home alone so that I could sleep.'

'You're terribly late. I ought to punish you,' she said, handing
a towel to Sally. She tidied Martin's shirt at the waist. 'Your
mother says you're to come in and say good night to the visitors.'

'What! Into the drawing-room! Like this!'

She smiled and with the little primness of the chin said: 'Yes,
for once. No, don't put on your shoes and stockings, it's not worth
while.'

Mrs. Vincent was singing and they waited outside the door. She was singing, 'Fain Would I Change That Note', and silent in the cool hall they listened to the familiar melody:

> 'Oh Love! they wrong thee much
> That say thy sweet is bitter
> When thy rich fruit is such
> As nothing can be sweeter. . . .'

The notes and words pierced him; he could picture her in there at the piano.

> 'Fair house of joy and bliss,
> Where truest pleasure is,
> I know thee what thou art,
> I serve thee with my heart
> And fall before thee!'

And in a blurred moment of emotion he was drawn into the room and there she was, head bent to the last sounds, her fingers sloped to the black and white keys. Beyond, in different places, were others and, by the mantelpiece, Uncle Brendan and Colonel Howard looking across at her.

She whirled about on her stool as they went to her, while near a window someone laughed and the man who had been turning her music gaped at them. They ducked, Martin a head, Sally a bob, and she leaned forward, her hands in the lap of the bluish dress with the creamy top. On the bare wide half-moon above the creamy top the black medallion hung, secretly holding Uncle Brendan on one side, the girls on the other. 'So dreadfully late,' she whispered and bit her lower lip and looked half reprovingly, half appealingly at them. They looked solemnly back at her.

'All right. Go and speak to anyone you know, then go to bed,' and she touched their arms and backs. 'You seem quite dry.'

Barefooted on the worn crunchiness of the carpet, they went among the people they knew. They were talking to Miss Thorpe, the curate's sister, when old Mrs. Carter's voice boomed across the room, calling them. They sped to her. 'What! You here, ma'am?'

'Of course. You don't think they'd dare leave me out of a big spread.'

'But you ought to be in bed,' said Sally, and added with great honesty, 'My God, you're marvellous, ma'am'—one of Mrs. Carter's many charms was that she expected one to use strong expletives often.

'Stop talking as if I were impossibly old! Bed indeed! I'm old, but not so old as all that.' She was eighty-three, had been born in the reign of George IV, and her father, as a child, had seen Robespierre in Paris, and, five years later in Ireland, had seen the '98 rebels assemble on his father's lawn.

'What a grand dinner your mother has given us! All in style, proper style! And such claret! There was trifle too. I think Aggie's been hiding some up in the schoolroom for you.'

'Miss Clare would soon spot it.'

'I'm afraid of your Miss Clare.'

'Why should you be afraid of *me*?' Miss Clare was smiling down at the group. 'Young as you are, you're a little past the age for being a pupil of mine.'

'Huh! No, I am not a schoolgirl; but all the same I'm afraid of you because I've always been afraid of freaks. An Englishwoman who is both handsome and a brain is a notorious freak. All Englishwomen should be either studious and plain, or beautiful and stupid—and hard as nails underneath. But you are a freak of nature a . . . what's the damned Latin for it, Philip?' she shouted.

'A—a—a *Lusus Naturae*,' stammered Colonel Howard.

'That's it! Thank you, Philip, a *Lusus Naturae*—but a damned agreeable one, my dear,' giving Miss Clare a wave of her fan.

Mrs. Carter took Sally and Martin across and introduced them to a tall man standing by the fireplace. 'Mr. McKenzie is a soldier,' she said.

'Have you been to India? Colonel Howard's writing a book about Irishmen in India.'

'Yes, so I heard.' The tall man began to smile; he seemed less shy now than he had at first. 'Unfortunately, even if I had been to India, I couldn't appear in the book. I'm not Irish. I'm English,' and he began to chat quite briskly to Sally and Martin, asking about salmon on the river and which fishing month gave the best results. Now that he had stopped looking wise and serious he was, Martin saw, very young, in spite of his moustache.

Sally was being cross-examined by a woman in a flounced dress who wanted to know why she and Peggy had loathed school so much.

'Ah,' said the fashionable voice knowingly. 'The rebel Irish. I suppose you objected to the discipline'; and in a large way she added conclusively, 'Always revolting against the despotism of fact!'

Martin whispered urgently through the side of his mouth, 'Matthew Arnold,' and Sally said innocently:

'We don't agree with Matthew Arnold in that, ma'am.' The lady gaped, and Sally went on: 'Besides, the school wasn't so very strict. At least, not when compared with home. But I'm never bored at home and I was always bored at that school.'

Martin turned to say good night to Mr. McKenzie and found himself saying without premeditation, 'May I ask you a question, sir?'

'Yes, of course. Delighted. What is it?'

'If Carson does set the Orange Volunteers fighting against Home Rule, will the Army fight him and see that he is tried as a rebel? Especially for bringing in German guns.'

There was a dreadful silence. Even before the question had left his tongue, Martin was shocked by the dreadful thing he was doing to this nice, shy visitor. From behind him, he heard Uncle Brendan's voice say sternly, 'Leave the room at once, sir!' Uncle Brendan who never interfered!

He could feel Aunt Kathleen's eyes on the side of his face and knew how angry and disgusted they would look. From the awful silence around him Mr. Vincent's voice came again: 'Did you hear, sir! Leave the room at once!'

But young Mr. McKenzie, who had turned very white, intervened. 'No, please.' He began to speak very slowly, almost as if he were learning the words as he said them. 'I took an oath to serve the King,' he said, 'and if I am ordered in the King's name to attack the Northern Loyalists, I shall do so'; then, with a deep breath, 'Whatever friends may say.'

Colonel Howard's voice said, after a sigh, 'Good man, McKenzie.'

But Mr. McKenzie, as if unaware that anyone had spoken, added, 'But I hope to God I never have to!'

Soon afterwards Martin and the girls said good night. When he

came to Mr. Vincent the latter looked at him reproachfully.
Miss Clare, who was standing nearby, said in a low voice: 'He's
tired out and it just popped out. Wasn't that it, Martin?'

'Yes, yes. You know I wouldn't mean to be rude, Uncle
Brendan.'

'All right, Martin,' he said patiently.

When they came to Mr. McKenzie he pulled at his little black
moustache. 'Good night . . . er . . . er . . . oh, Sally, I suppose,' and
he laughed contentedly. He beckoned Martin to him. 'Look here,
I'm awfully grateful to you for asking me that question.'

'Oh, no! I've been waiting for a chance to apologize.'

'Good Lord, you mustn't do that. Besides, I really am *glad*
about it. I was funking that very question and worrying most
terribly about it. Now it doesn't worry me any longer.'

Understanding this, Martin said, 'Word of honour?'

'Absolutely! I assure you. Word of honour.'

'I think you're splendid.'

'Good Lord, you mustn't say that.'

'Oh, yes, you are,' said Sally seriously.

Mrs. Vincent watched them as they went up the stairs. In the
moonlit schoolroom, far from all sound, they leaned against the
table and drank their milk, ignoring the bread. On the cracked
blackboard the letters '. . . ama' glimmered down into a dark
corner. That was where Miss Clare had written 'Vasco da Gama'
with a flourish that morning. All the hot day the three letters had
lain there deserted, all through the cooling evening, and now
would lie dusty and glimmering through the night. Vasco da
Gama. The '. . . ama' was inspiring because it was filled in by a
memory of Miss Clare in the sunlight flourishing it down into a
corner. 'And now—Sally, straight up—he reached Madagascar,
called the Island of the Moon.' Only five hundred years ago.

Sally twisted her eyes at him across the side of her glass of milk;
he twisted his eyes at her. Thus, watching one another and watching the dusky flow of milk in their glasses, they drank.

They linked arms, wearily supporting one another, as they
moved dreamily along the passage behind Peggy, through the
brightness below the Gothic window and into the cold moon-
radiance of Martin's little room. Their linked arms dropped
easily apart, and Sally, pulling at the neck of her frock, moved on
into the greyness around the communicating door and emerged

far off, sharp, familiar, in the lesser radiance of the girls' room. A moment she stood, her petticoat a startling whiteness in the whiteness about her, until she stooped to pick up her frock.

Standing at his window, he saw far below him the river like a silver blade among the trees. On his right the smell of the flowers in 'Kathleen's Garden' came into the room; behind him he could hear the splashing in the girls' room.

Kneeling by his bed, he prayed with great assurance. After his usual prayers, he prayed that all in Keelard might never have the opportunity to learn the True Faith, so that they could continue to be Protestants in honesty, and thus go to heaven when they died; and he crushed down his doubts about the sinfulness of this prayer. Then he prayed for Ireland, in a confident serenity which accepted that not in this present time nor in any future time of the world, but only in God's own time, would there be an explanation of the purpose which had denied his prayer for Aunt Mary in that distant March. And having prayed thus confidently for Ireland, he said a prayer for Mr. McKenzie.

Back in bed, he looked in at Peggy's shadowed bed and the edge he could just see of Sally's. The scent of Aunt Kathleen's flowers came faintly to him, the breeze sighed faintly—he opened his eyes! The whispering and rustling in the girls' room came towards him and he lifted his arms to Miss Clare's shape, to Aunt Kathleen's shape, and faint scent; but the two rustling shapes pushed his hands back under the clothes. He was slipping down again, and as the shapes receded upwards from him he made a great effort and got the words out and up to them:

'I know thee what thou art
I serve thee with my heart
And fall . . .
and fall . . .
and fall . . .
And fall before thee!'

2

A few weeks later half Europe was at war. No one at Keelard had given much thought to it when the newspapers had headlined the murder of an Austrian archduke—whatever an Austrian archduke might be—at some unpronounceable place in the Balkans. Even Miss Clare had only seen in it an opportunity to point out that there were still a few corners of the world left which were not wholly civilized. She did not dream that the mask was going to drop from the face of the whole continent. And when it did drop, though a statesman could say, in a moment of intimacy, that the lights were going out all over Europe, the general mood in all countries was one of elation rather than despondency. That mood touched Ireland as well as everywhere else. It too resounded with cries of 'gallant little Belgium'. It too raised its hands in horror at the crime committed against Catholic Louvain. The flags of the Allies appeared on traps and asses' carts. Mr. Redmond had offered the services of the Irish Volunteers to the Government to protect the shores of Ireland; the British and the Irish flags hung, crossed in amity, in Irish streets. It was being said that Ulster would drop her opposition to Home Rule when the war was over, after this display of Southern loyalty in England's moment of peril. People spoke of a 'Union of hearts'. In some places Unionist and Nationalist volunteers were said to have publicly shaken hands.

From chimney-pot to chimney-pot the banners spanned the streets of Ballow. Gold-washed in the light of a September evening, the windows shook to the drums of war.

Three hundred of the Ballow Companies of the Home Rule Volunteers, obeying the call of Mr. Redmond himself, were going to the war for Justice, and now they marched away at the head of the local British garrison, their Green Flag bearing Eire's graceful body on her harp. For Justice and Liberty!

In the Leinster Arms Hotel, Sally, Peggy, Norman and Martin cheered from the fourth window of the Ladies' Tea Room. Down at the door, Miss Carmel Brannigan, still unmarried, still refined as when she had pulled the corks of bottles of stout on the day of Mr. Redmond's meeting, waved a little penny flag.

Martin turned to Sally but hesitated. In these recent weeks she had occasionally astonished him by a broody crossness; once or twice her voice had held the half-adult quality which had startled him on Dan Murphy's barge and sometimes now she would want to sit over the schoolroom fire, chin cupped in her hand, silent and alone.

'Sally! Mr. McKenzie says the Volunteers are so well trained that they need hardly any more.'

'All right, Martin,' she answered shortly. 'But you know there are just a few of the Army in this war too. They're not *all* Home Rule Volunteers. And it isn't *Mr.* McKenzie any longer. You might try to remember that he's a captain now.'

Behind the Volunteers, the troops marched at ease, their singing lines fringed by the figures of swaying girls. An officer on his horse bowed to the waving hats, saluted the window where Mrs. Vincent and Miss Clare waved handkerchiefs. The drum sounds double-thudded back from the grey-brown houses.

Four voices called loudly: 'Captain McKenzie! Goodbye again. Now don't forget you promised to write from the war!' He looked up, watched shrewdly by the fat Cockney sergeant who during the month just past had so often come whizzing up the avenue on a motor-bicycle with a note for Miss Clare. Captain McKenzie turned his glance from Miss Clare, waved to the four leaning faces, then looked again at the next window and formally saluted, his smile a little stiff, his eyes on Miss Clare. Once he looked back, then he was hidden by the moving banners and nothing left of him except remembrance and the refluence of his, 'I took an oath to serve the King and if . . .'

Again, the little tables of the Ladies' Tea Room were drawn up to the plush sofas and stiff ottomans; as on the day of the Redmond meeting, again, the hall and passages below were thronged by noisy men.

'Think of it, Norman! Marching off to France! Flanders and all. It's just like the Irish troops marching off to France after Limerick. Colonel Reilly, my great-great-great——'

'Martin, do dry up,' said Peggy patiently and with a kick under the table called his attention to Sally's exasperation. He wanted to stop, but by now he was caught in a nervous roundabout which hurdy-gurdied him along against his wish. Besides, people at another table were admiring his vivacity and he exaggerated it for them.

'Oh, stop it, Martin!' It was Sally. 'You are for ever showing off now. Showing off for any Tom, Dick and Harry in an hotel! We never have a minute for quietness.'

His excitement went stale and distasteful inside him and he slipped away to the passage where he sat with his face hidden behind a newspaper while people came and went. Why could he not be like Norman, always gentle and nice to everyone? And Norman never showed off.

He went back and looked through the glass panels of the door. Sally was glancing to and from the door, and when his face appeared there she came unobtrusively out to him. He drew her aside. 'I'm a pig, Sally.'

'No, you're not. I was beastly.'

'No, you weren't. I was.'

'No, I was.'

They smiled half-heartedly.

'Martin, since the war we never seem to be quiet together. And besides, I'm sure Mr.—no Captain—McKenzie wanted to propose to Miss Clare. I feel sure she'll marry Mr. Turner. And she'll do it only because he's waited so long and is going to the war now, and I think she shouldn't. It makes me . . . Well, last year I thought I'd never be grown-up and now I don't think I even want to begin to. I'm sorry I was snappy and horrid. But the world is queer, isn't it?'

He nodded. 'Gertrude in Glenkilly said something like that.' He stared uncertainly at her. Could she be right about Mr. Turner, the long solemn man who had twice visited Keelard, who had wanted to marry Miss Clare before ever she had come to Ireland, who thought she was 'wasting her time and training buried in Ireland'?

'So you see?' said Sally. And he said he did. She took his arm with quiet, graceful dignity and they went to buy sweets to bring back to Aggie and Betty.

In the hall a big man in the uniform of a Volunteer officer was saying: 'Yes, it's a great chance for any chap that'd like an army career. There's many a fellow getting a commission now that wouldn't have got within smelling distance of one before. Well, here's to them. It's for the old sod and the old flag they've gone.' The figure turned about and it was Mr. Tim Corbin. His glance rested without recognition on Martin to whom he gave a good-natured nod. 'Must be great for a boy, a day like this,' he said good-naturedly to his companions. Then his glance turned to Sally, and he allowed it to rove up and down her figure.

Martin said quickly: 'Listen, Sally. Perhaps, after all, you had better go back to the Ladies' Tea Room. Miss Clare was in none too good a humour this morning.'

'Yes, it might be safer.'

Mr. Corbin, glass in hand, moved to watch her going up the stairs. Looking up, he suddenly gave one of his companions an excited nudge, then, changing his expression, said reprovingly: 'Now isn't it queer that they'd send a great big girl as old as all that out in a bit of a baby's skirt. She has the real Proddy cut about her, whoever she is. Ah well, their day is done here; they've ruled the roost here a damn' sight too long.' He nodded sagely. 'It's a fact, men, the more stand-off they are, the less decency they show in turning out their children and that long red one gone up is no child. We really oughtn't to let such things pass without protest; it's high time they learned that this is a Catholic country!'

'A pup, an infernal pup.' Uncle John had called Corbin that in the drinking-parlour below the Ladies' Tea Room. But he had called James Edward that, too, on that night of Josie's song. No. He would not go to stay at Glenkilly for Christmas; he would find some way to get out of having to go. Yet, he would like to see Aunt Eileen and James Edward—and of course Mary Ellen. But Father Riordan gone, Josie gone—vanished indeed—and no letter from Gertrude for over two years. She would be a woman now while he was still only a boy. The treacherous power of time dismayed him, and the dismay passed back through the shame of Corbin's words about Sally's clothes.

The evening sunlight was gilding the spires and roofs of Ballow in its valley as he and the girls squashed themselves into the back of the old Swift, and drove back in it through the wafts of newly cut corn. As they drove up the avenue and passed beneath the green pallor under the sycamores they saw, in the field near the gate, the cricket stumps forgotten after last evening's game

when the postman had hit a boundary; and now the sheep were
lined about them like weary fielders in shabby flannels greyed by
dusk. Still the afterglow of the sunset flamed nearby on the copper
beeches. It was the hour when hall and rooms would be blown
fresh and cool. As they came to the half-moon of lawn, there was
Hanrahan in his shirt-sleeves, pushing his wheelbarrow, his little
hard hat atop of his long head, his shrivelled pear of a beard
aggressively out-thrust. All that long afternoon, while Ballow
watched the troops, he had been tending 'Kathleen's Garden'.

For one more week young and old, male and female, helped
with the harvest before any break in the weather. The war for
justice remained a far-off glory in France. Norman went back to
Tory Hill for a last few days with his family before term began.
The harvest moon had begun to bevel off into its oval, when one
evening Mrs. Vincent summoned the girls and Martin to her.

'I have something to tell you. Miss Clare is going to be married!'

'Captain McKenzie?' they said without much hope. She shook
her head—regretfully, they thought. It was solemn Mr. Turner.
'She did not know whether she wanted to marry anyone for years
yet. She wanted to stay on here until you were all grown-up. But
now that Mr. Turner is going to the war she is going to marry him
before he goes. Here—in a few weeks.'

'And us? School?' She told them that Mr. Vincent, believing
that his presence was not essential to the farm which could be
managed by Mr. Binnay and Tom Prendergast—Tom would
say by himself alone—had thought it his duty to offer his services
to the War Office. He would have to be in England or France,
England more likely. He would leave soon after Miss Clare's
wedding; the girls would go with him and be put to boarding-
school for the coming term; she herself would see the house shut
up, then follow and try to get a cheap house or flat near to Mr.
Vincent and to a day-school.

'Since it must be school, it's going to be day-school if possible.
We shall be together, not scattered over the place. What could I
do here with you all away? I can do some war-work in England.
It'll be only for a year at the very most.'

The girls' heads leaned to hers as they talked and Martin felt
sick fright in his belly. They were all forgetting about him. Where
could he go if Keelard were left empty like that?

She looked up over the girls' heads. 'And when you come for
the Christmas holidays, Martin, you'll be able to teach those
English boys some of your Irish history.' The words dissolved the
clamps around his heart. She had not been forgetting him; she
said it quite matter-of-course. And he heard the girls speaking to
him of things they would do together in England.

He would see the lights of London, the Tower and Thames
barges, the places where Goldsmith had talked to Burke. He would
travel on the mail-boat from Kingstown! With a rug over his
arm, his scarf blowing jauntily and Kingstown boys and other
Dublin Jackeens looking enviously at him. He would have a meal
on the boat—the waiters on a ship were called stewards. And now
there would be no more question of that visit to Glenkilly at
Christmas—things could not have turned out more luckily.

Miss Clare was married shortly before the end of the holidays.
Alone among the guests Martin and the girls had the privilege of
seeing her and the bridegroom off at the station.

She waved from the moving train and they called and heard
her last, high call: 'Goodbye, goodbye. Christmas.' There was
nothing left but the smoke drifting across the fields, and already
the station-master had taken off the official braided things and
was pulling the old soft hat from his pocket. Several times on the
drive home they said, 'Well, it's not really long till Christmas.'

Much tidying up had already been done by the girls who were
to leave in a week with their father. 'Mother says we're to bring
only the things we feel we simply couldn't live without, because
it would be silly to carry much when we'll only be away a year at
most.'

They gathered together Sally's drawings and water-colours,
many of them showing views of the house, its fields and river—
she never tired of working at her pictures of the place seen from
all sorts of aspects. They put them with the collar of her dead
Airedale, her coloured plates of 'Wild Horses of the American
Continent', her rosettes for jumping prizes won with her pony
when her dark red hair had gone glinting out behind her bow
and her blue velvet jockey-cap, her illustrated Shelley, her Strauss
waltzes, her print of Van Dyck's 'King Charles'. They made
another parcel of Peggy's model house, her book-binding tools,
her dog-eared John Bunyan, but they put on one side her list of
medicines for her brindle bitch and the list of her old men and

old women protégées, which she had written out for Colonel
Howard, who had promised that during her absence he would
arrange for the distribution of the ju-jubes, knitting wools,
tobacco and yesterday's newspapers. They parcelled up Martin's
records of rugby and cricket scores, his collection of ancient maps,
a rowing riband he had won, school prizes, his dramas which
they—with conscripted Colonel Howard and conscripted postman and children—had acted in the oat-barn. But, with his
histories and dictionaries that he would take away with him, he
put his diary and photographs. This putting-away of things
recalled to him the things he had packed from the tea-caddy in
Glenkilly and left in the care of Mr. Burns, and he planned to
send for them one day.

Behind moved furniture they found lost pencils, old penances
and a cabalistic sheet of which all they now knew was that it had
once hidden an involved plot against Hanrahan. They took down
from the wall the Green Flag and the Union Jack which they had
formally hung up there since the beginning of the war. They
rolled up the shiny map of the world and put it in a corner with
the rolled flags. Then, in that corner they put the cracked blackboard and, later, put the boat's lantern there also.

They made their tea, but the tidied room gave back echoes now
to every sound and therefore they remained for the most part
silent. With Miss Clare not there and Mrs. Vincent occupied,
they might, with impunity, do all the things upstairs which they
had sometimes wanted to do. But they did none of them. Instead,
without mentioning it, they did all their duties as Miss Clare
would have had them done. So Martin cleaned the knives, fetched
up their washing-water and filled their lamp, while the girls un-
laid the table, swept the hearth, brought night clothes to air at the
fire and gathered the bread scraps for the economical and boring
bread pudding. They went then to put on their party clothes for
the celebration dinner downstairs, at which they were to be
present. Some of the wedding-guests were staying in the house, but
the others were coming up from Mr. Humphries' house, and
from Mrs. Carter's.

Dressed and ready in their old party clothes, they sat for the
last time together by the fire, waiting to go down as so often
before. But tonight they let the fire die away because it would not
be wanted again. And so, when the tubes from Malay jangled

harmoniously, summoning them to dinner, the glow had paled from the girls' faces, the shine from their black silk knees, and the room was dark.

After the thrill of a special dinner and its delicious ritual, they sat obscurely, while other people were arriving; some of the younger ones quite evidently in hope that the evening would end in a dance. Many had already joined the Army, others were about to do so and those who remained were feeling—some to their own surprise—how sorry they were to be about to lose the Vincents for a year. Even the Stillmores came, Alice Stillmore who was, Peggy said, 'the female land-monster who could lie in the shade of her own feet', and her two brothers, with the same kind of feet. They were even pleasant to Martin; but he was not going to let himself be patronized, so late in the day, by 'snobs and bigots'. None the less, he had to admire the way the elder Stillmore boy went off bare-headed on a sleek carriage-horse, his coat-tails flying, to fetch a cornet for the impromptu band that was to provide music while they danced. Stillmore put the animal to the moon-lit fields amid cries of 'You'll kill yourself—*and* the horse!' Martin would remember that moon-lit scene when, far from Keelard, he read in a newspaper of the posthumous honour awarded to dead Lieutenant Sydney Stillmore who had at Suvla Bay 'rallied his Company with great coolness' on the death of other officers and, though wounded, had 'held an exposed position under heavy fire until reinforced'. There would be a special amnesty then for the snobbish bigotry of the Stillmores and a salute to Sydney Stillmore, lying not in the shade of his own feet but in the darkness of his grave.

The dining-room was cleared by many hands and soon a band was playing and the Grand March of a Sir Roger de Coverley curving with ever-growing linkages. Later they sang the first song of the war, 'Tipperary', as well as various songs of victorious home-comings. And when for the last great sweep and linkage the band struck up the 'Minstrel Boy', even the English visitors seemed to know most of the words. All voices sang it, even the Stillmores'.

> 'Land of Song,' said the warrior bard,
> 'Though all the world betray thee,
> One sword at least thy rights shall guard,
> One faithful harp shall praise thee.'

When the waltzing and the sitting-out flirtations had got under
way, Sally and Martin found Mrs. Vincent.

'May we go down to the river, please?'

She wrinkled her forehead apologetically. 'Aren't you enjoying
it?'

'Oh, but we are. It's just that Peggy's gone to give her bitch
her night crust and we'd like to go to the river.'

'All right. Put something on, Sally. Martin, take my big gold-
and-red shawl for her; it's outside my day-room but don't make
a noise; Colonel Howard is taking a doze there. He wants to see
the party through.'

When they went outside, he put the gold-and-red shawl around
Sally and her dark red hair shone in the moonlight above the
gleaming shawl. The laurels were stiff and dry tonight; a faint
breeze blew coolly on their warm cheeks, but up in the sky the
wind was wilder and scurried the clouds before the new moon that
was going down to the western horizon. They looked for a while
at the crescent smouldering along the edge of a ragged cloud.

'The new moon in the arms of the old,' she said.

'Yes, Astarte.'

'Astarte?'

> 'With these in troops
> Came Astoreth, whom the Phoenicians called
> Astarte, Queen of Heaven, with crescent horns.

I'm all Milton tonight, like Ned Connolly—the chap I told you
about, often. He's going to the war, I hear.'

'Yes, I remember. The big boy who was so nice to you and
Norman your first year at school.'

'It's the huntsman's moon, Sally.'

'Yes, the harvest moon is over.'

This end of 'Kathleen's Garden', separated from the dancing
dining-room by the passage to the side hall-door, was pale white
in the night, but the far end was bright in the light which
streamed out from the back windows of the drawing-room. Now
and then they could hear a murmur of voices coming from those
windows. They stood at the central intersection of the garden
paths and looked far down at the river shining before the trees
of the Long Island.

'That's what you call the Virgin Mary, isn't it? Queen of Heaven?'

'Yes. One of her names.'

'Your favourite saint, and Norman's.'

'But look here, Sally, I've explained before. She's not just a saint. She's far above saints. Our Lord had to do what she told him when He was young even though He was God and now He'd do it to please her and honour her, so we often just ask her to ask Him for what we want. It's perfectly reasonable and logical. But we do not *worship* her; we worship God only. I've told you that dozens of times.'

She rested her hand inside his arm and said nothing. They went down then diagonally towards the river. All the land was cracking a little in the cold night.

'Winter will soon have his knife in it,' she said.

'Yes. Still, next year everything will come up again. And you want the winter for that. No frost, no harvest, you know.'

'Yes. And we'll be back by then. But I shall hate missing the spring. The lambs and then the foals and then the daffodils.'

They walked upstream along the firm bank to listen to a good-bye from 'the rapids'. From the stripped fields there still came a slight tang of corn and living grass but at one place the air held a doubtful memory of burning weeds.

'Are you cold, Martin?'

'A little. But it's nice. Are you tired?'

'No.'

They were silent for a while and could hear their thin shoes moving on the close turf of the bank. Then they heard the rupple-dupple of 'the rapids' and stopped to listen. They went into the thicket-patch which led to that secret 'useful way of getting in and out'. There, the half-sawn tree-trunks lying moonlit on the grass looked not heavy but fairy-unsubstantial.

They came back to the boathouse, opened the door and peered in at the shadow of their boat beyond the family boat. They listened to the lapping of the water at the prows and the gurgle around the river-door. Replacing the key in its theoretical hiding-place, they went up the bumping slope beneath the blossomless elders and, beyond the back-avenue, the night stock in 'Kathleen's Garden' was still giving a weak scent to the autumn night.

Sally looked across at the moon, now very low in the west.

'Astarte, Queen of Heaven. You always say such wonderful things, Martin. How you remember everything!'

She stood straight and slim, and, in her gleaming stiff shawl, looked like a young priest in his cope with head erect at the Elevation of the Host. Then she turned her head and no longer looked like a young priest because now the darkness of her hair was lit at each side by silver, and her hair-bow stood out stiffly on either side.

'Your eyes are so bright in the light, Martin.'

'So are yours.' He fingered his wide collar.

'Is your collar hurting again?'

'No.' But she put her hands on either side of it, easing it from his neck. Her fingers became joined behind his neck, her breath was warm on his cold face.

'Do you remember one day on Dan Murphy's barge when Peggy talked about how everything, even a saddle or a book, really comes out of the land in the end. Norman said it was really the sun. Chlorophyll was God.'

'Yes. I remember.'

She looked up at the crescent moon, and smiled rather enviously at him.

'Tonight it really looks like the new moon in the arms of the old, Sally.'

'Your special Queen of Heaven.'

'But she's *everybody's* Queen of Heaven. Not Astarte; I mean the Blessed Virgin. She's for everybody, all nations and peoples. Blacks and Red Indians. Astarte was just for the Phoenicians.'

'Yes. Isn't it strange to think of them looking up at the self-same moon?'

'Yes. They used to come to Cornwall for tin. Miss Clare was in Cornwall once.'

'Yes.' And then: 'Supposing a Phoenician boy and girl . . . Well, they might have gone out for a walk like this and seen her, and said "Queen of Heaven"!'

They looked across at the crescent among the running clouds.

'It really fits—the huntsman's moon. Look at the way she's galloping along. Out on the hunt.' He hesitated. 'I wish I wasn't a year younger than you, Sally.'

'It doesn't matter. And if I'm kept at school for two years, then you'll only have one year after me. Then we'll be the same again.'

Beyond them they heard occasionally a dim pulse of music from the dancing in the house.

'Sometimes when I'm with you, Martin, I feel . . . I feel . . .'

'I know. I know what you mean. Sometimes when we've just said good night I want to be the best and most honourable man in the world.'

'I know. I know *exactly*, Martin! Exactly!'

After a moment, they stepped back from one another and the loosened shawl slipped from her shoulders so that suddenly she stood all white in her simple muslin dress.

He was putting the shawl around her when both stiffened in alarm because there in the darkness of the laurels something white had moved. They held their breaths. A white figure came into the light and it was Peggy, bare-headed and without cloak or coat.

'Have you seen Mother? She slipped away not long after you went out.'

'Perhaps she went to "Kathleen's Garden". But it's getting cold for that.'

They went into the garden, walking towards the brightness at the drawing-room end and calling softly: 'Are you here? It's only us.'

The moon, sailing into a clear space on the horizon, flooded the garden with light and threw their shadows far along the beds. The river leaped with lances of light. Suddenly, they were aware with a little fright that somewhere behind them there was a light where it should not be. They whirled about and saw that all this time there had been a light in Mr. Vincent's office-study.

They went to the french window and stood in a row, looking in. Mrs. Vincent was in there, writing at the bureau, the lamplight streaming across her. They tapped on the window and instantly her head jerked up, one hand to her breast, the other covering her writing as if to hide it. The startled look went from her face and she came to open the window.

'You startled me. When I saw your white faces and your dresses.'

'It was stupid to tap like that. We forgot how alarming it might be.'

'It doesn't matter. But you stood so still. All in a row.'

She drew them in. 'Are you cold? You look lovely; your eyes are shining. You have nice eyes, all of you, thank goodness.'

'Such a night outside, Mother,' Sally said. 'Such a night!'

'I know. I had a peep.' She went to the bureau and folded up sheets of writing; there were several of them.

'Isn't the moon marvellous? The hunter's moon. But you should hear Martin's name for it. Astarte—Queen of Heaven. He says it's what the Phoenicians called her. He got it out of Milton.'

'Your memory, Martin!' said Mrs. Vincent. 'I wish I remembered more. . . .'

'Oh, well, I forget lots of things, too. Often for ages and ages. Now, if you wrote things down as I do in my diary, you'd remember them, too.'

She looked away from him, gave a little laugh and said: 'Well, you have all stayed up late enough. Go to bed now. Don't be seen again by people—and certainly not heard. Have your supper in here,' and as she went she took with her the folded sheets of writing. When she returned she was flushed from dancing, but seemed at once abstracted and restless. As she said good night to them, the way she looked at Martin puzzled him slightly, and when he closed the door after the girls he saw her about to sit again at the bureau, those sheets in front of her.

They slipped deferentially past the sitters-out in passages and hall, past couples on the stairs, and, for the last time, picked up their candles inside the green door. When he awakened, later on, to wafts of cheering and singing coming from downstairs, he heard the girls jumping from bed. Scrambling into their dressing-gowns, all three raced to the landing and, crouching in the dimness below the dying landing-lamp, they looked down at Mr. and Mrs. Vincent side by side in the middle of a great circle of people singing 'Should auld acquaintance be forgot'. Looking down, they saw her fingers pressing the inside of his arm. His usual reserved gravity seemed lit by something else. He looked younger, and for once it was possible to guess what he was thinking and feeling, to see that he was pleased and strongly moved.

The circle cheered three times. 'And another!' They drained their glasses. Some were drinking the toast in hot soup or trying to do so. 'Speech, sir! Speech!' He shook his head but they kept at it. 'Speech, sir, speech!' louder and louder, and at last Mrs. Vincent slipped away from him and, returning with a glass of wine, gave it to him and whispered in his ear. He nodded and all down there

waited and went silent. He lifted his glass; she put her hand inside
his other arm. Thus Martin would often see them, clear in his
head, side by side and that great circle of faces.

'Ladies and Gentlemen. The King!'

The silence grew queer and deep. Glasses were raised, and here
and there men's voices, Colonel Howard's among them, murmured 'The King!' But before any could drink, the song began
and in an instant it swept around the circle.

'God save our gracious King . . .'

Down there they were singing with devotion in every face. And
up on the landing the girls and Martin, scrambling to their feet,
sang, their voices lost in the great sound below.

'Send him victorious, happy and glorious,
    Long to reign over us,
    God save the King.'

For Justice, Justice! And death to a bully.

People turned away from one another, finding places for their
empty glasses as they moved. Already some of the ladies were
coming towards the stairs, so Martin and the girls scurried out of
sight. Pausing to shut the schoolroom door which was creaking,
they looked in on the tidied room, the black hearth, and saw a
gleam of their boat's lantern which they had put in the corner
before the flags and the cracked blackboard.

3

O N T H E day of his return to Dunslane he waited as usual at
Ballow Junction for the doubtful 'stop at every pub' train which
was bringing Norman to join him from Bencourt. That evening
they went together with cheerful hauteur to lay their hand-bags
on their beds amid the respectful silence of some new boys—
'Freshmen'.

Of those who had been with them in Bridgid's Dormitory in
their first year, some were grown-up and gone; others had now
been moved to other dormitories, among them Mullins and
McNally who, with Seumas Conroy and O'Mahoney, were
beginning their last school year. Perhaps because of their youthful
appearance it had never occurred to anyone to promote Norman
and Martin from a dormitory which was erratically and uncertainly reserved for the smaller boys, and they were glad to
retain their old beds and the habits which custom now venerated
as rights.

Before going to see Long Dick, they strode cheekily into
Matron's room. 'Hello, Matron. The brains of the place are
back again.' Thus, it was from her they first heard the news. The
Dean was going as a chaplain to the war; in five or six weeks he
would be gone and he would be succeeded by 'what amounts to
two Deans' she said grimly.

'*Two* Deans, Matron?'

'Well, one is to be Dean, and the other a Joint-Dean under
him.' With asperity, she added that not only would the priest who
already assisted Father O'Neill remain, but that the newcomers
would bring yet another assistant priest with them. 'And that
will make four priests in the place! The next step will be to have a
nun for Matron. This war's giving the Holy Joes their chance at
last.'

The new Dean, Father Lloyd, was already known to the school by sight. His open fastidiousness had won for him the nickname of 'The Duchess'. It was known that he had spent some of his schooldays at Dunslane, had sat under Jimmy Curran, and known Mr. Bourke. But the Joint-Dean, Father MacTaggarty, was unknown. 'All I can tell you is that he grew up half the time in America and has a bald head, and a limp he got a few years ago. He's terribly anti-English, whereas Father Lloyd is all for Mr. Redmond and the war.' Both men had 'great degrees and qualifications', and had studied all the best authorities on education, and, unlike Long Dick and Matron, who were not experts on anything, the newcomers were 'Experts on the Young'.

In a few days the boys had settled completely in. Much of the summer kept filtering through to the autumn. Far across the playing fields the Dean's dog-cart flickered sunnily between the trees of the avenue. It stopped and from group to group the call rang frostily clear. Norman and Martin, with two smaller boys, who had also been called, ran.

'Caps and topcoats fairly handy?'

He was going to the village nearby.

When they came streaking back to him, he agreed that Martin should drive on the way out and Norman on the way back. The two tiny boys got up behind on the 'facing-back' seat and away they went along the berry-sprouting lanes, Long Dick sitting up between Norman and Martin. In three weeks he would be gone.

While the Dean called on a friend, and the mare had a feed and a shake without her harness, the four boys bought sweets and sent post-cards for the pleasure of sending them out of school. Martin's post-cards went to England to 'Mrs. R. Turner', and one to Aunt Kathleen that ended with a phrase now familiar— *Have you found a place where we can all go at Christmas?*

When Norman drove back, the sun was setting, but threshing engines were still shaking the berried hedges, the heads of horses and men still nodding to their plodding journeys. They whirled into the avenue and there, all set and serene, the Bigger House was bathed in the sunset. It was just as it had been on that September evening when Danny, his jarvey, had suddenly said, 'Well, here ye are now!' and swerved between the gates.

When Willy took over the dog-cart at the first triangle of flowers, Martin slowly walked after the others, hearing his own feet in the gravel and the car creaking away to the left. In the doorway the Dean reappeared, his hat waving Martin onward. The sun struck red and gold lights from the sweeping lock of hair. Above him, he heard the old, coaxing, 'Well, what is it?'

'Nothing, Father. Only I was thinking of the first day I came. There was only the wood-quest and the weir, and I didn't know what a new boy—a Freshman—should do, or if I'd have enough to pay my jarvey. I was standing just here looking in and then down at that corner someone said, "Well, what is it?" And it was you!'

'Get my old soutane from my bedroom for me.'

In the bedroom, he saw the slippers, the jar of flowers, the shaving mirror, a race-card, just as they were when he had come to fetch the strap, the day Frankie Regan had sent him up. If only Time could now stand still! God had stopped the earth's revolutions for Joshua, although Joshua thought it was the sun which had stopped in the heavens. Why could not God stop the war here and now? God knew what was best for us. But Aunt Mary? One must merely say 'God's Will be done', knowing that finite human reason could not weigh the infinite purposes of God.

'I want to talk to you, Martin. My successors, Father Lloyd and Father MacTaggarty, I'm sure they'll both be very nice. But . . . if you happen not to like certain people, don't look at them quite so haughtily. And . . . and . . .'—it was well known that the Dean hated giving this kind of talk—'realize this: it's not enough to be submissive to your elders when you like them or just put up with them. The real duty is to be submissive to those you may not like or approve, but who are placed over you in your station of life; you know that. And for schoolboys and schoolgirls, their station in life is only the first station—like a railway train getting coal and water put into it and being polished and hammered by everyone. You'll be shooting out from now on, you and Norman and others,' then in a shy, half-apologetic way: '. . . don't be intolerant, don't be *too* contemptuous of people who aren't everything you think nice and right.' Looking sideways at Martin's serious face, he said, 'Mind you, I feel just the same myself often.'

It was exceptional for him to talk like this. Most shyly, most gently and, for him, most surprisingly, the Dean spoke of men and the world, and of goodness. Men had to eat and drink, had

to earn their meat and drink, and yet they would often throw
away food and clothing and warmth merely to serve some idea
or 'just to be themselves'. Some people were more likely to do
that than others, and must be specially careful and wise. He
spoke of the noble impulses which he said most boys felt more and
more as they neared their manhood, and he said that the better
the boy, the stronger would be those noble aspirations, but the
stronger, too, might be the feelings pulling the other way. 'You
understand, don't you?'

And Martin whispered, 'Yes, Father.'

'Well, in any difficulty, either to do with others or a private
one, in any struggle to be good, one great help, after prayer, is to
think of the people one respects and loves.'

As he talked, twilight dimmed the room and the familiar smell
of books and tobacco in the room seemed to wax greater. A boy
could always live up to those he honoured, until he was a man,
ready to live up to himself, and to God's universal order—'or try
to, which is all any of us can do'. For himself, when he was a boy,
he had always found that those he honoured came most clearly
to him when he went to the Blessed Virgin, 'even just to say her
names. Tower of Ivory, Vessel of Honour, Mother most
Admirable.'

After that, they were silent for a while. Tea came, and lights;
Norman was sent for from Study, and they talked of people who
were going to the war, of things which had happened in other
years, funny things and dramatic things, the day a window had
blown in and cut Ned Connolly and Great Mars, both of them
now off to the war.

When they had finished the cake and all of the biscuits except
one, left on the plate for politeness, Norman said, 'If the war is
over before a year, you'll be back before we know where we are.'

'No. I wouldn't be back here, anyway. You see, I am not very
good about education. I often meant to read up about it, but . . .'
He shrugged apologetically. 'Now, both Father Lloyd and the
new Joint-Dean, Father MacTaggarty, have really studied the
whole thing. They're authorities on it. I'm not qualified to be in
charge of young people at all, only just I liked being here and
clung on to it. Besides, I don't keep all your noses hard enough to
the grindstone.'

'Listen, Father, if it isn't rude, tell that to the Marines! As if we weren't half killed for the smallest thing. And what about all the prizes and honours which the school gets?'

He looked down at them where, squatted on the floor, they were jockeying one another away from the most comfortable position against the sofa-head. 'Well, anyway, you'll find things will be greatly improved in all sorts of ways. And then there's the matter of degrees. The Head of a school ought to have more qualifications than I've got.'

'Why? Lots of stupid people have degrees. Father says the lowest creature on God's earth is a pass B.A. He says the only thing it shows is that the fellow didn't idle.'

'Idle! Well, you two are authorities on that, anyway!'

'Ah, go on, Father. Tell the truth and shame the devil. When you were at school yourself, didn't you do just as much idling as any boy would do? That is, not too much, you know, just ordinary.'

'I'm afraid I did do a certain amount. It seems only yesterday that I was like you two there. I often feel that I'm not grown-up at all. And now here I am going off as a chaplain to the war.'

Thinking that this sounded like a good joke, they looked up, ready to lark him, but saw that he was not joking at all. He was abstractedly rolling one of his dark cigarettes, and they jumped up to jostle for the pleasure of lighting it for him. He held them, squeezed one on each side of him, and said: 'Ah, sing a song. But quietly, for goodness' sake.'

'Did you ever hear this one, Father?' and they went over the French words to give him 'the hang of it' before they sang of the man who had never got to nearby Carcassonne.

> *'On dit qu'on y voit des châteaux*
> *Grands comme ceux de Babylone*
> *Un évêque et deux généraux*
> *Je ne connais pas Carcassonne!'*

'A bishop and two generals, Father! Worth seeing, eh?'
'Yes, but did he ever get to see it?'

> *'Ma femme, avec mon fils Aignan,*
> *A voyagé jusqu'à Nargonne*
> *Mon filleul a vu Perpignan*
> *Et je n'ai pas vu Carcassonne!'*

The song continued, telling how the old man's chance had
come at last, how another man had taken his arm to lead him to
Carcassonne, how he had set out and died on the way.

'Aye, that's it,' Long Dick said, when it ended. But when they
looked inquiringly at him, he laughed the inquiry away.

The remorseless days passed. Nothing could lighten the oppres-
sion which spread among masters, boys and servants with a conviction of irreparable loss. The new Dean—Father Lloyd, 'The
Duchess'—was sometimes now to be seen on visits, lilting with
careful dignity along the halls, the gown of his degrees billowing
about him, his pointed face giving a tiny rise and fall as if he
were counting each deliberately harmonious step. But of Father
MacTaggarty there was yet no sign.

They saw little of Long Dick in those last weeks, for he was very
busy, and they had only scrappy meetings with him. When they
serpentined their way into his study, hoping to be asked to stay,
he had other boys with him. Once it was Seumas Conroy, a long
young man now and in trousers instead of the kilt.

'Long Dick always had a regard for Seumas Conroy,' said
Norman.

'Well, I bet he doesn't lecture him on Gaelic Civilization, or
tell him what "my father says".'

'I'm not so sure,' said Norman. 'Seumas Conroy is capable of
telling the Pope himself that he ought to talk Irish on St. Patrick's
Day, or have the Vatican at Tara.'

The day came for Long Dick's departure. He went during
Study, choosing that time to avoid the risk of a farewell demonstration. Masters did not even pretend that they were pretending
that boys were working. The school knew his wishes, and all sat
quietly in their places, listening to the sounds at the hall door.
Then, after a silence, his old dog-cart was heard creaking. They
heard it move slowly, knew when it was passing the last triangle
of flowers, heard it get into a trot, until at last it died away along
the avenue.

A little later, the study-hall door gave a click. Startled, all
jerked up their heads and saw a great figure, taut-set and motionless, inside the closed door. It was Father MacTaggarty, the
Joint-Dean; it could be no other. They saw that his large head
was very bald with some hairs plastered across the baldness, they
saw him limp slightly as he entered. All stared at him, disturbed

by this way of making his dramatic début. They were accustomed to Long Dick's swooping entries in lazy haste or smouldering wrath.

The door opened again and 'The Duchess' joined him, more fastidious and refined than ever beside Father MacTaggarty's hewn look. They moved down the central aisle in a great silence, 'The Duchess' lilting gracefully, with his gown billowing. Father MacTaggarty's even finer gown did not billow; it rose and fell slightly to the pad-pad of his limp. Eyes slewed uncomfortably up to the passing of these powerful presences. They saw 'The Duchess' smiling tolerantly with his small mouth amusedly pursed; they saw Father MacTaggarty's huge mouth wide in a grave and very different smile. It was as if both of them were anxious to show that they thoroughly understood how important to boys were their studies and all the attendant joys and pains which went with them.

The school gradually learned to be less startled by the click of the door and the pull of Father MacTaggarty's presence inside it.

At the rustling entry of 'The Duchess' himself, hearts rose in hope of another dramatic speech, another performance. The lilting step, the nodding face, the swirling gown, went along the aisle.

He would first bend understandingly at other boys' desks before squeezing in friendly intimacy between Norman's and Martin's to comment on their work. 'I'm sure many of the big giants of nineteen could not have done that!' And he would smile invitingly. The remark offended their sense of the permissible. It was proper that they themselves should keep older boys in their places by occasional references to stupidities performed, to indignities endured, but a master, of all adults, should maintain the outward forms of the hierarchy. After all, a bishop would never invite a sub-deacon to belittle a deacon.

Unaware of the intolerant judgements going on in the growing human being on either side of him, 'The Duchess' would keep an arm around each of them and squeeze them companionably. But instead of liking it and feeling flattered, they were embarrassed.

One night when the door gave the little click and eyes slewed upwards below bending foreheads, they saw inside the door, not only 'The Duchess' but also big Father MacTaggarty himself. Both advanced to the head of the hall.

'Later this evening,' said 'The Duchess' solemnly, 'Father MacTaggarty will give you the first of a series of Spiritual Addresses. Please note that to these addresses I attach the greatest importance. . . . Another matter. The method of distributing letters will be different in future. Father MacTaggarty and I know how much boys can be hurt by seeing things important to them treated in a roistering way.'

It had been Long Dick's custom, swooping through the Refectory at breakfast, to send letters whizzing towards grasping hands. When he sent a letter fairly into scrabbling fingers, he laughed, and the table said 'Good shot, Father' to him, 'Well held, sir' to the boy. When he sent wide, he called 'Awfully sorry, Jimmy' and the table called 'No harm done, Father, it missed the milk!'

There was worse to come. The school colours were to be changed. They exactly resembled those of a Protestant school who played matches against them. This was not seemly. Then there was the matter of corporal punishment.

'Neither Father MacTaggarty nor I could bring ourselves to inflict corporal punishment, which, as you know, is now being carried out by Father Gunne or Father Callaghan.' He made a moue of outraged sensibility, shivered speakingly, and the school applauded cheerfully.

Father MacTaggarty intervened in his disturbing, compelling voice: 'The very way you greet that statement is itself very indicative. It is not a laughing matter.'

'The boy or girl,' continued 'The Duchess', 'who will not work or behave properly without corporal punishment has no sense of dignity.' He dropped his hand dramatically. Seeing that no strong impression had been made, he added sharply, 'And no self-respect!' Still no one seemed impressed. 'And no manliness!' he added.

A boy behind Martin whispered fretfully: 'How can a girl have manliness? He said boy or girl. Where's the man's logic at all?'

'I do not go so far as Father MacTaggarty who hopes that one day such punishment may be abolished entirely.' The hall

cheered enthusiastically, but Father MacTaggarty stood powerfully unmoving and the cheerful applause died.

'To inflict it myself . . .' 'The Duchess' shuddered in distaste,
'would destroy the sympathy and trust that should exist between
us.'

Then in a low tone he mentioned once more the Spiritual
Address which Father MacTaggarty would give later that
evening, and billowed away. Father MacTaggarty's limp padded
down to Martin. 'I'll take your Latin grind, now.'

He had begun to give Martin private lessons in Latin, although
Martin and Norman were already receiving extra work from
Lennie Bourke. The lessons took Martin to the Joint-Dean's cosy
room, sometimes—when the Dean was absent—to Long Dick's
own study, that familiar hearthside. Nearly always there were
biscuits or sweets, for Father MacTaggarty was fond of these
things and was generous; hard work was unnecessary, because
Father MacTaggarty believed in giving a lesson somewhat on
the lines of a university lecture, with much mutual politeness and
never any question of penalties. It was the kind of class which
Martin and his friends had sometimes pictured when wandering
in the more delightful glades of fantasy. Yet, it bored him. He
even rather disliked it.

In the hall, to his distress, he saw Mr. Bourke, who had not
been consulted about these private lessons. The old master was
pacing up and down with Jimmy Curran, who huddled his neat
figure within the ragged gown, one hand frailly beating a rhythm
to his own words, which Mr. Bourke leaned to catch, one hand
to his deaf ear. The masters stopped as their former pupil and
Father MacTaggarty greeted them pleasantly.

Martin, waiting apart, thought that, if ever he became a
schoolmaster, he would like to have his own old masters under
him, and that, if they were so under him, he would call them 'Sir'
and show in every way that they were to be more honoured and
more important than himself. He tried to catch Mr. Bourke's eye,
to will into the master's head the knowledge that he was still the
honoured Senior Classical man, that a boy could not help it if the
new Dean and Joint-Dean gave private lessons without consulting
the masters, that the lessons were dull because Father MacTaggarty
did too much explaining too carefully, and with never a musing
repetition of a fine-sounding line such as those which in Mr.

Bourke's voice could ring through the head and heart until the line, its dead author and his vanished Roman world were bone and flesh of a boy's understanding.

Really, it was not fair that Lennie and Jimmy could never become headmasters simply because they were not priests.

On their way upstairs, Martin looked back and saw Lennie Bourke wagging his head up at him. In that wise, homely, every-day kind of wag there was full assurance that Lennie understood. Up went Martin's own arm to release the grateful rush in his heart. He gave a little wave with his hand beside his face, as he had often given to Mary Ellen, to Miss Clare, to many. Lennie acknowledged the wave, and Martin, turning, his hand still near to his face, saw Father MacTaggarty looking down at him from the landing beyond the big windows. He went up and the compelling voice said: 'You waved like a girl. Not like a boy.'

Martin blushed, and looked away.

'I've seen you do several other things that way.'

The lesson began and soon Martin was wondering if Aunt Kathleen had yet found a place where they could all go at Christmas. At the thought that in five weeks he would see her and the girls, a pre-party thrill squirmed through him. He would have that meal on the mail-boat and say 'Steward' like Uncle Brendan.

If he went by the night boat the lights would be put out because of submarines; that would be exciting. Perhaps a submarine would come, and he be the first to see it. If that happened would he get a medal?

He came out of his dream and heard Father MacTaggarty saying: 'You have great gifts, Reilly. I wonder what you'll become. I'm sure you are a hard-working boy. Have you really no idea what you will be?'

'I don't know, Father.'

'But really, at sixteen you ought to. You ought to be developing very rapidly.' He stretched his hand towards a big textbook, changed his mind. 'You are far too childish in many ways for your age, both you and your friend. I have noticed you—it's absurd. And, by the way,' he said solemnly, 'you will be glad to hear that if a vacancy occurs elsewhere, the Dean will give you both your promotion at last from St. Brigid's Dormitory. It was hard on you to be left in a dormitory with lads so much younger.'

Martin protested that neither he nor Norman minded.

'But at your age you ought to. Why, you're an adolescent! You know what that means, of course.'

Uncomfortable, Martin said, 'Yes, Father.'

'An adolescent is a person under twenty-one, but past the age of puberty.' He said this with great satisfaction, and as if it contained a revelation, and looking solemnly, almost owlishly, at Martin, he said, 'You know what that means, of course?'

Martin said, 'Yes, Father,' and rose, pretending that he thought himself dismissed. On his way downstairs, his nervy discomfort flooded through him an angry wish that Father MacTaggarty would leave him alone and not ask him to define 'adolescence' and 'puberty'. He stepped into the Refectory and went to the picture of the Blessed Virgin 'in half-tones like Rembrandt', Herr Heiner had told them.

There he did what Long Dick in that last talk had said that he himself had done when he was a boy; he called up the thought and names of many people, until he had come back and back to his Aunt Mary.

In hall Study that night 'The Duchess' announced: 'Father MacTaggarty and I deplore the fact that the school has not had a Sodality of the Blessed Virgin. We are going to establish one and every boy must become a member, except those debarred by bad conduct.'

A Sodality for boys—how Aunt Mary would have laughed! And how she would have wrinkled her nose at most of the new moves that were being made. The boys who knew Irish fairly well, for example, were to form groups with other boys, and 'converse' in Irish!—for twenty minutes a day. Only the first of many steps 'to ensure that every boy could speak the pure tongue of Ireland'. That would have amused her too. But she would never be heard laughing again—never. He must not dwell on it. Say 'God's Holy Will be done' three times. How hard he had prayed and then she had died like that. Why? Why must there be a war? Man's folly and sins—but God made man like that. Why?

'Father MacTaggarty has proposed that we should move the picture of our Lady in the Refectory to some place reserved to her own Sodality, to be a rallying point for the devotion of those worthy to be boys in her pure Court.'

If there had to be a war, why should Long Dick have to go? Why couldn't someone like Father Riordan take his place? Why should God always make things difficult? And why should the headmaster have to be a priest? Why not someone like wise old Lennie Bourke? Why? Why?

'Now, if our minds and hearts are fixed upon our Lady, we will ask Father MacTaggarty to come to us.'

Ah, stop this 'we' and 'us', pretending that you're the same as we are, when you're a man and we're only boys. Like the doctor with his 'and how are *we* today', as if it were he who had the bellyache.

In the dying afterglow which was the only light in the hall, the crucifix gleamed ruddy white, and Father MacTaggarty spoke of the principal reason why every boy should be enrolled in a Sodality of the Blessed Virgin. To keep a pure body was most difficult, to keep the mind pure almost impossible. Boys more than all other people were susceptible to the insidious snares of Impurity. Those snares lay in ambush in the simplest things around a boy's eyes and ears. Something which might look to him like the innocent flower might really be the serpent under it. A boy could never, never be sufficiently watchful of his every thought to ensure that in it there did not lie the deadly snare of Impurity. To sin against Holy Purity—how terrible! How specially terrible for an Irish boy. Because Ireland, which had lost everything and was even now only half-way back towards her rightful place, had never lost her native Purity. To sin against that Holy Irish Catholic Purity! By a word! . . . By a thought! . . . By a deed!

The voice droned on, as in the sky the first glories of a late autumn night were lit. 'The angels' bedtime candles, Martin dear,' Aunt Mary had often said, shaking her little curly head, tinkling out the merry laugh. But now she was dead, Long Dick was gone to the war, and there was only this mincing, droning voice, announcing that this must be changed and that must be altered.

4

Tugged by the under-current of the Spiritual Addresses, mind and soul would sometimes cry: 'Oh, leave me alone; why can't you just leave me alone?'

He would say her names then: 'Vessel of Honour' and Long Dick's 'Special Protectress of Boys and Girls', and he would ask her to make him think, as Long Dick had said, of those whom he honoured. From the ambushing question behind Aunt Mary's name, he would pass to the roster of the living, ending always with Aunt Kathleen.

So his letters to her became longer and with green ink he would mark in his diary the days when her letters came. Each of his own letters ended with the plea: *Will you have a place for us all to go to at Christmas?*

It seemed uncertain. As Mr. Vincent had been sent to Rouen, Aunt Kathleen had not yet taken a flat. She was with friends in England. When the letters from his Aunt Eileen began to talk of his spending the Christmas holidays in Glenkilly, he wrote imploringly to Keelard. The answer came, but not by letter.

To his astonishment, he received a visit from Mr. Peters, the fat man with the monocle in Kingstown, whose house he had visited with Aunt Mary and where, sitting on the terrace overlooking Dublin Bay, he had studied Vienna in a stereoscope under Miss Peters' prim, excited guidance.

Little Mr. Peters, who loved town and hated the country, sat chillily buttoned in his creaseless overcoat, held on to his folded umbrella and gave uneasy glances at the furniture of the visitors' parlour. Even the lineaments of obstinate good living in his plump face looked shrivelled.

'Now, my boy, I have kept my jarvey, so I must be off in a few minutes.' He explained that Mrs. Vincent, knowing that he had to go down to Keelard to discuss the farm finances with Mr. Binnay, had asked him to endure a second day in the country in order to break the news to Martin that he was not to come to her for Christmas.

'She has no place yet and the girls will go to their Irvine aunt in Surrey for their holidays. Besides, your aunt and uncle in Glenkilly are objecting to your going to England in war-time and their view is not unreasonable, especially as they have seen little of you. Mrs. Reilly would, I fancy, agree. But Mr. Reilly strongly objects. So you are to go to Glenkilly for Christmas and come to us in Kingstown for your Easter holidays if by then the position is unaltered. By the summer, Mrs. Vincent will bring the girls back to Keelard, if it is clear by then that Mr. Vincent is not going to be in England. Wherever they may be, you will spend the summer —or most of it—with them.' Then, noticing Martin's dejected face: 'I'm afraid that's final. I've had enough letters about your affairs, my boy, not to want any further changes.'

He glanced at the furniture of the parlour and the few chill religious pictures, then looked out at the icy sky.

'I must be off. It's getting dark already. No. No, thank you, I'm afraid I haven't time to see over your school. Thank you very much. I'm sure it's very nice. I scarcely think it's necessary, is it, to say goodbye to one of the . . . er . . . clergymen? Well, goodbye, my boy.' He pushed some money into Martin's hand. 'Don't forget to write—oh, heavens no, not to me! I'm too busy. Write to your two aunts. And work hard, of course, and . . . yes, play hard . . . and play the game. . . . Goodbye.' And off he went, short, plump, neat and monocled, and looking very miserable up on the side of a jaunting car with his folded umbrella held stiffly upright between his knees.

That evening, Martin wrote to Tory Hill, asking to be asked there for the Christmas holidays. The letter and a supporting letter from Norman went to Agnes who had to be more and more the mistress of Tory Hill, Mrs. Dempsey needing complete rest and seclusion.

When an invitation to Tory Hill arrived, Martin sent it on to Mrs. Reilly with a covering letter. She replied that she would be sorry not to have Martin for Christmas but that she wanted nothing except that he should be happy. Martin, touched and ashamed, tried in a letter to explain to her the reasons for his unwillingness to go to Glenkilly, but could not name his Uncle John among the reasons.

When she wrote again, she said: *Don't worry about anything; I am sorry not to have you but I think that it is probably for the best.* There was a P.S. to her letter—there always was. *Pray hard that James will not go to the war.*

The term went by, the grass shrank in on itself, the land grew quiet on top, its year's work turned now into flour, hay and meal, into wool and bottled peas, and hot roasted apples. Martin wrote regularly in his diary, remembered the various anniversaries, everyone's birthday, every commemoration. He passionately clung to the past. The giant shadow-barrels of the trees lay athwart the barricades of hedges when he and Norman went off for Christmas. He found changes at Tory Hill. The second of the grown-up girls was now married, the next girl already had a suitor—several suitors—and Agnes herself was engaged. Of the three younger girls, only one was still at school, and Molly, who had once been the plumpest and gayest of the three, was now a serious young woman of twenty-one, studying medicine. Agnes was 'managing', doing war-work, fetching books on Egypt from the library for her fiancé, who was a doctor home on leave from France, and playing golf with him.

The boys spent most of each day as they pleased and often made the main street of Bencourt quiver between terror and delight when, with the last 'Tomboy' between them, they pounded up the street behind the big gelding. Much of their time was spent with Mr. Dempsey who sought their company even more than formerly. He looked much older, mentioned his wife's ill-health more often, and had stopped speaking at recruiting meetings.

'When I realized that it would last until Norman would be old enough to go, I knew that I could not want him to go, although it would be his duty and I could not try to stop him. So I won't lecture any other young man now on his duty if he doesn't know it himself. I only hope I'm doing right.'

'But surely it will be over next year, sir? Wait till the Russian steamroller gets going properly! When Norman is old enough, I will go too. I'd like to have a smack at the bullying Germans.'

'This war is not a smack, Martin. It's a foul business. All we can do is to turn to God and ask Him to take this plague from us.

We must offer up every Mass for that now. And whatever does happen, you must promise me to look after Norman. Even here—well, supposing any trouble came here.'

'Here! In Ireland? And how could I look after Norman?'

'Martin, I'm worried. I'm very, very disturbed about the future here.'

'But why, sir? With everybody united now! Why, it's all wonderful. Nationalists, people that were Unionists, all on good terms: everyone except that cranky little part of the Volunteers that split away from Redmond because of the war.'

'That's it. Look at the arguments the British are handing over to that same cranky minority.'

'But how, sir? With Home Rule actually on the Statute Book and signed and only waiting until the war's over to be put into force.'

'Aye, but it's getting harder to give a real heart-and-soul answer to our extremists when they say that it never will be put in force, that it'll be just another broken treaty like the Treaty of Limerick, that after the war England's die-hards will encourage our other extreme minority—the Orangemen—to threaten war again rather than let Home Rule come into force. Martin, my father served the Crown, my young brother died for it in South Africa; I served the old Queen; I served Edward and I'm serving the present man, and I've seen fifty years of peace, progress and all-round improvement here. But I've lived also to see the King's law defied by people who said they were loyalists, and I've seen their open treason encouraged by British statesmen: encouraging them to arm, to bring in guns from Germany, to say they'd shoot the King's soldiers if they tried to enforce Home Rule.'

'But now that everyone's united because of the war?'

'Yes, yes, I cling to that. But will it last? To go and put Carson and the other leaders of that Orange treason into the Government—that's been a shock, Martin. And what answer have I when our own extremists point out that those same Orange rebels were given their own Division, most unjustly called "The Ulster Division" as if they were all Ulster instead of only a section of it, while Redmond is refused all his requests for a corresponding Nationalists' Division with its own flag and its own officers. How can we answer our extremists when they use these things to prove that the top pressure in England hates and despises Ireland, and

will never let us have an inch? I'm worried, I'm worried, I'm
terribly worried. Look, they're even blocking gallant young
Nationalists from getting commissions. How can I go on speaking
at recruiting meetings? If a young man comes to me for advice, I
tell him it's his duty to go, but I won't any longer seek them out
to lecture them.'

He walked up and down in silence for a long time. Then he
sighed. 'I'm so tired these days. If it weren't for Norman's future,
I'd just go back to my books and hunting and let someone else
take care of the world. But there's Norman. Martin, if trouble
does come here, you'll look after Norman, won't you?'

'Me? How could I look after Norman?'

'You could prevent him getting drawn into all that Kathleen-
ni-Houlihan, God-Save-Ireland business. It'd break his mother's
heart altogether if she thought he would ever get mixed up in it.
Look at their manners, and dressing up their girls in uniforms
like Boy Scouts, and their impudent abusing of their betters, and
sneering at His Majesty in front of my face. Whatever their
opinions, they needn't be so bad-mannered about them!'

'But I can't stop Norman reading Irish history and so
on.'

'You could dampen him a bit. I know it's just young foolishness in the two of you, but you must try to tone it down.'

'All right, sir. If you don't like it.'

A week later the holidays ended and Martin said goodbye to
Tory Hill.

Down in the town, the big gelding once again struck fire from
the stones in the main street. The ivy along the railway-station
wall slid out of sight; and the train carried them away to Dunslane.

In the darkening January evening, Norman and he, rushing
along the school corridors when they got back, loud to proclaim
their presence to all, nearly collided with a plumpish, prosperous,
gravely twinkling young man who walked between the Dean and
Father MacTaggarty. It was Mr. Tim Corbin. Martin remembered with relief that Corbin had not recognized him on the day
the troops and Volunteers had marched away from Ballow, but
he feared that he might do so now, seeing him side by side with
Norman. But Mr. Corbin's twinkling gaze saw only two apologizing schoolboys and they ran on. They soon learned that Mr.

Corbin had come to arrange about a lecture he was to deliver to the school. The Dean and Father MacTaggarty knew for certain, beyond fear of contradiction, that 'it was good for boys to hear men speak who play a part in the big affairs of the world'. Nevertheless Martin stared in troubled silence at the title of Mr. Corbin's lecture: 'Catholic Principles in Public Life'.

When the night of the lecture came he sat with Aunt Kathleen's latest letter crinkling in his pocket, and looked along the platform from Corbin to the Dean, to Father MacTaggarty, to Father Callaghan, to Father Gunne. 'Many of you, I am sure, are familiar with the reputation of our lecturer this evening . . . one of the most prominent Catholic figures in the county.' Four priests and Corbin—they must know about him? Even Mr. Burns away in Glenkilly long ago had known how to name him to Father Riordan—'Mr. Tim Corbin—the Slave-Heart'. The Dean was a silly little man and although Father MacTaggarty was not a silly man altogether, he was very silly about some things, always saying that he understood what was important to you and why, when he was not within a mile of being right. Yes, it was probable that the priests were being bamboozled by Tim Corbin, like so many others.

The lecture was full of high-flown sentiments, but Martin was amused to hear, as they came out from it, quite a junior boy say to a companion, 'I think that man's a humbug.'

On Martin's calendar, a green circle marked not the first day of the coming Easter vacation but of the summer one when he would be with Aunt Kathleen, far from lectures, spiritual addresses and talks about manliness, reason and honour. The girls had been unable to write to him very often. They reported that their mistresses regarded much letter-writing as 'rather sloppy and not quite healthy'.

But really, wrote Peggy, *I'm sure it's far more healthy to sit writing to you than to jump into a cold bath first thing in the morning. They take away conduct marks for being a slacker about the bath and I've already lost all my marks for this term. I find it is convenient to be Irish because they rather count on one to be a slacker. They expect nothing else from me but they are not sure yet that Sally might not be less of a slacker if she were properly encouraged. They are really quite decent in their own way and I should not like to think that my being such a slacker worried them.*

Sally's letters, although short, contained much about a new friend and soon Martin began to resent the existence of this Marjorie Bingham, of whom Peggy wrote:

I admire her for being clever about the slacking. You see, over here, a girl who is very fond of hockey cannot be called a slacker. So she can slack with Sally about certain other things without losing the respect of the mistresses and other girls. Her brother has only just left school and is in training camp near here. He will be in France this summer and sometimes we are allowed out with him to visit his aunt, which is a great relief for me. He is specially polite to Sally which shows that he is forming a temporary attachment for her, don't you think? If the mistresses find out, I am afraid they would stop our outings, because I am sure they would think it sloppy and unhealthy, especially as they have their eye on Sally. I don't mean only because she hates hockey, but also because of the things she laughs at and because she draws the curtains of her cubicle like me. Some of them look as if they were thinking it sloppy. We cry for Keelard often. I know better and better now how very nice you and Norman always were. Cousin Harry was nice too. I often sit up behind my curtains and send my love to you and nice Norman, and imagine Keelard.

When next Martin wrote to Sally he forgot about Marjorie Bingham because he had something to tell with pride: *My big cousin in Glenkilly, James, is getting a commission in the Irish Guards and I'm sure he'll soon be Captain Reilly like Captain McKenzie.*

James Edward, when he paid a visit to Dunslane, seemed as shy of Martin in the visitors' parlour as ever in the old Glenkilly days. 'I never wrote, I know. But now that I'm going to the war, I just thought I'd come.' He spoke of 'money worries at home', of 'bad business methods' and of his mother. 'Look—write to her often. She has a lot of feeling about you. And she'll be worried now about me. Mother is a hero. She's always been in the thick of it with one thing after another. The Reillys didn't want her to marry Father. And I rather think it was your father, Uncle Mat, who championed her before the marriage came off. Once she said to me, "Poor Mat Reilly was a noble man to the heart's core." So write to her often.'

Martin promised and a rather sad silence fell between them. They had come out of doors and James stopped, looking across the fields, at Muire's House, at the trees budding now above their seats; he listened to the weir. 'It's nice here, isn't it? I never thought I'd find myself in the English army. But now that all the best of England is fighting for the decent and right thing, they'll begin to see that they ought to be on our side here in Ireland. Yes, I think everything is going to be different, I think it's going to be a better world in all sorts of ways: I think Ireland and England are going to be friends at last; real friends, and together we could show the world.'

'I know, oh, I know! All at Keelard are quite ready to accept Home Rule now. Isn't it wonderful to think that we are going to do what Grattan wanted—the King, Lords and Commons of Ireland; and to be real friends with England.'

'Yes, but it isn't only Ireland and England. The whole world is going to be a better place, Martin.'

'I wish I could go and fight too. I wish I was older.'

'No. Just keep on at your schooling. And don't grumble later at having been kept a schoolboy, with your knuckles rapped for you. I wish now that . . .' He looked around, and said for the second time, 'It's nice here,' and then: 'You'd never think there was a war going on over there. . . .' He nodded towards the east.

Martin took him and showed him the great hall. Once James said awkwardly, 'I'm pretty good at Spanish now,' and Martin remembered that in the old days of James's dignified, unschoolmastered studies of American Business Books he had also done Spanish with the old man who lived in a caravan and said he was a relation of King Alfonso.

The term ended. The Easter vacation came and went. Three weeks with Mr. Peters and his sister in Kingstown did not seem to have added anything in the least memorable to life. When he returned to Dunslane, at the beginning of the summer, Martin found a somewhat changed Norman, one that refused to stretch out his hand in the darkness between their beds at night, who condemned demonstrations of affection as 'babyish', and who seemed to feel that it was time for both him and Martin to move elsewhere now that Dunslane had become such a different place under the new regime.

'It's not really Dunslane any longer, Martin. Will you never face reality? Sodalities, Addresses, Irish Conversation Groups— ach! Being sent to someone else to be slogged instead of going

properly for it to Long Dick . . .' Norman's face set half grimly,
half petulantly, and he had never before been petulant. 'How can
you call it the same place? The colours changed, priests all over the
place now, yards of Apologetics, everything different. I'd sooner
go now, Martin, than sit here watching them go on with their
stuff.' Out of the darkish light, his voice came with much of the
coaxing, dimpling Norman in it. 'If we went now, we'd always be
able to call ourselves Dunslane boys properly. It'd be Long Dick
and Ned Connolly and plain nice chaps like Great Mars, and no
swank and aping of bigger schools.

'Ah, don't "but". You always "but" about things. To put it at
its smallest, you don't want to feel ashamed for Dunslane because
its heads are such silly asses.'

'I don't want to leave it, that's all.'

Whereupon Norman with an angry gesture, said, 'You will
never face facts—never!' and walked irritably away.

After this conversation they were sundered still more, although
they went everywhere side by side and still Norman seemed to
find Martin a shelter from other people. Occasionally the old
intimacy would link them; as on one night during an absence of
the Dean, who was away for the day, and also of Father Mac-
Taggarty, who was attending a Conference on Education in
Dublin, Norman suddenly said in a low voice as they sat together
in the Refectory, how good it was to know that for once the Dean's
study overhead was empty and that therefore they could imagine
that something of Long Dick might tonight be hovering about the
familiar room.

When, later, rain drove the school in from the evening fields,
Martin played billiards in the play-hall, then read in the library,
knowingly pulling a book from behind all that swinging glass
which once had seemed so grand. He went to his old shiny place
beside Norman in the study-hall, relieved to think that tonight
there could be no private lesson with Father MacTaggarty. But,
not long before bedtime, the message came that Father Mac-
Taggarty had just returned and would take his lesson.

Up at the familiar door, Martin, glancing towards the Oratory,
saw the red sanctuary lamp burning before the Tabernacle, and
he went in and knelt in his place. Except for the starlight and the
steady glow of the sanctuary lamp, there was no light and, on the
walls, the garments of Jesus and His mother gleamed pallidly.

Below him he could hear occasional sounds in the study-hall; a distant cart ceased to rumble, somewhere a dog stopped barking and the sounds of the trees mingled with those of the weir.

He prayed that the month now between him and Aunt Kathleen, Sally and Peggy might go quickly, he prayed for Long Dick, for James Edward, for Mr. McKenzie, Ned Connolly, Great Mars and Harry Vincent, for all whom he knew at the war; he prayed that Norman might again become 'the same friend as before', the Norman who had sworn to discover himself always in Martin and to delight in the discovery.

Father MacTaggarty was seated before a small fire with a magazine across his knees and the topcoat with the furry collar across a chair. The Dublin evening paper was beside him which made Martin think of a crowded railway carriage and the lights of the city flashing past.

'Ah, Martin. I did not want you to lose your lesson even though it is so late. No, come here to this hassock.' He seemed eager, not like himself, anxious for company and talk, and he almost looked 'nice', Martin thought. 'Such a queer day,' he began excitedly. 'The way I ran into one old acquaintance after another whom I had not seen for years. . . .' Suddenly he pulled himself together and with rare curtness said: 'Come. Let us start.'

Perturbed by the curtness, Martin said, 'I haven't it all prepared, Father'—he had not as much as one line prepared.

Father MacTaggarty sharply said, 'I sometimes think that you may possibly idle at times,' and Martin began to translate without hope, thinking that he had relied once too often on the mutual politeness system and that he might now prepare to face Father Callaghan's room. But when he found that mistakes and evasions appeared to be unnoticed, he settled down to the exciting task of wriggling through a lesson in complete ignorance of it.

Hurriedly getting 'the smell of the context', he schemed up what he called 'a very *free* rendering, Father, a sort of literary one —a bit ambitious, you know'. Father MacTaggarty loved that kind of talk from a pupil, but every time Martin or the girls had tried it on Miss Clare, she had reacted strongly against the treatment. He was enjoying the risk of this game when he glanced up and saw Father MacTaggarty's eyes staring at him with a look that was travelling upwards along him slowly towards his face. The eyes looked hastily away and Father MacTaggarty, lighting a cigarette, began to talk of his day and of the city, of praise he had received for his paper at the Conference, and of the war news—with a few ironic remarks about 'the gallant Allies'.

'But there,' he said, stretching himself almost luxuriously, 'I know you're a great Redmondite and all for the Allies, like the Dean, and I've had such a wonderful queer day, that I can almost feel well disposed even to old Britannia.' Again and again, his talk came back to the old school acquaintance who had been so surprisingly excited by the meeting and who had brought him to luncheon in his comfortable home with a young wife and three children. 'We had scarcely known one another even at school. Yet he seemed quite delighted. Said it was years since he had met anyone from those days.' Father MacTaggarty continued to talk repeatedly of this encounter until the cigarette went out in his hand.

Along the corridors the school rumbled past towards the Oratory. They would all be in there now, his place empty beside Norman. He was hoping that Father MacTaggarty would talk the lesson away, when Willy came in with a tray of tea and toast which he put beside Father MacTaggarty.

'Thanks, Willy. You may go to bed now. Good night, Willy.'

'Good night, Father.' Willy had never seemed to get a day older since the afternoon when Martin had first seen him down below in the Refectory.

The rumbling movement came from the Oratory, broke into lesser rumbles, some going upstairs, others away to Muire's House. Now Norman would be looking at his bed upstairs and wondering why he was being kept so late, wondering if he was in for trouble.

Father MacTaggarty sat back, not saying a word now, and the silence of night crept over the whole school. Out of the silence, there came a little tap at the door and Martin started to his feet, frightened by that little sound coming into the silent room.

'It's all right,' Father MacTaggarty said in a low voice and put a hand on Martin's shoulder. He walked to the door and went out. Someone's voice whispered outside and Father Mac-Taggarty answered. 'No, turn it off as you go down.'

'Yes, Father. Good night, Father.'

Father MacTaggarty came back to the fireplace, put his arm

round Martin's shoulder and stood looking down at the glow of
the dying fire. Peeping timidly sideways, Martin saw the beginnings of the reddish hairs which streaked across the baldness
and on the big cheeks he saw flakes of skin showing powdery.
He looked down at the fire and waited for the Joint-Dean to say
or do something.

Suddenly the light went out, instantaneously, blackly, and
Martin jumped. With a soothing 'Hush!' Father MacTaggarty
steadied him with his arm, pressed him, held him close. 'You're
as quivery as a girl. Did anyone ever tell you that?'

Silence now and Martin wondered if he had really heard words
coming from the darkness where Father MacTaggarty's nostrils
were breathing strongly. He peeped across the ridge of the arm
along his shoulder and, in the upward red glow from the fire, he
saw that the priest's lips were strangely parted as he stared down
into the upward light. Martin was a little frightened by the fixity
of that stare, the noisy breathing and the tightness of the arm
around him. He was trembling and was ashamed of the trembling,
thought too that he ought to stop it, that it might appear rude to
a priest.

He made to withdraw apologetically from the arm but the arm,
shifting in the dimness, held him and he was being drawn closer
to the black wall of Father MacTaggarty's body. He tried to put
a hesitating hand between himself and the pressing body, but he
could not push, because he was held in an embrace which bent
him back and the black shape was hooked above and around him,
his head held back in the crook of an elbow, his eyes seeking
explanation in the vague shape of a white face which was bending
down to his, while a hand in the dimness, like the hand of a third
person, pressed his waist and thigh. Suddenly, just before he was
kissed, he understood.

Had he really heard that voice fluttering through his mouth to
his head? 'There's something about you, you're often plain, very,
but there's something about you.' Had he really heard that?
'And your eyes sometimes.'

The hand was touching his neck now, strokingly, sickeningly;
the kissing crushed his lips, stopped all air.

And then, suddenly, the arms released him and he turned towards where the door ought to be. He caught his feet in a rug,
splayed his hands out before him, and at last he had the door

open and there all the time were the big windows and the stars
above the weir.

He stopped and looked back. Dimly outlined before the red
glow, the priest's figure stood motionless. He could not leave like
this, something must be done or something said. 'Good night,'
he said at last. No answer came from the black figure. He spoke
again, trying to add 'Father' to it this time. The deep voice
answered, blurred, wavering, and what it said he never knew.

He went up to the dormitory and undressed, listening fearfully
to the breathing which rose and fell along the white beds. The
Joint-Dean of Dunslane! A priest!

The thought that he was the only boy in the history of the
Church to whom this had happened panicked through him until
his spirit sought discharge in sounds which he stifled with his
handkerchief. Groping for Aunt Mary's torch, now a battered
old thing, he cautiously brought the light on to Norman and saw
despairingly the clenched hands, the little dampness around the
roots of the tumbled fair hair. Norman, why are you so sound
asleep?

Better leave him asleep. He could never be told. No one could
ever be told. A priest! The Joint-Dean of Dunslane!

He sat on his bed and stared through the grey light from the
night outside. That was the way a man would kiss a girl, he knew
it now as if he had always known it. And not the easy, harmless
'terrible' way of poor Tommy Fagan's 'sins at dances', he knew
that also now.

Was there really hidden somewhere in him something of a girl,
secretly, for only some to see? Gertrude had often said it with
delight. But it was 'your eyes sometimes' which those whispers
had said in the darkness. And suddenly he thought of his Aunt
Mary's, 'Well, they always said I had a small touch of a boy,
Martin.' 'And they say I've a small touch of a girl.' 'Well, so you
have, thank God!'

Sitting on the end of his bed, reluctant to lie down beneath the
imprisoning bedclothes, he looked diagonally down towards the
weir and thought with longing of that hour when the night had
struck against his legs as he came up along that same direction
from the river with his new and overawingly 'different' Aunt
Kathleen beside him. She was four weeks away. But anyway he
could not tell her; she a Protestant.

He tiptoed carefully to the door, went down to the door of the Oratory, hesitated, then sped without a sound down the next flight to the hall. Slipping into the Refectory, he stood beneath the picture of the Blessed Virgin and joined his hands with care and order. 'Mary, Mother Most Admirable, pray for me; I can't pray.' He peered up into the shadow, trying to see the picture, but could see nothing. Was she up there at all? Could they have moved the picture for their Sodality this very night of all nights? He fetched a chair, climbed up and felt the picture.

He flitted up the stairs but at the Dean's landing he halted stiffly—a bar of light was now coming from under the Dean's door, a lamp had been lit in there. He had ever been among the most daring and skilful in skipping across the territory by that door, when bent on a forbidden journey, but now he faltered. Crouching there, he heard a soft, sighing sound. It was the sound of steps along a carpet, softly soughing up and down, up and down. The unchanging measure of those steps, up and down, up and down, in there behind that door once so familiar and friendly, drove his fear into reckless panic. He fled past and up to the dormitory.

He lay tautly for a long time, listening to the weir. Towards morning, with a weight in his chest, he slept.

5

A t t h e altar the acolyte's hand already held the bell, already
Father MacTaggarty was bending over the Host. So he was about
to say it then?—*Hoc est enim Corpus Meum*, This is My Body.
Martin bent his head. One must distinguish the man from his
office; what the man did could not touch the priest. Once a
priest a priest for ever according to the Order of Melchizedek.

Father MacTaggarty's hands held up the Host. Martin said
the worn adoration, 'My Lord and My God.' Those hands held
up the chalice. *Hic est enim calix* . . . the chalice of My Blood, of
the new and eternal Testament, the Mystery of Faith, which shall
be shed for you and for many unto the remission of sins.

The summer morning was cool and sweet in the Oratory, cool
and bright along the clean pews, sweet on the cool linen of the
altar, on the still flowers.

He kept away from Norman. He stood under trees by himself
and looked mindlessly about him, postponing a task he must do—
to get his books from that room where he had left them last night,
forgotten in his stumbling for the door.

Before trying to get the books, he went to Matron seeking
something for his headache which was nearly as bad as in his
Faithful Brothers days. Looking knowingly at him, she said:
'Well, I know you've sometimes run a little temperature for
nothing, me lad, but all the same I'm going to take it now. I don't
like the look of you this morning.'

His temperature was down, not up. 'Well, isn't that just like
the contrary young divil you are!' But, while her tongue chivvied
him, her eyes were studying him.

'Please don't send me to bed. I tell you I'll get really sick if you
put me to bed.'

'And just the very lad that might, too! All right, I'll let you

stay up till the doctor shows up.' She gave him a powder, told
him that it had been relieving headaches for years, got him to tie
some parcels for her, casually put him down to a cup of fragrant
tea, chit-chatted and chivvied him, then sent him away, and he
thought that the headache was better when he left her.

Then he scouted about the stairs, watching for a chance to get
his books without meeting Father MacTaggarty. The Dean himself, who was due back this morning, had not yet returned. His
scouting showed that the familiar door was ajar, it would take
only a few moments to skip up there, get the books and be gone.
But he wavered about the stairs, shrinking at every sound, many
of them imaginary. Finally, he gave it up and, when Lennie
Bourke's Latin class came towards mid-day, he shared Norman's
books in the small room where Lennie sat recovering his breath
after the exercise of walking half the avenue from where he had
pushed his bicycle into the hedge.

Yesterday, Norman and Martin had had the copy of Virgil
on the river, and now the picture of Pallas Athene, helmeted and
wise, gave forth the ripple of running water, the smell of sun on
the page drawing forth the essence of a schoolroom desk. Looking
through the window, he saw 'The Duchess' himself billowing
across from the Bigger House, Martin's books under his arm.

He billowed in, the little head giving the nodding rise and fall.
As he entered every face went serious and the prompting stopped.
Because of Lennie's slight deafness, whispered prompting was
used with discretion in his classes. But, just because of his deafness, boys had an unwritten law that in oral work 'an extra
decent' amount of work must be done for Mr. Bourke.

'The Duchess' swept in. 'Your books, Martin. The first thing
I find when I walk into my study is a pile of books littering a
corner.' And at the thought of the untidy sight in his neat room
from which Long Dick's untidy comforts had been banished, he
became plainly irritated and said: 'They might quite easily have
scratched my . . . Well, no matter, but this carelessness must
cease.'

With a bow to Mr. Bourke, he swirled towards the door and the
class began to breathe again. But the boy who had been constru-
ing was silent, waiting for a prompt when the Dean would have
gone. The Dean looked across to him humming and hawing over
the test, and said, 'Well, continue, Tommy.'

Lennie looked up sharply, then said quietly, 'Go on, Tommy.'
But the boy was foundered. At the corner of the Dean's mouth
a little smile showed understanding of the situation. 'I see,
Tommy. You will go to Father Callaghan's room after lunch.'

He spoke in a low voice and at first it was not certain that
Lennie had heard one of his class sentenced to punishment over
his head. But he must have heard something, because a blush
deepened in his cheek, he said, 'You may stop, Tommy.' His
eyes sought round the class for a boy who could put up a first-
class performance. 'Norman.'

Into the tense air came Norman's light, unaggressive voice
translating, steadily and certainly, and the class relaxed.

But the Dean had moved over to stand directly behind the
master's chair. Lennie looked around at him, fretfully, uncomfortably, but 'The Duchess' carefully looked over Lennie's head.
Lennie looked down again. It was the boys, not the master, who
first understood what the Dean was doing to one of his own
former teachers. He was waiting to show that Lennie's deafness
and the whispered promptings needed the rebuke of 'efficient'
younger ears like his own. All waited for the moment when
generous, sensible Lennie would see the thing. At long last he saw
it. When his face began to go white, every boy bent his head and
looked down at his desk. They heard him say: 'That will do, boys.
Write the analysis of it.' Rising without a look at the Dean, he
went to the window and with his hands holding the window-ledge
hard, he stared out at the sunlit squares and the robin puffing his
belly in the trees.

In the dreadful silence the boys' pens scratched. The Dean
flushed, bit his lip. He gave a glance towards Lennie's back, and
said, 'Er . . . Mr. Bourke . . .' But Lennie made no answer, kept
his back turned to the room and the Dean with compressed lips
swirled from the room. All the time until the bell rang Lennie
stood staring out through the window. Then he pulled the gown
up on his broad shoulders and turned about. They held the door
open for him as usual, but today everyone wanted to have a hand
in holding it. 'Mind the step, sir,' they said, for there were two
wooden steps down to the hall and for more years than anyone
knew Lennie had been inclined to slip on the bottom step where
it was worn into a groove by his own feet and the feet of boys and
masters before him.

'Would you like me to carry your books, sir?'

'Would you like your paper from your raincoat, sir?'

'Be careful where you sit today, sir. Some of the seats were painted yesterday.'

He stopped at the foot of the little steps, and looked back at their hurt faces crowding the narrow door. 'Good boys,' he muttered. 'Always, good decent boys.' Then he made his way slowly across to the Bigger House and up towards the Dean's room, and after lunch it was learnt that he had resigned.

Before the week was out, Jimmy Curran also resigned, whether because of his colleague Lennie or because of his own dissatisfactions none knew. It was said that on his way down from the Dean he was seen wearing some bright thing pinned to his torn gown, and boys confidently asserted that the bright thing was a bow made in the old, inartistic colours banished for being the same as the colours of a Protestant school.

By then, Martin had decided not to post the letters he had already written to his Aunt Eileen and Aunt Kathleen, begging not to be sent back to Dunslane. He would wait until he saw Aunt Kathleen. Soon, soon he would see her.

The last boy separating him from the moment of Confession came from the vestry. Time had come on top of him with his problem still unsolved. Why should he confess it? It was Father MacTaggarty's sin, not his. But he did not feel sinless.

In the tiny vestry with its familiar freshness he knelt on the prie-dieu. 'Bless me, Father, for I have sinned.'

Only one priest had visited the school to hear Confession this evening and he was in a hurry since he had twice as much to do as usual. None would come this night week because the examinations would be over then and most of the boys would have gone home; it was his last Confession in Dunslane.

'. . . *mea culpa, mea culpa, mea maxima culpa* . . . through my most grievous fault.' He always said the Confiteor in Latin. The priest's body slanted broadly down to his feet on the box stool and his boots were broad and dusty, not richly shining as Father MacTaggarty's had been in the glow of the dying fire.

'Well, well, my child?'

It was not his sin, he would not tell, he would forget it. He said that he had taken God's name in vain, that he had been tempted by 'bad thoughts' and 'bad images', that he had wished for another boy to fall and hurt himself. He said that he had been inattentive at Mass, he had fallen into the sin of anger. He paused.

'Well, my child, anything else?' The tired priest turned his splotched face towards him impatiently.

'Yes, Father, there is something else.'

'Well, come, come—what is it?'

'One night . . . one night I did not pray for the departed ones of my house.'

The priest looked sharply at him. 'Do you mean you forgot to pray for your dead relatives?'

'Yes, Father,' said Martin, whose way of putting it had come to him from his grandfather praying in Lullacreen.

'Well, you should always remember the dead, you know. Anything else, my child?'

'Yes, Father. It was one night when I did not say any prayers at all.'

Now! To receive Absolution without Full Confession was a heinous sin. His sin? My sin?

The priest stirred. 'Anything else, my child?'

'No, Father.'

The priest stirred quickly. 'Say three Hail Marys for your penance. Tell God how sorry . . .'

Above his head he heard the murmurs of the priest preparing for the Absolution, he heard his own murmurs and the murmur of the weir. 'Oh, my God, I am heartily sorry for having offended Thee and . . .' But a flame of resentment leaped up in him even as he prayed. Why should God have taken Long Dick away? Why did Father MacTaggarty's train arrive on time that night? Trains often were delayed, sometimes even they had accidents that killed people; but Father MacTaggarty's train must arrive on time. Why was there war? Why were Faithful Brothers allowed to have schools? Why . . . why . . . why . . . ah, God, why should Aunt Mary have died?

He heard the Absolution begin, saw the priest's arm move in the healing sign of the Cross. He rose and, with '*Ego te absolvo* . . .' ringing in his head, he went for the first time from Confession without peace. If he told anyone, it would be Aunt Kathleen— only her. Three weeks would pass, he could wait three weeks.

Yes, she was a Protestant. Perhaps all the better, all the better.

On his plate at tea-time there was a letter from her. She confirmed the arrangement that he was to stay with the Peters while doing an Institute examination in Dublin, after the more important intermediate examinations were over, but after that fortnight, instead of going to her, he must spend at least a month in Glenkilly, and only then would she know whether she and the girls would be coming to Ireland.

He came sweating out of his Glenkilly dream, in which Uncle John urged him to join the Sodality and not to tell things secretly to Gertrude Jamieson, as she was a Protestant. He savoured the relief to know it to have been only a dream, and his mind flowed back to the dream's unsubstantial beginning, to the unknown, nameless girl.

It was the cold hour before the dawn. He turned on Aunt Mary's torch and, with relief, saw Norman curled on his side, his hands beneath his chin. Tomorrow they would go. They had waited over the week-end after the school break-up to take one remaining special examination paper. The only others in the dormitory, two tiny boys, were fast asleep. Elsewhere in other dormitories, some boys, mostly final year, lingered on, working for other examinations or posts.

Father MacTaggarty, over in his room, was he perhaps awake too and thinking? To sit up and think of Father MacTaggarty's thinking—to lie down and dream? He got up, dressed, pinned a note to Norman's pillow, then tiptoed down the stairs.

At the rain-swollen window which Norman and he could always open from inside or outside, he climbed out into the dewy coolness before the dawn. His own bicycle was punctured and he took the first one to hand, which belonged to Mullins.

Dawn was stretching thin fingers of light over the land as he went swiftly towards Rodesbridge. Pausing on the bridge, he thought with longing of the day when Norman and he on Jimmy Curran's message had leaned arm-in-arm across the parapet eating Long Dick's apples. Everything looked the same as on that day: the reeds, the water-hens, the distant tops of the sawmills. Down there, a barge was halted, its two horses browsing near to the trees. Who, cheering Mr. Redmond that day in Ballow from the window of the Ladies' Tea Room, could have foreseen that a war would come and everyone go away?

At the village, where all still slept, he halted beyond the huge police barracks and hammered on the door of the little shop-cum-post-office. The old woman who kept it was very cross when at last she put her tousled head out of a window and saw a school-boy leaning against a bicycle in the dawn and shouting up to her that he wanted to send a telegram.

'Well, write it out and lave it on the window-sill with the money and I'll send it bime-by when I've dressed and fed the hens. Has someone died on ye that ye want to send a telegram?'

'Oh, no!'

'Ah, well then, sure there's no hurry.'

He wrote out his telegram to Aunt Kathleen. *Must see you. Cannot return Dunslane. Something else also. Please come Kingstown.* Even that much would make an appreciable hole in his existent pocket-money but he spent a few more pennies on: *Love to all. Martin.*

He was speeding back towards the bridge, when he was nearly thrown from his bicycle by a girl who rushed out from beside a cottage, wearing a sack and shouting at him. Slithering into the ditch, he looked angrily at her. She was plump, red-headed and sweating. Her legs, bare in unlaced hobnailed boots, and her arms, bare to the strong biceps, were greasy with a sticky, greyish slime.

'Ah, God,' she panted, 'could you ever give me a hand? There's me uncle in bed with his broken leg, me aunt's rale delicate and me cousins are only bits of childer. The bloody red cow's gone and started to calve.'

'But what do you want me to do? When did she . . .'

'When! It's maybe this instant she'll be dropping it dead on the ground. Couldn't you help me to pull?'

'Veronica Eily!' a fragile woman said severely from the gate. 'Mind yer manners, miss! What would they be knowing over at the college about pulling a calf!'

'Certainly I know!' said Martin contentiously. 'But you shouldn't pull unless the calf is getting locked and there is no vet or good cowman. My uncles would be furious to hear of people backing and hauling and . . .'

'Ah, here—come on,' shouted Veronica Eily and he followed her, her legs bare to the kilted sacking all glistening with slime. Choking down his disgust, he went into the dark, hot shed where the cow stood with sacks spread about her. Already part of the forelegs could be perceived and in spite of his protests Veronica Eily rooted in with a rope to them, while he stripped off jacket and shirt. 'I tell you it's wrong to start pulling without necessity. Now firstly, you should . . .'

Veronica Eily gave a whoop and clutched the rope. 'Come on. She's working.'

'Well, it's your cow and your calf, so if you want pulling I'll give you pulling. But all my uncles . . .'

'Lean on it. She's working.'

They pulled, sweating and slithering along the floor littered with droppings and urine, while the cow straddled lazily, scarcely squeezing the calf from her.

Then they paused, wiping the sweat from them and staring in at the blind face which looked out towards the world. The cow began to rampage a little and they pulled, but that mask of a face remained motionless, looking out unseeingly through its opening into the world. The cow tried to go down on her knees. They were dizzy, drunk with the heat and effort, as they swayed with dirt splattering about them.

'She's coming! She's coming!'

'This is no way to treat a calving cow. You never even washed your hands before pawing in with that rope.'

Swivelling and twisting, the blind face moved and the head was screwed out in a beautiful movement. 'Stop pulling!' Flinging her aside, rope and all, he received into his arms the long weak body as it came curving out faster and faster. It gained speed against his restraining push, its oiled flanks shooting eagerly through the opening to the world. As they laid the shining body down on the sacks the cow gave a roar. Only then did they hear steps clattering along the yard and a figure shut off the oblong of light and air at the door. 'You're just in time to be too late, Jummy Burrin. Sure, we might as well have left you snoring.' The man came in apologetically—a little resentful because the calf had been safely delivered without his help.

A small boy was left to watch the cow while she licked the beastings and to call if she showed signs of injuring the calf.

They tried to make Martin stay for food but he knew that he might now arrive at Dunslane too late to avoid discovery, and although discipline was relaxed during these last few days, he feared that he would have to suffer for his serious offence. A basin of warm water was brought to the cottage door and he washed quickly.

Travelling back along the road towards Dunslane, he still saw the calf staring blindly out at the world from the womb and he could not shake off the mystery of that blind life which he had released into the world to start its breathing there. Two breaths gone into the past, never to be breathed again. Two more breaths, four breaths, thirty breaths! Even in the moments when he had been lowering its weak body to the sacks, the calf had been already travelling into the eternal Future which one day would be the dead Eternity of the Past. In the empty study-hall, later in the morning, alone, seated at his desk, he looked into the unfathomable mystery, saw mortality as a personal fate. He shivered, and the spiritual shiver set up the shivering of the feverish cold which he suspected he might be getting. From far away, through the flood sounds of the weir, he heard the smack of someone's bat dealing with Norman's leg-break. Norman, too, must die one day, take the last of all the breaths of his life.

He had not restored Mullins's bicycle to its place in the shed because to his astonishment when he got back he found that some-one during his absence had locked the door of the bicycle-house and he therefore had to leave the bicycle outside the door. Not only was everyone up, but the Mass was over and he had met the little group of boys coming down to breakfast, followed by the Dean counting the heads—the two prefects had gone home. Fortunately the Dean had not asked if everybody had been at Mass and prayers.

He continued to overlook telling Mullins about the bicycle until the late afternoon, when Norman, he and the two tiny boys were returning from a hunt for wild strawberries. Coming at a run into the yard, they saw Father MacTaggarty speaking to Mullins who fidgeted sullenly in front of the group of final-year remnants.

'Come now, Paddy. You're surely not suggesting that some other boy used your bicycle today and is lying low about it?'

'I'm suggesting nothing, Father.' Mullins was a huge person now, as big as Father MacTaggarty himself, and very proud of his size. To Martin, the lip, the eyes, seemed just as stupid as on the far-off morning in the dormitory when Mullins, wakened by

himself and McNally, had laboriously thought of ways to disturb
Long Dick in order to annoy Norman and Martin.

There were dark streakings around Father MacTaggarty's
eyes and his voice was tired and patient. 'It must be either one or
the other, Paddy. It was used this morning that is certain. The
Dean, knowing that any boy tempted out by these bright mornings would almost certainly take a bicycle, has been slipping
down each morning just before Mass to lock the bicycle-house.
Thus, any bicycle out would be discovered.'

Norman muttered in a low voice: 'The detective! What is
Dunslane coming to!' But Father MacTaggarty did not hear, or
perhaps heard and ignored. In his tired, expressionless face, the
boys could not read whether or not he disapproved the trap.

Martin stepped forward. 'I was out on that bicycle, Father
MacTaggarty.'

The deep-set eyes looked with an inner reproach at Martin,
as if the priest resented this confrontation. The group of boys
drew closer. Martin knew that his chance of escaping punishment had now vanished because questions would reveal that he
had not even returned in time for Mass, but what he feared most
was that Father MacTaggarty would insist on knowing where
he had gone and what he had been doing on that morning jaunt.

Father MacTaggarty said in a low, almost gentle voice, 'Did
you do any mischief while out, anything wrong apart from the
grave wrongness of going out like that?'

'No, Father MacTaggarty.'

'Very good. If the Dean inquires further, I shall tell him that,'
and he turned away, while all stared in surprise at the disappearing back.

There came a tug at Martin's arm, and Mullins, red and
embarrassed, drew him aside. 'Here,' he began roughly, 'if Mac-
Tagg can't stall off "The Duchess", you'll be asked if you were
back for Mass.'

Martin nodded; Mullins pawed the ground with a foot.

'He'll have you slogged for that.'

Martin nodded. Mullins scraped again with his foot. 'Here, I
want to say something.' He struggled to get it out. 'It was decent
to step out about that bike. I mean we were always—well, not
friendly.'

'Anyone would have had to do the same.'

'Begod, I'm none too sure that Sly McNally or Fox O'Mahoney would have done it, and they're supposed to be friends of mine.' He grew redder. 'You remember the day I said something about ivy, and about a dead aunt, long ago. And Conroy slated me about it. He was quite right, I'm sorry!'

Martin's hand went out impulsively. 'It's all right. Maybe it was partly my fault.'

Shaking hands, Mullins summed up. 'Of course, you read a lot, maybe that's what's wrong, eh?' Now that he had made his hang-dog apology, his manner changed back to the new air of self-assurance and briskness which had grown upon him in recent times and which he called 'Business smartness'. 'Well, you poor devil, you have still two years of school ahead of you?'

'Yes. What are you going to do now you've finished?'

'First thing, I'm going to have a great month somewhere. Bray maybe. Up the prom, smoking all day and clicking with the bits of stuff! Then my old chap's putting a lot of money into an Irish insurance company and there'll be a fat little job there for me. When you're a professor or a poet or something, come to me— I'll get you good terms for an all-round policy—here, wait!' and producing a neatly kept notebook he wrote: *M. M. Reilly. Age next birthday—seventeen. A Dunslane contact*, and, explanatorily to Martin: 'Just to memo you about a policy in five or six years' time.' And very efficiently he snapped the notebook shut.

'And the war? You're not bothering . . . ?'

'What's the war got to do with me?' said Mullins in surprise. 'That's for England and Germany to fight out between them— the pair of robbers. Well, I mayn't see you in the morning. So, goodbye now in case.'

'Goodbye. And good luck, anyway, Mullins.'

'Same to you. You're a queer divil and damn' irritating, but I see that maybe you're not a bad bastard really.'

Martin ran after Norman. 'Do you know, Norman, even the worst people have good points.'

Norman looked sideways. 'Corbin of Ballow?' he said dryly and Martin was silent.

He told Norman about Mullins and Norman sniffed.

'So he discovered that much grace? He'd never have done even that had it not been for Seamus Conroy, I bet. He's a common fellow.'

'Look here, Norman, I wonder if Conroy is right, if you really are riddled with Anglo-Saxon middle-class snobbery, as he says.'

Norman stopped. 'I thought you always understood,' he said, 'this has nothing to do with money or a person's job or what his father is or was or any of those things—*that's* the rotted Anglo-Saxon stuff, and you know it damn' well. It's just what a person is *himself*. And I hate, absolutely loathe, coarse or common people. And that's what Mullins is. The way you've changed. You are just being a cod now. Just being high and mighty . . . impartial, all of a sudden, merely because Mullins has apologized after two or three years.'

'Oh, well,' said Martin testily. 'Possibly Mullins isn't a bad bastard really.' And at Norman's look of surprise and sudden distaste, he added: 'Now, don't look like that. It's really a quotation.'

'From where? It doesn't sound much like a quotation. It sounds just like Mullins himself!'

'Well, it is. It's a quotation from him.' He laughed because he had fooled Norman and justified the word 'quotation'. 'He said I wasn't a bad bastard really.'

For an instant, Norman's eyes flickered with a highly distressed look and he turned his face away to hide that fugitive embarrassment. But the original look had been involuntary, full in Martin's eyes, and it had instantly tugged deeply down into some one memory in him. It was of a winter evening at Keelard, when they had been reading *The Winter's Tale* with Miss Clare. Aunt Kathleen had joined them. She had taken Miss Clare's work-basket, and had pretended to hand Perdita's flowers from it.

> For you there's rosemary and rue; these keep
> Seeing and savour all the winter long.

Presently she came to the words:

> . . . and streaked gillyvors
> Which some call nature's bastards . . .

She had stopped and her eyes, full upon him, had widened with the same embarrassed look which had flickered just now into Norman's eyes. It had surprised him because she never minded much worse words in Shakespeare or the girls' Bible lessons. Now the whole incident came back to him.

Nature's bastards. Was he one of them himself? Had Norman discovered the secret from his mother in the Easter holidays and was that why his manner had been so different when he returned at the beginning of the summer term?

'You go on,' he said. 'I forgot something,' and he ran to the house, slinking around corners, fearful of looking into knowing eyes. He cowered at his desk in the study, wondering where to hide; he opened his dictionary to look at definitions, but could not bring himself to do so.

No wonder so many had been laughing up their sleeves at him all these years! The accumulated shame of those years overwhelmed him.

Had he been born a bastard with a special queer mark on him so that he might be the cause of a priest's sin? Something which had never happened until now in the history of the Church. Back in his old shiny place in the study-hall, he sat trying not to think, and there stole through him the thought, at once a hope and a fear, that perhaps other boys might share terrible secrets with priests. Instead of consoling him, the thought terrified him and he slunk out and ran towards the river. He broke all rules by pushing off unaccompanied in a boat and without permission. In a feverish anger, he insisted on rowing against the flood and did progress for a few yards against it but was so worn by the effort that he had to tie the boat up and lie exhausted. Wondering if he would bathe to cool himself, he looked down into the flood current and saw in it the wavering image of himself.

The water flowing over his own face down there wooed him to hide, to rest for ever. One of the boats was moored to a big weight lying on the bank. He fastened that boat to the others and dragged the weight towards a thicket where the subsoil of the bank had crumbled away, leaving a shelf of earth overhanging the water. All the warmth of the afternoon was held here in the odorous, close thicket. He fastened the rope around his waist and, seeing ivy on a tree, he tucked a piece of it in his waist-band.

Then he lay down, closed his eyes, and, with a stick, began to crumble the shelf of earth from around the great weight. He felt the earth giving and he worked more quickly with closed eyes. There came dimly to his ears the distant sounds of the bell, ringing not sharply, not quickly, but in a measured pattern of pauses and renewals. It was the Angelus and it would be Seumas Conroy who would be ringing it up there in the absence of the prefects. The call of the bell went over the fields and water, the melodious pattern flowed into his mind and with it the sin of what he had been about to do.

'. . . Hail, our Life, our Sweetness and our Hope. To Thee do we cry, poor banished children of Eve . . .'

For a few moments he lay still, unable to understand how he had come to be doing this dreadful thing. Opening his eyes he looked with shocked amazement at the rope coiling from himself to the weight. He reached to pull back the weight but, to his hazed vision, it seemed already to be sliding through the crumbling earth and he was afraid to touch it. He began to unfasten the rope from his waist. He had the rope almost off when he thought he saw the weight sinking; he made a grab at it and, with a moan of terror, rolled after it into the water. His hand, going out, clutched a rotten root which jutted out from the bank, and the weight, halted in its fall, dragged the loosened rope down around his loins with a painful jerk. The root was breaking away from the bank; he made a great straining effort, narrowed his loins and kicked. The weight shot from him and he himself shot upward with a bobbing rush, but at that moment the root came away and he was swept out into the flood.

The flood roar of the weir seemed almost beside him. He lunged up at a thin, overhanging branch, caught it and his legs went streaming down to the pull of the weir. He tried to shout but could only whisper; he was lost, the weak branch was giving way.

As hope died within him he saw Norman running towards him from upstream. In a matter of moments he had swung himself on to the stouter branch from which Martin's shoot sprang and leaning out had grabbed his wrist and was drawing him slowly to safety. Gradually he drew him into shallower water, and up on to the bank. Then they lay for a moment, side by side on the grass, exhausted.

Hardly a word was exchanged between them until Martin, having managed to slip back unobserved to school, had got a dry change of clothing and they had come out again into the sunlight.

Then Norman said: 'I got worried. I felt queer looking for you. What would I do without you, Martin?'

Martin longed to say, 'But since Easter you have been keeping me at arm's length.' But he did not say it.

'Norman, I want to ask you something. I must ask you now. What do you think . . . my mother and my father . . . ?'

Norman glanced towards him and his glance seemed to say, 'So that's the explanation.'

He waited a moment and then said: 'I think that possibly your mother and father may not have got married until maybe a short time before you were born. I think there was possibly a scandal about it at the time. I'm sure no one else we know knows; I only got the idea from something that Mother said one night.'

There was a note almost of relief in Martin's voice as he said: 'But that would be quite different, wouldn't it? I mean, a boy like that would not be . . . you know the word.'

'Quite different. And even if he were, it would make no difference to me.'

The summer sunset beams were almost horizontal along the land, and the light glistened on a faint, golden down now showing on Norman's cheeks. The flood was subsiding, but as the breeze was blowing up the river they could still hear fragments of the weir's sound. Looking not at Norman but away from him, Martin said: 'What happened this afternoon wasn't altogether an accident, Norman. I mean . . . at first . . .'

'I wondered. Somehow it seemed unlikely that anyone who knows the river bank as well as you could have slipped.'

It was their last evening meal at Dunslane. Aunt Kathleen had written to say that he need not return if he felt so strongly about it. They would discuss his next move when they met, early in the holidays.

Norman and Martin had supped late. The other boys had already eaten and gone out, so they had their meal alone together in the Refectory. Through all the years now, the Blessed Virgin's picture would be looking down at their places and they would not be there. Other boys would stand behind their chairs for Grace after Meat.

They went to say goodbye to Jimmy Curran whose light was shining up there among the trees. They crossed the deserted yard, under the two odorous trees, and went up the creaking stairs. They found him kneeling bewildered among books, cloth-

ing and piles of cuttings from the country newspapers, the accu-
mulation of years, far too much now for the old-fashioned boxes
which no doubt had been an adequate travelling outfit when
first he brought them here. They offered to help with the packing
but he said that only he himself could find a way through the
confusion. Looking down, they saw on top of one box a photograph of a girl smiling out at them over a fur-edged collar.
Blushing slightly at the thought that they might be uncovering
his secrets, they glanced at one another, then away, wondering
if this was the girl whom—people vaguely said—Jimmy had
nearly married years ago.

He was going to England. 'No France, no Italy for anyone just
now. Perhaps it is only fitting, seeing that there are so many
changes.'

'Do you remember, sir, telling us what you saw in the village
shop when you walked down into Italy? The Renaissance and
. . . Murphy's Starch from Ireland.'

He coloured and shot them a suspicious look. 'Er . . . yes, I may
have said "walking down into Italy". And I *did* see the starch.'

He opened the window, waited until his ears had picked up the
sound of the weir and then listened a while. He turned to them.
'Well, anyway, he'll be hard put to it to find brains next year
among pupils or staff.' Then, biting his lip, he said shamefacedly:
'No, I should not have said that. We must always wish Dunslane
well.'

'Do you remember Ned Connolly, sir, with Milton?'

'Of course I remember. Clever boy but indolent. He's out in
France tonight.' He looked out at the stars in the deep blue sky.
'In the trenches. We must remember that. It makes our own
troubles bearable.'

'I suppose you'll be getting an important post in some big
school now, sir?'

His face seemed to contract, he put his hands to the movement
of huddling his gown around him, then finding that he was not
wearing it, clasped his frail hands.

He gave a very superior sniff. 'A school post? H'm, more likely
university work for the future! No doubt it may have to be one
of the provincial places for the moment.' Sniff! Suddenly, the
corners of his mouth crumpled, he looked blackly ahead of him
and said to himself weakly, 'Perhaps London might remember

me and do something.' Then after a pause: 'Why should one
have to look to another country, not one's own? At the same time,
I ought also to want all empires to be beaten sufficiently to teach
them what it means to be worthy and helpless. But I can't wish
it because I need a rich England. It's a wretched world!'

Martin said timidly, 'I suppose London University would give
another big dinner for you like the one you told us about?'

He went quite white, then flushed, looking at them with bitter
suspicion and shame. As he studied their expressions his shamed
suspicion went, he averted his head and said in a shaky voice:
'You are good boys. Good and loyal and trusting.'

They told him: 'When we leave tomorrow, we're going to
wear our old caps. The old colours.'

He said 'Ah!' and, in a moment: 'Yes. That is in character. I
am glad.' He scribbled on a piece of paper, then said with great
loftiness, 'My movements are uncertain but this address will find
me for some time,' and with an attempt at a haughty sniff: 'Purely
temporary convenience, of course.' They saw on the paper: *Poste
Restante, Charing Cross Road, London.*

The trees were giving forth a smell to the night and from behind the handball court there came wafts of glees; the dozen big
boys, the two tiny boys, were down there singing and some of the
big ones probably smoking. They went away from the sounds
into the silent Muire's House and passed from one unlit classroom to another, looking at certain things and seats in the semi-
darkness.

When they came out they joined the circle of boys who
squatted beneath the trees, some faces glowing in the light of
cigarettes. They joined in the songs but not much in the talk
which was about medicine, jobs, the law, university scholarships,
'being a vet on the Curragh' and similar topics. Some were going
to do their priestly studies in Spain, others were going to the war,
but said little about it.

Dislikes and enmities were shrouded now. The ugly mind and
the quarrelsome spirit seemed to be as gently blurred as were the
bodies in the velvet night. When McNally, leaning forward on
one elbow to offer sweets around the circle, looked hesitantly
towards Norman and Martin, they put out their hands and
accepted the offered sweets from him. He was a tall, thin youth
now, and was going to the University in the autumn.

'Well, Seumas,' said someone to Conroy, 'I suppose you'll spend all your time running debates in the University and telling the Lord Mayor how to run Dublin?'

From the half-darkness Conroy's voice answered, 'I am going to spend my time preparing to be an efficient soldier in the next insurrection.'

They laughed. 'Insurrection! At Tib's Eve—eh?'

'All right,' said Conroy confidently. 'Wait and see.'

All laughed again. Someone complained that Martin and Norman had made no contribution to the concert. Both pleaded the excuse of breaking voices.

'Arrah, one little song won't hurt, man.'

Norman whispered, 'Sing "Down by the salley . . ."' He stopped as if he too had remembered the lines about grass on the weirs and had understood that Martin would not want to sing of that tonight.

From the darkness, Conroy's voice came. 'Something we all know, Martin. Something Irish.' There was friendship and confidence in the voice.

'I'll sing " '98" if you like.'

Everyone joined in the song, and the words went up through the sighing fretwork of the trees.

> 'Alas! that Might could vanquish Right.
> They fell and passed away.
> But true men, like you men,
> Are plenty here today.'

All sang it, boys for seminaries in Spain, for farms or city jobs, boys for trenches in Flanders, all sang it.

It ended and all looked sharply round, feeling someone's presence near to them. It was Father MacTaggarty, standing among the trees, motionless, listening to the last echo of their song.

He stepped forward and bent to the circle. 'Prayers now,' he said in a startlingly gentle voice, and without a look at the lighted cigarettes he went.

The prefects being absent, it was one of the boys destined for the Flanders trenches who read out the night prayers in the unlighted Oratory. The little group was clustered in the front of the Oratory, two pews being enough for them—strange to see the Oratory so empty, no one kneeling in his familiar place.

Magnificat anima mea Dominum. Et exultavit . . . and my Spirit hath rejoiced. Even more than in the magnificence of High Mass or Benediction Martin had always felt the unwavering power of his Church in quiet prayers like these at night, in the clear order of the nuns' private Mass before dawn.

In bed that night he watched Norman stand upon his bed and put out the light. He waited to hear him say good night. But, instead, a few moments later in the darkness, he heard a once familiar sound. It was the slight, signalling click of fingers. He put out his hand, it met Norman's and once more they shared pain to pain, seemed to be united, flesh to flesh and bone to bone, making one hand of their two hands in the darkness.

Next day they brought out their old caps and went to say good-bye to Matron, carrying with them a farewell gift: a handsome work-basket. She made no comment on the fact that they were this time taking away their cutlery, table silver, bed-linen and winter underclothes. She had bullied them, given them threats, nursed their colds, sometimes got them punished, sometimes got them out of punishment; she had sewn on buttons for them, joked with them and given them advice which had often proved useful. Now all they could do was to wring her hand, say, 'You were an absolute brick, Matron,' and hope that the grand work-basket would say all the rest.

Later that morning, in the train, in a compartment to themselves, he told Norman of the incident with Father MacTaggarty. Norman, his own tongue loosened by this burst of confidence on Martin's part, told of the sort of questions he had been asked in Confession at Easter. Martin could only say unbelievingly:

'He asked you about the fillies? Your own sisters! Thoughts from them? Norman, the fillies?'

'Yes. I couldn't even take their arms afterwards.'

'The priest asked you that?'

'Yes, everyone, everything . . . !'

'Do you think he might have been a bit . . . well, touched, queer in the head?'

'No. He was a young priest. Very young. Listen, Martin, *after* he had asked, it all seemed as if it could be true. I could see it all then. Everything became different, even ordinary things. I kept looking for things in everything. That's why I told you not to be sentimental when I came back at the beginning of the summer.'

'What are we going to do?'

'Pray, of course, but . . .'

'Gosh, the fillies!'

They sat staring at one another.

'Listen, Martin. Did you ever think—you're born and grow up and die. And if you have a son he simply does the same thing all over again. And for the temporary world in which we do that— *eternal* damnation or . . .'

'But you know the answer to that one.'

'Of course I do. Dash it, you're not answering in Apologetics examination now. Finite and infinite purposes, for example, won't seem much good to the birds if there's a hard frost next winter. Answers—always answers—perhaps anyone can give an answer to anything. Free Will, Pre-destination—oh, answers galore! I suppose prayer is the only thing. Pray, pray, pray and don't think. They're right there.'

Again they were silent, but suddenly Martin said: 'Long Dick! We'll go and see him, Norman. We'll try and go and see Long Dick in the holidays. He's still in barracks. . . . He'll put us up for a night maybe and we'll write to everybody from the Mess and they'll think we have joined up under age.'

'Gosh, of course—Long Dick. And he knows some of the trainers down there, so he'll surely have a few good tips and we'll make a few bob. This day fortnight, after your other exams, you come to stay at Tory Hill—we'll fix it then with Agnes.'

At Ballow they parted. Norman's train for Bencourt went first. As they waited for it Martin caught sight of a cheap reprint on the station bookstall.

'How much is this, please?'

'One-and-sixpence.'

He bought it and standing side by side they turned the pages of great names from far back. The book was a series of short biographies; the '98 men were there, and Parnell.

'They say you can't be a great man, Martin, unless you're a good man first.'

'Whatever else we believe in or don't, we'll always believe in Ireland, Norman.'

'Yes, always.'

'Look out, I think this is your train coming.'

They had just time to get Norman's luggage and his old bike into the train and Martin ran alongside while Norman leaned from the window. 'This day fortnight. In Kingstown or with us at Tory Hill. And then, if he hasn't been sent abroad, Long Dick.'

'And maybe Keelard! Aunt Kathleen's coming, she's coming!'

A porter was dragging at him.

'The fillies, Norman—my love. And your father.'

Their hands were broken now; the porter dragged him back. 'Begorra, you'd think it was your sweetheart going away.' The train puffing vigorously, rounded the bend, that old 'stop-at-every-pub' train that they knew so well. Martin waved his cap and Norman waved back. So the train carried him away, his fair hair blown by the breeze, his old Dunslane cap held up.

A telegram was awaiting him at the Peters'. Aunt Kathleen was coming at the end of the week. The next day a letter to Mr. Peters said that she was waiting a few days longer, since Mr. Vincent, who was expected on leave, could then come with her.

Miss Peters, disturbed by Martin's rather drawn appearance and the signs of a cold, sent him to bed. On Sunday evening he watched from bed the long plume of smoke as the mail-boat mounted the horizon, using its speed as its best defence against submarines. Tomorrow or the next day, the plume would be her signal!

On the third day he coaxed Miss Peters to let him up, and he sat on the terrace with Mr. Peters' racing-glasses, waiting until it would be time to be watching for her plume signal.

Perhaps Sally and Peggy would be with them? Perhaps they would all go down to Keelard, if only for a few days. The river, their boat, Dan Murphy's barge. He kept thinking of Sally out under the huntsman's moon with him the night of the dance for Miss Clare's wedding.

And Peggy! Dear sober-sides Peggy with her own forms of divilment obstinately carried out to their ending behind a smug smile of satisfaction. Uncle Brendan, so quiet, so patient, nodding his head to show that his silence did not mean lack of interest. Aunt Kathleen herself. He could not bear waiting; the thought of a possible submarine attack terrified him. But no, not even the

Germans, the bullies of Europe, would do such a thing as sink a passenger ship with Aunt Kathleen on board.

Mr. Peters came through the room behind him and put a hand on his shoulder. 'My boy . . .' He was breathing hard. There came a scurrying sound in the dim room and Mr. Peters whirled about. 'Go back, Elizabeth. I begged you to leave this to me.'

There was whispering out in the hall, the servants also whispering—most rare and strange, because Miss Peters did not permit her servants to whisper.

'My boy . . . be steady now and good. Mrs. Vincent . . . your aunt and Mr. Vincent . . .' All the lineaments of obstinate good living in his face were streaked and drawn 'I want you to be calm. You must prepare yourself for bad news.'

At long last, grey, unable to postpone the moment any longer, Mr. Peters told him. It was the Swift; Aunt Kathleen had taken it with her to England, she used it much in her war-work. He had been telephoning, sending telegrams, trying to get more information. As far as they knew the Swift had overturned, and then gone on fire. Two men, wounded soldiers from a nearby hospital, had tried to help, he gathered. Only one thing was clear and Martin must be brave, very brave! She was dead, both she and his uncle were dead.

Miss Peters was there now, saying, 'Try, oh try to think of it as something to bear for our dear Lord!'

'For pity's sake, Elizabeth! This is no time for your dear Lord!'

Mr. Peters was lying back in a chair—finished! It was all Miss Peters now. It was she who shepherded him back to the room upstairs and advised him to go to bed.

He saw her sitting on the side of his bed in the room she had made so nice for him. Once, nearly a year ago, she had said, 'If there were another boy, we could call it "the boys' room", that would be nice.'

He saw the harbour lights burning in the summer night, so blue, so warm; he saw the night boat go back to England, a moving shadow, its lights dimmed against submarines, using its speed to make safe the journey to England.

He woke and saw the dim harbour lights burning in the dawn, so cool, so uncertain. He got up, dressed, went out into the cool, slow dawn and began to walk quickly as he headed for the sea.

In the dim light of the lane a man was shouting up at a girl

who leaned from a window in her night-dress and called the man
foul names which Martin had thought were used only by the
coarsest of men; it was the first time in his life that he had ever
heard a woman using foul language and he had always thought
that a clean and fastidious tongue was a natural possession of all
women. But he had not time to be shocked now.

He leaped on to the sea-wall and ran along it until he came to
the turning into the back lane to the convent. The half-opened
door revealed the lay-sister's white face and wimple.

'I'm Martin Reilly, you remember. I had permission to come
to the nuns' Mass when I was here for my Easter holidays.
Reverend Mother Angela is a cousin of my aunt, Mrs. John
Reilly in Glenkilly.' He had remembered that this was Sunday
and he must go to Mass.

'Yes, I remember. You should have got the permission renewed. However, you may come in.'

As he went up the polished stairs, the black-and-white figures
rustled on their aloof coming and going. In the Oratory, warm
with the incense of many years, he watched each sequence of the
ordered service. Now and then the nuns' voices rose in the *Gloria*,
in the *Credo*, and the Gregorian chant was gentle yet plangent in
the quiet chapel.

The moment of Consecration came, he saw the young acolyte
prostrate along the altar steps, waiting to sound the bell of
Adoration. It seemed to Martin that his belly was falling away
from him, he was sliding over and heard disturbed, frightened
rustlings from the nuns. Then he pulled himself together; his lips
ceased trembling, but down his face there crept, one after the
other, a slow, involuntary succession of unrestrainable tears.

6

Slowly, half awakening, Martin heard the early working-
men's train for the city distantly puffing through the foggy
October dawn. The heavy air of the dormitory, charged with the
exhalations of fifty boys, carried the sound in waves. What was
that train doing in the fields of Dunslane? Or was it Keelard?
The questions wakened him fully from the amnesty of sleep; this
was Knockester, and though he had been there only a few weeks
he was already beginning to think that even the new regime at
Dunslane had a few points in its favour when compared with the
academic setting in which he now found himself.

The air of the place closed around him for another day and the
weight settled in his chest. Turning on his side and looking along
the beds jammed head to foot in double rows, he saw the prefect
standing down there as he had stood every morning and every
night, silent, black, immobile, his hands folded under his soutane,
his unblinking eyes watching. 'If I didn't see him go into the
cubicle, I'd swear that he never went to bed.' In each dormitory
a prefect slept, behind curtains which permitted peeping as well
as hearing, and the key of the locked dormitory door was under
his pillow.

He turned over from the sight, thinking to drag back from Time
the moments when there had been no danger of his hearing the
puffing of a train in a breath-laden gloom. He would pretend
that he was on the opposite side of Dublin Bay, sitting with Miss
Peters, or that he was at Tory Hill, and that in the bed beside
him was Norman; or that Peggy and Sally would enter in a
moment saying, 'Get up—it's gorgeous,' from above the pleated
collars of their night-gowns, while Sally tugged at the long night-
plaits of her dark red hair.

Life seemed to have gone sour for him. One day he would pull himself together; perhaps at Christmas when he would have enough to eat and see people. Or if he could get down to the country for a few weeks. He ought, of course, to pray more against the sin; if only one could be sure that God was there to hear the prayer. Six terms, two years to spend in this place! This . . . this . . . He sought the word which might uncoil the core of wretchedness within him. This . . . fortress! This . . . Bastille of Soutanes!

Very cautiously, he sneaked his hand out and took from his coat his Aunt Eileen's latest letter, took his Aunt Mary's torch, now a forbidden thing, and putting his head under the stuffy clothes, turned on the torch and read the letter again:

. . . now, about those suits with short knickers. I wonder if you would feel too shy in them, or if you are willing to try and save your one knicker-bocker suit? We do not know yet about some money which we think may not be available for you now after Mrs. Vincent's death. Business is not good, and Rosaleen's fortune into the Crucified Saviour nuns was a drain. But of course if you would be too shy in them now, don't bother. Major Moran's nephew here is only a little younger than you, yet he never has anything else to wear. They are much too big to pass on to Patrick—besides, he never wore those short clothes and he would feel queer.

Well, he had made no bones about wearing them, but that and his youthful appearance had resulted in the strange mischance of his being dumped in amongst the Minors.

He had soon discovered that the mistake of dumping a boy of his age into the Minors did not occur very frequently. On the afternoon of his arrival he had been put to wait in a parlour where he had been glad to rest because the journey from Kingstown into the city and then the long journey through the North County to the school had left him not tired but satisfied to sit quietly.

He had sat in the parlour for a long time, looking the other way when parents whispered last words to other new boys. Now and then, one of the wheeping soutanes stopped at his corner and someone asked his name, looked at a list and went away. The room had become dark by the evening when the parents and new boys had all gone. Hearing the sound of a distant bell, and guessing that it must be for the evening meal, he had found his own way along great passages and had gone into the Refectory in a line of boys. As he had never heard of separating older boys from younger, he did not know that the line entering at the other end was composed of Seniors, some older, some younger than he, and when, very hungry after the meal, he had heard a prefect calling, 'New boys this way,' at his end of the large room, he had followed. His name had been added to a list and he had been given a place in this dormitory, where he had lain awake for much of the night, wondering, hungry and beginning to be appalled. When, next day, he had learnt that the school, in addition to having a railed-off section for 'Ecclesiastic' boys, was divided into Seniors and Minors, he had unquestioningly accepted the station which, it seemed, Authority had allotted to him. When, some days later, one of the implications of this division had been revealed to him by the mortified blushing of various Minors and the jokes which were being made about 'dolls' in the 'Harem', he had spoken to one of the senior prefects whose manner encouraged him. The prefect, without asking his age, had said good-naturedly: 'Many a Minor thinks he should be a Senior. However, speak to the Rector of Morals and Manners.' But Martin had given it up, not thinking a transfer to the Seniors worth all this trouble. It might be to his advantage to remain in the Minors where he could go his way without physical or verbal annoyance from bigger boys.

Silently, in single file, they went downstairs every morning. Silently, other Minor dormitories joined the file, emerging soundlessly from dark doorways, faces white above their clothes. They turned into the cavernous hall and there, along the opposite wall, was the silent line of Seniors, a few daring ones glancing across in the weak glimmer of the scattered lights. Everywhere, in chapel, study-hall, recreation yard, halls, what Martin had christened 'the Pope's line of demarcation' separated the *Pupilli Seniores* from the *Pupilli Minores*, who were, on occasions, called the 'Harem' by those among the Seniors whose eyes, as they glanced across at the forbidden world of the Minors, held a glittering curiosity, different from that of their equals.

Down the dim centre of the hall the prefects moved soundlessly on rubber soles; there was no noise except the wheep-wheep of soutanes in the dimness, and the subdued pitter-patter of house-shoes. Under the scattered glimmers the cavernous hall this morning seemed to him even larger and gloomier than ever, reminding him of a drawing by Miss Clare of one of the new underground stations in Paris. This in turn brought to mind the long prisons of the French Revolution; the bodies piled bloodily in the September sunshine outside the doors of La Force and Abbaye; and Princesse de Lamballe's head carried on a pike past Marie Antoinette's eyes. He smiled grimly, longing for his diary that he might write down this satisfactory coincidence.

A priest called the prefects to him. Something exceptional had happened. They followed him out of the hall.

At once the Seniors' tongues swept a current of talk through the windowless hall. Some talked with reckless loudness to impress the Minors, and soon, on the Minors' line, punches, giggles and antics began. A message whispered along both lines: 'Old Water-Float Finnerty has died suddenly. That's why we're being kept here.' Martin had never seen Father Finnerty, but had heard boys jokingly say that the old priest floated in his bed, so much water seeped through his dropsical skin. He was eighty-eight.

As the minutes passed the unsupervised boys grew daring. One Minor recklessly skipped across the hall to speak to his brother in the Higher Line and along the files other brothers spoke. Some of the known 'smuts' among the Seniors began to look wooingly across at the few known 'dolls' among the Minors, but one or two of the 'smuts' watched for decent, modest Minors because they would prefer to own the whole heart of a Minor, even a plain one, rather than share in the favours of the public beauties of the 'Harem'. Something wrapped in paper whizzed across to Martin's feet, a piece of toffee. He could guess what the note with it would be like, because he had already received others: *Is your name Jem Riley and what are your Christian names in full? Why do you never even give a smile back? Wear those clothes always. You look awfully nice in them this morning.*

Martin laughed. Ostentatiously, he tore the note up, giving what he hoped was a sardonic look in the direction whence it had come. Yes, it almost certainly was from that wealthy Senior with the large Adam's apple, the great footballer, the sleek-haired, well-dressed giant who watched him always as he filed under Senior eyes in and out of places. He scribbled: *Shall I put a ribbon in my hair tomorrow for you? My surname is Shakespeare and my first name is William.*

He whizzed this across and saw that it was indeed the one with

the big Adam's apple who picked it up. That huge creature wanting to—ugh, like Father MacTaggarty, only more of it and worse.
Just exactly what did they do? Just kiss and paw? But in an
insidious way it was flattering to know that that great Dublin
Jackeen with the sleek hair was spending his time thinking about
one's dark eye-glancing. Flattering for so long as no one else
knew. And he pointed the neat house shoe and made big eyes,
hoping that they would darkly glance in the weak light and
torment that brainless giant.

The prefects returned, the antics stopped, the silence came
again and the files entered the chapel, where the Ecclesiastical
Division boys had already been at prayer for some time. He knew
that they would one day go to the Seminary, come back to be
prefects, later priests of the Order, and he looked with distaste
at their stuffy clothes and at their faces, smooth young ones,
knobbly older ones, fifty or sixty of them. Priests! How could
they endure the specially wretched life they were led! Trained
from ten or eleven into the ways of the Order!

During prayers he vainly searched his pockets for a sweet or
biscuit-crumb and fell to brooding bitterly on his hunger, all
day and every day hungry. Supposing he could bring himself to
give Adam's Apple a girlish glance and point the leg for him on
the way out after Mass, Adam's Apple would probably keep him
supplied in some damn' thing to eat, biscuits or sweets.

Mass began. *Introibo ad altare Dei*—To God who rejoiceth my
youth.

This term, next term, another term and on and on. And every
day there would be evening recreation. He swore at himself because he had not succeeded in forgetting about the evening
recreation until at least after breakfast.

It was only an hour since the rising-bell, and in one tock of that
hour, one flick of God's mind, old Finnerty had died. Ended now
all the seconds of his eighty-eight years. All the thoughts and
deeds done now, not even drifting specks on the shore of Time—
'good phrase, that' he thought, and wished he had his diary.

With a start he realized that the Consecration had taken place.
He mumbled vaguely, 'My Lord and my God.' A piece of bread,
a little wind, changed, metamorphosed—was it really true? If a
small piece of that Host was broken off now and blown outside,
then, since matter could not be destroyed, God would be floating

about in one physical form or another from place to place. But
God was already everywhere and therefore could not float from
place to place. An immanent God floating from place to place!
How 'The Duchess' had loved saying 'immanent' in his Apologetics lectures!

The Last Gospel was said. *Verbum caro factum est*—and the
Word was made flesh. The Word? 'If there is among you one boy
who feels the call of words, who feels moved to learn words and
fashion old ones for expression, let him beware of the tremendous
power God has given him; let him remember that of all the means
of influencing souls, there is none so long-living as the written
word.' Could he himself be that boy? 'I know more words than
the others.'

In silence, the files left the chapel and in silence filed by the
walls back along the cavernous hall. He had forgotten to smile at
Adam's Apple.

In silence, they filed into the study-hall. Having vainly searched
his desk for biscuit-crumbs, he wrapped his travelling rug about
him, blew on his cold fingers and took a cautious look at the
prefect behind. He thought: 'They got you young, twelve years
ago or more; they've fed you, taught you, trained you, knocked
the stuffing out of you. Soon they'll make you a priest of their
Spanish code, put a silk hat on you via Holy Church; but they'll
never give you enough brains to make you sure whether a Minor
is deliberately cheeking you or not.' He put a book open before
him, and, making blinkers of his hands to hide his eyes, settled
down to the hour's struggle with sleepiness, hunger, chilliness and
the sudden ambushes of his indriven imagination and adolescent
body now recovering in spurts from his night.

Soundlessly, the swart-grey, tormented-looking Rector of
Instruction was inside the door. Soundlessly, he was behind a
contracted back; soundlessly, he stood above a bent head. He
went. The coughs, the scraping of feet, the rubbing of hands
began again and Martin imagined a hot drink in his throat that
was nearly always vaguely sore nowadays. The last half-minute
went, the files went to breakfast and all boys' tongues spoke at
last.

After breakfast they went out to the walled recreation yard,
Minors through one door, Seniors through another. Although the
raw morning air hurt his fractious throat he was glad to get

moving and stamp alone around the place until he felt warmer. Up in the sky, a dispersed radiance showed behind the grey clouds and he knew that it would be a hot day later, possibly a regular St. Martin's summer. He smiled and thought, 'My own summer,' then stopped smiling as he thought of the Crucifixion Convent nuns calling long ago in their garden: 'Little St. Martin, come back to us.' Voices high and sweet through the shrubberies: '. . . St. Martin . . . come back . . . back to us.'

The white mist, creeping inland over the four miles from the sea, made him cough, made him cold in the bones, and he tried to join in the ball-kicking but found it a greasy boredom that dispirited him, so he stood about near one group after another of well-behaved, agreeable-looking boys and tried to sidle into their conversations. But the groups were close-knit and exclusive; the falsity of his ingratiating manner was as clear to them as to himself and, when each group cold-shouldered him, he walked away with what he hoped was an air of 'interesting and dangerous irony'.

He went to the far end of the Minors' side of the yard and walked up and down there, going over in his mind the morning doings now taking place in Dunslane, thinking that perhaps just now, small new boys, high up on the shoulders of someone like Ned Connolly or Great Mars, were perhaps carving their names into the goal-posts and hearing the chant of the weir over the stripped cornfields and the sounds of birds and boys in the morning.

And now Ned and Great Mars were dead, in graves in Flanders and Gallipoli. He looked with contemptuous distrust at the crowds of Cork and Kerry boys, all calling each other by two or three Christian names every time, all with the quick eye and the smile of McNally and cunning of O'Mahoney from Kerry. He looked askance at the hordes of boys from the suburbs and the professional squares of Dublin, for, to his intolerant eye and limited experience, many of them seemed to be just the types of boys who had stalked with self-possessed impudence about the foyer of the Gaiety Theatre during intervals at Christmas pantomimes or Shakespeare, loudly ordering sweets with pocketfuls of silver; sniggering to see Sally, Peggy, Norman and himself counting their few coins; sniggering to hear them saying 'Sir' and 'Ma'am' and at their politeness to grown-ups; nudging their

sisters who, in bright, half-grown-up dresses, stared boldly over
their lemonade at the muslin frocks and white hair-bows of
Peggy and Sally and the Tory Hill 'Tomboys'. How they used to
look down their noses at the old Swift as they drove away in their
parents' more impressive cars!

Ah God—to sit under a tree with his arm in Norman's, to kick
up the red-gold leaves, to hear some quiet, enormous chap dis-
course upon the mistakes of the ploughman in the field across the
Dunslane avenue. Ah, to push Lennie Bourke's bicycle into the
hedge for him when he arrived in the morning! And, oh, to leave
behind for ever the evening recreation, walking alone round and
round in a circle, while the Seniors walked round and round in
their own circle and the prefects stood guard, out of doors or in
the cavernous hall. Walking alone, round and round, his eyes
seeing the backs of the talking group before him, his ears hearing
the talk of the group at his heels; walking alone because he had no
friend with whom to walk and one must not stand still, nor read,
nor rest against a wall, nor even run up and down, lest in the dim
light one might do some evil, perhaps even meet a Senior.

Dread of that evening recreation haunted him every day and
all day, and sometimes at night he would waken to an over-
toppling insanity of pitter-patter of shoes before and behind him,
talking voices before and behind him, round and round, only to
find that he was hearing the breathing exhalations of the packed
dormitory.

The bell rang and soon he was mooning along in the silent,
pattering file before sinking with relief into his obscure seat in the
back bench of his English class, with Senior day-boys and
Ecclesiastic boys. The priest looked with weariness at his class,
then took a consoling peppermint. Martin personally liked Father
Hareloss because he had brains and because he had not entered
the Order by way of 'twelve years' Slave-Education in the
ecclesiastic division'. When he looked down at the pile of corrected work beside him, now, his face brightened. 'Ah, yes,' he
said gravely, sternly, as he picked up the top book. 'Where is the
boy who wrote this?' He read the name on the book. *Reilly, M. M.*

'Yes, Father.' Martin stood up, uneasy and puzzled, because
he had thought his essay satisfactory. Although his shorts stopped
several inches above his knees, he was able to keep his bareness
hidden by quickly arranging his books in a big pile, as the boys,

not imagining that there could be a Minor in their midst, glanced back at the obscure person in the unaggressive back benches, who might be a day-boy, an Ecclesiastic boy or a fellow Senior of that inconspicuous sort who occasionally mooned through the school for a term without other boys noticing or caring where the unimportant one was sleeping, or at whose table he fed.

Father Hareloss surveyed Martin. His expression made the class uneasy. Holding up Martin's essay, the priest began with restraint: 'Some of you are terribly stupid. You've heard that before now. Most of you are just ordinarily stupid and will do all right in the professions. About four boys have brains of varying orders. But brainy or stupid'—he prepared to throw the exercise-book down the room—'there isn't one of you, nor one in the final-year crowd above you, who could produce anything as vigorous and genuine and polished as this. It has something one longs to meet with in your monotonous essays—feeling! Too much feeling, in fact,' and the book hurtled towards Martin. 'Honour marks for a fortnight.'

McConnell and his sort here won't love me for this, thought Martin. He despised McConnell and all 'the tribe' of those who struggled for classroom successes.

He picked up the book that had been thrown to him.

'Of course,' said Father Hareloss, chuckling, 'your essay was off the whole subject. Tell me, where did you get all your side-strokes? Who told you about the month having originally been "the moonth"? And your bit about Pamela Fitzgerald playing ball with Madame de Genlis, for example? Who told you those things?'

'It was mainly my . . . a woman . . . a lady.'

'Well, you're a lucky man to have someone to tell you things like that. Is it your mother, boy?'

'No, Father. Just . . . just a lady.'

In the intelligent eyes of a boy near to him, he saw a malicious gleam light up. In a loud aside the boy whispered: 'Governess! Sister's governess smacks nice boy if he doesn't know his lessons!'

The class roared and the malicious one added, 'Nice boy, very naughty today.'

Martin was about to reply angrily 'Well, it was! And I don't care!' when the priest's voice boomed:

'Of course not. Nonsense! Sit down, boy. Sit down at once and don't mind them.'

Martin, sitting down, thought: 'He's right. I nearly made a fool of myself. Up on my feet calling attention to myself—like Seumas Conroy in his kilt. How Norman would have loathed it.'

From Father Hareloss he passed on to 'Squizzy' O'Malley's class in Mechanics. Here he could not sit in the back row. It was the private preserve of H.T., and those very few whose existence he condescended to notice. He sat there so that he could read his mathematical journals throughout the class without disturbance. H.T.—H. T. Murdin, but he was never called anything except H.T.—had been in the school for ten years, Martin had heard, and it was said that he had never worked at anything except mathematical subjects and English Literature up to the death of Byron—he despised all writers after Byron. When he had been a little over eighteen, he had left school, 'to begin living like a civilized human'. Some months later he had reappeared among the astonished boys.

It was rumoured that the very oldest of the Seniors, a boy whom he occasionally addressed, had once dared to ask the reason for this remarkable return to school, and H.T. was reported to have said: 'If I obey my holy and publicly respected father in all things until I am twenty-one, I shall have an income of four hundred a year under my uncle's will. If I publicly disobey my father in a provable manner, the money goes to him! But it also goes to him if I die in the meantime. Therefore, my Pillar-of-the-Church parent, using as excuse that I have failed my matriculation'—he had failed in nearly everything except Mathematics and English—'gave me the choice between the gay, and short, life of a lieutenant at the war and the life of a schoolboy until I pass my matriculation. To his astonishment, I have made the obviously rational choice, thus heroically obeying him to the admiration of several idiotic, adoring aunts of mine and piercing him to the heart because he, like I, is well aware of the high mortality rate amongst subalterns in this filthy war. When many a nice subaltern is rotting in Flanders, I shall be enjoying a wholly unjustified four hundred a year and doing as much harm as I can to my father's pocket, reputation and comfort. We'll see if then he will find his daily Mass a consolation.'

H.T. lounged most of the day either in the infirmary rooms—

he had built up a reputation for being 'delicate'—or in Squizzy's classroom, sometimes correcting exercises for Squizzy and coldly allotting really savage marks, which Squizzy secretively and shamefacedly raised to a safe level. He treated the authorities with a smiling submissiveness and a frightening gentleness. His amused, far-off, yet altogether docile and 'obedient schoolboy' smile always gave Martin a mixed thrill of fear and admiration. Few boys ever dared to address H.T., and it was said that he scarcely knew the face or name of any boy.

The class had just begun when a message came to Squizzy, who regretfully spluttered: 'Oh, dear, I must leave you for a while —poor Father Finnerty, you know. We must all be sorry for Father Finnerty and pray for his soul. Work this out, if you can, without me.'

He wrote a problem on the board. The door had no sooner closed on him than a few boys produced cigarettes, and a boy sitting in front of Martin turned to him. 'Here, you, whatever your name is, get up and shut that window in case a prefect snoops by outside and sees the smoke.' Anxious to show goodwill, Martin stood up on his desk and had just shut the window when he heard a gasp of shocked astonishment:

'Holy Moses—look, everyone! He's a Minor! . . .'

He turned to find all faces staring up at him with outraged amazement. 'God, it is! In Squizzy's Mechs. Shorts in here! The whole get-up of him!'

Martin clambered down, hoping to sink back into his obscurity, but some of the talk must have pierced through H.T.'s far-offness; he lifted his head sharply. 'What's that? Did I really hear someone saying that there's a Minor in this room?' They nodded.

'It can't be—not in here,' said H.T. 'Only three or four times in history has there been the accident of a Minor in your grade. And in none of the cases did they allow the sweet thing in here,' and he smiled to himself.

'But, H.T., he must be. Look at the way he's dressed.'

'Show him to me then. Which of you is it?'

They pointed to Martin, who looked back and saw the pale blue eyes narrowing as they studied him. The smile on the wide, thin mouth showed brittle teeth, sloping inwards. 'Stand out and let me see the whole of you.'

Trying to grin as if he thought all this a good joke, Martin stood out. The eyes looked him up and down, the lean, fair head nodded. H.T. sniggered and said:

> '. . . His form had yet not lost
> All her original brightness, nor appeared
> Less than Archangel ruined.'

Then, observing Martin's expression, he said sharply, 'You don't mean to say that you recognize those lines?'

'Milton,' said Martin, who had heard them many times from Ned Connolly. It was the thought of Ned which had shown in his expression, because he had suddenly perceived why H.T.'s appearance had seemed vaguely familiar. The lean fair head, the set of the slender neck, the elegance of dress, were all rather like Ned's own. And now Ned was one of those subalterns rotting in Flanders. His name had come in during the summer. All during the summer the names had come in. From Suvla Bay the name of Great Mars, called Mars because he was so peaceable; from Cape Hellas the name of Harry Vincent leaping ashore from the *River Clyde*; and from Suvla again the name of Sydney Stillmore who would never again dance a Sir Roger de Coverley nor ride a carriage-horse bareheaded in the moonlight to fetch a cornet for an impromptu band, for now he was lying not in the shade of his own feet but in the shade of the same beach as Great Mars whom he would have snobbishly snubbed at home. That was how prayers were answered!

Worst of all Long Dick—the beloved Long Dick—was dead! He had been shot through the head within three weeks of reaching his battalion in France, in September. Martin and Norman had never paid their projected visit to him, and now they would never pay it.

'So!' muttered H.T. a little resentfully. 'A Minor who knows Milton! Or thinks he does.' Then he smiled. 'A real live Minor straight from her morning in the "Harem".'

For a moment the resemblance to dead Ned seemed so marked that Martin stared with a sad fright in his heart. 'Well, big odalisque, what frightened you that time? I wonder if you could perhaps be an interesting bird?' He grinned secretively to see Martin's watchful fear of him. 'Tell me, clever odalisque, did the gods put you here in my path, do you think?'

'I don't know,' said Martin idiotically, and the class sniggered, but the snigger died when H.T. did not smile.

Suddenly he seemed to become bored. 'Ah, sit down,' he said, and was turning to his papers when a boy was heard saying to his neighbour:

'That kid has a governess; we found it out in English class.'

H.T. looked up again.

'Yes,' said McConnell, who piously disapproved of H.T., but was very anxious to be noticed by him. 'And like all that type of precocious kid, he sucked up to Father Hareloss to get Honour marks for a fortnight for his essay.'

'I do not believe you!'

All stared to hear H.T. saying so much about anyone. He continued cuttingly: 'You, you with your mean, proper face, exactly like the sons of my father's friends, I know your respectable breed. You are probably a good deal of a coward, of a jealous nature and vulgarly anxious for importance without having the talents to deserve it. God, I've watched them, I know your breed. For these reasons, and because you have obviously just the working minimum of grey matter, I presume that you have chosen the road of the Church.'

Boys glanced at one another, shocked, but marvelling at this new example of H.T.'s frightening cleverness. For McConnell was indeed going to be a priest, and it was nearly certain that H.T. had known nothing of him until this minute. But Martin did not think it remarkably clever of H.T., because he himself, without knowing anything of McConnell except his class behaviour, had long ago marked him down as a future priest, a successful superior sort of priest, giving lectures on Church Art, perhaps, or Philosophy, in a well-to-do suburban parish like one of Martin's distant cousins did.

McConnell looked crushed. He came down to Martin and said in a voice too low to be heard by H.T., 'Could I see that essay?'

Martin said in boredom: 'Don't worry about your class marks because of me. Go screw your head crazy trying to win the English class prize if you want it—I don't.'

McConnell, disbelieving him, said airily: 'Oh—the old prize—who cares? But just let's show each other our work before we hand it in, eh? And don't think that I was sneering like the others because you have a governess. It was just that I was a little amused because first you said it was a lady who teaches you all that and then it turned out to be only a governess.'

For a moment Martin was too surprised to speak. Only a governess! Miss Clare!

He said: 'Listen here—she is a lady. And keep your tongue quiet, I'm warning you!'

McConnell smiled patronizingly. 'Oh, granted some governesses are nominally ladies, I suppose, but usually, well . . . I was just a bit amused, that's all.'

'You impudent Dublin Jackeen! Listen, if you open your mouth again about that lady, you, you . . .' His voice, cracked by the great choir, where he had been put to sing alto with a broken soprano, betrayed him again, and its sudden twist into a keyless shrillness drew all eyes to him and McConnell.

There were shocked calls of: 'Here, you! That's no way to talk to a Senior, you cheeky brat.'

McConnell said loftily: 'Oh, never mind, chaps, he can't help his country expressions! Such vulgarity! Of course, if a person has only been educated down the country by some common little governess . . .'

He staggered back against the desk, his lips split against his teeth by Martin's fist. 'Get up! Get up, you Jackeen, till I . . .'

Before he could get McConnell up for hitting, he was grabbed amid angry calls: 'The savage! And to a Senior! A dolly Minor if you please!'

They dragged him out. McConnell, whose lips were beginning to bleed, stammered: 'Mind you, I'm not *asking* for anything to be done to him but it was cowardly because of my glasses. And he's loosened a tooth. If I had had my glasses off . . .'

'Take them off now,' shouted Martin, 'I didn't aim at your glasses. I aimed at your mouth,' he called, as he was forced backwards across a bench.

'Apologize to McConnell and you can sit down.'

'Apologize? Why should I?'

'You hit him. You were absolutely savage. Besides, he's a Senior.'

'I'll hit him again if he comes within a yard of me. It's he who should apologize to me! You and your stupid Senior-Minor, Senior-Minor!'

'God, this is a brat all right, he just needs to be sat on properly

—did you ever see such a look! Make him drink ink-and-spit. What's his name anyway?'

Someone said, 'It's Reilly—M.N.'

And, as he was forced farther back, Martin called: 'It isn't N. It's M. Two Ms.'

Amid protests from a few boys, he was spreadeagled face-upwards on the desk. A mixture of ink and spittle was prepared, McConnell saying anxiously, 'Remember I have no part in this: I never asked for anything to be done to him.'

The heads craned over him in a dome of faces, the chalk dish suspended below the dome.

'Apologize! To all in the room now—to all Seniors.'

'I will not.'

'We don't want to do this, hear? But if you don't apologize we'll *have* to.' They tilted the dish and he could see the spittle floating on the ink like scum along the dark parts of the weir, and the chalk flakes like strips of foam.

'Well . . . ? Will you apologize?'

'I won't. He should apologize. I told him to stop. Two or three times.'

'Hold his nose.'

They tilted the dish still more, the scummy rim of it waiting up there for his mouth to open for breath.

'Last chance! Apologize!'

He tried to speak and they said: 'Wait! He's trying to apologize,' and they took the grip from his nostrils. 'What were you trying to say?'

'I was trying to say "Slave-Hearts". Bullies! That was what I was trying to say.'

'God, give it to him for that.'

Sharply from the back there came a 'Stop it!' and H.T., advancing, looked down into Martin's eyes. 'Say that again, what you called them.'

'I said they were Slave-Hearts. They are! Slave-Hearts.'

H.T. smiled with intense satisfaction. 'Perfect descriptive epithet.' Then contemptuously: 'Let him up, you bores.' They did so and H.T. studied him. 'Look here, did Hareloss really waken up for something you had written? Hareloss is no fool.'

Martin nodded. H.T. said with a smile—not a frightening smile this time, a simple smile, 'And the governess is a lady, is

she?' Then to the others: 'Keep your hands off this odalisque
from now on, you lot of . . . ah, what he called you just now.'
And he sat down. Then, astonishingly, and almost passionately,
he snarled: 'Disgraceful to have a governess? Any lout of a man,
especially in a soutane, may teach you or wipe his boots on you!
But not a governess! *Homo sapiens! Sapiens!*—Give me cats
instead!'

Martin went back to his obscure corner and nearly collapsed
there. He heard a soft rustle beside him and H.T.'s voice reached
him from beyond his hands supporting his dizzy head. 'Listen,
big, well-read Minor. You heard Squizzy O'Malley saying that
we should all be sorry for Finnerty. Can you say straight from
Milton himself just the very lines that give a reason why anyone
should lament Finnerty?' The low voice sniggered softly. 'I'll
make it easy—Lycidas! Go on—if you know the smallest thing of
Milton you'll know this one.'

Martin kept his hands to his cheeks.

'Come along, answer me, you disobedient Harem-maiden!
Lycidas and watery, floating Finnerty. Damn you, you lazy-
minded thing, I've had to tell you it almost.'

In a moment Martin said:

> 'He must not float upon his watery bier
> Unwept, and welter to the parching wind,
> Without the meed of some melodious tear.'

'Yes, that's it. It's good, isn't it?' said the whisper.

Martin said nothing. His hands were drawn away from his face
by two cool hands, his head was tilted and the pale blue eyes
looked deeply into his: coldly blue like the edges of milk from a
cow on poor pasture. The lean head began to nod and Martin
felt convinced that those eyes now knew. Not Father Mac-
Taggarty's name, nor where, nor when. But H.T. knew, he felt
sure. Those eyes knew that Martin knew that H.T. knew that he,
Martin, knew that . . . He blushed and lowered his eyes.

'So, that's the way it is?' H.T. whispered. 'So that's it. And you
didn't like it, poor little slave-girl? My word, you *are* proving to be
an interesting bird.' He went back to his seat, and beckoned
Martin to follow him. Speaking in a low voice, he said:

'Odalisque, let me give you some advice. Firstly, learn your catechism; the good shall suffer and the wicked prosper. They actually put it down for us to read, as if we hadn't seen it already for ourselves. I knew it when I was twelve—I did, I say! My father prospers but I shall prosper more. Secondly, don't be half-and-half. Half-and-half is loathsome. Next, and above all—hide the truth. Hide what you think or feel. You give yourself away in your very expression and your eyes. That proves that you are only half clever as well as half everything else. You're a mongrel. But at least you're not a full cur like the others. And you're clever enough to be worth advising. Listen—when I wasn't yet fifteen I had seen that the last thing people want is the truth. Look at this war—the perfect example of a fine, big lie—people are idiotic. Even when the truth could do them no hurt, I think they would prefer a lie. Tell the truth only to those who can't do you either good or harm. Spit at *them*, show your scorn. They won't believe you, of course. But never tell the truth to anyone who is in a position to act for you or against you. In this place, for example, firstly, get out of the Minors. If your reason for staying there was to have a lazy quiet life, you're mistaken. In the Seniors, if you play your cards properly, cheer, praise, be enthusiastic, you'll gradually be able to make a soft corner for yourself. But not in the Minors. Besides, you'll have no peace there from foul, brainless clots; they'll go on thinking of you as a possible doll, and they'll get you sooner or later. Next, talk to the priests. Be a little distant with the prefects, but in a friendly way, and be sure to let each one of them believe that you think him cleverer than the others and socially superior to them. Ask their opinion now and then. But the priests—talk regularly to them. Next year, begin to have doubts about the Faith and—be careful about this—have a struggle to keep pure. You'll get privileges that way. And above all—praise the place. Praise, praise, praise. There's no end to the flattery people will believe. Really believe. It's the one pure pleasure—to see them swallowing it. I think I must have always known that. I certainly practised it always. Especially here. I was here for years without ever once getting lines or being slogged or losing a day out. Have you been slogged yet? Go on, answer me —don't presume. Don't forget you're still my captive Minor. Have you?'

Martin nodded.

'Fool. Totally unnecessary.'

He was silent for a minute. Then he continued in the same detached voice:

'I'd like to think there was some successor to me here and you're the only possibility I've ever seen in the place. I'll be gone at Christmas. I never intended to stay more than this term. I wanted to see just what my father would do. I knew they only agreed to take me at all because the fools, like so many other fools, are overawed by their own concept of my father's importance and influence. Now I'm getting them to fix it with my father. I'll work for matric outside. There'll be no more H.T. in here. Odalisque, tell me one thing. Who burned you? Answer me.'

'A priest, but he didn't really doll me; only just . . .'

'A priest. Excellent.'

He leaned his elbows on the desk and gave vent to a long, almost silent, sardonic chuckle, and it seemed to Martin that the shame of that occasion at Dunslane had been doubled for him in that moment.

H.T. was only one more thorn, a cynical, indeterminable thorn, in what was already a bed of thorns. His troubles as a Minor were over. The news must have got round, for next day the Rector of Instruction took him down to the study-hall and showed him his new place amongst the Seniors. And it was suggested that a change of raiment might be a good idea as soon as his guardian could arrange for it.

But it was just as easy to be hungry as a Senior; to be cold and angry and bored and contemptuous; to despise one's contemporaries and to take a savage pride in the realization that one was different from them. How perceptive it had been of H.T. to detect that the ardent Mighty Martin Matthew Reilly of other days had in him now not merely the cherished dregs of past enthusiasms but also a strong, latent predisposition to angry scorn. Long Dick had been equally perceptive when he said, 'Don't be too contemptuous.' But Long Dick was dead; his advice belonged to a lost world. Scorn of one's fellows seemed to grow greater every day. None of them read Montaigne; none of them kept a diary; none of them had a grandfather who was a Castle Catholic.

7

Half-way through the term a telephone call one morning from Mr. Peters summoned Martin to Kingstown. He went in some trepidation along the dusky corridors to get his exeat and found stout, round Father Halloran taking the place of the Rector of Morals and Manners, who had gone to Dublin on business.

'Reilly, M. M.?' The round red face looked good-natured, plain and simple like one of the men on the farm at Lullacreen. The priest translated the name into Irish—'O'Rathaillaigh, Mairtin'—and asked Martin if he knew Irish. When Martin said a few words in his schoolroom Irish, the priest was delighted and even tried not to be discouraging about Martin's accent: 'But no "blas" of course. The usual English accent.' Martin nearly laughed openly as he remembered how Irish this 'English' accent had sounded in the rooms of Keelard. He knew that some other Irish speaker would be saying that Father Halloran's accent was 'terribly English', and he began to enjoy the interview, but longed for his diary to write it down.

The priest spoke earnestly about 'the language', how noble it was, how cultured and, above all, how pure. ' "Purity" in a priest's meaning,' thought Martin when Father Halloran said that if Irish were spoken by all it would 'keep bad ideas from coming in from the other countries of the world'.

Martin should go to live in a cottage in an Irish-speaking district, go out planting potatoes with the cottagers, and thus get the 'blas'. Only there could one get the true accent. 'Indeed more than the "blas", O Mairtin, the true Irish life which still continues there for us all to copy.'

This Mr. Peters who had telephoned, was he a relative?

'No, Father,' said Martin, thinking how Aunt Kathleen had hated that word 'relative'.

No relative? Just business—h'm. Well, the Rector of Morals and Manners being absent, Father Halloran did not know what to do. But perhaps it was all right.

As he filled in the hour and Martin's name on the exeat, he said kindly: 'A treat for you, eh? But no use eating more than you can hold, it won't last until tomorrow.'

Martin refused to smile at the mention of his hunger. He said goodbye and ran. *Exeat*—let him go forth!

He swooped into the bright corridor, past the statue of the Queen of Heaven, Protectress of this House; he ran through the cavernous halls in search of the necessary authority who would sanction collar, clean handkerchief and clean shirt. But they were refused: it was irregular; 'not even some notice given, and just when we are so busy'.

He washed, brushed his hair, probed for his raincoat; found a prefect, saw his exeat marked; and said, no, he was not leaving any penalties undone behind him. Then he turned out into the sunshine of the St. Martin's summer.

He raced past the flower-beds and trim rectangles of lawn, breathless for the moment when he would see the gates and the world beyond. Let him go forth! If only it were Let Him Go Forth For Ever! Suddenly he whirled about and ran back, ran across the empty yard, through the empty halls, by stairs and passages and turns, as far as the lavatories and shinned up the side of a compartment. He crawled along the top of it and recovered from behind one of the cisterns the parcel he had made of his diary, his photographs, his old letters.

When he had been less than a day in his new school, he had wrapped these things in all the paper he could find and sought a hiding-place for them. He had put them here, hoped that they would be safe and finally dragged himself away from them. Every day he had asked permission to leave one or other class, and at those times, as well as other stolen times, three or four a day, he had sneaked here, climbed up and checked that the parcel was still there.

Recovering the parcel quickly now he cleaned some of the damp, smelly wall-mould from it and ran. With the stained, secret parcel under his arm he streaked past the public, pretty ways, using nearly as much speed as he and Norman had once used in their rugger games at Dunslane.

There, down there, were the gates and, beyond them, people, people moving freely, people dressed and bright. Even the wounded soldiers in their bright blue looked free, dawdling and smoking; there was a man striding along with a fine walk, and there were girls in clean frocks and nice hats all in the morning sunshine. And the gate-porter's wife was a woman; really and truly a woman!

She looked at his jiggings. 'All right. Patience! A great big boy like you jumping at getting out of school.' Then, as she looked him up and down, a shrewd puzzlement came in her look: 'Here—just what age *are* you?'

He did not answer, he could not—for the gates were opening. 'All right,' she said. 'Enjoy it while it lasts.' And he was out.

Before he looked at anything he thrust his school cap out of sight in his raincoat pocket. Then he looked. He looked at the fleecy blue sky, at windows with curtains to them, at boys who did not know how lucky they were, at a woman coming along the path, a little girl beside her carrying flowers.

He strode along the country roads that led towards the nearest trams; but would not at first take a tram, partly to save on fares, partly for the pleasure of swinging along in the sunshine, the breeze rippling against face and bare knees, his diary, letters and photographs at long last safe under his arm. Out of what he was saving on fares he bought chocolate and, hearing a flower-girl wail in the Dublin accent, 'Vi-ah-letts, twopence the bunch, the love-eh-ly vi-ah-letts,' he bought a bouquet, pinned it in the lapel of his coat and went swinging along, gazing at everything and sniffing the violets.

Even after he had taken a tram into the city and changed there on to another, and had come out on the southern side of the bay, he was still jigging impatiently on his seat. Nearing Kingstown, he got off the tram, partly to save his pennies, partly for some more striding along in the sunshine.

Towering, double-decker trams overtook him and passed him, swaying along, very much, he thought, as the galleons of the Spaniards must have swayed home to Cadiz from the New World. They were 'argosies', as they whined their way full of exciting-looking people.

Drugged by their rhythm, he found with a start that he had been walking almost on to a pair of mincing high heels. Above the heels he saw sturdy ankles and a navy-blue skirt flouncing jauntily, swinging from balancing hips. His glance, travelling up, saw the arc of a rose-swarthy cheek and black hair in gleaming coils under the hat. He hung back, watching the girl and her swinging blue skirt that was shiny where her behind moved slightly within it. When she went into a shop he turned into an archway and there, keeping watch on the shop, he hurriedly pulled up the turn-downs of his fine Keelard stockings to cover his knees, breaking one garter in his haste. He put on his raincoat which came down nearly to his knees and hid the ribbon of skin remaining between stockings and shorts. Following her off his route, he was puzzled to guess her age. She could not be quite grown-up, as she was showing a little of her legs, but it was a very odd turn-out, he thought, neither one thing nor the other; for one thing, her hair was up, so her skirts should be down all the way. And those heels! Or was she one of the new war-girls, a V.A.D. perhaps? A war-girl—the phrase thrilled him with a sensuous allure.

Looking perkily about her, she noticed him staring. He looked away, but had seen black, round eyes boldly glinting. He followed on, clutching his parcel and tugging at the ungartered stocking which kept slipping down over his knee. She looked swiftly back and something white fluttered to the ground as she turned the corner. Grabbing at his stocking through his raincoat, he ran to pick up the handkerchief. Quite a pretty handkerchief, too! Much nicer than her clothes.

Running round the corner, he was surprised to find her quite near and walking very slowly now. 'I say, I beg your pardon—you dropped your handkerchief.'

Between the rose-swarthy cheeks the round mouth moued surprise. 'Oh, fancy, really! I am always dropping things.' The black eyes looked boldly into his.

'Well, I'm awfully glad I found it. It's a very pretty one.' It seemed to take her aback a little.

There was a pause. Then she said brightly: 'Lovely day. It's like summer come back.'

'Yes, it's St. Martin's summer, you know.'

That seemed to take her aback completely. To recover her assurance she said jauntily, 'Do you want a hand with that great parcel of yours?'

'Oh, no, thanks. I couldn't have a girl carrying . . .'

She laughed. 'You're a queer boy. What's your name?' He told her.

'How old are you?'

He hesitated. He might be a queer boy, but it was not for her to say so. 'I'm nearly nineteen,' he said, adding on two years on sudden impulse.

'Crumbs! You're a year older than me!'

He was profoundly shocked. A girl of eighteen in those heels! Yes, she was a very common girl. 'Well, goodbye,' and he began to turn away.

'Goodbye, bright-eyes, if that's how you want it.'

He watched her flouncing away, her hips swinging the blue skirt jauntily, the sunlight on her rose-swarthy cheek. She looked back, laughed, and he ran after her. 'I'm going this way so we might as well go together perhaps.'

'Righty-ho,' and she grinned at him. She craned forward to look at him secretively tugging through his raincoat. That blasted garter. Why had it broken? 'What's wrong with your . . . ?' and she giggled. 'I mean you're walking so strangely.' She laughed and laughed.

'What *is* wrong up there?' and he saw her looking with curiosity at his stockinged knees. Hastily he said: 'I fell and tore my knickerbockers'—oh, damn! Knickerbockers were only less child-ish than shorts—'er . . . cycling knickerbockers of course.' She looked at his thin, fine stockings knitted for him in the Keelard days by Miss Clare. 'No, they're not cycling stockings; they're a sort of specially fine stockings . . . er . . . for hot weather.' She hummed a tune, looking sideways at him with an amused air.

'What do you do? You're a student, I'd say.'

'Well . . . yes, I study. Yes, I do study.'

'Oh, are you one of the Trinity boys? Are you one of the terrors that dragged two girls into their box at the Tivoli last Saturday night—oh-ho!'

'Well, I'm not precisely at a university. I . . . I just study.'

She again hummed amusedly. But, after a moment, her eyes looked less boldly at him, and more kindly, and she said: 'Here, sit down and rest. You look a bit peaked out.'

Saying nothing, he sat beside her. They had come to a quiet

part of the sea-front, overlooking the sea, and only for pedestrians. There was no one in sight. Her blue skirt, hot with the sun
and the warmth of her body, touched his hand. She leaned to
him. 'You *are* a queer boy.' He looked into the glinting dark pools
of her eyes and saw there his own small image wavering and
watching. The neck of her blouse hung forward and the blue-
black shadows from the branches of a tree on the pathway
slanted down into the blue-brown shade of her bosom. He looked
deeply into her eyes but could see there only the image of himself.
On the blue surface of the bay there was nothing visible except a
single, great sail standing up out of the Irish Sea, motionless and
white. He put one hand to her throat and instantly took it away,
but she took the hand and replaced it on her throat, and slowly
the hand slipped down into the dusky warmth and closed over one
stout, taut globe. She bent her head and they sat silently, his
hand on the firm-tipped orb, her heart-beat flicking his middle
finger. She raised her eyes to his, and in all the world he knew
nothing except his own image in those depths, the pulse of his
life and hers there in his hand, and out on the Irish Sea the sail
standing motionless and timeless.

She stiffened, paling as she looked into his gaze. She took up
his hand, tapped it and said perkily: 'You're quick off the mark.
I don't know what's come over me, I never let anyone get as far
as that the first time before.' She took her eyes from his and said:
'Here, don't look at me like that. Come on, I must cut home.' She
stooped to brush herself down and suddenly burst into peal after
peal of laughter, while he, not knowing that she had just seen his
school cap peeping out of his pocket, as well as a bit of bare thigh
visible through the gap in the coat, looked at her with embarrassed timidity.

'Brown-breadcrumbs! Well, that's the best ever! My, but
you're a holy terror.'

She laughed all the way back to the tramlines, refusing to
explain, refusing to say who she was. 'My name is Florrie, and
I'm along this road every Thursday about this time.'

'But I might not be able to be here.'

She laughed and laughed. 'Why? Sure studying with no one
over you, you can do what you like. Or . . .' her eyes shone
maliciously, 'is there someone who might slap you?' She held her
hand to her bubbling laughter, while he, puzzled and timid,

looked uneasily at her. She stopped laughing. 'All the same . . .' she said, and, leaning forward, kissed him. Then she bounced away, and he looked after the jaunty blue skirt.

Dazed and shaking, wondering how he could possibly get out on any Thursday, he walked on, tugging at the stocking, until he thought of rearranging his clothes and using string for a garter. Would Adam's Apple, who had thrown him the toffee, have a rich, important uncle, important enough to be allowed to take out his nephew and the young friend whom the nephew had met during the last holidays? But perhaps Adam's Apple would not let him have time off to meet Florrie? Adam's Apple must not know that it was to meet a girl, since he himself would be Adam's Apple's girl—no, no! it was all unthinkable, a hand on his leg and neck again like Father MacTaggarty's—he shivered with disgust in the morning sunshine of this returned summer.

He was trying to see some other hole of escape from Knockester on a Thursday when there came to him the thought of Norman and what he would think of Florrie and of himself sitting beside her with his hand . . . He knew that in a moment he would be asking himself what the Tory Hill fillies would think of him, what Sally and Peggy would think, or Aunt Kathleen, if she were still alive! What madness had got into his blood? Actually planning to let Adam's Apple . . . ! Maybe that was how girls became prostitutes?

He shook off all thoughts and quickened his pace, but the smell and warmth of Florrie were still pouring through his senses when he walked through the dim room towards the terrace where Miss Peters sat against the sunlight and the sparkling water. Far beyond her, that sail did not seem to have moved one inch.

He held his face up for her authoritative salute. Her second-hand motherhood was becoming very precious to her. He was the first person for years to do more than inquire with kindness about her health, speak very respectfully to her—and then ignore her. 'Such a dignified little person, rather a dear. Pretty too in her old maid's way.' So they said; yet kept away from her at the parties Kingstown gave for wounded Tommies.

She kissed his cheek now with a finely balanced mixture of tenderness and 'stiffness'. He knew that she felt obliged to live up to her own 'one has to be stiff, very stiff, with boys'. She would pack him off to Glenkilly if her conscience judged that she was not being sufficiently severe with him.

'I've lost a garter,' he said. She scolded him about this. She was shocked by his collar and shirt, and utterly appalled by his three-day-old handkerchief. She sent the maid, Gwennie, out to buy new ones, and she prepared to make a garter for him herself, putting on a cross air as she measured the elastic around his leg.

Looking down he saw the shining brown hair trying to cover the grey hairs. Over her head he saw that sail still in the same place. What would she think if she knew about Florrie?

'Well, I mustn't be too angry with you,' she said. 'A day out of school is a *"jour de fête"*, so you must eat a very big luncheon— *Fête sans gourmandiser, fête sans joie.*' In her schooldays she had been made to talk French at mealtimes, and, ever since then, food and French had gone side by side in her head.

While she sewed the garter, he opened out his diary and photographs to let the sunny wind blow away the mouldy smell. She talked of the view from the window, the view she loved so well: the bright bay, the curved granite arms of the harbour and Howth Head beyond. Then with a fluttering of the eyelids which indicated that she was about to engage upon a topic of some importance, she said: 'Martin, your letters never tell me a single definite detail of your new school. Yet, even before you came fully under my charge, you would tell me innumerable things about your last school. Why?' And, with one of her blind, blinking stabs at the truth, which astonished him because they came so accurately from her whom he had once overheard described— justly but hatefully—as a 'dear old maid without the brains of a fly', she said: 'You *hate* that school. And you won't tell me. Is that because I am a Protestant?'

'Well, partly . . .' he began evasively, then honestly: 'No, Miss Peters, it isn't that. I will tell you one day on condition that you do nothing about it. I will not have everybody, especially Aunt Eileen, worried all over again about me and my school. I will finish my time where I am.'

Into her eyes came a slight gleam of jealousy: 'But your school is definitely a matter that I must know about. I made it absolutely clear to Mrs. Reilly that if I was to be a sort of guardian to you, I must have complete responsibility for decisions. Of course if there is going to be a change we must tell her. . . .'

'Exactly! Listen, please—I'd just hate to have anyone up-setting Aunt Eileen all over again about my school. After all the fuss and trouble already. And . . .' He hesitated, then said shyly in a low voice: 'I want to go on staying here with you. You have no idea how much I want it.'

She kept her head bent to the needle. After a few moments, she said, without looking up, 'I want it too.'

On the iron table of the terrace—Aunt Mary had once sat at it—he spread a sheet taken from his pocket.

My World-Wide Connections. M. M. Reilly.

England—Sally & Peggy, Harry Vincent (dead now—Cape Hellas), Niave McDowell.

Niave now a schoolmistress! With boy pupils like himself as well as girls!

Malta—Gertrude. A V.A.D.
America—Miss Clare.

Her husband had been seconded to a government mission to America.

France—James Edward, Captain McKenzie, Ned Connolly (dead now).
Dardanelles (near Troy)—Great Mars (dead now).

Looking up he saw her little face flushed and pretty, her hair glossy in the sunlight. 'When I was a girl I always made their garters for the boys. Even at that time my brother Tom was a rather plump creature.' It had started a train of thought and she began to speak of her old home, the Rectory in County Water-ford, and of the days when 'dear Mamma and Papa were alive'.

Presently she said shyly: 'Would you like to read Longfellow for me? Or recite it the splendid way you do?'

He would never let her guess what he thought of her favourite authors. He fetched her leather-bound Longfellow from the little table on which it lay in the drawing-room; and on the terrace, after one secret gulp like someone about to take nasty medicine, launched forth on 'Excelsior', doing it as dramatically as possible which he knew was what she wished.

'You are a dear boy. No one but you has ever read that for me the way I wanted it read. You read it just as I've always wanted it done.'

Gwennie, coming with the newly bought shirt and collar, found them trying to count the seagulls in the sun-bright air, 'and the mistress laughing, laughing out loud!'

Taking Gwennie's purchases from her she bundled him upstairs and hovered near the bathroom as he bathed, coming in when he was sufficiently covered for one who was not of her flesh, but sufficiently disarranged to assert the rights of her second-hand motherhood.

When he came down, cleaned, spruce and with new handkerchief and collar, Mr. Peters, who had just come in, gave him a glass of sherry and even spoke to him for a few moments without the embarrassed manner he used for schoolboys. Mr. Peters could talk to anyone, even a schoolboy, even a Catholic schoolboy, about wine and he was glad of an excuse for opening a bottle of claret for the meal.

There, on the table, were the flowers as always, cool and still; there, at his elbow, Gwennie's clean starched apron and cuff reappeared from time to time; on the stiff cloth the solid forks looked pleasant and strong and cool; on his plate each thing was an item to be remarked and savoured: soup to begin with; meat whose appearance was immediately appetizing; decently cooked vegetables. When his favourite 'Queen of Puddings' was placed before her, Miss Peters bridled happily and from a full stomach he smiled his grateful love.

But the hours of his exeat were passing, and when the meal was over he followed Mr. Peters back to the dim room behind the terrace. There, Mr. Peters jigged nervously, swaying his short body and polishing his eye-glass before setting it firmly in his eye.

'Will what you have to say take long, sir? Because I'd like to have time to ask a few things, please.'

Mr. Peters said uneasily, 'What exactly is it you want to ask about?'

'Well, about money, for one thing.'

'Ah, money! Quite,' he said. 'I was coming to that in any case,

myself.' As a solicitor and family adviser, he loved talking about
money, anybody's money.

The death of the Vincents, he explained to Martin, had left
things in this way: Keelard automatically went to Sally and her
children, to Peggy after her and Peggy's children, if Sally had
none. Mr. Vincent's personal money went mostly to Peggy but
—'There is not a great deal. Too many schemes, public halls and
what-not. Helping those people! Might as well try to help—well,
no matter.' Hanrahan was caretaking the house, keeping fires lit
and so on, 'and of course spending all day in "Kathleen's Garden".
Can't get him to get on with the other work.' He came back from
that to the irritating absurdity of Tom Prendergast sending his
sixteen-year-old son to school. The boy ought to be at work, knuck-
ling down to life in time. 'Now, my boy, to come to your own
financial future. It's a pity that it should be necessary. You
shouldn't have to worry about such things yet.' He explained
that 'a long time ago, money was left to Mrs. Vincent for you. A
young woman in the prime of life'—he paused dramatically—
'left no will! The same old story—people put these things off and
off. And your money, ridiculously left to her, passes now to the
girls!'

'But they'll give it back to me. So, no matter.'

'You assume too much,' said Mr. Peters testily. 'Supposing,
firstly, that there were brothers or sisters of hers to share in her
estate? Or supposing someone objected on the girls' behalf, where
are you then? However, everyone is agreed. Mrs. Curton—she's
the Surrey aunt—is no friend of yours, let me warn you. Neither
are the Binnays down at the brick factory. But they are con-
scientious people and I have satisfied them that this money is
morally yours.' And so, he said, it would be legally settled on
Martin, with Mr. Peters as trustee, until Martin was twenty-one.
That done, neither the Curtons nor the Binnays wanted ever
again to hear a word of him or his affairs.

'But they can't forbid Sally and Peggy to see me?'

'The Binnays have no say. But I am afraid Mrs. Curton has,
and I can't lay down the law to her about how to bring up two
girls! Between you and me, they'll keep the girls as far away from
me as from you. They want to cut the painter finally. But come!
Sally will be twenty-one in less than three years and you'll be
locked away at school for two of them.' He said it happily like

one solving a difficulty. 'Now, for a long time, in fact until after you had gone to Dunslane, the interest on your money was never used. The capital, thus increased, should bring you in a little over eighty pounds a year. But I am very sorry to have to inform you . . .' he paused gloomily, 'that that is every single penny you may ever look forward to.'

To Martin the news seemed far from catastrophic. 'And you will send most of it every year to my Aunt Eileen? I have to get different clothes now that I'm a Senior. I have three whole out-fits like this one and I can still wear them in the holidays. So of course you'll have to deduct something for clothes and,' he added shyly, 'of course, something for keeping me here. . . .'

Mr. Peters laughed, and said with genuine conviction and kindness, 'Why, Martin, I think I should pay you for being here and giving Elizabeth a new interest in life.' Determinedly he began to gather his papers together.

'Mr. Peters, please—wait a minute! This money was left by my mother?'

Mr. Peters, squaring his fat little body obstinately in his chair, nodded and shut his pursy lips tight.

'And the interest . . . why would the people in Glenkilly not use my mother's money in those days?'

Mr. Peters made a valiant effort to treat the question as trivial. 'Oh, religious differences, I suppose, and so on.'

'They would not have hated her just for that!'

Mr. Peters jerked his head up. 'Hated? Oh, surely . . . ?' he said in a distressed way. 'Hated poor . . . oh, no, don't say that. Surely they couldn't.'

'They never even told me her name.' He watched Mr. Peters closely. 'You knew my mother, sir?'

'Look here, my boy, I am not going to be cross-examined like this. Besides . . . I'm in a hurry. I . . .' He caught Martin's pained expression, sank back in his seat and said, 'Yes, I knew her.'

Although the sun had still far to go before its setting, its light was now leaving the terrace and the room had grown a little darker since they began their conversation.

'Mr. Peters, please, was there a special reason why some of my father's people—leaving out Aunt Mary—should have hated my mother?'

Mr. Peters rose and came to him. With a miserable look in his plump, selfish face, he said gravely, 'The mere idea that anyone could have hated your mother is simply incredible to me.' He shook his head. 'And very painful; she was a sweet girl.'

'Would you say that she was'—he used Aunt Kathleen's phrase for her—'lovely and good?'

'Most certainly I would.'

'Mr. Peters, please, I'm not strictly a bastard, am I?'

The monocle dropped from Mr. Peters' eye. He goggled.

'I don't mean to be rude, sir. . . . But it's the right word, I mean; it's a proper old word, even though it's used . . .'

Mr. Peters said weakly: 'Oh, I understand. That's all right.'

'Well, I'm not, am I? Not legally and . . .'

The little man made another valiant effort to brush the question off. 'What's all this nonsense? Where are all these extraordinary ideas suddenly coming from? We all understood you . . . Look here, just supposing—only supposing—that such an unheard-of thing could be true, why, Mrs. Vincent would certainly have told you.'

'She might not. She *would* not, in fact.'

'Why not, indeed?'

'Because she always wanted me to be happy and proud.'

The vinous-streaked face seemed to lose its lineaments of obstinate good living; he nodded slowly. 'Yes, that's just like her. I admired her. Yes, I admired Kathleen Vincent.' He looked down at Martin. 'She was extremely fond and proud of you yourself, let me tell you. Look here—why shouldn't you be what you said just now—happy and proud? You're a decent type of boy as far as I see.' He coloured faintly. 'And young people ought to be decent and honourable and all that.'

Martin said nothing.

'Well, then, here you are. This is your home. Elizabeth looks on you as a god-send. The war may be over before you're of age to go. You must finish your two school years. What then are you worrying about?' But his satisfied look died under Martin's gaze.

'Mr. Peters, please—how long before my birth was my mother's marriage?'

A flicker passed across Mr. Peters' eyes. 'Her marriage!' he muttered. 'Now, look here, my boy, all this when and where and how and . . .'

'Can't you see, sir, that it's not fair to put me off. I'd like to know something. A little will do. What I most particularly want to know, after the date of the marriage, is what part of Ireland my mother was born in; and if she grew up there or in another part of Ireland. She might, for example, have had an ancestor who went out in '98, like lots of Protestant Irish. I could be planning in Knockester to go to see her parts of Ireland. It would be something to think of in evening recreation.'

Mr. Peters meditated. 'Wait there,' he said and, going into the narrow oblong annexe, he began to open his safe.

On the terrace there was only a little direct sunlight now, but the bay was all shining in it.

Mr. Peters came to him. 'You had better have these now. I opened the first one by mistake. You see, there was only this little "M" in pencil, up in a corner, and I couldn't imagine what it meant until I opened it.' He walked out to the terrace.

From the opened envelope Martin took a strongly sealed envelope to which was clipped a sheet of Keelard note-paper with his Aunt Kathleen's writing. From that sheet and the inner envelope came, either actually to his senses or imaginatively to his memory, a faint essence of the scent she had so liked.

On the sealed envelope he read: *Private to Martin Matthew Reilly, the boy at this date a pupil at Dunslane College and living here under me. If it cannot be delivered to him, it is to be destroyed unopened. Kathleen Vincent*—and then the date: *15/10/1914.*

That date—his last night at Keelard, Miss Clare's wedding-guests dancing, Sally and he out under the huntsman's moon, the new moon in the arms of the old.

He read the sheet clipped to the envelope.

Dear Martin,

You have just gone up to bed. You were all in here telling me names for the new moon tonight. When you tapped at the window how you startled me. I saw your collar and the girls' dresses all white and all your white faces in a row. But when you came in I only thought how good you all three looked, with your eyes so bright and decent. I want to keep you all three like that, decent *and* good, *until it will be so deeply in you that it will stand against the things that will come to you when you are G.U.'s, 'Jews'.*

I have just written you a letter and now I do not quite know why I did, or what to do with it. I was upset—all these people dancing who are going to the war, and Margaret Clare married and gone. When Sally and you asked permission to go down to the river, you looked so like the first day when you opened the door of your Dean's room in Dunslane—bigger but very like that day. Probably you will never see the letter, because I shall have told you all that is in it. It is about your dear mother. If, however, it does come to you, I forbid you to open it until you are twenty-two, at the earliest, unless you believe it essential. How silly, I forget that, if ever you do see this, you will be beyond commands from me. It's all so difficult because I have just been writing about the past. But the war will surely be over in a year and we shall all be back here and I shall laugh at feeling so upset tonight.

God bless you, always, wherever you are. We have many times told you of your many faults and lectured and counselled you. But, if I had had a son, I should have wanted him to have the fine and noble things we all see in you, dear Anne's own boy.

Your loving Aunt Kathleen

It was decent of Mr. Peters to give him plenty of time to sit there at the table and read that sheet of paper not once but several times.

He slipped up to the bathroom and bathed the tear-marks from his face. In his own room he put the sealed letter and clipped sheet in the desk where he had already locked away his diary, letters and pictures, including hers. Before closing the desk he looked again for a moment at the old snapshot of Norman and himself in football things, arms round one another, laughing because they were so cold, and Long Dick behind them, laughing at their laughing.

Downstairs he stuffed his pockets with small cakes against the unpleasing future. Miss Peters, carefully not asking if Mr. Peters had tipped him, which he had, gave him the second half of his term's pocket-money. He said his goodbyes and poked his face forward for her goodbye kiss. He took a final au-revoir look at the terrace and the bright view beyond, and far away among the evening colours along the rim of the sea he saw the plume of smoke as the mail-boat mounted on the horizon.

He would never see, never touch, Florrie again; he would never again dishonour the dignity of any woman; and he would remember what Aunt Mary had said when asked about Parnell and Mrs. O'Shea: that he was never to let anyone speak ill of any lady in his presence, when he was a man. Tonight, if he did not sleep, he would think of Sally and Peggy and Norman; he would write regularly to Sally and Peggy now, and he would shame his own body no more.

The afternoon sun shone warm and clear, and from the top of the swaying tram, Spanish galleon, he could see all the bay; motionless, coloured and tranquil. Suddenly he thought of Great Mars and Ned Connolly. How good they had been to Norman and himself. One day he would do something for all who had been so good to him, those who were alive. For those who were dead he would pray. And how wise the theologians were to say that if you once allowed your mind to argue about religious problems, you never knew where it might lead you; Norman and he had been going too far on that road. Perhaps after all he would not buy that copy of Voltaire on the Quays.

By the time he came to put on Knockester's cap and take a last look around, the sun was approaching its setting, and, as he went up by the public ways, he got a better view of the sky, judged the wind and was certain the weather was on the turn— it would rain tonight or tomorrow. Well, one couldn't expect this weather to last for ever and by now all the harvest at home would probably be gathered in.

Tonight, he would ask for permission to go up to the priests' dusky corridors. He would first say a prayer at the statue of the Queen of Heaven, and then he would go along those dusky corridors to the room of some priest who knew little about him, not his classes, perhaps not his name. There, in Confession, he could cleanse his soul of his sins. He would come back along the dusky corridors with the Confession peace inside him, and in the morning he would go to Communion, and after that he would sin no more against God and against his own Holy Ghost, and no more think of problems which only theologians had the grace and training to master. He would be good, he would be decent and good.

So, he decided to enter by the corridor where the statue stood, and therefore continued along the pretty ways to the forbidden quadrangle and the peacock preening among the flowers. He turned into the bright corridor, lined to the ceiling with pictures of the important men whom the school had trained, and, having waited to make sure that no soutane was wheep-wheeping along the dimmer passages ahead, he stood before the statue, and read her legend painted about her feet: 'Protectress of this House'.

'Mother most Admirable, Vessel of Honour, pray that I will always be decent and good. Like Norman. Pray that if I do not sleep tonight I will think of Sally and Peggy and Norman. Pray that I will work hard a good deal of the time anyway.' He paused, then, in Long Dick's phrase: 'Special Protectress of Boys and Girls,' he said. He stood a while, looking at her, with her palms held outward in abnegation, in acceptance of all.

He turned to go, but out there among the flowers, where the sun still lingered, two women were walking, and the walk of the taller woman was somewhat like the glorious walk of Aunt Kathleen herself. They went round the corner of the quadrangle. He did not like the airs of the younger woman, not much more than a girl in woman's clothes, too expensively dressed and prodding ungracefully at the ground with her umbrella. But the other, with that walk—ah, he must have one more look at her before he turned into the place. He went jumping across the flower-beds, then stopped as the blast of a prefect's whistle smote his ears. On the other side of the quadrangle a prefect was waving at him. It was his own dormitory prefect, and he went slowly towards him.

'What do you mean by being out here? Jumping across the flower-beds out here by yourself!'

'I was just coming in, sir. I was out and I was just coming in.'

'That's an untruth! You were already in. I saw you come deliberately out of that door and start jumping about.'

'No, sir. I was just following someone.'

The prefect's eyes flickered sharply. 'Those two ladies? They're not relatives of yours. Why were you following ladies secretly about the place and into places where you have no right to be except with visitors of your own?'

Martin saw that it would have been better to have left the prefect's first impression uncorrected.

'H'm,' said the prefect in a meaning way, and Martin blushed under those eyes. 'I set you some lines yesterday and I've never seen them.'

In dismay, Martin nearly blurted out that he had forgotten all about them. 'I thought after tea would do to hand them up.' The swarthy young face studied him, then made a sign of dismissal. Martin ran to the study where he hastily tore sheets from the first exercise-book his hand found in his desk. He could get the lines done now in a lavatory, he would have time. He would not be expected in evening recreation. The door opened and the prefect walked straight down to him, the soutane wheep-wheeping, the rubber soles noiseless, the black-browed eyes piously expressionless, except for the bright hunting light which now showed.

'Look here, Reilly, you are making a fool of me! Here you are again where you shouldn't be! Why didn't you go straight out to the others?' He said watchfully: 'Why are you always keeping out of sight? Always keeping alone to yourself?'

Martin said nothing.

'Well, give me the lines now that I'm here.'

'I . . . well, I was just going to do them.'

'Just so. I suspected you were lying yet once more when you said you had them to hand up after tea. I followed you. So on top of all else you won't even do lines, won't you!'

'I was out, sir. I had an exeat.'

'I know you had. And when you were showing it to Mr. Corr you lied also to him, saying that you had no lines to do!'

'I forgot, sir; honestly I forgot. I forget lots of things.'

But the prefect's dark eyes were staring down into the open desk. 'What does this mean?' He picked up the open book from which Martin had torn the sheets and he studied the drawing revealed on the page. It was a plan of Dunslane, including the river and the roads. Each room, each field, was numbered and an index gave names to the numbers. Next came plans of the Dunslane study-hall, Brigid's Dormitory, the Oratory, the Refectory, each carefully and neatly done with its index of names to numbers.

'My word! These must have taken weeks to do!'

A map of the river from Rodesbridge at one end to Keelard at the other, with a chart of the fall of the river at locks.

'The Rector of Instruction will have a fit when he sees how you spend your time in Study. How is it you have never been caught until now?'

Keelard numbered and indexed, the boathouse numbered; Moydelgan, Lullacreen, all done during Second Study after the evening recreation round and round, all done in a vague effort to hold on to the past.

'The Rector of Instruction will just collapse!' He turned the pages. 'Poetry now! H'm!' He paused and slowly the swarthy face with the knobbly forehead blushed darkly. He raised accusing eyes and tilted the page so that Martin could see his own verses.

> With earache I went to Sally's bed,
> We sat there resting head to head,
> The pain soon went, I felt no fear,
> No harm could come while she was near.

Martin, ashamed of the doggerel, said: 'It's nearly two years since I wrote that. Even then I knew it wasn't good verse. I just only copied it out a few evenings ago. It's my cousin.' Then looking into those suspicious eyes, he blurted out angrily: 'It's shameful to look at a person's private things. It's a . . . it's a low thing. Only a lane-boy would do it!'

'Nice kinds of writings! Nice thoughts at night-time.'

The prefect, brushing him aside, began to search the desk methodically. He found nothing to interest him until he came to the jotter at the bottom of the desk. He looked grimly at one page and said, 'I thought so!' He had seen on the page:

Norman. NORMAN. N for Norman. "Wherefore I loved him; because it was he, because it was myself."—Montaigne must mean the same as Cicero's discovering oneself in another, and delight of that discovery—"It is a great and strange wonder for a man to double himself, and those that talk of tripling know not nor cannot reach unto the height of it. Nothing is extreme that hath its like." Wherefore I love Norman to the height of it and he the same for me.

Martin had seen this in an anthology; now, not knowing what might be on any and every page of his jotter, he merely stared with curiosity to see the prefect tearing out that sheet and putting it inside his soutane, with the verse about Sally.

'These will have to be seen by someone else. And those map things will be for the Rector of Instruction.'

He gave Martin a note to take to him. Putting on his house-shoes, Martin read the note: *This boy tries all the time to keep out of sight. He talks to no one. He is very secretive and cunning. He has an impudent way of talking out to prefects. P.J.K.—(I fancy he is not very popular with the other boys.)*

He took the note and it was the beginning of a complete

inquisition, all about nothing. A very gentle priest looked despairingly at him and wearily signed him to his knees. That priest and
others whispered for a while in anxious voices with the Rector of
Morals and Manners, Father Lindom himself, who looked sad and
appalled. At length the Rector of Morals and Manners asked,
gently and patiently, if Martin would tell the truth without fear
of any other boy implicated in this affair. Martin merely nodded.

No, that boy Norman was not a Senior here. No, it was neither
a pet name nor a false name, it was his real name and they could
cross-examine any Normans in the school. Yes, he could swear
that that boy was not a Senior here, not here at all, he was at home
with his father and mother 'and the fill—I mean, his sisters'.
Yes, he had sometimes got into—he tried to change it, but saw
that he was too late—he had sometimes shared a bed with that
boy Norman. No, no one in the house or anywhere had said that
he mustn't. Yes, that boy was a Catholic but no one had ever said
a word. No, not his father. No, nor that sister—yes, Agnes was the
name he had said—yes, she had charge of them all, sisters and all,
but she never said a word. Oh, no, she was strict really, even
severe. But never a word about her brother and him, no, never,
never! No, he had not understood what a sin it was. Yes, he knew
now.

No, he had not understood before that it was a terrible thing
to write such things, to think such things, about another boy.
Oh, yes, he understood now.

That girl Sally, in that verse, was a cousin. Well, not a first
cousin. Well, no, not even a true second cousin. No, he had never
understood before that it would have been bad enough even with
a sister. No, he would never think such things again, write things
like those again, especially at night-time. Yes, he knew that from
the evening recreation until breakfast next morning he must not
speak so that he might think only about his morning and evening
studies and his prayers.

Yes, he could swear that her mother had known. Yes, known
about the verses and all. No, he was not lying, sure everyone in
the house knew, there was only a door between and it was hardly
ever closed and anyway her mother had often been there and her
governess even more often. Besides, he would probably tell her in
any event. Yes, yes, if necessary he could swear that this girl's
mother had known.

No, she was dead.

No, a Protestant.

Sometimes he had to pause before answering because his tiredness made him stupid, so that the names of H.T. and Adam's
Apple kept coming on to his tongue.

No, he had not seen the sin of all this.

Yes, it would be different in the future.

They took him to another room where they agreed that he was
not really a bad or immoral boy. It was merely that he had a very
unformed sense of sin, most strange for his age.

No, he had not read Montaigne, only bits in anthologies like
the one he had copied. A man called Howard had been fond of
reading Montaigne. Yes, another Protestant. Yes, in future he
would never open a book without first asking a priest if he knew
whether it was a good book or not.

They agreed that there was one thing in his favour. H. T.
Murden had been talking about him the other day and had said
how loyal Reilly was about the school and how enthusiastic.
In view of all this and his own clearly expressed sentiments, now,
he would be forgiven.

They gathered then around the fire but left a space through
which he could see the proof that the past would now be forgotten
and that for the future he would be a very different kind of boy.

Above the flame the gentle priest held up his verse about Sally
and the earache, which he had long known to be doggerel, and
the priest dropped it forgivingly into the fire; the pages where
Norman's name were written two or three times, once in capital
letters, were also dropped forgivingly into the fire. Thus, they
said, he could see that all was not only forgiven, but would also
be forgotten; everything would be forgotten.

But he, too, must play his part; now that he understood, he
must firmly resolve to forget all this sort of thing.

As for those maps and charts, they persuaded the Rector of
Instruction to deal leniently with him for all that amazing idling
in Study. The maps, of course, would be confiscated and they
need scarcely assure him that he had seen the last of those charts
of places and names.

He was led through the corridor where the Queen of Heaven,
Protectress of this House, stood with her hands held out in
acceptance, and, as his only small punishment, he was put to

stand in the place of disgrace, an alcove off the priests' dusky corridors, where a boy, apart from the world, would yet be seen by all who walked those corridors, by a priest, by one of those queer menservants, perhaps by a boy going to seek God's penance and pardon in the Sacrament of Confession. Through the big window there, he saw the crescent moon now focussed in a ring of haze and he knew that he had been right to think that the summery weather was over.

Tiredness and weakness drugged him into a desire for sleep and he leaned against the grubby wall. But a restless excitement maintained itself in him and he could not doze. He walked the few steps round and round the place of disgrace but stopped suddenly in a fear far sharper than the moment of having to deliver the prefect's note. At last he dared to look again at what had frightened him. He saw it still there, watching him, the white face on his right, staring in at him from beyond the priests' dusky corridor. It was so frightening with its cold look and glittering, dark eyes. Then he saw that it was his own face reflected from the moonlight into a mirror. He stepped forward until his face was close to its unsubstantial self in the glass, and for a long time he looked at the incorporeal image of himself, held in the glass and watching him, as he had seen it watching him in Florrie's eyes.

He tried again to rest against the grubby wall of the alcove of disgrace. But the hatred and excitement in him were greater than his tiredness, and he walked round and round, round and round, the impotent hatred churning in him. What fools they all were with their suspicions and their accusations. Well, he would beat them H.T.'s way. H.T. had never been a fool. H.T. had seen the lie in everything long ago. Yes, he would play his cards carefully and be enthusiastic and loyal; and think what thoughts he chose in the solitude of his own heart.

He had been clenching his hands and biting his lip until the blood came. He dabbed the little trickle of blood with the new handkerchief Miss Peters had bought today. Then, because his bare knees, creased by kneeling in that room, were cold, he dragged up over them for the second time that day the turn-down tops of the fine stockings from Keelard, which Miss Clare had knitted for him in what seemed now to have been another lifetime.

III

Initiation in Love

I

THE smell of lilac came up from the Peters' garden on Easter
Monday morning. 'Amazing,' thought Martin, apathetically
dressing in front of the open window. 'Summer in the last days
of April.'

Out on the bay a yacht had raised its bluish-white sail. The
breeze stirred the chintz curtains; the sunlight touched his three
Medici prints, his gleaming book-titles, mostly second-hand from
the Quays, the Voltaire among them.

He looked at his design for the cover of *The Athiest Torch*, a
magazine which, he hoped, he would one day establish; and at a
memorandum on the piece of paper beneath it.

Time-Sheet of Convict M. M. Reilly

Time served: 2 whole terms. 4 terms to go.
Behaviour: Exemplary; enthusiastically loyal.
*Last Term's Great Sight: The eyes of the Rector of Instruction when
Important Visitor announced M. M. Reilly winner of an award
much coveted by the loathsome tribe of schoolboys.*
*Big Ass Visitor beaming, but in Rector's eyes—baffled disbelief, outraged
realization. Has brains, and has lately begun to guess that M.M.R.
is really a secret enemy of dear Alma Mater.*

He filed last night's notes under careful cross-references. One
note read:

*It is said that the soul is (a) revealed in the eyes; and (b) is made in the
image of God.*
Examples:
    1. Eyes of Prefect smelling boy's breath for nicotine.

2. *Eyes of Bath Monk standing under crucifix, silently watching four silent boys having silent baths. How did they devise these cubicle openings so that Monk could see all four boys and they see him and the crucifix but not one another? Did they consult an Architect who had taken a course in Purity? A lesson in the Luxury of the Bath. Is that why we get a bath so seldom?*

He locked the fine writing-bureau which Miss Peters had put here for him, and looked at the flower-vases, the extra book-shelves she had arranged, at the curtains tied back in bows like those long ago in Gertrude's hair, in Sally's. Ah, there in that clogged dormitory—yes, there he could at least pretend to himself that his lapses were in a sense a defeat for the controls of the Bastille. There it was fine to carry his black, silent thinking as he stood in the file and covertly watched his watchers. Fine to cheer, and watch them receive his lying praise. But here, where scorn and pretence were equally unnecessary, one was faced solely with the embittered self.

Into the looking-glass he said: 'Yes, you will die young, M.M., like Byron and Mangan!

'Tell thou the world when my bones lie whitening
    Amid the last homes of youth and eld,
 That there was one whose veins ran lightening
    No eye beheld!'

Proudly meditating the tragedy of his own early death, he went downstairs and was kept standing for several minutes for a scolding from Miss Peters. There she sat, bright but 'stiff', behind the coffee-pot as it flickered in the sunlight from the window that was wide open as for midsummer.

'No, Martin, I will not have you coming down late every morning and looking so tired. This night reading must stop. And all your grunts and yawns, which make Gwennie laugh when she brings up your shoes. Stand stiller and listen. I am going to enforce my rule about your light being out by half past ten except on your theatre nights.'

'I'm sorry, Miss Peters.'

He would sometimes bid himself to wonder why he, so far above the detestable tribe of schoolboys, he the secret atheist, submitted to being 'governed', even in public—'like any brat of sixteen!'—by an old maid who believed that Jonah had spent three days of twenty-four hours each in a whale's belly and that it was the inspired word of God that Tobias's dog had wagged his tail when he saw Tobias returning. Yes, she was entitled to pack him off to Glenkilly if she thought that she was not governing him properly; yes, she had a right to authority; yes, he loved her. But he would never pass on to the thought that she enforced real moral sanctions like Aunt Kathleen, who would have expected this submissiveness from him, counting it part of his being 'decent and good'.

She suggested that this afternoon, when everyone else would be away enjoying the Easter Monday holiday, he should remain in his room, as a punishment, from tea until dinner. But, remembering that every afternoon he stayed in his room reading and writing, and that only a little daily 'stiffness' could get him out of doors for 'fresh air and exercise', she hastily changed her mind and said with unhappy reproach: 'No, not that. I'll think of something else. First have your breakfast at any rate.' She gave him a still more severe look, then added, 'And you may come and say good morning to me.'

As she kissed him, he touched the brownish lace collarette that stood up so frivolously, ribbed like brown scallop shells at dinner. 'That's nice,' he said. 'You look awfully pretty here in the sunshine.'

'Do I really? . . .' she began; then firmly: 'No, Martin, I don't want compliments. There can only be a formal good morning between us until after I have punished you.'

'Yes, Miss Peters,' and from the sideboard: '*Must* I have the porridge? *Must* I take . . .'

'You may leave the porridge since it's such hot weather. But put at least two sausages on your plate. *L'appetit vient en mangeant,* sir!'

This was too much and he said sourly, 'I am trained by my school not to want to eat.'

'Martin, please! You might be an unpleasant old man!'

'I suppose it's useless to ask you let to me off going to Mrs. Craig's garden-party thing tomorrow for her wounded Tommies?'

She hid her delighted surprise and said judicially: 'Quite useless! It will be very good for you to be compelled to go.'

'Well, there will be one pleasure about it, one *big* pleasure—
the pleasure of escorting *you*.'

It was not a leg-pull. He meant it. And it was worth saying
things like that to watch their effect upon her. She looked almost
like a girl just then, and Mr. Peters, entering and making his
flying peck at her cheek, said:

'My word, Elizabeth, you're getting so pretty—well, not
getting but like old days at home really. Remarkable! Good
morning, my boy, sit down again please. But it *is* nice to see that
some young people have still got manners. Last Thursday a
lady—well, a woman—walked right by without so much as a
bow or a smile while I held Tyson's door open for her. Really
she did. It's the war-work, I suppose. And the other day one of
my own clerks passed me in the street with a cigarette in his
mouth. It's socialism, of course, and that fellow Larkin and his
Citizen Army.'

At the sideboard, while choosing carefully and copiously among
the dishes, he said: 'You should go bathing today, Martin. It's
hot enough and . . .' Then afraid that this might have involved
him in a discussion of Martin's day or any other 'domestic
matter', he withdrew quickly behind the *Irish Times*, reading
its news in his invariable order—Casualties, Communiqués
(British and French only, he never read the other Allies), law
reports, stocks, the new London play, an article on the French
Impressionists, and then the racing page, for today he was taking
to Fairyhouse Races a party which would, Martin expected,
include those merry, fashionable ladies whom he had seen one
night of the Christmas holidays up on a side-car, with Mr. Peters,
like a small, monocled idol, among them. One of those ladies
had been to the house once, to dinner, but she came no longer
since the day when Miss Peters had discovered that she had
made the mail-boat crossing without absolute necessity on a
Sunday.

To drown thoughts of other Easter Mondays at Fairyhouse
with Tory Hill and Keelard there, he thought instead of the
brownish-faced lady who had leaned down to him from Mr.
Peters' car-load on that occasion. Wandering about before the
theatre, he was passing the city's best restaurant and trying hard
not to remember the night of a pantomime visit when Aunt
Kathleen had shown him that restaurant, saying, 'When you are

twenty-one you must take me and the girls to dinner to celebrate.' His surprise at seeing Mr. Peters had changed to smiling
delight as he stared at that brownish-faced dark-eyed lady. She
had seen his stare and he had bowed, but could not raise his
hat because Miss Peters would permit him only a schoolboy's
cap—hard hat on Sundays!—and he went bareheaded rather
than wear Knockester's cap. The lady had bowed back, and had
spoken to Mr. Peters who, turning cheerfully to her signal, had
gaped down with dropped jaw into Martin's solemn face.

'Good God, boy! You!' Then, puffing out his cheeks to get rid
of his guilty look: 'I never thought Elizabeth would allow you
into the city at this hour.'

'She allows me to go to the theatre twice a week, sir.'

'Twice a week! Elizabeth? Twice a week for young people!'

'Yes, sir.' He had laughed and tried to talk in the tone which
would be, he knew, the worldly tone of that party. He had talked
to keep himself near to the scented, merry naughtiness of that
car-load, all misty-haloed against the city's night sky which was
pierced by St. Andrew's spire; that car-load up there behind the
jarvey who looked proudly down and back at his clients.

'But I'm not to let the servants see the programme unless it is
Shakespeare. . . .' The brownish-toned face was laughing now
and he had talked on, the ladies' ankles and dresses close to his
face. He was being a success! It was just barely possible that he
might be allowed to cling to the fringe of that naughty gaiety for
an hour or so. He said wickedly, 'She says that as I am a Catholic,
it is not quite the same. . . .'

Swiftly that lady had leaned down to him and said: 'Oh, are
you a Roman Catholic? I was . . . once I was . . . I had a friend
who was a Catholic. He's out in France now, I heard. He was
very attached to his religion and very . . . very . . .' She abandoned
her attempt to find the right word.

'Yes,' he had answered. And because he saw that she would not
let him into that gay wickedness, and that her interest in him had
been only a grown-up lady's interest in a schoolboy who had
admired her and was a Catholic like some remembered person,
he had added 'ma'am', in the manner of the old Keelard rule
for boys and girls, and mockingly thinking, 'Now let her wonder if
I think she is the Queen!' The car had driven away with Mr.
Peters looking back a little anxiously. Mr. Peters and he had

behaved as if the meeting had never taken place, but he sometimes thought of the scented nearness of that brownish face as on
harsh winter days he walked about the Seniors' side of the yard
with an acquaintance or plodded in crocodile past and past the
shrubs, his bones aching, his chest just about to succumb to
another cold.

He was still brooding when suddenly Mr. Peters said: 'Martin,
you remember that letter I gave you some five or six months
ago? I think it would be better if I kept it in my safe.'

Upstairs, getting out the letter, Martin had to move the diary
and photographs which he had locked away that day six months
ago. He had never looked at them since that day. An inch or
two of photograph peeped out—Aunt Mary's. He could see the
bent corner of the diary cover, cracked during one Christmas
visit when Peggy had kept it under her pillow because he distrusted their host's son whose room he shared. Yes, here was the
sealed letter and he carried it downstairs to Mr. Peters.

'I have thought of your punishment, Martin. No reading or
writing today! I am going to send you out to bathe, it's quite
warm enough. And then you must stay out in the fresh air all
the morning.'

Thoroughly appalled, he said sulkily: 'A bathe! And stay out
all the morning—oh, Miss Peters! Well, if I am to be *made* to
stay out all morning, I don't see why I shouldn't be *allowed* to
stay all out day and go to a theatre tonight!'

To his surprise, she nodded, her eyes showing a little alarm at
her own daring. 'Why not? One whole day out of the house for
once; no poking about and fugging indoors. You may take one
very small book with you and you must promise to bathe.' She
was blushing with excitement. 'I'm sure you will enjoy it once
you have started. Look how beautiful it is.'

It was indeed beautiful, the blue water white-fringed in the sun
where it broke against the granite sea-wall, the swooping seagulls,
the winking gaiety of the distant houses on Howth Head.

Going to her desk, she brought a pound note to him. 'This is
partly an extra Easter gift, and partly for food today. Get yourself
a proper meal. It's iniquitous what they charge. I have often
thought of asking the *Irish Times* to protest that poor people
cannot take their families out for a day without paying scandalous
prices for food. *Sans pain, sans joie.*'

Looking remorsefully from the pound note to her, he said: 'But I have a few shillings in my book fund. I don't really need it.' Then suddenly, putting his arm round her: 'I promise to bathe and get plenty of fresh air and come back positively sunburned!'

'Tom will be away in the country. I shall have some of his pictures down for dusting.' When Mr. Peters went to a race-meeting, she called it 'being away in the country'.

In the hall she called up the stairs after him, 'Wear your nice grey suit.'

'Yes, and I'll wear it tomorrow when I escort you to the Craigs'.' He had relented and was almost looking forward to it.

'It will be so nice having you. People always congratulate me about you, you are so attentive and . . . well, entertaining also.'

A bar of sunshine from the fanlight was falling across her shoulder as, fingering her collarette, she smiled up at him. 'Why not take your diary today and write in it as you used to do? I feel so excited, Martin—this summer weather, your whole day out; going with you to the garden party tomorrow. But we mustn't over-excite ourselves; that is a very common mistake. I am going to walk up and down in the garden for ten minutes.' And, pulling herself together, she turned away.

He chose for the 'one very small book' his latest purchase along the Quays, a Catullus interleaved with an English translation. Recalling her suggestion about the diary and vaguely irritated by her remark, he took it with him. It might be illuminating to look at that childish stuff.

He counted his money—it came to nearly forty-five shillings. With that much he would be able to entertain a girl, if he could find a girl gay enough, wicked enough and high-soaring enough for him! But she must be a lady and have spirit—he wanted no more Florries.

The bright day, the money in his pocket, the good breakfast which Miss Peters had just compelled him to eat, put him in a holiday mood, like those people who were already hurrying for trams and trains and laughing back at one another. But the sight of a jaunting car bowling along made him think immediately of swinging along to the Horse Show, high above the world, with Sally and Peggy, wide and stiff in their starched things; and

Miss Clare's long grey waist; of Aunt Kathleen's lace cravat; and of the smell of ammonia as together they entered the hall. 'Are you never going to be able to stop remembering?' And he resolved that today at least he would come back to Miss Peters with a face less pale and with stories of long hours spent in the open air. But he would also, when dusk came, seek out that gay, high, wicked girl. He could take her to the D'Oyley Carte at the Gaiety; or even to the revue at the Theatre Royal. A letter in yesterday's newspaper had denounced the 'wicked exposure' of the chorus-girls in it.

Turning a corner, he shrank back against the wall because there was advancing towards him a black crocodile of ecclesiastical students tramping from some seminary to bathe. He stood against the wall to avoid contact with their glistening black shoulders and, in the revulsion that flowed along his bones, he remembered how he used to crouch in a doorway at Glenkilly until the black boots of the Faithful Brothers had passed by. They had looked like great, black cockroaches, and he murmured to himself the phrase he had coined to symbolize all the imperfections of life: 'Turnips in "Kathleen's Garden", turnips all over the world.'

The unquestioning shoulders swept by, the feet smacked down on the pavement—beat down, it seemed to him, over all his country. And, as he looked after the line coiling along the sunny road, he thought: 'If we had any men now like those who kept the Bridge of Athlone; if anyone could cry aloud today, "Are there ten men who will die with me for Ireland?" then we might have our own 14th July, like the French, and a great crowd with guns and butchers' knives might pull up the railings of all our Bastilles.' But this land was a bog of Slave-Hearts. The boys at school—they even laughed at fellows who ran away. Fancy boys running away—and clever boys! Yes, dear prefect, stand still and dark, on watch to hear some evil, even though it be only the offspring of your own imagination; yes, dear Father, a stupid boy might run away, but fancy a clever boy doing that, and then yet another clever boy! Let's all join in the laughter at their misery, and thus keep in the good graces of power. Cowed syco-phants licking the trainer's whip. Or waiting, like Norburton, their turn to use the cricket stump. Ah, God, was it just the same all over the world, all either bullies or Slave-Hearts? All voting for Tim Corbin everywhere?

'But Long Dick? Father Riordan? Mere exceptions to prove the rule,' he growled, and heard behind him the tramp of marching men. Turning, he saw a group of Volunteers marching down and emerging on to the main road from one of the long roads that led in from the hills. They belonged, he saw, to that 'cranky' minority who, refusing to support England in the war, had broken away from the majority in the Volunteer movement and from Mr. Redmond. James Edward had been very angry about them.

The group was led by a young officer in Volunteer uniform. The head, erect and set, seemed vaguely familiar. Yes, there could be no mistaking it; it was the set of Seumas Conroy's head.

'Well, by all that's wonderful, if it isn't you, Martin!'

Conroy, who had given his men the order to stand at ease, seemed to be as much awed as excited by their meeting. 'Why, it was of you I was thinking, not two minutes ago! You and Dunslane. It's like an omen . . . like a confirmation!' He wrung Martin's hand. 'You look queer. What have you been doing to yourself?'

Averting his face, Martin said: 'Oh, just indoors too much. Stewing and fugging.'

'You should be with us. We've just done a twelve-mile march to get back quickly into town.'

He told the men to fall out and some of them settled themselves on the low wall at the side of the pathway.

'But why? I saw in the newspaper that your manœuvres for today had been countermanded.'

'They're on again,' said Conroy grimly. 'That countermanding will have to be investigated one day. As it is, only fifteen of my Company have turned out. And we were in our week-end camp when we heard the truth of the matter. I may be able to collect a few more of the lads before they go away somewhere for the day.' He spoke rather bitterly.

Martin asked if he might hold one of their rifles. A big working-man with a Chinese drooping moustache showed him how to hold the rifle at attention and all laughed. While this was happening Conroy noticed Martin's bathing things, and gave a high cackle. 'How queer! Today of all days! To be going for a dip in the briny ocean! While—while—but I forgot. Of course people will be going to places just as on any Easter Monday.'

A tram came along but Conroy told his men not to board it.

Three of them were in full Volunteer uniform, the others wore such pieces of equipment as they had been able to buy. All had bandoliers, but only seven had rifles. Some had revolvers, but two scraggy little 'Dublin-tykes', slum-lean, slum-white, had nothing but one bayonet, shared between them, and they looked very funny sitting there with the bayonet across their knees, as if each refused to let the other have full charge of it. It made Martin think of a description of Washington's first army, which he had lately read.

Conroy had a revolver in a holster, field-glasses and, as far as Martin could see, everything big or small which any officer in any army had ever carried. He was smiling at Martin in a hesitating way, and looking very handsome with his brown head and his bright green uniform. They spoke of Dunslane, swopping news of boys and master. Conroy had heard that Jimmy Curran was teaching in England. He gave Martin the addresses of some Dunslane people now in Dublin, among them McNally's and Mullins's. 'But they're no use, those two,' he said sharply, and then: 'Yes, I had been thinking of you and then, there you were suddenly on the pathway. I'd been thinking of what clever chaps like you will be able to do as a result of——' He stopped himself sharply.

'What do you mean?'

'I mean when we have a new Ireland with no middle-class snobbery. Tuppence looking down on penny-ha'penny, and threepence looking down on the tuppence. Snobbery of any kind kills the soul, Martin.'

Martin laughed. 'Same old Seumas.'

'Apishness and pretentiousness are eating into the soul of Ireland, Reilly. But with God's help, today we'll . . .' Again he stopped midway in his sentence and, after a pause, said curtly: 'Where's Dempsey now? He was a bad influence on you.'

Angrily, Martin said: 'You're intolerable, Seumas. Talk of something else or we'll quarrel and I don't want to do that.'

'If it hadn't been for Norman Dempsey . . . well, no matter, but you were like putty in his hands.'

'What! *Me!* Putty . . .' He stopped; there was too much truth in it. Then coldly: 'If you mean that I saw Norman's superiority to us . . . to me, I'll accept that.'

'Superiority? To you he was the tops of the world.'

'If you mean more brainy, better, more patient, gentle . . . oh, let's leave it, you simply do not know him.'

'He's a West Briton, Martin. You're too susceptible. If you like someone you give all you have and are. You *give in* to them.'

'He's not a West Briton. In every letter that I get from Norman he talks of what could be done here, and of the way the Old Gang in England would almost sooner see Germany win than let Ireland have her rights. It's all making him dislike the English very much. He's beginning to think they never give anything except to force.'

'And isn't he right? Haven't they shown us for fifty years that peaceful methods get nothing from them? We don't want our people to dislike other countries. We want them to love their own so much they'll have no room for hate of any other nation. England is fine and I admire Englishmen; but not in Ireland. That goes for every people that interferes with any other people's country or freedom. In killing another nation's freedom, they kill their own soul. Because in their hearts they know that what they are doing is a sin, and they have to pretend not to know it. That's what Englishmen are doing to themselves here, and it's as bad for them as for us. We've told them over and over again to clear out of here . . .'—the head settled itself in the old Dunslane gesture—'we've told it to them in arms often, and we'll never stop telling it *and* telling it in arms.'

'Arms! A tiny country against the greatest empire in the world!'

'Ah, there you go!' Conroy's eyes lighted. 'Listen—"any man who tells you that an act of armed resistance, even if offered by ten men armed only with stones . . ."' He smiled proudly as he turned to look at the two skinny slummies with their one bayonet between them. Then he turned to Martin to continue but Martin silenced him.

'No, don't say any more. I know it. The very day we left Dunslane—I gave Norman a book with that quotation in it. At Ballow Station. It was called "Proud Hearts of Ireland".'

Conroy studied Martin. 'You remember the night that you sang "Who Fears to Speak of '98", and sang it as if you meant it? Well, I do too, and I'm half inclined to give you the chance that hundreds of Irishmen have dreamed of, the chance to . . .' He meditated a moment, then said: 'No, finish your schooling. That's more useful.'

Martin said irritably, 'What riddles are you talking now?'

'Never mind. I'm glad you told me about giving that book to Norman Dempsey. I know that book. You, and he, and a few other chaps, have gifts which will be wanted, things I haven't got, although I'd like to have them. But I was never jealous of you. I was glad—because the more gifts that are spread around among Irishmen, the better.'

'But jealousy is the last thing anyone would associate with you, Seumas.'

'Well, one day, soon now, you and others will have the chance to use those gifts for Ireland. Often at Dunslane I thought . . . well, you could get people to listen to you, to follow you.'

'I?' Martin felt flattered and a little sad.

'Ten men with the right gifts will be enough to waken Ireland.'

Grimly, Martin said: 'The things I'd like to waken people up to are not your things, Seumas. I don't want merely to waken people here. I want to waken all men everywhere. All peoples!' And then jocosely: 'Tell me, Seumas—you're not thinking of blowing up Dublin Castle today, are you?'

'Oh, you never know,' replied Conroy in the same joking way.

He sat silently looking down at the people passing out of the city on bicycles, jaunting cars, motor-cars, the girls bright in summer colours. He told Martin that he was marching his men as far as Blackrock, where they had a rendezvous with another unit. From there they would all take a tram into the city.

'Couldn't we arrange to meet somewhere after your manœuvres, Seumas?' Conroy shook his head and held out his hand. Before Martin, puzzled and curious, could detain him, he had stepped to the head of his men and told them to fall in. As they did so he looked back, saluted Martin in formal military fashion; then, settling his head in the old gesture of making ready for ridicule, misunderstanding and chastisement, he marched his little armed band away.

2

DECIDING that the duty of bathing would be less unpleasant in the afternoon, Martin boarded a tram for the city, his absorbed brooding occupied first with Conroy and then Norman. Norman and he were planning to spend August together, some of it at Tory Hill. If he went there, he would have to pretend to go to Mass and Sacraments. This pretence was easily maintained in Kingstown, where he sat on the sea-front for an hour on Sunday mornings and assiduously bored himself reading Voltaire as compensation for the pretence of being at Mass. After doing this on Christmas Day, he had written his delayed Christmas greetings to Sally and Peggy. Peggy regularly sent him her detailed, solemn letters; but in all this time he had received only a few short notes from Sally who never now mentioned the subaltern Bingham, although Peggy had told him that Bingham had used two days of his short leave from the front in coming all the way to Scotland to see them.

It was nearly midday and Dublin was astir with country people arriving to stare at the city's monuments and buildings of interest, and with city people heading out into the country. He caught a glimpse of some Ballydore cousins and stepped hastily into a doorway, mortified and intolerant of their peasant ways and bonhomie; that ploughboy uncouthness, those ready-shaped opinions, earthy cuteness and superstition. How they had feared and watched Aunt Mary and her Charles. Let them till the ditches and grow their turnips.

Moving away he walked about, looking at the sights of the holiday morning: the flag-sellers, the cheap, crowded cafés, the groups of Volunteers and of Citizen Army men marching to their meeting places for manœuvres which all had thought abandoned. This evening there might be baton charges, perhaps even some shooting, if Dublin Castle at last made up its mind—as Mr. Peters had hinted was about to happen—to disarm the Volunteers and the Labour Citizen Army. 'High time, too,' Mr. Peters had grumbled. 'Letting them parade openly; absolute madness.' Well, there would be excitement of one kind or another in the city tonight, at the very least all the excitement of Dublin on a crowded Bank Holiday night. That would be something fine to see even if he did not meet a girl high enough of spirit to be his companion.

He stood awhile at O'Connell Bridge, watching the jarveys poised upright on their jaunting cars, with pointing whip touting for passengers to the Fairyhouse Races, to the hills or to the sea. When he passed boys of his own age, or a little older, he scowled, especially if they wore the cap of some big Catholic school. Otherwise he liked everything he saw. Sometimes he followed a group of girls, lured by a touch of elegance in their walk, or in someone's long black glove, a quick meeting of eyes as he passed, the turn of a head. But the girls met young men; the jarveys drove them away; the bands carried their music into their halls; the Volunteers were vanishing and high noon was approaching.

Walking along the old Quays and seeing the bluey, fleece clouds in creases around the sky, just as in a Malton print, he found himself near to an hotel where he had once had luncheon with Aunt Mary. He decided to rest there, have a meal, and not bathe until the very late afternoon. But outside the hotel the name Ballow suddenly rang from an argument among men hiring a jaunting car to catch an excursion train for Ballow. Martin called, 'May I share your jarvey, please?'

'Sure, sure! All aboard for Ballow!'

But he was not going so far as Ballow. He would leave the excursion train at a station which he knew to be near a part of the river where he had never been. There he would keep his promise to Miss Peters, he would see the river again but see it without tormenting memories.

In the crowded compartment, he stood tense and eager, trying to peep between shoulders at the landmarks of the familiar journey: the lush water-meadows; the Hill of Allen; the stretches of bog; the tillage which seemed already to be swelling up to meet this summer come back so soon. He came out from the smoke and laughter of the carriage into the drowsy warmth of a wayside station, not very different from the little station for Keelard. A public house by the roadside made thick sandwiches for him and pocketing them he followed the white road, which, patterned by the shadows of budding leaves, led to a bridge beneath which the river flowed.

A barge had gone by not long before; he saw the new hoof-marks and the reeds freshly frayed by the rope. It might quite easily have been Dan Murphy's barge, Dan's horses, Dan's cabin. He leaned across the parapet and ate his sandwiches. There was no one in sight, up river or down, on bank or water; nothing but the flash of a magpie, the dimpling insects and the heat lying along the rich fields through which the river wound, binding them, not dividing.

Beside the river he came to a boat-shelter with one boat in its darkened shallows. As he hesitated there, a man with a dog crossed the fields towards the house. It was almost certainly he who owned the boat and he must live in the long cottagey house which lay back a few hundred yards from the river. The man, seeing him come towards him through the fields, waited, and his eyes watched gravely as Martin asked if he might use the boat for an hour or two. 'I would take great care of it, I'm very good with a boat.'

'So is my son. It is his. He's out in France. He is not much older than you.' He stood unmoving, with his dog, equally motionless, beside him.

'I'm not eighteen yet, sir. And even when I am they say I must finish with school first; and that's more than a year away.'

The stern expression softened. 'I let my boy go when he was eighteen. I hope it will be over before your time. Please use his boat.' He nodded abruptly to Martin's thanks and went with his dog towards the house.

Untying the boat's moorings Martin pushed out from under the penthouse tunnel of the shelter into the sunlight, and, as if time had dropped aside, he heard the clug-clug of the oars in the row-locks and the rippling under-song of the water. He had not been in a boat since his last day at Dunslane when Norman had saved him from the weir.

He rowed downstream until he came to a wide quiet stretch. When he had stripped to bathe, he stood on the bank looking down into the water at the broken image of himself and hesitated because he was afraid to trust himself to a river which had once nearly swept him to his death. But he must keep his promise to Miss Peters and he knew, too, that if he failed to go into the water now, he would always be afraid of a river. He plunged down towards that wavering, uncertain image of himself.

He came up and there, against his chin, was the pull of the current as if there had been no time, no Knockester, and the tang of the river water in his throat was unchanged. But he was tired when he came back to the bank, and, in the old days, he would not have been tired. Crawling out through the muddy, cold bases of the reeds, he lay on the warm earth and looked up at the slowly changing patterns of the sky. Frowsting indoors; angry with life; at war with oneself; bored with one's fellows— that was what explained why one should be so tired after so little effort. Once Sally and he could swim the width of the river twice and not be tired in the least.

Pulling out into the current, he shipped oars and let the boat go with the river. It carried him along through a world that seemed familiar and certain, although holding no landmarks notched in memory with names and doings. This rare summer was as yet too young for the dragonflies to come and, with their impudent spurts, bend the reeds into bows, but otherwise it was indeed crescent summer itself, the young leaves showing, the last catkins fallen.

He came to a hollow of hazel trees known to him. There he pulled the boat into the bank, he would go no farther. In a few miles there would be the telegraph office at Rodesbridge, the sawmills, the huge police barracks, then the boreen up to the yard where the calf had been born, beyond that the bridge, the wide stretches to Dunslane, the miles onward back to Glenkilly, the longer miles to Keelard.

He took out Mary Ellen's Easter letter which, when it came this morning, he had barely heeded.

Never a word from Josie all these years but she was seen by someone in Dublin getting off a tram. There's only me now in the kitchen and that's more than enough with no one here and money so scarce. The mistress finds the house queer these days, all empty like, with Miss Bridget away and Master Patrick off at school. I often notice her listening to the Crucifixion nuns' bell with Miss Rosaleen in there a holy novice. Every night we say an extra decade of the Rosary for Mr. James Edward out fighting the German bosh, the mistress and the master and me. All them terrible battles, the lists read out in the chapel on Sundays would break your heart, lads killed that were only children a year ago, six months even. All the same it's a shame for the British to be making such a fool of poor old Ireland all along the line, with Carson and his Orangemen chiefs in the Government. Mr. James and the lads ought all come home and not fight for them any more. I have glass and a frame with flowers on it round that grand snap photo of you and Master Dempsey friend in your football suits laughing up there on the mantelpiece and so I often think of you in here with your songs and old stories and Josie saying me hearty to you. They say you've got terrible different in your ways. I don't like to think you're different and people maybe castigating you in that big place for your lessons or because they don't understand your old talk and ways. Tommy Fagan always asks for you when I go in to buy notepaper, he still has all the Columcille Prophecies and now dear Master Martin, I put down my pen hoping you're not the way they say terrible different. Soon I'll be having a special news for you but I must wait quiet and easy-like another while yet. And now dear Master Martin goodbye and I mention you high up in my prayers every night. Yours kind and respectful.

Mary Ellen

From the pocket of the diary he took envelopes and paper and when he had answered Mary Ellen's letter he wrote to his Aunt Eileen, and told her of his jaunt to the river. *I shall be spending all of August with Norman Dempsey but I should like to spend a week or two in Glenkilly with you at the end of July. Will you write to Miss Peters about it? The end of July.* His Uncle John would not be there then, he knew.

He closed the diary again and opened his latest purchase from the Quays, the Latin-English Catullus:

> *Qui illius culpa cecidit velut prati*
> *Ultimi flos, praetereunte postquam*
> *Tactus aratro est*

—the poet's love which, by the fault of a woman, had drooped over like the last flower on the meadow's edge when once it has been touched by the plough, Catullus's love for someone who was worthless. The last flower on the meadow's edge. He could see it drooping over, that flower, see the horses at Keelard or Lullacreen and the flower drooping over the loamy swathe behind the ploughshare—*prati ultimi flos, prati ultimi flos.*

No, it was not the moment for Catullus. The man had felt too much, had exposed himself to too many of the barbs of unkind fate. He put the book back in his pocket and sliding the oars once more into the row-locks began to row slowly back upstream. When he reached his starting point he tied the boat in its shelter once more and crossing the yellowing fields he made a bunch of primroses and the scentless pale blue dog-violets which Peggy had always praised, against the indifference of others, just as she had taken under her wing the ignored old men and old women and had carried to them the ju-jubes, tobacco, knitting wools and yesterday's newspapers. He left the starry anemones where they were but spent some time seeking shady hollows for bluebells and it was drawing towards sunset when he struck a road and headed in the direction of the railway line.

He was tired and stopped at a cottage to ask for a drink of water. They gave him milk and soda-bread and he went on refreshed, while the sunset spread its banners afar and the warm twilight approached so slowly that it seemed to him as if it might indeed have been true summer and not a false one which had yet to feel the frosts of May. He saw the railway line, the telephone wires black against the rosy flush. The wires led back to Dublin and Knockester, to the silent, oppressive hours, the cavernous hall, the evening recreation, the chapel of his hate.

He had wrapped his damp bathing things around the flowers and, as he walked on, all of the chords of his being seemed strung to the pain of '*Prati ultimi flos . . .*' rather than to that promise of spring which he carried, already a little wilting, in his hand.

A hooded motor-car gave him a lift, and left him down not very far from Dublin. But when he turned into a side-road towards a railway station he met groups straggling aimlessly in the half-light, then larger groups talking excitedly by the ditch where their womenfolk hushed weary infants.

'If it's for the train you're looking, you can save your legs,' they called to him in cantankerous satisfaction.

'What do you mean?'

'There's red murder in the city.'

Every sort of rumour was offered him. The Germans had landed at Cork, the Americans had declared war on behalf of

Irish Independence. A Spanish admiral called de Valera was 'blowing hell out of everything in Ringsend'. In any event there would be no train to Dublin.

'But what's wrong?' he asked.

'Oh, nothing at all! Only the biggest insurrection ever. Only all Dublin captured behind our backs. Only roaring murder and arson, that's all. Nothing to speak of. Nothing much at all!'

They had to repeat 'insurrection' and 'a rising' many times before he could believe it. 'Seumas Conroy,' he muttered to himself. So that was where he had been heading with his little band.

'But, look here, how are people going to get back from Fairyhouse for example?' All the army officers would be at Fairyhouse. And Mr. Peters.

'How the hell are *we* going to get back?'

What would Mr. Peters do with his elegant, merry car-load of ladies now?

The light was almost gone. Along the hedge, older people rested wearily, but the younger folks, delighted with this exciting end of routine, frolicked out in the roadway, not caring if they never got home. One youth was flashing the light of a bicycle lamp along the dusky hedge, drawing giggling screams from girls and protests from their elders. His light focussed on a mane of dark red hair and for an instant it seemed that there by the hedge was Sally's hair, hanging free. But the girl, half turning to the light, said with shy protest, 'Can't a girl do up her hair in private?' There was a little of the flat Dublin accent in the voice, but a pleasant flatness, gentle and shy behind musical overtones. Her face and the neck made a lovely line between the dark red hair and the dark hedge. Pausing to look, he saw beside the dark red hair the face of Florrie grinning impudently back through the light. He whirled about before she saw him, but the thought of that mane so like to Sally's lured him to one backward glance, the light of the bicycle lamp came full upon him and Florrie with a gasping giggle ran up to him.

'Oh, it's you of all people! Can't you get us home somehow? We'll catch it hot if we're back late; at least I won't, but my friend will. She was told to be home by nine. And I want to be back for a party a few of the lads are having after the races.' He allowed

her to draw him towards the hedge and towards the girl with
Sally's hair.

'Better let her finish tidying herself first,' he said.

'It's all right now, thanks,' a voice in the dimness said, and
the girl who had protested stepped out from the darkness of the
ditch into an after-light which was dusk-milky here because of
the filtering branches. He saw the pale shape of an oval face;
the dark line of her lips was wide, a brooch glimmered at the neck
of her saffron-coloured blouse; and the hair was up now behind
a neat hat turned back in a little swoop above her forehead.

Florrie whispered a few words of explanation in her ear, obviously not for him, and then said to Martin, 'This is a friend of
mine.'

He said, constrainedly, 'How do you do?'

'Very well, thank you. How are you? Pleased to meet you.'
Her voice and stance there in the luminous dimness were full of
grace. 'Do you think you could get us into the city at all?'

'Of course, of course,' he said airily, then less airily: 'We had
better get back to the main road as a start, and then try for a
lift. Waiting around the railway line is obviously the worst policy.'

The girls walked one on either side of him, Florrie giggling
across to her companion, whom she called Millie. The girl let
Florrie do most of the talking but he knew that she was glancing
sometimes at him from time to time. Florrie would run round
behind his back and draw her aside to whisper to her once more,
with giggles. He caught snatches of the whispering.

'Didn't I tell you he . . .'

'Go back. It's rude.'

Along the main road the high trees and demesne walls framed
in the sky an indigo roadway leading to a rosy dome above the
rebel city. Florrie swung familiarly from his arm, her hand and
hip touching his, like a claim on their past caresses. The unseen
girl on his other side was silent all of the time.

'It's rough here,' he said to her. 'Can I give you my arm?'

Florrie laughed in an unpleasant, knowing way but the unseen
girl said, 'Yes, please,' and her hand crooked cautiously inside
his arm.

'Don't let her cod you,' Florrie mocked, 'she's just afraid of
you, playing up to you. Why, Millie could *teach* me and she six
months younger than me.'

So, he thought, she was eighteen? But she seemed—well, so grown-up.

Ahead of them a gig turned from a gateway towards the distant sky-glow over the city, and he ran after it and found that the driver could give a lift to one person. At his call, the two girls came pattering through the half-light, and when the swerving of the pony brought the light of the car lamp on to them, Martin saw the eyes of the girl Millie looking at him. She said: 'You take the seat, Florrie. You've to get all the way out to Monkstown after getting into the city.'

'But sure I've no special time to be in by. And . . .' She began to laugh . . . 'And it isn't me that'll get pandied you know where for being late home,' and she laughed and laughed in just the same way that she had laughed that first day above the sea when she had said, 'Sure, studying alone you can do what you like.'

The girl Millie said nothing and Florrie, although still counselling her to take the seat, admitted that she herself wished to take it. 'It's that party of mine that I'm thinking of. If this rising or whatever it is doesn't spoil everything on me tonight.'

'You go, Florrie. Another car's sure to come along.'

'All right! I can see when I'm not wanted. Ta-ta. And remember what they say, if you can't be good, be careful!' And, as the trap drove away, she leaned out and called to Martin, 'Don't forget, you owe it all to me!'

The echoes of her farewells and the sounds of the hooves died away, leaving only the stirring of the trees, the invisible tapping of the feet beside him, and now and then a scent of hair when he turned his head to glance at her.

'Are you tired, Miss . . . ?'

'Bannon. Miss Bannon. Millie Bannon. Yes, I am, a bit. But it doesn't matter. Are *you* tired, Mr. Reilly?'

'No, thank you. And I'm not "Mister". I'm only a sch—I mean, everybody just calls me by my name,' he said, never suspecting the trend of Florrie's whisperings.

'Yes, of course. Just by your name. At home, everybody calls me by my name too.'

They walked on for another mile.

Then he said to her, 'We're both tired, let's sit down and rest for a few minutes.'

He spread his raincoat on a bank at the side of the road, carefully put down his flowers, and they sat side by side in silence.

'Have a smoke while you're resting,' she said.

'I don't sm—I mean, I left my pipe at home.'

He heard her fingers plucking at the grass, knew that she was glancing at him. 'Are you a close friend of Florrie's?' he said.

'Well, I know her, but she's anything but what I would call a *friend*, like.'

The trees, the land, the last birds, all were settling down for the night after this summer's day, so early-come, so warm.

'It's queer,' he said, 'to listen to those noises and . . .'

'What noises? It's as quiet as quiet.'

'Well, the grass and the birds, the trees and so on.'

'Oh!' she said.

'It's queer to think that those sounds have happened every night for all the years this country has been in existence. A hundred, two thousand, years ago, people must have sometimes stopped to listen to them. And here we are listening to them and down there . . .' they both looked towards the purplish glow in the sky far ahead of them, 'men are fighting for this country and among them there is a boy—no, he's a man now—with whom I've often quarrelled and whom I met only this morning.'

'They're mad, aren't they! Look at all the upset there'll be. How will everyone get home tonight? Fancy choosing a holiday night for their rising! They ought to get a few months in jail, that'd teach them to be quiet.'

He remained silent and she politely added: 'Of course, if one of them is a friend of yours, I shouldn't have said all that. You're not one of the Sinn Fein crowd yourself, I'm certain.'

'Good heavens, no! I'm a Redmondite. But are the Sinn Fein lot in this? I thought it was only that cranky part of the Volunteers who split away from Redmond over the war.'

'But sure they're the Sinn Feiners, or nearly all. And I bet Jim Larkin's old Citizen Army is in this too; we ought to have guessed that something was up when we heard that Theobald Wolfe Tone Murphy had gone to Confession on Saturday night. . . .' She had begun to talk in a laughing, careless way. 'It's a wonder the Confession box didn't go up in flames at what he had to tell.' She checked her laughing tongue and said in a careful, demure voice: 'That's Mr. Murphy. He's a tin-can soldier in Booths.

He lives in our street, with his old-maid sister. She does the books in a butcher's nearby. There's six-pounds-ten a week going into that house.' Her tongue began again to run away with her discretion. 'We have great gas with him, him and his political views. When he goes off to his drill in his bandolier and turned-up hat like a Boer War man you should hear all the kids shouting "Kruger" after him.'

'I'm wondering what James Edward will think when he hears of this out in the trenches. He's my cousin. Where I lived when I was a youngster—years ago, of course!'

He would have been willing to sit for a long time with this half-seen presence beside him as company to his watching of the city's night sky, but she said, 'I'd like to go now, please.' He rose and she took his helping hand, put her hand inside his arm, and without a word they walked on.

As the first straggling lights of the suburbs appeared, he walked faster, drawn on by the exciting thought of the rebel city ahead. 'I may be able to find a jarvey and leave you home. Then I can have a good look around and see the whole thing before trying to get out to Kingstown—er, I'm staying there, but please don't tell that girl, Florrie.'

'A jarvey! Do you mean a side-car? But that would be terribly dear,' and giving a little gurgling laugh: 'Fancy me driving up to the door on a side-car, they'd think I'd come from a wedding.' After a silence, she said insinuatingly: 'Of course, if you like, I could stay with you and look around with you a bit. Of course, only if you like, like. Then you could leave me somewhere in the city, and I'd be all right. Once I get near O'Connell Bridge, I'm all right.'

'But it will be late by then, and, even if there were no trouble, I couldn't let a girl go home alone through the city at night.'

'Couldn't you, then! I know a few fellows who . . .' She checked, and said carefully: 'No, of course not. I just thought that under the circumstances . . .' Then: 'Do you often see girls home at night?'

'No, not very often. But I have been my aunt's escort, her *only* escort, late at night. I was fourteen and she wanted to walk back to the hotel after the pantomime.'

She muttered dazedly: 'Escort! Pantomime!'

And he, wondering why she sounded so flabbergasted, politely explained: 'Yes, the Gaiety pantomime. Coming up for it was one of our great treats every year. That and the Horse Show and Fairyhouse Races. School term unfortunately made Punchestown impossible. I remember it was *Cinderella* that year. Perhaps you saw it?'

'Oh, a treat, of course,' she said very hastily. 'Yes, a treat. The Gaiety always has the best pantomime, hasn't it? The Royal and the Empire are a bit cheap and rough. All the nobs go to the Gaiety.'

'Do those places have pantomime? They're just music-halls, aren't they?'

This seemed to crush her and they went on in silence till they came to a long street where groups at doors talked excitedly. They slowed their walk. The trams were not running; yet everything seemed peaceful and they began to think that there might be no more trouble than a few baton charges, the traffic held up and perhaps troops firing over the heads of the crowd. That was said to have happened earlier in the day.

'Would you call this escorting *me*?' she said, after a pause during which she had been looking down at her own moving feet.

Thinking this might be a kind of joke on her part, he merely laughed.

'But it is, isn't it?' she persisted. 'I mean you are my escort now. Like you said for your aunt. My *only* escort.'

'Yes, of course. Obviously. But what's the joke?'

'It isn't a joke at all.'

Once or twice, as they went through the light of a street lamp, he glanced at her and she, catching his look, smiled and looked down, and all the while her hand rested lightly and gracefully on his arm.

'I could go on like this for ever—with you escorting me.' He only laughed.

'But I could! and those noises you heard in the country—and the things you said—and now the lights.'

As they swung down towards the Quays, people called, 'Don't go down there,' but, ignoring the warning, they went down a street like a canyon between the brewery and Kingsbridge railway station.

'My station,' he told her coolly, 'for home.' When they came out of the canyon they stared amazed at the wide spaces, at the lights on bridge after bridge, at the river holding the lights reflected like golden ear pendants. They looked farther afield towards the domes and spires downstream, then stepped closer together and held each other's hand, for in all those places not a man nor an animal was to be seen. Over bridges and all places there was a silence so great that they could hear a gull pecking below them in the mud-flats.

They went down the Quays and stood on the next bridge. It linked older streets, Norsemen's and Danes' alley-streets still crannying their routes up from the river past convents and under arches. The lighted city waited silently under its canopy of indigo night, breathless as a true summer's evening, with the shuttered houses giving back from their mellow bricks the warmth of the day. The house-tops caught the last of the after-light, which made ruby and gold of their old bricks, and in converging lines all the tall old buildings waited in grave and jewelled dignity, silent and with their marks of poverty all hidden. Not a sound came from the humped, switchback roofs on either side of the river, but there were lights in windows and in some of them mattresses had been placed for protection.

'What'll I do? It looks grand. I'll never get home. Kitty'll give it to me for sure.'

'Who?' he said.

'Kitty. My step-mother. She only gave me until nine.'

'But I'll take you home and explain that you were with me.'

'Are you mad altogether! Sure that's the very last thing . . .'

Her perplexed explanations died away into silence, as she looked down into the jewel-reflecting river. Presently she said: 'She won't do anything if Da takes it in good part. Maybe he will too. Da's not bad, the old aggernostic.'

All other surprises from her talk and all criticism of her speech were swept away in the delight of hearing that her father was an unbeliever.

'I'd like to meet your father. I'm always on the watch for men like that. Is he really and properly an agnostic? He ought to be an atheist. I'm an atheist—like Shelley—only in secret. To be an agnostic is to be evasive.'

'Ah, poor old Da is everything. Socialist, aggernostic, flute-player, the whole bag of tricks.' She was musing now over these matters, tenderly musing, and smiling.

'Flute-player? What do you mean?'

'He plays the flute in the St. Joseph's Faith and Temperance Band down our way. It's a rag of a band; but they're good sports.'

'Look here, that sounds a very Catholic kind of band. An agnostic shouldn't be in a band like that.'

'But sure that's the only band that'd have him as flute-player. He wouldn't have anywhere to play his flute if it wasn't for the St. Joseph's Faith and two-pints-of-Guinness-please crowd.'

He looked astonished. 'Temperance, is it!'

She laughed gloriously. She was forgetting all about being careful, and Martin, turning to look at her, was enchanted by that laugh, both musical and tender, by her grace and the free movements of her head. 'Ah, I like to see poor old Da having a good time. Kitty, too, is a sport sometimes. She doesn't often do anything to me of her own accord; it's mostly only when Da's in a growl at me. Because she's very fond of him and she likes to pretend he's the boss of the house. She and I used to knock around a bit together before they got married—just before Christmas. Many's the time she was out with me and a couple of fellows.'

'What! A woman old enough to marry your father?'

'But sure Kitty's only twenty-three. She's a sport even if she is now my step-mother. I nearly died laughing when she said she was going to marry Da. Faith, she often makes me laugh the other side of my mouth now.'

As she mused half humorously, half tenderly, he studied the side of her face, at first with curiosity to understand this strange world of hers where a former companion was now a step-mother and her agnostic father played the flute in a religious temperance band whose members were 'two-pints-of-Guinness' men. But curiosity died before the delight that stirred in him to see her graceful, lady-like stand, her upcurving, corner-of-the-mouth smile. Although her hair was that dark red, her cheeks had not the russet light which so often lay behind Sally's paleness; they were clear-pale; her face was longer than Sally's and her regular features would have given her a severe look had it not been for the upward tilt of the eyebrows, the free, graceful movements of her head and that corner smile running up into her cheek. The mysteries of her talk fell into unimportance compared with this mystery of her grace, alone there against the balustrade, in this exciting, frightening evening, with the city waiting in an un-worldly silence, as if he and she were alone in a great capital

made only for them, lighted on all its carved bridges only
for them, and all the jewellery hanging in the water only for them.
Looking down at those spiralled reflections, she said:

'Doesn't it look like a banquet table, a banquet in a castle?'

The reflections of the granite quay walls became the walls of
a room that held that spiralled table, candlesticks, hanging
chandeliers, tiaras around the heads of ladies unseen down there.
They began to plot out the plan of that banquet table, laughing
and selecting their own places at it.

'My aunt—the one I mentioned—sometimes went to castle
parties.'

'I'd love to do that. Just once,' she murmured. 'The aunt you
escorted?' She flashed a look at him, took the risk and added
invitingly, 'Like me?'

'Yes,' he said seriously and they stood looking at one another.
Brown eyes, she had, under that broad forehead and the brown
hat upturned in a swoop.

Suddenly, all around them stones rattled along the balustrade of
the bridge, but in a moment they knew that it was the noise of
bullets, not of stones. They could see neither shooters nor targets
but all around began to ring out the sounds of rifles, revolvers
and even a machine-gun. Holding hands, they ran, not sure
whether they were running into the firing or away from it. 'This
way,' called Millie and she led him quickly into side-streets
which brought them to the back of the Four Courts where people
stood about, staring at the occupied building and at its dome now
a dark bronze in the sky.

From the crowds they heard rumours which they could not
believe, but which alarmed them. Distant firing continued and
they walked on, wondering 'why the solders don't put a stop to
this nonsense'. Millie guided him partly by knowledge, partly
by city-bred instinct, until they came to the great, central
thoroughfare and the crowd like an endless sluggish animal
staring with hundreds of eyes at the occupied buildings, at an
overturned tram, at the lights blazing behind the broken windows
of looted shops and at the dead horses of a cavalry troop,
routed that noon in a gallant but ridiculous charge up a street
which had become a hostile fortress with a rifle at almost every
window.

They stepped to the middle of the roadway, where, sheltered by

Parnell's statue, they could have a clear view of this centre of rebel activity.

'The night I told you about, I brought my aunt here after the pantomime. She had never known that there was a statue of Parnell in Dublin—imagine that! You see she was a Unionist. She was wearing a wonderful evening shawl, and I read out for her what I'm going to read out to you now.' Turning to the statue, he read: ' "No man has a right to fix the boundary to the march of a nation. No man has the right to say to his country, 'Thus far shalt thou go and no farther.' " Parnell himself said that.'

She did not seem interested.

'Was she pretty, your aunt?'

'Pretty! Why, she was beautiful! She was graceful, proud and good . . . I tell you, she was dignity and grace itself!' Then, looking at his companion quite simply, he added: 'She would have liked your graceful ways. Your clothes and your ways.'

Her eyes on his grew brighter and a colour slowly crept along her cheeks. He turned again towards the statue but she said quickly: 'No, don't look at that writing again. Anyhow, the priests killed him, Da says.'

'Yes. They and their Slave-Hearts'; and he told her of his grandfather turning the priests back from Lullacreen door when they had come to talk against Parnell. 'And he sat on Parnell's platform and never stirred even once while all the turf sods were flying. The parish priest had preached against Parnell that morning and you may say it was his turf sods they threw—the Slave-Hearts.'

He found he could talk to this strange girl as he had not talked to anyone since he had parted from Norman at Ballow. 'You've heard of the Parnell split, of course? When I asked my aunt about Mrs. O'Shea and Parnell she just told me never to let anyone speak ill of her or any lady . . .' He stopped, astonished to find himself mentioning these matters to this girl. Her glance rested speculatively on him, then away.

Looking along Sackville Street at the General Post Office, they saw a flag at either end of the great building. They floated out in the slight evening breeze. One of them was the Green Flag with Eire and her harp; the other flag was a tricolour. 'That's the new flag,' she said. 'Green at one end and orange at the other with white for peace in between them. The Sinn Fein flag.'

'Have they a flag? Those colours come from '98 and the French Revolution; it's like the Republican tricolour. But Ireland was always a kingdom! It was the Fleur-de-Lys and the Green Flag that my ancestor Colonel Reilly fought for.'

Almost all the shop windows in the street had been broken and looting had been going on for several hours. Looters, dragging furniture away, banged against them but they scarcely noticed the bumps in the excitement of seeing an officer in the green Volunteer uniform come out under the Ionic portico of the Post Office and call through a megaphone to the crowd. No, it was not Conroy! The crowds could not understand his commands and the officer went inside. A moment later a volley crashed from the Post Office and all fled. Volley after volley sounded as Martin, holding Millie, ran, not knowing that the rebels were firing over the heads of the crowds to drive away the looters.

They tried some of the routes that would take them towards Millie's home, but turned back each time, alarmed by the stories they were told of the dangers ahead and by the sound of firing. People said that her district was 'one of the hottest places' and that this strange 'Spanish fellow called de Valera' was still down there 'blowing hell out of everything'. It was just as though old alliances with Spain and France had been renewed, and the foreigner was more once fighting for us.

'Some of those men in the Post Office have only old shot-guns. Think of it. Against the greatest empire in the world, greater than Rome's. And some only a bayonet between two. I saw that this morning. Just Dublin working-chaps, cheap little faces, gutties, a lot of them. Well, they're not Slave-Hearts anyway.' He had forgotten that she and her friends might not like his 'just Dublin working-chaps'. But she was not listening; she was smiling happily to herself, swinging more freely on his arm now, always with that graceful way of hers. Constantly he found her glancing at him.

He had tried to telephone to Miss Peters. But, although the Exchange girl answered as usual, she either could not, or would not, put him through to Kingstown.

'Let's get something to eat, even if we can't get home.'

She guided him through safe side-streets to a little café-bar where, behind a zinc counter, a man whom she addressed as Anthony, and whose face only showed over the counter, made a clucking sound of greeting to them in his throat as they came in. They waited until one of the cramped wooden compartments was vacated. When she said that she would take only tea and bread-and-butter he, not understanding that she was trying to save him expense, agreed to this diet, being willing to eat anything on this magical night or to eat nothing at all.

'You're tired?'

'Aye, I am tired,' she said; and, leaning back against the high pew, she raised one arm to draw her hat from the dark red hair.

Before the lazy power of that gesture had dropped away, he said: 'Beautiful! The way you did that!' And, instinctively, he tried to imitate the gesture.

She stared, then said:

'You do it a bit like a girl, yourself!'

He flushed, their eyes looked deeply into one another's, then each smiled shyly. They smiled also every time their hands touched on the plate, scarcely hearing the talking all around them or the gramophone blaring at the counter where boys and girls clustered cheek to cheek, almost drowning the music with their chatter.

3

W<small>HEN</small> they had finished eating, they went out into the streets where the air seemed even warmer than before, the pulse of this new life more powerful. Again he tried to telephone Kingstown but now not even the Exchange answered, and back once more in the central streets they fled hand in hand from more shooting and came gradually far away from danger into streets which even Millie did not know. On a street lamp where children swung on a rope in the cone of light, they saw one of the Proclamations of the Insurrection:

'In the name of the dead generations . . . The people of Ireland, through us, strike again for her freedom.'

When they saw him reading it the children began to gabble the words which now they knew almost by heart. But he shooed them away and their shrill cries of play circled once more in the cone of light.

'In the name of the dead generations . . . The people of Ireland. . . . Six times in the last one hundred years they have asserted it in arms. Again asserting it in arms . . . we pledge our lives to the cause of its freedom, of its welfare and its exaltation among the nations.'

'Excuse me, mister.' The children were trying to edge him out from their field of play.

' "In the name of the dead generations",' he muttered. 'It might be Conroy who had a hand in drawing that up.' She did not ask who Conroy was, but said sharply:

'Come away from it now.'

When, from a distance, he heard high, importunate cries he looked back; but nothing was to be seen, only the children flying through the air like birds round and round in the cone of light.

The last of the afterglow had gone and the night which closed down on the summer day came itself so warm and sweet that it drew a last heat tremor from the tall patinas of brick above the Italian doorways of tenement houses that had once been the mansions of Ireland's Georgian gentry. In these long, teeming streets the pulse of summer was stronger than the distant thud of rebellion. But that far-off daring in other streets spiced the glamour of the night.

Silently, he and she moved between the people, moved through the warm air whose towny redolence could not altogether overbear the elusive breath of flowers which had been pinned into girls' coats that afternoon in sunny country fields. They watched the youths swaggering with a wild assurance about the fish-and-chip saloons, or drinking lemonade in crypt-like shops where hanging oil lamps hung yellow, shedding their light down on cabbages and cards of nail-files. Out sauntered the youths, their padded navy-blue shoulders touching their plastered hair, the sign manual of this strange Bank Holiday; while in mocking wit, made pungent and sad by desire, they called to the other side of the street where girls in a line, linked waist to waist, moved arrogantly in their best clothes, singing as they went.

The young men whistled and voiced their longing in clumsy witticisms; but Martin, with this girl beside him, could see that those girls were armoured for a while against the thrust of male desire, armoured by the night and by a transient feminine unity. They made no answer to the wistful gibes, but sang with untroubled clearness, released from sense in a brief moment of spontaneous camaraderie.

The singing line went by doors once made by craftsmen from Europe itself; the voices were higher than the far-off tattling of a machine-gun as they passed those doorways where mothers watched with shrewd, spancelling looks. The line came past the tall windows dimly glowing from the red lamps on Bossi chimney-pieces, where the acquiescing eyes of the Queen of Heaven looked down tonight on little bowls of freshly gathered flowers, first fruits of this summer which might well be false, since it had come so early.

The line came on unwavering towards Millie and Martin, the line of eyes looked unchallengingly, intimately, into his; the line broke in two about him and her, whirled to return, and on his side, on her side, a hand was held out. She took the hand on her side and he took the hand on his side and away they went in the singing line.

The young men called, 'Oh, nice boy!' and 'Jasus, look at the Queen of the Fairies!' But little by little the singing drew the young men into a mimic movement on their own side of the street and soon even the mimicry went from the swaying and they were lured into the rhythm of the girls' movement. When that happened, all sang; on both sides of the street all sang.

No sound of bullets came through this wave of song. At the doors, the mothers, each with a keen glance at her daughter and the girl who was a friend of her daughter's, nodded their heads to operatic arias which once their own voices had pealed in the gallery of the Gaiety and the Royal after the early door had let them in.

Suddenly all the singing stopped. The line of girls broke its unity and all ran to a corner where three Volunteers with rifles over their shoulders had appeared. The three men stood inspecting a closed warehouse, while the crowd pressed close, but left always a clear space around the men, except for some urchins who leaned forward to shout: 'Hi, mister. The police barracks is down this way and they're all locked in the canteen, drinking and frightened out of their pelts—you can come and look in at them through the window.'

When the three men began to push their bicycles away, some people called mockingly, some good-humouredly, 'Wait till the Dublin Fusiliers get at you tomorrow!' and 'Up the Rebels, I don't think!' Others called with vicious hatred, one man shouting savagely: 'Bloody playboys—doing the Robert Emmet! Wait till they blow hell out of you tomorrow!' The three men looked angrily back at the man, but did nothing.

The people began to disperse. Mothers came to seek the young women and drive them homeward sternly or jovially. Very sedately, Martin gave his arm to Millie and walked primly away with her.

Sometimes they saw Volunteer groups hurrying on bicycles through the night. Once he stopped to read another copy of the Proclamation. 'No, come away from it,' she said again insistently.

But he stayed there reading: 'In the name of the dead generations . . . again asserting it in arms . . . we pledge our lives to

the cause of its freedom, of its welfare, and its exaltation among
the nations.'

They had circled the great central space where rebel activity
seemed concentrated. They came now by side-streets again to the
river and, too tired to care about danger, they leaned on the
quay wall.

'Will you be seeing Florrie again? She's a talker, Florrie . . . I
mean she says things about people.'

'Oh,' he said haughtily, 'I merely met that girl once or . . .'
Then, ashamed of himself, he said: 'No, I shan't see her again, I
hope. Why?'

'Oh, no why.'

Reckless with tiredness, they walked now right under occupied
buildings and saw at one boarded-up window a Volunteer
sentry, a youth, peering over his rifle, his face a little drawn by
homesickness. At last, in a drabbish side-street, Millie stood
against a wall. 'I'm dead tired. But it doesn't matter, it doesn't
matter a bit.'

Higher up the street he saw the globe of a hotel lamp. 'Don't
worry,' he said, 'I'll look after you.'

'I'm not worrying. I'm just dead tired, but it doesn't matter.'
When she saw that he was guiding her to the hotel, she drew back.
'Oh, but look, that's an hotel! Look, it has a lamp with "Hotel"
on it and all.'

'It's a third-rate place but we must get in somewhere for the
night. It's just the kind of place that manages to be dreary without
being cheap.'

'But an hotel? There'd be servants, waiters, girls . . . and look
in at the palm in the hall and all!'

He could see that she was awed by its tawdry grandeur. At
the hotel door she halted and looked down at herself.

'You'll be the only nicely dressed person in the place,' he
said gently. 'There'll be no one half so nice as you look just
now.'

She looked swiftly up. 'Do you really mean that? Really and
truly?'

'Really and truly,' he said.

Through the pallor of fatigue, a flush spread in her face and a
smile ran up into the flush. 'All right,' she said. 'But . . . well,
listen,' and she drew him aside. With bent head she murmured:

'I haven't much money. Only one-and-ninepence. Kitty wouldn't let me have more than a half-crown this morning.'

'But it's my place to pay for you.'

'Well . . . well, you'll have to! I'm sorry. But won't it be too dear? I mean Florrie told me you were only a . . . sch—I mean that you studied privately. So, if you're not earning, like.'

'Oh,' he said proudly, 'I have more than enough on me.'

'I see,' she said in a queer way. Then, with something half tired, half defiant in her tone, she said to the ground: 'Well, I haven't! I only have one-and-ninepence,' and for a while her head was bent, the nape of her neck curving beautifully before the black pillars of the Georgian house degraded now to an hotel with its pillars of granite from the Dublin hills painted black to the hotel-keeper's fancy.

'You'll *have* to pay for me,' she said to the ground. 'One-and-ninepence won't get me a bed,' and looking with resentful challenge into his eyes, 'I don't ever have much money!' He said nothing. 'I work,' she said angrily, 'so now! I work in a factory. So now!'

'Please come along. You're tired out.'

'I know I'm tired! I know well I'm tired. I work in Jacob's Biscuit Factory, now! You'd better know that I'm one of Jacob's girls, that's what they call us, as if we never did anything else only work for old Jacob. We're there all day, like we were sardines in a tin. And then when the day's over, God, fellows think that all they have to do is say: "Come on and pick up a girl. Pick up some shop-girl, or one of Jacob's girls." I'm fed up with fellows. I'm fed up being . . .' She dabbed at her eyes and said: 'It's all right. It doesn't matter.'

'Well, come on, please. I never said that. So why blame me? And I never picked up . . . well, only Florrie.'

From behind the handkerchief, she said: 'You didn't. Florrie picked you up, I bet—I know Miss Florrie. And her mother's worse, for the way she lets her go about. I'll let you pay now. So long as you didn't mind being an escort for a factory-girl.'

'The way you keep harping on things. We're both in the same boat tonight. We are like . . .'

Before he could think of a suitable simile she had taken his arm, and said with a tearful laugh, 'We're like a pair of stray drunks, if you ask me,' and had followed him giggling into 'the hall with the palm and all'.

In the glass booth the well-brushed, shiny-faced proprietor watched with one eye the girl writing up the books, with his second eye scanned the newcomers, and with some third eye counted the glasses passing on a tray, while his tongue primly rebuked the porter for something. Millie whispered: 'Tell Waxy-Chin we're brother and sister. I wouldn't like . . . well, perhaps you wouldn't mind saying I was your sister just for now.'

The tariff prices on a card said 'Bed-and-Breakfast, 6/6', but Waxy-Chin explained sadly that he must charge them six shillings for bed only and four shilling, for breakfast because of the unsettled state of the city and the run on food and accommodation.

And would the gentleman sleep on a seat in the billiard-room and the lady on a sofa in the drawing-room? A whisper came into Martin's ear, 'Don't pay him four shillings for any breakfast.' Yes, they could have something to eat. And they had only to order their drinks.

They went into the coffee-room and sat side by side, watching one another, and hearing but vaguely the popping of corks, the shouting and laughter along passages, and in billiard-room and bar. They had 'tea with bacon and eggs', which was the alter-native to 'tea with cold ham', and Millie looked with delight at 'All that lot of rashers and eggs in one dish at one time. That's one thing Da wouldn't do without for anything, his rasher and egg every morning.' He began to be aware that she was watching what he did with table things and he was hurt by the thought that she should be impressed by this under-appointed table, she who sat there so gracefully, so pretty, with so much more of elegance and ladyhood in all her ways than anyone else in this room she feared.

They were so hungry that they laughed in whispers at the quantity of food they devoured. The meal over, he forced a way for her through the groups drinking in the hall, and various newcomers also looking for shelter, and had some trouble on the stairs with a drunken man who sang 'God Save Ireland' with loud assurances, telling everyone that he did not 'care if all the bloody British in the world heard it'.

In a deserted corridor upstairs, they looked out across the roofs towards the old Green Flag and the new flag drooping in the

breathless glow of the city's summer night. Below them echoed
the rough sounds of the overcrowded hotel.

'I heard a man saying that your factory was occupied.'

'Good. Maybe Miss Watch-the-Clock was there, waiting to
catch one of us late in the morning. If she has her Woolworth's
penny Union Jack up in her coat, maybe they'll shoot her.'

'You mustn't make jokes like that. I'm quite certain that
they'll treat prisoners honourably. And, anyway, she's a woman,
so they'd treat her properly.'

Her face turned to him, pale and serious, as so often Sally's
face had turned to him. '*You* think everyone would treat a
woman nicely?'

'Well, everyone would.'

'All right it doesn't matter.'

They descended to the drawing-room floor where he gave her
his raincoat to be a dressing-gown. 'Then you can take off your
blouse and your skirt without minding those other women
in there. Anyway, your clothes will be much nicer than theirs.
I used to see that sort on the beach at Tramore when I was a
youngster; really expensive clothes outside and safety-pins and
ugly things underneath. Honestly, really dear clothes, and then
bits of old tape instead of proper garters!'

In the doorway, with the breath of many women in the
darkness beyond, she shook her head wonderingly. He held out
the bunch of flowers which he had plucked by the river. 'They're
not altogether faded yet,' he said. She took them, nodded and
went into the room.

Down in the billiard-room he lay on his share of a cushioned
seat, his diary and bathing things tucked between him and the
wall. Staring into the darkness, he thought of her upstairs and
of Conroy outside in some barricaded building under the Green
Flag and that tricolour from the French Revolution. He dropped
off into a troubled doze, but woke to hear women screeching in
the hall. Giving up hope of more sleep, he took his rugs and diary
and went towards the hall where people were sleeping on chairs.
There he was waylaid by the singing drunk who was now whining
about 'Two bloody English chorus-girls jeering at poor old Ireland'.

The two girls in question were singing mockingly, 'Irish and
proud of it, too!' But a third girl sat apart on a stool and looked

before her with weary self-respect. 'Stand by a brother Irishman,' implored the drunk of Martin, as one of the girls high-kicked in his face, at the same time turning to screech at the girl on the stool:

'That's for you too, Miss Phillida P. Hesseltine, I don't think —Maggie Doggin. You don't like showing your thighs to the two-bob stalls and their bits of stuff beside them! But you draw your three quid a week for it same as us, see!' She whirled round with her back to the drunk, and, with a whoop, flounced her skirts up from her backside.

'Ah, no Irish girl would mock you with her posterior,' wept the drunk.

Outside, the night was shaken by a volley. A cluster of terri-fied women began saying prayers for the fighting out in the city and the fighting down in the hall. And then the drunk flung his arms about Martin. The masculine embrace nearly sickened him with fear and disgust and he struck out at the big jaw. The blow staggered the big drunk, and Martin, disentangling himself from that male hold, ran upstairs and gained the landing where he saw his raincoat in the middle of a group of women. Millie's hair shone out amidst that general frostiness, and, gripping her hand, he tugged her away from them and they sped up the next flight, her knees flashing in and out of the raincoat, her hand in his. In the deserted attic corridor they tried several doors but sleepy voices within drove them back until, opening the last door, they saw a bathroom.

'I knew an hotel would have a real bathroom,' whispered Millie. She went in and, standing by the glimmer of the bath, she ran her fingers along the cold enamel. Half mischievously, half longingly, she stroked the bath. 'At home we have baths in the kitchen.'

She looked around the room. 'A towel on the rail and all! Fancy that now! This room is only for having a bath in.'

He whispered—they were both whispering although no one could hear them: 'The water's hot. Have a bath. I'll keep guard.'

Her eyes shining with excitement, she nodded. He went into the housemaid's closet where he had seen a broom with its handle broken short. He knocked off the head of the broom, and, armed with the stout handle, he squatted outside the bathroom door, listening to the recurrent quarrels downstairs, the occasional sound of volleys outside and the splashings behind him. Almost he wished that some of the drunks would come up to this passage so that he might use the broom handle and show her how well he would guard her.

There was a noise behind him, and he saw her standing there with his coat about her, the lower curves of her hair-loops a little damp. 'It was perfect,' she said. 'Just perfect, that's all.'

'I'll have one too. You can call a warning to me if old Waxy-Chin comes upstairs.'

His bath over, they decided to spread their rugs up there and stay together. She had found it impossible to sleep on the sofa downstairs. But first he led her down to the hall and looked among the sleeping people, seeking the girl who had sat apart on a stool. Her two companions were now drinking quietly at the bar hatch with some men. He found the third girl trying to sleep in a corner and told her that there was a sofa free in the drawing-room.

At the drawing-room door, when they had retrieved Millie's coat, blouse and skirt, the upturned hat, the bunch of flowers, the girl spoke: 'Thanks very much. We only got here yesterday, and I was out for a walk with two young ladies of the company when the shooting began. I'm an actress, but just now I'm doing mainly dancing—it's useful for an actress to be able to do different things.'

'You must be tired,' he said. He was thinking that once perhaps she had been one of the Princess's attendants in the Gaiety pantomime—Sally, Peggy and he had stared at them in delight.

'Aunt Kathleen, do they spend most of each year looking for so many beautiful girls?' Had Aunt Kathleen known that it was a case of three quid a week for showing your thighs, when she bent her head and gave him her answer: 'Yes, perhaps they do look specially for them.'

The girl looked from him to Millie, bit her lower lip and went inside.

'Actress indeed!' said Millie as they went away. 'She's just a chorus-girl.'

'Yes. But how did you know?'

'Oh. The square behind our house is full of their digs. I could tell one a mile off since I was that high.'

They wrapped their rugs around them and sat in the corner on the floor and looked out obliquely through the window. The spurts of shooting were getting fewer and fewer.

'Some of those men have no rifles, almost no weapons, yet they're challenging the biggest empire in the world.'

She said nothing, just looked up at him from his shoulder where her head rested.

'They're wrong, of course. It's a crime against the Allies. But all the same . . . well, they're not Slave-Hearts, anyway!'

She put up a hand to draw the rug more closely about him, while he stared out at the points of Cassiopeia's chair fading beyond the drooping flags. Watching him, she said, 'Tomorrow—no, today now—we'll get home somehow, and then I don't think you ought to see much more of this rebellion.'

'But why not?'

'No matter,' she said, and soon they dozed. When he awoke, he would not stir for fear of disturbing her sleep. Sometimes he pressed gently with the arm which was round her, because he could not become accustomed to the wonder of her strong young body resting so trustfully against him.

Cassiopeia faded, all stars faded and the streaks of a fair dawn showed beyond the distant roofs of O'Connell Street. There was not a shot anywhere now. The wide streaks spread, the sun would be rising soon over the rim of Dublin Bay, mounting the eastern horizon as the mail-boat would mount it coming from England. But this morning it would be troopships of the greatest Empire in the world coming in to fight Conroy and the men with one bayonet between them.

At last she stirred down there on his shoulder, her cheeks rosy from sleep, a faint aromatic freshness still seeming to emanate from her after that bath of the night before. Her brown eyes, looking up at him, were dark with sleepy affection. She raised an arm, pressed down his head to hers and they kissed. He had read of the sweetness of women's kisses and had thought the phrases exaggerated, but now the sweetness of this kiss dizzied his senses and, when her head again lay quietly on his shoulder, that sweetness, along with his own wonder that her grace and beauty should be enfolded by his arm, flooded through him and he wished with remorse that he had never summoned to his Knockester pillow the creatures of his nightly imagination.

If only they and all the smouldering, in-driven, embittered thoughts that crowded his mind in the silent file could be obliterated from the past, and if he could bathe mind and body clean of their memories.

She was lovely and that was all that mattered. She would soon stop saying 'Da', and 'pleased to meet you', stop adding 'like' to sentences, and stop holding her knife like a pen. The innate snob in him winced at such things but his heart did its best to tell him that they were an irrelevance.

The coat had fallen back from one bare arm and he saw in the firm flesh near a shoulder-strap the red imprint made there where it had pressed the wall. He stooped and kissed her passionately.

She whispered, 'I never knew there were really boys like you except in books, and I thought it was all a cod, the way no one in a book ever said a bad word or did anything bad.'

'But you've got it all wrong. If you only knew what I was really like.'

'Maybe girls know more than you think,' she whispered. 'Girls I mean who don't have families well-off enough to keep them kids for years in strict schools.'

They rested, half dozing, cheek to cheek. At last he said: 'Everything is very quiet outside now. We might try our chance soon.' They stood up and she stretched herself magnificently, unrestrained, confident and accepting. She saw the delight and admiration in his eyes, and they stood gazing in joy at one another.

When she had dressed and put on the little brown hat with the turn-up—'like a tiny Napoleon's hat' was his comment on it—she took the bunch of flowers from the tumbler of water which she had put on the floor and they went downstairs without making a sound in the house which had long ago sunk into rest. Only the proprietor seemed awake. They had paid him the night before, but now they coaxed him to make tea for them and, to their surprise, he did not charge exorbitantly for it.

When the hall door had been chained and bolted behind them, the first thing they saw was a platoon of swallows cutting masterful sweeps against the milk-blue streaks of a summer's dawn.

'Look, Millie! Now who said the summer won't last! Who says it's a false summer!'

Up along the street, the high, thin bell of a convent rang the

call to Prime. They listened to its lonely echoes and waited for
the sound of shooting which must, they felt, follow that sudden
breaking of the silence. But there was not a sound over all the
city.

'The Government are waiting for reinforcements from England,
I expect.'

The sun surged up, it shone full upon them. All around the
sky the fleecy clouds were piled tier upon tier, like amphi-
theatre seats looking down into the waiting arena of the city.
The sun of this amazing summer shone on the golden words—
'No man has a right to say to his country, "Thus far shalt thou
go and no farther." '

They went then in safety through the silent, armed town.
They passed the looted shops and she led him by long ways to a
small and shaky double-door drawbridge with railed-off ways for
pedestrians and traffic crossing one of the basins that linked
the city's port to the canals of the countryside. There she halted.

Beyond the bridge, a long grubby street ran away between
high mills, aerial trolleys of factories, terraces of cramped little
houses with pretentious villa doors, and reeky warehouses.
She asked him to come no farther. 'No, no farther, please. I'll
be all right now.'

Although they did not know it, this shaky wooden bridge
was the centre of a very dangerous area and eyes along rifle
barrels were watching them standing there, he with the broom
handle which he had forgotten to restore to the housemaid's
cupboard before they left and which the proprietor had never
noticed; she with the small bunch of withering flowers, both of
them exposed on all sides. They leaned over the basin, hurriedly
trying to plan future meetings. 'There'll be no chance until this is
over,' she said.

'And after that I'll be back in . . . I'll be away studying,
you know.'

She looked gently at him. 'Yes, I know.' Then: 'Tell me, no
one will be unkind to you—I mean people studying sometimes . . .
I mean,' she fingered his coat, 'no one will hurt you or anything
or . . .'

He longed to tell her the truth, not knowing that she already
knew it; longed to tell her that he was still at school, that next
birthday he would be eighteen, not the twenty which he thought

Florrie thought him. But he was afraid to tell; she was eighteen.
And not Sally's kind of eighteen.

'Of course no one will touch me,' he said loftily. 'But you!
Your step-mother. I wish . . . I wish I could . . .'

'Kitty's all right, she's a sport, nearly always. And Da can't
be in a growl at me for this; he'll be too glad to see me safe back,
for one thing. But you? I wish . . . I wish . . . I wish . . . ah,
what's the good of wishing!'

He tried then to explain, without giving himself away, that
he might not be able to write very often. He gave her his address,
c/o Miss Peters. 'And I'll hope to see you in four weeks.'

'I know, I know,' she said ardently. 'Anywhere you say.
Any day you say. I'll just take sick leave, or put them off somehow.'

'We might go down the river—my river. Look!' He pointed
to the barges moored in the basin, and spoke of Dan Murphy's
barge, of the cabin and the chair of Cassiopeia seen beyond the
hatch; spoke of the smack of water against tarry wood, the pull
of oars against leg muscles, the flowing current.

She said several times, 'Aye, I'd like that with you.'

She was going at last, resolutely begging him not to come any
farther.

'Listen. Every evening between half-seven and eight, I . . .
well, I knock off studying and just walk round and round. Er . . .
a kind of exercise you know. Will you think of me some evenings
at that time? Every evening I'll be thinking of you.'

She promised it.

'But promising's not wanted. Sure, won't I be thinking of you
all day!' Still they could not part. They looked at the sky, at the
basin, the oily reflections of the sunlight on the scummy water, the
flounce of weedy scruff which time had hung like a fringe on the
hems of the gaunt buildings that lined the rectangle of the basin.

At last they kissed goodbye, clasped tightly on the little bridge
in the growing sunshine. She gave him back one of his faded
flowers for a buttonhole and he let her go, their hands dragging
to the last breaking touch. He watched the graceful, strong figure
and the neat brown hat grow smaller and smaller between the
lamp-posts and the grim buildings. Far away, the tiny figure turned
about at the corner of one of the dingy side-streets. He waved
goodbye. The tiny figure waved, then turned into the side-street.

He made detours to avoid sniping on the long walk to Kings-town. He came to a Volunteer barricade at Ballsbridge and they let him through. He asked about Conroy but these men knew nothing. 'Conroy? Who's he?' A cigarette shop was open farther on and he bought some cigarettes and walked back to the barricade with them.

'But we don't want gifts from anyone.'

'Go on, please,' he said. 'Just a present from me even though, mind you, I think you're crazy and wrong.'

They took the cigarettes. He looked at the few rifles, the shot-guns, the faces of the men, then went on his way.

When he reached Blackrock, with the last coppers of the money which yesterday morning he had planned to spend, he bought biscuits in a shop thronged by the poor and the servants of the rich. All feared shortages of supplies, and all had been terrified by stories of civilians slaughtered in the city, and when he said that he had come unharmed out of the very heart of the Rebellion they did not believe him, and he did not care.

All night Miss Peters had sat in the room behind the terrace, waiting and praying. She knew his ring and knock and was at the door before Gwennie could get to it. She swayed there a moment, looking at him. She could not speak; her little face, shrunken by weariness and strain, quivered, crumpled and for the first time he saw her weep. He put an arm round her and drew her to a chair.

He knelt by her chair, patting her hands and passionately hoping that Millie now might be clasped and welcomed home like this.

His place had been laid for breakfast because, despite the stories of slaughter in the city, she would not admit that he would not return.

'You will stay with me now until this terrible thing is over. What must the dear King and Queen be thinking of this? Stabbing the Empire in the back in its hour of danger!'

That was how it seemed to most people. That was how it seemed even to him. After all, England had promised them Home Rule and now when she had her back to the wall it seemed hardly the moment to strike at her. The rebels had seized strongholds all over the city: the G.P.O.; Jacob's Factory; the South Dublin Union. The thing was serious.

Morning after morning he went down to the harbour to watch the Imperial reinforcements arriving. He stood apart from the crowds who gave tea and cigarettes to the bewildered, anxious Tommies, some of whom thought that the cannonading was the first roar of Flanders, and he looked at their rifles and equipment, at the lorries, the armoured cars, the machine-guns and all the power of a great army, huge and rich. They came continually, thousands of them, and he began to think, 'Well, anyway, the greatest empire since Rome has had to send thousands to fight a few hundreds,' and when he saw among the watchers a resentful face it re-awakened the rebel in him and he went to stand beside that man or woman. Generally it was a boy or a very young man. They would agree: 'The Rebellion is wrong. But can't they at least give the rebels a fighting chance?' In this way he spoke to many, walked home with some and took tea, once in a comfortable study-bedroom with a boy whose eyes smouldered when his bridge-playing sisters downstairs spoke of the rebels as 'riff-raff'.

All day the artillery boomed like distant thunder, hammering the streets where he had walked with Millie. He sat at his window with Mr. Peters' racing-glasses and watched a gunboat going towards the river-mouth to join in the bombardment. He watched the red canopy widen over the city, widen, deepen, pillared with smoke columns by day, by night a purple-red plain caverned with black pits, while the great guns of empire hammered.

At breakfast each morning Mr. Peters said in astonished rage: 'Not surrendered yet? Well, they can't stand up long to that. Another day and they'll have to come crawling out of their holes.'

Down at the harbour, young women in high-powered cars were calling the soldiers 'heroes'. The rebels were 'murderers', and he longed to say: 'They are not murderers, they are very brave men, and chivalrous, which you are not, when you talk like that. At least have the decency to acknowledge that artillery is being used against half-armed men.'

Each night he wrote down for Norman a report of all he had learned of the day's fighting, making a record for when the mails would travel again. Each day he wrote a letter to post later to Millie in which he said little or nothing of the Rebellion.

He could forget it all by thinking of Millie, by vainly trying to
call up her image. But then he would gaze again at the distant
canopy of smoke over the river city that was now on fire. Down
in that furnace was Conroy, blazing away with rapidly dimin-
ishing ammunition, unless he was already dead. Ned Connolly
had died in France and Great Mars in Suvla Bay. With
divided loyalties and tormented heart, he did not know what to
think.

He was glad when it was over and the rebels had surrendered
unconditionally. Two days after this had happened he was sent
back to school and had to lock away his diary once more. And
now halls and classrooms rang with violent arguments for and
against 'the rebels'. For even in here life had been shaken out of
its old, assured ways and bubbled with an undercurrent which
authority could not control. For yet another day or two, Martin
was with those who, while praising the rebels' courage, condemned
the Rebellion. But the courts-martial had begun and morning
messages began to whisper along the pattering files: 'Two more
executed this morning,' or 'Only one this morning.' The names
of the executed would travel along the files with the ranks they
had borne in what was called 'the fight'. Every morning Martin
woke early, long before the prefect had stirred, and would look
across towards the suburbs, trying to hear the bullets of the
executioners, wondering if perhaps, this very morning, in the
dawn of a barracks yard Conroy might be marching out to his
death.

Each day in classes copies of the Proclamation passed secretly
about. It was related that Connolly, the Labour leader, wounded
in the fighting, had been carried out and executed, seated on a
chair, because the rising tide of indignation, both in England and
Ireland, had made it possible that the blood-bath would be
ended by the politicians before the military had taken their
vengeance upon all the leaders. It was told how one of those leaders
had gone on writing poetry until the death dawn, how another
would not be blindfolded before rifle barrels, and how a third
had assured his court-martial judges that since they were officers
of an empire they would understand the words of an Imperial
poet, *dulce et decorum est pro patria mori*, 'tis a sweet and agreeable
thing to die for one's country'. As the daily killings continued,
the bubbling undercurrent founted up through the surface of

school discipline, so that halls rang with arguments, and now it
was the boys with Imperial emblems in their coats who blushed
and turned away when others said: 'Murderers! Butchering men
who, right or wrong, fought like soldiers for what they believed
was right!'

Stories even began to arrive of Irish officers and men in Flanders
refusing to honour the King's name when they learned that their
fellow Nationalists had been executed for following the example
of rebellion set to them by their Orange opponents. Had not
Carson, now a member of the Government which was ordering
these executions, been the original rebel, with his talk of calling
in German aid if Home Rule were enforced? To hot bewildered
minds it seemed that all justice was thus mocked; and one day a
boy, who was to have followed his father and grandfather on to
the battlefields of the Empire, publicly burned a letter from his
grandfather's regiment.

From a list of court-martial sentences he learnt Conroy's
fate—twenty years' penal servitude; he swore that Conroy
would not stay for long in an English prison. 'And next time,'
the growing little groups at school were already saying, 'next
time we will not wear uniforms, we will not show a flag, we
will fight in the only way a small, unarmed country can fight.
We won't hoist a flag to be bombarded by big guns that we haven't
got; next time it is we who will do the executing, do it whatever
way we can. And there will be no surrender.'

By the time the generals with their courts-martial had been
called off and the executions had stopped, it was too late. Martin,
like many others, was by then a rebel. Even Norman had been
alienated by the executions and spoke as if his sympathies were
with Sinn Fein. When he wrote he signed himself: *Your friend in
the cause of Freedom.*

Sally and Peggy were a different matter. Sally's first letter
after the Rebellion shocked and appalled him—he did not know
that Ronald Bingham had been 'missing' on the Western Front
since the very week of the Rebellion. He sent a bitter reply to
*your ranting repetitions of every honest inaccuracy and every deliberate
lie you have read in the great English propaganda machine.* He was
beginning to wish that he had written less violently when her
answer came. She was so astonished that she wondered if *this
can possibly be a jape in the very worst of taste?* . . . *Siding with the*

riff-raff of Dublin who stabbed the Allies in the back, disgracing Ireland in the eyes of all civilized people.

The letters came and went but neither of them would yield an inch.

Dear Martin,

I do repeat every word I said about them. How can you write these dreadful letters! Have you lost all respect for Mother and Daddy? You need not fear that I shall write to the Peters, since you seem to have enough shame to want to keep these terrible things from them. Pretty news for Miss Clare to hear out in America! And would you say such things to Colonel Howard? I never want to hear from you again until you apologize and write decently. And now Ireland is keeping all those troops and guns in the country which might have saved men in France from being taken prisoners and missing.

So it went on:

Dear Sally,

How can you hint that I would help the Germans in any way in the war! I loathe the way they think Might is everything. In the war England is on the right side—but not in Ireland. Here they have become Germans themselves—Might is the only thing that counts. Nothing now is of any importance to me except to make Ireland a country where everyone, especially the poor, will have Justice and comfort and everyone be proud.

Martin

Very dear Martin,

What have you been doing to Sally? And what is all this muttering about you helping those dreadful rebels? Now Aunt Ethel has forbidden me even to write to you. I must obey her but every three months I shall tell her that I am going to write a letter to you. So please write often to me. Everything is dreadful. It is dreadful about Ronald Bingham. Sally cries nearly every night and some of it is about you, so please write her a nice letter to make up. I wish there was no war and no rebellion or fighting anywhere, and I just will not think of all the men being killed and sleeping in dug-outs with rats and skin diseases.

Going back to school is going to be more depressing than ever for me. I am growing up and the mistresses are not. Neither are the other girls. I see more and more how very nice nearly all the people at home are in ways I never noticed before; and how very nice you and Norman Dempsey and dear brave Cousin Harry always were, I have learned many things about boys and I shall want your advice since you know about boys as well as about Sally and me.

I am going to be very bored and lonely this term. Even the punishments are boring instead of punishing. Please get a photograph taken. The only one I have is that one of you between Sally and me. You are small in that and now I want to see you big. Please write a pleasant letter to Sally now. Do not mention the war or the dreadful things in Dublin. I have started an album for Mother and Daddy, so please tell me things they said. You always remembered so well.

Your loving cousin, Peggy

He did not know how to answer Peggy. He knew only that he would not 'deny Ireland'. Instead of writing to Peggy, he sent an angry answer to Sally's bitter words, and was answered in kind.

Dear Martin,

I will not endure these letters from you. 'Solemnly dedicating all our lives', you and Norman. I simply cannot understand how you two can have become such beastly, vulgar prigs. When you and Norman have 'kicked the English out bag and baggage', I suppose then you will help Prendergast to pull up Mother's garden and plant turnips? Then Ireland will be happy—your 'Proud Ireland'.

Sally

P.S. It is settled that I am to be allowed to join the V.A.D. So that's the end of school for me.

Dear Sally,

I shall never forgive you for what you have said about Aunt Kathleen's garden. In our new Ireland everyone will have a garden and therefore people like Prendergast will understand that turnips are not everything.

Martin

Dear Peggy,

Please believe me that I love you—just exactly as always—but what you say shows that you do not understand about the rebels and therefore you might say something as bad as Sally has done. I do not want that to

*happen so I am going to stop writing to you until Ireland is free. Honestly,
please try to see why I must. Please do.*

*I admit Aunt Kathleen would not agree with me, but she would come
to understand that we only want freedom and justice for everyone. She might
even understand that I am really going to fight for Keelard. Keelard is
Ireland.*

*I don't see why you want to find out things about boys. You are only
sixteen and a half. You just be careful what kind of boys you allow to
escort you or talk to you. I hate to think of some kinds of boys even talking.*

*I am very glad that you have not said anything unforgivable and it is
honestly better to stop now before anything too bad is said. In that way,
we shall be able to be the same as ever when Ireland is free. It will take
a few years. I shall always, always, always be*

your loving cousin, Martin

P.S. I do love you, Peggy, I do. Please try to understand.

*P.P.S. Tell Sally I am just forgetting what she said. Tell her she will
be sorry one day.*

They were not his only correspondents. One morning he found
on the breakfast table an envelope addressed in Mary Ellen's
round and careful hand.

Dear Master Martin,

*The mistress had a letter from Mr. James' hospital in Eastbourne.
He will have a false foot but now he is coming home and can't be killed.
Isn't it Eastbourne where your great pal Miss Jamieson was at school?
Poor Mr. James they say is furious about all the executions and when he heard
they used the artirallary on the city he was wild and he and three of the
Irish officers at a party would not drink the drink for the King. And now,
dear Master Martin, I am going to get married in a year or two. We have
a good bit saved and he is a very nice man, nice and quiet like. He is
foreman in the Cork branch but now they are making him the under-
Manager and maybe in five years they will promote him to the Dublin
head branch. With Mr. James settled back home I won't mind leaving the
mistress but I hope Miss Bridget won't get married and go before then,
she's that tall and long. And now, dear Master Martin, never a word
from poor old Josie. I often look at the grand snap photo on the mantelpiece in the frame with Master Dempsey so fond of you there and all in
your football suits, so I am waiting for the day when you will walk in
the door there and sing a song for me like the old days, only poor Josie*

won't be here. And now I hope, dear Master Martin, they're not right
what they say about you being terrible different in your ways and I mention
you high up in my prayers every night.

Yours kind and respectful
Mary Ellen

When her three months of obedience had passed, Peggy wrote
to him again. She said nothing of war, Ireland, Justice or Empire;
she did not mention Sally and she asked him to write. He hesitated, longing to write to her, but his summer holidays passed in
writing articles for the revived journals, in collecting for the
prisoners' National Aid, in Liberty Clubs and in rooms behind
tobacconists' shops where men and boys talked of Constitutions
and the Rights of Men. This and occasional meetings with Millie,
which, however eagerly awaited, left him farther than ever from
Keelard in spirit.

He did not write.

At Christmas, Peggy sent greetings. He replied with New
Year greetings. Encouraged by this, she wrote a letter. He
hesitated, longing to write to her, and to Sally, but afraid of
quarrelling about 'Ireland' and 'Empire'. In the end, he did not
write, and Peggy wrote no more.

4

O<small>N</small> <small>THE</small> Easter Monday anniversary of their meeting Millie and Martin had been cycling back between the orchards of Meath towards the luring sky-glow of Dublin. The day had been warm and now in the beam of the bicycle lamps the dew showed opalescent on young buds, as they entered the great avenues of the Phoenix Park.

In the twelve months that had elapsed the whole mood of Ireland had changed. For every rebel heart then, there were at least twenty now. The English Government had vacillated, interned hundreds of prisoners; then sent the Prime Minister to visit them behind the barbed wire and—shifting foot on to a policy of mercy—had released many of them, including Conroy. But it was too late for gratitude. The daily executions had done their work. Sinn Fein, that had been a tiny minority, was becoming the dominant political party. The Home Ruler and the Nationalist were creatures of the past. If there were an election now Sinn Fein would sweep the polls.

Martin's thoughts were divided between politics and Millie. At Christmas, and during the weeks of the previous summer, it had been enough to come too early to their meeting places so that he might see her hand waving at him from the tram, her strong graceful figure leap lightly down and her eyes laugh into his across all the traffic; enough then to kiss, to dawdle with her along the book-stalls of the Quays or pretend they were buying furniture in the quayside auction-rooms amid the ringing handbells of the auctioneers; enough then to stand with her in the gallery queue for the Gaiety Theatre, the pit queue for the Abbey Theatre, to lean beside her on the quay wall above the river, and enough to walk with her hand in his through picture galleries and the national museum. Enough, and perhaps most sweet of all, to be her teacher and to see her learn.

But now these were no longer enough; now, on many nights, he lay clenching the pillow or the edge of the mattress, while his whole being craved for her.

She must be hungry now, after the long bicycle ride, drowsy too like himself with country smells and the tang of swelling earth where they had dozed in the sunlight.

'Put your hand on my shoulder. Norman and I often did that for Sally and Peggy when they were tired.'

She muttered fretfully over her shoulder: 'Oh, Sally-Peggy, Sally-Peggy! Norman, Norman!'

Then, dismounting on the grass verge, she said, 'I wonder what you would have done this night twelvemonth, if my hair hadn't been the same colour as your Sally's.'

He took no notice of her remark. Instead he said, 'Funny to think that in some of those farmhouses back there in Meath today cousins of mine were sitting as we passed and I don't even remember their names.'

'So there *is* something you don't remember!'

'Millie, don't be like this. I told you I forget a lot of things.'

'Forget a lot of things? I think you remember the Garden of Eden itself, and what the Father, Son and Holy Ghost looked like the day they were making it!'

Suddenly she put out her hand and pressed his arm urgently.

'Listen, Martin. I'm *myself* and I want to be myself. I'm not always thinking of relations and people I once knew . . . For some people what's happened in the past would be best forgot. But for you the past is still there alive. Well, you're welcome to it. But don't be always ramming it down my throat. I'm tired, that's what I am.' She mounted and cycled on, silent, nor did she put her hand on his shoulder.

But when they had crossed the Fifteen Acres and passed the bounds of the Vice-Regal Lodge, they began to see the silhouettes of lovers, still and sad-looking against the twilight; and she put her hand on his shoulder with something of a child's movement. He bore the touch of her hand burning through his veins and, close together in a silence which scarcely trembled before the whirring of their wheels, they sped down towards the city. They halted at the bridge where on the night of the Rebellion they had looked at the city lit only for them under its indigo-and-violet sky. Her hand stole into his. 'The night you were my escort.'

'Yes.'

They rode on to a side-street where she waited while he went into the National Aid office to fetch the bag in which this morning he had brought the money he had collected for prisoners' relatives.

They went to Anthony's. On the fixed table, as narrow as a bench, they leaned elbows and talked almost mouth to mouth, she drawing him on to tell her why he had been so depressed earlier in the day.

'I was thinking of Conroy,' he said, 'doing time.'

'Ah, it pulls the heart out of you, the people you're fond of, I mean. Maybe you think too much.'

'I couldn't think too much of them any more than I could of *you*.'

'I didn't mean your friends. But just of . . . ah, Ireland—England, France, Timbuktu and the Stars and Stripes. Look, Martin . . .' Her face, eager and wooing, leaned even closer to his. 'Listen, I want us to be ourselves, Martin. I want to cut down the time till we can get married. God knows it will be years at the best, but with this politics-for-Ireland business there's no knowing anything. You say that Frenchmen and English and Americans gave up careers and friends and all, just to fight for their country and Right. But all those fellows were paid a salary for being officers; and they got medals and presents and what-not. You and your like are going to *pay* to be officers.'

'Officers! The way you insist on us being officers!'

'Well, I can bet my life you never thought of yourself as a private!'

She laughed at him; and he, looking at her loving laughter, did at last laugh at himself and admit, 'You're right, Millie.'

'Martin,' she said timidly. 'Supposing you and me . . .' With a shy look she changed 'you and me' to 'you and I'. 'Supposing we decided we would live—at least for the first while—in some place where our friends and acquaintances couldn't come interfering and talking. Supposing we started off in England, say—for the first year or two anyway? Or America, if you like. Or Australia even. Not here.'

It was torture to think of it, the time when they would live together; and her talk of where it would be was scarcely noticed by him. 'I can't wait, Millie. And yet I must. I must even do another term . . . I mean, another spell of studying, you know.'

'Yes, I know,' she said gently. 'Tell me, will it really be over for good this summer?'

'Yes. God, yes!'

June, June—no more lying and pretending. No more having to go to Sacraments, which almost choked him.

'Millie, I wish you would give up going to Confession and so on.'

'Ah, but sure I only go once in the blue moon. And when I do go I don't tell them everything. Only as much as I think good for them to hear. Sure they have to tell people a lot of stuff and invent sins. That's their job.'

That made him laugh. 'You calling yourself a Catholic! If the theologians heard you! You've turned it into something altogether private to yourself.' And then very soberly: 'Of course you'll have to put it all overboard before we're married. No Confession to priests from *my* wife.'

'Ah, sure, I only just like to keep them on my hands.'

Then she added more thoughtfully: 'I wouldn't like, Martin, *never* to say a prayer. Don't you ever feel you'd like to say a prayer, Martin? Go to Mass, or just say a prayer?'

'No, never. You'll find yourself dropping all that altogether soon. Look—Pascal said he shuddered even to see his sister embracing her own children. He should have been a priest. They hate life, they hate people like us, they hate love. They must in honesty hate and fear everything—things we like, Millie—the theatre, books, everything. Their love of God simply must become hate of life. Lock us up, don't look at this, don't hear that word, don't read that book—don't live!'

'Oh, aye, there's lots of them with very dirty minds all right;.I wouldn't have them inside the door. But you can always pick a nice one if you look about for him.'

He shook with laughter. 'You remind me a little of the way Aunt Mary used to talk about the Sodalities. Aunt Mary would have taken you straight into her heart, Millie.'

'I like her,' she said wistfully. 'I like the way she looks in that photograph you showed me.' And then remembering a promise he had made her: 'Did you bring that photograph of your ten-pound Norman?

He took Norman's photograph from the bag and the blood swelled the veins around his heart when he saw her neck bending over the picture, the pectoral muscles drooping her blouse between shoulder-bone and breast. The browny tinge down her throat, the lie of her fingers along the photograph, clouded all vision, speech and thought. 'H'm, I knew,' she murmured over the photograph. 'He looks a proper snob and swank.' She studied the picture. 'Aye, I knew,' she said again with something of sad acceptance in her voice. Then, with bravado: 'Well, let's forget about your ten-pound Norman for once. It's a pity one of you wasn't a girl, then you could have been sweethearts properly.'

To change the subject he begged her once again to let him meet her family.

'They'd be suspicious of you, Martin, from the word go. You'd seem all queer and dangerous to them. Also, Kitty's dead against girls getting mixed up with men any way above them, students above all. And you should hear Da—my father—about "so-called gentlemen students playing about with working-girls". Even if we got over that, Kitty and he would laugh at the idea of me waiting maybe years and years. And even if they didn't stop me seeing you altogether, we'd be a marked pair and could go nowhere free. As it is, even supposing I'm ever seen with you on a tram or anywhere, I can just say afterwards, "Oh, a chap I know," and be done with it, for I know hundreds of chaps off-hand like.'

For a moment he looked jealous until she said weakly, 'I love you rightly, Martin, and best of all.'

He could not stand it. There, before him, her face; and her words humming into his head. He stammered out his passion and the burden of his desire of her.

'I know,' she whispered to his mouth.

'You don't. A girl couldn't know. I can't go on like this for ever.'

'Neither can I,' she whispered.

He looked up and saw in her brown eyes the flame of his own desire. That revelation filled him with relief and gladness. They whispered their plans. On Thursday in the hills above the city they would find some place for their love.

They went out into the night, collected their cycles and rode back to the river.

With their heads hunched over the stone coping, away from people who brushed past their backs, they kissed and repeated the plans for Thursday.

'Tell me again how to find the stars. Tell me again where Cassiopeia is. Did I say it right this time?'

He showed her the Lady in the Chair, then watched her up-tilted, watching face. If only he had not done the things he had done; if only he had never gone to Knockester.

As always, they said they must part now and did not part. When at last she made resolutely to go and their fingers' touch was breaking, she stepped back close to him and, looking modestly into his eyes, she spoke of the risks an unmarried girl took in love. 'And I don't know whether you know anything at all about how to . . .'

'Of course, of course,' he lied; hastily taking over from her the burden of that necessity. But his heart gave off a frightened curse at the world which had kept that sword in ambush.

'All right then,' she whispered and their eyes looked deep into one another.

'Thursday.'

'Thursday.'

And with a shy, backward smile over her shoulder, she went. Thursday, Thursday, Thursday.

He stood in a doorway, thinking of what he must learn before Thursday, and he searched his memory for scraps of talk at Knockester in days when pride had made him scorn the queasy exchange of confidences between older boys. 'Aye,' he thought, 'H.T. would be the man to tell me, H.T. would enjoy that joke.' Knockester had soiled everything, and now his own imagination had turned into the same paths. Pulling aside the bandagings which pride had wrapped around his mind, he looked at himself on his knees before priests while they begged him to see the sin of his love of Sally, the worse sin of his love of Norman, and he renewed his vows that one day he would help to make it impossible that such things should be said and done to other boys after him. In a free Ireland!

But Thursday, Thursday, Thursday. The minutes were passing and he was still ignorant. He knew Jimmy Curran's Principal

Writers of the Pastoral School—sniff—but he didn't know what
he must know now. Young men bustled past the doorway confidently and he thought: 'For sale! The poems of Virgil and Horace
and all the irregular Latin verbs without a mistake, in return
for one small piece of information! For sale, the names and tastes
of several French wines and some Rhenish. For sale, how to keep
a boat prow on to a flood.' Elsewhere, a man, a boy, could find
some mercifully anonymous, impersonal shop, walk boldly in
and pretend to know, or learn! But not here.

He was standing under the Four Courts when he thought of
searching his wallet in the weak hope of finding an address, the
visiting card of some grown man whom he might, daringly,
approach. There, among the addresses of Dunslane boys given
him by Conroy this day twelvemonth, he saw Mullins's name. It
was just the kind of knowledge Mullins would authoritatively
have; Mullins in an examination would get more than a mere
pass in that.

With a savagery deliberately invoked to fortify himself for a
call upon the aid of Mullins, he said: 'Damn them. They keep us
ignorant, half starved and overworked, while the parish priest
feeds himself fat so that he won't feel the cold when he goes
hunting boys and girls out of the ditch—the only place they have
left to us at all. Great, black bullies—I am going to Mullins.'
He swung away and, crossing the river, saw to right and left the
lights which last year had been lit only for her and him, the tall,
huddled roofs, the domes and spires and, far away at one end,
part of the rubble heaps from last year's bombardment. He said
to the spaces above the water, 'I will love her and honour her
always.' And having said that, he went to Mullins.

His route took him a long way, through the moneyed Georgian
squares, past houses whose parties and young-lady daughters were
already beginning to bore him because of Millie and of politics;
already he had spoken during holidays under an assumed name
at a big by-election meeting, already had felt rising within him a
power that had seemed to flow out to that great crowd of people
who had not seemed to remember that he was only a boy. 'Real
people,' he said now to himself, 'not second-raters like those in
there.' He laughed to the amber night above the graceful
Georgian squares and he cocked his lip as he passed the granite
door-pillars carved out of the Dublin hills where he would go with

Millie on Thursday, Thursday, Thursday. Arriving at the address
which Mullins had given him he found that it was a boarding-
house. He rang the bell.

'Gentleman to see you, Mr. Mullins,' and on a gust of talk
a burly figure swept confidently into the hall, then, seeing an
unrecognized visitor, hesitated with an air of alert but friendly
business trustworthiness.

'Hello, Mullins. Don't you know me? Martin Reilly—from
Dunslane.'

'Well, be the hokey! Well, fancy *you* coming to see *me*!' The
big, shiny face beamed. 'Fancy you looking old Mullins up!
Bedad, this is damned nice of you now.'

Martin whispered that he wanted to speak to him in private.
When the living-room door had been closed he revealed his reason
for coming and Mullins slapped him on the back. 'Man, you're
the deep one! Fancy you getting a good thing with only the
holidays to find her, and myself can hardly get one at all with
nothing else to do every evening but scout round. Where did
you get her?'

'She was working in a factory when I met her, if you insist on
knowing.'

'And, be God, haven't you more sense than myself any day. No
wasting your time with some bloody clerk that's hoping you'll be
fool enough to marry her. My old chap's offices are full of that
sort, all with an eye on the boss's son.' Then with an access of
honest manliness: 'You're still at school, you know, I sort of think
a fellow ought to stay pure till he's left school. For ever of course—
if he's the sort that can. Now, I'm no saint but . . . Ah, well,
sure I'm not my brother's keeper. I wouldn't see an old Dunslane
chap stuck for want of a helping hand from old Mullins.'

They went upstairs together. The electric-light bulb threw
gleams on Mullins's fat, efficient-looking face. There he learned
what Mullins had to teach him, received what Mullins had to
give him.

There he heard also the tale of Mullins's business triumphs, the
big institutions that had taken out insurance with Mullins's
Irish Company; the nuns' hospitals, the home for penitents, the
churches and the schools. 'And why wouldn't they back us instead
of a lot of Protestants and English! Catholics should all stand
together, shouldn't they, Martin—old man?'

He conducted him back to the hall again.

'Tell you what, old man, I'd better take you to the shop and introduce you personally. Then he won't be afraid to serve you any time you go along to him.'

'Oh, no, thanks. I'll just go now.'

'And come running to me again next time?'

There was no answer to that. Indeed, better the shop than another visit to Mullins's hall and bedroom.

Along the Quays, the houses might never have been ruby-and-gold in the after-light, so blackly notched were they now against a sky that was washed pale blue by the moonlight. The verdigris of the copper dome of the Four Courts shone with a strange uncanny gleam. All around the rim of the sky a scalloped frill of cloud enclosed the city and only the river tunnelled a way in under that flounce of darkness. Far off, below and beyond that fringe, were the roads to the places he had loved; in Glenkilly, the night streets would echo the sounds of footsteps and the bell of the Crucifixion Convent sound far over the roofs, while in Lullacreen, Moydelgan, Keelard, the doors would be closed and the cattle down on their knees in the gloom.

They turned into a street towards Dame Street and 'Here we are,' whispered Mullins like a boy raiding an orchard. In the shop he whispered to the youth behind the counter who fetched his father, a big, stagey-looking man with dewlaps pushing forward between the wings of his collar like the prows of two barges coming out of lock-gates. He gave Martin a fleshy hand, sucked his mouth into a pursed circle of radiating flesh and said that any friend of Mr. Mullins would always be 'as welcome as a sod of turf'. That genial countryside expression, coming so sibilantly in a Levantine voice from that pursy corona of bloodless lips which had never whistled over a turf fire, revealed to Martin a whole world where tongues were ready to be all things to all men, and to talk of turf to Mr. Mullins.

They came out. 'Now you'll be *persona grata* with him,' said Mullins. A moment later he said *persona grata* again as though to draw attention to the fact that his Dunslane days had not been entirely wasted. 'He has to be careful. The National University fellows smashed the place up twice.' Martin said good night.

Shame, self-hatred and hatred of the world, which was as it was, lay like a stone in his chest. He made his way to Westland Row station. From the train he watched the suburban lights flashing past the windows. If the bicycle lamp had not flashed on Millie's hair this night twelve months ago he would not have known her.

Miss Peters sat with him while he took his supper, scolding him a little for being so late. He told her of the look of County Meath in the spring. One day he could tell her about Millie—one day, one day. From her bedroom, she rang her little silver handbell and he went in and read Longfellow to her as she sat, upright in her straight-backed armchair, in her woollen bed-jacket. Then he kissed her good night. Ready on the night table beside her were her face cream, her spectacles and her prayer-book. Last thing before she slept she would read the Prayer for All Sorts and Conditions of Men.

In bed he could not sleep. The rhythmical flashing of the light-house brought the evocation of the night when he had seen the going-away of the mail-boat which ought to have returned with Aunt Kathleen. Huddling in his dressing-gown, and drawing the curtains against the flashing, he read Aucassin and Nicolette. When he pulled back the curtains again, the stars were paling in the blue-grey end of night, and he smiled to think how always when they stood on the shaking bridge over the canal lough Millie would ask him to show her once more the roadways of the heavens and Cassiopeia riding in the golden chair.

Mais que j'aie Nicolette, ma très douce amie. It was only a story. But it was true, always true. True even now in 1917! He would tell her the story of Aucassin and his Nicolette; and she would say: 'It's just perfect, that's all.' *Mais que j'aie Nicolette, ma très douce amie.*

In bed he smiled. *En paradis qu'ai-je à faire?* Yes, indeed, what had he to do with their pale Paradise! And he put his watch upon a pad lest it might keep him awake with its ticking of time, time, time—Thursday, Thursday, Thursday.

Walking their bicycles up past the last trees and birds, they moved on to a mountain world, empty of everything except furzy gorse and the little wind that wheeped through it. Once they turned and saw far below them the Bay of Dublin pushing back into the land the crescent of the city whose horns, beaded with townships, curved in distant brightness to Howth Head on one tip, Bray Head on the other. They turned their backs on it, found a place for their bicycles and then walked on into a world where they were the only living things.

They did not speak while they searched, nor after they had found a deep, hollowed place. They stood looking down from the brink of that sun-bathed hollow. In silence, they went down there and found a slope of dry spring moss.

Down here where they lay, not a sound came to them except the thumping of their hearts and the thin, distant wheep of the wind stirring the gorse at the brink of their sunlit bed. Sometimes, faint trickles of wind stole down to them and moved a tendril of her hair. Once she said: 'Maybe it might be like this up in an aeroplane. Away out of the world.'

'Yes, only you and me.'

She whispered his words back to him, 'Only you and me.' As they looked up at the canopy of sky above them and back to one another their love spilled over from lips that could scarcely speak. Some mute pleading in her eyes signalled him away from her, and when he returned he saw the sunlight full upon her, lying where he had left her, and on the slash of white that she had drawn across her as a girdle.

In the peak of their hour of union, his passion and clumsiness betrayed him. Their separate selves could not mingle beyond the crumbled fortresses of separate flesh. Smitten by a thunderbolt of defeat, he felt ashamed, mocked by that electric light which he had seen gleam on Mullins's fat, efficient-looking face.

But beside his head he heard a whisper. 'It'll be all right next time—just wait and see.'

He looked into her eyes at the very face of her spirit, and bending to her bosom, he said, 'Why must it be this way, why has it to be this way at all?'

At long last she said, 'I suppose you'd like me to put on my clothes now?'

He remained silent, ashamed to admit his real feelings, ashamed to say 'Yes'.

And she, with a little note of bitterness in her voice, said dryly, 'It's all right,' and they dressed.

A shared impulse seemed to prompt them to turn their backs on their lovely hollow. Even when they had taken their food packages from their bicycles, they went still farther away from their hollow bed and ate their food in silence, side by side in the shelter of two great boulders. That done, he rose and, without a word to her, walked away from her. He walked about the gorse, and by the brinks of pools, and now and then he looked back at her distant figure, small and dark, waiting there with her back against a boulder.

He went back to her, sat beside her and said: 'I have some things to tell you, Millie. I've been letting you believe a lot of lies. Or not telling the truth anyway.'

He did not look at her and she, with her head lying back against the rock, said nothing.

'I'm not a little over twenty now. I added on two years when I first met—well, when I picked up Florrie. I'm a little over eighteen. Nearly a year younger than you. Not quite.' She said nothing. He said: 'And that's not all. I don't study privately. I'm only a schoolboy still. I'm in Knockester College.'

Still she said not a word; and he did not know what she was looking like now, with her head against the rock round which the wind crept to her face.

'Studying in the country—a lie. And the reasons I would give for not being able to meet you—all lies. I was just locked up in school. I was thinking of you out in the city, and I could not get out to see you for even an hour, I could hear hooters and things from the city. When your evenings were barely beginning, I would be going to bed in a dormitory and hearing prayers. I'll be finished with all of it this summer—that part was true. But I must go back in eight days.' He waited.

She said nothing. He began again: 'You see you told me you left school before you were even fifteen. I was afraid and . . .'

'Listen, Martin, is this more about your being only a boy at school?'

'Well . . . er. Well, yes.'

'But sure I knew about that, all the time,' she said tenderly. 'Didn't Florrie see the school cap peeping out of your pocket. And didn't she see through the gap in your raincoat, and when you weren't noticing pull your parcel up against the bottom of the raincoat, just to make sure you really were in bare knees.'

'And all this time you knew that I was letting you believe lies?'

'Yes, but I knew that you'd tell me the truth of your own accord. I knew why you were doing it. I wanted to tell you that it didn't

matter, but I thought it nicer for you probably to do it your way.
I didn't want you to feel ashamed by me knowing.'

'Millie, there's another thing you ought to know. It's about
my . . . my birth. I won't know exactly until I am twenty-two.
There's a letter I'm pledged not to read. But it's quite likely that
I may be . . .' He stammered and her voice beside him said easily,
gently:

'Ah, I sometimes wondered if you might be a love-child.'

A love-child! He had heard that name when he had been a
child and had not known its meaning. Now it came so easily, so
affectionately, from her.

'A love-child,' he said. 'I never thought of it that way before.
A love-child.'

When he asked her in wonder what had made her think this,
she said:

'The night we met, the night of the Rebellion, you said your
aunt had said you were never to let anyone speak ill of Mrs.
O'Shea and Parnell or of any lady. We were under Parnell at the
time and you looking up at him with a pair of eyes like a girl
yourself and . . .' She turned her face to his and looked into his
eyes. 'And all evening I'd been afraid to open my mouth for
fear I'd put my foot in it and send you chasing away from me.
Well, you said then that maybe your own mother—and then
you stopped and looked shy, like the way you do sometimes. So
I thought then that maybe you might be a love-child yourself. And often since then I thought you had the marks of it,
because I heard once that they're the nicest and kindest and
truest.'

'And all this time you . . .' He could say no more, he held one
of her hands between his two. She might say 'Da' now always;
say 'like'; say what she chose; how had he dared to correct a
word of hers!

'I knew from the first that you were a girl in a million, Millie,
but I didn't know how fine you are. I don't deserve you.'

'Ah, hush,' she said hastily. 'Deserve! Don't talk of what we
deserve. And anyway the boot's on the other foot.'

'It isn't. It isn't. How can you love me, Millie?'

'It's just that, from the very first, the way you looked at me and
all your ways and—everything; it's just yourself. I think from
the first minute I saw you it was just yourself, and I often can't

believe I've really and truly met you until I come and feel your
bones again the next time.'

He could feel the bones of her own hand beneath the pressure
of his.

'You're real enough, Millie.'

'And the things you've taught me. I never even knew that some
pictures were painted with oil and others with water; and now I
know the names of half the men in the National Gallery and
Harcourt Street Gallery. I can learn, I have a head on me,
haven't I? You said so yourself.' He laughed.

'Some day we'll travel,' he told her. 'We'll go to France.
French books don't pretend about people and things. The French
ones they give us at school are all a cod! But even they are different
somehow. Italy, France and Italy, Millie—imagine it! We'll see
all the Renaissance things that never came here, we'll talk to
everybody in the cafés. We'll walk down from the Alps into Italy
one day together, one really sunny day, and maybe we'll see a
packet of Murphy's Starch in a village window like Jimmy
Curran.'

'You're right. We'll do that. The schoolmistress said I could
learn anything. She said it was all wrong me having to leave school
but of course I myself was peppering to leave then. We'll start
all over again; no past, no . . .' Suddenly she clung weakly to him.
'Oh, Martin, Martin! I love you rightly and best of all.'

While the sun moved down its mountain arc, they talked, building above the empty world of gorse that triumphant future when
Martin would have house and money, and Ireland would be free.

'Ireland free!' She laughed. 'If we wait for that, we'll wait till
Tib's Eve.'

'Just you wait and see. This time we're going to do it,' he
assured her.

Walking down they came to trees on which young buds were
already trying to burst into life, and they saw far below them the
city transfigured by evening light. Like a glowing medallion strung
on its beaded necklet of coastal townships, a necklet looping from
Bray Head to the Hill of Howth, the city lay tucked back by
the satin curve of the bay into the foliaged shelter of the mountains. As they stood looking down on it she told her plans. Kitty,
her step-mother, was to be away in Greystones over the week-
end, visiting a sister there.

'On Saturday I'll know if . . . my father . . . is going with her, he often does. When he does, they ask a woman up the street to pop in occasionally and see if I'm all right, and I'm supposed to pop in to her and show myself a couple of times. But sure I know the times she comes knocking! If my father does go, I'll send a note to you at Anthony's on Saturday. Come the back way. There's a lane at the back, it'll be the fifth door there and I'll put a cross in chalk on the lane-door and leave it unlocked. For God's sake don't let any of the neighbours notice you; I mean, see what you look like. Between nine and ten, there's generally not a soul around; they're all down town for the Saturday night.'

Standing among the young trees, they worked out their plan. Then they rode on through the fogging light down to the city. In Anthony's they sat silent, listening to the gramophone, watching the various flirtations going on around it. But they had no wish to be part of that world which they were glad to see so bright and cheerful.

Later, at the canal bridge, they leaned across the pedestrians' railing above the basin and whispered their last plans. All the time, something seemed to keep on bringing a shy and troubled expression to her face. And at last, looking down and fingering his coat, she said: 'Listen, Martin. It's just a very small, cramped little house. It's comfortable enough and bright and clean, but terribly cramped. I didn't want you to see it for a long time to come.'

'I know. What does that matter? I know your people haven't much money and all that—but one day!'

'Aye, one day!' And she looked swiftly up. 'One day we won't have to go behind the door with anything.'

Their trembling hands met, and she whispered: 'My room, it's . . . Well, it's only a box of a room really. But I keep it painted. All bright and matching.'

'I'll bring flowers.'

'Yes, do that,' she clung to him. 'Do that. Bring flowers and I'll have a nice supper ready for you.' She turned away and went and as she went she looked back suddenly over her shoulder with the shy, backward smile, deep now with new meaning and unity.

He told Miss Peters that an old Dunslane acquaintance wanted him to stay the week-end. He reminded her that at Christmas he had made no fuss when she had sent a refusal to Agnes Dempsey's invitation asking if he might spend Christmas with Norman at Tory Hill. But the reason why he had made no fuss was because he had been unwilling to leave Kingstown even for a week while Millie was in Dublin, just as in the preceding August he had broken the plans made by himself and Norman for spending the month together. He had asked Miss Peters to invite Norman for Easter, and when Norman could not come he had solaced himself with the thought that the postponement of their meeting could not be for long and that this time it was not due to any act of his.

On Saturday afternoon he went into the city, but there was no message at Anthony's. Later, there was still no word from her; no message, no sign by the late afternoon. He went again an hour later and the note was there, bidding him to come.

So, when the houses were shrouded by night, he walked between the bawling fruit-women, the glittering shops, the Saturday-night crowds, and he heard as in a dream the clanging of the trams. He came to the bridge and the inland harbour, withdrawn equally from the dim, deserted places beyond and from the crowded city streets behind him. There, a barge's porthole showed lighted, yellow like an orange—yellow like Dan Murphy's.

He buttoned up his overcoat collar. He had bought a cheap cloth cap, and this he now put on, and pulled well down over his forehead. He wanted to look indifferently into the eyes of the passers-by who made such secrecy necessary. But Millie must be secret. And so with upturned collar, with disguising cap, and with his flowers hidden in paper, he went like a thief to his love.

5

He left Knockester, he welcomed Conroy home from prison, he left Miss Peters. He told her no more than that he was not going to join the Army, that he was getting a university scholarship and must leave the house since Mr. Peters could not sit at table with a 'shirker' while his friends' sons died in Flanders. When he would have said more, she lifted a hand as if to ward off all information and she asked none of the questions which hovered in distress behind her eyes.

He packed and, bit by bit, the room she had made so nice for him grew bare. Inside Aunt Mary's dispatch case he put his diary, and he took a last look around his room, then went down to the cab. From the stairs he saw her in the hall, a shaft of sunlight across her face above the frivolous, ribbed lace collarette.

'Food in lodgings is not always nourishing. I shall send a special sum to your bank each month to be spent on nourishing additions to your diet,' and she looked imploringly at him. 'I have not only that right but that *duty*.'

He hesitated, then said, 'Yes, Miss Peters.'

In the city he drove to the lodgings which Conroy had found for him. The Misses O'Canavan—Miss Flo, thin as a reed, her younger sister, Miss Agnes, fat as a maggot, each with the rebel tricolour hidden behind the striped blouse—met him in the hall under Queen Victoria's picture, hanging high above the photographs of many Sergeants O'Canavan, Band-Masters, Corporals and one O'Canavan in a morning coat. Soon that royal portrait and little gallery of loyalists would help to make this house one of the safest places in Dublin, all the more so because Miss Flo and Miss Agnes were known to keep in their superior boarding-house only quiet Civil Servants and the like. But the rebel flag was pinned beneath each striped blouse because the Misses

O'Canavan, too, had had their sympathies inflamed by the drastic suppression of Easter Week.

In his little attic room, the cheapest in the house, he laid out his books, the prints, the photographs. On the mantelpiece he put beside Millie's picture the picture of Norman and himself in football togs, and Long Dick behind them, laughing at their laughing.

From his new digs he went to his first Volunteer drill and stood in the ranks with men well fed and hungry, with some who had come, he saw, from streets far poorer than Millie's, with labourers, students, drapers' boys, one son of the landed gentry, but no son from Dublin's professional squares. There, in a quiet part of the Dublin mountains, he formed fours with sacrificial accuracy and devotion; there he heard Conroy read out the vow and there he swore his oath to 'maintain and defend the rights and liberties of the people'. Afterwards he would go back to his attic room, his books and his prints and his photographs of the living and the dead.

The doors of Tory Hill were closed against him nowadays. Norman's was another heart which had turned rebel, and Mr. Dempsey had written to him:

. . . Without your influence this would never have happened. I asked you to look after him because I knew your influence over him. I try to forgive you, because it is my duty as a Catholic; but the most I can manage is to avoid wishing you ill. . . .

Norman himself wrote:

I have promised not to see you for a year. Father has not asked me not to write because he knows I would refuse. They think I may gradually withdraw from the movement. One day they will understand, and then you will come here again. And nothing will stop us meeting after the year.

For Millie the movement was a threat to all her hopes. Sometimes she would say: 'It isn't the waiting, Martin. It isn't the dodging and story-telling at home. I'd wait any length, dodge any way for you, if I saw the end of it coming in three years, five years. But we can't go on like this for *ever* and you getting nowhere in life.'

Then he would say: 'Wait. A few extra years don't make so much difference to us. Ireland must come first.'

'Martin, what difference will it make to you and me who's passing laws in Dublin Castle? Most of them, if you ask me, just want to do the bossing themselves instead of the English. I tell you it'll be a fine funeral if all that lot get their own way!'

Occasionally there came a night when he would have neither drill, nor committee, nor speech, nor article. Yet when he did have the night and the few shillings for theatre seats, she, who loved the theatre, would often say: 'No. It's a lovely night; come out to Howth Head and say poetry instead. Sure, you're a whole theatre yourself.' They would go away from the streets of the city with its cheers or boos, its processions, its baton charges, its welcomes to returning prisoners and all the growing signs of the work she did not share in, and lying high above the star-lit bay at Dublin, he would quote for her things from many countries of the world. Often he would discover from her talk that she saw things differently but with quite as sharp a vision as his own. She would range back and forth about places familiar to him but in a focus entirely different from hers. Passing some children playing 'hopscotch' along the street, she would know that their prize would be a half-penny for chips in a fish-and-chip saloon. She would talk of the 'lads up on their bicycles to bathe at the Half-Moon where the sewers wouldn't get at them', or about the girls heading off towards the Half-Moon to meet the lads on their way back—'by accident on purpose, Martin'. She would say of someone, 'Ah, he wouldn't dream of stepping down to the pillar-box without a hat.'

With a woman's tendrils she would draw him away to tell her of the things he had loved, of the stall-fed cattle in winter, their flanks gleaming in the lantern-light, of the great wheel turning to pulp the meal, of Christmas parties and plays and mixed hockey in Glenkilly; of Gertrude and Niave, all outward primness in the street under the stern maternal eye and all inward divilment of whispers, nudges and schemes. He would tell her of racing out into the morning mist at Dunslane and of the football shaking sparkles out of the dewy grass; of Norman's first try with the ball under his arm and his fair hair waving in the breeze. He would tell of night coming to the barley fields, still, golden night; of starry winter evenings with the hooves of fat Billy under the governess cart hitting the hard road and Sally's

eyes, bright under the shape of her tam-o'-shanter; of winter
mornings and the frost-jewelled turnips winking in the sun; of
Peggy's medicines for her brindled bitch, and her pony, and the
spring lambs which would not stay still when she tried to draw
them but went nosing crooked-ways into the milky teats of the
ewes, bumping their bored mothers who never bothered even
to look at them. She had never seen a walking sower scattering
the seed to right and left as if to music, alone in a field. It was
all marvellous in her eyes, he could see the marvel there, even
if he spoke only of the sun coming up and the sun going down.

The war was over. A general election was coming and it looked
as though the Home Rule party of former years was already a
thing of the past. The new party announced: 'We do not ask
your votes, we *demand* them. We are going to establish our own
Parliament without asking anyone's permission and we will
recognize only the laws, police and army of that Parliament. If
the police or soldiers of any other Parliament interfere we shall
resist their interference.'

Less and less patient grew the 'men of action' as no answer
came from the great world; more and more certainly they snarled:
'You and your moral persuasion! Where's it getting us? We're
oiling guns and drilling and making bombs and God knows what!
But when are we going to use them and teach those fellows that
we've had enough? The only principle any of them understand,
above all big Britannia, is the smack of a bullet. To hell with
Parliamentary sanction, we are going to start—and start soon.'

From the moment the shooting began he knew that from now
on he need try no more to find a free Saturday afternoon for a
visit to Miss Peters. He faithfully used her money on eggs and
butter and such things, as if that small loyalty might one day be
known to her. '*Qui mange bien dort bien,*' she had been used to tell
him, but he slept but little now, and more and more with instinct's
eyes wide open for danger, like a hare who expects the coming of
the dogs.

More and more he had come to act as an automaton to Conroy's
calls upon him. As the sounds of guns spread wider and louder,
his count of days became blurred, the calendar of his mind being
marked only by the approaching meeting with Norman and by
his appointments with Millie. Even those hours with her were no
longer secure to him, since often he had to go down into the

country without getting word to her; and often he was unable to return to Dublin in time for an appointed meeting. When they did meet, the old rhythm of their intercourse was shaken by searing memories of the things from which he had just come and by her silent repressed horror of the bloody deeds done by both sides in a struggle which had once merely bored her but now dismayed her.

She knew the danger he was running. Sometimes an assignment would take him into country that he knew. In a town not far from Ballow the police had adopted the foolish system of sending an armed escort to meet the local mail-car whenever its load included official mails. It was decided to make a raid on it. Conroy, Martin and another bicycled all through the night hours and, not long after dawn, they and the local Volunteers surrounded mails and escort. The rifles and revolvers were taken, the prisoners locked up for the day in a barn, and Conroy and Martin, having stamped the civilian mail 'Censored by the competent Irish Authority', gave it to young Tom Prendergast, who had become an ardent Sinn Feiner, to leave near a post office. Then they released the prisoners, fed them and sent them on their way. Twilight was falling when they began to head warily out of the area now streaked in all directions by searching troops and police. They were silent and sullen with one another because, during the labour of searching the mails, Conroy, coming across a love-letter from a local girl to the District Inspector of Police, had begun to blush angrily and mutter: 'I'll read no more; there's nothing official in it, and it's not good for one to read that kind of thing. He has a very nice wife, that fellow, and two children. He ought to be shot!'

Martin had rallied Conroy jokingly: 'Really, Seamus, when you're like that I don't know whether you bore me or disgust me. Can't you even read about love-making without feeling your delicious sense of sin!'

Sullen and contemptuous of one another, they came round a bend to see two military lorries bearing down on them through the twilight. Even while the soldiers were being thrown against one another by the sudden braking of the lorries, Conroy and Martin were through the hedge and racing up a high slope of field towards the shelter of its crest. When the bullets began to hit the earth behind their heels, they turned as they ran and fired back at the squat figures trying to lumber heavily across the hedge black against the last rim of light, while far away a ploughman stood staring from beside his unyoked horses and the crows and magpies rose scattering behind him. Two of the bulky encumbered figures were in the field, and one on the bank was taking aim at Conroy. This man's face was lit through the dusk by some light from the sky; and when Martin fired he saw the face tilt forward and the little squat body sag down on the bank.

The next morning Martin was astir early, but before he could get away he was commandeered to act as one of the judges in the local Sinn Fein Court. He had to spend the morning learning the Rules of Evidence from a kindly but very aged and boring barrister who would be his fellow judge. That afternoon, the court had barely passed its sentence in the first case when troops and police swooped down on it, so that the ponderous barrister had to run with the rest. When Martin got back to Dublin he went straight to Anthony's in the expectation that Millie might be there. And there in the last pew she sat, hoping that he might perhaps come.

But though at sight of him she banished the troubled look from her face, he had seen that grave, frightened look and saw the evening paper lying beside her. Looking down from her brown eyes, he saw the usual headlines: 'Audacious attack on . . .' 'Desperate affray at . . .' 'Detective shot dead . . .' and then amongst the news items in smaller type: 'The soldier wounded in the skirmish yesterday, when troops challenged two men believed to be connected with the Mail hold-up earlier in the day at Ballow Railway Junction, has died of his wounds.'

He looked into Millie's watching eyes and nodded miserably. 'Yes,' he said, 'yes.' And the expression on his face as he said it told her everything she needed to know.

Three days later a letter arrived from Norman. His mother, who had been ill for so long, had died, and the doctors had advised Mr. Dempsey to spend the rest of the winter out of Ireland. He said that he would go to the South of France but on one condition —that Norman came with him. Norman suspected that his father's object was to take him away from dangerous Ireland. He did not know that both police and military had privately warned Mr. Dempsey to get his rebel son out of the country. They had even named a week-end when Norman, who for some time had been 'on the run', could slip home safely to hear his father's proposition.

Norman wrote: *What is your advice? Can I in honour leave Ireland now?* He took the letter with him when he went to meet Millie at Anthony's.

'What should Norman do?'

'In the name of God!' she said angrily. 'What should he do? Should! Go with his poor father, of course!'

He wrote to Norman, and scarcely had Norman gone with his father than Martin learned that in the spring Millie was to be 'packed off' to London for a stay with a dressmaking aunt—and to be within courting distance of 'a man with the good job' in a chemical factory. It was Kitty's idea, and there was no gain-saying it. Out of this disappointment, Martin was soon building an exciting plan. Since Millie would be away from him, why should he not have a fortnight walking with Norman some-where in France, and, on the way home, bring Norman and Millie face to face at last in London?

Soon there were passing between them maps, plans, charts of their walk and the names of towns, as once cricket catalogues had passed and the secrets of the Conjuring Department of Gamages, Holborn, London, E.C.2. In his letters, Norman told about the pamphlets he placed in the lounges of Riviera hotels, how he had spoken at a meeting of French ex-servicemen, and how some English residents had complained to the Prefect of these 'outrageous activities by some Irish Sinn Fein murderer'. But the Prefect, whose wife had once been snubbed by an English doctor's wife, replied that this Irish visitor, this *'individu'*, this *'étranger'*, had as much right as anyone else to speak his mind so long as he observed the reasonable, logical, systematized laws of the Third Republic, home of Freedom and asylum of the prosecuted.

The days passed. Millie was 'packed off' to London, and Martin set about finding a few pounds to finance his fortnight with Norman.

He pawned the dinner suit which Miss Peters had got for him in his last school year; he pawned an overcoat; he even thought of selling some of his books; even parcelled up for the pawn shop Aunt Mary's dispatch case and the watch Colonel Howard had given him, both of which were valuable. But he unpacked the

parcel again, and began instead to meditate ways of getting to
France without having to spend on the journey the few pounds
he had now collected.

Stiff on his bicycle along dark roads at night, mud-caked,
wind-dried, with his pockets often holding fifty or sixty pounds
of country subscriptions to the Republican Loan, he would
meditate that journey to France. Let his foot once touch the soil
of France and his own two legs would carry him down to Norman
and Carcassonne. Then a sudden solution to his difficulty came
from an unexpected quarter. Returning to his room one night
before reporting to Conroy, he found Conroy already there
waiting for him. He was none too pleased that Conroy, who was
well known to the Secret Service, and might have been seen by
Secret Service men, should have come to his safe O'Canavan
retreat and perhaps aroused suspicion; but Conroy said patiently:
'I had to see you. I'm going down the country tomorrow for a
few weeks and I've heard of something that might interest you.
Martin, your nerves are beginning to show the strain. You need
a rest.' He explained that in Paris a Monsieur Gourdet, a well-
to-do manufacturer of shirts, wanted a holiday tutor to spend a
month giving his children English lessons. The gentleman was an
ardent Anglophobe, had no use for the political machinations of
'Perfidious Albion' but through a friend on *Le Temps* he had got
the addresses of some Irishmen in Paris, one of whom received
him in an hotel bedroom, told him with the confidence of genuine
conviction that the best English was spoken in Dublin. In the
end, word of the post had come to rebel circles in Dublin. Conroy
had heard of it and had thought of Martin.

'It would mean six weeks away, Seamus, and if I went I would
have to have a fortnight to myself after the month's teaching.'

'I know. But what you need is a break. You will do all the better
work for us when you have had it. Here's the address anyhow.'

Conroy's suggestion would have seemed providential to him,
had he still believed in providence. Now he could see Millie
in London. Now he could get to France and see Norman with
hardly any expense to himself at all.

For one long, long day—almost nineteen hours of one day—
from the grey dawn when she ran with hand up along the platform at Euston to meet him, until her last bus near midnight,

Millie was once again his guide through streets already becoming familiar to her, when, with her hand resting on his arm, she trudged with never a plea for rest all over London in order that Martin might see the great places of the rich, powerful enemy. But looking at the Tower, the Houses of Parliament, the Galleries and all the tourists' sights, he forgot to remember that he was in 'the enemy's' land, because the past and present of the land, the pulse and colour of its thought, were so intimately part of his own connective tissue, and because too many a street of 'the enemy' was the place where so-and-so had written such-and-such, or said this-and-that with gallantry and with an echo of man's indestructible heart. With never a complaint Millie hurried along beside his questing feet and looked happily at the tireless eagerness in his face.

'You're like a kid again, Martin. Sort of half and half a kid, and half your high and mighty self like the night of the Rebellion, the night when we met.'

'Your escort,' he smiled, 'your only escort.' And then, with compunction and self-reproach: 'I want to see Swinburne's house, but it will mean taking a bus out to Putney. Would you sooner we didn't?'

'No, no, no, no! I'd sooner be tired and be with you than be sitting down without you'; and off they went. He had planned that they were to sit down to a 'a real dinner, dinner properly and nicely, for you and me'.

'You and me.'

But he did not tell her that to atone for the expenditure on the dinner he was going to save the price of an hotel by walking the streets all night, or sleeping on the Embankment. They had the dinner, and the first glass of wine he had tasted since leaving the Peters', the first Millie had ever tasted, and they clinked their glasses and were happy in the enemy's great capital. Then they went out to walk by London's river, above a larger and richer banquet table of lights than the Liffey could furnish. They sat near Blackfriars Bridge, her tired head on his shoulder, he telling her stories of the Thames when London was the Londinium of the Romans, and of Tudor barges carrying noble prisoners to the Tower. At last she had to go. When they were kissing goodbye in a doorway, she said, 'Will you bring me something from Paris —any little thing, so long as it's straight from Paris to me?'

'Of course. More than one thing. And one day we'll go there together.'

'Aye, one day. And wasn't today like old times? Tonight and the river and all. I never knew London was as full of things, it's three or four Londons you make out of it. Ah, Martin! There's no one like you!'

'It's funny. I want to feel a foreigner here, but I don't. I ought to, but I can't.'

'A foreigner! In England? Oh, Martin, that's a scream!'

Still they lingered, although it was already an hour over the time limit given her by her dressmaking aunt. 'There'll be a shindy tonight when I get in. But who cares!'

She had told him nothing of the 'man with the good job', who had been one of her step-mother's motives for sending her to England.

'And this man Gus, the fellow with all the curls in his hair in that snapshot you sent me . . .'

'Ah, Gus. He's all right, he's a sport. I told him straight out about you. Not who you were, or your name or anything; but that I loved no one but you, and that I was waiting to marry you, so it's his own look-out if he insists on coming round to see me. Ah, forget Gus, poor Gus is all right, but when I listen to him and think of you . . . ah, God!' she began to laugh. 'It isn't really laughing I feel like. If only we could stay the night somewhere now, Martin. I don't want to go.' Though they knew she must go, they went, clasped together, back across the road to look at the river once more as if, out of its flow, they might fish some marvellous tale which could be telephoned to the dressmaking aunt to explain Millie's absence for a night.

'I must go. It'll be the last bus now. But, Martin, if we could only have a few days without dodging and watching.'

'We will. More than just days. Always. Only wait and see.'

She went and he walked the streets, slept with tucked-up feet on a seat, took coffee many times at stalls and saw the great city all hushed and graceful by its river in the early dawn. Sleepy-eyed but eager in the train next day he tried to imprison in his diary jerky notes conveying in some measure his impressions of England and his hopes of France. France had always been the friend of Ireland. He felt like an infant at whose push a barred gate has surprisingly fallen, releasing him into an illimitable meadow, enchanting and belonging to his father.

That night, from his room looking over the Parc Monceau, he wrote to Norman: *I have so much to say to you that it would take a year*; and, putting aside the diary, he erased on the calendar another of the days which separated him from the time when Norman and he would go on their walking tour arm-in-arm in Nîmes or Carcassonne.

To that calendar he would return each evening at the close of the happy days which followed. He was the enthusiastic foreign guest. He did not realize that it was his own enthusiasm and naive unconcealed wonder which had swept the Gourdet family themselves into an affectionate and gratified excitement, which covered the *salle-à-manger* with reference books, histories and maps unearthed from M. Gourdet's shelves. Everything was new. Everything was interesting: the prints, the reproductions, the catalogues of museums unearthed from the bookcases, the queer pans in the kitchen, the casseroles, the grills; elegant Gounod in stone calling music from the heavens into the *parc*. M. Gourdet was becoming more and more pleased with his un-English English tutor, his high-minded revolutionary who shared most of his views about 'Perfidious Albion', his arbiter of what was chic in *le Sport*. Madame Gourdet, on the other hand, not only refused to share her husband's distrustful fear of Albion, but zealously imitated her own extraordinary miscomprehensions of Saxon female fashions and English customs. She dressed her two sons, for example, in outfits which she called Eton suits, the most recognizable part of these outfits being a collar of remarkable width, whiteness and stiffness. Out into the Parc Monceau the two boys would proceed, beside them their two pale lanky sisters in skirts of brilliant tartan design, entitled 'le Scotch plaid' by Madame Gourdet, who seemed to think that English ladies never dressed their daughters in anything but the materials of Scotland.

Sometimes in their quiet walks beneath the chestnut trees Monsieur Gourdet would talk himself out of Paris back to himself as a small boy chaffing the gendarmes as they fished from the village bridge, and having talked of these things, he would suddenly say with solemnity, 'Monsieur Reilly, there is between you and me the separations of so many years, but we are good friends in spite of the years, is it not so!' Then, when the regular clock in his stomach twanged the hour of dinner, he would make towards his car, casting satisfied, protective glances at his good bargain of a tutor, now dreaming no doubt—for Monsieur Gourdet had known what the heart is—of some woman in that strange Atlantic island, that turbulent and warlike misfit, lost out there in the frozen North.

Once he took Martin in the car to visit some of the battlefields. The latter returned, filled by a wonder and fear before the implications of those unending graveyards of men, who had died for the names of nations, unlike the Greeks and Trojans who had fought only for Helen, who had looked so beautiful when she walked upon the wall; unlike the Crusaders who had died for the birthplace of a god. Doubtfully, he looked up at Norman's photograph; what would Norman say to that?

But he wrote in his diary: *It is queer to think that there was a time when the world was without the idea of nationality. Without it for a much longer age than it has had it.*

Only two weeks remained unabolished on his calendar. Only one week. Four days. Three days. Two! He had his things ready; they had exchanged their last instructions, the maps of the route, the lists of towns where they would linger; and that night, walking with Monsieur Gourdet by the Luxembourg, he planned different ways of first seeing Norman at the meeting place, which was to be the Café Riche, Cannebière, Marseilles. Norman had chosen it because he found something funny in meeting at a place called the 'Rich Café'. Would he arrive late and see Norman already sitting at a table? Or pretend not to recognize him? Or be there first and watch Norman arrive? So he played all the games with which long-separated friends tease the heart in the exquisite hours before reunion.

He came down the next morning to find to his delighted surprise a letter from Millie, who wrote so seldom and usually only tiny notes. But this was a fat letter. Escaping quickly from the table, he read that she had *worked out the chance of a lifetime, the very thing we've always wanted.* She had won consent to her spending a fortnight with a friend in Falmouth. The friend was *young and a sport and knows about you, and her husband is English and a good sport and doesn't care what anyone does so long as he has his whippet and billiards. The two kids will think we're married. You would have to pay just a little because usually they have a lodger from the spring on, and I could buy something for one of the kids. Only it's all off if you can't come before the end of the week. So come. Come. Your own Millie.*

As he wrote to Millie, explaining why he could not go, he cursed the ill luck which had brought this suggestion at the one moment when he could not accept it. But he did not post his letter at once. He wandered miserably about with the letter in his pocket. A honeymoon with Millie, no skulking and dodging, a honeymoon with Millie in Cornwall. It would never come again, this chance, and he could meet Norman in Ireland at any time, now that the ban no longer held. He took the letter from his pocket and walked with it straight to a letter-box. He hesitated, did not post it.

That afternoon he sent a telegram to Norman calling the walking tour off and said that a letter of explanation followed. The whole Gourdet family came to the station to see him off, the lanky girls in their whitest socks and best Scotch plaid in honour of the parting guest, Madame Gourdet mistaking the stares of the English at the station for glances of admiration at her sons' 'Eton suits'. Monsieur Gourdet, with the air of a man who takes a great resolution, signed to him that he might embrace the boys, might even embrace the demoiselles. Last of all, Monsieur Gourdet himself gave the accolade of friendship to his un-English English tutor and Martin saw that Monsieur Gourdet suspected that the English tutor was going to his mistress, that woman from the strange turbulent island which irritated 'Perfidious Albion'.

A postcard from Norman was forwarded from Paris to Falmouth. Norman said that it seemed less stupid to do a walking tour alone than to stay on at Mentone after so much excitement and planning. He did not ask for an explanation of Martin's desertion, and he made no mention of another plan for meeting.

Each morning, bright sunlight wakened Millie and Martin. Each evening, when the sands were darkening, they would return, drowsy, richly tired and glad to go to bed a little later than children. Sometimes when she was asleep, her head on his shoulder, Martin would lie wakeful, watching the brightening night beyond the curtains, listening to the sound of her breathing mingling with that of the tide, and thinking that perhaps just now Norman was taking a late walk alone in Nîmes or Carassonne.

IV

Initiation in Hate

I

At the end of his holiday he returned to an Ireland where conditions were rapidly deteriorating. Guerilla warfare had been supplemented by a policy of assassination and counter-assassination. Each side had spies in the camp of their opponents. Every murder led to savage reprisals, which in turn led to further reprisals. Loyalists were dragged off trams and shot in broad daylight. And youths, suspected of doing the shooting, were tortured and their fingernails dragged out. Each side had cause in abundance for savage resentment: each side gave cause in abundance for similar hate.

Hurtling lorries, fringed with pointing rifles, roared along the roadway to and from raids and searches, hooting at the pedestrians, at lovers, at silly young elegants, at old ladies who scurried at the mere thought of a lorry, at messenger boys who looked up at the netted coops to shout: 'Hi, who are you pushing off the road! This is our city, not yours!'

Without a sign of recognition other than a flicker of the eye, Martin might pass Sinn Fein Members of Parliament now on the run; whom he had helped to elect, and who were now part of the Government-in-Hiding of the country. He scowled at the thought of their evasive rulings, their woolly willingness to do what they were told, their emotional hypnotism—the Republic. Banishing the thought of them from his mind he turned into a café, seeking Conroy among the young elegants, the chess players, the tango dancers, the Secret Service spies of both armies, the gunmen, the toughs and touts, 'Fly-boys', 'Chancers', barristers who prosecuted in British courts and at the same time were judges in rebel courts, English and American women trying to be more rebel-Irish than the Irish themselves. He wound his way through room after room, the 'Ye Olde Cottage Room',

the 'Tango Room', 'Smoking Room', wound past scrubby
French journalists seeking human intelligence in this guerilla
war, past a Yorkshireman in an Irish kilt and a coat adorned
with the countless rebel badges which even the stupidest Black
and Tan laughed at. Here and there he saw men from the inner
ring which was Conroy's. One of them knew his appearance but
made no sign. At another table, he saw, with a pang, a suspected
English spy, the man who claimed to have been at Haileybury
but who had not recognized the Haileybury colours nor the
name of Harry Vincent's House. He had not left the country;
there he was still trying to pick information, this time from a
pretty young woman student, all unaware that the hospitable Mr.
Reilly whom he now saluted had long ago handed over to Conroy
the first nail for his coffin.

'Yes, I think he's a spy, Seumas. But give him a chance to get
away. He knows nothing worth knowing. I'll send an anonymous
note to him, telling him to clear out, that he's spotted.' Well,
he had had chance after chance, and there he was now; and
somewhere at a table, someone would be watching him.

He walked out from the music-saturated comedy of death and
breathed the damp air of the streets where the newsboys were
gloatingly shouting to the hurtling lorries: 'Hi, mister, Stop Press.
Three British shot dead in city ambush today.'

He had to seek his various contacts in one 'office' after another,
going from the drawing-rooms of wealthy minor poetesses to the
back rooms of motor-tyre agents and building contractors.
Periodically there would be a hold-up in the road by Auxiliaries
or Black and Tans, and if one were caught with a gun then it
was likely to be the end. It was easy enough for the Auxiliaries
to explain to higher authority that a prisoner had jumped from
the lorry and been killed in doing so.

Once Martin found himself trapped in a side road during a
search. A workman, lazily filling in the hour before lunch-time,
looked at him and said, 'Oh, begob, have they come for ye, lad?'

'Where can I dump this?' Martin said, producing his revolver.
The man nodded lazily towards a heap of sand-and-cement.
Wrapping the gun in rags, Martin pushed it deeply into the
heap and went to the end of the laneway where he knew the
Auxiliaries were waiting. The red-headed workman had promised
to take his mother to the pictures that afternoon but he offered

to come back later and retrieve the gun and leave it wherever Martin directed him.

For people went to the pictures, went to dances, life went on as though it were normal, and murder went on at the same time at the very elbows of those who danced. To someone like Mullins it was a matter of keeping out of trouble, away from places where trouble was likely to be. To the committed, like Martin, it was a matter of living from moment to moment, uncertain always what was going to happen next.

Sometimes he felt inclined to harden his heart against Conroy. Had not Conroy the sweet balm of the Confessional, the benign ancient words touching the shrivelled and hungry soul like summer dew.

Ego te absolvo . . .

It did not trouble Conroy's mind that he must seek the uplifted hour of cleanliness and peace in the Confessional of a priest whom the serpentine wisdom of Mother Church, winding backward from the lances of lay theology, had left free to choose 'guerilla war' not 'murder' as the appropriate term, and to place within the simple haunts of country boys the stored ointments of Europe's mysticism.

Ego te absolvo . . . Wear this relic of St. Michael in the next attack . . .

He sneered to Conroy at the wearing of such relics. Nevertheless the latter could say to him: 'Martin, it's a queer thing. You and I don't really agree about much, do we? And yet you're the only person I can say certain things to.' He looked up, looked away again and added: 'I never had a sweetheart, Martin. But I can tell you.'

Martin was a little embarrassed by this admission.

'I took a chance last night,' Conroy continued, 'and went to see my people. They are heart and soul with us and yet I was a stranger, a frightening stranger. I could see it.' He shook himself. 'I think sometimes I'll be glad enough to be plugged when the time comes. I think you and I will both be plugged—if the time comes.'

Martin said nothing. Conroy went on, reflectively: 'There was my mother looking at me and smiling, but I knew she could not see her son at all, at all. She was afraid of me. If ghosts can come back, that's how they must feel, able to see their friends just as

they are and were, yet knowing that they themselves seem a terror
to them and a strange awful thing.'

A sad foreboding lay on Martin. Conroy or he, Conroy and
he, would soon be dead; and, if they lived, they would one day
be enemies. He glanced sideways. On Conroy's fair head, on
his lean jaw, a beam of sunlight fell through the trees, lightening
his face, so that he looked more boyish than ever he had looked
in his boyhood in Dunslane.

'Seamus,' he said gently. 'We agree about one thing anyway.
We'd both give anything we're asked for, if we thought it would
be a help to Ireland.'

'Yes,' and they smiled at one another, but it was a sad smile.

'You're a hard fellow, Martin. I used to think . . . People,
some people, say you're too soft and wandering in your ways, too
womanish, but I think now that you are the hardest of us all
inside you. I think you'll go your own crooked way wherever
it takes you until the day of——' He stopped sharply, not to say
'the day of your death'.

Though he had matriculated at University College before
leaving Knockester, Martin did no reading and only went to
lectures when they offered, as they did occasionally, a safe and
plausible way of escaping the attentions of Black and Tans. It was
being rumoured that participants in the national movement
would be conceded attendance at lectures and possibly even
exams in the same way that ex-soldiers had been by the British.
Hearing of this Martin went to see a professor who was known
to have the ear of the Master. When he had obeyed the call to
enter, he heard the 'Well, what is it?'—Long Dick's words
but not Long Dick's manners.

Stung by the boorish greeting, Martin said viciously, 'I merely
want credit for lectures I have not attended.'

'Well, really! Upon my word . . .'

Martin looked with dislike at the long figure swaying slightly on
its heels, the weak, watchful face, trying to express authority.

The Professor, with a deep, noncommittal 'Ah', sank negli-
gently into a chair while he appeared to consider the matter.
He left Martin to stand, and appeared to become absorbed in
important papers on his desk as if forgetting his visitor. Bored by
this by-play of authority through whose façade he, in common
with other young men, had pierced to the moral cowardice be-

hind it, Martin began to feel a little pity. 'He's sixty and I'm not quite twenty-two. But even if I was that age it would not seem worth while to me to try to preserve my dignity that way.'

Mollified to see this rebel—and presumably tough—young man waiting so quietly, and satisfied that authority had been sufficiently emphasized, the man began to smile and talk. As he talked and Martin answered, he became witty, genial, forgot any longer to be on his guard against youthful impertinence, and even began to hint politely some of his dislike of this rebel movement, which was shaking the values of his Catholic middle-class world. 'And, you know, Reilly, it's all very foolish of you for your own sakes, because a man's first duty is to himself.' Seeing Martin's sharp look, he repeated vigorously: 'Certainly. A man's first duty is to himself. You know that yourself.'

'No, sir. I never even thought it.'

'Oh, come, come, you don't ask me to believe that.'

'I never even thought of it until this moment. No one in all my life ever told me that.' There was a silence. 'In fact,' said Martin thoughtfully, 'I was taught the very opposite by everybody.'

'But come now, Reilly,' he said quietly. 'Everyone has that knowledge instinctive in him.'

'That his first duty is to himself? No. Everyone hasn't. I know lots who haven't.'

'Oh, these times,' he said hastily, as if anxious to forget what was going on outside the door. 'Abnormal. Quite abnormal. You know very well that you are here to get a degree, so that you can get on in the world.'

After a silence, Martin said: 'And the men who went to the war in France? From here, from England, from Germany? No one said to them that their first duty was to themselves, and to get on in the world.'

It was only when he saw the man flush that he remembered that his voice had been among those which had told young men that it was their duty to forget themselves and go to the war. Indeed he had heard him almost weeping once, as he spoke of the young men killed in the war.

'That was quite different,' the Professor said coldly. He paused. 'It was . . . er . . . quite different. In ordinary times a man must think first of himself, especially of his career and prospects. If he does that and sticks faithfully to his religion, he's all right. No bigotry. It doesn't matter what religion a man is born into, so long as he sticks to it.'

'Must he die for it?' said Martin coldly. 'Forget himself and his career for it, for a religion which he was born to?'

'Don't be absurd, Reilly! People don't have to die for their religion nowadays. Formerly it was different, quite different.'

Aye, thought Martin grimly, but only thanks to unbelievers who forced mercy and pity into your religions. 'Sometimes I think that nothing is different.'

The Professor twinkled. 'As a Catholic—and an intelligent one—you naturally understand that. Only the reformed conscience can imagine the perfectibility of human nature. In that sense nothing is different. But I was speaking . . . er, not philosophically'.

He whirled about with his back to the window to catch the expression on Martin's face in the light. 'I am often puzzled by some of the men who support this . . . er . . . wild political movement. Intelligent, well-mannered men, associating with that crowd who will destroy all . . . well, all manners and . . . er . . . decent society . . . Also . . .'—he walked to the window—'I hear that many of them are secretly anti-clerical.'

Martin kept a stolid expression and said: 'The people in our movement, the best of them, the young people especially, are tired, looking at the people who have been running this country. They are tired of all the shams in what is called Society in Ireland. They want to run this country on the assumption that those who govern can themselves live up to Justice, to Freedom, to Truth, as well as prating about them. This is not a rebellion, it is a revolution.'

'That was said before, Reilly, in history!'

'It is being said again now!'

'Really? Come, come! Said by whom, for example?'

'By me, for one!'

'Well, upon my word . . .' he said with something like awe, 'I wonder if you see your arrogance.'

Martin shrugged slightly. 'And it needs to be said again, as it needed to be said then. There is more liberty, more fraternity, more equality in France today because it was once said there.'

'There may be more what you call liberty, which is usually only licence to sin. But has there been any fraternity in Europe since the betrayal of the order of Christendom? There was political fraternity, then, of a kind; there was no fraternity of the mind and heart. No fraternity of acceptance, only licence to sin and——'

'Excuse me, sir, but I must interrupt because every word is an assumption. Sin? Sin according to whom? According to Augustine? Or to St. Francis? Or Pascal? Is it worth while to mention according to Jesus Christ? A Buddhist might say——'

'Your impertinent display of reading does not——'

Martin gaped at him. 'Display of reading? But I have read very little,' he said honestly. 'This after all is a university. Everyone would have read of those things.'

'I sincerely hope not!' He stammered angrily. 'You have talked, young man, glibly of fraternity. Your reading, however undisciplined, should have shown you that there has been no fraternity in Europe since the order of Christendom was broken and betrayed by the same intellectual disorder which you call Liberty.'

'The Fraternity of Christendom? I have tried to find the thing itself behind all the repetitions in books that it did exist. I found only a fraternity of dogma imposed from above. There was no fraternity of minds and hearts.' He meditated a moment. 'There was no love.'

'What? When the glorious Middle Ages erected in pure love those edifices to the love of God, Chartres, Rheims . . . why, the love of God animated every man's life with——'

'With the rack!' said Martin hotly. 'With the fire and the whip if he stirred by even a hair's breadth from the formula! Love of God! Ah, I have seen their love of God; any boy in school can soon feel the weight of their love of God. Fraternity. A compulsory conformism does not make a Fraternity. It makes a Corporation.'

'Exactly. The Corporation of Christendom. Can you honestly say you prefer the vulgarized commercialized corporations of today? Big Business? Illustrated papers? The commercial theatre?'

'Their vulgarity is less at least than the vulgarity of a love of God commercially coarsened to be a parody of what it pretends to be, less than the vulgarity of a love of God which relies mainly on the same terrors as any advertisement about rheumatism. Cling to me or you won't be saved. And, if that does not work, then "cling to me or you will lose your job". It is this relentless compulsion . . .'

'Nonsense. The only compulsion is the gift of Faith . . . I . . . er . . . speak of course of our own times.'

'Till our movement gave men courage, Ireland was rotten with cowardly hypocritical submission to all kinds of compulsions, moral, social, financial. Half the young men in Ireland were cowed. In the name of truth, could any man have dared to hope for a post in this building if he revealed one iota of revolt simmering in his heart?'

'Stop. I cannot allow such remarks. If I thought you really believed a word of all this, I should feel obliged . . . well, of course I know you don't. Naturally, this university has a very special obligation to safeguard the moral and religious principles of its students.'

'Safeguard? No, to hammer them into one single pattern. Is this, sir, the national university of a nation, the home of minds, or is it a training institution for secretaries?'

'How dare you say these things to me! Reilly, you forget yourself and where you are. Let me tell you that this confirms something I had frequently been told about you so-called republicans and . . .'

'Am I a republican? Why not ask me before making these immense assumptions? Republican has become a catchword, like Bolshevik or "mad dog". In fact, I am a King, Lords and Commons man, of the school of Mr. Griffith. . . .'

'Ah! That man Griffith! His radicalism and hatred of the Church have come to my ears. It is becoming well known that many of you so-called Irish patriots are riddled with anti-clericalism . . .'

'Anti-clericalism? Oh, nothing so old-fashioned as that, sir. We are riddled with the hope of seeing truth and freedom at last in Ireland.'

'Are you aware that if I were to take your remarks for anything more than the inconsiderate and uninformed remarks of a foolish young man your continuing in this univesity would be impossible.'

'It would not! You know, sir, as well as I do, that not all the bench of bishops could at this moment eject a Volunteer from anything on the grounds of his religious or non-religious opinions, actions, propaganda or what you will. Freedom has got that far in Ireland.'

'This interview is ended, Reilly, but you will hear more of your triumvirate, liberty, fraternity and equality before you finish, and you may not like all you hear.'

Martin had been upset by the interview. He decided to take the tram to Blackrock and to walk on to Kingstown by the sea road. The air and the exercise would do him good. He might even take the risk of paying a call on Miss Peters.

He had left the tram and walked a few hundred yards when a motor-horn tooted a message at him, and a shiny, fleshy face leaned out towards the kerb. It was Mullins. Martin had not seen him in the streets since that night . . . that night. He flushed now, and waved a vague greeting.

'Don't you want a lift? Hop in. I'm going as far as Dalkey.'

But Martin hesitated. Mullins, confidently misunderstanding his hesitation, said: 'Come on, man. It's not a bother at all. As a matter of fact I've our agent working that area this week, and I want to see what he's doing. I may catch him out in some trick or other, perhaps wasting his time in a pub. Two birds with one stone, old man, come on.'

Martin got in. He felt grateful, and he was forced to admire the nonchalant skill with which Mullins drove the car.

The powerful engine did not vibrate as sometimes the old Swift had shaken, the seats were deep and plump and there were pockets, a flower vase, a mirror.

'Is this your father's car?'

'No sweet fear. Mine, sir—ree!'

Mullins spoke of his insurance society's progress, and his own importance in it. 'I put across a bloody good one this week.' A rival company it appeared had been 'after that big new laundry run by nuns, you know, a penitents' place, grand insurance mark because nuns never have a fire or a robbery and it's worth giving them policies for half-nothing for the sake of the big investments which you can lead them to, once the connection's established. Rolling in the dough, of course. No wages to pay the penitents, no hours, just fire ahead, and rope in the work. Can you imagine the impudence of those fellows, Protestants and English to a man, trying to snaffle a thing like that from a good Catholic company? Well, I walked in personally, yes, old Mullins in person, and I bagged the whole shoot—fire, accident, burglary, everything.' He speculated a moment. 'No. No use thinking of a life

policy for you. Sinn Feiners are no mark. Ah, well, it is a relief
to be able to have a chat with someone, without having to nurse
him as a prospect. As a matter of fact, it was old MacTaggarty,
down in Dunslane, who got a Monsignor pal of his to work the
open sesame for me with the nuns. Of course I keep in touch; I
go down there sometimes to Mass on Sundays, and I gave them
a picture for the Sodality: a nice print of the Sacred Heart to
go with the Blessed Virgin picture. You remember the one?'

'Yes. I remember.'

After a silence, Mullins swerved past an old woman bewildered
in the middle of the road and not hearing his tooting horn.
'Jasus,' he roared with delight. 'Look at that old one, she's as
deaf as a beetle. Well, Martin, old man, how's the good old
cause going? Man, the British don't know what way to try next.
Though mind you now, Martin, you won't mind me giving you a
bit of advice. You chaps . . . well, I don't care about the others
but an old Dunslane pal like yourself ought to be careful. I'm
all for Ireland's rights, yes sir, as good an Irishman as the next,
and better; but a man's first duty is to himself.'

'Say that again, Mullins,' said Martin dryly.

Placated by this mark of attention Mullins said: 'Yes. A man's
first duty is to himself. Sure, everyone knows that.'

'How wise you were, Mullins, to know that it was unnecessary
to study under our university doctors. All their wisdom and
culture you have learned for yourself in your one-hundred-per-
cent Irish company. I beg your pardon—Irish and Catholic.'

'Bedad, Martin, that old sarcastic note of yours is bloody
good, you know. And it's a relief to talk in a social, clever way
with a chap like you. Most of these parish priests expect you to be
well up in coursing, and I don't know enough about hares to
hold my own with them. Though, mind you, some of them are
very cultured men and you have to be careful. I'm often sorry
I don't get more time for reading and so on; only the other day I
nearly lost a good prospect, one of the theology teachers in May-
nooth. He was all for poetry and there I was pretending, and
nodding my head in approval over the lines. Rhymes of a
Rolling Log, I think, or Rolling Stone; but if he'd asked me who
wrote them I couldn't have told him in a hundred years. Knew
good Irish poetry too; "Fontenoy" and that sort of thing. Wish I
could remember "Fontenoy", they all know it, even the coursing

ones. When I stay a night with one and we have a jorum or two, they get lit up and give it out in great style.'

A deep, new thought lumbered into his mind. He picked his right nostril and said: 'Tell you what, Martin, you'd make a damn' good insurance man with some of the more cultured prospects. That dry, sarcastic note would go down well with a lot. If you didn't get angry; you're inclined to get too hot. Martin, old man, as one pal to another, I'm going to tell you straight out that you'll never get on as long as you keep your queer ideas and your old savage way of suddenly bursting out at people. Do drop all that side, old chap. Use the dry sarcastic, that's good. But don't be unduly bitter. You want to be too different from other people. Honestly, you have a kind of complex about being different. You make yourself labour under a sense of grievance. And . . .'

'Continue, Mullins. Reveal me to myself.'

But Mullins was pointing ahead to a young woman on the pavement, going in the same direction. 'Hi, look, Martin,' he said. 'Nice-looking bit of stuff. All on her own. And sir—ree . . .' He winked towards the mirror. 'Have we or have we not everything she needs,' and he revealed under the mirror a little cupboard with powder-puff, pins and other feminine accessories. And a glistening transparent packet labelled 'Sterilized towel'.

Long before Martin had begun to understand why these things should be there, Mullins was slowing, as he overtook the girl. He leaned out, his big lips glistening in a liquid ingratiating smile. 'Lovely day,' he cooed, like a sucking dove, and then: 'Look back now, quick, Martin and see how she took it.'

'She's still alive and on her feet, Mullins. Let me out.'

He felt that the last thing in the world that he was willing to witness was Mullins making an assignation.

'Shut up, man. We can share and share alike. I know the very place. Just as good as real country but only a mile up the other road.' He had stopped the car, the girl was nearly abreast of him.

'Lovely day,' he cooed.

'Mullins, drive on or let me out. I insist on you driving me to Dalkey. . . .'

'Lovely day, lovely day. Grand weather,' breathed Mullins to the girl with her nose up with ostentatious lady-like hauteur.

And off along the road they went, the girl mincing like a turkey on the pavement, Mullins breathing and cooing, Martin pounding on the floorboard and shouting, 'I insist on you driving on at once.'

'Lovely day, lovely day, lovely day.'

'You ought to be arrested, the pair of you. Insulting a lady.'

'Mullins, drive on, and don't behave like a complete cad.'

While in from the sloblands the seagulls swept squawking, Martin, furiously punching Mullins, knocked the one hand which lightly held on the wheel as he cooed through his liquid smile. The wheel stirred out of his grasp, the car bumped gently on to the pavement and bounced back from the sea-wall and stopped. The young woman turned to call with lofty ladyhood: 'Serve you right. I hope it's burst,' and she pranced away.

Mullins turned a sulky fat face to Martin. 'Christ, you ruined that on me. You might have been more sympathetic. I was sympathetic enough to you the night you came to me, and you only a schoolkid at the time and . . .'

'Mullins, let me out! Stop your tongue and let me out.' But Mullins was already driving once more past the girl, this time with his head held very haughtily away from her.

'Mullins, let me out of your car.'

'Ah, go on, man, forgive and forget is Mullins's motto, I'm not going to bear ill-will. Stay where you are. Besides she probably had wool bloomers. That home-made-by-mother jumper looked suspicious. Some bloody clerk off to strong tea and poached egg for lunch. Might even be a friend of one of my old man's typists. That'd be awkward. Hard enough to keep the bitches respectful and proper, as it is.'

'Mullins, let me out of this car!'

He pushed open the door to get away before the intolerable moment when Mullins would again speak of 'that night you came for help'. There it was in the past, his going through the respectable squares, hand on the bell, sound of bell, introductions to the fellow guests downstairs, and then upstairs and the light on the belly of the water-jug on the washstand and on Mullins's gleaming cheeks. There it all was, the whole occasion, in Mullins's head, and in his own head, revolving for ever on the arc of the unforgettable past. . . .

He pushed so violently that Mullins, alarmed, slowed down the car, and stopped. Martin fumbled at the door handle. 'Let me out.' He pushed the door violently, and nearly fell out on the pathway. His companion had got out also and he heard steps behind and Mullins's angry voice. The steps ran back, the car drove ahead, stopped and Mullins, advancing on him, grabbed his coat.

'You bloody snot. You might have damaged the car, opening the door like that. And then walking away without a thank-you to a chap that's done you a good turn. Do you think you can do this to me, and get away with it?'

'Let me go. Thanks for the lift.'

'God! "Thanks for the lift", the way you say it as if... as if you were talking to a bit of dirt. Jasus, that day you owned up about the bike at Dunslane, I thought maybe you weren't such a bad little bastard.'

'Yes, I remember. You said so. I remember. Let me go now.'

'Ah, go, and go to hell. You're just the cocky upstart you always were. Your butty, Dempsey, was a mean little scut; but at least he wasn't a bloody hypocrite. He'd never have run after a shop-girl or factory-tart on the Q.T. and come crawling to me for help. But you . . . ! Ah, you're only half one thing and half another; half everything, and the whole of nothing! You're just a bloody mongrel, just a mongrel, that's all.'

Before the shiny face which he had called the face of a fool, he felt abashed now, helpless, chastened, as the measure of truth behind the coarse words passed sluggishly into his undenying spirit.

'I want to be alone, Mullins. Leave me alone. Goodbye.'

He pushed aside the hands and walked on. When he was out of sight, he sat on the sea-wall and put his head between his hands.

A Babu land, a Babu university, a race draining the bogs of this outcast island that their sons might be priests and held in honour; might be Tim Corbins and exploit their fellow countrymen, might be Mullinses and insure them. Even his own high aspirations were forgotten, and the expectations of youth. Of all of them, memory could scarcely recall anything save that Gertrude and Miss Gifford were to have lived in a beautiful house in perpetual love and beauty.

He would leave it all. He would go back to France. Monsieur Gourdet would get him a good post; Millie would like it, leap to it, since it would end her mysterious terror of strange deep fears

of their future at home. To live among free men, to love Millie
and to study. To bring up a son in manhood and honour, no
dirty nails to place even one scratch on his mind, scratching a
sense of sin into the soft wax, the nourishing wax of the heart.

The roll of the tide against the sloblands changed its murmur,
and beat high. The tide of memory rose, bringing faint high
voices calling, 'Little St. Martin come back to us.' Sweet and
clear the voices before dawn, rising in the *Gloria* and the *Credo*,
passing over his head in the hierarchy that led up the altar steps
to Father Riordan, most careful and dignified on his rung before
the altar of God himself. Ah, how sweet and clear.

What had been only a childish acceptance could not now be
the nostalgic solace of a grown man. 'I am grown-up now. I
am a G.U., a Jew.' So, forget that sweet, ordered, calm hier-
archical universe of a child's soul. . . .

He smiled grimly. 'When I was a child, I spake as a child,
I understood as a child, I thought as a child; but when I became
a man . . .' He could hear his Aunt Kathleen's voice as she read the
passage aloud to them. But He, up there, had burned her auburn
head in petrol. 'Oh, hateful God, I defy You, one day the whole
world will rise in weariness and anger and cast You from its
heart. Are men fools? Are the animals wiser? Suns may set and rise
again, but, for us, once the short light has set, there remains to
be slept the sleep of one unbroken night.'

Above the city's pretty pendant the haze of smoke rose from
thousands of houses and among them dear Millie's house.
Between those huddled houses of her street, clamped to the railway embankment, that ran behind them, by damp backyard
walls, there was no room for her agnostic old father to plan a
bathroom as life ambition, as old Prendergast had done. Where
was Ireland, what was it? What was he himself?

Out there the haze was still hanging over the huddled city
and Millie's house. She had painted a green border around the
sticky cupboard which was her wardrobe and dressing table, and
on the box-seat jammed between her bed and the window she had
put a vase to hold his bridal flowers. There in her cramped
room, during the fortnight when her father and Kitty had been
away, the whispers of their love had been lost sometimes in
raucous night sounds from the street; but each morning the flowers
were there and a beam of the sun touched her sleeping and rosy

beside him. It was the only hour when the sun came into her room.

He would not go to Kingstown after all. He would return to Dublin. As he came to the suburban roads, to busier places, he looked enviously at the people who could walk with careless laughter to tea and the pictures.

How was it that a nation could live for months, for years, on the very threshold of murder and sudden death and yet pretend to forget it? He thought of a scene which he had witnessed at the house of a loyalist friend only a few days before. The tea party was drawing to a close when from a distance they had heard a noise which could only be the sound of a Crossley tender. There were voices and heavy rapid steps in the hall, the door was thrown open; a maid with a white face was trying to say something; and into the room swept two lean, long-jawed Auxiliaries, worse than the Tans, more intelligent, since they were trained ex-officers of sufficiently robust disposition. Their jaws were out-thrust to the hunt, their hands down to their holsters swinging on their thighs. He had stepped quickly back, wondering if they had come for him. But he need not have worried. The Auxiliaries' hands were swinging their Glengarry caps—and Auxiliaries with their caps not their guns in their hands were a sight to make him gasp with relief.

'Hello, hello, good afternoon. We've come to steal Ruth from you, Mrs. Lefroy.' They strode cheerily forward, slapping the caps against the thighs, winking wickedly at the girl, Ruth. 'Hello, hello, we've come to steal you, Ruth.' The two brick-red, lean faces grinned happily. Ruth went to fetch her coat. She was being taken to supper and the theatre. Martin turned his face away, not wishing to remember their appearance or to note under Mrs. Lefroy's roof their Company number, their names or any information about them. He heard them murmuring their goodbyes. 'No, thanks, we must buzz off now, and so sorry for bursting in. Always burst in on Ruth, you know. Terrible person, Ruth. Come on, Ruth, not afraid of the I.R.A. are you, the duckies have a special bomb waiting all for you. Who wouldn't ambush Ruth!' Martin, gripping a chair to steady his trembling hand—for their sudden entrance had been a shock—had nodded goodbye to them as they led Ruth out.

A few days after this incident he had been in Ballow and met

young Tom Prendergast whose father's life ambition had been
at last fulfilled. The cottage now had its bathroom. Whenever
he met young Tom, Martin tried to get news of Keelard. Hanrahan still kept the house warmed. Mrs. Binnay and Tom's
father were still in charge of the farm; it had made money during
the war, even more money than during the five good years before
the war. Mrs. Carter was dead, Martin had known it. There
had been rumours that Mr. Peters and others had advised selling
the place. 'But they say Miss Sally and Miss Peggy would never be
persuaded to sell. They want to come back any day now, I hear.'
He looked awkwardly at Martin. 'But maybe you know all about
that, of course.' Martin said nothing.

'Miss Vincent—Miss Sally—would never sell, everyone knows
that. They say she's been in France, in Paris, this last year.
But she's expected back from one month to another.'

Hearing that, he had felt a stab of pain to think that Sally might
have been in Paris perhaps when he himself had been there,
planning to go to Norman. He wondered if she was still a V.A.D.
Would she look well in their uniform—her hair up—what was
that like?

'Of course, you know Miss Peggy's supposed to be learning
some welfare business or something in England. Looking after
girls in offices and factories, they say. She'd be good at that, I'm
thinking.'

She would indeed. The ju-jubes, the knitting wools, the
tobacco and yesterday's newspapers of her childhood had trained
her for it; he could see her setting off down the back-avenue
on her pony.

Young Tom said that having got the afternoon off from his
office to attend the committee he would have to work on the
coming Saturday instead of going to see his family.

'I bike over occasionally on Saturdays and back on Mondays.
It's a long pull. But God knows how long more that'll last; I
might have to go on the run any time.'

Martin looked enviously at him, thinking of him cycling down
the dusky slope by the little post office, round the walled bend
in the fall of evening, past the 'easy way of getting in and out'
where the wall gave place to the railings on the high bank.
From his father's house, young Tom, if he cared, could see the
distant window of the schoolroom; from that window he himself

had so often looked out at the scaffolding of Tom senior's ambition. Now, the bathroom was built at last. 'But he has yet to
put up a tank like for water now,' and young Tom smiled
deprecatingly.

'Does Hanrahan still ask about me?'

Young Tom shook his head. 'He saw your name in the papers
a long time ago. And anyway, I daren't go near him myself, since
the scrap started. He goes nowhere at all now, to none of the
neighbours or anywhere, just all day in "Kathleen's Garden".'

He had dreamed that night of Hanrahan, of the sour darkness
of the boathouse, of the house bright above the river. He rose
weary-eyed from a morning dream of France where Monsieur
Gourdet with Sally and Gertrude in V.A.D. uniforms had watched
the unending graves of men who had died for nations and justice.
Rain fell in endless files and the thought of cycling back to Dublin
was unbearable. Taking the risk of going by train he went to a
station where he would not be known, went cautiously to the
guard's van and found, as he had hoped, that the guard himself
was one of the volunteer despatch-carriers. The guard put him
into a first-class carriage where he would be not only more
comfortable but protected to some extent by the aura of law-
abiding respectability surrounding a first-class traveller. While
the train was halted at stations he had to be on the alert, for his
own safety and for any information that might be gathered. In
between stations, he stared out at the rain falling on the darkened
Midland fields. No honeyed breath came up from the rich heart
of the land under the endless falling of the rain. He dozed and
the beat of wheels and rain became a lullaby of crying coming
to him from the brown darkness around his grandmother's
bedpost.

2

HE MIGHT be away from his lodging for days at a time. When he returned to it, fat Miss Agnes and thin Miss Flo would come up from the basement to meet him in the hall. In their obscure world of basements, Sunday joints, grocers' and butchers' shops, the once-better-off Misses O'Canavan read the news in the papers and accepted its dreadfulness as the necessary work of the men 'out fighting for poor Ireland'. Of all their phrases 'out fighting for poor Ireland' was almost the only one not made for them by others, by *Home Chat* or the daily paper. For the men 'out fighting for poor Ireland' they said the Rosary in their basement, subscribed their savings, praised and mourned. It was their share of magnificence.

With sadness he saw the pride and relief in their eyes. With sadness he knew that nothing would ever persuade them that the fight for 'poor Ireland' could easily continue without their great lodger, M. M. Reilly.

'Shut up for the night, and better, too, put out the lights in the front of the house.'

They stiffened with alarm but asked no questions. They chained and double-locked the door, went up to arrange the boxes under the open skylight which, in the unlikely event of a raid on this respectable house, would lead Martin to the roof, the shelter of the parapet and so to the skylight of the next house left open for him, while the Misses O'Canavan, having closed their own skylight and removed the boxes, would go to meet the raiders under the credentials of the Sergeant-Major O'Canavan and Queen Victoria and her royal orb.

Millie, back once more in Dublin, would wait for him every evening in Anthony's, hoping, fearing. Often he would not come. Then she would write him a note: *I try not to look up whenever the*

394

door opens to see if it is your step. I can't stand it much longer, afraid to look at a paper in case your name is there. She spoke of the position in her home, the pressure that was coming from all sides about her future. *We can't go like this for ever, even if things in the house weren't getting awkward.*

From her new home in the south Mary Ellen wrote. She liked Waterford and her *nice, easy man.* He was to be moved to Dublin on promotion: *So now I'll be seeing you at last and I hope you're not much different. Never a word from Josie all these years.* She had paid a visit to Glenkilly and *the mistress was well but shook and worried terrible about you all, and all the best of the furniture moved out of the house and no one sleeping there nights in case them murdering Tans come to burn it. They've raided a dozen times for Mr. James Edward and they asked about you too, and put the mistress up against the dining-room wall with two guns in her face but never a word would she answer them. She hid all the photographs long ago, so they got no information. I remember you high up in my prayers every night.*

As he read her letter he could hear the rising burst of bombs, the thuds of revolver bullets, then distant shouts.

When the screaming lorries, the armoured cars and the tramping of search patrols had begun to die away from the principal streets on either side of his safe side-road, he went to the window. The rain was still falling. He drew his curtains. It was falling on Tory Hill, it was falling on all the houses, all the motor-cars, falling on the fields of Ireland and of England, on their men, women and children and animals. All over the city, quietness and night spread. And all the time the soft rain fell, its sound speaking persistently of the marriage men loved to make between the gently falling rain and the mercy of their God.

The whole country was in travail. Waiting at Ballow station one day he watched the train entering the vault of the station and out there on the platform were lines upon lines of bayonets and steel helmets gleaming under the foggy bluish bulbs. Behind the files lorries waited, and crowds of civilians were running to join a great throng around two rows of the belted Sinn Fein women volunteers drawn up in file. He grimly guessed what had happened. He had heard that two wounded prisoners were to be moved to Dublin and that they would be rescued. But the arrival of the women volunteers, to make a salute for the prisoners, had brought crowds, thus frightening the British military into sending for a larger escort, thus drawing more crowds, more escorts, more crowds, and there would be no rescue now. Martin's sympathy was divided between the two prisoners and the British troops standing in bitter embarrassment with rifles and bayonets before a collection of women, pretty and ugly.

Beside him, he heard a quiet question: 'Will there be shooting, do you think? Is this dangerous?'

He tried to smile reassuringly at the questioner.

The train had slid past the squat khaki figures who moved down the platform to form cordons around two carriages. The military girls wheeled in pursuit of them; the crowds, now filling the width of the platform, surged after them. A low rumble like a sea withdrawing from a cavern rolled along the vault and in a continuous wave, like wind across grass, the great crowd knelt. Far down there, near the wan gleaming of bayonets, one of the belted girls had stood up on something and was saying the Rosary in Irish.

The netted advance lorry fringed with pointing rifle muzzles began to snort a way through the kneeling crowds, clearing a way for the hooded lorry which held the prisoners. The eyes of all the people stared towards the depths under the hood and a new sound poured out. For now they were praying in English. Far down there, the girls still determinedly said prayers in Irish but the people on their knees—the shawlies of the slums, the clerks, workmen, shop assistants and railway porters—had put that aside and now in English they prayed with passionate reality to the Queen of Heaven.

'Hail, holy Queen, Mother of Mercy! Hail, our Life, our Sweetness and our Hope. . . .'

Looking back at the lorry, he saw an officer watching him as he stood conspicuous above the kneeling people. Unlike the troops and the other officers who looked on the scene with embarrassment, this man showed in his face the supercilious amusement with which he regarded people saying their superstitious prayers for a pair of rebel murderers. The heavy jowl, the stolid, complacent lack of knowledge in the face, filled Martin's eyes with the memory of Norburton. He looked at the dangling revolver, at the uniform and insignia of legalized right to kill, right to power, and he renewed his vows to the liberties of his people.

'Hail our Life, our Sweetness and our Hope. To thee do we cry, poor banished children of Eve. . . .'

He stared back at that officer; their eyes met and centred like the eyes of caged animals and for moments they held that centring, blazing challenge. The prayer swelled high, and above the heads of the people each pair of eyes sent to the other a message of undying enmity.

The escorting lorries went by, netted against bombs, fringed with pointing rifle muzzles, machine-guns swivelling. They gained speed at the exits and the crowd swept after them with a roar of pain and rage: 'Up the rebels! Damn you, England! Up the rebels!'

From the gloom below the hooded lorry came a thin, faint answer, it was the sound of song. The doomed men were singing in there.

They lived in completely different worlds, the people of the ascendancy, and the people who knelt on Ballow platform. Conroy had encouraged him to maintain his contacts with the few ascendancy people whom he knew in Dublin. It might enable him to pick up useful information. One afternoon he was invited to a party at the Shelbourne Hotel.

The hotel porter swung the door open, bowing, a file of searching soldiers had made a gap for him. He went up the steps from the sizzling of tram wires and the whine of armoured cars into the attuned atmosphere of music and voices, through which moved, without impinging on it by as much as a flicker of flesh or spirit, the soundless waiters, the soundless whitebound waitresses. The maître d'hôtel bowed greeting to some habitué of the hotel and then went his way, tuning the atmosphere with an imperceptible touch or nod and an occasional ungentle word sent discreetly at close quarters to one of the whitebound servants like the sound of a rifle bolt going home after ejecting a cartridge. Hall and lounge were thronged.

When he came from the cloakroom he had to search for his hostess among standing and sitting groups. There had been racing at the Park, bloodstock sales somewhere the preceding day, and a dog show somewhere else. He moved between standing tweedy groups obviously from the country: and avoided the sitting, towny, silk legs. Army officers in civilian kit laughed into lustrous eyes, before going back to their lorries, their raids and their good or bad treatment of prisoners. They admitted by a glance their masculine acceptance of the passing tribute of these eyes as they allowed their own to rest, but not too long, on the powdery bloom of their companions. He could not even find his hostess. Her large party had apparently been absorbed into other parties who were jointly concerned in the occasion. A deep, amiable voice boomed with a husky placid flatness at his elbow, 'Come and sit here, Mr. O'Reilly,' and he went to a big woman in tweeds, green by age or from home-dyeing, a hat that would have been Tyrolean if it had flaunted a feather, and the general appearance, Martin thought, of the non-playing president of some women's hockey club. She was vaguely familiar to him but he could not even remember her name. In a stolid, amiable way, she began to surround him with muffins and cakes while he said several times to people about him that he had not been to the racing, to the bloodstock sales, to the dog show. 'Came with Mrs. Detrey's lot, Mr. O'Reilly did, let him have his tea. Men love their tea in peace, don't they, Mr. O'Reilly?' Near him was sitting a short lean girl with dark cropped hair like a boy's and eyes that were almost almond-shaped or at least painted to look almost almond-shaped. With her was a burly young man who kept his face turned eagerly to her until seeing her almond-shaped eye send a half-mocking, half-friendly look in the direction of Martin, perhaps in sympathy for his having been captured by the green hat, he looked aggressively down the table. In hostility, his eyes and Martin's centred. It was the officer who at the station had swung from the lorry, dangling his revolver and looking down with complacent ignorance at the people praying to their superstitious Queen of Heaven. Each remembered the other, each remembered the look of undying enmity.

'Oh, I've just heard that you're terribly clever, Mr. O'Reilly,' a shrill, nervous voice called down to him. The speaker was a woman. 'Are you a writer? You look as if you might be a writer. I love clever men. But I hope you don't write poetry.'

Although somewhat flattered at being mistaken for 'a writer', he felt obliged to deny the distinguished claim. He had said at least three times in a perfectly clear voice that he was not 'a writer', and was about to intimate that his name was 'Reilly' not 'O'Reilly', when the big woman in the greenish hat and greenish old costume said good-naturedly: 'Well, since you're a writer, I suppose you must be a relative of Sir Hector's. It runs in the blood, you see,' and to the shrill matron who screamed with delight, 'Oh, what did Heccie write?' she explained: 'Beehives! An extremely good book too. It cost him a clear five hundred, but that was the expense of reproducing his own drawings, the publishers said. Very good drawings, I believe, but difficult to follow. He spent twenty years on that book; devoted to it he was,' and with a ponderous half-turn towards Martin: 'So, I suppose you can't help it either. It's in the blood, you see.'

Before he could find any way of answering these remarks, she passed him a large plate of bread-and-butter. 'Don't talk, I know you men like to have your tea in peace,' and he heard someone far up the table explaining to someone else: 'Oh, some nephew or other of old Hector O'Reilly. He's selling beehives for the old chap now. Hard-up, I suppose.'

The young woman with the almond-shaped eyes was smiling in his direction. The smooth lids came down to hide the expression in the brown eyes. He looked challengingly back, then felt a violent pain shoot through his side. The big greenish woman had jogged him amiably with her elbow and was presenting him to a ferrety-faced little man, lean and chirpy as a bird. 'You must meet Mr. O'Reilly, the well-known writer. One of Sir Hector's lot.'

With a frightened look, the perky little man said hastily: 'Oh, yes. How d'ye do. Grand books. Loved every one of them,' and sidled anxiously away while Martin looked helplessly towards his companion who merely shrugged and smiled.

For a while he was able to eat and drink some tea but not for long. He was about to raise his eyes under the compelling certainty that he was again being watched from the other end by the girl's stocky companion when the great husky voice beside him said: 'Oh, you're being neglected. Here, Terry, come and talk to Mr. O'Reilly, Terry, you'll have a lot in common. Mr. O'Reilly is a famous writer. Sir Hector, you know. The beehives. You know.'

'What? What did you say, Agatha?'

'I said beehives! Your deafness is getting worse, Terry. You ought to try a tube, got to come to it one day.' And shaping her lips into the word 'Beehives', she hurled the sound at the man Terry, now struggling towards her in great haste as if he thought she had a good tip for him for the next Baldoyle meeting.

'Yes, come along here. Come and talk to Mr. O'Reilly about
books. You can tell him about that Koran you found in the
lavatory at Basra.' And with a kind smile to Martin, she said,
'I always have to remember that it's the book, their Bible, and
not the place where they keep all the concubines and drown them
in the Bosphorus.'

Terry had just caught the word Bosphorus, and came in with:
'Sick men of Europe! And no wonder! Disgusting self-indulgence.
Well, we'll hear no more of them for a long time; they can chop
wood like Little Willie and his vulgar old father.' The massive
figure beside him drew her mouth back into a laugh like that of
a sleepy old terrier. 'We're still top dog and it's all because we
have morals, don't you think, Mr. O'Reilly?' He nodded desperately, wondering if he could sidle away to another chair. He heard
a voice saying '. . . and there was Cecil standing fingering his tie,
you know his way, and he was just wishing, he says, that he had
put up a carnation. He always puts up a carnation when he
doesn't put up his decorations. And this little man comes up to
Cecil and says, "Say, my man, are you aware that I've been
standing here looking for a table. Get me a table at once!" Ha,
ha, ha! Took Cecil for a waiter, ha, ha, ha!'

It passed, it flowed, the story of Cecil taken for a waiter, and
out of it flowed other high moments of life when this one or that
one had been mistaken for a servant, a detective.

'Yes, my dears, it's shanks' mare for us now. They took the
poor old tin Lizzie and gave us a receipt on their Republic!
Ha, ha, ha!'

'A receipt on the Republic, ha, ha, ha!'

'Say, did you hear that! Took Letitia's Ford and gave her a
receipt . . . ha, ha, ha!'

The laughter suddenly dropped into a silence shot through
with strain when someone spoke of a barracks burned. Someone
else mentioned an ambush on a familiar road. But a third
speaker restored the high laughter with the information that
'the Republic's agent, their Ambassador or what you will in
Spain, pays his calls in a taxi-cab. A taxi! A taxi all washed up
for the occasion. Ha, ha, ha!'

The big greenish woman dug her elbow into Martin again.
'Dirty things, taxis, don't you think, Mr. O'Reilly? Rotten smell.
I like the smell of horses in a town. Good for the lungs, too, my

grandfather said.' But the chirpy, bird-like little man who had
said 'Grand books, loved every one of them' did not laugh; he said
with the thoughtful air of one who is the informed member of a
group: 'It all goes back to letting the tenants buy out. Once you
give those people an inch, they'll . . .' and with a gush of laughter
several woman said in a chant, 'Good old Stephen, they'll take
an ell, ha, ha, ha.' But down there at the other end, the girl
Ruth was not laughing. The slanting eye looked sometimes at a
face, slanted away, and sometimes, when the eye met Martin's
glance, he thought there was weariness not mockery in it. Beside
her, that Norburton face—Captain Furlong was his name—
did not laugh and his eyes were often on Martin.

'And the man who signed the receipt said he was the Captain.
And do you know who he was . . .' The vivacious, shrill young
matron paused dramatically. All leaned forward anxious for the
high communal moment. 'My dears, he . . .'

'Wish Kitty Ussher wouldn't say "my dears" like an Englishwoman.'

' . . . My dears, the Captain was the son of the little draper
where Great-Aunt Hilda used to get her elastic-sided boots, ha,
ha, ha!'

'I say, did you hear that one? Elastic-sided boots! . . . He was
the Captain, ha ha, ha!'

'But that's nothing. Our coachman's cousin is a lieutenant I
believe. Ha, ha, ha. He'll be the next Ambassador in a taxi,
ha, ha, ha!'

Into a momentary silence, a clear voice called, 'And what
does Mr. O'Reilly think of the situation?'

Looking swiftly up from the table, Martin saw the stocky
captain leaning forward, his dark, insolent eyes, awaiting the
answer to his question, watching intently as he repeated, 'What
do you think of the rebels, Mr. O'Reilly?'

There was silence while some looked expectantly at Martin,
anxious for a new note of laughter; but others looked embarrassed, disapproving of this direct rude question. Beside Captain
Furlong's imperialistic jowl, the slanting almond-shaped eyes
looked fully into Martin's and the long look seemed to signal:
'Say nothing! Whatever you are, you are at least in earnest
about it, not like these scoffers.'

Not sure that he had read that expression, those eyes, aright,

he made a slight inclination of his head, saw then that he had
read aright, and ignoring Captain Furlong's waiting, he said to
his massive neighbour: 'I'm afraid I must leave. I must find my
hostess and thank her for this interesting party.'

The big woman said good-naturedly: 'But what a small tea.
Men of course can never take their tea with a lot of chatter going
on. She's in the outer lounge, I think, with Mrs. Detrey'.

She was not there and when he sought her in the hall he saw
a group clustering on the steps around the porter and looking
curiously at something up the street. A faint sound of distant
tramping grew slowly louder, it was the sound of steady military
marching. He went quickly to the steps and saw a child's coffin
being carried through the ill-lit street, past the trams, the cars,
the netted lorries. It was slung on webs carried by some working-
men and behind it marched a group of men, women and children,
some in their best clothes, others still in their working-clothes and
unwashed as if they had come straight from their day's work.
Among the faces that were white and stiff were others bloated by
tears and others bloated by drink and tears. They had formed
roughly into a kind of military order and the tiny coffin was
covered by the new flag which first he had seen flapping in the
purple night of the Easter Week rebellion. Standing bareheaded
on the steps, he looked down on the untutored defiance of that
clumsy military cohesion which the netted lorries forbade and
looked at the flag wrapped around the coffin of a child who had
never been a soldier.

'Really! How these kind of people love to make display of their
griefs!'

'And a military funeral for a child, my dear. And what a
military turn-out, ha, ha!'

The porter, who had just given a surreptitious salute to the
passing coffin, now heard the voice of power and place, and
whirled about with a tactful assenting smile for the speaker.
Striding past him, Martin strode down the steps and into the
street and stepped in among the faces white or bloated. Two
men, their clothes smelly with the dust of slag, bran and cement,
looked curiously at him, then made a place for him in their
ranks. He hoped he could be seen from the hotel, among the
shawled women, the coats glistening with saltpetre, the girls
in their crackling finery and in shoes as cheap and glossy as those

that had tapped on the pavement and on the lamp-thrown shadows of young buds on that Easter night of false summer, when he had swung with Millie into line with the band of girls singing with unbound hair and linked waist to waist.

The little cortège turned into a side-street, slowed, and with a shock he realized that the coffin would be left in a church for the night.

He stood aside in the dark porch and the faces went past him into the church. From his shadowed place outside he looked in on the distant sanctuary lamp. Down there, the people were standing and the little coffin was being received by a small fat priest. Watching from the cold, dark porch, Martin saw that the fat priest was not one of those who gabble the services of the poor, but that he moved with care and dignity like Father Riordan and received the cheap coffin as if he were remembering at every moment the body it held had but lately been the temple of the Holy Ghost. The priest remained with the people and led them in a prayer. The sounds came with rhythmic urge down the nave to the cold, dark porch.

'Hail, holy Queen, Mother of Mercy. Hail, our life, our sweetness and our hope . . .'

He turned away and went quickly through the streets, not noticing for once even the symptoms of danger round a corner. He had forgotten his coat in the cloakroom. Moving on to the hotel steps, he lifted his head to find Captain Furlong poised up there on the top step, looking down at him.

'Been taking a walk, Mr. O'Reilly? Cold without a hat or coat!'

Martin said nothing. He went up the steps and as he passed Captain Furlong spoke again: 'Enjoyed your walk, Mr. O'Reilly? Getting to know the plain Irish at close quarters?'

Martin looked into his eyes, turned away and walked on into the farther lounge. Seeking his hostess and a last word with her, he approached the party, now smaller in size, and heard Captain Furlong moving swiftly behind him on the carpet. He saw the eyes of the girl who had sat near him at tea, looking past him with a watchful, strained look. At the touch of a male hand upon his shoulder he shivered and, turning, looked straight into the smouldering anger of Captain Furlong's face.

'I asked you a question, sir!' Captain Furlong's eyes were those of an angry bull. 'I asked you a question, sir!'

'I heard your question, sir!'

The 'sirs' might have been given to refractory dogs or school-boys. All at the table looked up, pulled quickly into this emotional whirlpool.

'You did not answer my question!'

'Exactly! I did not answer you.'

'Exactly, sir! With the manners of your kind!'

There was a gasp from someone at the table; someone said sharply, 'Good God, is Furlong drunk?'

In a strained voice, Captain Furlong said: 'And, by the way, could we know just what is your kind? Or is it a mystery? I'm not the only one to think so.'

For a moment he stared into Martin's white face, he began to smile insolently, shrugged and turned back towards his seat beside the girl.

'Wait!'

His own voice seemed to Martin to betray him into a keyless note which belonged to no admitted scale. 'Wait. You yourself have answered that question. My kind are the plain Irish at close quarters. The coachman's cousin, who is a lieutenant for freedom, the son of the shopkeeper where your great-aunt, ma'am, bought her elastic-sided boots, the road labourer, who no doubt would make you laugh if he wanted a bathroom. You make my heart sick. Your great-great-great-grandfather probably robbed that man's great-great grandfather of his land, therefore it is funny that the road labourer should now want a gramophone or a bathroom.' He turned towards Captain Furlong, forcing the shaking pitch of his voice down. 'Your impertinence, sir! My people, my kind, were gentlemen in Europe when yours were on their knees tugging off the riding boots of their masters and mistresses. A Reilly thrashed many a Monro and Grey, and many a Hessian, but it needed only that Reilly's servants to thrash you at Fontenoy. The impertinence of you, stalking into this country, you English upstart who began at best in 1700. You won here, for the time being, but you made the mistake of leaving some of us with our heads just above the mud. And now we are working to hold them erect before all the world. And, by God, we will! The plain Irish. You yourself have said it. Thank heavens I am Irish!'

He saw a quivering haze of staring white faces, mouths open

as the gaping mouths of the lane-boys in the Faithful Brothers school after the crashing of the slate.

He turned away, not a sound followed him from the table. Dazedly, he found himself remembering to tip the cloakroom attendant who squirmed about him. Returning through the hall he saw his hostess, her ungloved right hand held up near her breast in a gesture of bewilderment and recall. He took the hand, looked sadly into her bewildered eyes and stooping, bending low over her hand, he touched it gently with his lips. Swinging about, he saw the gaping snigger on the porter's face change immediately to an obsequious smile, as he held the door open for him.

'Good evening, sir.'

'Slave-Heart,' muttered Martin to himself, and strode down the steps.

He sought Conroy in the Old Cottage Tea Room, the Tango Room, sought him in 'offices' and the rooms behind public houses. When he found him, he said harshly: 'You can pass on the word that the blockhouse idea is on the mat again. More than that, it is almost definitely decided upon.'

He refused to say where or how he had learned this, though actually he had learned it at the Shelbourne, earlier in the afternoon. 'God above, man, don't torment me. I have learned it. Isn't that enough for you? Learned it from a source that surely knows. I'll meet you tomorrow night and hear what this new job of yours is. And, of course, I'll keep my word about helping with the Ballow operations.'

He had promised to help in the first of Ballow's 'military' operations. The Ballow men wanted help from Dublin men, preferably those who knew the area. Conroy had therefore been told to pick some men and had come first to Martin. The latter's mind was made up. Once this operation was over he would marry Millie, go away for a honeymoon and when he returned get transferred to civilian work.

'But of course! Who ever said you wouldn't!'

'Oh, nobody, nobody.' Martin snarled and went away, hurrying through the streets to a tobacconist's shop to see if by any chance Norman had addressed a letter to him there. No letter from Norman, no sign or flicker from Norman, not a shade of a word or a smile from Norman. Not a syllable had arrived

since the postcard which had come to Falmouth. He had written
several times, but in vain. All he knew—and that was hearsay
from a casual acquaintance—was that Norman had been long
back in Ireland and was on the run, probably with one of the
new active-service units. Often he wished for Norman's presence,
the clear blue eyes of his friend, his clear mind behind them, the
smile that could be dimpling and intimate as a woman's, dis-
dainful as a great lady's. A letter might be there. It was not there.
But there was a letter from Millie asking him to meet her on the
morrow, to meet early so that they might have enough time to
settle everything.

He turned his eyes from the headlines in Miss Agnes's evening
paper to the back page and there a paragraph suddenly caught
his attention. 'The late Miss Peters. A short appreciation.' It
was his Miss Peters. She had died two days ago. The 'appreciation'
told of her kindness, her many charities, her pious works for
Christian negroes and unconverted Chinese. It spoke of the line
of admirals, scholars, clergymen, country gentry; it spoke of the
sympathy which would be 'extended' to Mr. Peters who held so
high a place in the professional life of his country. 'The death of
this gentle lady at so early an age will cause sincere regrets not
only among her many friends in Kingstown . . .' He put down the
paper, knowing that it was about to speak of the regrets of all who
had known her long ago when she was a girl in the Rectory in
County Longford.

The next day he took his flowers to the newly made grave.
Standing on the trampled grass, he wondered if she had found
anyone to read out 'Excelsior' dramatically for her before she
put on her glasses to read for herself the Prayer for All Conditions
of Men.

Coming from the graveyard, he saw the bay all tranquil
and cold blue, as it had been on that October day when he
had broken his garter on the way from Knockester and she had
sat on the terrace sewing a new one and telling him that she
had always made the garters 'for the boys' when she had been a
girl. Never in all her life had any man's hand closed over her
breast as his had closed on Florrie's that day.

A few days later, in a solicitor's office, he learned that she had
bequeathed to him, firstly 'the sum of one hundred pounds to
be spent at his discretion on nourishing additions to his meals

as long as he remains in lodgings without a female relative to look after him'. In addition, the bank was to act as paid trustee of fifteen hundred pounds, paying him the income until 'his twenty-second birthday when, if he demands it, the capital sum is to be placed freely at his disposal'.

She had left a little to Mr. Peters 'solely as a token of my sisterly affection since he does not need more money', a little to distant relatives, and the rest to Protestant charities and missionary funds. Martin knew that he would probably have had most of it had he not been a Sinn Feiner and the companion of 'traitors and murderers'. Looking back, he could now see that he had been the only person in years to do more than call her 'a good and charitable lady', or say how 'nice' she was and then leave her. But he too had left her.

He spoke coldly to the suspicious solicitor who smelt a rat somewhere and tried to pump him, and who was clearly adding up two and two to make five until Martin said harshly: 'No, I am not Miss Peters' illegitimate child. Miss Peters really was all the things which you and others are going around saying she was.' And he asked to see what she had written about himself.

At the window, away from the solicitor's eyes, he read it. She said nothing of any wrong-doing by him, of his desertion of her, mentioned nothing but her 'confident hope of his final resurrection in the Lord'.

He paid his debts; he bought more 'nourishing additions to his diet', but they choked against the grief in his throat, when he thought of her 'L'appetit vient en mangeant'. Yet, even while he railed against life because it had made him desert her, he was thinking that now with her money he and Millie could get married. They would be poorer because of their more expensive needs; but at least they could manage.

He had a plan to spend some of the money now. The disapproving bank manager gave him an overdraft of twenty pounds on the strength of his expectations, and among the spies, the touts and the gunmen he went to and fro, between shops where hushed young women in rustling black silk nearly forgot their liveried submission in the struggle not to smile behind their hands. That done, he could scarcely endure to wait.

3

THE afternoon of their meeting glowed in a late autumn sun that was nearly as warm as high summer's. There had been rain that morning, and as they swung through the Phoenix Park and out along the winding roads to Lucan it became a whispering kind of afternoon with the grass blades flickering upwards in slow motion under the weight of pearly drops, the hedges rustling and the birds creaking after insects among the quivering undergrowth. He knew that she was leaving until later all talk of their future and marriage. All she had yet said of that was, 'Martin, I've got to talk to you later.'

And all he had said of his own plans was, 'Just you wait.'

They came round by the strawberry-beds of Lucan when the sun was beginning to flame golden, lingering on the trellised cottages beyond the sloping lawns and gardens. They were the only customers in the tea-rooms and beneath the sun-lit table their feet touched while their eyes sent glances full of the mutual knowledge that lies in the bodies of lovers.

The long beams had not gone from the flowered trellises and brightly painted doors when they came out and turned towards the city. It was as if this autumnal summer was reluctant to leave the world to the hints of advancing winter. They left the road and went down to the slopes by the river. There the Liffey's look of a dimpling country stream tempted them so they took off their shoes and stood in a creek, laughing at one another. The feel of cold water around the ankles, the sound and look of a flowing river, lured them to silence, and he glanced often at the grace of the way she stood in the water, her elbows to her sides as she kilted up her skirt about her knees.

They sat on the bank, and fingered the books she was returning to him and those she was borrowing. He taught her more of his knowledge; she taught him more of hers, and he forgot the pain of what was past. The future was going to be different.

'Say me some poetry. Say Goldsmith. No, say something in Latin.'

'All right.'

'And no death or sunset in it. Not for you and me now.'

The coloured rivulets of sunset were beginning to flow around the sky when he said that it was time to go on to the city, that they were going to a theatre She, who loved the theatre, was all eagerness at once, telling him that she had not gone to a play since he had last taken her. 'It's no fun now going without you. And if it's the Abbey, we must hurry or all the pit seats will be gone.'

'We're not going to the Abbey And we're not going to a pit. We're going to the Gaiety and to the dress circle.'

'The dress circle! But the money, it's terribly dear, it's . . . And how could I . . . ?' Half scared, wholly excited, she began to talk of the other girls who would be there with 'their proper dresses' and their bare shoulders. . . .

Then he told her about the taffeta dress of peacock-blue that looked the deep blue of midnight in one light and sea-green in another, which he had bought for her in Switzers a few days before; told her how lovely it was in itself and how much lovelier it would be on her. He did not say that he had chosen it because Sally had once worn that same colour in tableaux vivants at one of their Christmas entertainments and everyone had said how well it suited her and her dark red hair.

'An evening dress specially for the theatre,' she said with bright eyes.

'Specially for *you*! And for tonight!'

'But . . .' she whispered with alarmed excitement, 'but I couldn't dress up and go to the dress circle.' And then: 'Is it terribly bare down the back?'

He described the top of the dress as well as he could and she said: 'But I couldn't, I'd be cold. Well, wouldn't I? And suppose anyone I knew saw me!' It was said with delighted awe. Suddenly her face fell and with bitter disappointment. 'No, that settles it! The only way I could manage not to have things show, with a top like that, would be to slip home and get my dance underclothes, that I could fix not to show. And I can't. Because Kitty would know there was no dance for me to go to.'

Laughing to see that of all her objections only this one really had power, he told her that he had bought everything that could be wanted to go with the adornment of that dress of peacock-blue: shoes, stockings, underclothes, everything. He reminded her how once when he had joined her outside an expensive shop, he had seen her looking longingly at the things in the window.

'Do you remember what you said? "It'd be nice to wear things like those: just for once: *real* underclothes—not made at home." I've got everything. It's all with the frock itself. I found a very nice woman, and opened the box and showed her the dress and explained what I wanted. She said I could leave it all to her. I asked for the head woman because I guessed she'd be older than the others, and anyway the others were giggling. She was very helpful, I told her how much I could spend. I explained that I wanted to do this on my own because it was to be a surprise present. I expect she thought it was a secret surprise for a sister, a sister just coming out of school, perhaps.'

Suddenly she flung her arms round him. 'Ah, Martin, in the whole, wide, blooming world you did all this for me!'

With locked fingers they went up the slope towards the road. The colours which had been overlaid by the bright daylight flamed now in the sunset and all the evening perfection of autumn was blazoned there before them. It burned in the russet of bricks, in old stones and walls, in the reflecting green of the grass, in the gold of turned leaves. There was no pallor in all the world: not in Millie's cheeks, nor in the worn slim birch trunks; everything was rosy and glowing, and the song challenges of the birds began with many loud calls of triumph. They walked hand-in-hand and saw in the corporeal things around them only assurances of the world's great beauty, panoplied in this hour. They stood silent by the roadside until the foreign-looking Lucan tram came swaying through the evening. They were still silent as they sat on top of the tram.

Once she whispered: 'Where will I put on all those clothes? I couldn't dare take them home.'

'In my room,' he whispered back. 'Don't forget, it's Tuesday.' She nodded, blushing shyly. On Tuesdays the Misses O'Canavans' maid had her night off and the kitchen fire was let go out; Miss Flo and Miss Agnes were going to spend the evening with a friend. Of the few lodgers who came in to eat a cold meal, almost all went out again, so that often on Tuesdays the big house would be empty except for one elderly, though still junior, Civil Servant, and he was very deaf and very self-absorbed, keeping for the most part to his cheap return room. Millie had therefore come sometimes to the house on Tuesdays, because they could not often find the money or the lies for other accommodation and it was seldom she was left alone in her own home.

She bent her head shyly, and he told himself that the days of their contriving were nearly over. Soon she would be his wife.

At the first of the bridges the flowing water changed instantly from a country stream to a city's river, deeply caverned within its walls of granite brought from the darkening hills which they could see from the tram-top. The places which they had seen silent and ominous on the night of the Rebellion were now busy with the sounds of cars. But they scarcely heard the sounds as they glanced at one another, then looked at the curving bridges that had been lit only for them, the ruby-and-gold bricks of the house-tops, swinging into view, the candle-extinguishers of Christ Church, and the Four Courts' verdigrised dome. They were carried close to the windows of shadowed rooms above little shops filled with walking-sticks, sweets and rebel song-sheets, close to bare-armed old women leaning out from hot shadows over bright flower-boxes, past the barbed wire placed between the city and the pointing guns of military barracks.

She was startled when he told her where they were going to eat. He was taking her to the best restaurant in Dublin. She whispered, 'But can I go in as I am?'

'Yes, of course. The Misses O'Canavan won't have left the house yet and if we wait we won't have time for a meal. When you do change into the new frock I'm not going to look at you until we go up the stairs to the theatre.'

'Why not? What's the notion in that head of yours now?'

'Oh, just a wish of mine, that's all.'

Sometimes between courses her shining eyes, instead of looking into his, would look at the table, the silver, the shaded light, and after a hasty glance to ensure that no one could hear, she would murmur, 'Lovely, lovely,' and sometimes: 'What gives it all the tastes it had? I wonder if I could cook that? Frenchmen must think our food grass.'

She demurred to the suggestion of having a second, different, wine.

'I won't be drunk, will I, if I have a little more?'
'No.

> '*Blanc avant rouge, rien ne bouge*
> *Rouge avant blanc, tout fiche le camp!*

'Do you know what that means?

> 'Red after White, everything right
> Red before White, everyone tight!'

And he smiled happily, for it all seemed wonderful and witty and cosmopolitan.

Outside in the night where a delicate, coloured mist was beginning to shimmer between the lights, a jarvey touched his hat to them as if the look on their faces had broken through the prevailing drabness to recall something of the days of the vanished, high-hearted parties. Martin was feeling elated. Tonight he would tell Millie of Miss Peters' money and they would plan their marriage.

When they came to the northern square, once the mansions of Georgians, she dawdled behind, while he made sure that no one was in the house except perhaps the old, deaf, self-absorbed, unsuccessful Civil Servant in his room. Taking care that the lock could not function when he banged the door after him, he sauntered down the steps, and, for the benefit of any prying eyes in neighbouring houses, he saluted Millie in her ascent as fellow lodgers, or distant acquaintances, might salute. Five minutes later he sauntered back with the evening paper noticeably in his hand. With the door now locked behind him, and the familiar musty smell of the hall in his nose, he waited, listening to the creaking emptiness of the tall old house, long since declined from its original grandeur.

From the lucent gloom far above, the shape of her face looked down and his name came echoing, 'Martin.' The light in his room would not light. 'I'm afraid to touch a thing in the dark, I might tear something.' He went down, put a shilling in the meter and returned to light the gas bracket for her, while her shape stood motionless in his attic refuge. He had asked the shops to cover their printed boxes with plain paper and now he took off that plain paper and arranged the boxes in order leading up to the last box with the taffeta dress of peacock-blue.

As he was lighting the bathroom geyser for her, he heard a sound behind him and, turning, saw her standing at the door.

'I haven't dared to touch a thing as yet,' she whispered. 'I'm waiting and waiting.'

'Don't wait too long.'

Though there was none to hear them, they whispered.

'They're terribly dear, those shops you went to. Did you have to use all your savings?'

'Don't worry about that. I'll explain later.'

Propping a mirror against the landing balustrade, he dressed there, wishing that he had tails, and thinking that everyone would know that his shiny old dinner-jacket, rescued from the pawn shop, was only a schoolboy's. Waiting sentry in the un-lighted hall between the dim glimmers of all the military O'Cana-vans under the dimness of Queen Victoria, he heard her softly coming down the upper flights. On the lowest landing she paused, a faintly gleaming shape.

'Can I wear my coat?'

'Yes, of course. I wanted to get you a proper cloak, but my money ran out. Put it on up there, I don't want to see you until we get into the theatre itself.'

'I don't wear any hat, sure I don't?'

'Not unless you want to.'

He kept his gaze away from her deliberately. He would see her when they were inside the theatre door; he would take her coat then; he would look at her and then go beside her in all her beauty to the lights and the overture.

When she came close to him in the dim hall, she put her face to his and whispered, 'I've put one of the flowers you gave me at supper in my hair.' He saw the gleaming of a golden gladiolus. When he had fetched down the dress-box in which he had put all her clothes, she nodded towards it and whispered: 'I haven't a thing on that's not new. Not a thing made at home! Not one thing!'

The night outside was pearly with the mist and the many reflections from windows. Once out of the square he found a side-car and the jarvey, giving a look at them, let down the upturned side with a noble flourish. They swept down the hill towards the statue of Parnell into the dull world of people in trams going about their ordinary affairs; bowling along between the ruins of the bombarded thoroughfare and passing the empty shell of the post office where the two flags has flapped on the night of their first meeting. She looked at him as they passed it. The joint store of their heaped memories came toppling out through her look.

As they came near the river, the jarvey suddenly swerved down the Quays off their expected route because he wished to keep well away from the files of soldiers who were stalking and watching along the street ahead. A couple of more left turns brought him round again to College Green and they spanked up Grafton Street, whisking by the shoulders of the gunmen, the touts, the rival sets of spies, the sweethearts and the unfashionable evening strollers in fashion's afternoon haunts. Between the two crowded cafés at the top of the street, where he had often looked for Conroy on his return from Ballow, the rectangle of light flooded the roadway, and the music came out to them, with gusts of laughter, from the tea-tables where two secret armies watched one another and planned the deaths of those betraying go-betweens whose steadfast hope was to make money easily.

They turned away from the theatre to go along one side of Stephen's Green to the tobacconist's shop where Martin's messages so often went. Here, the big clubs and private houses stood aloof above their balustraded steps, until the street narrowed beyond the Shelbourne. At the tobacconist's he left the box with Millie's own clothes. When he came out, she leaned down from the car and whispered that she would like to walk from there to the theatre, and they walked in silence back along the Green towards the spot where the distant name of the theatre burned like a signal call. As they came towards two men, standing in the shadow of a wall, he gave a sharp look at the stance and cut of them, then saw that one of them was Conroy. There was the unmistakable settling of the head to meet something, familiar ever since the days of the Dunslane classroom, out of a rather gaunt tired face. Conroy did not see Martin, and the latter hesitated, noticing two other men waiting a little farther on. He gripped Millie's arm. 'Quick, Millie, hurry.'

He looked across the wide roadway, trying to peer into the shadows before the railings where the shrubs and trees glistened in the delicate vanishing mist. There, on the kerb, by a tree, a man stood, another near him. A woman's figure began to slink away through the shadows, presently it began to run. Another woman followed; and then another, running furtively but swiftly, and looking back over her shoulder. People said that the prostitutes of Dublin could smell the approach of danger.

'Quick, Millie, don't mind why, but hurry, hurry.' And at that moment he realized that this was no ordinary ambush or people as important as Conroy would not be engaged.

There, ahead of him, about to descend the balustraded steps of a club towards a hooded car, were two men, and one of them was the man who had made his first slip when he had not recognized the name of Harry Vincent's House at Haileybury. It was he, Martin, who had first suggested that his activities should be watched. Now, his hour had struck. Suddenly a netted lorry zoomed screeching round the farther corner and a Crossley tender came in a screaming parabola after it, its Thompson gun swivelling.

'Run, Millie!' he screamed above the noise. 'Run for all you're worth!'

What was to have been an ambush by Sinn Fein looked like being ambushed itself. He dragged at her, but before he could get her to an archway ahead he saw that it was too late. Already the four original figures were swooping, two of them turning to meet the unexpected lorries, but the other two swooping implacably on the foolish one who had risked the vocation of spy. 'Down,' he screamed, 'down flat!' and threw her to the pavement and flung himself on top of her, covering her dark red head with his arms, crushing the golden gladiolus, spread-eagling his body to shield her and wishing that he was not a slim student in a shabby dinner-jacket but a filled-out, large man.

Two explosions crashed behind him and out of the corner of his eye he saw the first lorry going sideways across the road, its driver flopping over the wheel, its officer standing on the brakes and grabbing the wheel. Through the bursting of the bombs that were thrown at the lorry and the tender he heard other sounds, the sounds of revolvers riddling those two who a moment before had descended the steps.

Up out of the mist-wet trees the birds rushed; a tram, spattering its broken glass, hissed through the ambush, the driver crouched down over the controls, the passengers screaming above the din, while up and down the Thompson gun splayed its bullets, and the rifles splayed theirs. Fathers in motor-cars lurched backwards to pull children to the floorboards, and running figures flung themselves flat, or, foolish with panic, ran among the bullets.

Her ribs were breathing there against his, she was warm and alive beneath him, and it was nearly over. Single shots were coming clearly now, so the bombs must be used up. But the maddened, terrified men in the lorries fired blindly up and down the street, wanting only to kill any man, woman or child of this treacherous race that struck out of nothingness and darkness.

Above his head there came a whirring rush, almost like the sound of birds' wings, and he saw a bare-headed woman, neat of hair and blouse, running without a sound, holding to her the sagging form of a boy in her apron while from the starched whiteness of the apron dark blood dripped. Without a sound, a cry, she ran like a wind through the bullets, her eyes fixed on some place she saw in her mind.

The attackers had gone, but still, up and down the street, the Thompson gun and the rifles sent their bullets among the living and the dead.

When he heard reinforcing lorries approach, screeching through the street, he helped Millie up. 'Quick. We might get through before the cordons are made.'

But she pulled him into a doorway. 'Have you anything dangerous on you? No gun, no papers?'

He remembered then that in his overcoat pocket there were notes particularizing Black and Tan reprisals, which he had been making for a man who was to be interviewed by the *Manchester Guardian*.

'God, they'll kill you for that if they get them. Didn't you say they hated that paper? Or they'll hold you, and then find out who you are. Give them to me.' She snatched them from his hand.

'No, give them back; there may be women searchers along here any minute.'

'I'll chance that. They won't worry about us. They'll be too busy with the men.' And, turning aside, she hid the papers in the top of the new stockings.

They stepped out from the doorway, but a very young officer

ran at them, brandishing his revolver, his boyish face strained with hatred and bewildered fear.

'Put them up, you Paddy bastard!' and he shoved the revolver into Martin's face. Then, as if driven crazy by the sight of some-one with his hands up, he roared, 'Irish bastard,' and, in a kind of sob, to Millie: 'You too! You're all the same sneaking cowards. It's you bitches who carry the guns for them.'

Over the youth's shoulder, Martin saw in the roadway a tall army captain who looked a little like Mr. McKenzie. 'Hi, sir,' he called. 'Can you come here a moment, sir, if you please.'

The tall officer came across the road. 'Can't you see those people are in evening dress!' he said to the younger man. And then, to Martin: 'Going to a party?'

'Yes, if this sixth-form prefect will stop being a Hun.' It was a brilliant inspiration, he thought, but the tall officer did not seem pleased. He flushed a little, and murmured something about the extraordinary circumstances and the strain under which his men had to work.

'I quite sympathize. But he's disgracing the King's commission when he uses that sort of language in front of a lady. It's just the sort of thing that those Sinn Feiners like to make capital out of.'

The tall one called a soldier and told him to escort the lady and gentleman outside the cordons. He saluted pleasantly, and Martin raised his hat haughtily, and went with shaking knees and chill ankles after the soldier.

Once outside the cordon, they walked on and on in a daze, not seeing where they were going, not seeing the name of the theatre burning and luring. Millie suddenly leaned against a wall, her face white, and said: 'My knee, it's cut, I think. It got cut when you put me down. But it doesn't matter.'

While he supported her, she said, 'That woman—she had a boy in her apron.' And then she was sick. He helped her into a little shop where she sat, while he hunted for a car to take her to a hospital where some of the resident students were known to him.

Outside the hospital, two gaping lines of sightseers studied him and Millie as he led her past them. A resident whom he knew took them towards the withdrawn, quiet dispensary, instead of to the overcrowded accident room.

'We have a child dead here,' he said. 'The boy's mother just

won't believe that he is dead. She says he can't be dead because he was just asking why do the gulls fly when the shots
began.'

In the corridor a trolley passed them noiselessly and swiftly,
a student leaning down to soothe the wounded man, a nurse cool
and restraining by his head. The man was a coalman. Martin
could see the lines of black grained in his face.

'But, Doctor, darling,' he kept saying up to the student,
'you won't let them take me leg off, I couldn't work without me
leg.' The nurse pushed back the pleading coal-grimed hand. 'I'm
a coalman, Doctor, what would they do in the house at all if I
hadn't me leg. I have three children, Doctor, and I couldn't work
without me leg.'

The stalwart student pushed down the shoulders. 'Now, now,
Sir Henry himself is going to look at you and you know he's the
best surgeon in the three kingdoms, so you see, you'll be fine.'

'But you won't let him take off me leg—I'm a coalman.'

Silently, the trolley slid into the lift, moved swiftly upwards,
the nurse cool and steady beside it, the big student nodding down
to the frightened eyes, his healthy country-boy's face shadowed
by pity.

Millie's eyes met Martin's and darkened with reproach before
she looked away from him.

The injury to her knee was not serious but it had to be dressed
and by the time they left the hospital the moon was mounting
in the sky. The sightseers had gone and in the dreary street
there was only a tram rumbling peacefully along. A little group
came from the side door of the hospital. Two men and a woman,
followed by a child, were leading away the woman who had
rushed like a wind through the bullets. The bloody apron had
been removed and a coat loosely placed round her shoulders.
The light of the heavens and the street gleamed on her smooth-
drawn hair, and her unseeing eyes. When she reached the corner
she tried to turn to the right.

'No, Allie, poor Allie, it's this way.'

'What's wrong with ye all? Don't I know my own way home?'

At last she turned obediently away from whatever disordered
weaving of memory had been drawing her in the wrong direction.
A low mutter came from her; her unseeing eyes sometimes looked
up at the silence of the infinite spaces; and as she passed Millie

and Martin they heard her muttering: 'God's everlasting curse on everything. God's everlasting curse on everything.'

It was long past nine o'clock now. Their seats at the theatre were wasted. In silence they went to the tobacconist's shop where Martin left his companion in the back room to change her clothes, the shopkeeper's son who was in charge saying clumsily and resentfully that he supposed his father would not mind. 'It's just to change a dress, is it?'

As he closed the inner door on her Martin saw for a moment the peacock-blue dress; it was all bedraggled at the hem and beslimed in front with the grease of the city.

In Anthony's they tried to warm themselves with coffee in the tense, silent pews, where no music from the gramophones blared tonight, where the boys and girls clustered at the door, ready to spring back from sudden shooting, as they listened to the growing madness which swept the lanes and streets, when the armoured cars, the Lancias, and the Crossley tenders netted against bombs, moved slowly up and down, searching, prowling, their searchlights swivelling, while from hallways and windows the heaving slum world ventured an occasional defiant shout of 'Up the rebels!'

The lorries turned and re-turned, seeking some tangible enemy amidst the dark, burning hostility of the city. Uncomprehending, half-ashamed Tommies peered from behind their netting at small boys who yelled: 'Wait till *we* have Thompson guns! We'll blow you out of that!' Old slatterns shook their fists and pretty girls curled their lips in hatred at the young English faces which looked out on streets that seemed no different from the warm home streets of Manchester or Leeds and yet were the streets of a foreign city quivering with contemptuous hatred.

Through this snarling passion Millie and Martin wound their way in silence. He had had no time to tell her his wonderful news, and when he tried to do so now she said: 'No, no! I can't talk now. I can't. And, anyway, I daren't stay a second.'

At sight of his unhappy face she put her head to his shoulder, and with frightened woe in her voice said weakly, 'Ah, Martin, Martin, where's it all going to end?'

They kissed and clung to one another, each saying to the other: 'Go home and rest now, you're worn out. We'll talk next time.' Their hands broke apart at last and she turned away. He watched

her as her departing figure dwindled beyond the lamp-post, and
between the high drab buildings. Long after she had gone, he
stood on the little canal footbridge above the sheeny water, fas-
cinated by the lights from the portholes of barges moored there,
as Dan Murphy's must be moored now somewhere, before going
its way tomorrow peacefully between the fields at home.

4

It was a week before they could meet again.

Millie, turning into Anthony's from the street, paused a moment between light and shadow exactly as, long ago, Sally, when he had first seen her, had paused between the shadow of the hall and the light on the half-moon of lawn.

They sat silently in the private publicity of the cubicle. Although she took off her hat with the strong upward gesture which he knew so well, there was a weariness in the familiar movement; and although she smiled to see him watching it, it was a quick worried smile, which died into tired thoughtfulness and a silent preparation for something she had to say.

'Let's go somewhere quiet Martin. The Phoenix Park. It'll be a bit like the real country.'

The mist of late autumn clung to the dark patterns of the tree branches and stilled the sounds of children playing in the park. They walked quickly to get far away from people, and then in a narrow walk between the cold wide fields they stood embraced, silent and holding one another closely.

They sat down.

'Well, you got my letter?' She nodded and listened while he told her all that he had been unable to tell her the night of their planned visit to the theatre. 'So now we can get married. I have to go down the country again, but when I get back, then, immediately! A few weeks now at most.'

She said carefully, 'Martin, could you ever get a scholarship into an English university?'

'I don't know. I suppose I could. I imagine so, but why?'

'There's the university in London, isn't there? The one your Curran man got the dinner from?'

'Yes, but what's all this about?'

'Just wait a minute, Martin. And, with or without a scholarship, you could, anyway, give lessons there, and earn a little that way until you were finished and had a degree?'

'Yes, but look here, you are not suggesting, are you, that . . .'

She turned fully to him, and took his hands between hers.

'Martin dear, be guided now by me, listen to me,' and she gazed with imploring fear into his eyes. 'Come to England and we'll get married and live there, at least for the first, Martin. It need only be till you're finished. It's our only chance. If it's needed I can get a mannequin job or something of the sort. With or without a scholarship, you must get finished, that's your life, Martin.'

'But what's all this about living in England? I couldn't do that.' He paused, then added: 'Not yet, at least. We'll go away, of course, for a holiday, another honeymoon, Millie. But it wouldn't be right to stay away very long. We must find a flat here too before we go and——'

'Oh God, no! A flat here in Dublin! No, no, I couldn't, Martin.'

'Why on earth not?'

'For hundreds of reasons. And one last one—it wouldn't work. It wouldn't work, that's all!' She beat down his words with her imploring, 'Ah, listen, listen now and be led by me, Martin, or . . .' She stopped, began again, like someone who has much rehearsed their arguments. 'Martin, as long as we are here, the first thing will be Ireland; Ireland all the time, and never us two. Besides, living here, you'll never get anywhere, and even if you did they'd try to pull you out of it. I'm telling you, Martin, oh God, I'm telling you, can't you be led by me this once? Don't you realize, on top of everything else, there's your people and there's mine! People talking, Martin, about both of us . . . I want to live your way, not the way the people I know live, and if we were here that would be impossible, unless I shut the door in the faces of everyone I know. And I wouldn't do that. You don't know them as I do. God, I can see them dropping in and stopping us in the street for one of their back-hand chats with all the spite in it. Telling things, hinting and . . . Oh, lies, Martin, lies! Come away from this place. You'll make new friends. You always liked the decent English and I'll know how to talk to them by then and do everything the nice way. We'll not write back to

anyone here until we've made our way; then we can come back
and face them different, if you want to. Let the past be the past for
both of us . . .' Her wide lips trembled and drooped. 'I love you,
Martin,' she muttered passionately. 'I love you, I love you, I love
you, the way no girl ever loved anyone before. I'd look after you
and love you always. I'd be a good wife to you, I would!' and her
head came down to his shoulder and rested tiredly there as if her
mind were tired of working. 'It's now or never, Martin. At home
. . . it's no longer a matter of putting them off and off. Kitty wrote
to Gus and asked him point blank if he wanted to marry me or
not and he said of course he did. But I don't want to marry him.
I want to marry you.'

He held her, hushing and soothing her, and she, feeling the
yielding softness in him, raised her head and said solemnly:
'You'll just be led by me and not ask any more questions about
it? You will, won't you?'

'But, Millie, I can't leave Ireland in the lurch all of a sudden,
just like that. Wait a little while. In a few weeks we'll be married,
and have a good holiday together, and come back feeling quite
differently.'

'Ah, wait, wait,' she said despairingly. 'Martin, as long as we're
here, it'll be "wait, wait". It'll be "wait until Ireland is this, or
until Ireland is that or the other". . . . And anyway, there's no
question now of being able to wait. It's now or . . . Come away
with me now, Martin . . . we'll be happy away from them all,
away from this place.'

'But I can't! Millie, I can't. It wouldn't be right.'

'You're not responsible. You were only a kid, you didn't know
what you were doing when you joined them. You had no one
like Kitty to strap it out of you.'

'Kitty! I'm going straight away to see Mistress Kitty,' he said.

'Oh God, no! You keep away. Whatever you do you'll ruin
everything if you do that. They've heard about you and they're
after your blood, Martin. Ah, come away, come away from this
blasted country. If ever you put your foot near any of them,
Martin, we'll be ruined! That's the very thing I'm trying to
avoid.'

'But why?'

'Haven't I gone over and over it many a time? Haven't I
tried to explain? . . . Ah, if you knew what it was like at home

now with Father, that said he was an agnostic, threatening me
what he won't do to the fellow that doesn't believe in God!
That's what he calls you. Someone's been doing the usual Irish
trick, talking to them; how much they know or don't know, I
daren't try to find out, but that's how the whispers and talk
will come to your ears too one day about me. . . .'

'About you? Who would dare? What whispers?'

'Ah, come away, come away from this awful country.'

'But I can't. It wouldn't be right! We'll manage here.'

'I can't. It wouldn't work.' She raised her white, anxious face
to his. 'Can't you just take it from me that it would be the ruin
of us? I'd sooner never see you than see you thinking one smallest
bit different about me than you do, I'd sooner . . .' Terror broke
through her eyes. 'I'd sooner be dead and gone, than hear that
you'd been called out one morning and later found flung on the
road outside a barracks, prodded to death with their bayonets.'
And, weeping helplessly, she said again and again, 'Like that man
in the paper the other day, like the man in the paper the other day.'

He held her tightly, hushing the man's name on her lips.
He had despised that man for an ignorant gunman, and was
ashamed to think how easily he had scorned someone who was so
soon to bear, without treachery to others, the long tortured hours
before death. He held her head on his shoulder and stared out at
the misty park lands, the drifting wisps of greyness in the sky
beyond the tree patterns.

'Listen, Millie, I'll do this. When I get back from this work I'm
committed to we'll go straight away. I'll stay off the job longer
than I had intended. We'll talk everything over and you'll see
then that I must come back here, at least for another while. Then,
if the fight's not over, I would feel I had done enough and could
go.'

'In your heart you want to go now. Your real friends are all
on the other side. Come away. We can't wait. Come to England
with me!'

'I can't! It wouldn't be right! We must try here first!'

Through sheer weariness, they rose and walked aimlessly
about among the damp grass, the trees, the wide fields and the
harmless, unalarmed deer. The fall of evening was approaching
when, worn out, they turned back towards the city.

When they had come in sight of the gates, she drew him aside among the shrubberies and said desperately: 'We're nearly back! Listen to what I'm telling you. Oh God, Martin, if you don't . . .'

'How can I? It wouldn't be right!'

'I knew in my bones, I suppose, that you wouldn't. I suppose I knew. I suppose I did.'

He pulled some tufts of wet grass and held them to her aching forehead, then to his own. With the aid of the vanity bag he had brought her from Paris she tried to freshen her tired face.

As they made to step out into the avenue, she held him back and, looking at him with a sombre intensity, said, 'Whatever happened, Martin, you would try to see that it was because I loved you rightly, and wouldn't have it all ruined and dirtied.'

'I love you, and I know you love me. But what is this?'

'Nothing, don't worry. Ah, Martin, Martin, don't worry and break your heart.'

'In a few weeks, when we're married, you'll see . . .'

She put up a hand to stop him.

'What's wrong?' he said, and she answered:

'Nothing. It's all right.'

As they went down the avenue she kept turning her head towards him and studying him with long glances. They walked to the tram at the first bridge of the river, where over four years ago they had arrived to find the city waiting for war. They sat in the rushing wind on top of a tram; the lamps were not yet lit and her banquet table had not yet come to life under the water. When the tram came to the farther bridge, where they had stood hand in hand watching the city, she put down her head and, after that, she looked no more at him or at the places they passed. By the time they had reached the central streets twilight was turning into darkness. When they stood for the last time on the shaking bridge above the inland basin that linked the city's river to the canals of the countryside, the moored barges were dark, no port-hole showing an orange of light.

She said in a low voice: 'Just check that I've got all the different ways of finding your Cassiopeia. I want to be sure that I've got it right, and can always find it.'

'But the stars are not out yet. I can only show you where they will be later. If this mist clears.'

Looking at her he thought he had never seen such misery in a face.

'What is it, Millie? Why do you look like that?'

'It's all right, it doesn't matter, Martin, don't worry.'

'You're worn out, you're just worn out.'

They stood clasped on the narrow footpath of the bridge, strained cheek to cheek, body to body. Footsteps clattered on the other pathway of the bridge, which echoed to the heavy tread.

'Ho-ho, having a good last paw at her?' And then, as a final good-natured joke, 'Well, up the rebels, anyway!'

They stepped swiftly apart, her face wrung with anger and pain, while the steps went on into the echoes of all the steps in the great busy streets beyond. She made to hurry away, but when she gave that well-known look backward over her shoulder, she turned about and, coming back to him, she held him in a silent, strong embrace. Then, without a word and with bent head, she went.

The line of street lamps sizzled into light. He saw her figure getting smaller and smaller until, at the accustomed corner, she turned. She stood, a small, dark, distant figure. He waved to her, a reassuring, brave wave. She raised her arm to wave in reply, but it fell back to her side with weary helplessness and, turning away, she went back into her own street.

Left alone on the bridge, he stood for a time, disturbed by the quality of farewell in that helpless gesture. 'It's just that she's tired out,' he said.

He went back quickly through the city. He went first to the tobacconist's shop. He had never collected the box with Millie's finery from the inner room.

The owner of the shop, hitherto so friendly and so proud to be a secret letter-box for Mr. Reilly, looked at him sullenly from under resentful eyes. He had evidently been prying. 'That box ... I don't want it here any longer. I don't want things like those around. I'll not have my place turned into a brothel. . . .'

Martin stalked into the back room and stalked out with the large box into which Millie had put the peacock dress and all that went with it. He had to hurry to be in time for a late meeting with Conroy arranged the day before.

'What's in the box, Martin? Are you travelling for Hoovers?'

He ignored the question.

'What's this job you want to tell me about?'

'Well, you know that owing to the breakdown of the enemy's

civil administration, especially the normal policing of the city, we've had to take certain matters in hand?'

'For heaven's sake, Seamus, don't lecture me! I'm not a Lithuanian journalist!'

Conroy went on imperturbably.

'The criminal classes have been getting out of control, and our own Republican police needed stiffening. I've been on the job now for a fortnight. I've been asked to recruit help from intelligent officers willing to give up a few hours a week to the job. I'm on my way to visit one of my street patrols now.'

'Do you mean that you want me to do policeman's work? Really, that's too much! I'll not touch it. Besides, it's mainly only eyewash for propaganda purposes.'

'On the contrary,' said Conroy gravely. 'Since I took over, you won't find one pickpocket or confidence-man from the Parnell monument to Stephen's Green. I cleared them all out in a week.' Then, even more soberly, 'I don't undertake any job in the spirit of eyewash.'

Martin looked sideways at the lean face with the young-old look which showed now on the faces of so many enemies and friends, who had leaped straight from schoolboyhood to leadership.

'Pickpockets, confidence-men, "fly-boys"—Scotland Yard will have to deal with them now.' Conroy chuckled, then said solemnly: 'We got rid of them. We deported them. We sent word to the enemy's police here so that they could warn the Holyhead and Liverpool police of what was arriving for them. But for the last few nights we have been tackling the next job . . .'

He paused, and in the light of the street lamps Martin saw him blush as he settled the head.

'The streets,' he muttered. 'Immorality . . . women on the streets, you know what I mean. We've already given them a big fright.'

'Do you mean prostitutes?' said Martin bluntly.

'Well, that is the *official* name,' said Conroy very reprovingly.

'Official! Well, I declare to heaven . . . Official! Really, Seamus, you make me tired! Anyway, I won't be a policeman to spy and pry on people. And women! Prying on women, even if they are prostitutes! I once saw two policemen manhandling one of those girls and . . . no, I wouldn't touch your filthy job. Can't you

leave them alone? They leave *you* alone! They keep out of the
way of anyone who doesn't want them.'

Conroy blushed.

'You're silly, Martin. Listen to me. Now, firstly! Do you admit
that society has to be protected against people who prey on it?'

'Prey! Society! Society is people, and people aren't cotton-
wool babies! Protect against a few big things, murder, robbery
and the like. After that, a man must look after himself. You want
this place to be one big schoolroom governed by a simpering
miss, with a non-existent Holy Gael for her dream-man. Damn
you, you're like a clean, girlish schoolmistress! Prey! What do you
mean? How many women would lead that life of their free will?'

'Good women—no,' said Conroy solemnly. 'Bad women—yes.'

'Good women! Bad women!' muttered Martin, and saw again
the weary anger in Millie's face when those clattering steps had
passed on the bridge and that mocking Dublin voice had called
out to them.

'What do you know about women, any woman? You stand
there classifying women, and you've never kissed a girl in your
life.'

He saw a puzzled, sad expression come into Conroy's face.
He did not lose his temper, but said gently: 'Martin, when we
come back from the Ballow job, you ought to take a rest. Go
away for a holiday. They say I need a rest too. Would you . . .'
He hesitated, muttered: 'Would you come with me? You could
show me things you . . . well, places and so on, eh? You could read
your pagans in the hotel, while I was at Mass, praying for you!'

'Ah, Seamus, if it could be 1913 again and the two of us back
squabbling by the weir!'

By common instinct, they turned to look at the pedestrians
on the other pathway, the people passing in cars, the courting
couples, the young men so obviously proud of their clothes, their
brains, their looks, the impression they were making on the world.
Looking at one another, Conroy and Martin each saw that the
other would like to be for a little while as young and ridiculous
as those young men of their own age.

They had reached the street patrol Conroy had spoken of.
A red-haired youth came up and surreptitiously saluted him. He
nodded diagonally across the roadway towards the shadows of
the railings. From the shadows a young woman dashed. With

a sound between a laugh and yelp of fear, she ran from shadow to shadow, while the patrol, halted by a line of passing traffic, first made to head her off, then resumed their advance towards the shadow from which she had come. A big shape of a woman came out of the shadow and, with a scornful, clumsy swagger, moved slowly down the pathway towards the tree where Martin and Conroy stood. Once she turned, looked back at the patrol in the roadway, then spat on the ground and resumed her ungainly, swaggering walk. Her short coat, her bulgy skirt, only accentuated the raw, bony cut of her. Around the collar of the jacket there was a mouldy bit of fur and from her queer hat there tossed with arrogance, high above her head, a feather which plumed upwards with a terrible, old-fashioned declaration of finery.

Peering into the shadow of the tree where Martin and Conroy stood, she looked them up and down, made a sound like a horse with a cold, and swaggered contemptuously away, her bulgy skirt flattening itself in places against her knobbly limbs. The patrol made to pursue her, but Conroy called them back. 'We'll get her later. Make a round of the Green in the other direction.'

Farther on, in the full beam of a lamp, he and Martin came on her, preparing to throw one leg over the loops of the chain slung between the little pillars along the kerb. She swung a big leg across the chain and straddled astride there, snorting loudly and tilting hat, feather and face full into the light. The beams of the lamp threw soft lights into coarse red hair.

'Ha! Dublin Jackeens playing at being policemen! Give me an honest-to-God, old-fashioned peeler any day of the week!' and she swung into the traffic.

For a few moments Martin stood staring. 'It's Josie,' he whispered to himself. 'Josie!' he shouted, and ran.

He could see her far away beyond the traffic as she neared the other pathway; he could see the bit of fur and the tossing feather.

'Josie! Wait! It's me!'

He rushed diagonally across the roadway, but suddenly cars and trams seemed to be coming from all directions. He dodged amidst the hooting lines of traffic, trying to get through to where she stood hesitatingly on the pavement. Looking across the traffic she saw him coming and threw back her head in a great snort of laughter. She put her hands on her hips and called something savagely at him. He could not hear. But some fragments of her words came to him, and in the shape of her lips, the bitter contempt in her stance, the fragments of her call were completed.

The lines of cars tailed away and he ran across the rest of the road. He could see the ridiculous feather flaunting above the heads of the pedestrians, many of whom turned to look after the feather and laugh. Others, however, did not turn to laugh, and even when they came to pass Martin their faces were still set in disgust and condemnation.

The feather went quickly round the corner and, at the corner, he ran to the roadway to see how far she had gone along the pathway, watching to see her pass through the rectangle of light between two cafés. There was no sign of her. Careless of the traffic, he got out into the middle of the roadway, searching both pathways for a sight of her. Cars hooted at him, pedestrians began to look at him and people coming out of the picture house, seeing groups gathering, clustered timidly around the big commissionaire, wondering was there trouble afoot.

He could not see her. When he came back to the footpath, some small boys and their sisters followed him, an old lady came bustling after him, and caught his arm.

'Poor fellow. Try to remember your tram number and I'll put you on it,' and, instantly, the small boys and girls were around him in a circle, staring hopefully at him.

'It's all right. I lost someone, that's all. Thank you. Thank you.' He raised his hat and hurried away, pretending that he did not know that the children were still at his heels. He turned into a side-street, to shake them off, but some of them straggled hopefully after him, and he rounded on them at last. 'Get away, you intolerable little pests!' To escape them, he rested for a while in a public house, then went out and began a systematic search for Josie.

Along the streets and laneways which were the haunts of prostitutes, faces smiled whitely out at him from alleyways and dark mouths in the white faces trickled out a vocabulary of tenderness, naming their recommendations and sometimes using the word 'love'. Young women, old women, one with a face raddled, another with a frail perverse beauty almost of a child, but no face like Josie's, no matter how close he went to peer into the shadows.

Now and then he stood against a wall to rest. Soon it would be the curfew hour, but the theatres had not emptied yet and the pulse of the city was sunken in a monotone of dreary footsteps, as the people walked the streets, preferring the risk of an ambush to the drabness of home or bed-sitting-room. The great central population of clerks, students, servant-maids, typists, factory-hands, moved sluggishly past the wall where he stood, and he looked on them without sympathy, seeing in them only Slave-Hearts and lane-boys who would be the first to laugh at Josie or draw back from her in disgust.

Once more he made his rounds and when, worn by tiredness and the shock of this knowledge of the dark places, he would have abandoned the search, some picture of Josie long ago would spur him on, making it impossible to think of going back to his attic eyrie, leaving her out here to walk these streets, do this business.

'D'ye know what I'd like now, me hearty Master Martin? I'd like to be sweeping me own kitchen and me own son ating hot buttered brack be the fire. Aw now, one day you'll be Mr. Reilly and Anastasia Josephine will still only be Josie.'

Big, bony Josie, gasping to hear 'the latest' about Big Mick Lannigan who had courted so many pretty girls in his time, but without marrying, so that all hoped he would marry Josie in the end, and 'wouldn't it be a blessing and a wonder if anyone did!'; Josie and her jigs, her wild eye ready for fun and life, too ready, people said, not quiet and easy like rosy-cheeked Mary Ellen.

The box under his arm made his muscles ache, his feet were swollen, but he tramped the rounds once more, looking into the rancid hallways and the scabrous archways whose darkness quivered with an unseen life beyond them.

He stood in a gateway and looked up at the silent, purple heavens. 'If You are up there in those burnished halls of yours, You, Conroy's God, listen now to me! Look down on Your work!'

What folly, he thought, to hurl defiance at a sky that only men had peopled with the creatures of their fears, turning away from their bare human destiny.

'And courage never to submit or yield,' he muttered. He would not yield to them nor to their smoke—nobody; not even if that

sky up there could open now to show him the face of their Almighty One. For if that happened, he would out-eye the Mighty
One Himself; he would clamber up on the necks of the adoring
multitude and stride through the ranks of strong Archangels
within the shadow wall of their powerful outstretched wings and
he would peer straight into the infinite pools of Jehovah's eyes.

He smiled then to think that the heavens would not now rend
to the roar of God's anger reproving him. He smiled and forgot
that even from the earthy gods of his boyhood, from Aunt
Mary, Long Dick, Miss Clare, Aunt Kathleen, reproof had not
come until after chastisement had run its course, and then had
come not in a thunder of wrath, but with a murmur of love's
reproach.

Once more he made the round, although it was now nearing
the curfew hour. It occurred to him that it would be just like
Josie to return to the Green and stalk insolently past Conroy's
patrols. On his way there, a voice called from a doorway and
he hurried on, but heard, 'Well, give us a fag, anyway.' He went
back and handed his packet of cigarettes to the shadowy figure,
raised his hat and turned away. As he did so the figure stepped
out of shadow and he saw a simple, countrified face looking at
him, the only attractive face he had seen.

'Do you know a girl, no, a woman really, called Josie? Anastasia Josephine McDonnell?'

She shook her head, giving him a flickering, apologetic smile,
and stepped back into her shadow place.

'Do you think you could ever find out about her for me?
She's a friend. Or was a long time ago, when I was a boy. I'd
like to meet her again.'

After a moment, the voice said: 'All right. If you're around this
way some night, ask for Katty, I might just hear something.'
A soft young hand came out, and touched his. 'Thanks for the
fags,' and the hand withdrew.

He went on towards the Green and, not wishing to be seen
again by Conroy or his patrols, he prowled along in the shadows,
keeping one eye out for Josie, one eye out for the Irish police.

From the dark places where he moved alone, he peered out
like the hunted prostitutes themselves. The crowds were coming
now from the early closing of the theatres and pictures, using the
last half-hour to get home before the terrors of curfew hours fell

upon the listening city. In a car halted opposite where he stood, the roof light was turned on and he saw the face of a girl he knew. She was laughing at her companion, her pretty head snuggling into the down of her wrap like a kitten in a soft corner. If he went to them, she and her brother would invite him into the car, a trifle flattered to have with them the strange, difficult young man who scorned their friends' houses. They would ask him to stay the night, because their father liked nowadays to put up Sinn Feiners, if they were of the less rough sort and not important enough to be hunted down in his house by the British. He would be given a glass of cheap sweet Graves, there would be no religious pictures in the dining-room, only in the bedrooms; the son would show his books on Thomism, and read him poems about gaso-meters or the soul. The mother would talk of gardening and the father ask him how things were going and who did he think would form the first Irish Government when this movement of blood-shed had finally won what years of argument and reasoning had not been able to win. And the girl's music when she sat down at the piano would be turned by the manicured fingers of a priest from a good district or from the University.

Even after we have won they will all still be there unchanged. Conroy's police will have a green uniform and a green flag. The lamp-posts will be painted green, the street names will be in Irish which no one understands. That is all. No, not all! Those people over there in the car will have climbed into the saddle. They will be *all*-powerful and heaven help poor Conroy!

Miss Agnes was waiting up for him, and to please her he made an effort to eat the meal she had kept hot for him. Lifting his head from the unfinished food, he found her eyes upon him.

'It's old men it's making of you all, before your time,' she said. 'But you'll have your reward, all of you, when we see poor Ireland with her head held high before the nations.' She moved over to the mantelpiece and took two letters from where she had put them in a Lipton's presentation tea-caddy.

One was from Mary Ellen. The other envelope, a fat envelope, was from Norman. Seated at his table up in the attic he opened it. It contained some amazing news.

. . . *To explain things properly now, I must go back to that time in France. I went the walking tour alone, but after some days I changed the*

*route because I was finding it too depressing to visit alone the places I had
hoped to see with you and about which we had exchanged all that exciting
information. My new route took me to Avignon. There I made the acquaintance of an Abbé. You must have noticed that for a long time I had been
avoiding the kind of talk about religion which we used to write to one
another after we left Dunslane. I had been working and wondering, and
could come to no resolution. But this Abbé! In himself he was a revelation
of the intellectual perfection of the Catholic Faith. A human being at his
best, Martin, charm, learning, humanity, humour and love of life. It is
clear to me now, that many, if not most, Irish priests are doing great harm
to God's Church without knowing it for an instant. They have exalted
one virtue—obedience—above all others. And they have despised the in-
tellect. One day, you too, Martin, will see that the Catholic Faith is the
only valid assertion of an Universal Intelligence. The unchanging Mind of
the Universe is expressed only in the Catholic Faith and you are too intelligent not to see that for yourself eventually. Meantime, nothing is changed
between you and me. We shall talk about it if you wish or not talk about
it if you prefer it. But our meeting must wait because in a very little time
I am going on a Retreat. Meanwhile I shall continue my work with the
Flying Column. After the Retreat, I am ready go to anywhere with you.
But my decision already is definitely made. I am going to be a priest, and
one day I may be the means of bringing you back to the faith you have
abandoned. . . . '*

He felt dazed, baffled, defeated; his best friend to be a representative of all that he most hated and despised. He undressed slowly
and got into bed. From his bed, he saw something white glimmering beside the box that held the stockings, the clothes, the
taffeta dress of peacock-blue, that had been deprived of its planned début at the Gaiety. It was the glimmer of Mary Ellen's
unopened letter. The letter could wait until the morning, for he
knew all that Mary Ellen could ever say. She would say that she
liked living married in Waterford to her nice, easy man; she
would say that she hoped he was not 'much different', that he
would come one day and sing a song for her. She would say that
there was never a word from Josie all these years, that things were
going 'nice and easy' with herself as always. And she would say
that every night she mentioned him high up in her prayers to
God.

V

The Flying Column

I

D<small>AY</small> after day, while waiting for the order to go to Ballow, he postponed the ordeal of answering Norman's letter. Day after day, the order for Ballow was delayed, and at last he set off to tell Conroy that since the Ballow people had been so dilatory he thought himself now liberated from his promise to take part in the operation: that he was going away, might be away 'some time', in fact that he was going to be married. He found Conroy waiting to tell him the news that they were to leave for Ballow in the morning.

In the cold autumn dawn they rode down through the Midlands, silent for the most part, never mentioning that night in Stephen's Green. Towards midday they found themselves confronted by the outposts of a large British force engaged in searching several parishes. It took them nearly two hours to make a detour through fields and lanes, and when they again struck their road the clouds were piling up far ahead of them, lumbering over Mount Leinster and unrolling across the flat plains in fleecy masses. The rain belted them, lashed them; and they bent their heads to it. In the late afternoon the sun came out and stiffened their sodden boots, made ridges in their clothes, and for a while they sought rest in a farmhouse but the children bringing in news of the sound of approaching lorries drove them onwards.

In a serene starlit night they entered Ballow town; too weary by now to make a detour, they took the risk of cycling openly through the streets where scarcely a person was to be seen and nothing heard but an occasional footfall hurrying by in fear, because the Tans had been quartered in Ballow for three weeks now. There were Auxiliaries in the neighbourhood and already an old man had been killed, a woman's head cropped and a

437

twelve-year-old boy was in bandages. The Royal Leinster Arms was lit up and had the air of a place which knows itself safe, but there were no groups gossiping at its door. There was no light in the Ladies' Tea Room, no light in No. 9 where Aunt Mary had once waltzed with a chair as partner.

They cycled past the closed shops and with legs numb from the pedalling motion went down the road that led towards distant Keelard, passed the cross where one turned off for Moydelgan, and rode out towards the little patchwork hills. Then they made contact at last with the scouts and were led to a kitchen fire. Food and rest awaited them but they found that operations, other than the preliminary minor ones, had once more been postponed for several days. Later in the evening James Edward arrived, limping along on his false foot. He had not been in Glenkilly for months, but he was able to give some news of it. There were Black and Tans there, worse still, Auxiliary Cadets; but so far they had done little mischief 'thanks mainly to the regulars. The Tommies' O.C. in Glenkilly is a determined fellow and has managed so far to keep the Tans and Auxiliaries in the background.' Martin learned that his Aunt Eileen and Uncle John never now spent a night in the house and that most of the furniture had been moved to Dr. McDowell's house for safety. There had been raiding and looting several times, but the only really dangerous happenings had been bullets through Bridget's bedroom window one night and a Mills grenade flung through the dining-room window another day. Bridget was engaged to be married, but would not leave her parents alone 'until the troubles are over'. She always got on cheerfully, James said, with the younger military officers conducting day-time official raids.

'It was Bridget who used to tease Rosaleen once about sending cards to British army officers in the barracks. Do you remember?'

'Yes. I remember.'

He remembered Bridget's black hair flowing over Rosaleen's mousey plaits, the lamp-light on white pinafores, on Aunt Eileen's needle and account books and Mary Ellen, shy, behind wild Josie in the doorway, and the unseen rain touching the dark window-panes beyond the blinds while he sang Aunt Mary's favourite song.

'Yes. I remember. And Rosaleen?'

But of Rosaleen James could say only that she was alive and in health and nothing more, since of a Poor Clare there could never be any worldly news other than that she was alive or dead. Seeing the trouble his false foot gave to James, Martin said suddenly, 'It's not fair, James, that you should have to fight in two damned wars.'

James shrugged his shoulders. 'It can't be helped. This is Ireland's last chance. If we're licked this time, we're licked for ever. They're out to hound the fight out of us for ever this time. Mind you, I'm not one of those who are ashamed of having fought for England in the war. They did mean all that about small nations and freedom, the ordinary English people, and the lads I met in the trenches,' he said. 'We all thought then there would be a new world, but . . .'

'I know. They've forgotten it now. It doesn't suit them any longer. Sometimes I feel I could cut the throat of every English diehard living.'

'There has to be moderation in everything, Martin, even in war. Decency and . . . er . . . humanity, moderation and tolerance.'

'Oh, no, James. It's evident that you have not been mentally disciplined in our higher Catholic schools. If you had, you would know that while error is in the ascendant one must cry for moderation and tolerance towards the defeated Truth. But once Truth is in the ascendant then it would be a sin to show tolerance to error or to be moderate in crushing it.'

James said sharply: 'Look here. Do you really think these things? Or is it just . . . well, intellectual theorizing?'

'Intellectual theorizing! That's good, James.'

They stood awkwardly silent. James, glancing at him, said: 'Have you had a break lately? You ought to take a rest.'

They smiled at one another with the resignation of men who know that their deepest thoughts will never mingle and turned to take their places at the meeting of officers to discuss the plans of the coming action.

Around the table the rectangle of faces, shadowed above the light of the oil lamp, watched and listened to Conroy, to James Edward, to the Commandant of the Flying Column which would bring to the operations their experienced bombers, roof-men and a new kind of land mine which was expected to blow in the main door of the barracks to be assaulted and taken. It was Rodesbridge barracks.

'All garrison towns in a circle stretching as far as Killcar will
be cut off by continuous road trenching and trees. But on one
road the obstacles will be arranged so that the reinforcements
along that road will get through within a couple of hours. They
will get through and drive into a perfect ambush. Let's hope they
come in force, that's all.'

The rectangle of faces nodded. 'That's it. Hit them every time
harder than the last one they hit us.' Martin looked at the
speaker, a former school-teacher. He knew the man to be at once
sentimental and brutal. A man like that was capable of hurting
an English prisoner. Perhaps even torturing him. He saw him now
snubbing young Tom Prendergast and putting the mere country
boy in his place.

In a nearby cottage he lay in his rugs listening to the breathing
of other men around him. The sound was like the sighing of a
foreign and ominous sea. Now, over there at Dunslane, the
breathing of the Blue Dormitory would be mingling with the
murmur of the weir which he had left behind him less than six
years ago. In those years men had carried guns over all Europe,
over much of Asia and Africa; their bones were giving phosphates
to many continents or lying polished at the bottom of the various
oceans. There had been nothing like it since the whole Mediter-
ranean world had gathered to fight at Troy.

A week passed to the remorseless treadmill of bicycle pedals.
Up into the eaves a mother or sister would climb to bring down to
him fifty or a hundred pounds of collected money, or they would
unpick a mattress to hand him a brother's or a son's report. Twice
he came within cycling distance of Glenkilly, along roads where
he had driven in Dr. McDowell's car or cycled with Gertrude and
Niave. Once he crossed the river far below Glenkilly, not many
miles above Johnny Patterson's lock.

Two years earlier the houses willing to shelter him would have
been few and far between; but now almost every house was ready
with food, shelter and information; and in the towns it was not
behind hucksters' shops he sat but in the drawing-rooms of richer
people, linked with the others either in fear or in angry revolt.

It passed, a week of pedalling, of strange doorways by night,
strange tense faces by day, fingers pointing to the bullet holes in
the bedroom wall, to the grave of the dog blinded by Tans in
senseless hatred. To all he said the official things that were 'to

hearten the people's resistance to terror'; he said the things to steady the people.

More than once he got off his bicycle and stood looking down at his boots, asking himself why he did not cycle straight back to Dublin and to Millie. Twice he began an answer to Norman's letter but put it away each time. He would send his answer from England when he went there to marry Millie in a few weeks' time.

The young moon was rising when he came back to the house in the patchwork hills beyond Ballow. Two rings of scouts were out, the house full of fighting men. The Flying Column messages said that the Column would enter the area in the morning. All was ready for the assault on Rodesbridge barracks and the big ambush that would follow it.

He sat, trying to read, watching over his book the neighbours arriving, the men and officers gathering in a huge circle facing the hearth. Behind them, on forms, were others; and in the dark recesses of the hearthside the eyes of old women gleamed out on the young, on the children gaping between stool legs, the girls with arms or heads reclining on the knees of the boys who would fight tomorrow night for 'poor Ireland'.

The Flying Column Commandant and two of his unit, who had already arrived, told tales of their wandering battles; but James Edward, resting his false, Flanders foot, smoked and said nothing of trenches or of Germans rising out of the mist beyond No Man's Land. Those of the district who after tomorrow's battles would leave homes and work permanently to travel on with the Column had brought their few necessities in little parcels, and in their eyes were the mystery and danger of the new life opening before them for however long or short a time.

Sometimes Martin, glancing up from his book, found Conroy's eyes upon him, but he had nothing to say to Conroy now. Nothing to say to James Edward either; and when he heard the chairs scraping and talk of the Rosary he went unobtrusively to the door. The horned young moon was up, and he went out into a whiteness which struck his fevered face with a cold shock, as if he had been engulfed in a soundless cataract of light frozen all about him. Far beyond the icy whiteness the rhythm of the Rosary came rolling over the unmoving Michaelmas daisies. The deep-voiced music reached him from a distant other-world, as aloof as the star world of Cassiopeia's chair up there. He walked

down through the white garden pursued by the waves of prayer
and even when he had come to the gate and could see some of the
inner ring of scouts the sounds of the prayer came to him. He
looked up at horned Astarte.

> . . . with these in troops
> Came Astoreth, whom the Phoenicians called
> Astarte, Queen of Heaven, with crescent horns.

From behind him the sounds of prayer swelled—Hail, holy
Queen, Hail our Life, our Sweetness and our Hope. . . . He laid
his cheek against the cold stolidity of the gatepost and rested
there. He dozed, and when he woke again the sounds behind
him had changed to the lusty rhythm of song. He stepped back
through the little white garden and stood bent to the window,
peering in through the gap beside the curtains. In there, the men,
women and children were singing now of freedom, having prayed
for it. They sang new songs made out of the new fight, and in
their verses names of dead men he had known made music.
They sang of tomorrow's fight and of death's grey honour that
was come to some.

> 'We'll drink a health to every man
> Who walks in death's pathway.'

With his face pressed to the cold glass he peered and crouched,
while in there in the firelight they left the new songs which some
did not know and went to the old songs which all knew so well:

> 'Alas, that Might can vanquish Right.
> They fell and passed away.
> But true men, like you men,
> Are plenty here today.'

He turned away then from the window and went to the bank
from which he could look far across the moonlit plains and see
the circle of the places where he had grown. Far over there on
the left was Tory Hill, with Norman's father and the last of the
unmarried fillies fretting with shame about the dangers over-

hanging rebel Norman, or reading with relief and joy the news
that he was going to be a priest of the One, Holy, Catholic,
Apostolic Church outside of which there was no redemption.
Farther still, on the right, by the river and the massed trees of the
long island, Keelard stood dark, his name burned deeply there
between Sally's and Peggy's. Now in this moonlight a gleam might
steal into the shuttered schoolroom to shine on the cracked blackboard, on the map of the world and their boat's lantern, which
they had put with those things in the corner for company's
sake and as a sign of something. And between those far-parted
two, Tory Hill and Keelard, were all the locks of the river, all
the roads he knew, and Glenkilly, Lullacreen, Dunslane and
Moydelgan.

Oh, Aunt Mary, why did you die that time!

When all was silent in the house and the cows beginning to rise
from their knees in the restlessness before dawn, he went back to
the kitchen and found a place among the sleeping men. There
he dozed until he was awakened by a faint, secretive creak upon
the stairway from the loft overhead. He sat up sharply and saw
a small white shape on the stairway. It was the son of the
house come from his bed to stare down at rifles stacked in his
father's kitchen and his country's fighting men asleep on the
floor.

The next afternoon he sat by the kitchen window watching the
fall of twilight. There was nothing to do now but wait for the
night. Everything was prepared. He, supported by young Tom
Prendergast, would have charge of a small group which would
form the extreme left wing of the line of riflemen and bombers
attacking the front loopholes of the barracks; but their special
duty would be to smother the fire from a penthouse attic which,
jutting up from the barracks roof at that end, overlooked the
barracks yard where Conroy and others, having climbed an
exposed wall, would try to batter down the yard door with a
sledge-hammer. The other and right-hand end of the barracks
faced the by-road which at that point made a wide junction with
the main road. From the houses lining the side-road, men of the
Flying Column would attack while their comrades got up on the
barracks roof to break it in and hurl down burning rags. The
Column men had entered the area that morning, and scouts had

reported their arrival within striking distance of Rodesbridge.
All then was 'going according to plan', Conroy said.

Some of the poorer men, not wishing to accept more food from
the people of this house, had slunk shyly away to neighbouring
cottages; a few had gone not for the food's sake so much as for
the sake of some girl they had seen during the singing last night.

Martin wanted no food. The feverish cold which ever since the
winter terms at Knockester had lain in ambush inside his chest
seemed about to overtake him and made the thought of food
repellent.

The squads were already beginning to cluster in the barns to
play the last few hours away with cards; the officers in the kitchen
were sitting silently by the fire when a frightened messenger
dashed up the darkening boreen.

That afternoon, Tans and Auxiliaries, swooping more or
less blindly, had surrounded a large area which cut across the
line of retreat chosen for tonight, and in the house where the
wounded were to have found shelter the raiders had come across
some Volunteer papers. They had smashed up the house, arrested everyone in it, including the doctor who was to have seen
to the wounded.

Operations, he felt sure, would be cancelled. Now he could go
back to Millie; he would not be killed tonight! Now, with no line
of retreat, no place for the wounded to go to, the attack must
be postponed, perhaps for weeks, and he could go with her to
England to be married. But Conroy stood white and grim in the
middle of the room. 'The civilian trenching parties are already
making for their positions. All the organization will go for
nothing. We can pick another line of retreat from the ambush.
Here's the map. . . .'

Someone said: 'But what are the wounded going to do? There
won't be a road fit to travel on; even if it wasn't a death sentence
to take them any farther by road than the trenches.'

'War is war,' was his reply, 'and this is one of its bad fortunes.
The wounded must take their chance with a general line of
retreat across the fields.'

The taut-sprung will behind the voice chilled the lamp-lit
faces in the kitchen. James Edward limped forward and said
quietly, 'We'll vote on it,' and he began to tear paper into voting
slips.

The silent embarrassment of men, handing in secret votes, ended. James Edward said: 'All have voted to carry on except one. There is only one "no".'

'It is mine,' said Martin. He watched through the window and saw it come at last, the pale benevolent night-time symbol, like the candid look and the serene brow of calm and purity. Its quiet starry order overbore for a while the clamour of his heart, and the clamour of men's minds which he could feel in the air about him; and he wondered if it could be something more than mere human foolishness to see in that formal display up there the assurance of a universal harmony.

Young Tom Prendergast's face was stiff and white in the light of the young moon, as they moved off in the main party behind the scouts. There were lights in many of the cottages which they passed, and Martin knew that behind those orange squares of windows some would tremble and others say a prayer for the footsteps going by on the business of Freedom.

Leaving the boreens, they went over a slope and saw far below and behind them the lights of Ballow twinkling in the milky plain. Once, a man who had stooped in the ditch to fasten a lace muttered to those passing him, 'Begob, 'tis all terrible well planned; there's scouts coming in every tick of the clock with word in front.' No one answered him and he ran to his place as if abashed by the sound of his own voice.

Once a whispered message came back along the single file and they lay down in the shadow of a hedge and after a few moments beams of light swelled over their heads, while the grinding roar of lorries swept past them. That swift reality of a hitherto unseen enemy stirred all pulses, and when they rose again there was a quickening of the pace which was soon checked by the officers in front.

The horned moon was sinking when at last they climbed over a wall and saw far below them the river like a silver blade between the trees. They went down towards it and joined the river road about two miles above the bridge. If he could step apart now from these men, and walk back alone to the bridge, he might possibly hear a fragment of the weir's sound because the rains of several days were having their effect upon the river and its hurrying flood would be making a mighty sound on the weir.

The smooth surface of the water was in places rippled up into a series of wide, curving necklaces, and from the direction of the glittering curves he saw that there must be a sporadic breeze blowing down the river, though no breeze could be felt along the hedges of the road. Would he ever now come here with Millie or would he die tonight? Never, never again to see her up-curving smile, her arm's lazy power sweeping her hat from the dark red hair? Never again to move his little finger by the un-noticed purpose in his brain? Thoughts like that were the first symptoms of panic, and he bit his lip against them and walked on.

The file left the road and went down to the river bank in order to approach Rodesbridge behind the long back gardens of the houses whose fronts faced the barracks. When they saw in the distance the dark shape of the houses higher up against the sky, they halted, letting groups of three or four go forward at a time. Waiting there with his own group, he heard young Tom whisper to one of the men, 'It's terrible for poor old Flanagan'; and then he learned that when the Tans had come to Ballow old Ser-geant Flanagan in his cuteness had got himself transferred out to Rodesbridge for his last few months before retirement, thinking that he would be safer out there away from a post of Tans.

The young moon was now low on the horizon of the malevolent heavens which had played that trick on Flanagan. Soon she would be gone, the young heavy Queen, loaded down with all the wasted talents, the broken vows, the unanswered prayers. Down, down she must go, and no matter who had died in the night, old Flanagan or himself, the sun would rise tomorrow, for suns may set and rise again. *Prati ultimi flos.* It had all been said long ago, the world was worn with age and nothing new.

Soon all the groups had gone forward except that with Martin and young Tom. As they waited in silence, nervousness touched the men with querulous doubts about their officers' leadership. They began to see mistakes in the plans, asking why the telephone wire to the sawmills was to be left uncut. He spoke reassuringly as an officer should, telling them that one wire was left to keep them in touch with the night operator at Ballow Exchange who would report events in the town when the Very lights went up at Rodesbridge. But he had no sooner reassured them than they stiffened nervously again as a faint popping noise came to them. All took cover among the shrubs and, peering down the river, saw a motor-boat breaking the silver necklaces into tossing jewels.

It moved slowly because of the powerful flood current against it. Far up near the road there was the sound of a door being roughly opened and steps clattered down a rocky boreen towards the river. It was the boreen from that very house outside which he had helped to bring a calf into the world.

A man's figure plodded on to the bank and snatches of his angry words came to them as he pulled a girl roughly from the boat, striking her heavily, while a youth burst away from the boat and ran up the boreen. 'You're worse than her,' shouted the man after him, 'playing gooseberry for your own sister,' and he banged the girl roughly towards the boreen. The sounds of his thumping on the girl's back, of his angry self-pitying voice, trailed away. ' . . . sooner see you dead at me feet . . . shameless . . .'

None of the men made any comment on the scene, and not a word was said as they went along the bank and turned up into the field towards the wall which, continuing the line of houses, faced the greater part of the front of the silent barracks. Already Column men, it was said, had got into the houses on the by-road at the other end of the barracks; and now the frightening message would be going along the village's houses, bidding the people get down into the back rooms.

As they stood looking across the field towards the positions which they would hold at the wall, there came a creaking behind them. It was James Edward, crawling swiftly through the hedge in spite of his false foot. All was 'going well', and he went rapidly over the whistle signals with them once more. He turned to Martin and said hesitatingly: 'We'll be in action in a few minutes. So . . .' He held out his hand. 'Good luck.'

'Good luck.'

Still James hesitated, half turning on the artificial foot. Martin whispered, 'If the reprisals stretch as far as Glenkilly, James!'

'I know! We mustn't think about it, that's all!' They looked at one another in the dimness of the hedge. 'Dash it, Glenkilly ought to be safe enough. They'll scarcely go for places so far away. It's Ballow and nearer places they'll shoot up.' He sighed deeply. 'You ought to write to Mother more often. All the strain of everything now comes on her head.'

They nodded at one another, but James turned back to Martin and whispered: 'Oh, I nearly forgot! Wasn't Dempsey the name of your great friend in Dunslane? The chap in that snapshot you sent once upon a time? Mary Ellen had it on the kitchen mantel-piece in a frame. Was it Dempsey?'

'Yes. Why?'

'Nothing. Only it must be he that's over with the Column lads. They were saying that they had a chap who knew the district well because he had been at Dunslane. Norman Dempsey, is that it? I was wondering why the name sounded somehow familiar. I'll tell him you're here. I must hurry,' and he crawled away through the hedge.

From the shelter of the wall came the single quick flash of a torch and the line of figures stole forward in silence through the stiff grass. At the lean-to shed built against the wall, Martin, young Tom and their group took off their boots and cautiously climbed up on the galvanized iron roof, cautiously laid out the bombs in rows, the home-made coffee-tin bombs in front, the four real Mills grenades, like dark chocolate Easter eggs, behind them. They saw to their revolvers, the safety catches, the magazines; then, crouching below the top of the wall, they waited, their orders being not to reveal their presence until the whistle signal which would mean that Conroy's section were about to face the risk of climbing into the barracks yard under fire from the penthouse attic.

In the silence of waiting they heard gusts of the strengthening breeze in the hedges make noises like those of a dog or a man upon broken twigs. On the left a horse whinnied nervously, blew through its nostrils and moved unhappily about. Louder than any of these sounds was the thudding of his own heart. Far away on the left a flock of sheep had stopped running and now stood in a grey arrow, looking back at the vague things from which they had fled. Did Norman know that old Sergeant Flanagan was in there in the silent dark barracks, Flanagan who had coaxed the lovely girl Suffragette away from the boys' grandstand? Or was he thinking of the days when he had wakened from sleep in the Blue Dormitory and stretched a hand out in the direction of Martin's bed?

The shapes of the riflemen waiting behind the gate in the wall were motionless below him. The distant dog had stopped barking, the sweet cold wind strengthened. Then, up out of the silence burst the first detonations, the gate was flung open and the rifle-men knelt. The birds squawked frantically all around in every direction, and far away the arrow of sheep ran and ran. From the far end came the clattering of slates; the Column men were up on the roof already.

'God in heaven! What's that?' gasped young Tom, as a rippling flame widened around them, burning yellow and red along the galvanized roof and lapping at their toes.

'It's all right. It's only the Very lights going up from the barracks.'

Now looking vertically up along the wall they saw the lights fall away against the sky and the roof was dark again. Through the bursting of home-made bombs, the clatter of slates and the ping of bullets on the other side of the dashed wall, they could hear the sound of cheering and shouts. Through the cataract of sounds came the blast of a whistle; along this road and the by-road the attack suddenly ceased and a moment later the police bombs and bullets also stopped.

'Surrender!' roared a voice along the wall. 'Surrender in there, ye peelers! If not, we'll burn ye out!'

After the sound of that voice a silence lay along the wall and fields. It was broken only by the terrified plunges of the horse going round and round the field-hedges nearby. Once a child howled in terror in some back garden and was soothed. Still no answer came from the doomed barracks. Crouching on the roof, he begged in his heart that they would have the sense to surrender. Why should they die in there for Downing Street and Dublin Castle? It was different for Mr. McKenzie, he was an Englishman, and his oath . . .

'For the last time, surrender in there!'

The answer came then: 'We won't! Ye pack of murderers!'

For a few moments following that answer the silence continued; the horse's gallopings had stopped, the screaming birds had become quiet again.

Then once again, out of the heart of the silence, the cascading detonations burst, and the sky was laced by flashes and by the spray of the Very lights blazing to the heavens for help. From beyond the gate the signal whistle shrilled.

'Ready,' said Martin, and lit the candle-stump. They held the fuses of the home-made canister bombs to the flame.

'One, two, three.' They rose up into the clangour and the lights, and saw straight before them the penthouse attic. Down on the

2F

left the men around Conroy with the sledge-hammer were shelter-
ing under the barracks-yard wall and looking across and up at
them. In unison they hurled their bombs. They ducked and rose,
ducked and rose, and at each rising they sent five seconds of
death-bearing time locked within the coffee-tins that hurtled
against the weak roof of the penthouse. Although the attic windows had armoured shutters its roof was old and weak, and the
slates were yielding not only to the explosions but to the blows of
the heavy tins. Bullets pinged plaster out of the wall up into their
eyes, bullets wheeped past them, and, at each rising, they came
up out of shadow into a growing glare of light made by the flames
that had begun to shoot from the other end of the barracks roof.

Now in the attic roof there was a hole through which they
could see slantwise and the whitewashed wall inside showed like a
framed target. Hurling more tins across, into that cracking hole,
they signalled down to Conroy who at once began to climb the
wall. There was no shouting now from the penthouse, no sign of
movement within the gaping hole, and they crouched down again
into shelter. Martin began to think that he was wounded. He did
not know where, and he could see no blood and feel no pain.
It was his imagination. They heard the hammer blows quite
clearly above all the noises and cheerings. Then suddenly he saw
a dark stain on his left hand, felt dampness, felt that all his sleeve
was sodden with blood.

'I'm hit in the arm,' he said, just as there came calls for more
fire against the attic. They rose up and hurled a round, then saw
that Conroy must have gone back over the wall, for now he was
entangled on the top of the wall, his leg caught in something.
Through the hole in the attic, Martin could see the side of a head
and shoulder bending in the direction of the yard to aim at Conroy on the wall. His hand went down and closed over the pine-
apple markings of a Mills grenade; pulling out the pin of the
grenade he felt it spring like a live thing as he launched it, not
in a lob but in a fast throw, straight at that shoulder and head.
The darkly shining oval went direct towards the hole, a face
peeped up behind the shoulder of the firing policeman and
it was the face of old Flanagan. The dark oval struck into
Flanagan's face, fell, and even as the explosion burst up in a cloud
of dust cheering swelled all along the line and there were shouts
of: 'They're surrendering. Cease fire.' Beside him on the gal-

vanized roof the men were jumping. 'Look, look! They're surrendering'; and he saw down there a white thing drooping from
a rifle barrel held out through a loophole.

Staring sickly across at the battered penthouse, he heard
someone say, 'Where's Tom Prendergast gone?' and, turning,
saw young Tom huddled on the roof against the wall. His shirt
was thick with blood, there was blood on his mouth and he was
trying to squirm upright, trying to look up at them through the
glaze in his eyes. He made an effort to speak, but the blood
bounded out of his mouth and soaked them. His eyes strained up
at them with a wide, long look of amazement and anxiety, a
big bubble of blood grew slowly out of his mouth, his head bent
gently over to one side, and they saw that he was dead.

They handed him down to the man who had come to the shed
and who laid him down on the grass and closed his eyes. All
around them rang cheering and singing and even the voices of
girls running out from cottages at the news that the barracks had
surrendered. The men knelt to say a Hail Mary beside young
Tom, and Martin, turning away, went weakly to the gate. He
leaned there and asked a man whom he had never seen before to
bandage his arm.

'God, it's covered with blood y'are.'

'It's mostly young Tom Prendergast's. He's dead. Absolutely
dead.'

The man cut the black mess from his shoulder. He said that the
bullet had gone clean through the flesh but had missed any
artery; and, with his field dressing, he bandaged the wound, while
Martin looked out from the gateway at the figures running into
the barracks with petrol, or running out with the captured arms
and ammunition. The shadows thrown by the spreading flames
of the blazing barracks danced so much that it was hard to distinguish the shadows from the running figures, or from the village
people moving with cups of tea among the men.

2

He set out in search of Norman among those shadows and men. Faces shouted exultantly at him: 'Machine-guns! We got two machine-guns!' He went through the yellow glare, past the roaring crackle and saw the line of policemen standing along a wall with parcels and suitcases. At their feet three bodies lay, their faces covered. The middle body was old Flanagan's, surely? As he moved away, he saw a police constable making a half-defiant, half-pleading motion of drinking and he turned towards a group who were giving tea and biscuits to some Volunteers. He asked the girls to give the police a drink. They whirled about, screaming: 'Tea! Poison would be too good for them'; but the men said: 'Shut up! Get them a drink'. The girls still refused, but two old women said that they would bring tea to the police, and two Volunteers went up to the line of prisoners, clumsily holding out biscuits and saying roughly, 'Here's biscuits.'

He found James beside two pony-traps, one to take the wounded, the other for the captured ammunition and guns. The Ballow Quartermaster was greedily counting the boxes of ammunition and bombs while the Column Quartermaster watched him suspiciously, jealously checking the share which would fall to his Column.

'James, I can't see Norman Dempsey anywhere.'

They told him that Norman was in the second house at the end. 'He's helping to get down a wounded man from the roof there, I think. The casualties are heavier than we hoped,' said James. Then he added, 'I hear that you saved Seumas Conroy's life.'

'Young Tom Prendergast is dead. Died just like that.'

'Yes, and it's going to be hours before we can get the wounded far enough away for them to rest in any kind of safety at all.'

'Is there a Sergeant Flanagan dead?'

452

'They have a Flanagan dead. Yes, a sergeant. They put up a good fight all right.'

He walked dizzily across the flame-lit junction of the two roads, passing on the way those village people who had crept out to see the sight, but who would not be seen mixing with either police or Volunteers. What was he going to say to Norman now? It was more than five years since that day at Ballow station, when they had resolved together to take their problems to Long Dick. Long Dick was dead and now Norman was going to be a priest.

He stood by the kitchen door of the house listening to the noise of feet above and muttering voices. He would wait here until the men came down with the wounded man from the Column, then he would pluck Norman's sleeve and draw him aside. There were enough of them up there to carry the wounded man without Norman's help. Listening to the low mutters overhead, he tried to make out Norman's voice, then went slowly up the stairs and saw the head and shoulders of a man framed in the oblong of the roof skylight as he carefully lowered a helpless figure to the two men reaching up their arms around the skylight ladder. The beam of a torch moved along the ladder, moved on to the helpless figure; it shone on Norman's fair hair all tumbled and on Norman's face pale as death itself.

He dashed forward to the ladder. 'No, no. Give him to me,' he said, and stretching upwards he received Norman into his arms.

Norman's clothes were bloody in the middle of his body and his face as it touched Martin's cheek felt cool.

'Careful. Mind the bandages. It's through the belly. He'll be all right if we're careful.'

He let one of the biggest men take the head, he himself helping with the legs, and, as they wound slowly down the stairs, he thought despairingly of that drive of three or four miles to the first block on the road; then of the wounded being carried across fields and ditches to lie for hours in some hillside cottage with raiding Tans all around; of the doctor who might not get to the wounded for hours and hours.

'Haven't you any arrangement at all?' he snarled. 'It's a nice way to think of your wounded.'

They said gruffly that they had relied on the local arrangements and when they had laid Norman down on the kitchen table they stood looking gloomily at one another. The Column Commandant came in. 'How is he? That bloody pony-car is the only transport. And we must move off to the ambush right away. The others are falling in outside.'

Norman opened his eyes and said: 'Am I badly hit? I don't feel any pain. But I'm thirsty.'

While they were giving him a drink, Martin leaned forward to show himself. Despair rose in him at sight of Norman closing his eyes weakly and unable to speak. He crushed his head between his hands trying to make it think of some plan and, leaning his face against the cool glass of the window, he muttered, 'O God, I'll believe in You, I'll *make* myself believe in You, if You'll save Norman now.' Beyond the reflection of the lamp-light on the window there was another and fainter gleam. It was a dull sheen on the river below the garden. Out there, how cool and quiet it would be on the water flowing down to Dunslane and Glenkilly. Flowing down to Glenkilly! He whirled about, for a plan had opened suddenly and clearly before him. He would take Norman to Dr. McDowell in Glenkilly. If it were indeed God who had given him a straightforward sign at last, he would believe and pray against his unbelief.

He dragged the Commandant with him as he ran calling, 'James, where are you, James?' and when he found James Edward he asked about the night operator on the Glenkilly Exchange. 'Is he all right? Is he a Volunteer?' It was spreading clear before him and he could not endure the bewildered questions of the other two.

'Are you mad, Martin! All that distance. And the roads, man! And the Tans! Man alive, are you mad!'

'The river! Don't you see, no one's thought of the river.'

He had them running beside him as he raced for the sawmill and the uncut telephone wire. 'No shaking on the river. No noise on the river, and it's miles shorter than by the roads. Miles.'

'But you could never row all that distance, no matter how much shorter it is, it's still——'

'I know of a motor-boat! Oh, hurry, and don't talk about what you don't understand.' Were these questioning two, these damned military geniuses, to delay him now by even one second? He shouted at them as he ran.

'Be quiet. You don't know a thing about it. I can do it in two hours. Less, with this wind and flood.'

They argued no more but sent a man to delay the cutting of the sawmills' wire, and James, having got through to the Ballow operator, got the Glenkilly man next, spoke to him and handed the instrument to Martin.

'Listen. Ring up Dr. McDowell's house.' He had spoken in a whisper as if there were danger of being overheard, but the voice which answered was clear and precise, though distantly faint.

'It'll take a few minutes. He doesn't keep the phone upstairs at night, he keeps it in——'

'I know *exactly* where he keeps it. Hurry.'

Through his mind there was unrolling the chart of the river, the snags and bends, the locks, the places where he must pass close to roads, and be overlooked.

'Here's the doctor now. Don't be too long. Everything quiet here so far.'

And then in his ear Dr. McDowell's voice, startlingly familiar.

'Listen, Dr. McDowell. This is Martin Reilly. You remember?'

'What did you say? Who is it, please? You know I never go out at night nowadays except to my old patients.'

'Listen, Dr. McDowell. This is Martin Reilly. Martin Reilly who went away to Dunslane. Niave's friend. . . .'

'Martin Reilly?' And in a moment Dr. McDowell's voice said quietly: 'What is it, Martin? You're a long way off. Why are you ringing at this hour?'

In his other ear James was whispering: 'We can't wait. We must move on to the ambush. But how can we leave him to this mad plan of yours!'

'Oh, go. Go away for goodness' sake and leave him to me. I don't want any of you now. Go away.' Then, hastily, to Dr. McDowell: 'No, not you, of course. It's people here bothering me.'

He glared at James and at the Commandant who, after whispering to one another, said: 'All right. Maybe it is the best way.'

James pressed Martin's arm encouragingly. Noticing only then that he was wounded, he said, 'Oh hell, you too?' and followed the Commandant out to the road.

Carefully, passionately, Martin spoke again into the telephone, explaining his need, explaining who Norman was.

'Oh! Is that the boy in the snapshot you sent long ago?'

'Yes, yes. In football things,' and he went on pleading and explaining. 'I know you never cared much about Nationalism and all that; but this isn't for Nationalism or anything. It's just for me. He's the only friend I ever . . .'

'But, apart from bringing him here, I'm not a surgeon, Martin. Wounds are different now—treatment, I mean—from Boer War times. Abdominal too. I know a man in Dublin who would try to get down to you if I asked him.'

'He couldn't, there will be only one road free and there's going to be the hell of an ambush on that. I must get him out of this area, the Tans will be blazing demons tonight. Rodesbridge barracks has been taken and the ambush is going to be the worst they've ever struck.'

'My God! And there are Auxiliaries here. They may break out.'

'But your house would be safe, you know it would, and . . .' He argued and begged and at last: 'Listen, is Niave there?'

'Yes, and Michael.'

'Well, ask Niave. She'll tell you to do this for me. I won't let them get Norman and I won't let them take him to lie in some cottage in the hills. It's not like in your days, Doctor. These fellows nowadays are quite different; they'd torture him. You don't know them the way we do.'

'Yes, I do,' said the voice grimly. 'I saw something of their handiwork last week. All right, Martin, bring him; the river is a good idea, Martin. Best possible transport. What do you propose at this end?. They won't suspect me, but the more secret we can be . . .'

'Listen. I have it all worked out; down there. The old fishing wall below Gertrude Jamieson's window, Mr. Jamieson's, I mean. I can land there, where the wall's broken, and there's a path that comes out behind the marshy bits on to the Feather Lane and . . .'

'Is there? I never heard of it.'

'Ah, grown-ups wouldn't know it! I mean, Niave and Gertrude and myself knew it. It goes right up to the Feather Lane.'

'I see. You want me to drive straight up to the back lane and the garage?'

'Exactly! Niave will tell you the place in the lane. There's a gate with the two bottom bars loose to come up and down but

Niave will remember all that. Ask her.' They spoke of Norman's
condition, Martin telling what he could; they spoke of the timing.

'Is there plenty of water in the shallows above the tile factory,
do you know? There should be with this flood. Never mind, I'll
manage somehow. I know every yard of it.'

'But will you remember?'

'Yes, I'll remember!'

He ran back towards the sinking flames that burned steadily
now, bending like flaming grass stalks to the wind. Many and
many a man had lain out in No Man's Land for three times as
long, and far more dangerously than Norman now, and had
lived to tell the tale.

Everyone seemed to have left the village but there at the flare-
lit junction was James, waiting with a bicycle that had a strap
fixed to one pedal for his false foot.

'I waited to see. Now I must dash.'

'James, you've seen worse cases in France, haven't you? He'll
be all right, won't he?'

'I think so. I think he'll come through all right. Don't show
your face out in Glenkilly, don't go near the house. Send word to
Mother to come to the McDowells'. Tell her I am well and that
I don't need money. There's no money there now anyway, only
debts, I fancy; but if she thought I wanted . . .'

'Yes, yes. Go now, James. And good luck,' and he helped
James on to the bicycle and saw him speed away, a shadow
towards shadows. He ran then through the village where there
was complete silence except for the humming of the flames
bending behind a tricolour flag stuck in triumph in a barrel.
Everyone had vanished from the street: the Volunteers, the girls
with tea, the more timid onlookers. He rushed into the house,
caught a glimpse of Norman's face turned sideways, his eyes
closed, his hair glinting between the shoulders of the people
looking down at him.

'Carry him down to the river. If you can't get straw, gather
rushes, fir needles, anything. Everyone, children and all. Lots
and lots of rushes and needles. I must have a blanket too, and a
pillow, and hurry! But don't shake him.'

He pounded down the road away from the humming flames
and into darkness. There was a light in one window of the cottage
beyond the yard where the calf had been born, but as he scrambled

noisily over the gate the light was instantly extinguished. As he
hammered on the door, he was sure that there was breathing
beyond it. 'Ah, don't be afraid, come out. I'm only taking the
motor-boat. It'll be sent back to you or you'll be told where it is.
But don't attempt to report that it was taken.' There was no
answer, only the certainty of people holding their breaths in
there.

He ran past the calf's shed, down the hedge-lined boreen, and
there the river flowed. But when he crouched to the shape of the
boat he nearly overtoppled into the water, so giddily did his
head throb, always with the one central thought of Norman's
safety within it. The thudding giddiness yielded to the slushing of
water against a boat, and its lapping among reeds. He knew the
things which he had to do and that he could do them.

Seeing to the row-locks even as he untied, seeing that the oars
were there, for if the motor failed they would be needed, he
thrilled to think that it was all the better that she should be
clinker-built with a wind and a flood behind her. The stern
swivelled round, the flood bore him broadside to a stony creek.
But he pushed calmly away from it, jerking repeatedly at the old
string until the engine started, when he turned the prow up
towards the glare in the sky and soon found the worn place on the
plate where the throttle lever got the best results from the engine.
Turning to come in on the flood to the group on the bank, he
pulled up the centre rowing seat. Over sacking and a blanket
he spread rushes in a honeycomb and down through the cells of
the honeycomb he poured loads of fir needles. A woman handed
him another blanket and a pillow, and he thanked her warmly,
knowing that she could ill spare them; but she said, 'Musha, it's
little enough to do for him.'

He patted the bed, happily reassured by the feel of its gentle
resilience. The best bed in the world, they had long ago known
that. Niave, Gertrude and he in Glenkilly, Sally and Peggy in
Keelard. 'Now,' he said, and knelt with his hands outstretched
for Norman.

As they brought the legs round, Norman opened his eyes and
said calmly, 'What are we doing on the river?'

'Hush. You'll be all right now. It's me—Martin!'

But Norman had already closed his eyes again and lay as if
he had not heard anything.

Martin whispered to the faces bending from the bank, 'Did he
say if he was in pain?'

'No. He said he wasn't at all. He'll be all right now. God is
good.'

They were all bending, all the plain, rough faces and the
gaping childish ones, looking down at that pale face with the
closed eyes and the lips firmly pressed as if against some inner
strain.

They had put water into a bottle, and he thanked them
eagerly, for he had forgotten about drinking water. He tucked the
second blanket over Norman and, over that, he put Norman's
own blood-soaked overcoat. He reloaded the chambers of his
gun, and waited a moment to make sure that he had thought of
everything.

'Now,' he said, 'shove well out.'

In a moment he was out, swirling about in the flood and
pulling at the fly string. The engine popped, he got the prow
straight down and then he heard the under-song of a boat in full
movement and the song of the breeze blowing full against the
bow as it splashed through the water.

Looking back as he passed the boreen to the calf's yard, he
could no longer see the people on the bank and already the glare
of the barracks was only a stormy sunset in the sky. Now he had
Norman away from Volunteers and fights and fires, snugly
bedded in a boat with the strong clean wind all about him and
the fine flood bearing him along the river.

It was carrying deep water in almost all of its width so that he
was able to cut the corners and, on the straight stretches, take full
advantage of the flood current. And never a shake for Norman in
that resilient bed.

Beneath the bridge the boat drove onward in a powerful curve
and when he looked back he saw that there was not even that
midnight sunset any longer in the sky; only a rosy glow was there
now, strange to see at night, but not dreadful.

Suddenly the engine spluttered a couple of times and stopped
with a thrashing of the propeller: the petrol had given out.
Cursing his forgetfulness, he clambered past Norman to the
forward rowing seat. It was difficult to row from that seat, the
contractions of his wounded arm muscles were agonizing, and at
every pull there seemed to beat up to him the smell of drying

blood, his own blood, young Tom's and Norman's. But when he looked at Norman peacefully breathing there beyond his feet, he got fresh strength and won back the long, steady stroke that gave speed to the boat without jolting. How good Norman had been at that stroke; he and Sally had been the best regatta pair for their age on the river.

Norman's eyes opened and looked at him. They were bright in the grey night.

'Is that you, Martin? I heard you talking a long time ago. I knew it was you.'

'Yes, yes. It's me. Don't talk.'

'What are we doing in the river? Am I badly hit? I don't feel anything at all. Just a bit cold.'

Martin put his raincoat over Norman's coverings, then got painfully out of his jacket and tucked it across the raincoat. The clothes were heavy with blood, but the wind would blow the sickly smell away from Norman's face. The clean sweet country air would be going into him all this time while he rested. Surely that must be good for him?

'I'm going to stop at Dunslane for petrol. Sleep now.'

'Dunslane?'

'Yes, but sleep now, won't you.'

'Yes, I'm sleepy.' But instantly he opened his eyes again and said sharply, frighteningly: 'Listen, Martin! Listen!'

'What is it, what's wrong?' He strained his eyes for the sounds of lorries or shooting.

'Listen!'

Distant and intermittent came the chant of the weir.

For a moment or two they listened to it, their eyes on one another; then Martin stopped rowing for a moment, leaned over until his face touched Norman's cool face and kissed him.

'God is good, Martin.'

Back in the forward seat and again rowing, he saw that though Norman's eyes were closed he was restless.

'Try to sleep, Norman.'

'Sing something.'

He forced his cracked voice to come and he sang the lullaby which he had loved to hear sung long before he ever went to Dunslane or met Norman.

> '. . . and Holy Mary, pitying us,
> In Heaven for grace does sue
> Sing O, hush-a-bye, low, low . . .'

Norman rested, a little smile on his mouth, the shade of his old dimpling smile. Once he murmured reflectively two lines of a song they had been accustomed to sing together at school.

> 'Row, brothers, row, the stream runs fast,
> The Rapids are near and daylight's past.'

They had sung that together, squatting on the floor of Long Dick's study and jockeying one another away from the most comfortable place against the sofa-head.

Clug-thump went the oars, the starlight flashed on his dripping blades. The chant of the weir came continuously now, louder and louder, and he knew almost every different shade of graduated darkness along the banks. He steered in, heard the knocking of the school boats as their gunwales touched and glided in beside their ghostly gleaming under the trees. Holding the prow taut with the boat hook, he fastened the stern rope. But when he went to tie the prow he had to find a strong root, because nothing had been put there to replace the weight which had dragged him into the water that day when he had come to the riverside in such a mood of despair.

He raced up the alleyway beneath the trees and was astonished to find that the gate there was locked. That gate had always been open in the old days, when lads slipped down there for a smoke. He ran round to the stile that led into the yard, saw the chimney of old Jimmy Curran's lodging among the trees before the conifers and wondered what master, if any, lived there now. At the water tap he held his throbbing eyes under the water, wiped some of the dried blood from his cheeks, then ran to the corridor windows and smiled to find that neither 'The Duchess', since departed to another sphere of activity, nor MacTaggarty, now Dean, had ever discovered the swollen window which left a tiny gap at the top. He climbed in, where he and Norman had so often climbed in and out. On tiptoe he sped along the corridor towards the Bigger House. He was not sure of his plans, but was making for the servants' quarters in the hope of finding Willy or some other servant

who would remember him. He knew none of the present masters
and he knew that Matron had married and gone from the place.
But when he went down through the Refectory he found to his
dismay that the service door to the kitchen was locked, and he
cursed the new ways introduced by 'The Duchess' or Mac-
Taggarty.

Running soundlessly on tiptoe his eyes went from force of habit
to the shadowed place where the Virgin hung in 'half-tones like
Rembrandt'. For a moment he felt like stretching up a hand and
touching the picture. So after all they had never moved it for
their new Sodality for boys! He shot a glance at his own old
place beside Norman's and sped out to the hall, intending to get
outside again and run round the front to the kitchen yard. Above
his head there came a well-known sound, the sound of the Dean's
door being thrown open, as Long Dick had often flung it open in
lazy haste or smouldering wrath. Steps hastened across the landing and down into the hall came Father MacTaggarty's voice.

'Who is down there?' and in a moment: 'Some boy is moving
about down there. Let me have his name at once and come up,
till I get a light.' From the foot of the stairs, Martin whispered up
to the vague shape bending over the banisters, as the wan light
fell from the windows on the stairs.

'It's me. Martin Reilly! Martin Reilly who was here.'

Out of the shadows above there came a long frightened gasp:
'In the name of the Cross! Who are you? What are you?'

'I'm Martin Reilly,' he said, beginning to mount a step.
'Martin Reilly who——'

'In the name of the Risen Christ, not another step. How do you
get through locked doors? If you are a soul come here for prayer,
I will pray for you.'

'I say I am Martin Reilly,' and he moved up into the hazy
light of the great windows, the smell of blood moving with him
in this clean atmosphere.

Up on the landing the priest's figure straightened, made the
sign of the Cross and he said in a clear voice: 'In the name of the
Father and of the Son and of the Holy Ghost! Leave me in peace,
I have repented my sins. I will beg God for yours. God is good.'

Martin tried to push back his hair and to wipe some of the dirt,
water and blood from his face.

'Father MacTaggarty, look, I am not a ghost. I am Martin

Reilly alive and I've come here for help. I have Norman Dempsey wounded on a boat.'

After a moment he heard a sighing, 'Norman Dempsey too?'

Martin went up and the priest checked his first movement of shrinking from the smell of blood. He beckoned and, inside the well-known door, the familiar room was greyish in the light of the big window where Aunt Kathleen had first stood looking down at him, one gloved hand on his shoulder.

There by the mantelpiece and the empty grate he told his case to Father MacTaggarty.

'Wait there,' said the priest and put one hand reassuringly on Martin's shoulder. At that touch on his shoulder beside the fireplace, Martin shrank, then instantly controlled the movement.

He went away, came back with brandy and said: 'Drink this. I was right, I did hear shooting. I thought so: but I was half asleep.' He told Martin that he himself would go in search of a doctor. If the doctor would not or could not come he would drive until he found one who would. And Norman could stay at Dunslane until he was well again.

'Impossible. There's to be a big ambush. And it would be fatal to be found wounded.' In any case he was resolved not to have Norman handled by some country dispensary doctor. 'I can get him to Glenkilly before you could ever get a doctor here, even supposing you were not both arrested or killed on the roads.'

'Well, perhaps what you say is right and it's the best way, after all.'

He heard the Dean whispering outside to someone. It was like Willy's voice. 'He says they need petrol.'

Looking round the room, he noticed that not a thing of Long Dick's furniture was here except one small cupboard where he had sometimes kept the strap. The crucifix gleaming on the bureau was not Long Dick's. Father MacTaggarty came back with a tall young man, who turned out to be not a young man but a pupil called Kirwan, who had been only three years younger than Norman and Martin in the Blue Dormitory. He had been the comedian of the Dormitory, given to voicing witticisms after lights were out. All this time he had been here, the sound of the weir in his ears, learning lessons.

'Reilly, I presume he has been to Confession and Communion? Is it a case for Extreme Unction?'

'Oh, no! He's going to get well!'

'You know that's not the point. This seems a case where Extreme Unction may be given.'

After a moment Martin said, 'Yes.' He flung out the good arm angrily. 'We have no time. We've already lost ages.'

'Nonsense. You haven't been here ten minutes yet.'

He beckoned and Martin went with him towards the Oratory, but stepped aside into the Dean's bathroom to wash his hands. When he reached the Oratory, a light had been lit there, beyond the red sanctuary lamp. Well, if it was to be, it was to be; and he must do what he had done so often before. From the glimmering vestry he took an altar cloth, unrolled it along the altar, lit the two candles and moved a vase of flowers on to the altar. Back in the vestry he handed the stole to Father MacTaggarty, then went before him and knelt while the priest unlocked the Tabernacle, took out the Ciborium, and prepared the Viaticum. He carried one of the candles before the priest until, meeting Kirwan in the passage, he handed him the candle and, stepping into the Dean's study, took the crucifix from the bureau. At the foot of the stairs, Willy, who had been down to the boat with blankets and petrol, joined the procession and they went out by the back door of the Bigger House through whose opening Martin, peering long ago from the hall door, had first glimpsed Muire's House beyond the shadowed lawns and the robin puffing out his belly in the tree.

They went down the alleyway behind Muire's House where Aunt Kathleen had walked on his arm. Martin went first with the crucifix, Kirwan came behind him with the candle which had blown out by now, and Willy was behind the priest. They came to the river and the boat where Norman was lying, Father Mac-Taggarty's blankets around him, his eyes watching the procession as it mounted the slope of the bank. They helped Father Mac-Taggarty to get down into the boat, where he knelt beside Norman. When they heard him whispering, 'Well, just make a General Confession,' they moved back out of earshot.

Willy whispered: 'I never thought this'd be how I'd see you again, Mr. Reilly. I put in about a half-gallon, will that be enough?'

'Yes. Thank you very much, Willy.'

They shook hands and said no more. Over in the boat the

whispering had ceased, Father MacTaggarty's arm went up and down in the grey light beneath the trees and through the roar of the weir came a whisper of the Absolution! ' . . . *ego te absolvo . . .*'

They went forward, Kirwan holding the unlighted candle. The silver of the Ciborium flashed, the water grey-white about it, and Norman said clearly, in a strong, healthy man's voice: '*Dominus, non sum dignus . . .* Lord, I am not worthy that thou shouldst enter under my roof. Say but the word and my soul shall be healed.'

The wind scattered the words of the Extreme Unction as Father MacTaggarty anointed Norman with the oils. '*Per istam sanctam unctionem . . .*' Leaning forward, Martin handed down the crucifix and it was placed against Norman's lips.

Then Martin made to go quickly down into the boat, but Father MacTaggarty, getting back to the bank, said: 'And you, Martin? You will be in great danger perhaps.'

'I'm all right, Father,' Martin muttered constrainedly.

'Well, in that event,' said Father MacTaggarty and, raising his arm, he made the cross of his blessing above his head.

No one spoke and the chant of the weir mingled with the whine of the wind among the trees. Martin got into the boat.

'Push me well out. Get the stern clear. There will be roots sticking out all around her. And thank you all. I knew I could come here for help.'

Father MacTaggarty answered: 'Where else would you come for help but here? The whole school will pray for you both at Mass this morning.'

Kirwan and Willy bent to the boat.

'Well, then,' said Willy, 'in the name of God,' and they pushed him out into the flood and the starlight.

The current swirled him so rapidly towards the weir that he thought he might have to take his oars but the engine started in time and he drove across the powerful flow to the weir. Glancing back, he saw the three little figures watching from under the trees, he saw a bit of Jimmy Curran's house and, beyond that, the light in the Oratory.

He went down the quieter water and saw at last the blackness of the lock athwart the sky. When he had towed the boat into the cavern, he knocked on the cottage door, crying, 'Come out and give me a hand.' But no one came. As he ran to the lower gates he thought he saw a face peering behind the gleaming window-panes.

He was afraid to open the lower sluices more than a very little. Running back, he drew both stern and forward ropes each through a coping ring and then paid out the ropes to keep the boat close to the wall. He opened the sluices a little more, gasping, 'Oh, come out and help me, Slave-Hearts!' Running to and fro, from ropes to sluices, he felt all the time the sensation of being watched from behind the window. When he came to push the great lever arm of the gates a weakness of his legs and arms overtook him and cottage, trees and fields went swivelling to the sky. It was the old nausea which used to come on him in Knockester towards evening in the last weeks of the Easter term when winter was over. It passed, and he lay on the lever arm, his legs beginning to work for him again. The black mass moved, and he made it move still more.

He towed the boat out of the lock and being now in windy reaches he stepped up the little mast in its tabernacle, bellied out the small sail, and restarted the engine. The boat settled down to make speed on the miles of good going between them and the next lock.

'Martin, am I as bad as all that? Why did you tell him to give me Extreme Unction?'

'I didn't. You know well the conditions for Extreme Unction. It's just to cover every contingency that they give it to someone like you. Don't talk. You're all right, and you're going to be all right.'

'I feel I will. I don't want to die, Martin.'

'You won't die. You'll be all right. It was all my fault that you're here at all.'

'It's not anyone's fault. You made an Irishman out of me, Martin.'

'Don't. Go to sleep.'

Norman closed his eyes. Martin sat by the tiller, holding the sail rope.

'Go on, go to sleep,' he said. 'I'm going to recite "Carcassonne" for you.

> 'On dit qu'on y voit des châteaux
> Grands comme ceux de Babylone,
> Un évêque et deux généraux.
> Je ne connais pas Carcassonne. . . .'

To right and left the banks opened before him, the breeze blew and the little belly of the sail filled, blanketing out some of the stars. Norman slept at last. The boat sped along; it might have been an animal homing, or one who understood that speed was needed. But now they were approaching a place where road and river came close to one another. He shut off the engine, but they still kept moving fast with the aid of the wind. Suddenly his heart leaped ſin terror as he came round a bend and saw quite close to him first one upward radiance beyond the bank, then two upward radiances moving about. There were lorries halted on the road. He got down the sail, wheeled in close to the bank and, crouching to keep hidden, he drew the boat along the bank with his hands, nosing the prow along to feel for roots, stones or any obstacle that might make a noise. Peeping over the bank's rim, he saw the figures in groups before the headlamps. They were Auxiliaries; he could see their neatly waisted shapes, their glengarry tam-o'-shanters.

Along and along he propelled the boat in the shelter of the bank, along and along, while the voices out on the road began to grow weaker behind him. Along and along, until he had gone round a second bend when he took the risk of slipping out a little way into the flood. A little more and he was round yet another bend and putting up the sail. And now, as if forces were turning to his help, he saw that the upper gates of the lock were open and the lock full, waiting ready for him. A man, half dressed, came out of the cottage and without a word began to help him with the gates. The man spoke only when Martin was passing out in the boat under the footbridge: 'Watch out! They're all over every by-road for this last half-hour. God be with you.'

The voice was already dropping behind away into the spaces where the wash whited in a crystal arrow. Down here the animals had not been disturbed by noises of men fighting in the night; everything slept: beasts, plants and men. Sometimes dogs barked at his passing, but the birds and river-hens were quiet, as if they knew that the boat meant them no harm. Norman was asleep and breathing nicely. The Milky Way was paling now, but still bore Cassiopeia in her golden chair. Was there indeed a good God, standing over him and Norman now, with Holy Mary beside Him, pleading, 'There is none other that fighteth for us but only thou, O God'? Were they all aware now of where he was,

and what he was doing, all the souls of his beloved dead? Aunt
Mary, Aunt Kathleen, Long Dick, Miss Peters? He looked down
at Norman peacefully resting.

The stars were much paler when the next lough-cavern opened
before him. Here no one came to help; but he managed swiftly,
having got into an efficient routine with the ropes, even though
his arm was becoming stiff. Now place after place spoke the past
in the darkness before dawn. He bent his will to keep steady now
for the last lap and the winning post. Bats were still flitting about
beneath the trees but the stars were nearly out.

Here was the house with stairs outside, not inside, 'rather like
Italy', Father Riordan used to say. And there the creek where
Niave, Gertrude and he used to undress for their 'mixed bathing',
far away from all wandering busy-bodies, so that Uncle John's
Sodality friends might not hear of it and a storm of horror be
raised. He shut off the engine lest its sound might be carried on
the wind to Glenkilly. The first amber tinge of dawn was lightening the sky. It grew as he approached, it became rosy, blood-red,
covered by dark drifting clouds. And it was not the dawn! That
was not the east, that was Glenkilly. They were burning houses
in Glenkilly; the reprisals had begun.

He pulled down his sail, steered close in to the bank as the out-
lying gardens began to swivel into the arc pointed between his
prow and the strong glow of the sky. He heard shooting and
looked down to see if it had disturbed Norman, but Norman
slept on.

Deep in the darkness beneath the bank he slipped past the out-
lying houses, went round the bend and saw the bridge. He saw
flames between him and it; two mills were blazing horizontally
before the wind and the arches of the bridge framed a glow of
burning gold on the water beyond. Far to one side there were
distant glares, one of which was surely above his Uncle John's
house. It would all be burning over there: the dining-room, his
window-sill, the parlour, all.

The balloons of smoke from the mills swept across the farther
glares, and their shadows rolled through the golden brightness on
the water. In the shadow of the bank he crept past that stretch
of burning water into a space of darkness before the bridge.
Another sheet of gold on the water beyond the arch would surely
be the glow from Mr. Burns's house. He had taken of recent years

to sleeping in the cottage of an acquaintance beyond the town, so that he himself might have escaped them. But that glow would be from his burning house for sure.

As he crept nearer and nearer to the bridge, drawing the boat along the wall with his bleeding hands, the noises of shots and drunken shouts wakened Norman. Martin bent to the questioning eyes. 'They're shooting up Glenkilly. Reprisals. But don't worry, we'll get through, I know every inch of this.'

Now he could see the tight-waisted figures prancing on the bridge, shooting bullets into the air and into the water which splashed golden drops. He struggled back into his jacket, buttoned it high over any whiteness of shirt, saw to his Webley, and, creeping ever nearer and nearer, watched for the moment when he might risk the passage of the few exposed yards which lay between the curve of the wall and the nearest arch of the bridge. As far as he could see there was no one on either bank.

Now he was so close to the bridge that only by leaning perpendicularly over its parapet could anyone see him, even in the exposed few yards into which he must now go. He pushed the wall from him, went out into the glow and turned to meet the advancing corner of the arch. He pushed it aside and slid into the shelter of the arch. Now he saw Mr. Burns's house, flaming low and casting a flat sheet of gold across the spaces below the bridge. Beyond that golden plate he saw the dark spaces where he would be safe, down past Gertrude's window to the old fishing wall and a clean bed for Norman. Bandages, lint, the best of everything, and Dr. McDowell.

Above his head he heard the bridge shaking to the passage of a lorry, then the vibrations of song and shouts. They were leaving the bridge now. He wiped clean his right hand which would have to hold his gun. From beside Norman he drew rushes and knotted them around the blades of his oars to prevent flashing reflections and noise. Then he waited until he felt sure that all had gone away up the town; he could hear the far-off shouts and shots. He would push out into that burning plate of water and in five strokes reach the apex of a reed island which jutted out diagonally from the wharf, where its base began, close to Mr. Burns's house. He would lie in the darkness by the apex of the island and watch for the moment to attempt the second passage to the dark water below Gertrude's window.

He whispered to Norman, 'I'm going out now, Norman.' He
had one oar in the water, and the other ready to slide out. He
took a breath, released his grip on the wall and the flood swept
him out into the bright sheet of water. Out slid the off oar, he
pulled. One pull, two pulls, and still no shot, no sound. He heard
the murmur of the low flames dying down around the red socket
that had been Mr. Burns's house. He pulled the third long stroke.
No shot, no shout. He saw the wharf steps and two Auxiliaries
sitting on them, one with his head between his knees, the other
tugging jocosely at him as one tugs at a drunken man. In terror
he pulled the strength out of his body in a fourth stroke. The rush-
bound blades gave neither betraying sound nor flash. One more
painful pull and, whirling about, he crawled to the prow in time
to break the force of their rush into the reeds and mud of the
island.

There he lay panting, holding the gunwale in, tight to the
island, against the pull of the flood. The light on the next stretch
was weaker than the one he had crossed, but it was strong enough
to reveal a boat to a sober person looking down the river intently.
Down beyond that golden plate of water was darkness, Gertrude's
window, the fishing wall and Dr. McDowell.

Waiting for breath and nerve, he saw the dark shape of the
Poor Clare Convent, silent amid its flat fields. He was about to
steady himself for the move out when he stiffened in every muscle
and listened, because down there at the base of the reed island a
bird had risen with no sound except a slight rustling of the reed-
tops. In a moment, two water-hens swam out from a point farther
from the base. Someone must be moving down there.

A second later he saw their caps, three at least. They were being
deliberately silent and cautious; he was trapped. They must have
seen something, a passing flash of the water perhaps behind his
oars, as he shipped them.

They might be afraid to venture far on the treacherous foothold
of mud, twigs and reeds, especially as they must be uncertain
whether they had really seen anything. If they had been certain,
they would surely have summoned others. But they must be both
very determined and completely sober to come at all on to this
treacherous island and search there so silently.

He groped among the smelly foliage until his hand felt a
taut branch locked among the knotted undergrowth. He worked

the stern rope around the branch, and, using the branch as a pulley, played out the rope until the prow behind him was hanging downriver towards the apex of the island and swinging in its shadow. He crouched down in the stern and, with his feet on either side of Norman, shifted about until he found a comfortable rest for his Webley on the transom board. The moment the reeds parted and a face peered out at him, he would fire before anyone could say 'knife'; he would let go the rope and trust the boat, himself and Norman to the mercy of the flood.

With such steering as he would be able to do lying in the shelter of the gunwales he might get the boat so far into the darkness that he would have time to lift Norman out into some garden, Gertrude's perhaps, and send on the boat as a blind before pursuers could have made the wide circuit around the banks. The fellows on the reeds would be stuck there with a dead comrade and a rotten foothold ready to drown them, and, before others could arrive, he would with luck be already safely hidden with Norman. But the flood might drive him into the far bank too soon, or bullets might get him or the boat, as he was swept through the bright patch. If so, then Norman and he would be drowned together.

They were not far from him now, he could hear the rustling in the reeds. There was not a word from them, they were coming, questing and careful. He began to let the rope saw around the branch, aimed his gun along the transom board, ready for the face that would at any moment peer out at him from the reeds. The reeds were moving, the cracking of feet was close now and came clearly above the humming of flames. He watched his aim and heard a wild yell of laughter from the wharf side.

And right over his head a voice said 'Damn!'; and then another English voice: 'Oh blast it, they're right. We've been making laughing stocks of ourselves. Even if anyone could possibly have swum in here, he could not be here all this time.'

So they had thought they had seen a swimmer.

Many figures were running down the steps pointing to the island and making catcalls of derision.

'Let's get out of this messy trap. Those chaps are tight. Damn it, I wish we could carry out reprisals properly without sots like Mordall. Listen to him.'

'I'll give these Shinners one credit, they don't drink on duty

and they know what they're doing and why. I'm fed up with this
job, I wish I'd never heard of Ireland. If I were a bloody Irishman, which heaven forbid, I think I'd be a Shinner too.'

'They're going to win this scrap, too, if you ask me.'

'Unless we blow the whole place to bits.'

The groups straggled up the steps, a lorry started somewhere,
drove away, and the shouts died, leaving only the sucking of the
flood at reeds and boat, the low crackle of the flames eating the
last of Mr. Burns's house. It was all gone: the pictures of Wolfe
Tone and of the gentle Davis, the books, the grocer's calendar,
the map of Ireland above the flour bin. Gone too, in all likeli-
hood, his uncle's house, and all the things from his tea-caddy; the
silks and ribbons that had given such pleasure to pretty girls.
The house where Mr. and Mrs. John Reilly had talked about
Tramore with their nephew Master Martin Matthew Reilly, and
where the latter had made his speeches to a free parliament in
College Green, all ending 'Gentlemen, I have done!', was
probably a blackened ruin now.

When all was quiet around the wharf, bridge and banks, he
pulled swiftly through the dying light on the water. The lighted
parts seemed to flow with him implacably until he saw that he
was passing the Jamiesons' garden and remembered that from
under the bridge he had not been able to see anything down here.
He rowed less cautiously then and whispered down to Norman's
watching eyes: 'We're all right now! You'll soon be safe in bed.'

Keeping in the darkest places he shipped oars and peered until
he could perceive the broken top of the wall. He did not know
what he would do if the outbreak of the Auxiliaries had prevented
Dr. McDowell from getting down here. He decided to risk a low
whistle. Faint but clear an answering low whistle came upriver
to him, and he slipped swiftly along under the wall, until he
dimly saw two shapes lean out to grasp the boat and, looking up,
found the dark muzzle of a revolver pointing straight at his forehead.

'God in heaven!' he gasped, and struck out at the revolver.
A hand clutched him.

'Steady, man! It's all right.' It was Dr. McDowell's voice and
the dark muzzle at his forehead was Dr. McDowell's pointed
beard.

On the bank he felt the doctor's hands putting him into a big

coat, and he heard the men, who had lifted Norman out, whispering about hiding the boat in the rushes lower down, beside a
gardening shack which Tommy Fagan had for a little plot of land
where on summer evenings, after shutting his shop, he went to
garden and to re-read Columcille's prophecies.

'Yes. Beside the shack where poor old Burns is.'

'What's that?' whispered Martin. 'What has Mr. Burns to do
with Tommy Fagan's shack?'

They told him then that Mr. Burns was 'in there, in the shack'.
They had found his riddled body where it had been flung into a
field and they had put it into the shack and covered it with sacking.

When they had wound along the path and up to the car
waiting in the Feather Lane, Dr. McDowell would not let Martin
sit behind with the man who was holding Norman.

'You'd better be in front with me. We're pretty sure not to meet
anything up this back way. But if we do, don't move or speak.
Leave it to me, they salute me in the street.'

'All right. My Aunt Eileen and . . .'

'They're all right. They have been sleeping elsewhere for weeks.
But the house is gone, I'm afraid, Martin.'

When the car had gone up the lane Dr. McDowell boldly
turned on his headlights and drove swiftly up the back street
towards his own back lane and straight into the garage whose
doors were opened at their coming by a young priest waiting
there. Staggering out on to the garage floor, Martin saw that the
priest was Michael McDowell. As they carried Norman in through
the greenhouse to the return passage, two women met them. The
door was closed behind them and the lights turned on. One of the
women was Jennie, the McDowells' old nurse.

They carried Norman into Niave's bedroom, the old breakfast
room which had been turned into a bedroom for Niave long ago,
when she had been frightened by a story about people trapped
at the top of a house in a fire. The pale-faced, handsome young
woman in there was Niave herself whom he had passed one
evening at the top of Grafton Street when he had been skulking
through the shadows looking secretively out at the people and
Conroy's police.

He saw her coming towards him, he saw Dr. McDowell's
trolley laid ready, shining and with antiseptics in bottles; he saw
stiff cool-looking bandagings, stiff cool-looking sheets, and seeing

the room so sweet and clean he broke into dry helpless gasping and let them lead him from the room. Upstairs, when they began to undress him, he said: 'Go away, Michael, Father Michael I should say now. But go away.' But the young priest took no notice and remained. They undressed him and rolled him naked between the blankets with a hot bottle while he apologized for bringing his filthy clothes into the clean room. 'But Norman's all right now anyway. We were at Dunslane together, you know. Young Tom Prendergast is dead; some of that blood is his. You don't know what it was like. They set fire even to the water. The water and the sky too.' He became quiet as someone cut away the filthy dressing and washed his wound. Then he seemed to doze. He woke to see a grey light along the edges of the window blind and Dr. McDowell whispering to Niave at the door. They came to him and told him that Norman was asking to see him.

'If you want to be any use now to your friend you must be very brave and steady,' and they told him that Norman was sinking rapidly to his death.

'It's my fault. It's my fault. I took too long. But I had to go into Dunslane; I had to wait under the bridge; people would not come out at the locks.'

'Listen now. No one could have believed that you could get here so quickly. And, secondly, it was hopeless from the first. If you want to be any use to him now, be a man and pull yourself together. Even the best of surgeons in the best hospitals could only have taken a forlorn chance. You have nothing to blame yourself for.'

'I have. Everything, everything; right from the day I met him.'

They went downstairs, the lamplight shining on the same old faded roses in the stair carpet. In Niave's room with Jennie and Father Michael were the men who had come down to meet the boat. Martin stood by the bed until, seeing Norman open his eyes and try to move, he went to the corner where Dr. McDowell sat wearily.

'He wants to turn on his side. He always liked to lie on his right side. Would it be bad for him?'

With a helpless shrug, Dr. McDowell said: 'All we can do for him now is to let him do whatever pleases him. I stopped the pain anyway. I did all I could.'

'I know that.'

They went together to the bed and with Niave's help gently turned Norman on to his right side. His eyes signalled and Martin bent to his whisper.

'I gave my messages for home to Miss McDowell.'

Martin nodded, knowing that Mr. Dempsey and the fillies would hate to receive Norman's last messages through himself.

'But later on, when it's all over, they'll understand at home and you must write to Father then. Go and stay with him at Tory Hill. He'll be terribly lonely.'

Martin nodded weakly.

'Besides, I'd like you to go to Tory Hill again. You will, won't you? Promise.'

'Yes. I promise.'

Norman's eyes signalled to him to come still closer.

'Don't worry, Martin, don't. I can't die happy, thinking of the way you'll fret your heart out. I know you.'

'I'll be all right.'

'Don't forget me, but don't fret. I'm ready to die, and I might never again be so ready. And I'm proud of dying for Ireland, since I have to.' He whispered: 'There's only one thing on my conscience now. I once joined with you in blaspheming against God. You must promise me now that you will pray for God's grace to bring back the Faith to you.'

Martin half closed his eyes to avoid Norman's.

'You must promise me that, Martin. At least that you'll try. You're too clever not to believe in God, and once you believe in God you have to be a Catholic. Will you go to see that priest in Avignon? I told him about you and . . .'

Martin shook his head. He would not go to that French priest who had stolen Norman.

'Well, promise me that you'll pray. That much.' His eyes looked meaningly over Martin's bending shoulder, and, following the glance, Martin saw Niave's picture of our Lady with the Seraphim bounding about her.

'Remember? Pray to her, anyway, you can promise that much.'

'Yes,' he lied.

'Promise.'

'Yes. Promise,' he lied.

Norman's hand worked its way over the sheet and Martin put his own hand to it. They locked their fingers deeply into the sockets of one another's fingers, and made one hand of their two hands, and shared pain to pain and bone to bone.

But soon the pressure of Norman's fingers relaxed. His eyes were closed and it was plain to anyone that he had used up the last of himself. All were kneeling now, except Dr. McDowell, who went out to the hall to sit there with closed eyes. Michael McDowell read the prayers for the dying and then the soughing murmur of the Rosary rose and fell.

Once Norman opened his eyes and seemed to be trying to look at the streaks of dawn around the blind, so Martin turned off the light and raised the blind, then drew the curtains fully back. The soft kind light of dawn came into the room. In Norman's eyes there passed a flicker of thanks and Martin knelt as Niave's voice led the other voices.

'Hail, Holy Queen, Mother of Mercy, Hail our Life, our Sweetness and our Hope. . . .'

The eyes were filming over now, the bright blue eyes. Brighter and sweeter the dawn light washed the room.

'To thee do we cry, poor banished children of Eve . . .'

Norman's lips were trying to say something and Martin crouched forward to catch the words. But his courage failed him and it was Niave who, coming swiftly forward, put her ear to the moving lips.

She caught the sounds which Norman was trying to make, and putting her mouth close to the dying ear, she called loudly, clearly, 'Into Thy hands, O Lord, I commend my spirit.'

The shade of a shade of Norman's old dimpling smile passed across his lips. It stayed there, it did not go.

He was dead.

Martin saw Dr. McDowell step in between him and the bed and bend over Norman. He heard old Jennie sobbing, saw the tired faces of the men who had been at the river to meet him.

'I'll be good,' he said, 'I won't give you more trouble,' as Niave and Michael led him from the room. At the door he turned in their arms and saw Norman lying there, as he had so often seen him in Tory Hill, in Dunslane, in Keelard, comfortable on his side in the light of dawn, his eyes closed and a little perspiration around the roots of his tumbled fair hair.

3

Towards the first dusk of afternoon he heard the coffin being brought in through the greenhouse in secret and the sounds of hammering in Niave's room. Later they would move the coffin to the church.

More than a dozen persons now knew that 'one of the lads from the Rodesbridge attack' had died in Dr. McDowell's house, and that Martin Reilly of Killcar was lying wounded there; but, even if later on the news did come to the local police, isolated in their barracks and hamstrung between their duty and their revulsion from what their helpers had done to the town, they would never make trouble for Dr. McDowell, to whom they owed so many kindnesses in the peaceful past.

When Niave dressed his wound, she told him that Mr. Burns's body had been taken to the church. There had been no other place for him since his house was gone and the Town Hall closed by the military. So a great crowd of people had brought him to the church and, though no priest was there, none came to object, and the people themselves had put candles around the bier, said prayers and done all the things that would have been done for a believer.

Thinking of Mr. Burns and Norman side by side, he lay inert, his mind stupefied by the conclusions of the grave.

When Aunt Eileen came he saw they had been warning her not to excite him. He could see her being deliberately cheerful and when at last she spoke of the burning of her home she dwelt more on what had been saved than what had been lost.

'We had moved out a lot, long ago, but it was the goodness of God put it into my head last week to move the grand piano.'

Aunt Mary, who had only a little upright piano in Moydelgan, had never smiled when Mrs. John Reilly from Glenkilly, having

resuscitated Mr. Redmond's reference to 'the merchant princes of
Glenkilly's ancient city borough', had happened also, a few
minutes later, to allude to 'the grand piano'.

'And you'll be glad to know that I saved your old mahogany
chest'—it was the eighteenth-century tea-caddy which had been
his storehouse; but Aunt Eileen had never been able to imagine
that so large and solemn a piece of furniture could ever have been
a mere tea-caddy.

Her white face, for all the strain marked on it and the new lines
across her handsome forehead, still wore its look of reserved
dignity, and she held herself as straight as ever.

'Aw, begob, the mistress houlds herself up well,' Josie had said
in the old days.

'Where will you and Uncle John sleep tonight?' he asked gently.

She bid him not to worry about all that. 'We have plenty of
places to go to, plenty of good friends. Soon we'll have to look for
some little place to rent . . . or . . .' she hesitated, 'or lodgings.'

He guessed that there would not be enough money even for
renting a place. It would be lodgings for her now at the end of
the thirty years which had passed since she had taken her bridal
lessons in book-keeping.

'I have your father's photograph safe for you,' she said quickly.
'You must have it one day, of course.' She looked over his head
into the shadow beyond the invalid's lamp and almost for the first
time in history said something more of his father than her
warning 'John! John!' or her 'God forgive us all'.

'The first day I saw him was the first day I ever set foot in Lullacreen. There was no engagement between John and me as yet,
and they'd all turned up, cousins and aunts and all, and there
were many of them had their reasons, good reasons enough, for
not wanting the match. It was a bright cold day, I can see it all
still.' He thought she had stopped but she spoke again. 'And
before ever the car had stopped, the first thing I saw was Mat
Reilly, I knew him on the spot by John's description; he was
coming right out to meet me with little Mary beside him.'

'Aunt Mary?' he whispered.

'Yes. I knew her of course because she was only a child, only
twelve, and so pretty with her little curls. She doted on him and
he was bringing her out by the hand to meet me. And the two of
them brought me straight to John's mother.'

'Grandmother?'

'Yes. They took me to the orchard and the gardens and the barns and all the animals. And they showed me a picture of John when he was a child, and all the old things, the old hunting horn and their great-grandfather's saddle, still fit to be used. That evening Mat Reilly brought me outside and walked up and down the lawn paths and said he was glad I was going to be his new sister. We went in then and he showed me pictures of France, and he played and sang for us, and little Mary sang with him. And when it was time to go he called me his new sister out in front of them all, and kissed me.' Far away she stared into the shadow. 'No one anywhere was ever nicer to anyone than Mat Reilly was to me that day.'

He held her hand, feeling, against his own fingers, the ridge on her finger made by years of needle and thimble, years of the pen doing accounts.

'No matter this and no matter that, I never believed that at the very last moment God didn't find it in His great goodness and mercy to . . .' She stopped, stirred sharply, and said: 'Mat Reilly was good. He was a gentleman to his heart's core.'

He would ask her no questions. She had been glad to speak this much, he could see that. For all the rest he would wait until he opened Aunt Kathleen's letter and read it in her words, as she had wished it to be.

Behind Aunt Eileen's white, tired face, there, in her memory, his father lived and had prepared for him a welcome among the Reilly children, prepared a welcome there and in Moydelgan, just in the same way that his mother, living on in Aunt Kathleen's memory, had bade him welcome to Keelard.

Trying to give her cheerful news, he spoke again of James Edward, insisting on James's excellent health. Before his weary head could stop, his tactless tongue had added, 'And it's marvellous the way he gets about on the foot. . . .'

'Ah! That foot!' she said. A spasm of pain crossed her face. 'Why should James have to fight here as well as in France? Why should there be fighting at all anywhere? When I think of the men dead and the shelling and the gas-masks and the things that are being done to chaps in barracks all round here, I think there ought to be no such thing as a human being. God ought to destroy us.'

Her eyes, dark with pain, baffled and passionate, looked into his. 'I often think it would be a blessing if no one ever again was given a child. Gas! Pumping gas at one another out of pipes. Men going round with those mask things on their faces. Burning houses that never harmed anyone in the world. Sure men have turned into something worse than beasts.'

She made to draw her veil, but with deep, bitter helplessness, she said: 'Who started it all? Was it that Kaiser war-God fellow with his medals and uniforms and moustache? Or was it Carson? He has a bad, sour face, the face of a cruel man. God's curse be on whoever it was. God's curse be on him now for every home that's burned and every fine lad who's lying in his grave too soon.'

Never before in all his time with her had he heard her wish ill to anyone. Never had she called anyone 'bad', or said anyone had a bad face.

She knotted down the veil; then, hesitating over her glove-buttoning, said, not looking at him: 'I went to see the Poor Clares today. To tell them about the house and about yourself being here.'

She had seen Rosaleen: 'Sister Mary Aloysius she is.' She had seen her through the grill beside the revolving barrel, touched the few fingers that could be passed through the opening at the bottom.

'And Reverend Mother and Sister Cecilia Bonaventure, Kitty Carey that was—you were crazy about her when you were her page, and no wonder, for she was the belle of the county—and Major Moran's daughter. . . .'

'Yes, I remember.'

Still tugging at veil and gloves, still not looking at him, she said: 'They're all praying for you and for your poor friend. I had a little note from the Sacred Heart nuns too. They know you're here, and they said they never had anyone to serve Mass for them as nicely as you did.'

'Yes, I remember.'

'And when Father Riordan hears that . . .'

'Yes. I remember,' he said sharply. And then, turning his head to the other side, 'I'm tired.'

'Listen, Martin,' he heard her hurried voice above his head. 'Niave told me that your friend, that poor boy, you'd have done anything for him, wouldn't you? Well, she said he died like a saint and . . . and . . .' She was pushing something into his hand. 'It's our Lady. You were always great for our Lady and I often heard that a person who doesn't pray any other way can still pray to her,' and with the old-fashioned sound of a firm, lady-like step, she was gone.

If Uncle John had guessed as much as she had obviously done, he would exorcize him from the body of the Reillys and get Tim Corbin to help with bell, book and candle! He pushed the medal away from him among the things on the night table and cursed the malignant God who had played cat and mouse with him from Rodesbridge to Glenkilly. If ever, in the future through which he might now live, he came to laugh again, his first laugh would be a defiant echo back against the mockery of the heavens watching him on the river.

When Niave and Dr. McDowell came up, they were alarmed by his restlessness. He steadied himself and promised to be a good patient. But it was mainly because he wanted to prepare the ground for his getting up on the morrow to follow Norman's funeral. They told him then that Mr. Dempsey had come with one of the fillies. They said only 'Miss Dempsey' and he did not know which of the unmarried fillies it was. In order not to call attention to the McDowells' house they had gone straight to the church where Norman would soon be moved, when it was quite dark. They would stay in an hotel tonight. In their own neighbourhood not even the Tans or Auxiliaries would interfere with the funeral of a son of Mr. Dempsey, 'well-known loyalist and former magistrate'; but here in Glenkilly there might be trouble yet before the body could be got decently away. In accordance with promises already given him, the McDowells were keeping from the Dempseys the information that Martin was here; they would say simply that 'the Volunteers' had brought him to Glenkilly along the river.

Later he heard the sounds of the coffin being removed, the careful shuffling out through the greenhouse where, with Gertrude and Niave and sulky Michael, he had acted Macbeth and William Tell. He lay awake long after the steps had returned.

Far over the roofs of the silent, anxious town, the bell of a convent rang the call to Prime and he thought of the tiny ovals of fog around the candle flames on the altar, and of the dark figures slipping into their stalls to pray for him and for Norman's soul.

Morning began to show greyly beyond the blind and he was still awake, still thinking how Mr. Burns and Norman had met at last, Mr. Burns the atheist side by side all night with Norman, peacefully before the altar of God.

When the McDowells refused to give him his clothes he took a coat and trousers from the next room and swore that he would go to Norman's funeral in those. They yielded at last with many reproaches and gave him his clothes, which they had washed, and over which he wore one of Dr. McDowell's old overcoats. It was baggy and long on him, but would pass for a voluminous travelling coat.

Trusting that his shabby, battered appearance, when added to his worn look and the changes of the years, would keep him unrecognized, he went towards the railway station by back lanes, the quarters of the dirty lane-boys.

In spite of the danger of a raid by Tans or Auxiliaries many people had come to see the coffin off. Looking far down the platform he saw that the 'Miss Dempsey' was Alice, the next eldest to Mollie. Married Agnes was there too, she must have come to Glenkilly that morning. Then he looked away, shocked by the sight of Mr. Dempsey who was nothing now but a grey, broken, old man.

He saw the coffin lifted over the heads towards the van, the tricolour flag on it and a Volunteer officer's cap from the old, peaceful days of drilling for Home Rule. He knew that they had put an officer's uniform on Norman and that Mr. Dempsey had let uniform, flag and cap go unremarked, when they had raised the lid of the coffin in the church to let him have his last look at Norman. Surely that would have been enough to ask the old man and the girls to accept, without having them see these lines of belted political women whose every look and way was so distasteful to Tory Hill.

He sat in a carriage a long way from the Dempseys' compartment and the coffin van. The train puffed through the well-known fields and at Ballow there was the usual change and wait for the train down Norman's line. Here there were no crowds to salute the passing coffin because it had not been expected to pass this way today, and because many people were away beyond on the other side of the town, burying young Tom Prendergast in secret.

Seeing the Tory Hill party going into the refreshment buffet he went to the end of the platform to stand near the siding where the coffin van had been shunted. There, too, he was near to the fields in the event of the military with their machine-guns behind sandbagged posts taking an interest in him. But the military either did not know about the coffin van or thought it none of their business. Thirsty and shivering he hung about outside the refreshment-room. But the Dempseys were in there, Alice coaxing her father to drink a cup of coffee, so he walked up and down, watching the trains go by with the racegoers off to the Curragh, and thinking of other waitings here for Norman's old, doubtful, stop-at-every-pub train.

As usual, it was a quarter of an hour late, but at last it set off through the sunny fields, dragging that van behind it. The afternoon was fading when it came to Bencourt. The first sight of the station had always been the ivy along the outer wall but now the ivy was hidden behind faces packed row upon row and he could scarcely get the door open against the pressure of the crowd. Standing jammed among them, he could see that all the square beyond the station was black-and-white with people and heard some mutter that 'this is nothing to the crowds there'll be tomorrow for the funeral itself'. Tonight the coffin would rest in the church.

The officer commanding the local military garrison had let word get about that the troops would neither interfere with the funeral of Mr. Dempsey's son nor search people coming from it, provided that the Volunteers did not send a firing party to the grave. The local Volunteers, in return, had sent word to the barracks that there would be no arms at the funeral but that a bugler would certainly be there to play the Last Post. So from miles around the people had come, although it was feared that the Black and Tans or Auxiliaries from neighbouring towns, who were a different proposition from the regulars, might swoop down tonight to shoot up the dead man's home town.

Trying to stand on tiptoe, Martin got glimpses of the coffin as it was carried to the station doors. It took a long time before the hearse moved away but the train driver refused to continue his journey until the funeral had 'a decent distance' from him. Later the tramping crowds, filling the width of the main street, heard from the station three mournful blasts of the engine's whistle and the salute pierced shiveringly through the noise of tramping feet.

Up in the organ gallery of the church there was a little triangular seat in a back corner, out of everyone's view, and often, on the excuse that the Dempsey pew was full, Norman and Martin and one or two of the fillies had packed themselves in there, and had been able to play noughts and crosses and draw caricatures during the sermon. Behind that little seat there was a dark unfilled niche and, climbing in there now, Martin saw the coffin far below him and the muted evening beams from the stained glass, mingling with the colours of the flag.

It was the old Canon himself who spoke to the people and Martin was glad of this because the Canon had always been fond both of Norman and himself, and very easy-going with them.

'Death is not the time and God's altar not the place for politics. You all know I'm no Sinn Feiner but a priest must stand with his people and you know I have always stood with you in trouble and in joy. So therefore you'll know now that I have only your interests at heart when I counsel you to go home now and keep your sons and daughters all indoors tonight. Let there be no groups hanging around the streets to give even the shape of an excuse to murdering Black and Tans, if God lets them come here. Colonel Grierson up at the barracks is a gentleman and he's passed his word to me personally that if those scoundrels come here tonight he will bring out his troops and do his best to see that no wanton devilment is done here. So go home quietly, put your trust in God and let your prayers rise up tonight from all your homes for the eternal rest of this young man who died, they tell me, in the way you all saw him live here, a sample of an Irish Catholic gentleman.'

The funeral was to be early next day. Down below at the gallery door, he stood back when he saw the departing crowds clearing a space for the Tory Hill dog-cart and the old Dodge motor-car. When most of the crowd had dispersed he went to the one hotel, but they looked askance at him and finally said that they had no room. They would probably remember his name, if he told it; but that would only make them wonder why he was not staying up at Tory Hill and they would soon guess the reason. He could not blame them for refusing to have him, for, if Tans or Auxiliaries did come, the first place they would make for would be the hotel bar and if they found a wandering Sinn Feiner in the hotel they might smash it up or kill someone.

He tried to eat a meal but he sat worrying about his night's lodging, about his money which was running very low, while the proprietor hovered near to him, anxious to get him out of the place and bolt the doors behind him. As he shut the door behind Martin, he said with compunction: 'Ryan's in Benburb Street is maybe the place you want. Not a boarding-house, you know, but they sometimes, I'm told, take in . . .'—he gave Martin a meaning look—'chaps on their travels,' and he shut the door.

In the darkening evening he went up and down the ill-lit streets, seeking the house of the Ryans. Nothing moved in the streets but himself and a few cats slinking between the occasional patches of light from the windows. He knocked at several doors without getting an answer; nearly every house was heavily curtained and shuttered, some quite lightless, and the little town had settled down to wait through the hours of darkness which might bring the Tans with their petrol, their bullets and their bawdy songs.

At one house a head appeared behind an upper window and a suspicious voice said very cunningly, 'It's queer you'd be asking for the Ryans on a night like this and not know where they live, eh?' and the window was shut.

At last from one window a voice whispered hurriedly: 'Benburb Street. But they're not there. They're not sleeping in the place tonight.'

He thought then that the only thing to do was to go out of the town and find a shed somewhere or perhaps a cottage whose door would remain open long enough to let him request and explain. But when he came to the fringe of the main street, the country beyond looked so dark and lonely that he felt weak and afraid. From a window on street level yellow light poured out into the roadway, enhancing the loneliness of the darkness beyond it. Peering through the gaps in the curtains, he saw a portion of a dresser with plates and cups and a bit of Wolfe Tone's picture beside it. Emboldened by that sight, so like a corner of Mr. Burns's room, he knocked and the voices within instantly ceased. He knocked again and, hearing whispering, called quietly through the door: 'I'm quite alone here. Come to the window and look. I'm neither a robber nor a Tan. I just want somewhere to sit for the night.'

There was no answer.

'Don't be afraid. Can't you hear that I'm not English?'

A man's head appeared between the curtains and Martin tapped gently on the glass. Instantly the man backed away from the window, drew the curtains close together and more whispering could be heard in there. Tapping and asking, he leaned to the glass, trying to make himself felt through the window. The curtains were parted, a middle-aged woman opened the window a crack and when he asked again for somewhere to sit for the night, he heard her say to the room behind her: 'I'll let him in. There's only himself. I'll let him in, in God's name.'

'No, Ma! No, don't!' a younger woman's voice squeaked. The door was partly opened against the chain, the face of the young man looking out at him from behind the older woman's shoulder.

He said to the older woman: 'I came for the funeral, the hotel says it's full, Macinnerney's say they're full, someone said the Ryan family are gone for the night. I'm very tired and I'm not well. I must have somewhere to sit.'

'The hotel is never full,' said the young man with an air of great finesse.

'Be quiet, Johnny,' snapped the older woman over the shoulder; then, still not unfastening the chain, she studied Martin.

'On your mother's name, are you telling the truth? There's nothing to rob here.'

'Do I look like a robber! I'm not.'

'The time's that's in it, there's no knowing what anyone looks like. Tell me on your mother's name that you're telling the truth and I'll let you in.'

'On my mother's name I am——'

With a scream the younger woman cried: 'Look! Look at his hand in his pocket all the time. I said not to open the door, it's a Tan on his own. I said not to open the door.' Even as he took his hand out of his pocket, the young man leaned over his mother's shoulder, banged the door, and the bolts shot home.

'Oh, you fool, it's only my left hand,' he said weakly; he had been keeping it in his pocket to rest his wounded arm. He knocked again, but now not even whispering went on inside and realizing that they would not open again, he turned away.

He stood hesitatingly on the edge of the last houses looking through the greyish darkness of the country roar. Far ahead and above him he saw lights in Tory Hill. He turned back into the empty streets.

He went to the locked church, and crouching down in the corner of the porch he held his clothes tightly around him. In spite of the cold he dozed there, half dreaming of galloping the big gelding home to Tory Hill from Mass, Norman flushed and erect beside him, Molly, Alice and the last of the Tomboys, with their hair-bows flying in the wind. Afraid lest the Tans might come he bid himself not to fall asleep. But he slept and dreamed of the sky burning above him and the water burning below him. He thought that he was in the centre of a vast circle. People were singing. Ladies and Gentlemen, the King! Speech, sir, speech! Speak it up.

'Send him victorious, happy and glorious . . .'

In a flash he was awake and on his feet, crouching back into the corner, his heart almost stopped within him as he heard the long-drawn notes roaring up the street:

'Long to reign over us,
God save the King.'

The Tans! The Tans had come!

For a few moments he crouched, mindless and nerveless, while the pounding died in his ears and he knew that he had heard the singing only in his head and it was not the coming of the Black and Tans. Too frightened now to sit down again, and chilled by the night frost, he set off and forced himself to leave the town and walk along the dark roads beyond, where he got into a field and sat in the hedge, smoking, dozing, watching.

When at last he could begin to see the greyness of his hand moving against the darkness of the hedge, he went back towards the town, seeing Tory Hill a darker blur on the slope to his left and hearing his footsteps ring with hollow echoes. At the church door he stood with a few creeping old women who were waiting for the doors to open for the first Mass at six. During the Mass he dozed in a back seat and when the worshippers had gone he went forward to sit in the pew that was nearest to the coffin. The old

sexton came to fuss about with the candles around Norman's bier.
Moving the officer's cap, he raised the flag and, with Martin
beside him, looked down at the plate on the coffin:

Norman Francis Patrick Dempsey
Only son and seventh child
of
Frances Alice Dempsey (decd.) and Patrick Dempsey
at
Tory Hill, Bencourt
Died October 25th 1920
Requiescat in Pace

Beyond the base of the plate someone had fastened a card to
the coffin and some neat hand had written the things which
Norman's family would not record.

Adjutant and later Intelligence Officer
of
Bencourt Company, Irish Volunteers
Nobly dead
of wounds received in victorious action
in
the Battle of Rodesbridge
against
The foreigners' Army of Occupation
'To the Glory of God and the Honour of Ireland'

Doors and windows were being thrown open now, the night
of fear having gone. In the barber's shop he had himself shaved,
and washed and tidied himself. In the hotel, huddling over the
fire to warm his chilled being, he ordered only tea and bread, for
his money was running low. He counted out the price of a third-
class single ticket to Dublin, then went to buy some flowers.
Higgledy-piggledy among vegetables in the greengrocer's there
were only a few over-blown chrysanthemums, blowzy-looking and
dirty, and he thought that he might do better with wild berries
and leaves, that would cost nothing. He walked hesitatingly
under turning beech leaves; pulled some; but the stiff tinkling
of the russet leaves disturbed him, and beyond a wall he saw in

a garden many tall Michaelmas daisies and some late begonias.
Without thinking he turned up the short drive to the house, a
low grey house rather like Mrs. Carter's. The starchy maid, who
answered his ring, gaped when he said: 'Ask your mistress, please,
if she would sell or give me some of her flowers. Say I want them
for a very special purpose and that there is nothing to be had in
the town.'

'Oh, no, sir. Oh, no, the mistress would never do a thing like
that.'

'You don't know whether she would or not. She might. Go and
ask her.'

The maid hesitated and a thin middle-aged woman advanced
inquiringly from the hall. As Martin stated what he wanted she
studied him with grave bewilderment. He was already beginning
to regret the impulse which had led him to this house where he
would be held at bay like a dangerous beast if they could guess
who and what he was. He began to apologize for his unusual behaviour and to make ready to go, when the woman with a slightly
quizzical look and a suggestion of faint humour at the corners of
her mouth asked him to come in. He thought by her air that she
now imagined that he wanted the flowers for a girl. Following
her, he was uncomfortably aware of the odd figure he must cut
with his blear-eyed look, Dr. McDowell's baggy overcoat and the
hat which had once been a cheap Paris purchase and now
looked it.

Leading him out to another garden at the back she began with
scissors and gardening gloves to move among the flowers while
from an upper window came the muted sounds of two or three
children's voices repeating lessons. When they turned back
towards the house he saw children's faces pressed against the glass
up there, looking down at him, but a hand drew them back from
the window and at that moment all the air above the garden
trembled to a deep booming sound. It was the boom of the church
bell tolling for Norman. She whirled about, looked at him and
said grimly, 'May I ask what exactly you want my flowers for?'
and the bell tolled again. He nodded towards the sound, and her
face set hard.

'For this funeral which is being held here today? For that boy
of poor Mr. Dempsey's who turned out to be a murderer and a
common Sinn Feiner?'

'Yes. For his funeral.'

'*My* flowers for that!'

She looked him up and down, turned on her heel and went towards the house hurriedly, as if afraid of him, or seeking some-one's help. He made his way up the steps and along the hall, clumsily fumbling at the catch of the hall door.

'Wait a moment!'

He turned and saw her looking at him from the return passage. Taking string from the cupboard, she tied the flowers in a neat arrangement, brought them to him and opened the door. He tried to say something by way of thanks, but standing stiffly in the door she said: 'For Mr. Dempsey and the girls I am sincerely sorry. It must be terrible for them.'

'One day you will understand. It was very kind of you to give me your flowers in spite of . . .'

He raised his hat and went, aware that she was there in the door watching his back.

The bell clanged him onward, louder and louder, as he joined the streams making for the church. In a shop where the owner, already in hat and coat, was about to close the door, he bought a plain white card and hurriedly tying it to the flowers he wrote hastily: *Norman. In memory of Dunslane.*

The Dempseys were already in their seats beside the coffin, so he gave his flowers to one of the young men who were keeping the aisles clear and watched anxiously until he saw them safely placed with the great heaps on all sides of the coffin.

Up to the dark niche behind the triangular seat for boys and girls the mournful cadences swept; they wailed along the walls, beating to the roof with the frail but plangent undertone of hope, which in his boyhood's ears had trembled always behind the liturgical laments of his Church.

The Mass for the Dead was sung. Black vestments, black pall. His heart did not hear now the unequivocal though fragile tones of eternal hope behind the gripping chords of grief. Suns would set and rise again a million times but this was the end of Norman, this was the very end. Lazarus, come forth! But whatever else was certain it was certain that Norman would not come forth, that the trumpets of all their painted angels on the ceiling would not make a sound now to tumble the walls of this Jericho.

Around the coffin the old Canon went, sprinkling the holy water, saying the prayers. All the while he was clearly in great grief. He had baptized Norman and cut his christening cake that day up at Tory Hill in the dining-room.

When they carried Norman out all the churchyard and the street was black-and-white with people and their faces. Far away at the gates he saw the coffin high up and the glint of sun upon brass, for the local band had come out to head the funeral. All the faces stared one way, towards Norman, alone and high up in his hearse with the flag and the cap.

Only trickles of the priests' prayers came on the wind; but the answering responses were loud and deep.

'*De profundis clamavi ad te* . . . out of the depths I have cried to Thee, O Lord. . . .'

Trying to get somewhere nearer to the hearse he was pushed backwards instead of forwards, his wounded arm was dragged along against the roughcast of walls, while the tramp of hundreds and the thump of the drums shook the pulsing of his blood. He could get occasional glimpses of the coffin far away, high up, alone, and when the head of the funeral went round a bend he saw in the distance Mr. Dempsey behind the hearse with all the fillies walking with him, thus breaking the custom that kept ladies in their carriages. But they had always broken rules. Had they not ridden with him, four on one tandem bicycle, through the streets, and a woman at the National Health Committee had said that if anyone but a magistrate's daughters had done such a thing they would be 'privately excoriated'?

He could recognize Agnes. She had two children of her own now. She and the others would rally round the old man and look after him; perhaps they would sell Tory Hill and take him to live elsewhere. Anyway, they would always be good to him for they were good girls, the fillies.

Thump, thump, thump. Big drums and kettledrums rolled the low thunder of the dead. They went past the shuttered police barracks. There, when they had driven in with Mr. Dempsey on Session days, Norman and he used to go in to look at the carbines on the rack and admire the constables' biceps. From every other place faces looked down at the passing of the coffin and the long line of people walking to the roll of the drums. Children, boys and girls, were joining the procession far up in front, singing now

beside the hearse, and, before the noise of all the feet began again,
fragments of their shrill voices came back:

> 'Host of armour, red and bright,
> May we fight a valiant fight
> For the green spot of the earth,
> For the land that gave you birth!'

The road narrowed towards the cemetery. The fragments of the
singing ahead were lost in the rumbling prayer: 'Eternal rest give
unto him, O Lord.'

The sounds passed like a wind along the lines. 'May light perpetual shine upon him.'

In the cemetery he had one clear look at the distant coffin before
it was lowered among the heads.

He heard, before silence fell on the massing people, the last
echoes of the children's song:

> 'Have them in Thy holy keeping,
> God, be with them, lying sleeping.
> God, be with them, standing fighting,
> Erin's foes in battle smiting.'

Some of those around him were tall enough to see something of
what was happening at the graveside, but he himself could see
only heads and above him the fleecy, wind-blown sky. Now and
then a faint trickle of prayer was carried through the wind in the
cypresses, russet-tipped in the sunlight.

He would not be there to throw his handful of earth on the
coffin and he had wanted to do that.

Now there was complete silence except for the weeping sigh of
the wind in the cypresses. Into the silence a thin, hard voice came
with metallic faintness from the distance and between the heads
Martin saw that a man had risen above the others at the graveside. It was Conroy.

'Once again we bury a soldier of Ireland. Remember this dead
man and what he died for—the sovereign, independent Gaelic
Republic of Ireland.'

And as the notes of the Last Post rose chill and far, Martin
angrily tried to move forward. How dare they tell these lies about

Norman, who could not answer back! By what right was Conroy standing at the graveside to tell the people who and what Norman was?

The pressure of the crowd eased quickly as the people began to think of the unfinished day and the danger of a raid. Soon he was weaving his way rapidly towards the grave; while the band, the children and the hurrying crowds passed him by. By the time he reached it there was left only the family, the grave-diggers and the caretaker turning away some hovering boys. He stopped behind a tree. All grew quiet except for the soughing of the wind and the scraping of the spades as the grave-diggers cleaned them in a place apart from the grave. Watching from behind the cypress he saw the girls placing the family's flowers at the head of the grave and putting some order into the other ranks of wreaths and flowers which stretched on all sides along the trampled grass.

He recognized them all now, for they had turned up their veils as they moved among the flowers and spoke to the caretaker. Molly, who was about to put one bunch of flowers far away on the edge of the circle, paused, lifted the flowers again and looked at the card. They were his flowers, the asters which that woman had given him. He saw Molly look up towards her sisters, look again at the flowers and he saw that she knew whose flowers they were. She looked about as if seeking him, then going to the head of the grave, she placed his flowers beside those of the family.

His heart checked him. So she understood and, moreover, forgave. He saw her go to speak to her sisters. She was telling them about his flowers, he saw, because they went to look at them and at his card. Then, with their father, they knelt by the grave, while the caretaker and diggers stood far back. They rose and went slowly away and Martin came forward to stand by the grave.

Soon a cross would be put up with Norman's name and age, and Molly, who had always been so good with a garden, would see that the place was well kept. There was nothing to be done, he must go now. But he could not go, wondering at the folly of his fellows who must tell their customary lies even over Norman.

He walked so swiftly in the end, with bent head, that before he had reached the outskirts of the town he was back amongst the last stragglers of the cortège. Rounding the bend into the main street, he saw hundreds of people lined along either side and

Auxiliaries dashing here and there with guns out. Neither his
head nor his body would act for him; he stood rooted there, conspicuous and alone.

Two of the Auxiliaries came dashing towards him, whooping
like boys who have spotted a hunted rabbit out in the open. He
felt almost relieved to know that this was the end.

As they came, jabbing their guns at him, he saw with little
interest that they were the two whom he had once seen in Dublin
come swooping into his friend's drawing-room in search of the
almond-eyed girl, Ruth. They would not recognize him, he
knew; it made no matter. He had taken care that day not to note
their unit, their names or any information against them. Now
they were alive to kill him or have him hanged, what matter! It
could so easily have been any other two.

'Oh-ho, what have we here?'

His hands were above his head and in the upraised arm the
tell-tale wound throbbed. The fat one looked as if he liked plenty
of beer and fun, but the lean one looked as if neither a smile nor
a drop of drink had ever softened his lips. They were cold sober
now and deadly intelligent.

'Your name, Quick!'

'James Cooper.'

'Nothing doing! What's your real name, soldier?'

'Soldier? I'm not a soldier.'

'Sorry. I meant officer! Name and rank, come on, quick!'
They were patting him down, feeling for a gun.

'I have no rank, since I am not in any army.'

'Of course not. You've forgotten your name and at most you
are only a plain ranker, and not an officer. You've forgotten
where you were born, and where your parents live and all the
rest of it. All Ireland has that story off by rote. We've heard it
before.' The lean one was watching his face intently, and, as he
watched, his grim smile disappeared and for a moment there
flickered in his eyes a look that might have been one of bewilderment and might have been a flicker of understanding and fellow-
ship. He looked at his fat, well-fed companion who, following his
glance, also scrutinized Martin's face; then shot his comrade a
glance and with a jerk of his head in the direction of the cemetery,
said, 'Friend of yours, eh?'

'Yes.'

The two of them looked at one another, then looked back at Martin.

'Relative?' snapped the lean one.

'No. Just a friend.'

Again the fat one looked at the taller one, who did not see the glance because he was looking at Martin and looking down his nose.

'Er . . .' The fat one scratched his neck. 'Er . . . an *old* friend, I daresay?'

'Yes.'

The lean one looked over his shoulder, shot a glance at his companion, then snapped at Martin, 'Tubby and I were at Mannistown.' Martin knew that in that ambush the wounded Auxiliaries had been bandaged by Conroy himself, and their unwounded ones given cigarettes and a pony-trap to take their wounded to a doctor.

Martin said nothing, the two watching his face said nothing. Then, with a flash of his hand, the lean one signalled Martin to pass on.

Brushing past them in a daze, he muttered: 'Thanks. Good luck.'

'Luck!' said the fat one. 'It's coming to us all sooner or later. Friends and all.'

In a side-street, as far away as he could get, he loitered cautiously about, until he heard the lorries starting up as the Auxiliaries abandoned their boring investigation of hundreds of country people, and roared off into the country looking for 'real stuff'. He went then to a public house and sat as long as possible over a bottle of Bass. Having escaped from that narrow shave today, he might now live for fifty years, but in all those years, more than twice as long as he had already lived, he would never see Norman again, never write to him, never be reassured by the thought that he was alive somewhere under the sun.

Slinking cautiously round the railway, he saw that the station was quiet. He ducked in as the train arrived, and slipped into an empty ill-lit compartment. The train trundled along the miles to Ballow, but when he had found a quiet place in the connecting train for Dublin soldiers boarded the train, and night fell as one engine-driver after another, refusing to drive them, was formally dismissed. For over an hour the soldiers sat in the stationary train and soon Martin knew that he was about to be very ill; that his strength was gone. Outside on the platform he saw the face of a man who had been with him at Rodesbridge in his party with young Tom Prendergast and who was now watching the proceedings at the station. Staggering out with cold sweat pouring down him, Martin managed to get as far as the known face and gasp, 'Get me somewhere, I'm done.'

Three days later, they told him where he was; but the name of the house and people meant nothing to him except that he knew the place to be not far from Ballow. It was a snug room with a Lullacreen smell about it and bare branches tapping close to the window. There, in peace and cleanliness, he was able next day to sit up and to write a note to Millie, to say that he had been delayed yet once more but would be in Dublin within a few weeks. He was regretting that he had never arranged for her to send messages to him through Volunteer communications, and was sealing his letter when the son of the neighbouring house brought in a piece of news to shock and distress him. Conroy had given the local Volunteers a piece of information which Martin had brought him from Dublin, that the enemy was about to make blockhouses of suitable empty houses in the country. He and James Edward had chosen the most likely houses over a wide area and had had them burned to the ground. One of the houses was 'ah, a place you wouldn't know, it's a long way from here, a place called Keelard, belonging to people called Vincent, I believe, but they've been away in England this last while'.

A man called Hanrahan, 'a kind of gardener or caretaker', had resisted, and had been knocked on the head unconscious, and now it was feared that the old man's wits were gone and that he would have to be put in an asylum.

The day after the burning, the military, it appeared, as a reprisal, had burned down in each district some of the houses where the fathers or the sons were believed to be Volunteers. In the Keelard district the first reprisal had been taken against the home of a Volunteer killed at Rodesbridge. And so the military had burned to the ground Tom Prendergast's house, its new bathroom, the new rafters, the scaffolding and all.

4

His bicycle sped down the slope beneath the bared sycamores and passed the ruins of Tom Prendergast's house, new bathroom and all. The last half-mile from there to the gates left him with trembling legs, for he was still weak and had risen too soon from his bed. Hiding the bicycle behind the Six Acre gate on the other side of the road, he went across to the gates and pushed them. But the gates did not open to the push.

He stared at the great heavy chain which was strongly padlocked around the gates. Never on the darkest nights of winter had the gates been locked, rarely even closed. He looked in beneath the sycamores on the dim, glaucous curve of the avenue marked by the smears of moss, where Hanrahan, up to the last, had not succeeded in overtaking his tracks.

Beyond the tree trunks the morning's rain still glistened on the field where they had played cricket on Sundays, despite Colonel Howard's distress and a disapproving communication from Canon Masterson. Aunt Kathleen had stood under the avenue trees beside Mrs. Carter's victoria watching the postman hitting out for boundaries, and the tail of each eleven had been composed of cantankerous old men, who did not know the rules.

Hesitant and peering, he saw a figure coming along the roadway in the distance, and crossing the road he hid behind the Six Acre hedge. It was Colonel Howard and he carried under his arm the old black folder about all the Irishmen who had ever served in any capacity in India.

The silver hair was cropped as neatly as ever, but the head was bent and the shoulders stooped. As he went by, he turned his head to glance at the locked gates, shook his head from side to side weakly, then went on and shrank small into the distance.

Coming out of hiding Martin cycled back the way he had come, passing again the ruin of Tom Prendergast's ambition and the broken arches where once an owl could be made to hoot at himself, Sally and Peggy. Again hiding his bicycle, he clambered up the bank towards the branches above the railings, the 'useful way of getting in and out', which Peggy had soberly demonstrated to him on his first evening, another November day.

He went down the sloping fields towards the river making for the thicket path which circled the marshy bits on this side of the house. To his astonishment he had to search long for the opening of the little path. The years had choked it with brambles and branches. Once in among the thickets, he found places where the path was still fairly clear but he found many other places where it had been almost completely obscured by time. He was surprised, too, by the heavy silence in there, not recollecting it as having been particularly silent in among the thickets, but he remembered then that they had always been talking ahead to one another, Sally, Peggy, Norman and he.

Suddenly he emerged from the thickets without having seen the boathouse. There was the creek, the shelving bank, but where was the boathouse? In his bewilderment about the boathouse he had forgotten to look up towards the house, but now he turned to the right, looked up the bumping slope and saw the house. What ran back towards him was only one wall of the side—what he had once hoped might be called 'the wing' or, with any luck, 'the ghost's wing'. Nothing but that broken wall was left of Uncle Brendan's study below, the schoolroom and the two small bedrooms above, his room and the girls' room. The front of the house seemed to have more of a shell left, until he saw the trees through the empty window frames of the back wall. Seeing trees through the drawing-room back windows? They were the copper beeches, the front wall must be completely gone.

Turning back to investigate the mystery of the boathouse, he saw what had happened. The elder tree, the ivy and the brambles had crept over the boathouse and now hid it. Poking through the growth he felt the woodwork and putting up his hand he found the key in the theoretical hiding-place above the rotting door. The key was thick with rust. Pushing at the door, he found that it was hanging half off its hinges and he was able to peer in at the sour darkness of the boathouse. He could not see the boats, nor could he hear the customary lapping of water against them, so they were not there. He could hear only the sucking of the water at the door-jambs and its wash in the reeds outside.

Going up towards the back-avenue, he heard from a distance the sounds of someone tapping desultorily in one of the farmyards far beyond the dairy. The tinny tapping and the wind were the only sounds.

On his left was the low hedge between him and 'Kathleen's Garden' all scorched and littered with beams and rubble; and now, through the back window spaces, he saw that not a thing was left of the house but rubble. In 'Kathleen's Garden', beyond the black-and-brown waste of scorching, and of piled heaps of rubble, a few late marigolds still hung. So Hanrahan had still been tending 'Kathleen's Garden' as before, up to the last moment, nursing it no doubt against the day when Sally and Peggy would come back. And then they had come and knocked him on the head, James Edward and Conroy and their subordinates. It was beyond forgiveness, beyond punishment. Never in all his time here had he done anything which Miss Clare or Aunt Kathleen had thought too bad for punishment and forgiveness, not even when he had asked Mr. McKenzie plump out if he would fight against Carson's rebels.

He walked along the central path where he had gone to be given Sally's surprise, and looking towards the river he listened but could not hear the sound of the 'rapids'.

Over there Sally had stood in the moonlight when Aunt Kathleen's cloak had fallen from her, showing her tall and long, very long, in her child's party frock. And there, Peggy, in her white dress, had stepped to them out of shadow, and the faint sound of music and dancing had come to them from the house.

The still November afternoon was greying over. He moved round towards the side-hall door and the laurels, still heavy with rain, drip-dripped to his brushing shoulders. In front he saw that someone had uptilted a farm-cart right in the middle of the half-moon of lawn.

He stood on the cracked front steps down which Aunt Kathleen had swept to him with 'Welcome to Keelard'. From them he could look in on the meaningless rubbish which had been the drawing-room, the wide hall and the stairs. As he turned he saw that a young man in shirt-sleeves was standing at the farmyard gate, watching him. Who on earth was this person? And what was

he doing in there, tapping, and, no doubt, pretending to work at
something?

Martin called to him crossly, 'What are you up to in there in the
farmyards?' Then remembering that he had no excuse to be there
himself, he covered the question by muttering vaguely: 'I'm
taking a look round. How is Hanrahan, do you know?'

The sly-eyed, clever-looking face assumed a sympathetic expression. 'They say he'll not be clear in the head for a long time—
if ever! But the doctor will be in Dublin on Tuesday and will try
and get word at the office about him. I suppose you'll be Mr.
Joyce?'—cutely.

Mr. Joyce? Who was he? Martin made a noncommittal shrug
and moved on towards the coach-house gate, the young man
following him. There was something not far from impudence in
his manner and, with the resentment of one who thinks someone
has been trying to catch him out in mischief or in idling, he said:
'And I needn't be here at all today by rights, since I've got the
thresher fixed. Only I stayed on to let John O'Connor go home.'
John O'Connor! That was the man who had once been courting
Aggie. Were these two in charge here now or had this fellow come
to do some job on farm machinery? He had the look of a country
mechanic or half-skilled engineer.

'I was hoping Mr. Chater would come down himself. I have a
bit of news that might interest him,' the sly voice said. Who on
earth was Mr. Chater? Were all the strangers of the world swooping down on Keelard? 'I'd made sure in my own mind that he'd
be coming down from Kingstown.'

'Look here! Are you trying to talk about Mr. Peters?'

Sulkily and with a malevolent glance, the young man said:
'Well, I never saw the name written down. The fat gentleman
with the glass in one eye, the young ladies' guardian or agent, the
widower!'

If Martin could have laughed, he would have laughed at that.
Mr. Peters, the widower! Wanting to get rid of him, Martin spoke
of what had been saved from the house and instantly the young
man said over-assertively: 'Anything that was there is down on the
list, sir. If it's not on the list that was sent up to the office, it
wasn't there when I came.'

It was evident that he had stolen some of the things that had
been removed from the house before it was set on fire. Bidding

him show where everything was, and ignoring his 'I suppose you'll be Mr. Joyce?'—he remembered the name now as that of Mr. Peters' office manager—he followed the young man to the coach-house.

' 'Tis only left open when one of us is about,' said the young man, pushing open the door. 'Anything that's down on the list is there,' and, with a flicker of malicious pleasure: 'It's not much.'

It was not much. In the remembered dry gloom of the coach-house a few of the drawing-room chairs stood piled near the governess cart, which was the only vehicle there and had mud-marks on it as if it had been used recently. The smaller sideboard from the dining-room was there, a few chairs and many odd objects, including the easel from the drawing-room and the pampas-grass vases. There were some chairs from upstairs rooms, but not one thing from all the glowing things from Aunt Kathleen's day-room. In a box were some small objects including one of the silver coaches with its silver horses that had for ever waited ready to prance along the polished tables. Searching among the pictures laid against the wall, he soon saw that the Minorca Man who had hung half-way up the stairs on the landing was not there. He would smile down no more at dying Chinese lanterns in the hall, smile no more at a wide circle watching Aunt Kathleen and Uncle Brendan with admiration and singing 'Should auld acquaintance be forgot'.

Behind him the insinuating voice probed discreetly while he searched vainly for the damask frame that had held the miniatures.

'If it was there, it would have been on the list.'

Had this uprising bog-trotter stolen the miniatures, his mother's among them, thinking their lovely gold frames valuable? What use to ask? The fellow would sooner tell a lie than the truth.

He would never now have that picture of his mother as a child; it was not 'on the list'. Nor were any of his own boxes here; Sally could rescind her order that his things were to be removed from the house. Had the years made her regret those words? God, it were better now that she should never think of him!

He would have liked to search more thoroughly for things to rescue for himself. But the nearness of this man distressed him, in the presence of those speaking, useless yet terribly poignant objects from the house. Suddenly he moved straight to the shelf where the polishes used to be kept and stooping into the gloom beneath it he saw the cracked blackboard. Who on earth had thought it worth while to grab that and save it? He pushed his hand down to the long bundle behind it and touched the rolled flags and the map of the world. But the boat's lantern was not there.

'Ah, that's only a couple of flags, they're down on the list. They're from the Boer War.'

How these clowns got everything wrong! It was Prendergast who had made the poles for the flags in the third week of August 1914. It was Miss Clare who had sewed the cloth. It was Sally, Peggy, Norman and he who had tacked them to the poles and crossed them on the schoolroom wall, the Green Flag and the Union Jack, with the boat's lantern below them for a ritual.

'Aye, I thought I'd be seeing Mr. Peters himself. It's only a hint I could drop him, like. That is, Miss Vincent might be glad to sell and get shut of all the trouble.'

'Trouble? Sell what? The farm?'

Hastily the voice said—sharp one moment, soothering the next—'Oh, no! Not the farm! The house. If it was a case of selling the land some people might try to make trouble.'

They had come outside, the sinking sunlight was on this young man's face and there was something evil in him, Martin thought.

'Trouble? People here making trouble for the girls! What nonsense are you talking?'

'Ah well, you know some people are terrible greedy. They might think now that 'twould be better broken up.'

'What! Break up a fine farm of five hundred acres!'

'Five hundred and twenty-five.'

'Look here,' he said curtly—and got a quickly hidden vicious look back—'what is all this about? Can't you speak openly and stop this hinting?'

'Ah well, you know . . .' The inevitable opening led the voice on to say that he only thought that Mr. Peters might like to hear that there was a buyer in the market who would take over all the trouble of claiming malicious-injury compensation and a lot of trouble and delay. Sure Miss Vincent might be glad to be shut of the house and the claim that went with it, for ready cash, even if she had to make a fair allowance for the buyer's risks. 'Especially as she wants money badly, they say.' The farm question could be left aside for the present.

'What do you mean? Who told you that Miss Vincent was in need of money?'

'Oh, maybe not in need, sir,' the eyes flashed for a moment, 'but some that were comfortable and a bit over are not so comfortable nowadays.' And he went on to speak again of this buyer 'ready to put cash down. And that's not easy to find in these risky times.'

'You mean somebody who would rebuild here for his own purposes? Who could that be?'

'Ah, 'tis a long way from here. 'Tis a man over in Ballow. 'Tis a gentleman called Mr. Tim Corbin who owns the Royal Leinster Arms in Ballow now. He's a good mark for cash down I'm tellin' ye.' Staring into those clever eyes Martin saw that some game was being played between this sly fellow and Corbin.

'Aye, Mr. Corbin has the cash all right and when he was looking over the place this morning . . .'

'What! Do you mean to say that you allowed him to come here and stalk about . . . stalk about . . . ?' He turned and looked at the broken walls, gaunt now in the setting sun.

' 'Twas John O'Connor let him in. He came along with Mr. O'Mahony the new solicitor over in Ballow. He was very upset, he said, on account of all the hospitality he said he'd had here from the family.' And from the dry, humorous twist of the mouth, Martin saw that Corbin's fellow schemer had not been deceived by this piece of Corbin's patronizing. O'Mahony was in it too, probably, and this fellow, who perhaps had a few pounds somewhere.

'And maybe Mr. Peters might like to pass on to the young ladies that it mightn't be wise to come back now and try to hold on to the whole place.'

'Wise? What do you mean?'

But he saw the answer. He saw it all. This fellow and his like sending louts more ignorant than himself to drive Sally's cattle from her fields, to shoot Peggy's pony, and perhaps fire a few shots under cover of the green dusk of Keelard. The beasts of the field were better.

He told the young man that he wanted to be alone. But still he lingered, calling Martin 'Mr. Joyce', and saying a few last words for transference to Mr. Peters' ear.

'You see, the Faithful Brothers have been having their eyes
out for a place round this way to open as a boarding-school. Only,
with the troubles, they'll be keeping their horns in for the moment.' And he grinned. 'Trust the priests or a monk to mind the
dibs. But Mr. Corbin, if he got a good bargain—only of course
a real good bargain—might pay cash now and build with the
compensation money with an eye to a school's requirements.
Then he could sell when the right times came again.'

So there it all was! A few acres of ground for the Faithful
Brothers around their new boarding-school; a fat profit for
Corbin; fees and profit for O'Mahony; and forty or fifty acres of
the farm bought up by this fellow for a song under a campaign
of 'the land for the people'.

The young man, on whom it was beginning to dawn that
Martin saw through him and the whole idea, without being able
to do anything about it, smiled and turned away. Martin called
after him. 'By the way, what is your name?'

'James Pat O'Gonnerill.'

Sharply, Martin called: 'James Pat O'Gonnerill! Not the
mechanic in Meliville?'

'Aye, that's right. You saw it just now signed to the list.'

But it was not on the list that Martin had learned that name.
It was a name that had been given to him some weeks before as
'one of the shrewdest intelligence officers down the country'.

He watched his fellow officer move away before the black
ruins of Keelard. Whatever might be awaiting him in the years
to come he hoped he could never sink as low as this.

He went back to the coach-house, opened the door for one
last look at the remnants. He thought he saw a glimmer of white
on the dark blackboard under the polish shelf. He went to it
and dragged it out, wondering if it could be possible that through
all these years the board had kept some words, some letters at
least of a word, which Miss Clare in the sunlight had chalked
upon it years before. But there was nothing legible and he remembered Tennyson's line: 'For time brings not the mastodon
again, nor we those days.'

With bent head he hurried away, almost running down the
avenue, forgetting about the padlocked gates. He had come to
the curve by the copper beeches when he remembered the great
chain and padlock; it would be impossible for him to get out

that way. He must turn back and go by the route which the
girls had once shown him. And as though this had brought home
to him all the past elation of youth and the full realization of his
present deprivation, he leant his head against a beech and allowed the tears to fall, pierced by the knowledge of what all
mortality means.

The train thundered Millie's name as it carried him back to
Dublin, and beyond the dark, streaming glass he summoned her
image to move beside him through the flashes of the rain which
wailed from the darkness over all the stripped fields of Leinster.
Out there not a thing grew now on the land, and in all the farms
the harvest was gathered in.

When his swollen eyes could no longer summon up her image,
when beyond the glass the flashing reflections recalled the candle
beside Aunt Mary's head in the mirror, he lay back on his seat.
Now the wheels beat out another rhythm: *prati ultimi flos, prati
ultimi flos, prati ultimi flos.* No, not that! He would read Catullus
no more, read no more of the flower on the meadow's edge,
falling over when once it had been touched by the passing
plough.

In a strange land, among strange people, he would love and
cherish Millie. He would make a good home for her and they
would always be good to one another and true.

. . . *Prati ultimi flos, prati ultimi flos.* . . .

He shut his ears against the rhythm of it. They were all the
same, the poets, boasting that the grave was a fine and private
place, giving young brats at the university something to drama-
tize about; they wrote of darkness and death, they had seen
nothing of the grave, but he had seen too much. It was to warm,
living Millie he was going now and then away, away! He had
kept his word to Conroy and now he was free.

The small stations flashed by, the mail-train leaping on as if
it were an animal as anxious as he to delve into the lights of
Dublin. This morning she would have had his message and tomorrow her own message or she herself would be at Anthony's.
Ah! Anthony's! Let Millie choose where and how they would
start; Millie knew best, he should have heeded her long ago.

The train went into the cavernous vault, with its musty tang
and the bluish bulbous lights in the roof. This time there were

no shining bayonets, no prisoners in lorries, no people praying
to the Queen of Heaven.

As if a horse could bring him nearer to the morrow he took a
cab, and the clip-cloppety hooves drew him along past all the
bridges, myriad-lighted in the rain. On the Four Courts dome
the verdigris shone, and down below the deep quay walls of
granite from the hills Millie's banquet table would now be
spread with pendant jewels and grooved party candles. A netted
lorry slushed past, the fringe of dark muzzles looking in at him,
but soon all those things would have ceased to affect his life. The
hooves drew him along the Quays where Aunt Mary had led
him to the Dolphin Hotel, drew him on past the ancient shops
where the dead generations had bought their trinkets.

Clip-clop went the hooves past the new walls rising among the
ruins of the places bombarded in Easter Week. Clip-clop, they
went, clippedy-clop, clippedy-clop.

The Misses O'Canavan came to welcome him beneath Victoria's portrait, but their welcome died in their mouths as they
looked at him and listened to his abrupt words in the kitchen.

Miss Agnes watched him as, out of gratitude to her, he tried to
make himself eat some of the food she had insisted on preparing
for him.

'Miss Agnes, I shall be leaving here tomorrow or the next day
or the day after at the latest. I am going away to get married.
You have always been very good to me.'

She, who at any other time would have hopped with excitement over the wedding announcement of anyone, even a casual
acquaintance, could now do no more than offer some half-frightened congratulations. She noticed that he was shivering, and
would not let him go up to his room until a fire had warmed it,
and when she had fetched down a change of clothes he put them
on by the kitchen fire.

He went out and made for Anthony's on the chance that Millie
might have gone there. Behind the zinc counter Anthony gaped
at him with embarrassment and kept glancing sideways as he
muttered awkwardly that there was 'no message from Miss
Bannon'. No, she had not been in for a long time, not for
days. Yes, he had seen her once in the street. Oh, yes, looking
very well.

He walked to the little bridge to be nearer to her and stood for a while above the sheeny water and the moored barges. Then he went back, and opening the door of his attic refuge, saw the dancing firelight on Norman's face in the photograph that now thrust a knife into his heart.

Bewildered by the confusion of his attempts to begin packing, he went out again, thinking that Millie could come later and see to all the packing. He looked at the box which held all the lovely things to go with the taffeta dress of peacock-blue, the things which she had not dared to bring into her home. In her new home she would dare. Home! His and hers.

Tired and not knowing what to do with himself, not lively enough to like the smell of danger in the streets, he went into a picture house. Millie never went to films, she had seen only one in her life. But how she loved a play, how she would hold his hand in the gallery, crushing it in her rapt interest.

Finding comfort in being lost in here among all these gaping, withdrawn people, he dozed through the performance until a newsreel began to show pictures of Norman's funeral. Too scandalized to move, he looked at the coffin up there on the screen, while the orchestra leader, with a Manchester accent and dressed like a shop-walker, stood up in a spotlight, spoke in a churchy voice and began to play 'The Flowers of the Forest' for the Irish audience who paid his wages.

The audience sat tensely to the playing of the Scottish lament. Then they burst into a cheer when someone roared, 'Up the rebels!' On the screen a picture, taken over the heads of the cortège, showed Norman's coffin far ahead, being carried shoulder high. Struggling out of the darkness of the picture house into the street he breathed in some of the rain-swept air. Oh God, to get away from it all!

Back in his attic he heard the Misses O'Canavan arranging the house for the night. His going would make things more lonely, for a while, down there in the basement. Tomorrow he would get them farewell presents, something useful for Miss Flo, something pretty for Miss Agnes.

In the morning the old instinct for danger was dead in him, as he went to the bank. They agreed at last to let him have his next quarter's income in advance, and he arranged to call later for the box which held his diary, papers and letters, and which lately he had put there for safety in case his attic was raided.

He forced himself to wait until midday before going to Anthony's. Again Anthony's eyes avoided his as he said with embarrassment that there was no letter there. Nor had any message come, when he called again. She might not have got his letter until this evening, he knew; so he wrote a note bidding her come herself tomorrow, and, having posted it, he decided that if anything delayed her on the morrow, he would go to her house and demand to see her, saying straight out that they were going to get married. He would give them his name, Martin Matthew Reilly, son of . . . Ah, he would bring Aunt Kathleen's letter away with him and, in a strange land, among strange people, he would read about his father and mother.

Moving restlessly about, he kept away from places where he might see the patrols of Ireland's new police and be reminded of Josie and her like. At midday he was in Anthony's. Still no message, and he began to be frightened by the thought that she might be ill, despite Anthony's statement that he had seen her looking well. He waited for two hours. If this time there were no message, he would go to her house.

As he turned into Anthony's he collided with two running girls and was entangled in much over-gauzy finery. It was most odd to see at this time of year, for it looked like an imitation of garden-party finery. Under one of the stagey hats a girl with bold black eyes giggled, delighted with the contact of bodies. The face stopped giggling, looked in embarrassed amazement at him. It was Florrie.

For a moment her staring eyes were full on him and he saw his own image again in those depths. She tugged her companion and made to sidle out of the door.

'I say, wait a minute, please,' and he asked her if she had heard whether Millie was laid up with a cold or whether there was anything wrong at her home.

'Anything wrong at her house?' She gaped from him to her companion. 'Oh, lor'!' she gasped. 'Didn't you even know?'

And with a scared look at him she ran, and was jumping on to a starting tram even as he ran after her, calling: 'Hi, wait! What's wrong with Millie?'

The conductor saw him pounding along after the tram but would not ring the bell. A speeding lorry nearly struck him, and getting in on the pavement he swerved among the pedestrians, like a three-quarter who will not go straight for the line.

When, panting and with his wound-scar aching, he came to the little bridge, the tram had vanished long since. Racing down the long line of lamp-posts between the drear mills and buildings, he saw a cluster of people looking down into Millie's side-street, and when he came to the corner he saw at her door a cab and a larger group of people, some of them girls in over-gauzy finery.

He had never entered the house by the front, always from the lane behind, but that was her front door! Up there was the window of her room with her curtains and the corner of the painted chest of drawers which jutted half across the window.

A street musician shambling down to the cab began to play 'Love's Old Sweet Song' on a tin whistle, and as Martin went down the pathway opposite the house he saw a scurrying movement among the groups, the groups parted into a lane and there in the door stood Millie, unsmiling and very pale.

She had a new brown hat, new but brown like the first hat of hers he had seen, and with something of the same Napoleonic turn-up. She had, he saw, a new costume under her overcoat.

She waved rather wearily to the group, put down her head and ran to the cab while the people laughed and threw rice at her. Then the doorway was filled by a big man grinning and with a flower in his buttonhole. It was the man 'with the good job in London', it was 'the fellow with all the hair in that snapshot'.

For a couple of moments he saw Millie in the cab. She was sitting back in her corner out of sight of the groups and she had her head bent.

The cabby whipped up the old horse, trying to make a flourishing, wedding start-off and, followed by shouting urchins, the cab ambled round the corner, a shoe hanging behind it and a card with something about 'love-birds' scrawled on it. When Martin got to the corner, he saw the cab going up between the long lines of lamp-posts, saw it mount the low slope towards the bridge, go in between the compartments of the bridge and disappear on the other side.

Up to his attic nest Miss Agnes hastened after him with a letter which had come a few minutes after he had gone out that morning. He read it there amid the confusion of his half-packing, the open littered suitcases, the box that held the dress of peacock-blue, the stockings and underclothes, all that had been so fit to match with her own beauty.

Dearest Martin,

I tried to write but I couldn't. I am getting married to Gus; it has to be that way now. Maybe it was even for the best that you would not come away to England because it would not have worked there either. It would not work at all here, and I can't explain. Even then I would have chanced it here with you only that I knew that as things are now it would have been Ireland with you all the time.

You will not be meeting anyone who knows me here and I tell you from my heart that you are never to believe anything anyone says except that I love you rightly and from the night I laid eyes on you, the night of the Rebellion, when you said you were my escort I never let any other man's hand come within a yard of me.

Don't fret your heart out for me, Martin, please don't. Don't forget me but don't eat your poor heart out. Make it all up one day with your Sally and go back to that house and your boats and all. If only someone could make you get away from this awful place before you ruin yourself altogether. But no one and nothing can shake you out of Ireland.

If only I could know what happens to you. I can't bear thinking that I'll never know whether you are well or sick or what happens to you at all. Would you ever some day send me a word to say you're well and that those blackguards never got you? I wonder would you ever do that for me now.

I'll never again in all my life know anyone like you. No one can do anything to me now, I'll never again feel anything much. I can't say all I wanted to, I can't see for crying, it's dropping down on the paper. If ever you can think of me, do, if you do it, if you can think without hating me. God, to think that you may be hating me. Goodbye. I can't write. I love you rightly and best of all, I always will, that's all.

Millie

The Navigable Canal

I

Herbert o'grady, ex-corporal of the Royal Dublin Fusiliers 'Pals' Battalion, shivered snugly at the contrast between his own well-being and the icy slush beyond his little shop window where steely chips of sleet, shrilling before the east wind, lanced along the near-slum street towards the Parnell Monument. In the bitter February light the deposited lines on the houses were not veiled in a scrofulous haze but showed starkly beside windows grey with the steamy fug of the life which pullulated behind them. Herbert O'Grady looked on the scene with the cheerfulness of a repatriate studying familiar things from a pinnacle envied in childhood. He had a shop now, he had finished for ever with dugouts and shellings, he could afford to have plenty of drink, plenty of women, four newspapers in bed every Sunday morning, and breakfast three times a day—no marmalade, no porridge. Now he waited to hear the week's profits of his shop announced by his new-found lodger, guide and drinking companion, Mr. M. M. Reilly.

'Aw, just rough it out. What's a pound note here or there!'

'Turnover—thirty-one pounds odd; profit, ground from the faces of the poor—about thirteen pounds. Herbert, you're a profiteer! This place of yours is a gold-mine.'

'A man has to look after himself. Preservation is the first law of nature, ain't it?'

'A man's first duty is to himself, Herbert. Your wisdom would be approved by the best minds of our spiritually rich nation.'

'Whatcher mean?'

'Our university doctors, for example. And our bishops.'

'Oh, those so-and-so's!' said Herbert easily.

Martin looked out on the street and across at the newly painted public house where the publican's family entertained important rebels. He looked round at the indications of 'the Christmas Spirit', still evidenced in the shop in greetings cards and girls's pictures on chocolate boxes; and once more he shrugged helplessly at the thought of his own ridiculous return to Ireland. Here was down-at-heel Dublin with its unpainted, shabbying Grafton Street, and its badly dressed women, flaunting a few last elegancies; its loutish young men; its half-hearted brothels where never by any chance was there a woman to change lust to interest, except only ashy-cheeked Mae in Kitty Mac's. Here was the suppurating city, still heaving with the rumble of lorries and ambushes, as if the preceding four months had been four ordinary spaces measured on a calendar and not a chasm bisecting the heart of time.

Two days after seeing Millie's wedding cab vanish beyond the bridge he had gone to France. There was only one thing to do, to get away at all costs. Monsieur Gourdet had introduced him to an American business acquaintance who wanted to end his 'little European trip' by taking his wife and family for a tour in 'warm and sunny Provence'. Saying nothing of the winter temperature of warm and sunny Provence, which might have discouraged him, Martin had gone as guide, companion and tutor, and had been able on many nights to continue his own prowlings for disabused companions. He had been able to do this because his business magnate and family kept diaries.

He would watch them settling down to their diaries, then set off, not to silk and fine linen but to gabardine, cheap serge with a smell of Tunis still on it; set off to oil-stained leather and a cheap meal with the taxi-men; set off to the liveried muslin of caps and aprons in the servants' quarters of a rich house where he had a free meal with two young women, ladies once, in Russia, now full of wise, intelligible and sardonic stories of uprooted worlds. . . .

But he had kept his magnate away from certain places; from Nîmes and Carcassonne in particular; kept him mostly within striking distance of Marseilles; and there, on his way to his nightly companions, he had tried to avoid passing by the Rich Café.

He had been surprised to find that it hurt a little to say goodbye at Le Havre to the magnate and family. He declined their warm-hearted offer of his passage to America and the post of tutor to their children, and he had faced towards Ireland, vaguely resolved in mind to see his Aunt Eileen. A taxi-cab put him down in

what was almost Ireland—Euston station; the melancholy laughter, the belittling wit, the agricultural realism, it was all there in
the station, even to the parish priests putting down their feet
with authority and relief upon the platform. He had bought an
Irish newspaper, and, as if the chasm had not split time into a
past and a present, he saw the headlines: 'Barracks blown up at
. . . '—'Night of Terror at . . .'—'Protest against Mixed Bathing
at . . .' He was home again.

On his first night in Dublin he had made the acquaintance of
Herbert O'Grady in a public house and had gone home with him.
The next day his bedroom door had opened to a tinkling of
bangles, a crackling of satin; and, from under frizzed red hair,
Mrs. O'Grady, with a stretching of her great satin bosom, had
laughed her slushy good-natured laugh. He had not even written
to tell his Aunt Eileen that he was in Dublin; he had let week after
week pass at the O'Gradys', gradually coming to believe that
'Mrs. O'Grady' was a courtesy title. He paid nothing for board
and lodging because both Herbert and Mrs. O'Grady insisted
that he over-paid them by devising and managing a simple
system of book-keeping which put an end to the pilferings of the
long, melancholy shop assistant.

Now, turning from the sight of the sleety streets and the
superior public house, he sat in the warm back room drinking
with the O'Gradys and meditating the pastimes which this city
could offer by night in return for the earnings he intended to
scrape in that evening. His lassitude told him that the pastimes
would not pass the time. He would have gone to his room, but
Herbert, who could not bear to be alone, had begged him to have
a drink, adding for additional allurement that Mrs. O'Grady had
been keeping a story up her sleeve specially for him.

'Good,' he had said, for he enjoyed Mrs. O'Grady's stories. Her
expansive laughter, her good humour, her broad Dublin accent,
all contrasted so well with the expensive bangles, the frizzed hair,
the shining satin and the general appearance of a music-hall
contralto, that merely to sit and watch her was a better pastime
than reading masterpieces of literature for the purpose of detecting
great men being thoroughly dishonest with themselves and with
their readers. Besides, Mrs. O'Grady's yarns always told of successful roguery, or else dramatic manifestations of sexuality in
unexpected quarters; so he waited.

'Mind you, Mr. Reilly, I smelled a rat when first I heard tell of him. He only came there last term and what would an ould fellow with all that learning be doing in a bloody hole teaching cowld, long bits of over-grown babies that might as well have been nine as nineteen.' Then, with a good-natured, sympathetic leer: 'He'd done dirty work at the cross-roads somewhere before, you bet, and him a Catholic too, come down to teaching them Protestant, big-babby misses!'

'Ah, a Catholic! That's better!' said Martin.

Slowly, Mrs. O'Grady began to tilt forward until the shining carapace of satin across her great bosom overhung her glass of stout.

'Well, me old bucko was passing along the downstairs passage where the scholars keep their going-out hats, things like you'd see on Napoleon at the pictures. Oh, the ould divil, him and his pictures of the seaside resorts of Britain in France or whatever it is, I don't know.'

'Ah, Brittany! That shows he was a nice, cultured old chap taking a little holiday abroad every year at St. Malo or Dinard— whoops-a-daisy! Three-and-sixpenny print of the Gioconda over the chimney-piece—and ready at any time to out-Aquinas the Thomists. You're getting me into good form, Mrs. O'Grady.'

'Well, it was wherever you say, all right, so it was! And now, listen! Who should come along that self-same passage that very minute but . . .' She paused artistically, and the bursting breasts strained the carapace of satin as if thirsting to reach down into the frothing stout. 'Who should come along, Mr. Reilly, but one of the longest and cowldest gawks of all the big babbies! "Good afternoon, Frances," says he to her, and "Good afternoon, sir," says she, stepping aside respectful like just like you'd be passing an officer in a hall. Then without warning, without the sign of a sup of liquor on him, out goes his arm just like that . . .' and she shot her arm over her glass of stout and fixed Martin with her story-teller's gaze. 'His arm went out like that . . . and he took one good solid houldt of her and pulled her behind the door. Then didn't he put his hand on her neck and say . . . and say . . . well, no one but the headmistress knows the rights and wrongs exactly of what he said, but it was about her jewel of an ear and neck and what joy it would be for once in his old age to feel the sweetness of her lips.' She finished triumphantly and looked around for applause.

'And then as sure as I'm sitting here, he ups and kisses her!' She
licked her lips. 'Twice!' she said. 'And what did the long babby do
but burst out crying. And when he saw her crying like that, he
took his hand away and said, "My God, my child," and out with
him without hat or coat into the rain, and Maggie the cook saw
him going like a drunk with his head down and one arm waving
to himself like a pump-handle. And next morning, instead of himself, it was his written resignment that turned up with a boy for
his books and the pictures of wherever you say it was that he'd
put up in the classroom.'

She waited for Martin's admiring comments on her story.

'It's a good story,' said Martin. 'It just shows you can trust no
one,' and he went up to his room. There for a while he read; then,
tired by the murky light, he lay on his bed, half-somnolent,
visualizing the old schoolmaster saying 'My God, my child,' and
wavering away bareheaded in the rain.

Presently he turned over a pile of unlaundered clothing, vainly
seeking a shirt with all its buttons; then, muffling himself against
the bitter February, he went out and, turning round to Parnell,
entered the great thoroughfares where the winter dusk and the
shop lights put a decent veil over the city's shabbiness. He walked
between the new buildings now arising in place of those which
Millie and he had once watched in that pulsing night of Easter
summer. Although the passing lorries and the foot patrols were
now no concern of his, he would still be a concern of theirs if they
knew who he was. Therefore, beneath his bitter absorption, the
old instinct for danger worked faintly, bidding him either see his
Aunt Eileen and go; or else, without seeing her, go away at once
from the danger of death for past folly.

Once or twice he saw people he knew. He hastened to a tram
which took him to one of the nearer suburbs where he strode up
the steps of a Victorian red-brick villa, scene of occasional peda-
gogic activity on his part, into a hall completely bare of furniture
except for a second-hand grandfather clock. Hurrying out of his
overcoat, he was ready to smirk malevolently the moment the
clock struck the hour and the buttery hatch, to what had once
been the dining-room, flew up to reveal the stubby chin and big
nose of Professor Alix Prolitzer, founder, proprietor and only
beneficiary of Prolitzer's Academy. The latter was a gentleman
much too knowing to call his institution a 'Business College'. There

were already far too many of them in every street of the city. Looking mockingly from the striking clock to Professor Prolitzer, he bowed ironically to fellow professor Miss Prolitzer whose thin, unhappy, red-splotched face had now appeared beside her brother's at the hatch. For to Miss Prolitzer, as to her brother, the striking of the clock brought duty. It was her business to strike a magnificent chased gong—picked up at some auction or pilfered somewhere—and, pretending to close the hatch fully, peep out through a slit at the bottom to see if any of the teachers delayed in the hall. Waving mockingly at the slit, Martin strode across the hall and at the sound of his step a frightened voice within the classroom called: 'Nix, everybody, nix! Here he is, Mephistopheles!'

The rows of faces answered his roll call, rank upon rank of them; for the subject 'English' gathered to itself all the divisions of Prolitzer's high-class institution. He knew well that one of his assets in Prolitzer's eyes was his ability to dominate this huge class where ages ranged from eleven to nineteen and over, although the eleven-year-olds were almost the only ones who could be taught much since only they remembered the elements of grammar. Yet, during the five years since Prolitzer, dodging conscription in some other country, had set up the Academy, few of his pupils had failed to pass into jobs.

He began with genuine schoolboys and girls, then presently transferred his attention to 'the Young Business Ladies and Gentlemen'.

'Now, remember what happens to idlers, big or small, young lady or young gentleman. I draw money on the understanding that I will teach you something, and learn something you will every day!'

While the huge class hunched down to copying and learning without a moment's respite, he went around the stuffy room, correcting, teaching, hammering hard to drive some 'useful examination knowledge' into heads, and lingering longest with those boys and girls whose clothes and bearing spoke of hard-up homes, and cursing inside himself because he knew well that to earn Prolitzer's wretched pittance he was doing for Prolitzer what few qualified teachers could do—make this ferocious caravanserai learn to express themselves on paper.

Back in the hall, he breathed away the fog of nouns, verbs and

'Useful quotations', the smell of cheap gym tunics, of damp serge; and went to the Professor's face at the hatch.

'I want some money now, please. Two pounds, ten shillings.'

'Of course. Unless you would like now to leave it for another week? It will be here next week; bigger and bigger every week.'

'No, thanks. Two pounds, ten shillings now, please!'

Sadly the Professor counted out two pounds, nine shillings and tenpence.

'Two pennies for use of chalk, Mr. Reilly.'

'If you mean that you're actually charging me tuppence for chalk, I'll not come here again.'

The podgy hand weakly pushed one penny through the hatch. 'Well, one penny for chalk, Mr. Reilly.'

He went out, took his tram back to the city, and, striding through streets hazy with a breathless dampness, which had followed the sleet, he searched the public houses patronized by journalists—'the literary fraternity', Mullins called them—until he found the sporting sub-editors who owed him money for his 'expert reporting' of minor hockey and rugby matches, which they farmed out on him, paying about two-thirds of the amount allotted to them by their papers. Hawking himself from bar to bar, he extracted perhaps half of what they owed him, stood each of them a drink, necessary to keep in their good graces, and went away cursing them in his heart.

Above the hazed lights the house-tops bulged into a murky sky. He went swiftly between the picture-goers, the lovers and the lorries. He avoided as far as possible the streets best known to Millie and him; and, when he did come to a corner, a window, any landmark where she had done so-and-so, or said such-and-such, or had laughed—'it was just perfect, that's all'—he bent his head and hurried past. He had money in his pocket, and with money one could always get companionship, drinks and talk that might bring forth a story which would prick through the great smug blanket of lies which this country liked to wrap about itself.

Would he join Mullins at the Royal? Or go back with bottles to the O'Gradys'? Or to Kitty Mac's to see ashy-cheeked Mae smile as he fed her slow fire with stories? They called her ugly—the fools—but she was the only courtesan of any intelligence in Dublin. Ah, that wise, disabused sneer on her lips as her fingernail and her glance pointed to the newspaper speech of a bishop, or

the picture of a bride being given away in holy matrimony by a
slum landlord. From the cavern of her imagination a revealing
light would shine on his own dark caves, stirring up those scuttling
beetles in his heart, unnoticed by daylight or in the light of a
pleasant drawing-room.

Well, which was it to be? Get quickly drunk with the O'Gradys
or slowly drunk with Mae and her rancorous desires? Or Mullins?

The choice was made for him. As he turned a corner he saw the
street held up by searching Auxiliaries and troops, and as he
leaped on a tram going in the opposite direction he muttered,
'I must snap out of Dublin quickly.' He had stayed there too long
already. He would not delay or try to see Aunt Eileen. From the
tram-top he saw the city's landladies ferreting among the cheaper
joints and vegetables. Miss Flo and Miss Agnes might be down
there now, choosing the Sunday joint.

The tram took him to the river and from there he saw the cone
candle-extinguisher of Christ Church, the old domes, the higgledy-
piggledy switchback of roofs. Silently, darkly, the river flowed
beneath him, flowing away from its no-beginning, in the deep
past of the land, to its no-ending, in the timeless future of the
ocean.

He walked away from it. Back in the wide central spaces of the
bridge he felt again that the patient but relentless gods were tapping his shoulder when he saw the street on his right chock-a-
block with trams and pedestrians held up once more for searching.
Easily avoiding the foolish street hold-up, he made his way to a
music hall through a passage overhung with gables. It amused
him to see the gunmen of both sides, spies, touts and officers in
civvies, all crowding into the revue, while just round the corner
the street was lined by inoffensive clerks, stockbrokers, shop
assistants all holding their hands above their heads.

He found Mullins with his cronies in the circle bar, and called:
'Mullins, it's at the War Office you should be. You have just the
brains and the amount of imagination for the job.' Jamieson's
whiskey drove the wheels of his tongue, helped by the rattle of
talk around him, civilians and gunmen, including a man who
was to have been hanged that morning if he had not escaped from
a jail a few days ago. Into the oblivion of turmoil he swept himself; and around him was the helpful turmoil of popping corks,
and on the plush sofas the helpful idiocy of Dublin's imitations of

Bright Young Things. How furious Conroy would be, he thought, to see even Volunteers in this place, to see even some of the pet terriers of that romance-haloed body of men whom he revered so much. But Conroy would never know that this scene was going on less than a mile from the shadows where he watched for thieves and tricksters and for Josie. Ah, Josie. He put away the thought of her flaunting feather; he was out of it all now; not even for a prostitute could he do any service.

Following Mullins's party, he went past the reflections of himself in the gilt mirrors and out to the hushed dark circle with the great rectangle of the parterre beneath it, floored by heads all facing towards the distant brilliantly lit opening. There, beyond the moving lines of fiddle bows, shining limbs advanced and retreated in waves, rose and flashed to the beat of cymbals, of brass and the tinnier brass of Lancashire girl voices. Mullins was counting to himself—'Two, four, eight, twenty, thirty—not bad!' —he was counting the chorus-girls; both his sensual and his commercial instincts would have sulked, feeling slightly defrauded, if there had been fewer than twenty girls.

Head to head, lovers sat and stared at that wicked daring of flashing bodies, whirling beyond the purple of a royal box that would never hold royalty again. The tom-tom beat of cymbals and drum pulsed even faster; even louder beat the rhythmic crack of hands on thighs, ever higher the skirts whirled and Mullins's eyes began to bulge slightly. Dublin, half shocked, wholly delighted, stared from the darkness, and only from the gallery came honest yelps of encouragement mixed with the squeals of girls. But a persistent mutter from behind them began to irritate Mullins. A voice could be heard saying, 'It's a nice state of affairs that you can't bring a decent girl to an Irish theatre.'

Glancing back, Martin saw a young man and woman looking stern and modest; but with glassy-bright eyes. Indeed, the eyes beneath the dull hat of the 'decent girl' were bulging slightly, like Mullins's eyes. Even as the young man's long gullet began to work, like a serpent swallowing a ball, a storm of booing and counter-cheering swept up from below, crashed down from above. The unwise manager of the touring company had omitted to cut a line about 'good old England', and soon heads were being punched and challenges hissed through the din of cheers and boos.

In the wings the manager could be seen making signals to the

girls as he urged them to the only remedy he knew and, in response, the skirts went more wildly, the voices yelped more gaily.
But 'good old England' had released a power stronger than sensual
fun, and now, even in the respectable dress circle, a few here and
there were leaning from their seats to snap insults at one another.
Other theatres had stood on this spot; wild rows there had been
through the centuries, from the time of Sheridan and Goldsmith
on. In all the present maelstrom of emotions, only one voice remained unshaken in its original firm pitch, the voice of the man
with the decent girl. He was now averring in a firm undertone:
'Under the Republic we'll put an end to this kind of performance!
The encyclicals will make it impossible to have shows like this in
any Irish Catholic city.'

The attendants and chuckers-out had hustled the more aggressive challengers towards the exits, while, among the remainder,
the booing and cheering mingled in one communal yelp of enthusiasm as the girls gave a last upfling of limbs and a last backward toss of heads. In that yelp of approval, British and Irish
were one again, thought Martin; and a chain of chorus-girls' legs
might be said to have bridged the Irish Sea.

Now that any danger was over, Mullins was delighted, saying,
'A bit of a row like that does a show good.'

A burly cattle-dealer struggled along the row to the man with
the decent girl and said: 'Well, why the hell did you bring her
here at all? Shut your gob or else take her home to her mother out
of this,' and he gave the decent girl a look which said that he could
not imagine anyone wanting to take her anywhere since she was
pretty enough to be entertainment in herself had it not been for
the hat, the coat, the badges and the expression of one determined
to display conscious modesty on all occasions.

Up stood the young man. 'I insist on my right to express my
opinion of this—or any other—immoral spectacle. I call it a
festival of semi-nudity.'

The cattle-dealer, unable to cope with that, gave him a punch
in the jaw. The youth hit back like a man, while Mullins, terrified
of unprofitable publicity, crouched in his seat hiding his face
with his handkerchief. The attendants swooped down and having
by now neither time nor temper to sort the sheep from the goats,
bundled all three to the exits without further argument.

Into the huge, crowded building not a sound of the city's

shootings and ambushes could penetrate; it was all out there, waiting for the audience on their hurried way homeward before curfew. But curfew was more than an hour away and meanwhile the building shut in this tempestuous life: music, cheers, half-naked girls, passionate opinions and loyalties and hates.

'Mrs. O'Grady is probably down below in the parterre,' thought Martin, for Mrs. O'Grady loved 'the old Royal'. Soon he began to notice ripples of giggles on the far side of the circle where people were calling attention to a grey-haired old man who, gazing entranced at the distant stage where the young bodies flashed, held his hands perpetually together on the point of applauding like a child too excited to clap.

'Dirty old devil,' said Mullins good-naturedly. 'It's his grave he ought to be thinking of!' and at that moment there came from behind a familiar voice.

'Someone ought to protest! If you can't bring a decent girl . . .'

All turned and there in the gangway, rumpled, tossed, but victorious, stood the young man with the decent girl. He must have forced or sneaked a way back into the theatre and he now stood in the gangway, the decent girl behind him, doing his duty once more by 'morality'. The persistence and success of the fellow swung the crowd's humour into his favour and they cheered him mockingly, giving another half-mocking cheer for the unnoticing, entranced old man, gazing at the stage. From the set of the old head in the dimness, the set of the hands ever-ready, never-applauding, it was plain that he was oblivious of them and their cheers.

At that moment a big, meat-florid fellow, who had forced his way along that row of seats, began to tug at the old man and argue, apparently claiming the seat. The frail hands pushed him away, while the attendants, thinking that this was another political dispute, grabbed both men and began to drag them to the aisle. The meaty fellow went quietly enough, at the command of a uniformed attendant; but the old man, indignant at injustice and the disgraceful touch of menial hands, pushed the ushers back from him and, standing in the aisle, he appeared to be lecturing them, while they grinned as they shepherded him back towards an exit.

The old man suddenly became aware of his position and of the mocking smiles of the people. He looked here and there, then saw for the first time the gaping, laughing white faces, and, putting down his head, he hurried towards the exit. For a moment under a light in the aisle his face was lit clearly and Martin saw the face of old Jimmy Curran.

Muttering a vague excuse to Mullins, he hastened towards the passage.. He was in time to see the grinning attendants following the figure which hurried along the winding halls between the photographs of Irving and Bernhardt. Winking at the box-office girl checking her tickets, the attendants opened the door and the weak, wavering figure hurried along the pathway as if anxious to get far from that locality.

Martin strode after it, and to prevent his old master from suspecting that the scene in the theatre had led to the meeting, he ran across to the other pavement, outran the hurrying figure, then, recrossing the street, waited under the light of a street lamp.

'Mr. Curran! Fancy meeting you here!'

Startled out of his confusion and shame, Jimmy Curran lifted his head; then, collecting himself, he managed to give one of his lofty sniffs. 'Er . . . just a moment, please. I was . . . er . . . meditating! No doubt one of my old pupils?'

Martin, bare-headed, turned his face fully to the light.

'Martin Reilly!' said the old man. And then: 'You've changed a lot, young man, since the days of "the infants' dormitory".'

'I wasn't such an infant even then,' Martin said, a trifle piqued. 'After all, I was over sixteen when I . . . when we both left.'

'When we both left. Yes. Nearly six years now. I remember you coming to my room to say goodbye. You and——' He broke off and Martin saw that he had been about to name Norman. So he had heard!

The clouds of humiliation were parting in Jimmy Curran's mind, he smiled and nodded, held Martin's hands and stood in the harsh wind, saying, 'Well, well,' and 'I can't think of anyone I should have liked more to meet.' Martin, who had no intention of allowing his old master to see his sordid O'Grady background, spoke of·making an appointment for the following day. But Jimmy was going on the morrow to the country for some weeks.

'I shall almost certainly have left Ireland before you come back, sir. We simply can't let this opportunity go.'

With a sniff, Jimmy began: 'Are we, by any chance, close to your rooms? I take it you would have some way of . . . er . . . sleeping a guest? We must not forget the existence of curfew.'

'Well . . . er . . . I could. But . . . your own rooms?'

'To tell the truth, Reilly, I'm in the middle of a change in all my arrangements. Not yet finally on with the new but largely off with the old. I could offer you a comfortable fireside. But for sleeping, only a sofa. And . . er . . owing to the change in general arrangements, I am temporarily unable to offer either a meal or a drink. . . .' He flushed slightly when Martin suggested that they might buy a bottle of wine and sandwiches. The old master's eyes brightened greedily as he mused, 'Ah! a glass of wine!'; then, as if suddenly deciding: 'Yes. I know an establishment which has a magnificent Pommard. The proprietor took it as the only payment he could get from a bankrupt debtor; and he does not understand how . . . valuable . . . well, he charges decidedly less than one would have to pay for it elsewhere.'

On the tram which took them across the canal towards one of the wide, dreary exits from the city, Martin noticed with distress that the neatly pressed trousers were frayed at the ends, and that the overcoat was old and worn. But when the conductor came he touched his cap and said, 'Good night, Professor,' with the old-fashioned respect for learning which country people have; and Martin smiled at this man who had kept that old tradition through thirty years of tram-conducting in the city. Jimmy raised his hat in answer to the salute, gave an elegant sniff and stroked his moustache with a bit of a smirk.

He gave non-commital answers to Martin's polite questions. There had, it seemed, been for a time teaching of a sort in England; followed by some private venture which the master shrouded in the vague phrase: 'I returned to Ireland some months ago and consented to help an old friend, the headmistress of an Academy for Young Ladies. Purely temporary arrangements of course, to oblige an old friend embarrassed by the sudden illness of one of her staff.'

'Yes, sir. It was very kind of you to help her.'

'No, no. The lady had done me some kindnesses and one must pay one's tribute to the past.' He said it pompously, but the pompous teaching air went from him as he looked at Martin. Thinking how much Jimmy must loathe the bloodless conscientiousness of work of that sort, Martin asked him if he would stay long in the post.

'Well, as a matter of fact, that arrangement came to an end a

week or two ago,' said Mr. Curran, and tried to dismiss his past
with a little wave of the arm while he began to talk eagerly of the
future. He was going to have his own school—sniff!

'Are you really, sir! That's splendid!'

'Well, it's not really a school just yet—that will come in time.
For the moment it's a class of about a dozen pupils who are . . .
er . . . well, not quite up to the standard of their years.' Martin,
listening, began to fear that his old master was reduced to running
one of the hole-and-corner places where schoolmasters who have
missed the tide give lessons to stupid or pampered boys and girls
and uneducable failures, in return for beggarly fees paid by
underbred parents. He had seen one such shameful establishment at Mentone and as he looked sideways at the worn clothes,
the under-nourished cheeks, he bitterly recalled 'the spectacle
of Mr. Curran in the hall of Dunslane in the days of his glory,
when Martin, for one, had hung on his words.

In a suburban side-road Mr. Curran knocked at the door of a
closed public house, and, to a window which opened secretively
above, he whispered his name. A Dublin voice—more broadly
Dublin than Florrie's had ever been—ejaculated a pleased: 'Be
gum! The Professor!' The street lamps went out and window blinds
were drawn lest a beam of light might assist the prowling troops
and Auxiliaries during the long hours of curfew. The door was
cautiously opened and they were admitted to a yeasty hall by a
young man with upstanding hair and features any one of which
seemed larger than the whole face, his forehead, particularly,
being like a bulging cabin wall topped by an appropriate thatch of
hair. Secretively, Mr. Curran drew him to the end of the hall and
whispered. Martin heard some of the eager replies: 'Certainly,
Professor. I'll put it down on the slate meself and let the boss dock
it from me screw, if he likes.' He led the way into the fumed
mystery of the dark bar.

'Alphonsus! This gentleman is one of my former pupils.'

From under the battlement of the forehead, Alphonsus Liguori
Murphy gazed at Martin.

'Be gum!' he managed to say at last. Into the solemn, goggly
eyes there crept the sad, soft light of envy and he shook his head
with admiration and the sense of loss. 'Be gum! We must treat
this! You'll have to let me offer yez a drink on me.'

'No, no, Alphonsus. *I* am the host.' Sniff!

But when it came to treating, it appeared that Alphonsus Liguori was a teetotaller.

'Well, lemonade, then, Alphonsus!'

So, while Mr. Curran and Martin raised glasses pale in the dimness with the golden-corn look of sherry, Alphonsus lifted the bold, chemical yellow of his elected lemonade.

'Come, Martin. Give us a toast.'

'Well, sir, the New Year's not grown up yet. So here's to a Happy New Year for all of us.'

They drained their glasses and heard, through the silence, the soft purring of an armoured car nosing along the dark streets. 'Hush, listen,' and they tilted their heads and heard the pitter-patter shuffling past the shop door.

'Rubber soles,' said Mr. Curran. 'The greatest empire since Rome. And its soldiers creep about in rubber soles!'

'What about that other ecclesiastical empire?' said Martin, hearing the soutanes and soles wheep into silence along the cavernous halls of Knockester. 'Possess, possess. Do it by force, by fear, or by fraud. If that won't work, then by rubber soles and silence. But possess, beat down, beat down. God said—"Let there be order and few".'

Jimmy gave him a look, but Alphonsus merely gaped, then went out to get the bottle of wine. Unobserved by Mr. Curran, Martin slipped one of Prolitzer's pound notes to Alphonsus, and signalled secretively. There was cooked ham under a glass and they brought some of it, some cheese also, and a loaf of bread. Not for one moment would Alphonsus permit that the great Professor and his slightly less great companion should carry a parcel up the street—which was almost pitch dark. Dark and deserted as it was, Alphonsus went to dress for it. From a back room he produced a hard hat, a yellow walking-stick, yellow gloves and a very waisted, nap blue overcoat. Adorning himself with all these, he put the parcel under one arm, the yellow stick under the other and opened the door into the darkened, whispering street. Mr. Curran and Martin linked arms and off up the street went the procession, the two in front with the whiff of sherry still in their nostrils, Alphonsus behind proudly panting along with hard hat, stick and parcel.

They went up the steps of one of a row of dismally respectable suburban houses, through a musty hall and into a room which with its bright books, its pictures, Jimmy's old rugs and carpets

looked luxurious and richly sophisticated in comparison with the
musty hall and the dark streets. Putting down the parcel,
Alphonsus Liguori gazed along the rows and rows of gleaming
book-titles, from Parmenides to Voltaire and Newman; he gazed
at the photographs of Florence and of Rome, and at the angels of
Botticelli. With his hard hat and yellow stick in his mutton hands,
he gazed at a cheap print of Mona Lisa above the chimney-piece.
'Be. gum!' he said softly. Then he made his good-nights a little
reverently to the two men who could sit unawed amongst it all.

Opening folding doors, Mr. Curran admitted to the comfortable
room a breath of desolation from a larger beyond. 'This will be
my classroom.' The sherry, the excitement of meeting Martin,
had brought colour into the grey cheeks and his bearing was
almost jaunty as he stepped into the cold waste where the light
from the front room gleamed wanly on a few second-hand desks,
a map or two, the sofa where Martin was to sleep if he so wished.
Standing at the big back window, he tried to make Martin admit
that he could see the shape of a shed in the back garden whence
there came an odour of decaying nettles.

'That will be for physical exercises, a gymnasium—later—
when we expand. You have no idea, Martin, how much importance some people attach nowadays to these jerks and jumps.'
He spoke proudly of former pupils who were ready at any time to
put up money for his school; spoke of the time when he would
require the whole house, then the house next door, then the one
on the other side of the road. But ever and anon he returned to
the matter of these jerks and jumps, anxiously begging Martin to
say he could see the shape of the shed in the darkness, as if these
despised, ridiculous jerks and jumps, just because they were so
modern and so absurd, stood all the more clearly in his mind as
symbols for the success of his school.

'I can readily believe that many people find these jumpings
quite enjoyable. And in boys and girls they are often not without
grace, Martin. But grown people—there was a gymnasium mistress who wore one of those children's jumping garments, a full-
grown woman, and quite handsome, but—dear! dear!—it was
really more humiliating when she actually did the jerks than when
she stood still. Look! Surely you can just see the corner of the
shed now? There, just there!'

When he had stopped speaking of that hopeful new career of

his, he said, 'Talking all about myself,' and, giving Martin a look: 'You have had heavy troubles, Martin. I heard a little, and I can guess a lot more.'

'Guess? How could you guess? Guess what?'

'Something. But one thing I never guessed. That Norman Dempsey would die so young. They said the good die young. And goodness is what one remembers when one thinks of that boy's ways and speech. Yes, in this world the good shall suffer and the wicked prosper. All the old things are the true things.'

'So too a man called H.T. would say,' said Martin dryly. 'You say in *this* world, as if there were another,' and he smiled bitterly.

'I believe that there is, you know. Is it true what I hear, that Norman died in your own home town, Martin? I was told that the Volunteers made a desperate effort to save him. They actually brought him down the river, I understand.'

'I brought him. Not the Volunteers.' And he began excitedly to talk of Norman looking up at him in the boat, of the visit to Dunslane, of things he had seen on the banks, of the fires burning in the sky above him and on the water below him; of many things except the last half-hour and Norman's death.

'What can anyone say to young men today? I have met the same in England. Young men have always taken sides. When I was older than you are now I thought it passionately important to take sides between the Zolaists and the Symbolists. You young men now have the right to laugh at us. Your causes are a bit more serious than that.'

'I'd never laugh at you, sir,' said Martin naively. 'I have often and often thought about you.

They heard a burst of machine-gun fire not far off outside, and, nodding towards the sound, Martin uttered mockingly one of Jimmy's old favourite 'quotes':

> '. . . we but teach
> Bloody instructions, which being taught, return
> To plague the inventor.'

'Ignoring your mockery,' Jimmy said simply, 'what could be truer? All the old things are the true things.'

'All? The whole fantastic caboodle?'

'Caboodle . . . ?'

'Yes, the whole grand pyramid from children right up to God? A fairy-tale to make one happy as a boy.'

Jimmy remained silent, and Martin began to think that his old master might have been offended by the direct challenge in his last remarks. But Jimmy said carefully: 'I believe in the unchanging substance of God. I do not believe in man's changeable formulae for it—the whole caboodle as you somewhat vulgarly call it. You said Norman would have become a priest. What a pity! What a pity he did not live to be a priest. God knows His Church has need of more priests with gallant minds and clean hearts.'

'Long Dick! Do you remember telling Norman and me that he was a volcano but also a gentleman?' Both smiled.

'There are others as well as Long Dick, Martin. Not so many here; but this country is a private piece of barbarousness, best ignored for the moment.'

'I know. There was a Father Riordan in Glenkilly. I hope I never meet him, because I want to go on remembering him with the affection and respect I had for him then.'

'Romantic Martin Reilly! Just the same romantic. All that matters to you is the sunset-tinged glow of past events. Aristocratic revolt in the left hand, perfumed order in the right. But you will become your own self one day and leave both orders behind, because you were born into a clear, realistic order, the order that made Long Dick and your Father Riordan. Therefore you will never be too far from accurate sight of what really is. That philosophy and order is part of you, Martin, and you are a part of it.'

'No, no, never! I am myself. I will be myself wherever it takes me.'

'You can still follow your own star along the road of the old Church. Many do, you know. There was never yet a human organization which put manacles on people but it also gave them the files to saw through those manacles.'

'It's a sledge-hammer that's needed, not a file.'

'If so, then you will find that you have been given the sledge-hammer.'

Martin shook his shoulders impatiently to get rid of this oppressive folly.

'Look here, sir, excuse me, but what you are saying really

means that a man, having broken out of prison, should walk back into it of his own will.'

'Yes. Of his will. Then it is no longer a prison but his own citadel.'

'And, on those terms, you find it possible to . . . well, to pray?'

With a quick pressure on his arm, old Jimmy answered softly, 'On those terms, I find it *helpful* to pray.'

'Honestly, sir, and without rudeness, I do think that it is you who are the romantic.'

'That's good! That's good! A Catholic a romantic!'

'But why stay in a Church at all? Why step deliberately back into it, a Church which you have practically admitted to be dominated, certainly here, by the timid and the tyrannical?'

His why seemed to him unanswerable, in logic, in experience, in reason. And he felt sorry for having so bluntly exposed his old master's sentimentalism.

A little murmur came from the figure beside him.

'Because only there, in the Body of All the Faithful, can I hear a whisper of the Anima Mundi. My particular share of its whisper.'

The words themselves were a whisper.

'No,' Martin said. 'Never! Not for me! And it's not a whisper, not a sound at all. It's the smoke from a fire of weeds in the mind.'

'A light if you like. The little candle of the Anima Mundi that has never blown out! But it is idle to argue about it.'

'I'm not arguing,' said Martin pettishly.

Jimmy laughed. 'Well, what have we been doing?'

At the courteous 'we', Martin said with compunction: 'I'm an ill-mannered fellow, sir. Yes, I *was* arguing.'

'You say you might have been willing to believe again if your prayers had been answered and Norman had lived? But you can't bargain with God. God has always been a bad bargainer. And in any case what did you think you were offering *Him*? Your grudging assent in return for a miracle?'

Martin said nothing. Feeling the cold of the bare room, they went back to the bright room and shut the folding doors on the classroom of the future. They spread a white cloth on the table, laid tidy places with plates and glasses, laid out the shop-cooked ham, the cheese and the bread. In the middle of it all they put one of the plump Pommard bottles; then they stood back, looked at the table and laughed.

The glasses flushed a deep healthy ruby, old Jimmy's cheeks flushed and the glow of life brightened in his eyes. Sitting by the fire, they talked of the people they had known, where they had gone, what they were doing. They talked of the river and the weir. Old tales came from Jimmy's lips—St. Malo, the first port of France at which he had ever landed. 'Ah, Martin, France in those days!' He quoted bits of German lyrics picked up in the course of his original travellings; and all the while the lamp-light gleamed on the titles from Parmenides to Pascal and Voltaire. Was it in there behind those gleaming book-titles, that whisper of the Anima Mundi, that bell note which even he could not entirely silence in his heart?

'I'd better not join your singing. They cracked my voice after I'd gone to Knockester.'

'Nonsense. We both sing very nicely. Come on.'

They sang together and something thawed in his being, making him able to say such things as, 'Norman liked that one particularly.'

They spoke of Ned Connolly, of the battlefield where he was buried; of Great Mars and other casualties of the same generation. When the fire was dying beyond their toes, Martin proposed a last toast.

'To your success!' he said.

'Yes. To the future and success! And now, your health, Martin. The more of my old boys I meet, the more clearly I see that the boy is the best part of the man. Here's to the boy you were, and the boy you will be again.'

With rugs and coats they made a couch for Martin on the sofa in the bare classroom and then Jimmy gripped his arm. 'Look! It is not so dark now. Now you can see it.' It was true; the outline of the shed which was to give his whole project a modern slant showed faintly in the garden where the nettles decayed.

When he put out the candle, the room no longer seemed dreary. For, as Jimmy had said, the night was less dark now and its assuaging reflections glimmered on maps, on school desks, on a cracked blackboard. It was just a schoolroom by night and that in all conscience was familiar enough, to the boy he had been, the boy he would be again. 'A whisper of the Anima Mundi,' he muttered to himself; and slept there among the instruments of his old master's new career.

2

H<small>E</small> W O K E before the raising of curfew and moving quietly found a bathroom. Carrying the candle into the front room, he looked down at the divan bed where Jimmy slept with his breathing scarcely noticeable and his face as stilled as the faces of the nuns in the light of the candle beside Father Riordan's flashing Ciborium, as stilled almost as Grandmother's face in the light of her death-candles.

He tiptoed about the room, removing the empty bottles and glasses, brushing down the table and arranging the room so that it would show some order and repose to old Jimmy's awakening. The air was crisply cold and he went to the bed and began to draw the bedclothes gently up on the arm which lay outside them. In the skinny wrist below the frayed pyjama-sleeve the pulse of life was beating quietly. Very carefully he drew the arm under the clothes which he then patted into a nest around the scraggy neck bristly with its morning's beard. The sleeper smiled, and Martin smiled too, glad to think that some pleasant dream must be going on in there behind the sagged mask of the flesh. Might it be the murmur of the weir? Or an older sound, the sound perhaps of some voice from days long before Dunslane?

He wrote a note to thank Jimmy for the night and to say that he would write when he had settled his own future. He sat in his overcoat until the curfew hours had passed, then took a last look at his old schoolmaster, and, wondering when they would meet again, he went quietly out of the house and walked through the morning twilight. There was not a sound in the streets except his own footsteps and the chaffering of the house sparrows. The raiders of both sides had gone to their sleep, and for some hours the city would be at peace, because war in the city, unlike war in the country, seldom began until after luncheon. Here and there someone might be quietly killed in his bed; but the general routine of raids, ambushes, spy tracking, seldom got into its stride before afternoon tea.

Walking slowly towards the city he watched the rising light send its spy lances between the sleeping roofs, while the shuttered houses gradually released trickles of life after the resentful hours of curfew. Soundless on their cheap shoes, little daily maids flitted in the half-light, and now and then there came the ring of an unseen workman's boots on the pavement. Life grew and stirred. In the groined shadows of church portals, old figures stood bent, waiting for admittance, and sometimes a tram loomed big and surprising from the gloom. The lances of light widened, the sparrows chaffered, the breath of a horse vanished into the clearing air and he looked with the old awe at the spectacle of morning returning to the world. Before long the wren-like flittings of the little dailies gave place to the high-heeled pit-a-pat of shop assistants and clerks, mingled with the repetitive rondos of children's feet beating a graceful, reluctant way to school. When he came to the broad central bridge, he saw the sun sparkling on the brewery barges taking the morning tide, saw the grey gulls swooping, the old shabby, battered town with its bombarded buildings, its ugly buildings, all wearing a cleaned wintry face.

He had himself shaved, then bought a shirt, collar, a pair of socks and some handkerchiefs, and with the parcel under his arm, he turned down the southern quays towards the higgledy-piggledy of shining roofs.

In the Dolphin Hotel he changed his linen, breakfasted and meditated the matter of temporary lodgings to serve him until he had thought out the future and what he should do. He was sick of his present quarters. And besides it was not safe to stay in any one place too long. He would lodge at Miss Ussher O'Dwyer's; it would be very different from the O'Gradys'.

He went to Miss Ussher O'Dwyer's Georgian street where the granite steps of each house were scrubbed every morning by an aproned maid-servant, where the tradesmen's area bells were always in working order and the creeper along the russet bricks always neatly clipped around the tall windows and the spacious fanlights.

As long as he could remember, Miss Ussher O'Dwyer had been a 'reduced Catholic lady'. She was a friend of that cousin of his

Aunt Eileen's who had been—might still be—Mother Superior of
the convent in Kingstown where he used to hear Mass when first
he had gone to the Peters'. Even in those days, though only a
schoolboy, he had always been received with some consequence
by Miss Ussher O'Dwyer; it was unlikely that she would know that
he was a rebel, her house would be as safe from raids as had been
the Misses O'Canavans' house and he trusted that no stories about
her new lodger would come to Miss Ussher O'Dwyer's ears until
he was ready to jump away into the new life. She gave him a
prim welcome and it was arranged that he would move in his
luggage that day.

That afternoon he turned with embarrassment into the bank,
feeling that behind the clerks' politeness there might well be the
thought, 'So here's this mad young fellow Reilly, who's been over-
spending his few pounds in funny places like Padua.' On the way
to the manager's room, his belly sank nearly as gloomily as if he
were sixteen again and treading a reluctant way to Long Dick or
Miss Clare for chastisement. From the manager he quietly endured
a long lecture, most of which he could have told himself. But
knowing that authoritative experience would be more amenable
if it were allowed to enjoy the sound of its own wisdom, he
staged an attentive manner, and received his reward, when he
came to assure the wagging, worried face that he was going to
turn over a new financial leaf. The manager, having told a few
more stories of young men he had seen ruined by being left a few
pounds, said that Martin could over-draw another twenty pounds
until he had settled his plans. 'And I'll take that box of papers
which I left with you some time ago.' And leaving the manager
with the crowning comfort of Miss Ussher O'Dwyer's respectable
address, he went outside, called a cab and returned to his new
lodging with the box.

He felt restless and unsettled, sick of this moving from one place
to another lest the suddenly aroused curiosity of authority should
one day catch up with him, if his name should reach them in a list
of those who had taken part in such and such an action on such
and such a date. He put off the moment of going to the O'Gradys'
to remove his belongings. He wondered how they would take
his sudden departure.

Meeting a university friend, who had recently married, he
allowed himself to be taken off and introduced to the bride. He sat

with the young man and his wife in the bright, modern flat, wondering if he and Millie would have lived in such a flat. Millie would not have made it so determinedly bright, she would have made it more restful, cosier. He sat there until the hour when they might feel obliged to invite him to share a meal. Then he said cheerful things at the door, raised his hat, heard the door close and was alone with himself again.

He walked about rather than go to the O'Gradys' or return to his new aseptic room and that box of papers. Longingly he thought of his friend Mrs. Lefroy's drawing-room, her children's bow and arrows, her father sleeping by the firelit picture of a bridge he had raised across the Indus. Sometimes acquaintances saluted him; some heartily, some watchfully; others with that amused superiority which those who wander in their own mist must always arouse in those who move confidently from yesterday to tomorrow by way of a diligent and limited today. He met a group of men he knew; they had won a football cup that afternoon and were to celebrate. It meant little to him, only that their talk evoked in his ears the far-off thud of a boot on a ball, the smack of a distant cricket bat heard under insect-humming trees. As he prowled along, he sometimes tried to read in passing faces any answer, dusty or not, to the riddle of human nature. He tried to recognize in those hurrying beings one trait of himself; and from under his hat he peered out at the faces like some undomesticated animal peering out of its dark and secret cave.

When he turned off Grafton Street, there on his right, between him and the Old Houses of Parliament, was Jammet's Restaurant, and the pavement where Aunt Kathleen had walked, saying that when he was twenty-one he must bring her and the girls to dinner there to celebrate. Over there, the jarvey had held up his inviting whip to Millie and himself; there Mr. Peters had looked bemusedly down from his merry car-load, that brown-faced woman laughing wistfully beside him. He turned back and saw by Trinity College railings the line of hackney cars waiting in vain for the merry parties who would come no more. Even the horses seemed to know it, as they drooped their heads to the dung on the roadway where sparrows made busy. It was over now, all that perfumed gaiety, the new times would be purified of wicked, merry parties, and of jarveys shamelessly exalted by their frivolous fares. The best the jarveys could hope for now was death insurance from

Mullins or the job of driving Corbin to one of his new possessions. Ah! But Corbin is a faithful soul!

Ought he, he wondered, to go in search of Josie, or look for the girl Kattie, who had promised to inquire about Josie? But he would never find them. He came again to Grafton Street where now very few British Secret Service men dared to show themselves, only some of the more clumsy touts. That Grafton Street side of the war must be going in favour of Irish terrorism, because he noticed many Volunteer types striding confidently about as if quite ignorant that down the country it was English terrorism which looked like winning. Stephen's Green would be the safest place in Dublin, if Conroy were still in charge of the new police; for Conroy would insist that his men should not be disturbed by ambushes and consequent raids during their task of banishing all 'bad women and bad men'. Poor Conroy, he was like the Temperance people who show pictures of the alcoholic's hob-nailed liver. But who will show pictures of the patriot's castrated mind, or the areas of fatty degeneration in his heart?

He smiled bitterly to think how quickly a visit down the country would take that insolent military look from the faces of these Dublin Volunteer officers. To give his country, in its turn, that look of complacent power had been one of the smaller of his crimes against his Holy Ghost. Here were Ireland's own twenty-five-year-old Norburtons, and forty-year-old sixth-form prefects, with a cricket stump for their fellows! On the back of an envelope he wrote down a phrase, remembered from the poet A.E.—'We become like what we hate', but he did not pause to consider his own long hatred of dirty lane-boys and Slave-Hearts.

He turned away, went back to his new lodgings, and when he had lit the fire in his over-clean room there before him was the unopened box. At last he summoned resolution to open it, and handled the distant, familiar letters, the photographs, Aunt Mary's dispatch case. Each stain was a story: there was the corner of the diary, creased when Peggy had kept it under her pillow because they all distrusted their host's son whose room he himself had shared. That boy had grown up too and he, like Harry Vincent, had leaped ashore at Cape Hellas, but, unlike Harry, he had not died. There, in his diary, Sally, Peggy, Norman and he were still flowing down to Keelard, singing in the drifting boat.

There, too, were the last brief notes of days with Millie; there, his recollections of Miss Peters and reading her Longfellow; and of his Aunt Kathleen singing:

> O Love! They wrong thee much
> That say thy sweet is bitter,
> I know thee what thou art
> I serve thee with my heart
> And fall before thee . . .

He had served none, nothing; he had been faithless to all.

The sheets on the next bed, he read, *are marked 'Norman Dempsey'; that is the boy Long Dick, the Dean, spoke of to me.*

The Protestant poet in Dublin who wrote Aunt Mary's new favourite song . . .

The remaining pages fluttered back in a rush and he saw his grandmother's high, delicate letters. *To Martin, my warmest and dearest grandson.* And, under them, his own strange writing:

To the Glory of God and the Honour of Ireland
                                   Signed: Martin Matthew Reilly.

How had it happened? How had he come, stage by stage, to this hospital-like room; while Norman lay dead and rotting, and Josie was out there stalking men around Stephen's Green? Would there be a hint of an answer for him in Aunt Kathleen's letter? But he would not open it until the promised time had passed. Only days now. It had been years when first he had seen that inner envelope, in the dim room behind the terrace.

'She put me under pledge,' he said, using the Irish word '*geasa*'; as if an ancient vocabulary could ennoble this small loyalty by linking it to the heroic myths of his race's age of chivalry.

There in the corner of the outer letter he saw the familiar address, and the small-lettered *Railway Station; Ballawley, 3 mls.* He saw a bit of her neat figures: *15/10/1914.*

He took away from her letter the hands which had done things with gun and bomb; with pen and ink for printed pamphlets; with the fleshly case of his own first manhood for women's bodies. He dropped her letter from the hands which had scorched her garden and, dragging back the curtains to let the air come to his face, he saw the eternal silence which had terrified so many before and since Pascal.

Now if the heavens would open to the thunder of God's anger, he would merely bend his own head and say: 'Let me believe! Let me believe and I will pray for the order of punishment, and afterwards of forgiveness. Save me from this day after day with no meaning. Give me order, give me decent and good order.' In vain. The core of his being would not awaken to prayer, although the stained flesh was willing. Even the stained mind was more than half willing, or cleared at least of all explanations which explained nothing, all the clever words with which Reason had fortified the prior reasons of his heart. He cast them from his store, all that pretentious jargon of the magical vocabulary which required more unreasoning Faith than did the Mystery of the Trinity itself. 'Let me never again be that kind of fool. If I cannot believe in God's simple answer, let me remember that I then have none. Let me scorn to give "vital principle" as a name to Aunt Eileen's soul, as though that were an answer.'

No answer, no answer. Why should he go on to live for another fifty years? A job in Cochin-China had been suggested to him, but what did it amount to? Meals, acquaintances, long leaves in Europe, picture galleries, theatres—all unbearable. He would get up each morning, wash, shave, dress, knot a tie, raise the cover of the breakfast dish. . . . He could read, study? Better far such ju-jubes for amusement than read and think to no purpose! No doubt on his leaves he could visit the civilized places. England, France, Italy. Victoria-Folkestone-Boulogne, Paris, Rome. He would travel second class, later first class, if he did well in the job, taxi from the Gare St. Lazare, up in the lift to the hotel bed-room—oh, unbearable! What did men do when they did not know what to do? How did Montaigne learn to smile and shrug his shoulders?

Was there anyone he could visit? Mary Ellen? 'Ah, lovely! Master Martin.'

Conroy? All Conroy would now say was, 'Martin, deserter from Ireland in her hour of greatest need.'

All he himself could answer was: 'No, Conroy. Only the believer can apostatize; only the faithful can desert. Stay in your mirage and leave me in my darkness.'

Before him was the unanswering night, behind him the clean

room like an ante-chamber to unending emptiness, and he cursed
the priested men who, when the wax of the heart was still soft,
had stamped it with the die of hate instead of the love of God,
which had been scotched only for a while in Norman.

'I heard, Martin, that those who can't pray any other way,
can still pray to the Blessed Virgin.'

Could it be so? To her picture Norman's dimming eyes had
turned in signal.

Could it be so? Could the masculine order of a God permit that
an unbeliever should unbelievingly pray to her feminine compassion? Could she, in pity for one man's frailties, plait again the
life-line which he and Time had consistently unravelled?

'They always said I had a touch of a boy, Martin.' 'And they
say I've a touch of a girl, Aunt Mary.' 'Well, so you have, thank
God.' Bend then the girl's heart to her, leave God's masculine
mind to the future?

He hurriedly looked at his watch, saw that there was still more
than an hour before curfew, and began to tidy himself and wash.
Then he went swiftly through the streets towards a church where,
in a lady-chapel, there was a pleasing statue of the Queen of Heaven.

Not a sound came into the lady-chapel from the few fuzzly
old figures before the high altar. He knelt and prayed to Mary,
the depository of man's persistent tradition that the Anima Mundi
was an unchanging spirit of compassion and acceptance. 'In any
blasphemies of mine, I never blasphemed against you. Help me
now to find order. Take away the thought that I must walk, wash
and eat, only to do it all over again tomorrow. If you will give me
any sign, any touch of your spirit, I will try to believe, I will do
the hardest of all—pretend to forget.' His head bent to the grainy
wood, smoothened by many praying forearms, and words came
from him: 'Mary, our Life, our Sweetness and our Hope—make
me good. Make me decent and good.'

For a long time he knelt while the last trailing wisps of prayer
trickled away from his heart, leaving only the core of himself
stripped of all emotion. He knew then that to disbelieve he would
have to deny one-half of himself, and to believe deny the other
half. He sat up, looked at the gently smiling face of the statue.
'No, you cannot help me. I must make my own order even if I
only find it when it is my time to die.' He would accept whatever
rule there might be, even though he might never know it.

'Your smile is as high and serene as it was behind Brother
Finnegan's smiting hand, as it was in Knockester with the moonlight on your title "Protectress of this House".'

He took up his hat, meditated a moment. ' "And whatsoever
they have bound upon earth, it shall be bound also in heaven"?
Earth-bound even there? I doubt it. But if it is so, then let it be so,
Amen. I shall make my own purposes and I shall not pretend to
forget.'

He rose and for the last time genuflected towards the altar.
On his way out he gave one backward look of gratitude and
reproach and sympathy and farewell. Then, without disturbing
those who could worship, he walked quietly out of the church.
He thought it was for the last time.

3

Next morning, still reluctant to go to the O'Gradys', he was tempted by the thought of the river. He might never see it again once he had left. But in winter it would be so cold and dreary! Even so, even in the cold, dreary winter, he should see it before he went for ever. He made his way towards the shaking, wooden footbridge above the sheeny water. Far along stretched the line of lamp-posts between the dour buildings.

He stood above the unmoving water at the basin. 'I seen it on the water many a time,' Dan had said of the Will o' the Wisp. What had Dan seen? The reflection of the Anima Mundi whose whisper old Jimmy thought he had heard? He leaned over the railing where he and Millie had so often leaned to kiss, and looked down, but all he could see upon the water was the wavering image of himself. He saw again the long line of lamp-posts where she used to get smaller and smaller as he watched from the bridge. Still in all the time to come without her the barges would be moored there, as when he and she had stood before them, plotting the roads of the sky, marking the stars that hung over his distant river where one day he was to take her to have tea on Dan Murphy's barge, with the boat, that would be his and hers, knocking for them against the hull. Dan came to Dublin. There was just a remote chance that he might be at one of the basins now.

Making a detour to avoid coming near the bridge, he crossed the canal harbours, crossed and re-crossed locks and at last learned that Dan Murphy's barge was moored at the other end of the city near the Canal Company's basins. He crossed the city by tram and in the clammy dusk followed a boy along many narrow pathways between basins held beneath looming warehouses like dark rectangular lakes locked secretly between inland cliffs. Threading a path between yellow portholes, the boy pounded on a hull. 'Gentleman to see ye, Mr. Murphy.'

Up from the bright square of the hatch Dan's burly figure rose. Coming ashore he said 'good evening' reservedly, and peered through the dusk.

'Do you remember me, Dan? I'm Martin Reilly. You remember Martin Reilly and the Vincent girls down the river, down Keelard stretch.'

Dan stiffened and, without a word, turned on his heel and, keeping his head turned in Martin's direction, he went back and disappeared down the hatch. Reappearing with a lantern, he came and held it close to Martin's face. 'Well, this beats Banagher and Banagher beats the divil!' And he put down the lantern. 'Ye'll excuse me taking a lantern to ye, Master Martin, but ye never know what trickery might be afoot nowadays. It's not like old times,' and he held out his hand. 'How are ye at all, at all? So ye've gone all out of your way to investigate me up here in the city, and to find the ould boat.' Martin said nothing to that, being reproved by the thought that he had never sought Dan until he had need of him and 'the ould boat'.

He followed the broad, grease-shining jersey down the ladder and saw the cabin as of old, the bunk mysterious in shadow, the smoky lamp, the stove. Dan, flattered by his visit, was looking admiringly at this youth who had grown up and still remembered him, and Martin was looking admiringly at Dan, until both laughed; and Dan, apologizing for the deficiencies of his cabin, began to suggest hospitalities which finally came down to the choice between a cup of tea and a pint of porter out of the barrel at the cool end of the cabin. Pulling out the old padded box, Dan said: 'Sit down. It's not the first time ye've sat there, yourself and Miss Sally, and she with the Jack of Trumps waiting to kill me Ace of Hearts always.'

Martin said nothing and Dan suddenly, as though to the world at large, went on: 'Ah well, going up and down in the ould boat it's all one to me. And what's going on beyond the bank is nothing to do with me. And so there you are!'

He's heard something of my activities, thought Martin. 'That's the very thing I've come for, Dan. Just to go for a bit of a cruise with you. I wondered if there would be a corner for me on the old boat for a day or two?'

There was a constrained silence, and then Dan spoke with discomfort. 'I'll be open with ye, Master Martin. If it was just for yourself, you're as welcome to a lift as ever you were. But . . . well, I don't hold with the things that's going on and I wouldn't let the ould boat help anyone to bring trouble down the river for some-one else. Neither the bloody British nor the bloody . . .' in the presence of one of the 'bloody other side' he checked his tongue. 'Well, there ye are, Master Martin. If it was just for yerself, like, it'd be a treat to meself to have ye.'

'It is, Dan. Just for myself.'

'All right, Master Martin. Your word's good enough for me. Come and welcome.' He gave Martin a glance. 'And there's no hunting nor searching on the water. A man can sleep aisy on it.'

They said no more about that side of it, and, as Dan was to leave early in the morning, Martin arranged to come aboard that night and he hurried to the O'Gradys' to remove his things so that he would not have to go there for them on his return from the river. They welcomed him with boisterous mockery about his 'night out' and told him that they had been wondering if he had been curfewed or killed. Despite their protests and appeals, he packed his things, evaded their curious probings, and, while a cab waited surrounded by children, he went into the little back room for a farewell drink. He could see them eyeing his spruced-up appearance and knew by their knowing leers that they thought he was going away on an affair with a girl.

'Here's to Brighton,' said Herbert meaningly, for Herbert had often talked enviously of the wickedness which he imagined officers on leave had enjoyed on week-ends with girls at Brighton.

Mrs. O'Grady said with the huffiness which was her nearest approach to the fury of a woman scorned, 'You and your Brigh-ton!' and she lamented that now she could not have a 'hooly' for Martin's birthday. 'I know that it's in a few weeks now. But maybe it's in bed you'll spend your birthday'; and her eyes rolled lewdly, while Herbert muttered 'crêpe de Chine', and winked sadly at Martin, to whom he had often bemoaned the fact that, of all the girls he had known, he had never met one whose appear-ance in her underclothes bore the slightest resemblance to the illustrated advertisements in periodicals.

Martin said nothing, merely wished them luck, knowing that he would spend his twenty-second birthday with Aunt Kathleen's letter.

They came to the door to give him a rowdy, royal send-off, and the last he saw of them was a group in the light of the shop window, Mrs. O'Grady wagging the frizzed hair above a cluster of children, Herbert staring with envy after the cab which was driving away to high times in Brighton.

From the frowsty street, the painted public house of the superior family, the smell of poverty, dirt and cheap scent, he drove straight to the preserved atmosphere of Miss Ussher O'Dwyer's boarding-house. Saying that he had decided to visit a friend down in the country, he gathered a few necessities and escaped from the hall where already the servants were laying out a grim line of cocoa-mugs. He had a note ready to send to Professor Prolitzer warning him that he would not come again but saying that he was sending him a good teacher who would want considerably more than he had paid hitherto as he had a fine degree. 'If ever you stop a penny for chalk he will either beat you or sue you, probably both.' Prolitzer would half believe this, because, for all his cunning, he was a credulous and timorous half-wit. He took this note to a young schoolmaster who had been a boy in Dunslane with him and would be glad to get Prolitzer's few pounds for afternoon work. Then, making a cautious way through the city's snares of arrest and death, he came shortly before curfew to the rectangles of motionless dark lakes between the high cliff buildings and to the walks that were like pathways winding secretly between water and mountain to bring him far from the hum of the city. Amid the creakings of ropes and the soft slush of water he came to the barge, to the lamp swinging above the table, the bunk, the stove and Dan in his shiny jersey.

'God, Dan, I'm glad I found you today!'

He blushed for his impetuous greeting but Dan said: 'Ye haven't changed so much after all, Master Martin. Ye were always a quick, high pair, yerself and . . .' he grasped the nettle that lay between them, 'yerself and Miss Sally. Begob ye were a pair well met. I'd be calling her Miss Vincent now, but sure it's with her red hair hanging down her back I think of her and that eye of hers cocked up at me with a look that was as good as a court oath to prove that she had the ould Jack of Trumps waiting to kill me Ace of Hearts. Is there ever any news of her and the quiet one? I heard they were still away.'

'I heard that Peggy was to get some big post doing, or inspecting others doing, welfare work. Looking after girls in factories and offices and so on.'

2M

'Bedad, she'd be good at that!'

'She would indeed, Dan. Did you know about her old men and old women? She used to . . .' and he told of Peggy setting off on her pony down the back-avenue with the ju-jubes, knitting wools, tobacco and yesterday's newspapers.

'And Miss Sally?'

'I heard once of Sally. She was in Paris then.'

'In France is it? Paris! Bedad! Right beside that Hall of Mirrors where they codded Mr. Wilson out of his fourteen points and all. All mirrors, man; they say that three barges put end to end wouldn't fill it; and all mirrors,' he mused. 'Ah, that must be a sight to see. But sure I suppose you've seen it all yourself.'

They talked of old times until Dan's assistant came on board. The forward cabin had been specially arranged for Martin and from his bunk he saw the hatch frame oblong, not square, and away beyond the frame the stars of Cassiopeia hung. High over tomorrow's southern journey, Orion's great question mark bestrode the sky—'God's note of interrogation', he had often heard it called.

When Dan wakened him in the morning the locks of the city had been left behind, a smell of bacon was blowing along from the after-hatch and the barge was moored between flat grass lands where everything rustled as the sun dissolved the hoar frost from the ground. A cart was going across a field with a load of frost-jewelled mangolds, hens had been released for the day, horses released from their stables, the cattle from the stall-fed laziness of the night, and the children were taking the field paths to school past potato pits like blossom-studded burial mounds on the slopes. Out of the sky came tattered bits of impotent anger from a solitary old crow, squawking his self-hatred as he circled suspiciously above the sown fields where before very long the new green blades would push up from the unwearying earth. All things, land, animals, men, were showing fight against the grasp of winter; in the farmhouses the most rheumatic of the old men would be resting now with the blindest of old dogs beside the roasting bread oven, and all life waited until the summer should come again, and, after it, the harvest and 'good prices, please God'.

But far away, winding across the land, went a moving line of dark lorries, military, Tans or Auxiliaries. Dan said quietly,

'They're out early on their bad work today,' and he led the way to breakfast.

Martin looked back once at that black line moving, which was like salt rubbed into the inflamed gashes in his conscience, and muttered to himself, 'We but teach bloody instructions. . . .' It was a cryptic utterance which his host was much too polite to comment upon.

Despite Dan's warnings, he worked with an amateur's enthusiasm, swilling the deck, running along the banks to clear the rope and take a turn with the horses, back then to take a turn at the tiller, until Dan laughed when towards afternoon Martin's muscles began to stiffen from unaccustomed movements. They failed to reach a harbourage before dusk, but Dan did not care; he merely growled as he hung out a riding lantern: 'There's room there for another to pass. I've taken me own time on the water like me father before me, and I'll go on taking me own time as long as I'm left. Let them poor Company fellows race their schedules and time-tables.'

'What about the horses?'

Dan said mysteriously, 'Oh, there's a few decent people left in the country yet,' and, taking the feed bags, he and Martin led the horses along a track towards a by-road. Although the brutes were tired they rested their muzzles confidently against the human knuckles, without crossness or tugging, and the dog kept beside them a moving vapour above the freezing grass. Dan passed a couple of back gateways with a growl—'You'd be charged for as much as a smell of the dung-heap in there!'—but at one place he turned confidently into the back drive for carts and led the way to a stable where there was room for the two horses. Martin and he rubbed down the rough coats, scratched the parts that itched from the trailer harness, called the animals by their names and laid out food and drink for them while the dog watched, awaiting his own turn.

In the big kitchen where the fire of hard coal reflected a russet light from the rosy flags to the yellow lamp-light above, Dan and he sat making talk and news for the house. But when the talk turned to raids, shootings and death, Dan rose. They went back across the fields saying not a word except when making sure that gates were closed behind them. When they saw ahead of them the mound of the bank and the little glow of the distant hatch, Martin spoke.

'I've been thinking that you've been doing the same thing day after day all your life, Dan. Did you never take a hand in anything else? Politics, for example?'

For a while Dan trudged on, puffing sententiously at his pipe. 'The day I came back from burying Charles Stewart Parnell, I thought it all out and I tould me mother—God give her His light now—that ye'd put out one crowd to put in another, and sure the second crowd would turn out no different from the first, nor from any crowd that ever went before them. They'd maybe improve one thing; but, if they did, they'd worsen another and better old thing, that was there before them. From that day to this I've had no truck with any of them.' He stopped, faced Martin, his big face faintly lit from below by the reflection of the frost. 'And, Martin, ye've asked me my opinion! I think that there never yet came anything but mischief from people banding together for anything except maybe a dance or a bazaar. I seen it on the water over and over again. Seen it with the ould Canal Company, bad cess to them, and all. People are decent enough in ones and twos, and maybe even threes, but they're worse than a lot of bad-mannered dogs when they band together into a crowd. And above all . . . !' he raised the pipe—'Above all and before all, when they get listening to big notions at a political meeting!'

He said apologetically: 'Ye asked me opinion, Master Martin. I didn't offer it till I was asked.'

Stiffly Martin said: 'Don't apologize, Dan! I asked for your reproof.'

He remembered the faces he had seen upturned to him in the light of torches, the eyes burning, the expressions contorted, as they listened to the rhetoric of Freedom, and all the big notions of a political meeting.

'There ye go again, Master Martin! Always taking things to yourself, personal like. 'Twas just what we all used to say many a time after yourself and Miss Sally would be gone off in the dark in that boat: yez wouldn't take anything easy, neither of yez. Look at the way she used to bring the ould Jack down on me Ace of Hearts! Sure, she'd be bubbling with it inside her and bursting to get at it like . . . like . . . the red-headed princess at the Battle of Clontarf.' His tone deepened with affectionate reminiscence. 'Aye, yez were a pair all right!'

After a silence, Martin said dryly: 'If everyone had felt as you do, Dan, nothing would ever have changed in the world. There would never have been Catholic Emancipation, nor factory laws for children, nor free schools, nor . . . nor anything.'

Dan held up the pipe soothingly. 'Ah, all them things would have come in their own good time.'

'No. Not without someone badgering and hammering for them.'

'Listen, Master Martin, I seen it on the water many a time. All the badgering ever does is to hurry things up a bit and maybe that's the worst of it and not the best of it. Maybe it's in too much of a hurry we are, all the time, about everything. Look, I seen it with the ould Company, bad cess to them; and Guinness's barge-men; and the more I see, the more I know it's better to wait for ever for a good thing to come in its own time than to hurry it along by a bad deed. Or even to hurry it along by wearing yerself out blathering and arguing about it. Master Martin, I never yet on the water seen a good thing come but it spoiled an old thing that was just as good and often better. Look at the motor-boats and all the chaps taking the Company's regular pay. Aye, it's very nice, and often I think I'd like to have that regular pay coming in, or have a motor-boat for meself. But I wouldn't really. For look at all them chaps now, racing day in day out to a scheduled time-table, not able to answer back any impudent young fellow in a hard hat and gloves from the Dublin office, eh? Look at the way it's changed them all, sons of dacent men, become mean and on the make, dodging their hours and their bloody schedule that they sold themselves to. They have pay, I grant ye, and their childer have boots and stockings; but musha, I'd sooner be bare-footed again than be like them. And I knew what it was to be bare and cowld, Master Martin.' He stood meditating a moment, his dog patient beside him. 'When I read now about a man being made Prime Minister somewhere, or head of a canal company anywhere, or in charge of Guinness's barges or anything, I always mark him down in me own mind as a bit of a boyo and only half a man.'

'I see,' said Martin, half mockingly. 'The good shall suffer and the wicked prosper. Is that it?'

Ignoring or not noticing his mockery, Dan said eagerly: 'There ye are! Straight out of the Catechism itself! And isn't it only reasonable when you look at it? If I was God Almighty—God for-give the blasphemy for I don't mean any—I wouldn't arrange it any other way. It would be an awful world if everyone was taught to go out on the make for himself. 'Tis only the Catechism keeps a lot of us dacent. So, let the others prosper, and the rest of us be dacent.'

In a moment he laughed apologetically. 'It's fine impudence, me holding forth to an educated gentleman like yerself. Me that never learned more than to write me accounts and read the *Freeman*.'

'Maybe you were lucky, Dan.'

'No, Master Martin, I was not! I wouldn't of course expect a real schooling like yer own, but if I'd had the chance at something more than the National School, maybe they might have belted a bit of the Frenchmen's language into me and then I could read for meself all about that Hall of Mirrors. There was only a short bit in the *Freeman* and no picture. I'd have liked a picture of it . . . Man, three barges and maybe more, end to end, and all mirrors. And that Mr. Wilson sitting there being canoodled out of his fourteen points day after day. I'm sure they could have belted it into me as good as one or two I've met since—or maybe better.'

All Martin could think to say was, 'I'm sure they could'; and as they walked towards the watchful, guiding eye of the porthole, he looked at the big figure beside him. Let the other prosper and the rest of us be dacent! Was it murmuring there in Dan, some of Jimmy Curran's whisper of the Anima Mundi?

Back at the barge they fed the dog. Then Martin slipped unobtrusively away to a nearby village, returning later with a boy helping him to carry a half-dozen bottles of stout, some bananas, a box of sweets for Dan's young assistant, who neither smoked nor drank and thus had a tooth as sweet as a boy's, and lastly a tin of salmon, because Dan, who spent all his life floating above fresh salmon, thought the stuff in tins a wondrous luxury. The three made a strange meal in the cabin, each deciding for himself the sequence of foods in accordance with the fads of his own stomach or palate. Guessing that had it not been for his presence Dan would have returned to the farm kitchen for a game of cards, he proposed a game and soon became familiar again with the rules of Twenty-five, saw again the kitty of coppers gleaming on the table, and, beyond the hatch frame, the points of Cassiopeia.

On the afternoon of the day when they had leisurely left the

river junction far behind, he watched the widening, deepening
waters and the flow of the current. Beyond the banks with their
graceful bare trees the sound of rubber wheels on a road was over-
borne by that of heavy farm-carts. Above the sown fields the
crows floated downwind with casual ease, and on the loftiest
distant branch a heron made his evening halt, thin and angular
against the flaming evening sky. Yet, even when the first lantern
had begun to come and go in farmyards, a late sower was still
moving up a field, his bag nearly empty, his hands launching the
seed in the old rhythm.

Wrapped in overcoat and tarpaulin, he sat at the prow and
watched the current that, without petrol, horse or man, could
carry him down to the past. The flow tunnelled a way through the
closed box of his self and for a while it bathed with milk and
honey the jangled discord of his spirit. Must he really go away?
Never come here again? Here was his own corner of the world,
here his father's fathers had done the same things, seen the same
sky and land. Down there, just a short excursion for a swallow,
a Reilly had followed Owen Roe into St. Canice's, carrying the
flags captured at Benburb. Here his own flesh and blood had
wrung a living out of this land where the ancient ways still went
on; here they had done things which, though Josie and Mary
Ellen had not known it, were part of the ballads they had sung.
And here long ago, pagan Reillys had kept a Hallowe'en for their
dead, before ever the Round Towers had been raised to the Glory
of the new God.

But he was sick of it all. It had gone sour in the mouth. The
tides of pride were exhausted, and he would follow his mother's
tide. On his birthday he would learn from the letter what part of
his native land had bred her and if still here in the land he would
go to see those parts. Then he would follow her tide into the
ocean of exile and come no more to this flowing water but earn
his bread and comforts by the waters of Babylon.

All the next morning, while the barge trailed under rain-loaded
skies, he was revolving the places of the future. There was the
post in Cochin-China; Monsieur Gourdet had spoken of it. He
would trade, and the company named also built boats—that
would be nice. The idea was worth playing with. He gathered
together his parcel of things, because already the barge was
passing by the places where he had rowed on that Easter Monday,

and they had passed the place where he had bathed in obedience to Miss Peters.

When he had helped to get the barge through the lock above Rodesbridge he waited on the bank with his parcel until the young assistant would be out of earshot.

'It's a queer place to leave ye, Master Martin, here in the depths of nowhere and the evening coming on.'

'I'd prefer to go no farther, Dan.'

'Aye! Maybe it's best.'

They hesitated, Dan being a little anxious about him, Martin himself delaying the moment of goodbye because he was thinking that he would never see Dan again. So both were silent, the only noises being the lapping of the water among stiff reeds and the cawing of the crows flying low under a grey sky that curved heavily across the smoky trees like stained thatch over a cabin's rafter.

Dan said, 'If you ever meet Miss Sally or the quiet one, Miss Peggy; that is, if they don't come back . . .'

'Yes, I would tell them that you haven't forgotten them. But I'm not likely to meet them ever again.'

Giving him a wise look, Dan said quietly, 'Ah now, ye never know what time will bring to you in its round.'

They shook hands, and Martin, grateful because Dan had not asked any prying questions, said, 'I shall be going away, Dan, out of this country.'

Dan nodded as if he had already guessed that much, then began to look embarrassed. Glowering down at himself, he said, 'If ye were going to foreign parts again, I was wondering if you might maybe get me a little picture of that Hall of Mirrors, if it wouldn't be more than I could afford.'

'I will, Dan. I'll send you the best painting I can get of it.'

'Oh, no, please, not a painting!' said Dan anxiously. 'I'd sooner have a real picture, not a painting.'

'All right, but only if you let me make you a present of it.'

'All right, and thank ye kindly. I'll be on the watch out for it, for I know you're not the forgetting sort and you'll remember my picture.'

'Yes, I'll remember.'

4

THE barge was poled from the bank and the horses took its drag. Although the raw winter dusk chilled him as it dripped around him, Martin stood watching until the last of the barge had gone round the bend, with Dan leaning back against the tiller arm before the faint purple glow that went up from the cabin hatch. He went quickly then along a path which crossed the brow of the fields. Keeping well away from Rodesbridge, he struck the Ballow road after darkness had fallen, and, as he trudged along the dark road, he began to blame himself for having come into an area so dangerous for him, because he was so well known in it. Rain was falling when he turned down a side-road which led to a wayside railway station on the Dublin side of Ballow. He had, however, gone only a little way along the side-road when he heard the humming of lorries coming so rapidly behind him that he had barely time to get into a ploughed field before the search-lights were making pantomime stage transformations out of the rainy darkness, and, with a whine of angry power, the machines rushed through the tunnel burned whitely for them by their irresistible lights. Rather than take the risk that the lorries might wait at the little station, he decided to regain the Ballow road, plod on to the town and wait inconspicuously there for the night-express which would make only one halt between Ballow and Dublin and was unlikely to be raided. It was the train he had taken on his way back to Millie from the ruins of Keelard.

He had four hours to wait for the express, was afraid to shelter in the station waiting-room, and hotels and public houses were very dangerous places. Even the Royal Leinster might no longer be safe. The oily tact of its present owner, Mr. Tim Corbin, could not keep Tans from bounding in and out of the hotel bar. Besides, he was reluctant to enter the Royal Leinster. So he loafed about the side-streets until a combination of hunger, tiredness and rain drove him to take the risk of entering a Temperance hotel, where Tans or Auxiliaries were less likely to bound in and out. The full-bosomed proprietress looked at his soggy parcel, asked where he came from, said, 'Oh, Dublin!' in an alarmed, decisive tone, and told him that her hotel served meals only to 'residents and known commercials'. He left her and went out into the lamp-lit rain. Striding with bent head, he almost collided with a man coming out of a shop and found himself making his apologies to his Uncle John.

'Well, I declare to God!' said Mr. Reilly, gaping at him with dropped jaw and a startled, almost frightened expression.

Martin and he had not met for over six years, since the last of Martin's visits to Aunt Eileen's holiday quarters in Tramore. That was before the war. On top of the old embarrassments, rising again instantly between them, Martin began to perceive some new embarrassment; his uncle had all the air of a man caught at an unworthy moment, and in his eyes there was a new puzzlement, half defiant, half ashamed. With gruff bravado Mr. Reilly said: 'Well, you're the nice young man, leaving your Aunt Eileen without as much as a postcard all this time. And then you come stepping out of the pathway like a ghost.' Behind the bravado there was a certain defensiveness.

'Yes. I should have written. How is she?'

Mr. Reilly looked away, and said: 'She's waiting over in the Royal Leinster. We've been up to town today. She's had more than her share of trouble.'

'I suppose she never recovered from the burning of the house, and James Edward, too. All the strain she's had.'

'Aye! and that's not all.'

'Look here, Uncle John, there's something wrong. What are you and Aunt Eileen doing in Ballow of all places this dreadful night?'

Mr. Reilly's tall frame seemed to sag a little. The cheeks which age was veining tautened as he set his lips bitterly.

'Wrong! Why wouldn't there be something wrong! With my eldest running off to one war after another, instead of helping his father, and Patrick spending money learning engineering, making his career, as they call it, and one girl taking herself and her dowry off into the Poor Clares, and my nephew getting queer stories told about his doings and breaking with all his friends, doing shady business here, or galloping off to Honolulu, or God knows where after God knows what. The whole lot of you thinking of no one but yourselves. Wrong!' He laughed mirthlessly.

Martin looked embarrassed.

'And if that isn't enough the Black and Tans and Auxiliaries, pretending to raid us every day, sometimes twice a day, just to rob me under my eyes and then send me notes to say, if I wanted my property back and compensation for the other damage, that I was to get hold of my rebel son and give them a chance to interview him.' He stared into Martin's eyes but he was looking deeply beyond them. 'Wrong! And those damned, eternally damned, liars in the House of Commons, saying out as bold as brass that . . . ah, God, will you look!' And groping in his pocket he fished out a much-thumbed newspaper cutting and read (but he seemed to know it by heart): ' "We can obtain no official confirmation of these charges of robbery and wanton damage. These unending charges of murder, robbery and assault are very easy to level against our forces fulfilling the difficult task of maintaining Law and Order [loud Ministerial cheers]. The House will not readily believe that any Englishman would commit these crimes on defenceless people [Ministerial cheers in which many Opposition members were seen to join]." '

Martin stayed silent. It was like hearing the drunk man say, 'No Irish girl would mock you with her backside.' It was like hearing the patriots say, 'Ireland will not readily believe that the dead bodies of Auxiliaries could be mutilated by Volunteers who are heroically defeating in arms a terrorist force deliberately let loose by a so-called civilized nation.'

Over the wrinkled bit of newspaper Mr. Reilly's hot, puzzled eyes looked at Martin. 'There's truth and right in the next world, there must be, because there's a God. But there's none in this one. Leave me out of it altogether; but your Aunt Eileen deserved something better. She deserved the very opposite. You never liked me, Nephew Martin, and we'll leave it at that. But you'll admit that I was never the hating kind. And I always had a respect and a liking for a decent Englishman. But now I hate the very name of England and the very word "English" itself, and I'll hate them for ever, and I think I hate the name of Ireland too! You made your speeches and you wrote your weekly papers, the lot of you, and I hope you enjoyed them! But one day you'll realize where all your gab and tomfoolery have brought the rest of us.'

'Don't let's think of that now,' Martin said in considerable embarrassment. 'Will you come and have a drink with me?'

Mr. Reilly laughed grimly. 'Bedad, I thought you'd be too much the touch-me-not gentleman to take drink with anyone.' Stopping his unhappy gibing, he said with stiff formality: 'Thank you kindly. I'd be glad to. The Royal Leinster is safe.' Then, suddenly recollecting that he had an umbrella, he said: 'Well, isn't that a good one? Look at me standing in the rain with an umbrella shut in my hand,' and he repeated it, like one who finds in a small folly the familiar self which a large folly had submerged. 'Isn't that good? Standing in the rain with a shut umbrella!'

He opened the umbrella, Martin stepped under it, and, clinging closely together, shoulder to shoulder, they went to Corbin's Royal Leinster Arms Hotel. Miss Slattery, more leathery now, somewhat shrivelled around the eyes, but still bright and refined, ushered them into the private drinking parlour and served their drinks through the hatch where she once had peered in terror at Mr. John Reilly from Glenkilly hitting Mr. Tim Corbin of Ballow merely for asking: 'Was it a Dublin lady she was or from where? They died abroad, didn't they, or am I wrong in that?'

'I hope you're not too tired, Mr. Reilly. A business trip to Dublin is so tiring, isn't it?'

Mr. Reilly shot her a suspicious glance but Miss Slattery was merely claiming a place on the edge of the world of citizen merchants, in order to mark herself off from the under-dogs who have neither the freedom, nor the money, nor the reasons to make business trips to Dublin. They raised their glasses, and wished good health to Mr. Reilly who, after a sip, seemed to forget his glass in his hand.

'Uncle John, what are you doing in Ballow? What have you been to Dublin for?'

Mr. Reilly said nothing. In a moment he jerked his head towards the ceiling.

'She's waiting up there. In the Ladies' Tea Room. No, don't go to her for the moment. She won't want to see anyone.'

Martin studied the side of the face, wondering just what kind of man this, his father's brother, was, who used to say such things as: 'Books! Piano-playing all day! That's what sent Mat on the road to . . .'

To what? In less than a fortnight now he would read that letter;

his one small faithfulness would have kept its contract with Aunt Kathleen.

'You're a queer fellow, Martin,' said his uncle. 'Look at the way you've neglected your Uncle Charles all these years, after Moydelgan being all in all to you, when poor Mary was in it. I had to go over there a month ago and the whole place was that shabby, nothing painted for years. And poor Mary's piano and lamp-shades—it'd give you the creeps! Maybe now in the summer, with the girls back for their school holidays, it will be a bit more cheerful.'

The girls, he said, were at school in France. 'Your Uncle Charles is a cousin of Reverend Mother and got them in cheap with her, I believe. Young Mary must be turning to eighteen now. But it can't be as long as all that since you saw them.'

'Ten years last St. Stephen's Day.'

He lowered his eyes lest the pictures might be read in them: Grandmother's big four-poster, Aunt Mary swishing away with the apple-green frocks over her arm, the little girls holding him in the dark as he told them of the great Pope-to-be who once in Glenkilly had thrashed all dirty lane-boys and served Mass for the perfect priest, Father Riordan.

'Do they remember her? If only they remember her!'

'I don't know. It isn't to me that Charles would speak of such matters. Think of it! At your age I was marrying Eileen! And it's like yesterday sometimes. It was in May and your father Mat . . .' As of old, he stopped.

'Uncle John! What is your trouble, Aunt Eileen's trouble? There *is* something very wrong.'

Mr. Reilly nodded. 'I'm bankrupt,' he said.

Then, with an attempt at bravado, 'Ah, my lad, that takes the wind out of your sails!'

Martin scarcely noticed the bravado. He heard a long involved muttering as Mr. Reilly went over the road which his mind must have travelled morning, noon and night during the preceding months. The decline in business, the state of the country, the bad debts—'too trusting, I was, Martin'—the raidings and lootings, the loss of contracts, and so on; while from the street outside came straggling footstep sounds, once the sound of a raiding lorry, and, from behind the hatch, thin reverberations of Miss Slattery's gentility. Martin listened to the monotone of explanation, and

at the same time for a sound from the Ladies' Tea Room. Aunt
Eileen was there. It was over for her now, it was like an absurd
nemesis for once having been too proud of Mr. Redmond's sweep
of the hand and his 'citizen merchants of this ancient borough'.
No more bazaar stall, no more 'among those present', no more
Ladies' Committees for this and that, no more coal and food cards
for the poor.

Slowly he began to think of what might happen. A public
examination? 'Tell me this, Uncle John—Aunt Eileen—will they
want to cross-examine her accounts? They're good accounts but
she has worked lots of funny systems of her own into them.
Lawyers will try to prove anything, they'll prove any lie if it helps
to win a particular case.'

'Ah, there'll be none of that, thank God. Tim Corbin——'

'Tim Corbin here in Ballow?'

'Yes. Who else would I mean? I'm waiting for him now, as a
matter of fact.' And he went on to say that the creditors would be
paid 'a good bargain in the pound', but that it had been a near
thing because two of them had been holding out for a public
examination. But Tim Corbin had 'fixed those two', much as,
long ago, he had fixed the election of a county engineer to go in
favour of Aunt Eileen's cousin instead of the man Keelard knew
to be the better engineer. Corbin had 'fixed' one troublesome
creditor with whom he himself did business; the other, whom he
could not fix, he had bought out. He had bought up the debt,
keeping the transaction dark from the other creditors.

'Corbin! Corbin did that! The Tim Corbin here in Ballow!'

'He did. Of course, he'll do fine in the end. He knows he'll get
it all back from me with interest,' and Mr. Reilly wagged his head
virtuously. 'I'm going to a fine opening in Dublin. I'm going in
as manager-partner of one of the highest turf agencies in the
city! A gentleman's place, doing business in the proper way with
gentlemen!' he said very haughtily. Not sure that he was hearing
aright, Martin gaped at his bankrupt uncle who was going to
manage, of all things, a betting agency.

'But how on earth did you come in touch with such a post?'

It was Tim again who had 'fixed' it. Tim had a pull over one
of the two partners who owned the agency, indeed many agencies.

'Of course, at first it won't bring in an awful lot, and'—with a
wistful glance at Martin—'it'll be a change for Eileen. But wait

till you see how I'll expand things before long. I've got a few good ideas already for expansion and new commitments.' Then, with sulky hauteur, wagging the greying head virtuously: 'It's a very important, responsible post, let me tell you. I had to put up a thousand pounds and a bond for another three thousand.'

Ideas for expansion; new commitments; beautiful optimistic expensive ideas; unsound ones probably, thought Martin.

'But where on earth did you get the money and bond from?'

'Edward in Lullacreen is backing the bond along with your Uncle Tom, and Mary's Charles.'

Ah! So that was the reason for the recent visit to shabby, unpainted Moydelgan.

'And the thousand down? Is that coming from them, too?'

'No. From Tim Corbin.'

By the hearth littered with cigarette-ends Martin sat in a daze, listening to his uncle saying that fifty-five was not old, and that many a man had started again older than that.

'Why is Mr. Corbin doing all this for you? . . . ' He paused, then added with grim honesty, 'For us!'

'Ah, Tim and myself have always been friends in spite of one or two little differences.'

Did the one or two little differences cover that day of Redmond's meeting, and the 'Bedad, it'd be a good one if the pure and holy Reillys, God's first-prize Catholics, had a skeleton in the cupboard all the time!' By the time Uncle John came, if ever he did, to pay back Corbin's thousand pounds it would probably join the price got for Keelard, re-sold by Tim to the Faithful Brothers, at a huge profit, to be a boarding-school.

'And, of course, the Corbins always had a respect for the Reillys. A bit jealous and sneering sometimes, but that was only to offset the respect they felt. People are like that!' and for a while Mr. Reilly brooded over the paradoxes of weak human nature. 'It's a way of holding their own heads up, you know. When it comes to a hard push, the Corbins wouldn't like to see a Reilly go down. And Tim, too, always angled after your Aunt Eileen's good graces.'

Then, as if all the rest had been unimportant, Mr. Reilly said easily, 'Besides, Tim, with all his tricks, is not the man to forget his duty to the past.'

Martin's head jerked up.

'His duty to the past! Corbin?' he said shakily.

'Aye, Tim's a faithful soul under all his tricks. You see—it was Grandfather, your own great-grandfather, who gave Tim's grandfather his first backing in the world, when no one else would do it. And Tim is not the man to forget what he owes to those that went before him!'

For a long time Martin sat silent, while his uncle spoke of that morning's journey to Dublin to face the creditors' meeting. 'That's a nice church, St. Michael's and St. John's on the Quays. Eileen knew it when she was a girl. We went in there and said a prayer, and then one for James Edward, to bring him safe through this danger, like he was brought through that damned war of England's with nothing worse than that foot. Then we went to the meeting.'

Martin, sitting with bent head, saw not the hearth, untidy with the litter of Tim Corbin's citizen-merchant clients, but Millie's quays with his uncle and with Aunt Eileen trudging along beside him in her tailor-made, straight up, refusing to let him face the creditors alone.

'I must go up to her,' he said. And then: 'Look! We haven't touched our drinks.'

'Well, here's your health, Nephew Martin. I feel better. To tell you the truth, you were one of those I was most afraid to think of meeting, but you took it different altogether from the way I thought. Do you know what. . . . I'm glad I met you!'

'And I am glad I met you. Your health and success.'

He went up into the corridor that led to the Ladies' Tea Room. Standing outside the glass-topped door, he saw the very sofa where Norman and he had talked of their first disbeliefs, and of good and evil. The room was lit only by the flickering shadows of a fire and when he opened the door he saw her sitting down there by the fire. The light gleamed on one foot resting on the fender, and her lips were working in one of the secret calculations of ways and means by which for thirty years she had provided this for one, and that for the other, and both without offending the opinions of a third. Not recognizing him in the tricky light, she removed her foot from the fender and by a shy gesture she indicated that the stranger was welcome to sit by the Ladies' fireplace.

When her first tremulous, excited greetings were over, he saw that all her great troubles had not broken the firm comeliness of her face nor sagged the dignity out of the set of her head and shoulders. 'The mistress holds herself up well.' Josie had been right. And, looking at her, he realized that troubles would strike in vain against the inner worth of her spirit. There she sat now in this faded room, a Ladies' Tea Room which would not be any longer wanted in the new Ireland which was coming and which must, he thought, be far stranger to her than to himself, who had helped to make it.

'You're dreaming away to yourself, Martin, just the way you used to, sitting under the window at home.'

At home! Was that what she had been looking at in the fire? Her home in ashes now in Glenkilly.

'I'm heartily glad that you've met your uncle again. Now with this happening to him it is a comfort to me to see him with any friends he can have. You know he was really attached to you, it was only that he didn't know how to take you, and you were often a queer, difficult boy.'

Her soft voice continued the roundabout pleading, and began to go back to a young John Reilly, who was handsome and dashing. She talked of the picnics when the young men and girls had gone swaying on 'side-cars, dog-carts, gigs and everything', merrily off to 'all the old castles and old abbeys and all the things you yourself would like, Martin. All over the place, such fun we had!' And in September and October it would be off for hazel nuts, 'and of course that meant another picnic'. She told how more than once they had not stopped dancing until after the dawn, dancing the night away in those peaceful days. 'Once, at the Regatta Hall, John had the last waltz with me and the whole ballroom kept the waltz going and wouldn't let the band stop.' It was the Blue Danube, she said, and they had waltzed it until the Ball Committee put out the lights to drive everyone home. 'But stop we would not! Only the little fairy lamps were left lit over our heads and the birds singing for all they were worth outside the window, for it was nearly as bright as full morning.' Even then the gentlemen had refused to let the ladies go, and had swept them in broad lines down the stairs to see the morning sun at the door. 'Lines and lines of us, Martin. And when we were going down the stairs, old St. George Kelly, an old hunting man, ah, long before your time he was, caught my hand, as I passed by, and he kissed it and said, "Young Reilly will get you, me upright bright thrush."' She stopped ineffectually. 'So, you see, no one knows him the way I do, no one remembers him the way I do.'

2N

He held her hand, feeling the ridge made by thirty years of the
needle and the accounts that no shop-boy, shop-girl or clerk had
ever been allowed to do. 'If there is anything I can do for him.
For you . . .'

She gave him a queer, almost startled look and muttered, 'I
wonder . . . ah, no!' but in a moment: 'Still it is queer! I was
sitting here wondering how to . . . and then someone came in. And
it was you!' In a moment: 'Maybe God sent you into my path.'

When he questioned her, she said with embarrassment: 'Ah
nothing. Just an idea. . . . No, it wouldn't be right,' and then:
'Still it *is* queer! Just that moment of all moments when I was
saying to myself . . . ah, no matter.' Less than a year ago this kind
of thing would have displeased and irritated him, but now he
patiently led her on until, taking her courage in her hands, she
said: 'Well, it's this new business of your uncle's. I'm afraid,
wondering if he will make a success of it at all. It's all going to be
so different and strange and he's getting on in years now. You
know how easily he is led into optimistic schemes. And if anything
happened to this new start then I'd want to be able to keep a
home going for him out of my own pocket, and for any of the
children who might ever want some places to fall back upon.'
She brooded into the fire. 'Life is a queer thing and though they're
grown-up now and educated, you never know what time will
bring. If I had a place I could pay for by my own work, however
small it might be, that I could keep nice with what's left of our
own good things, then I'd know there was one home himself and
the whole family could always count on, no matter what. Then I
could leave Glenkilly with a less heavy heart. I'd be content.'

Under his questions she revealed her scheme. She had a friend
who was joint owner with another woman of a restaurant in
Dublin. Martin knew the restaurant; it had been a very good
place once, and still had a reputation for good food; but customers had been driven away by the grubby tables, slow attendance, servants indifferent or pert.

'Miss Caley's partner wants to sell out her half, and it was Miss
Caley herself who asked me to come in with her. She does all the
catering, and some of the cooking herself, and she does that well.
I'd see to the accounts, the tables, servants and so on, and I know
I'd do that well; of course we'd need extra money as well to re-
decorate the whole place, new linen and so on. If only I could lay

my hands on a thousand pounds, I'd chance the rest.' And, with a quick embarrassed glance at him and away: 'Or even eight hundred, I'd chance it! I *know* that place could be made to pay well.' Then, with pretended resignation: 'But where would I get the money! Pshaw!'

It was the old familiar 'Pshaw!' that he knew so well, and that she had used when her husband wanted to wait until Mary Ellen had come to join the Rosary or when Rosaleen grumbled that her stays were too tight, or Patrick said that his football boots must have cork studs not wooden ones. Thinking of that 'Pshaw, child' of hers, he laughed and she said: 'Oh, maybe it sounds a laughing scheme. But it isn't. I'd make that place pay. I'd make it! Then John and the children would be sure for ever of a home to fall back on.' She compressed her lips firmly. 'If only I could lay my hands on a little money.' And Martin, looking at her resolute face, felt that she would almost steal that money if the man she stole it from was very wealthy.

When he said that he thought that he could get the money for her, she began to protest weakly, saying that she could not take his 'little bit of money'. He let her talk round and about it, until she had talked herself into a half-belief that Martin was merely going to raise a loan for her, and he did not emphasize the fact that he must sell capital. Ah, how Tory Hill, Keelard and Kingstown would have shivered! The person who touched capital, especially when it was a small amount, would have been regarded as half a criminal and half a lunatic of the more unpleasant sort. One would be expected to sweep streets rather than to sell one hundred pounds of Birmingham Corporation Stock. But he knew that Aunt Kathleen, if she were alive to come sweeping down between the little tables of the Ladies' Tea Room, would nod approvingly.

'God direct me, it was Himself put the idea into my head. I must make sure of the future for John and the others. I'll be able to pay it back, I must have . . .' She looked at him, she let the fight go out of her and she bent her head. Sobbing a little she said: 'I was sitting here not knowing what . . . Your poor father, Mat . . . It can only have been the hand of God that it was his own son who walked in through that door tonight.'

She dried her eyes and spoke of the night when her home was burned. She spoke of James Edward, 'out there with that foot and only a little revolver against all their guns. Those terrible Maxims.'

He smiled to hear that odd, out-of-date bit of military knowledge coming from her. 'Who thinks of such guns in the first place?' and for a few moments she lashed out at all she could not understand. 'To think of a human being sitting down to invent a gun that'll kill a hundred men with a turn of a handle. And those newspaper fellows writing about it as if they thought it all a great thing. They called it an improvement! I often wonder if the time of anti-Christ is near and if God has turned His face away from us altogether.'

She asked him not to reveal to his Uncle John her scheme for the restaurant.

'I wish I could have Mary Ellen and Josie starting again.' He told her that he had seen Mary Ellen once since she came to live in Dublin. 'I'm glad. The man she married is rising and will rise more. Her husband will be one of the head men in his company before he's finished.' Of Josie all she said was 'poor Josie', and, from the way she said it, he wondered if she had suspected or learned what Josie's lot had been. Once he would have fancied that she was ignorant of those dark corners of life; but he knew now that not ignorance but goodness had kept her in love with life. And, glancing at her profile, he knew that in her, as in Aunt Mary, in Long Dick, in Aunt Kathleen, the refusal to cabin the lives of others, the failure to say 'sinful' to things whose intention was perhaps perfectly innocent, had sprung not from an ignorant mind but from a religious and upright soul. Neither she nor they would have burned his boyhood rhyme about going to Sally's bed, they would not have burned Norman's name written many times and in capital letters.

The rain had eased to a light mist blowing with the wind when Mr. Reilly joined them and all three set out for the station. Martin walked between them, sharing the shelter of their umbrellas. Once or twice they laughed at little remarks, and when Mr. Reilly grumbled about the poor meal they had been given in a Dublin restaurant that day Martin felt his aunt's elbow faintly nudging him and saw her umbrella tilted lightly backward for a moment and under it a smile like a girl's behind her veil and the gently beating mist.

Are they grown-up at all? Am I? he thought, listening to them. But he knew that their hardest hour had yet to come when they would shut the door on thirty years of life. Eight years more than all his own years and Norman's. What things his hands had done, had written, in that time, shorter by eight years than the time that had elapsed since Aunt Eileen had first gone a stranger to Lullacreen and been made welcome by Mat and little Mary.

He stepped into a doorway to wait in shadow while Mr. Reilly made sure that there were no British forces at the station. Standing in the doorway with him, Mrs. Reilly whispered, asking would he get a hot drink in Miss Ussher's? would he go straight to bed with a hot bottle? would he go to see Mary Ellen? would he keep a sharp eye out for danger, while waiting for his train; and all the time, until he got away from this country where he might be killed any day? He said that he would do all of these things. 'And . . .' she hesitated.

He said at once: 'First thing tomorrow I'll go and tie Miss Caley down definitely to it. I'll have to see the bank; but don't worry about all that side of it.' He did not say that he was going to realize more of his mother's money than the thousand Aunt Eileen had mentioned, but he had been thinking she would need some capital to tide over the period before the new state of affairs in the restaurant could begin to produce results.

'And . . .' Again she hesitated. 'You remember what I asked you the night your poor friend died? . . . Just to the Blessed Virgin.'

He said nothing, and, when he heard that there were no troops or killers at the station, he went there to see them off. Standing shoulder to shoulder in the window frame against the murky light of the compartment they looked down at him, nodding encouragingly, reluctant to leave him there in the rain.

'Sure,' said Mr. Reilly. 'If only we could ask you to come along with us. But it would be madness for you to show your face near Glenkilly.'

'Take care of yourself,' said Aunt Eileen. 'Remember now.'

'Yes. I'll remember.'

Guard and porters were hurrying, anxious to get the train on the move again before either side should come and raid it. He had shaken hands with his uncle and the train was on the point of moving when he saw her turn up her veil and bend shyly towards him. In the old days she had been too proud ever to ask for a kiss from her nephew. Now, at long last, they exchanged the salute of Hail and Farewell.

Bareheaded, he waved after their nodding heads, and while the rear-light of the train vanished into the darkness he stood watching from the platform, the misty rain beating in his face.

5

Iᴛ ᴡᴀꜱ his last night in his own country. He had decided to
take the job in Cochin-China, and tomorrow he was going to
France to sign the contract. He had already transported most of his
luggage to the station, including his diary with Aunt Kathleen's
letter which he would read tomorrow on the first part of his
journey to exile. For tomorrow he would be twenty-two.

He was reading when he heard the sound of lorries swerving
into the street and knew in his bones that it was for himself they
were coming. He swept into the fire the few letters bearing the
addresses of acquaintances, then dashing into the room across
the landing he put the cloakroom receipt for his luggage on the
chimney-piece. Already the rifle-butts were hammering on the
hall door and when he got to the stairs he saw the hall full of
Auxiliaries, some in uniform, some in civilian clothes.

After one deep shiver he walked down towards them, trying to
appear both surprised and upset, but not personally concerned.
They were swarming all over the ground floor, calling for 'the
landlady', but they had been much quieted by seeing a picture of
the King, photographs of some army officers and by the sight and
sound of the residents. The sober ones were now hushing the
drunken ones. 'Don't upset the ladies. That rat we're looking
for has been fooling them. Cute idea to come to a place like
this.'

There were three in uniform, coming up the stairs. One of them
asked Martin: 'Where's this fellow Reilly? He's a Shinner, a
murdering Shinner. Where's his room?'

'Reilly? That's the man who came here just the other day. But
he can't have anything to do with them, it's impossible!'

'What does he look like?'

Astonished by this, Martin said eagerly: 'Oh, red head! Great, huge fellow. I never liked the fellow really, thought he . . .'

Others joined them on the stairs, whispering about the roof and its possibilities for escape. Stepping down to the hall where all in silence were watching a group cautiously going up the stairs with guns ready, Martin said to one: 'Is it safe to pass out to the street? If that fellow is really up on the roof, and shoots down! We're doing overtime these nights and I simply must get along—the Ministry of Pensions; if you know old Phillips, you'll know that zero hour *is* zero hour with him.'

They grinned. 'Put me down for a pension,' said one, and Martin grinned.

'Put myself down for one, you mean,' he said, and they laughed softly.

From the dining-room two of the old ladies were gaping at him, their mouths held between dumbness and the shriek that would betray him. He cursed himself because he had left his hat and overcoat in his room and, taking a hat and coat from the hallstand, he hoped they would come somewhere near his fit. With a chuckling mutter of: 'Jolly good. Put me down for a pension,' he sauntered to the steps, pretending to be forgetting about putting on the hat and coat, as he sniffed the night air.

Down there at the tail of the second lorry was freedom and life. Just twenty paces, say, then twenty more to the corner. Once round the corner run like hell itself, hop on to a tram, then off the tram, into the side-streets as Millie had taught him, and away to the new life in Cochin-China.

He moved down the steps and heard behind him a bitter, dis-illusioned wail: 'Mr. Reilly! Oh, Mr. Reilly!' It was his landlady.

Even while he stood clamped by her voice they were on top of him, kicking and punching.

'Oh, the lying Irish bastard. Put me down for a pension!'

Having got him, they seemed to have but one desire now—to get away as quickly as possible with him. Some were hushing the drunken ones. 'Wait till we get back. The Army may be here for him any moment. We'd lose the bastard to Fraser's lot then.' He knew that Major Fraser was one of the most important of the military intelligence officers, and when he was put with tied hands out of sight on the lorry floor he began to suspect that these men were anxious to keep the military from knowing where he had been taken, or which company of Auxiliaries had taken him, and, though he could not explain this mystery, it seemed to hold some faint hope for himself. Some things from his room were flung in on top of him. 'Oh, hurry. We'll get all we want out of him later. Anyway, these beggars are too cunning to have anything in their rooms,' and two different feet ploughed about on him. When the feet stopped he felt the vibrations of the floorboards and saw up above him the fore-lengthened jaws, some starry patches of sky and the agonized face of the hostage tethered to the roof by his wrists with a card about his neck: 'Ambush now, I.R.A.!'

As the lorry blared along streets which he could not see, he had a weak hope that by an outer show of recklessness he might make them think it useless to torture him for information, make them think him too tough to be hurt. But among the faces looking down at him there was one whose eyes had already taken his measure. Those eyes were like H.T.'s cold blue eyes, and seemed to him to have looked deeply into his own self-distrust. That man was in civilian clothes; he was neither brick-red nor beef-red like any of the others, but had a queer pallor behind a tropical sunburn, and those eyes like H.T.'s! Fear splintered like a clammy worm through Martin's tissues until he had to bite his lips to keep back the yell of horror at the thought of being down here on these shaking floorboards above the streets where he had walked with Millie.

He could see gable-tops—narrow streets; he could see only the patch of sky—wide streets. His stomach felt a rise to a humpy bridge, and when he glimpsed a tower of the brewery he knew that they were taking him on a roundabout circuit, perhaps to cover up their tracks, and that he was close to Kingsbridge, the station for 'home'. Chaps might be going back to Dunslane now after a match in Dublin; a family party going home after a Dublin trip for the last of the pantomime before Lent. And down in the water nearby lay Millie's banquet table.

The sounds of traffic rushed by his head with the music of a street-musician playing 'Sweet Genevieve'. Then, after loud hooting signals, the lorry swerved in under a wide space of sky and he was dragged up into a darkness suddenly broken in three places. Not explosions, however, but the beams of searchlights had burst the darkness, and the next he knew was that he was standing on the ground in a circle of light fringed by shadowy figures, while through the outer darkness beyond the fringe of light a voice, shrill with passion, yelled, 'Let me get my hands on the ——!'

His face was held to the light by fingers dragging back his hair.

'Where were you on Bloody Sunday, the day you butchered those officers in front of their wives?'

He shouted back his answer to the fringe beyond the blinding light.

'I was in Padua when Bloody Sunday happened here.'

He knew that they were taken aback by that; he could feel the disconcerted silence; even a dirty Irish rebel could scarcely think up so good a lie as Padua on the spur of the moment.

'How did you get back from the ambush today?'

'I didn't even know that there had been an ambush today.'

Someone stepped from behind and struck him in the mouth. Someone else said, 'He's answering, Carmond, and it *might* be the truth.'

An Auxiliary, middle-aged—almost old, indeed, and very queer to see in the natty, waisted uniform—came out into the light and wiped the blood from Martin's mouth.

'Better answer up, lad. Two of our chaps were killed today in that ambush.'

'Don't waste pity on him,' a young, hot voice called. 'His name's not on Fraser's desk for nothing. . . .'

'Shut up! You damned fool! If Fraser finds out we've been studying his papers . . .' The rest of the muttering was lost.

Once, that name Fraser would have rung ominous to his ears, but now it sounded like the name of a friend, almost a guardian angel. The most that Major Fraser would do would be to have him hanged after a long court-martial and a good breakfast.

The little hope sank from the pit of his belly when he saw the figure which now advanced into the light. It was the one in civilian clothes with H.T.'s eyes and that pallor behind the tropical sun-burn.

'This hooded-men's stuff is no good with this bird. He must know more than the names of a few ambushers, and we'll get it from him,' and, turning, he led the way through a mass of figures leaping and prancing to get at Martin as he was bundled past them by some of those who had been in the lorry. 'Let me at him. Let me get at him, the ——.'

Someone was making the searchlight swivel about and in the flashing light the strange faces danced all around him. He was outside a closed door, standing two steps above them, and those clutching hands nearly had him now. Their hands were at his legs, and though his escort pushed them back, nothing was saving him for the moment but the very urge of that surfing hate, because those who got a footing on the lower step were pushed from it by those behind. While his escort fumbled at the locked door, voices from below shouted up at him the things which they had done to others, naming men he had known.

Once, information of such a nature would have been used as propaganda for the world. Now it was not information of the doings of an enemy but information of Evil itself. He had read in the history of men of the savageries done to men in the names of men's gods; but nothing in his traditions or teaching had prepared him for the knowledge that the human mind could invent an evil thing, over and above a cruel thing, to do to the human body.

As he was dragged through the door, he saw light from a window streaming on to the white face of the hostage hanging from the lorry roof by his wrists. The cheap suit gaped, the poverty-marked features were stained by dirt and twisted by pain. But his eyes met Martin's over the lost souls beneath him, as again and again he called some message. Fragments of his call came across the hate-lit faces.

'Up the rebels! God save Ireland!'

Down below they looked with bewilderment from Martin to the youth in the lorry, and the escort, taking advantage of the pause, pulled him in and shut the door between him and the now silent mouths of hell.

He was led to an ante-room which opened on to a larger room. There the lean leader—Anderson was his name—went away down a dark wide corridor. At the far end of the bigger room an Auxiliary, who was trying to read, glanced irritably now and then towards another Auxiliary, half drunk on a seat by the fire, and lolling with a maudlin air towards a tawdrily dressed woman. While the men around muttered something about 'Upstairs. Anderson's gone to see,' Martin saw the reader come towards him with his finger in his book to mark the place. The D.S.O. bar was on his uniform, his face was a young-old face, like that of many others, but he had something of Mr. McKenzie's air about him. The bright title of the book was familiar to him. It was a book of the lyric poets of England's war.

The puzzled eyes in the young-old face flickered to and from Martin, in whom hope stirred. If this man could still read without boredom the things in that book he might defend a prisoner.

'Who is he?'

'A prisoner. A murdering Shinner.'

'Have you told Army Intelligence?'

'Oh, Anderson's just gone to report the arrest.'

He had not, he had gone up a stairs round that corner, a wooden stairs, his steps had come echoing ominously back to this ante-room.

'You're sure Anderson's seeing to it . . . ? I mean . . .' The eyes flickered away from Martin's direction, looked at his book; he shrugged wearily and turned back towards his distant seat, while Martin, staring bitterly after him, thought that it would have been just as well for that man, little older than himself, if he had been killed when he won his D.S.O.

They shut the door between him and that reader. Soon from the unseen stairs came the echo of steps and, in the dim passage, the lean Anderson with H.T.'s eyes beckoned silently.

Along the stairs none spoke except one excited boy, the only young one. He was indeed a mere schoolboy, a rosier, livelier, older Norburton, with Norburton's jowl and a schoolboy's half-frightened excitement on the way to horror.

'Where are we taking him? Up to——'

'Shut up!' was the only answer they gave to his boyish nerviness.

They stood him up in the middle of a shuttered room lit only by reflections which, swivelling from the tops of passing tramcars, probed between the shutter gaps and made on the ceiling flashes as if from a revolving prism. There the six men muttered among themselves until Anderson's voice said: 'Better take the other one first, then this one. They'll both talk, you'll find,' after which they came and fastened his wrists high up between his shoulder-blades by a cord around his neck. They took off his shoes and socks and left him alone, shutting the door behind them. Their steps went across the passage and the door was shut over there.

The swivelling flashes from the tramcars came at intervals and he heard the soft beating of rain against the invisible windows. Fear wriggled around the walls of the room and at each corner it gushed out at him.

Now, sounds began to come from across the passage; they were low moans of someone in agony. The sounds mounted to a long scream which trembled in waves about him and swamped him. And then lower moans and silence. Not a stir nor a rustle could he hear, except only the floorboards stretching here and there, and the occasional distant rumble of the trams.

The door was thrown open to reveal a lighted room across the passage and all their faces there between him and that room.

'Now this one. He'll talk too.'

They stood there, big, bulky figures, and all of them, except the rosier Norburton, were far bigger and heavier than he, confident strong figures of mature men, full of beef and resolution.

They led him barefooted into the lighted room and locked the door. From behind a curtained exit in one corner, low moans came at intervals. Anderson was seated ceremoniously in a chair behind a table and the others ranged themselves with silent ceremony around him.

'Now, Reilly. We know all about you.' Anderson nodded towards the curtain. 'He could have saved himself a lot of trouble by answering up sooner. So you can make your choice.'

Instantly a low moan came from beyond the curtain and Martin, looking at the ceremonious ranging around the table like a schoolboy's fake court, suddenly saw through the trick and said, 'You can tell that fellow to come out.'

Some tried to look uncomprehending, but Anderson, his eyes on Martin said: 'All right. Yes, you're clever—all the better.'

He called and a fat Auxiliary shambled to a seat from behind the curtain and with a sulky look at the others, growled, 'I said not to pick me.'

'We'll waste no more time,' said Anderson. 'We have a few questions to ask you, Reilly.'

'I demand to be taken to Major Fraser,' he said, drawing a bow at a venture.

Anderson came round to him, fixed the cold blue eyes on him. 'Now, listen. If you answer our questions there will be no need for you to see Major Fraser or anyone else. I promise that you will go free from here, if you tell us what we know you know. If you don't answer—you still won't see anyone else. You will see no one else ever! Do you understand?' he said quietly. 'You're not a fool. You know you wouldn't be the first. You can see when you're up against it.'

He looked deeply into Martin's eyes, smiled confidently and went back to the table, where he made much show of looking at papers. Martin was sure now that there was no information about him on those papers. They had somehow heard or got his name from Military Intelligence, and all they knew was that his name would not have been noted if he was a very unimportant person.

'Now. Let me see. Yes, here—name and rank. Name: M. M. Reilly. Rank . . . now where is that sheet?' and shooting a look up at Martin. 'It was captain, wasn't it, on the Intelligence Staff?'

He looked brightly at Martin.

'Rank?' said Martin. 'Only men in an army have rank.'

Anderson acknowledged this with a dry grin.

'We'll see about that. Where do you live? Not the lodgings, of course. But where is your home?'

'I have no home.'

'So you're going to be a fool?'

'Give me back my shoes and stockings and untie my arms. I have no home; I said so and it is the truth.'

For the moment he was most afraid of showing how afraid he was.

'Where do your parents live?'

'My parents are dead.'

'Really? Both of them? Well, then, where *did* they live?'

'I don't know. It's the truth.'

'I warn you that this won't last long. Where do you come from, where do your parents live, where were you born? God damn you, who are you and *what* are you besides being the bloody M. M. Reilly?'

'I don't know.'

Anderson looked at him with something like admiring fellow-ship. 'By God, you're a cool one,' he said.

'I'm not. It just all happens to be true.'

'I see. Just a homeless orphan bastard, eh?'

'Yes. I think so.'

At that, Anderson rose and, coming to Martin, drew forward a chair and sat down, looking up at Martin.

'Now listen. This is your last chance. You must have information to give. But that is all we know. So, you see, I'm playing fair

with you. The Army Intelligence must have some special reason
for thinking that you might give them information. I want to hear
that reason and any information you can give. If you give it
voluntarily I pledge you my word that you can go scot free, as
far as we here are concerned.' He looked round at the others, who
nodded. 'Firstly, tell me if you believe me in that?'

Looking into the cold H.T. eyes, Martin saw that this fellow
did mean what he said. 'Yes. I believe that all right.'

'I knew you were clever. I *do* mean it. More than that, if you
tell us all you know—even, mind you, if it is not such a lot in the
end—provided I'm satisfied that you're not holding out on us
you can get on to tomorrow's boat and be off to a long, good
time of it, and we'll stage an escape for you if you like, so that
none of your lot will suspect that we let you go in return for
information. I give you my word. I mean it.' He waited a
moment and then added: 'But if you don't talk voluntarily we'll
make you. And when we have got the information then you know
where you'll be found—and how! So now it's up to yourself.'

The circle of faces leaned forward, watching, waiting. He
looked around the circle, seeking one human look of friendliness.
He licked his lips and said: 'I have told you the truth about myself. I have no other information to give. I know nothing.'

Anderson shook his head—almost regretfully. 'So you are
really a fool after all. You'll be lying stiff tomorrow morning when
you might be snug in the smoking-room of the mail-boat over
a whiskey-and-soda with trouble all behind you. Well? Last
offering.'

Martin shook his head. 'I haven't any information to give. Let
me go.'

Anderson looked up at him, shook his head again. 'Well then,
you are a fool,' and, leaning back, he took a service gun from the
table and began to swing it by the barrel between Martin's legs
while others unfastened his clothes. The sounds of the trams came
but weakly into this room, no flashes at all came, there was
nothing here but the wavering white faces, and the pain, and
the voice suggesting answers to unheard questions. When they
dragged open his eyes to meet the light of their torches burning
on them, he could not see.

Once, twice, the boots came down on his bare feet. They came
again and this time he moaned. The taps on the roasting weight

of his groin reached up to his chest, became the thuds of a great
pile-driver, and he heard his own scream go shivering around the
room.

'That'll do. He'll talk now.' It was Anderson's voice, very
confident and quiet. Anderson had taken his measure long ago
in the lorry; no more, not for anyone, no one could endure it, and
once more he heard his own scream shivering and shrieking.

They let him down into a chair where he stayed on the edge
while they untied his arms. Anderson and H.T. were right, he
was half a coward really, why pretend he wasn't? He would not
pretend, he would be himself.

'Does your offer still hold?' he asked.

Anderson nodded gravely.

'You'll let me go? You won't tip off the military to get me
outside the gate?'

'No. What I offered still holds.'

'All right.'

'Let's begin properly. Who gave you your orders and for what?
Where is his hide-out? What houses do . . . ? Wait. One thing at
a time. What was your own rank and duty and who is immediately
above you?'

The faces leaned to him, a curving semi-circle between him and
the naked bulb; and there in the very middle of the circle was the
face of Norburton grown-up and rosier but the same boy-prefect
face. And suddenly his whole soul revolted, as it had revolted
once at the thought of senior boys and cricket stumps, and he
answered their questions with, 'Poor Slave-Hearts and bullies,'
and sighed in relief. At times, beyond the corner of his eye, he
saw the glitter of the bayonet. He knew it all now, why faces had
been twisted black and ugly, not white and peaceful in death like
Grandmother's and Norman's. This he had feared more than
anything, feared it all the time in his secret bones, and now in
the end it was possible to bear it.

Soon he scarcely cared, he was beyond them, the pain was far
away in their world, not his. Opening his eyes he found himself
lying on the floor. The haze had gone from his eyes, he saw them
clearly and saw that they were tired of him and of themselves.
Anderson was not there. The others stood about as if they did not
know where to look or what to do. Soon he complained of being
cold, and one, the biggest and oldest of the six, helped him to a

bench by the wall and covered his blood-spotted shirt with the
too-big overcoat which he had taken from the hall of his lodgings.

'Why do you fellows do it? What do you get out of it?' It was
the oldest one speaking. He had brought a drink of water. 'What
do you get out of it?'

'Thanks for the drink.'

He heard Anderson coming back, heard whispering and
arguing about him, about Fraser and the military. Fraser, they
said, was furious, had sworn to search every Auxiliary depot for
miles, sworn to resign, if yet another prisoner of his had been
killed.

'Well, let him. Good riddance. Get a proper man in his place.
Get some results.'

Again Anderson went away, this time with several of them,
and the big, elderly one came again to stand over him.

'I'll post one letter. I'll have to see what you say but I won't
look at the address. Got to be quick.' Martin hesitated, tempted.
But he could not trust him not to look at the address. Poor Aunt
Eileen. It would be dangerous even to write to her. She would
cry when she heard that they had got him. But she would do well
in the restaurant.

He was alone and could hear a faint whine of the tramcars
coming from that distant world, where once he had ridden on
trams with Millie. Drowsiness struggled with the desire to lay
things out in order before he died. But he could not lay things
out, he could only see images dilating and returning and shrinking,
hear Millie's laugh, feel the pulse of Peggy's setter bitch as it laid
its muzzle against the bedclothes when he had a cold.

Languor overbore everything, tugged more insistently than the
thought of death, and, as he lay like a man on a high, dried beach
above a withdrawn tide at night, his mind wandered among the
past. Sometimes, however, fear leaped out at him, when his mind
whirled about to think of how death would come. A rush of feet
from the passage, shapes in the darkness and then oblivion? Or
his body in a ditch? Or the official 'shot while trying to escape.
The injuries to the face were caused by . . .'?

He had only one fear now, that at the end he might beg for life
and curl his lip to ask a favour of the powerful. Never! For though
there were many things he would have different, if he were back
again in a boy's big white collar, he would throw that slate all

over again at Brother Finnegan. He would be himself, his own half-and-half rather than anyone else's full man.

When they came back they were coated and capped for the outside world and all in civilian clothes, except only Anderson, who was wearing a British Warm. They would have led him away barefooted, but he resisted, saying: 'No. I won't go without my shoes and socks!'

'Blast you! You won't want them,' and they dragged at him, but he repeated: 'No. My shoes and socks,' and they fetched them from the other room and watched him and he forced his feet into the shoes which could not be laced over his swollen insteps. They helped him downstairs where, from the ante-room, he saw the drunken officer still sitting in the larger room, but the prostitute had gone and the officer who had read England's lyric poets of the war had gone, too.

They led him to the door by which he had entered and there in the rain a few paces from him a hooded Ford car waited. It was to be somewhere in a ditch, then! A lorry and uniforms would have been used for the official: 'Shot while trying to escape. . . . The House will not readily believe that any . . .' any of our own crowd . . . my crowd, their crowd. . . . He knew better, he had seen it all, his own and the others'.

When they bundled him into the smelly, damp gloom under the hood, he saw that the shape at the wheel was Anderson. God, never again would he see the back of anyone's neck! Never again recover from a stumble as he had just done. He managed to hold back the barbaric scream of terror even with his bloody mouth already wide open to make the sound. He tried to peer out at the world but could see nothing through the dirty and wet mica side-screens. He could see only ahead of him where the rain flickered past shining bayonets and rifles as the guard opened the gates to let the car pass out with him to some ditch in the north county, or up to the hills where it would be cold and dark. All cold and dark up there now, for miles around the lovely hollow bed which Millie had found that day.

Loud shouts were coming from the guards at the gate whence so much light was pouring into the yard that he could not at first see the shape of an armoured car behind the light and beyond that the shape of a tender with the steel helmets of Tommies. Soldiers—Fraser?

20

He shouted and was terrified because his shout was drowned under this clammy hood of a Ford car. But Anderson, with a little bored shrug, was turning off the engine of the Ford and a young army officer was coming to the car. Anderson was answering the officer half mockingly, half resentfully: 'Yes, yes . . . Reilly. M. M. Yes, arrested this evening . . . yes, that address . . . oh, take him to hell.'

He was standing out in the living, wet world and the rain was falling on him. In a month they might hang him by court-martial but he would not die tonight.

Rifles with glistening bayonets were being levelled at him and a sergeant very close to his face was saying: 'Prisoner! Fall in.' He did not know where to fall in and the officer who had spoken to Anderson was now beside him, supporting him by an arm and muttering: 'Damn it all. Oh, damn it all!' to himself and saying, 'Give him a hand, Cowper.' He could not focus the rain-shrouded faces around him, and he kept his head bent. He was ashamed of his unlaced shoes and his clothes flopping about him. When he was helped up into the tender he saw a small reddish glow come in under his eyes. It was a lighted cigarette, freshly lit, and the Sergeant's voice was saying, 'Bite on that!'

It was a Woodbine, its coarse bite in his throat was wonderful. Then he heard angry voices below the tender and saw Anderson, still in his British Warm, scowling into the face of the Auxiliary who had read England's lyric poets.

'Yes,' the latter was saying, 'I'm telling you. And I tell you again now, so that it can be quite clear for the future. I decided to save you the trouble of reporting the arrest. I reported it for you. More, I saw Major Fraser himself. Is that quite clear? More, that hostage is also going into military custody—look.' There, marching away amid a squad of Tommies, went the white, slum face. The white face of the English officer looked that way, looked up at Martin, then he walked away alone and Martin lifted his face to the lovely rain.

It beat on his face, the cool, lovely rain, as he was carried above the lighted streets now emptying of people because curfew hour was near. Tomorrow his little finger would move whenever his brain gave the unnoticed order. He could die in a month but he would not die tonight!

Tender and armoured car swivelled with hootings into Dame

Street and across to the Lower Castle Yard, whose gates opened
for them before a row of pointing bayonets. But he had been only
a few minutes on a stool in a room when the same young officer
came hurrying back and he was marched off once more out into
the rain. The young officer said, 'This must be pretty grim, buck-
ing about like this, but actually we're taking you now to get . . .
er . . .' He flushed in the rainy light. 'To get you seen to. Are you
hungry?'

'No, thank you.'

The young officer hesitated, said awkwardly: 'You mustn't
think, you know, that English people treat prisoners badly. They
don't. Really, you know. I mean, someone will ask a question in
the House . . . You know, the Germans, I heard, always wanted
to be taken by British troops.'

Martin said nothing. He was sick of national disclaimers. 'No
Irish girl would mock you with her backside.' 'No Englishman
would . . .' But, anyway, the same rain was falling in England,
his England . . . He fainted.

When he opened his eyes he was lying down near a fire while
above him a man in a raincoat was taking sticking plaster and
dressings from a tray held by a soldier so prim-looking, so reproving, that he might have been a pious clerk who had got into
soldier's clothes for a fancy-dress ball.

The man in the raincoat washed the prods, put cooling oint-
ment on nose and forehead and let lovely, soft drops fall on the
eyeballs distended by the tapping of their fountain pens in that
room high above the distant trams. Feeling the hands so gentle
along the mangled flesh of his lips, he thanked the man, saying,
'Are you a doctor?'

The man made no answer and soon Martin understood that the
raincoat was to hide rank and regiment lest the merciful deed
might bring trouble on its doer, if the higher wheels within wheels
found that inquisitive Englishmen, M.P.s, journalists and ordinary plain Englishmen were for once armed with information that
could not be silenced by the 'No official record of a prisoner of
that name having been treated by . . . The House will not readily
believe . . .' He had heard the same thing after the Cork ambush.
'Volunteers will not readily believe that the dead bodies of
Auxiliaries have been maltreated.' But that had not altered the
fact of the mutilations.

'Don't worry,' he said. 'No one will make propaganda out of me.' Back towards the city he rode again, away from the pearly rim above the river stealing in from the country. He went under the domes and huddled roofs, went round the side of the Four Courts and into the Bridewell yard. He was at once surprised and perturbed to find that he was not to be lodged in a military prison. What deep game lay behind this?

The high wooden furniture in the warm office recalled the office of the solicitor who had read out Miss Peters' will and its 'in the confident hope of final Resurrection in the Lord'. The big police Sergeant behind the desk was hastily re-fastening a few buttons as he listened to the gentlemanly, slightly hostile-looking officer—a different one—who now and then gave Martin a cold, contemptuous glance.

'Ah, he's young, he has a lot to learn,' thought Martin, who less than one year earlier would have looked just as coldly on many kinds of persons. He heard that he was to be 'for the present a military prisoner in civil custody'.

The old Sergeant, undoing a few buttons, gave a weary shrug to the departing back of the gentlemanly frigid one who had handed over his prisoner. Having told Martin to sit by the fire he scratched with a pen in a ledger, but now and then with a nudge invited the long constable beside him to take a look at the prisoner's battered appearance. Taking down a great bunch of keys, he said, 'It's not many of you fellows we've been getting here this last while and we don't miss you one little bit, I can tell you.'

'Don't worry. No one will come shooting to get *me* out.'

Mightily relieved, the Sergeant speculated: 'You don't look as if you'd want to give us any of your Sinn Fein bangings and hammerings and "Up the rebels". And as long as you're here, there's no one here that'll not do anything we can for you. But only . . .' he held up a wagging, paternal finger, 'only if you're quiet and respectable.'

They went out into a great echoing corridor of stone where from the many low openings in the cell doors white faces peered out at the newcomer, and from the women's end, behind them, came occasional oaths, laughs and songs. Giving sideways glances at Martin the Sergeant shook his grizzled old head. 'Ah, they're a bad, low lot.' From the women's end came a fresh series of terrible words, shrieked to the echoing walls, and the old Sergeant sighed. Another woman's voice took up the words, calling curses on the police, the magistrates, penitents' homes and nuns; but her oaths died as a young woman's voice began to sing 'Kathleen Mavourneen' in sad and pleasing tones. There were many cell doors without a pale face stooping to peer out through the low opening; Conroy's Gaelic police were so efficient that few of the land's rejected now fell into the hands of England's police to be lodged in this stone repository.

He saw ahead of him a stairs leading to the underground passages below the city and knew that those white faces peering from the darkness of the cells would go tomorrow down that stairs to the underworld and emerge up again into a side atrium of Justice, there to see the magistrate fresh from breakfast, the reporters picking for news values, the solicitors chaffering for defence fees.

He was led into a cell where by the shine from the sickly light outside the door he saw a wooden bed, wooden pillow and a lavatory sink in the corner. The bolts clanged shut but the Sergeant's steps were ferreting about the sounding halls and presently he returned with a steaming mug of tea and some buttered bread. 'That's from my own pot.'

Never had tea tasted so delicious and thanks were so warm that the Sergeant mumbled, 'Ah, sure, it's nothing at all for a decent gentleman like yourself,' and went away ferreting and came back with the mug refilled. There was silence now from all quarters, men's and women's, of the big clearing house, and the Sergeant, leaving the door open for light, sat beside Martin on the wooden couch, saying what a pity it was to see 'a decent fella like you from a nice home' letting himself be taken in by all 'that Kathleen ni Houligan blather'. Paternally he lectured Martin, who sipped the tea and only half listened to the sententious voice.

'Will there be anyone to bring you in a meal tomorrow? Those fellows mightn't let the papers tomorrow say where you were. But . . .' he hummed and hawed, 'there's ways of letting a decent man's family know, you know.' Instantly Martin thought of the letter, Aunt Kathleen's letter! He spoke to the old Sergeant of the letter, telling of all the years he had waited to read it and assuring him that there was nothing 'illegal' in it, that it had been written in far-off days, right back in 1914.

'Back in poor Mr. Redmond's time,' and the Sergeant spoke

of those piping days when the only trouble for a policeman was the Twelfth of July and 'the Orange divils in the North', days when it seemed that at long last the years spent in passing public resolutions were about 'to squeeze out a bit of Home Rule'.

'Mr. Reilly.' He stood up. 'I can tell one of the old stock when I meet him. You can have in any of your writings you like when I'm on duty, only just pass me your word that there's nothing in them to make trouble for any of us in here, if they were found.'

Martin had not a pen—up in that room of horror they had stolen his pen with everything else: the watch from Colonel Howard, the wallet from Miss Peters, the cuff-links from Millie, everything. He had not one thing of his own. The Sergeant fetched the little bottle of ink from the office and Martin, bending forward, wrote in the beam of light slanted in from the bulb hung at an angle above the door.

There was a reproach to his conscience in the strangeness of the once familiar 'Dear Mary Ellen'. Having told her where to find the cloakroom ticket for his luggage and his keys, he asked her to bring him the sealed packet and then asked her to ring up Dr. McDowell in Glenkilly and tell him to go round with the news to Aunt Eileen before she could see it in the newspapers. The Sergeant's ponderous steps died into silence after the clang of a distant door. Everything was silent then except for a woman's sobs which wavered weakly against the vault of stone and iron bars. The sobbing ceased and the woman sang to herself:

'I'm sitting on the stile, Mary, where we sat side by side
On the bright May morning long ago when first you were my
  bride.
The corn was springing fresh and green, and the lark sang loud
  and high,
And the red was on your lip, Mary, and the love-light in the
  eye.'

Outside the rain fell, fell on Ireland, on the tides of all the seas of the world, fell on England.

The city outside was curfewed now, and the last few, regular night-time shots were over; mind and body surrendered and he dozed to a lullaby coming down again to him from the darkness where his grandmother sang, while the rain kept falling, falling, as if the dead were weeping on the foolish world they still loved.

6

THE rain had gone, the barred sun was trying to lighten his cell when he crawled painfully from the couch to see what was causing the straggling sounds in the great passage. Peering through the low opening he saw the men and women being shepherded to the stairs that led down into the underworld from which they would rise only to a side atrium of Justice.

The morning warders were quick and curt but they helped him up the stairs to a larger cell and even left his cell door open on receiving his promise that he would not try to leave this upper passage. He had no money to send out for a breakfast, his jangled nerves would not let his stomach try to cope with the cocoa he was given, and he wished that policemen had more imagination, because it had not occurred to them to offer him a cigarette and he would not ask. Alone up here, he spent a long time dragging into his cell some planks and a box from builders' material lying at one end of the corridor. With their aid and by clinging to the bars and peering through a tilted vent in the frosted glass, he was able to peep out at the world. He could see the sky, the sun and some seagulls wheeling above the unseen river, and in a room of the Four Courts on the other side of the road the Civil Service typists were powdering their noses, opening the window, shutting the window, and powdering their noses once more.

Back on the floor of the cell, he had nothing to keep him from worrying about his fate, and he was depressed by the policemen who came now and then to take a look at him and speculate with him on his destiny. He had the sensation of being a curiosity, something to be seen, so that grandchildren could be told: 'Yes, I saw him only a month before they hanged him. Oh, man alive, you could see he was one of the brains of the whole thing.'

Since the hour when the Black Maria had trundled away, he

was the only prisoner in the place; it would grow dark in here long before the wintry light had begun to fade outside.

At last he did hear steps. It was the old Sergeant and after him an hotel Boots bearing a clean tray of food, with the evening paper and cigarettes. Neat parcels held a clean shirt and underclothes, a suit, his brushes; everything had been remembered down to cuff-links. It was Mary Ellen's doing. Indeed, he might have recognized her signature in the way the shirt arms were clipped back as she used to clip back the sleeves of his second-best surplices to keep them neat for the nuns' private Mass before dawn. The Sergeant had advised her not to come in until later, when only he himself would be on duty.

'And the letter?'

When the hotel boy had gone, the Sergeant then produced from under his coat the parcel which Martin had made when he had planned to read the letter on the first stage of his journey to the new life in exile.

With the parcel waiting beside him, he hurriedly ate some of the food, then painfully washed himself in the basin the Sergeant fetched. He put on the clean clothes and made what shift he could to rearrange his bandagings. He got rid of the tray, got rid of the Sergeant, heard the door clang and the first shuffling steps of the night's arrivals, while in the rectangular patch of light which fell slantwise in upon him through the opening in the door, he looked at the sealed envelope.

Now, when at long last the hour had come, the letter could after all tell him nothing which he did not already know, except one important thing—what part of Ireland had bred his mother.

He thought of his question years before. 'Am I like my mother?'

From the brown darkness of the bedpost above him had come his grandmother's answer: 'I think you must be sometimes like her. I never saw her, but I know she was very pretty. And she must have loved Mat above everything.'

He thought of the gentleness of her speech as she had said it. To her in Lullacreen there had never come the knowledge that every night of the year men and women shrieked aloud their bawdy defiance in all the Bridewells of the world.

'Anne—your mother—was lovely and good.'

Looking up at the barred window where last night he had seen the rain that fell on England, he saw now a share of starry sky.

He opened Aunt Kathleen's letter, and from within the envelope, sealed for so long, there came to the senses of his body or of his memory the essence of her faint, faint scent.

He read how his mother had married too young a man whose air of worth and strength she had found, as she grew more mature, to be only an enamel of unchangeable rules. He read how she and Mat Reilly had loved to walk and boat at a place he himself had seen, along the Marne beyond Paris. He read how for duty's sake she and Mat Reilly had parted when the current of their love-passion would have taken its flood, how she had been brought home by her husband to find that, because of the love she had denied herself, she was adjudged a woman unworthy to bring up her daughter. The latter had already been placed under the care of her husband's sister. He read how she had gone then to Mat Reilly, who had resigned his post and gone abroad with her to await the divorce. But her husband had refused against all appeals to divorce the sinner, because divorce itself was a sin.

Then Aunt Kathleen told him of two years' great happiness given to his father and mother, although often they had nothing to live on but her little money at those times when his father had been driven out from the small teaching posts which were all he could now get by way of work. In the evening of the day when she had given him birth she had died, asking that he be called 'Matthew after the dear husband God gave me'. He read of Lullacreen people arriving, of their refusal to meet Aunt Kathleen and Uncle Brendan, of a lawyer, a priest and a hurried baptism, and of his father's body found drowned. His father and mother had often said that they wished to be buried side by side when their time came; but the lawyer and the priest had continued to come and go, and in the end the bodies were buried far apart.

He turned the page to learn about those separated graves, but his eyes saw words at the top of a later page. Only after two or three readings did understanding of those words penetrate him:

. . . since by the time you read this, if ever, you will be grown-up, a full 'jew' at last, Martin, and will not mind so much, I am going to tell you this. You were not born in Ireland but in France; those separated graves of your parents are at opposite sides of Paris; you will never be able to go in search of the places in Ireland which made your mother. She was an Englishwoman, and you yourself are half English. . . .

He raised his head and there in the hall beyond the Sergeant
and the open door was Mary Ellen. When he stepped into the
beam of light she said with woeful acquiescence, 'It is you, is it,
Master Martin?'

She stood looking at his bruised face and wrung her hands.

'Ah, who could do that to you!'

Sitting beside her on the wooden couch he tried to keep her
mind from thoughts of his ominous future by making her speak of
his present necessities, messages to Aunt Eileen, food, clothes. As
her first emotion quietened he noticed that she too had changed.
It was not merely that she was older, paler, a little thinner. Nor
was it only the change in her style of dress—instead of the wide
hats with the wreath of cornflowers, she wore an expensive hat
resembling those worn by the wives of the solicitors, doctors and
the 'citizen merchants of Glenkilly's ancient borough'. She herself
had changed also: she was less simple, less shy, more aware of
herself, and he suspected that much of her present mind was
given to the task of impressing her new neighbours with her
rising status in their world. But when he spoke of Aunt Eileen,
the old Mary Ellen answered in the old, shy, unaffected voice.
'Wasn't she the first person I thought of when I heard. "The poor
mistress," said I.'

The Sergeant's tread sounded and he beckoned Martin out of
the cell. He seemed both embarrassed and worried. With marked
stiffness he said: 'There's another person asking to see you. She
won't give any name.' With a watchful look, the Sergeant said:
'I'm wondering if you'd know who she is. She has reddish hair,
for one thing. Darkish red, like.'

Martin was glad then that his face was in shadow. Had Millie
come to him?

'And she has a military pass!' the Sergeant said sharply.

But how could Millie of all people get a military pass? Only one
person with dark red hair would have the influence to get a
military pass! It must be Sally. Waiting to control himself, he
remained silent.

'And, 'tis this way. I'm fairly sure I've seen her before.'

Seen Sally? This sergeant? 'But how could you? Where have
you seen her?'

Curtly the Sergeant answered, 'In here!' and then: 'Aye, she's
one of them lassies. She's done her night with us twice at least, and

her spell in jail after it. Now if she has any hold over you to make trouble you'll have to be frank with me and that's a fact. Whether she knows I recognized her or not, I can't say, but I knew her big red head and the impudent swagger and lordy air of her as if she thought she owned the earth.'

Not Millie, not Sally, had come to him. It was Josie. He told the Sergeant what his contacts as a boy with Josie had been, and asked him not to tell her that he had another visitor. Not knowing how much Mary Ellen might have learned of Josie's life, he merely asked the latter to do what she could to set Josie working for his Aunt Eileen in the restaurant.

'I don't think life has been very kind to her, Mary Ellen.'

'Aye, if only that Big Mick Lannigan . . .'

When he heard the steps coming, he went out to the corridor and saw Josie's figure, half poised between truculence and defensiveness. He took her big hands in his and the rough defiance went from her.

'Me poor hearty, what did they do to you at all?'

'No matter now. It's fine to see you again.'

'First thing when I heard I thought what would the mistress say, if no one went near him to see if he had even a cup of tea. So I came along.'

She had put up neither the feather nor the unskilful face-painting of that night in Stephen's Green; and, as she stood there with her big coat hanging against her knobbly shape and with her hair fixed in pre-war coils up to her hat, there was about her a queer air of plain, old-fashioned decency.

Thinking that she would know only too well what his cell was like, he led her to the door. When he whispered that Mary Ellen was there, he checked her movement of retreat. She resisted a moment, then gave her head a toss and stepping into the darkness beyond the door, she said: 'Is that you there, Mary Ellen? How are ye keeping?'

'Grand thanks. How are ye keeping yourself?'

'Oh, pulling along.'

Although he asked her to sit on the couch, she remained standing against the wall.

'No, thanks, me hearty, but sure, you're not me hearty now, you're Mr. Reilly.' Then in a moment: 'I suppose it's late in the day to be congratulating you, Mary Ellen. I seen it in the Births, Marriages and Deaths.'

'Aye, and there was a bit in the *Glenkilly Liberator*,' said Mary Ellen. 'A bit that wasn't paid for, I mean,' she added proudly.

'I seen that too. I bet you made the right-looking bride in yer wreath and all.' The old hoarse laugh came out of the darkness. ' 'Twas the mistress gave you the wreath too, I suppose?'

' 'Twas her own.'

Martin saw that Josie was looking steadily down at Mary Ellen who had bent forward beside him to catch the beam of light on her gold wrist-watch. He too turned to look at the bending figure, and saw the curve of her belly big with child marking itself against her loose coat.

He looked up, held out his hand to Josie in the darkness. 'Come and sit beside me, Josie,' he said. She came. Mary Ellen began to whimper as if she had been unnerved by the loneliness and darkness in the cell, or by a whisper of life passing through her from her womb like a cold ghost passing through a forest. Or it might have been the remoteness of the barred oblong of stars which looked in on them. It was Josie and Martin then who encouraged her, as they had more than once consoled her in the past, when Josie had done her wild jigs for fun and Martin had sung his ballads. Bending to her body, swollen with the multiplying cells of new life, they soothed her and reproved her. While she dabbed at her eyes and composed herself, Martin in a low voice told Josie about Aunt Eileen and the restaurant. 'You will go and see her in the restaurant? Promise.'

She muttered: 'Yes. Aye, all right.'

The three sat so silently then that they heard the whine of trams on the Quays and the calls of young people, of children chanting in some game and youths chirruping after the swaggering bodies of girls.

They scarcely said any goodbyes, merely shaking hands and speaking of a visit on the morrow. The door and the bolts clanged on him, the steps died away and he was alone.

He took out the letter again and looked at it. If only he had known of their separated graves when first he had gone to those cemeteries in Paris for the sake of names signed to books and paintings!

He stood under his barred window, looking up and out. No rightful name belonged to him, no family, no Church, no country, no sweetheart, but when he lay down then on his bare prison bed he dropped into sleep more calmly than ever he had done since he had become a 'Senior'.

They took him away the next morning. With shining bayonets, shining steel helmets before him and behind him, he was carried above the sunny-cold Quays, past the old water-men gazing up at him with rheumy eyes, past Grafton Street's swishing young men and women on their way to morning coffee, and witty exchanges over the coffee-table. The lorries swept into a barracks of the southern suburbs, and after a long wait with a corporal and a talkative sergeant he was brought to another room where he found Major Fraser. He was told that there were 'grave, very grave, charges' waiting to be formulated against him but that 'at the same time' there was 'reason to believe' that he might now be willing to give helpful information. Major Fraser pointed out that the Colonies and Dominions were large and full of opportunities, that indeed 'steps might be taken unofficially—purely unofficially —to give a new start to . . . er . . . a man, who . . . er . . .'

All this sounded so very like Tim Corbin 'fixing' something that Martin might have smiled, had it not been for the gnawing anxiety to know whether the hangman's noose was dangling for him. The giving of information, he learned, could be regarded as 'by way of an atonement', but otherwise the 'grave, very grave' charges would of course have to be formulated for court-martial. Major Fraser seemed almost relieved when Martin interrupted him to say that he could give no information. With some blushing, the Major said: 'Well, it is a matter you ought to think over. These charges . . .' Seeing Martin give a definite shake of the head, the Major shrugged, shot Martin a look and said rather naively: 'We have to try, of course. It's our duty.'

Martin then asked if he might be told the charges against him and, after some hesitation, the Major revealed something of the unformulated charges, enough to set Martin's mind at rest about the hangman. They would not hang him for these things which they were adding up against him, some of which he had done, many of which he knew nothing about, but for which his court-martial would probably find him guilty. He felt sorry for Major Fraser when he noticed the embarrassment of this curt but kindly officer trying not to let the uncommissioned part of him take official notice of the unofficial bruises on the face of the rebel confronting him. He was not sure that he was not making himself ridiculous, yet he felt it incumbent on him to say to the Major, 'I have to thank you for saving my life.' And after this piece of parlour politeness he was led away.

While the Corporal scurried about the big barracks trying to get lorries and troops allotted for the escort journey to prison, Martin was given a good meal, and an officer came with polite inquiries about food and drink and the treatment he was receiving.

The Corporal returned without an escort and was sent off hot-foot again to find lorries and bayonets and troops somewhere, while the army Sergeant and Martin went out and sat in a shed open on one side where they could smoke unobserved and yet have a view of the sky and the life of the barracks yard. A few civilian clerks went out into the world beyond the gates, the Sergeant casting a bright glance at the tripping ankles of the female ones; the luncheon hour passed, the clerks came back, the Sergeant's eye followed the neat legs up the steps, and still no escort came. At first the Sergeant had been delighted with this lazy job of sitting smoking in a shed beside a prisoner who listened with interest to tales of Putney, Aldershot and Ypres, but soon he became worried by the delay and confided to Martin that he had 'a rondee-voo' with a girl for that evening, 'real Irish she is', and feared that a longer delay might make it impossible for him to get off duty and into his civilian clothes in time for the 'rondee-voo'. He had, however, thought of a plan, if Martin would co-operate. Among some undemobbed women of the W.A.A.C. there was one who was 'a lady—a good sort' and in any event a fellow wangler of the Sergeant's. She had been in the V.A.D.s but had been bored by it, and had got herself transferred to the humbler W.A.A.C. force. She drove a light lorry, and if Martin would give his most solemn 'parroll' not to try to escape, they could go off in the light lorry and the Sergeant could be back in time to change into civvies. He did not say the civvies were to keep him from being shot by the Irish while courting his real Irish girl. An escort would arrive sooner or later, and Martin could gain nothing by not co-operating. He gave his parole not to try to escape; if he refused it they would just have to await the escort, so what difference did it make to him.

Wondering if this 'good sport' who had been bored as a

V.A.D. might have met Gertrude or Sally in that service, he looked with interest at her when she swung her light lorry in between the pointing bayonets around the gate, with a corporal hanging out at the open back and signalling with the air of a successful conspirator.

Leaping jauntily down to tinker with the engine, she moved about with a cocky stride that seemed slightly bandy-legged under her short and dirty khaki skirt. At sight of that cocky waddle, the weather-beaten face and the knowing, rakish eye of her, Martin smiled to think of the contrast between her and either Gertrude or Sally. He could see that she would love the life of hooting about in lorries with a comfort-loving sergeant, a good wangler up to every trick of the Army, where girls or pubs were concerned.

Sitting under the hood, he heard the Sergeant tell her that 'this Shinner here', he too was 'a good sort' who had given his 'paroll d'onnair' to help the Sergeant meet his girl. Cocking an eye at him, she said: 'I hope to get a chance of a sit-up talk with a real, full-blown Shinner before they demob me. Why do you all do it? I always thought the Irish nice and independent, if a bit touchy, but I never thought they were absolutely crazy. What's it all about anyway?'

'It's a secret,' said Martin with a laugh.

'Oh, well,' she said easily, 'it keeps the job going. Postpones the properties of phosphorus.'

'Phosphorus?' he inquired with interest, and with comradely friendliness she explained:

'Yes. Phosphorus in the classroom all morning; the girls' character-development for lunch; interminable bloody hockey for tea; and damned tough beef for supper. My God! Back to it I'll have to go one of these days.'

'You mean you were a schoolmistress once?'

'Yes. But everyone has his or her crimes to answer for. You're a Shinner yourself, so don't you sit in judgement.' And, giving her cap a bit of a tilt, she slammed home the gears and, to her own whistling of 'Pack up your troubles in your old kit bag', she blew a few cheerful hoots and drove the rollicking little lorry out into the setting sunlight.

He saw a paper fall back from her pocket as she pulled an old rag out of her khaki jacket. As he picked it up, she called over her shoulder: 'Don't bother, thanks. Only an envelope!' and in a moment: 'From the old job. The dear old school writing to say they'll have me back.'

On the envelope was the printed address of the sender. It was from Gertrude Jamieson's old school and it was addressed to Miss Gifford.

Straight towards the city, Gertrude's rare and wonderful Miss Gifford sped between the long line of lamp-posts where Millie used to get smaller and smaller, past the place where she used to turn and wave. It went more slowly then along by the canal dock and he had time to see the barges moored there. Passing faces, looking up at him, were not sure whether to cheer a rebel prisoner or scowl at an enemy killer in civilian clothes. In the central places the ugly new buildings replacing those bombarded in the Rebellion were suffused by the sinking sunlight, and, far beyond the vista of the Quays, the parallel lines of the switchback line of houses met in an infinity of mellow sky over the station for home.

Miss Gifford, urged on by the Sergeant, sped quickly past Parnell and up the hill to the prison. As she drove him steadily up the hill, the light of the sun was overtaken and when the outer gates of the prison were opened before their coming he saw between the gates and the prison house itself a broad path of mellow sunlight that had a hint of coming spring.

He stood in that mellow-lit path while the gates were closed behind him and receipts signed for his body. The warder beside him signed to him that he must wait until a shuffling line of grey prisoners had vanished into shadows beyond inner doors of bars and steel network.

Maintaining his stiff stance of duty the warder whispered through the side of his mouth: 'Just keep your heart up and take things easy. Remember.'

He nodded, forgetting that the forward-looking warder could not see his accepting nod. Turning his head he saw the gates closing again behind the rollicking lorry as Gertrude's Miss Gifford drove away into the world.

'Remember what I said now,' the warder was whispering again.

Remember? He stifled a mocking sob. 'Oh, I'll remember,' he said.

He stepped on then, and his bearing was not without dignity, as he moved through the shade of his prison house, seeking at long last the old hammer of reality which might yet ring music from the anvil of a man.